Homo-Deus

BY THE SAME AUTHOR

The Human Arrow
Ouha, King of the Apes
Pharaoh's Wife

Homo-Deus

by
Félicien Champsaur

translated, annotated and introduced by
Brian Stableford

A Black Coat Press Book

Edited by Peter Gabbani

English adaptation and introduction Copyright © 2014 by Brian Stableford.
Cover illustration Copyright © 2014 by Yoz.

Visit our website at www.blackcoatpress.com

TABLE OF CONTENTS

Introduction

Homo-Deus, le satyre invisible by Félicien Champsaur, here translated as "The Invisible Satyr," was first published in Paris by Ferenczi et fils in 1924. The eponymous protagonist was featured again, albeit in a minor role, in Champsaur's next novel, *Tuer les vieux, jouir!*, issued by Ferenczi in 1925 and here translated as "Kill the Old, Enjoy!" for the sake of completeness in the examination of an inordinately strange invention.

The former book is advertized in the latter as *Le Satyre invisible*, which was presumably its original intended title, unchanged in the ad because of an oversight. The second is even more confused in its titling, having two different title pages, the first of which describes it as a "*roman narquois*" [a mocking novel] and the second as a "*roman vache*," which has more or less the same implication in vulgar parlance—the latter subtitle is the one reproduced in bibliographies, and both descriptions are supplemented with "*moeurs du temps*" [contemporary mores]. The designation is slightly odd, because the novel is not a satire but an angry indictment of the supposed effects of the Great War on the survivors of the generation who fought in it, although the introduction of the subplot in which Homo-Deus features does give it a strange twist akin to the more wholehearted bizarrerie of its predecessor.

Given that the composition of the first book set out with the title *Le Satyre invisible*, it was probably initially planned as an exercise in eroticism, and there is indeed a set of chapters which, if abstracted and run together, would constitute a distinctly steamy erotic novella. One cannot, however—not, at least, without lapsing into pure and simple pornography—make an entire novel out of a series of scenes in which a man takes advantage of a technology of invisibility to introduce himself into various women's bedrooms in order to play the voyeur— and, when the opportunity presents itself, to commit a curious kind of ambiguous rape, obtaining his victim's "consent" by encouraging her to believe, since what is happening is clearly impossible, that she is dreaming. Presumably, therefore, Champsaur thought it advisable to integrate those scenes, probably a trifle belatedly, into a broader and more complicated plot. In order to achieve that synthesis, however, the author was forced to improvise, moving into literary territory that was largely uncharted.

He elected to do so, not unnaturally, by developing two corollaries of the notion of a technology of invisibility. On the one hand, he attempts to explore the other possibilities for which it might be useful, giving the protagonist the opportunity to become a kind of crime-fighting superhero—in an era, of course, when there were no obvious models for that kind of character, although a curious fictional subgenre developed subsequently, which has flourished very abundantly since. On the other hand, he appears to have posed himself the speculative question of what other technologies might be possible if the theoretical basis of the hypothetical invisibility technology is taken for granted—again in an era where few literary models for that kind of exercise existed. Although neither of these other two plot strands is developed with any conspicuous logic, and both eventually dissolve into incipient chaos when they eventually embrace the later erotic scenes, the reckless mixing of the three aspects of the story produces something quite unique, and by no means devoid of interest, in terms of its groping toward narrative effects that were new at the time.

The notion of technologies of invisibility was, of course, by no means new. Indeed, the story that might be entitled to consideration as the very first *conte philosophique*, the parable of Gyges related in Plato's *Republic*, posits exactly such a technology in order to dramatize the question of whether a man with the ability to commit transgressions with total impunity would be likely to observe conventional moral rules. Although countless folkloristic and fakelorist deployments of cloaks of invisibility and similar devices subsequently used the notion as a narrative lever in entertaining plots, that philosophical question was bound to make a comeback as soon as the issue was addressed with any degree of seriousness, as it was in such moralistic fantasies as James Dalton's three-decker novel *The Invisible Gentleman* (1833) before being recruited to speculative fiction in a consistently prominent fashion, in such stories as Edward Page Mitchell's "The Crystal Man" (1881), C. H. Hinton's "Stella" (1895), H. G. Wells' *The Invisible Man* (1897) and Jack London's "The Shadow and the Flash" (1903).

The Wells novel was very popular in France, and helped to inspire a number of variations on the theme, including Jules Verne's *Le Secret de Wilhelm Storitz* (written 1902 but published 1910; tr. as *The Secret of Wilhelm Storitz*), Paul Besnard's "L'Épouse invisible" (1910), Louis Boussenard's *Monsieur... Rien, adventures extraordinaires d'un homme invisible* (1910), Henri Falk's "Le Maître des trois états" (1917; tr. as "The Master of the Three States" [1]) and *Joe Rollon, l'autre homme invisible* (1919) by "Edmond Cazal" (Jean de La Hire). Champsaur was presumably aware of at least some of these earlier works when he decided to do what most of his predecessors had delicately avoided doing, by suggesting that the first use for such a technology that would spring to the mind of many men would be to exploit its voyeuristic potential. It is unclear whether he was also familiar with Maurice Renard's mild admonition to Wells, "L'Homme qui voulait être invisible" (1923; tr. as "The Man Who Wanted to be Invisible" [2]), which points out that an invisible man would be blind because his

---

[1] Included in the Black Coat Press edition of *The Age of Lead*, ISBN 978-1-935558-42-2.

[2] Included in the Black Coat Press edition of The Doctored Man, ISBN 978-1-935558-18-7.

invisible retinas would be incapable of sensation; Homo-Deus' eyes are visible in isolation when he first appears in his invisible guise, but subsequently appear and disappear at the convenience of the storyline—always a more powerful motivator than logic in fanciful fiction. At any rate, Champsaur's novel was extending an established sequence, but consciously taking it in a new direction in order to transcend mere imitation.

Homo-Deus, le satyre invisible also extends a short sequence within Champsaur's own works in which he dabbled with speculative materials, following in the footsteps of *Les Ailes de l'Homme* (written 1914; published in revised form 1917; tr. as *The Human Arrow*) and hot on the heels of *Ouha, roi des singes* (1923; tr. as *Ouha, King of the Apes*).[3] The first of those two novels, which had the misfortune to be set in a near future whose possibility was torpedoed by the outbreak of the Great War and had then to be expanded in order to serve as a propaganda piece, and was twisted completely out of shape in the process, was relatively orthodox in both its speculative component, which deals with a new kind of ultra-fast aircraft, and its romantic component, in which the course of true love fails tragically to run smooth. *Ouha, roi des singes*, by contrast, is an account of a curious "missing link," resulting from a human/orangutan hybridization, which is intermediate, both temporarily and thematically, between Edgar Rice Burroughs' *Tarzan of the Apes* (1912) and Edgar Wallace's script for the movie *King Kong* (1933), and its "romantic" component is much more striking and uninhibited, featuring several graphic scenes of extraordinary interspecies intercourse.

Although Homo-Deus is far more personable than Ouha, the two do have certain elements in common, which might help to explain the imaginative genesis of the latter book, and which earn both works a special place in the history of speculative sex. The latter topic has precious few examples prior to the general relaxation of the literary standards of prissiness in the 1960s, and most of them are French, but Champsaur's contribution to the tradition was notably distinctive and original, even though the notion of superheroic satyriasis had been previously broached in Alfred Jarry's proto-surrealist speculative fantasy *Le Surmâle* (1902; tr. as *The Supermale*). The kinship between Ouha and Homo-Deus, which embodies assumptions about fundamental human psychology and "bestial instincts," is highly significant in terms of the *conte philosophique* aspect of Champsaur's plot, which seems to want to be taken seriously—although whether it can be is a matter of opinion.

The hypothetical metaphysical basis on which Champsaur constructs his imaginary technology of invisibility, as well as the other pseudoscientific no-

---

[3] The introduction to the Black Coat Press edition of *The Human Arrow* (ISBN 978-1-61227-045-6) contains a synoptic overview of Champsaur's career and literary production, which there is no need to repeat here. The Black Coat Press edition of *Ouha* is ISBN 978-1-61227-115-6.

tions featured in the plot, is a straightforward modification of Cartesian dualism, of a kind that had been used very extensively in both literary fantasy and occult lifestyle fantasy to "explain" various "psychic phenomena." Indeed, Champsaur takes those previous justifications entirely for granted, wanting to take the argument further, not only in terms of imagining an "alternative psychic fluid" conferring invisibility on the flesh, but in hypothesizing an innovative employment of the standard "soul-fluid" in shoring up a technology of resurrection, described and detailed in a fashion as strikingly melodramatic as the various manifestations of the invisible satyr. Some readers might feel that far more could and ought to have been made of that second notion—and probably would have been, if Champsaur had started from that point rather than merely incorporating it into a complicating subplot—and its extrapolation is rather odd, for reasons that are best left for discussion in a brief afterword in order to avoid spoilers.

The other subplot, which eventually expands to fill up more narrative space than either of the two strands introduced in advance of it, now seems far more familiar than it did in 1924, because crime-fighting superheroes, following in the mighty footsteps of the comic book characters Superman and Batman, have become a spectacular archetype of modern literature, amenable to enormous replication, variation and melodramatic inflation—to the extent that it is now very difficult to retreat, imaginatively, to an era when no such archetype existed. It is, however, necessary to do that in order to understand how innovative Homo-Deus was in that nascent role, and hence, perhaps, to understand why the manner in which he fulfilled it now seems so mind-bogglingly *wrong*.

Technically speaking, Homo-Deus was not the first mysterious avenger in French popular fiction to be equipped with a "superpower." Indeed, in the matter of his minor powers of mesmerism and fakirism, he had numerous predecessors, including the downmarket Sâr Dubnotal, whose adventures were chronicled anonymously, some say by Norbert Sévestre, in 1909-10.[4] In terms of more adventurous superpowers, he was not only foreshadowed by previous invisible men who dabbled in vigilantism, but also by the "Nyctalope," a creation of Jean de La Hire who eventually became a series character very much in the mold of American pulp and comic book superheroes. Although variants of the Nyctalope had been featured in two newspaper serials of 1908 and 1911, however, his ultimate incarnation as a serial battler of exotic evil only found its definitive mold in *Lucifer* (1921-22; tr. as *The Nyctalope vs. Lucifer*),[5] not long before the advent of Homo-Deus. Homo-Deus clearly had potential to be developed in the

---

[4] Available in a Black Coat Press edition as *Sâr Dubnotal vs Jack the Ripper*, ISBN 978-1-934543-94-8.
[5] ISBN 978-1-932983-98-2. Other Black Coat Press books featuring the Nyctalope include *The Nyctalope on Mars*, *Enter the Nyctalope*, *The Nyctalope Steps In* and *Night of the Nyctalope*.

same fashion, had Champsaur wanted to do that—and his subsidiary role in *Tuer les vieux, jouir!* is almost a feint in that direction—but Champsaur did not consider himself to be that kind of writer, deeming himself to be cut from finer literary cloth.

Even without such extension, however, Homo-Deus, in his crime-fighting role, represents an interesting precursory phase in what we can now see, retrospectively, as the evolution of superhero fiction. Because his superpower is so much more radical than the Nyctalope's ability to see in the dark, it inevitably engages the fundamental problem that superhero fiction necessarily inherited, at least tacitly, from Plato: to what extent is a person who can act with impunity likely to admit constraint by moral regulation? Again, though, the specific problems raised by Homo-Deus' actions in that regard are best left for consideration until the afterword, in order not to give away the plot of the novel in advance.

Tue les vieux, jouir! is much more focused in its *conte philosophique* aspect than *Homo-Deus, le satyre invisible*, but it too formulates the bulk of its actual plot as a story of crime and punishment, and also features a protagonist whose fundamental psychological impulses have something in common with Ouha the sovereign ape. It is interesting, however, that the vigilante role that ultimately stands up in opposition to his apelike tendencies is not played by Homo-Deus, in spite of his recruitment to the plot by one of the protagonist's henchmen, but by two very different characters. The brief subplot involving Homo-Deus is, however, nakedly speculative, developing another corollary of the version of Cartesian dualism underlying the speculative contents of the first novel, this one of much older provenance and much wider deployment since its first spectacular advertisement in Camille Flammarion's *Lumen* (1872; expanded 1887; tr. as *Lumen*). It is presumably because he was aware of its previous elaborate extrapolation that Champsaur did not feel the need to elaborate the notion in *Tuer les vieux, jouir!*, into which it is introduced primarily to provide an "alternative viewpoint" of the moral quagmire about which the novel complains, loudly and repetitively, and to which the last word can be given, in a literal as well as a metaphorical sense.

Champsaur obviously felt strongly about the "message" that he was trying to drive home in *Tuer les vieux, jouir!*, as he not only has most of his major characters recite it, one after another, but also includes an interlude mid-novel in which he reiterates it in his own voice. That interlude mentions in passing that Champsaur did not actually write his books, in the strictest sense of the word, but dictated them to a copy typist. That was not an uncommon practice at the time, when typing was widely regarded as menial work, and it had, in fact, been fairly common practice for many years before the invention of the typewriter, when even handwriting was often thought to be something with which high-minded (and sometimes clumsy) composers of fiction could safely leave to minions. The habit does have certain typical consequences, however, which are particularly obvious in Champsaur's work.

11

The most significant consequence of dictating a story rather than actually writing it is an oblique corollary of the old Latin proverb *verb volent, scripta manent*. It is a lot easier to forget what you said yesterday, or five minutes ago, than what you wrote yesterday, or five minutes ago, so if you are dictating—and thus composing considerably faster and at a steadier pace than you would normally write—you are more likely to make continuity errors and accidental repetitions, and you are far more likely to lose the underlying thread of a complex plot by following the momentum of immediate improvisation. Many gaffes resulting from continuity errors and unnecessary repetition can, of course, be eliminated when the work is read over and referred back to the amanuensis for correction, but some writers are remarkably lax about that kind of afterthinking, either out of consideration for the extra (paid) work that the copyist will have to do, or for reasons of simple laziness (also known as "having better things to do").

Naturally, most writers addicted to that kind of procedure adapt themselves to it, and get better with practice. Those who are genuinely expert are sufficiently fluent in production for it not to be obvious that they are working that way rather than writing or typing their work themselves. Champsaur, in fact, was normally very good at it, and it required unusual circumstances for such flaws to become as glaringly obvious in his work as they are in the two works under present consideration. In the case of *Tuer les vieux, jouir!*, the excessive manifestation of such flaws is probably due to the pitch of indignation that he felt as he mouthed off, again and again and again, about the fundamental argument of the novel. The fact that *Homo-Deus, le satyre invisible* suffers so much from it, however, has a different and more fundamental cause, which applies to speculative fiction in general, and helps to explain the oddity and unevenness not just of the novel in question but many other speculative novels produced by the same procedure.

Speculative fiction is, by definition, fiction dealing with the abnormal and the unprecedented, and are in direct contrast with fiction that is "mimetic" in the sense that its fictional worlds pretend to be identical to the real one and in which the fictional course of events, however exceptional it might be, is nevertheless "ordinary" in the sense that it is mundanely plausible. Because mimetic fiction deals, at least most of the time, with commonplace situations, those situations have, *ipso facto*, an innate momentum of their own, which the creative writer merely has to steer or modify. Whenever speculative fiction introduces innovations however—especially radical innovations such as invisibility and resurrection—that innate momentum is lost. The improvised situations still have, or ought to have, an innate logic that assists in mapping out their potential development, but the synthesis and extrapolation of that logic is an intellectually challenging business of an entirely different order of magnitude to the steering processes of mimetic fiction.

That challenge is particularly hard to meet if a writer is dictating, and thus attempting to work at the velocity of speech rather than the more modest and variable velocity of handwriting or typing. In those circumstances, the temptation to neglect the speculative aspects of a plot in order to devote the bulk of one's wordage to those aspects possessed of a more comfortably innate momentum—metaphorically speaking, to freewheel rather than pedaling uphill in high gear—is inevitably immense. The challenge is less difficult to deal with if there is only one innovation in hand, and hence a single linear process of extrapolation, but where there is more than one—as there is in *Homo-Deus, le satyre invisible*—the task becomes far harder, and the temptation to shirk it proportionately greater. Composing chapters out of sequence and fitting them together retrospectively like a kind of jigsaw, as appears to have been done with the novel in question, adds a further dimension of potential confusion.

That might be why, having bitten off more than he could chew in *Homo-Deus, le satyre invisible*, Champsaur was reluctant to try anything quite as ambitious again, even though he retained his personal predilection for the exotic in less complicated imaginative novels like *Nora, la guenon devenue femme* (1929) and *La Pharaonne, roman occulte* (1929; tr. as Pharaoh's Wife).[6] Flawed as it is, however—and partly because of its intriguing flaws—*Homo-Deus, le satyre invisible* is a unique and fascinating novel, interesting in the context of the general history of speculative fiction as well as the more specialized contexts of biomedical speculative fiction, superhero fiction and the literary treatments of invisibility and speculative sex.

Tuer les vieux, jouir! is far more marginal in the context of speculative fiction, in spite of the extraterrestrial visitor who lurks in its wings, but it has its own innate interest, which is perhaps renewed nowadays, as every passing year brings about yet another centenary in the awful development of what we now call (alas) World War I. We are a long way now from 1924, but it is not obvious that the phenomenon identified and bewailed by Champsaur is yet a thing of the past, or likely to be any time soon.

These translations were made from the copies of the Ferenczi editions of the two novels reproduced on the Bibliothèque Nationale's *gallica* website. I have corrected some trivial continuity errors but have left most alone and have only added commentary footnotes to the most blatant.

Brian Stableford

---

[6] Black Coat Press, ISBN 978-1-61227-156-9.

THE INVISIBLE SATYR

BOOK ONE: THE MYSTERY OF A SPRING NIGHT

I. A Walking Corpse

Two o'clock in the morning. Over Paris, a splendid moonless night. The overlapping crowns of the leafy chestnut trees in the Avenue Henri-Martin formed a kind of long opaque vault covering the roadway and the bridle path. Thick darkness and an oppressive silence reigned within that tunnel.

At intervals, gas lamps projected their timid gleam, but their wan light did not extend beyond the sidewalk and the railings of the little gardens that border the entire length of the avenue. No nocturnal strollers. At that hour, life has long since gone to sleep in that aristocratic quarter. On evenings of mundane celebration, the windows of small town houses and magnificent edifices are luminous, and an elegant activity surrounds them, but on the night in question, no file of carriages and autos was parked in front of any façade.

A manservant went by, with his arm around the waist of a soubrette, and then a taxi, traveling toward Muette. Then everything fell back into calm and silence.

On the third floor of a large building, a window opened slowly—hesitantly, one might say—and the silhouette of a man leaned out.

Soon, the window closed again.

In gaps in the verdure of the chestnut trees, stars were shining, strangely luminous in a sky like purple ink. Their yellow, green or red scintillation made them resemble thousands of gems hanging from the celestial vault, like precious stones sown into the robe of an enchantress. The nebulous phosphorescence of the Milky Way evoked diaphanous scarves unfurling in the immense expanse, or distant opal islands in a black ocean.

Beneath the splendid enchantment of the moonless sky, the door of the building in which the window had opened a little while before creaked. The same silhouette emerged through the narrow gap, traversed the garden and opened the door to the avenue. The man hesitated, darting anxious, seemingly anguished, glances to the right and the left. After having scrutinized the thick shadows under the spring foliage, he went back into the building. He came out again almost immediately, his shoulders slumped by a large packet, and set off, almost running, beneath the trees of the bridle path, in the direction of the Bois.

His burden must have been very heavy, because the individual had scarcely covered fifty meters when he seemed to totter beneath the load. He stiffened himself nevertheless, leaning against the trunk of a chestnut tree, and when he had recovered his strength, he resumed walking.

Soon, in spite of his physical resistance, it was necessary for him to stop. He breathed out noisily and looked round to see whether anyone had seen him or was following him. After another brief hesitation, he crossed the avenue, walked along the sidewalk of the even-numbered dwellings, and finally collapsed with his singular burden onto a bench placed at the corner of the Rue des Sablons.[7] He mopped his forehead with a handkerchief, because he was sweating copiously, and his haggard eyes explored the surroundings again.

Feverishly, he tried to install the long, heavy parcel—which had a vaguely human form in the gloom—on the bench. After that, he drew away very rapidly, recrossing the avenue. Soon, his silhouette, rather tall and bulky, was lost in the thick darkness of the tunnel of leaves and branches.

In the splendid sky, new luminous dots lit up at intervals: shooting stars passing rapidly through the constellations like rockets.

On the sidewalk of the avenue on the side of the even numbers, two policemen now advanced slowly, chatting. Suddenly, at the corner of the Rue des Sablons, they came to an abrupt halt in front of the bizarre mass lying on the bench.

"Look!" said one. "What can that be?"

"A drunkard," the other replied, placing a hand on the shoulder.

But the human package, poorly equilibrated, fell to the ground and the two policemen uttered an oath. Having leaned over the individual to seize him and bring him to his feet, they suddenly straightened up, their eyes haggard and their legs unsteady; they had perceived that the unknown man was dead.

The tremulous light of a gas lamp fell directly upon the man's pale face: it was livid, the features contracted, and they eyes retained, in the depths of vitreous irises, a kind of tragic reflection of fear.

The adventure disturbed the two policemen considerably. New recruits to the service, allocated to the surveillance of a wealthy and tranquil quarter, they had not yet had occasion to encounter a murder. Contemplating that dead face, retaining the imprint of fear, they were under no illusion about their sinister find. Until then they had scarcely accomplished any other tasks that giving directions to strangers, stopping cyclist driving without lights and picking up drunkards incapable of finding their way home, and this first contact with drama had horrified them.

---

[7] The Rue des Sablons no longer connects with the Avenue Henri-Martin because the name of a section of the latter thoroughfare was changed in 1941 to the Avenue George-Mandel, and it is in that section of the avenue that this scene is set.

"Jules," said one of them, timidly, "we need to figure out what to do."

"Yes, Hector."

They looked at one another, palely, and agreed that they ought to pick up the corpse and carry it to the commissariat. When they tried to lift it up, however, one by the feet and the other by the arms, they found it to be overwhelmingly heavy, and they were trembling so much, that they were unable to advance. Then, abandoning the dead man on the sidewalk, they conferred. Was it not better to leave the "stiff" where they had found it, in order that all the necessary observations could be made on the spot?

Their final decision was that Jules would go to inform the Commissariat while Hector stayed to guard the murdered man.

"Poor fellow! My God, he was young and handsome! Rich? Yes, for he's well-dressed. It's to rob him that he was killed, then!"

He leaned over to look for a wound. No trace of blood. No stains soiling the garments. And the body was still warm! One might have thought that he was only unconscious, if the eyes had not had that poignant expression of terror, betraying a dramatic end.

"Why was he on that bench?" he agent muttered. "It's an important affair; the newspapers will talk about it." Immediately, the policeman saw himself involved in a *cause célèbre*. He would make a sensational deposition; the dailies would doubtless publish photographs of Jules and him.

As he was daydreaming, a luxurious limousine appeared, driven by a chauffeur with a singular face. It was heading toward Passy, smoothly and silently, scarcely revealed by the imperceptible purr of a well-tuned engine. The driver perceived the peace officer watching over the cadaver lying on the sidewalk and, probably interested by the spectacle, stopped his machine. He considered the recumbent human rag. The policeman thought he could hear words exchanged with someone who must be in the back of the vehicle: strange, curt words in a foreign language—but he did not take long to persuade himself that he had been the victim of an illusion, for when he drew nearer, he observed that the car was empty.

The newcomer, however, did not pull away, seemingly having a strange interest in contemplating the cadaver.

"Are you looking at that poor fellow?" said the policeman. "My colleague and I found him dead on that bench." He said that because he felt an irresistible desire to speak, to chase away the emotion he was experiencing. In any case, the automobile was luxurious; there was no doubt that the driver was in the service of very well-off people.

To his great amazement, however, the chauffeur did not reply. Then, the worthy Hector saw that he had an odd, suntanned face, almost black, surrounded by a silk turban, with ascetic features and ears ornamented with golden earrings. He only just had time to jump backwards as the door, abruptly opened, had almost hit him in the face.

But that door had opened of its own accord, since there was no one in the back of the vehicle, and the Hindu chauffeur still had his hands on the steering wheel!

The policeman, vaguely anxious, returned to the cadaver.

Then something extraordinary, miraculous and tragically frightening occurred, which was to remain forever incomprehensible for the unfortunate peace officer.

One might have thought, at that moment, that the darkness beneath the vault of chestnut trees had suddenly become denser. The flickering light of the gas lamp was depressed by a gust of cold air, causing all the surrounding shadows to vacillate. And before the fearful eyes of the policeman, *the dead man moved.*

First, the upper body rose up; the man appeared to be sitting on the ground with his arms dangling, and his head slumped over his breast, slightly tilted to one side, as if asleep. Almost immediately, though, the body stood up with a supreme effort and with the head still hanging down, swinging to the right and left, like that of a marionette.

For a moment, the macabre vision remained upright, prostrate, like a lamentable rag. It took a step; the policeman heard a sigh, and the sinister remains collapsed onto the bench.

Not possible, thought the cop. *I'm dreaming.*

Having rubbed his eyes, however, and ascertained that he was not dreaming, that his sensibility was real and his hearing still keen—for he could hear the purr of the engine, which the driver was allowing to tick over—he had to accept the fearful certainty: the cadaver, doubtless uncomfortable lying on the sidewalk, had thought it as well to go back to sit on the bench.

So, *the corpse was alive?*

A formidable emotion caused the policeman's heart to hammer. Immediately, however, he had a generous thought: to help the unknown man.

Horror! The dead eyes retained their astonishing fixity, in which the reflection of an atrocious terror remained petrified!

So, the dead man really was dead! And since the policeman was not asleep and was not insane, there was some frightful magic at the bottom of this. The cop's hair bristled on his head.

Triumphing over his fear, and exasperated by the ironic smile of the Hindu, who was still at the steering wheel of the automobile, the sentiment of duty exalting his courage to the most dolorous sacrifice, he resolved to have the last word. And since that cadaver had been resuscitated in a macabre farce, he decided at the first move he made to put the handcuffs on him. He took them out of the pocket of his tunic.

The dead man had stood up again. Like a lamentable puppet, limp and devoid of sinews, he was upright on the sidewalk, even more horrible, with his head hanging down and shaking, his long arms flapping against his highs, his chest hollow, his knees sticking out, his legs wobbling and his feet at an angle, like those of a miserable cripple. He resembled those effigies of cloth stuffed with bran that are paraded on the end of poles on carnival day, and which, the day having ended, having been roughly handled, trampled and half emptied of their stuffing, collapse like sad, limp rags or deflated balloons.

But he walked, or, rather, dragged himself along, nodding his head and swinging him arms, as if he were sketching out a *danse macabre*, and, zigzagging all the while, folding up and straightening again. Like a monstrous scarecrow, he headed toward the limousine, plunged inside it—not without bumping his head on the rim of the door—and finally lay down on the cushions.

Then, his faculties suddenly returning to him, the policeman realized that the dead man was about to escape him. The characteristic noise of the engine changing gear left him under no illusion. He leapt toward the automobile and stepped onto the footplate, but just as he was about to stick his head through the window, he saw the horrible, frightened face of the cadaver loom up in front of him. The white and glassy eyes rolled back and stared at him. Then abruptly, the dead man's limp arm was raised, and the policeman received a punch in the face that sent him sprawling in the gutter.

He got up immediately, only to see the mysterious limousine pull away and disappear into the darkness. The head of the dead man was hanging out of the window, and sinister laughter chilled Hector with fear.

For a long time he rubbed his eyes, terribly tortured and anguished. He sat down on the bench where the ambulant corpse had been resting a little while before, because his legs could no longer support him. His head felt weak, and, wondering whether he might not have been living a nightmare, he turned his desperate eyes to the sky, a patch of which he could perceive through the mauve mass of the vault of foliage formed by the trees of the avenue.

Above that mystery, the indifferent heavens, beautifully somber, splendid and velvety, extended their infinite vellum, in which thousands of yellow, red, blue and green dots were scintillating like exceedingly pure gems. Amid their splendor, the Milky Way unfurled its immense sash of suns.

II. A Communication to the A.D.S.

The afternoon that preceded the mysterious spring night on which a cadaver of a murdered young man stood up and took a few tottering steps at about two o'clock in the morning under the foliage of the Avenue Henri-Martin, in front of a frightened peace officer, and then got into an empty automobile whose door opened by itself, which pulled away at speed, driven by a turbaned chauffeur wearing golden earrings, had been as lovely and bright as an April page preceding a tenebrous sultana Scheherazade in a starry robe in a tale from the Thousand-and-One Nights.

At four o'clock, in spite of the delightful temptation of the exceedingly mild and sunlit afternoon, inviting strolls, the most select audience was covering the steps of the amphitheater of the Académie des Sciences. To hear Dr. Jean Fortin, the vast hemicycle was filled with curious listeners, in spite of the beautiful sunshine and blue sky that made the spring magical, taking on the appearance of an elegant social gathering. There were many bright costumes, and feathered or flowery hats on women's heads set winged bouquets, rare plumes and miniature gardens, joyfully, among the morose patches of the somber dress of the men.

At four o'clock, after other communications of lesser interest and the *hors-d'oeuvre* service, Dr. Jean Fortin got up to take the floor. His was a face that caught the attention at the first glance, tanned and clean-shaven, with eyes that were malicious or cruel, according to the thought of the moment: the intelligent and refined face of a pope, evocative of a superior Innocent III, arrogant and authoritarian, which seemed, in the Académie des Sciences, to be presiding over a synod. The scientist's eyes had a hint of mockery in them as they scanned the assembly, and he smiled as he perceived familiar silhouettes here and there on the benches reserved for the public.

Dr. Fortin was the *enfant terrible* of the Académie des Sciences. His reputation, made by extraordinary discoveries, endeavors of a disconcerting audacity, calumnies and jealousies, was primarily popular. Colleagues inclined before his genius, but they were afraid of the man with the ardent temperament, the overabundant heart and the malicious verve. Fortin had a horror of everything official and practical; he admired the illuminati who spent their lives in pursuit of an elevated, ungraspable ideal. He did not hide his love of revolutionaries in art, science and even politics—and that attitude obtained him unusual relationships, by which his friends were alarmed.

Original in his brusque but good manners, disdainful of honors, recompenses—he preferred a rose in his lapel to a rosette—and publicity, but haunted by admirable chimeras, the great public loved him. That sincere admiration of the crowd made a distinguished scientist—which all the members of the Institut are, in a banal way—into a veritably glorious one.

With a remarkable suppleness, Dr. Fortin climbed the steps of the stage and began speaking in a clear voice.

"Messieurs, the subject on which I have to make you a speech today is too vast for me to hope to exhaust the anguishing question once and for all. I want to talk to you about the existence of the soul, a problem so grandiose that it seems at first sight to surpass human thought and intelligence. Thus, the endeavor about which I am going to talk to you is merely a commencement of studies, a set of observations from which we can extract information, but which you must be careful not to envisage yet as a definitive work.

"In any case, what do we know? As soon as we begin to study the manifestations of a healthy spirit—a soul, to put it better—we have the impression of finding ourselves confronted by a fluidic phenomenon, of a force of the magnetic or electrical order.

"Well, in the same way that, for a long time, we have been utilizing magnetism and electricity without knowing their true causes, we have been utilizing the fluidic forces of the soul without knowing anything precise about their origins. They are all, however, formidable forces. They have no weight, no aspect, no color, but, while some, stored in the air and the ground, seem to govern the world, others, more intimate, inhabit our brains and command our actions, our endeavors and our passions.

"And I do not see why, when we have domesticated electricity and enslaved magnetism, we should not become masters of our spirituality.

"That leads us, quite naturally, to research into the duality of our nature, the scientific analysis of that duality. To separate from a corporeal envelope the soul that inhabits it, in order better to treat and study that soul, and perhaps to change its aspirations—is that not a goal worthy of imposing its ideal on a man of science?

"Already, let us not forget, our great hypnotizers—Charcot and Luys,[8] to name only two—have enabled us to witness troubling cases of the exteriorization of the human soul. The experiment is facile, and I have repeated it many times, very often, with my daughter Jeanne, my collaborator, who has become so superior that in certain research, I have almost become her pupil..."

A few members of the audience turned round, trying to discover in the audience the young woman whose work had astonished the scientific world, but Jeanne Fortin was not at the session.

The doctor continued: "Such subjects lose consciousness of their individuality and become, in the hands of the master, an obedient and passive machine. The sense of things is transformed, tastes are modified profoundly, the body is

---

[8] The neurologists Jean-Martin Charcot (1825-1893) and Jules Bernard Luys (1828-1927).

21

insensible to suffering, and can even assume positions contrary to the laws of equilibrium.

"Why?

"Because the soul is absent, and nothing remains in the hands of the operator but an automaton.

"Thus, we are able to manipulate the soul, a subtle fluid, as the electrician manipulates the current from which he draws energy, light and heat; and it is possible—this is the most important point of my communication—to instruct that fluid to quit, for a time, the being that in animates, to animate another corporeal envelope. The subjects do not suffer any harm in so doing, as I shall have the honor of proving by means of a public experiment.

"This fluid is stored in the circumvolutions of our brain, and, like everything within us, is never at rest. You cannot have failed to reflect, Messieurs, about this world that lives within us and for us. Without that molecular activity, which is the fundamental constituent of all bodies, life could not be manifest. We each consider ourselves to be one being, but in reality we are an association of beings, to which are added chemical, mineral, gaseous and, finally, fluidic elements. Nature, after having composed a being whose mechanical movements are regulated by the play of muscles, nerves and bones, has given all that a fluidic motor, and our brain performs the function of a switchboard receiving and distributing sensations. Thus we utilize a few exterior forces: electricity, magnetism, waves, radiation, etc. You know as well as I do how the king of animals makes marvelous use of exterior fluids.

"From there we have, quite naturally, been led to the study of the interior fluids, the fluids of the spirit, of the soul. In the same way that we make use of electricity and magnetism without having been able to analyze them, we shall make use of the animal fluid without being able to define it: a strange fluid, in truth, of which we are both masters and slaves. For it permits use to direct our thought in a waking state, but wanders in the most bizarre fashion in the dream state. Thus, an individual who sleeps for six hours a day spends a quarter of his existence in an extraordinarily fantastic second life. In addition, if the subject is afflicted by morbid anomalies, his fluid loses its personality and obeys a will sufficiently powerful to dominate it; in that case, an inferior fluid is mastered by a superior one.

"Furthermore, that inferior fluid may be deceived, duped and constrained to act contrary to its own judgment and will. That human fluid, Messieurs, as you know, is subject to anomalies that are akin to maladies. The comparative study of various fluids and various means of influencing them has led us to surprising results—among others, to the conclusion that the fluid of normal subjects can be forced to passive obedience by a cultivated fluid having an absolute dominance over the others. From there to the exteriorization of that fluid and its vagabondage in the waking state is only a small step. That step, we have taken, and

I have come to submit to you today the results of experiments of which, I admit to my shame, the demonstration and analysis are not yet possible for us."

At that moment, there was a stir in the audience. Among the colleagues as well as the public, many people were wondering, given Fortin's singular character—whether he might be indulging in an extravagance. That scientist of genius was, in the opinion of some, a trifle harebrained, and quite capable of an eccentricity. However, he had already made so many sensational speeches that this one, on reflection, was no more troubling than the others. And when it was realized that the most renowned member of the Académie des Sciences was about to proceed with a permutation of souls, a slight frisson ran through the flesh of the "lovely ladies."

Smiling—with the expression of a sardonic pope—the doctor continued:

"Don't expect, Messieurs, that I'm going to read you the formidable report that treats this question. Apart from the fact that the revelation of my discovery would not be without danger if I rendered it public, it is too technical and far too long for me to undertake its reading. I have had a paper printed, which I shall propose to the A.D.S."—there was a movement of puzzlement and Fortin, still smiling, explained—"to the Goddess: the Académie des Sciences; but I believe that it is not inappropriate to proceed right away with a proof that will convince the incredulous. Mesdames..."

The members of the Académie des Sciences looked at one another, slightly shocked and anxious. It was the first time that one of their members, on the subject of a communication, had addressed himself directly to the public. Dr. Fortin was decidedly determined not to refuse himself any liberty.

"Mesdames," he continued, "I appeal to your good will. There is, in any case, no danger. Which of you would like to continue to speak in my stead—with my feeble spirit, of course?"

One professor whispered in his neighbor's ear: "He's addressing idlers, like a charlatan or a fairground wrestler in a public square asking for challengers."

Other colleagues opened their eyes wide, testifying to their emotion. They did not know what manifestation of genius or buffoonery they were about to witness. In any case, this was no ordinary session; it was turning into a spectacle, a circus performance.

The ladies looked at one another, a trifle alarmed—but none of them budged.

"Very well," said the scientist. "I shall be obliged to do without your good will."

Addressing himself then to the Marquise de Virmile, he bowed and said: "It will therefore be you, Madame, for you are someone that no one will accuse of being an accomplice. A part of my spirit—of my thought, I could say—is now sliding into your brain. You are already Fortin, and I am retaining of my personality only what is necessary to direct this experiment."

The Marquise, blushing deeply, sketched a gesture of refusal. Suddenly, however, to the amazement of the audience, she stood up, and assumed the decided and slightly Machiavellian expression of Dr. Fortin, while the latter sat down, with an attentive expression.

"That's prodigious!" someone exclaimed.

"She looks just like Fortin!"

"It's sorcery!"

"Shh! The Marquise is speaking!"

Indeed, Madame de Virmile continued Fortin's speech at the point where he had left off:

"The soul moves. A mysterious fluid, it never ceases to exist, without concern for the body that it inhabits and animates. If the body dies, it abandons it and seeks a new envelope. Thus it is with all fluids. An electric current is imprisoned in a long copper wire. A simple contact, a discharge, liberates the fluid from that conductive wire to escape into the air or the earth. In the air, accumulated at the poles of a cloud, it becomes lightning, a thunderbolt, and descends again, in that form or another, captured by a new conductor. Thus, nothing dies; everything evolves, is transformed. Matte returns to what it has been: humus. Living bodies fall to the ground, decompose, and turn to dust, but fecund dust in which new lives germinate."

At that moment, the Marquise stopped short and sat down. Immediately, it was a venerable member of the Académie, the chemist Bernardet, who stood up to continue the lecture. He was seen to be rejuvenated by twenty years, while the Marquise took on the weary air of an old man. Through the mouth of the chemist Bernardet, however, Fortin was still speaking:

"You have been able to judge, Mesdames et Messieurs, the docility of a fluid, of a soul, of which a part has passed successively from the brain of Dr. Fortin into the brain of Madame de Virmile and into that of the illustrious Bernardet. Let us recap: the intelligence of Madame Virmile is resident in Dr. Fortin's brain, and Bernardet's is resident in the Marquise's brain, while I, Fortin, am presently animating the body of my friend Bernardet."

The members of the audience looked at one another anxiously, for they were wondering, nervously, where these demonstrations would stop. The confident attitude of Fortin, however, convinced them that things would easily be restored to order when he decided to do so.

The spectacle of the trio, however, was enough to provoke apprehensions: Dr. Fortin was sitting down and arranging around himself an imaginary dress, while the Marquise picked up a corner of her scarf wearily in order to mop her brow and cranium, thus disturbing the entire expert edifice of a complicated coiffure; Bernardet, meanwhile, was stroking his chin with a gesture habitual to Fortin.

The doctor hastened to conclude by making a new transposition. With his hands placed on the table and his fingers going back and forth like those of an electrician pressing the buttons of a switchboard distributing lights, he seemed thus to be directing, with the gestures of a typist, the entire scene that was fascinating the anxious Académie and amusing the troubled public.

"However," he said, "this does not prove, as yet, that we are on the road to the immortality of the soul. These exteriorizations are too similar to those produced during sleep, in which our souls can lead several existences in a matter of hours. But I am only at the beginning of my research, and I hope that, in the near future, the mystery will have yielded further secrets."

He was obliged to stop: that interchange of intelligences, of souls, was threatening to create misunderstandings of a nature too amusing for the austerity of the location. In fact, while he completed his lecture, the chemist and the Marquise, placed side by side, were looking at one another with astonishment. The Marquise, wanting to make use of her lorgnette, put Bernardet's watch to her eye, while the famous chemist, thinking that he was mopping his forehead, continued to forage in the Marquise's coiffure.

Quickly, the doctor hastened to repair the confusion of intelligences by carrying out the mutation necessary to the harmony of the individuals. Fortin's two victims immediately resumed their ordinary personalities, without having the slightest idea of what had just happened.

As he returned to the stage, Dr. Fortin had something of the air of a conjurer who has just performed his tricks. He was smiling, visibly satisfied with the admiration of the public and the alarm of his colleagues. Like a performer of genius, he looked at the assembly and concluded: "That, Mesdames et Messieurs, is only one small aspect of the formidable problem that is posed to us, of which the sole objective, the only interest for us, is to discover what becomes of our personal fluid, our soul, after death. Does it return, like the matter, to the great All, or does it conserve its personality—which is to say, without all the confusion of human actions, at least the progress acquired scientifically and mentally.

"Now, this is the conclusion of my research, at the point that we have presently, reached, which is only the first step in the mystery. The human spirit passes from life to death as it goes from wakefulness to sleep. Have you tried to specify the absolute moment of that transition? It's impossible. It is, however, repeated every day. Thus, the intellectual fluid escapes life and passes into a new state. What happens to it?

"If it were a substance, even a gas, it would obey the physical laws of the Earth and obey, among others, the law of gravity, and would continue an evolution on the globe. As a fluid, however, it escapes that law and remains, in the universe, at the point where it is at the moment of death—which is to say that the Earth, carried away by its velocity of almost a hundred thousand kilometers an hour, continues in its course through space and that the soul, nor longer obedient, as a fluid to the laws of gravity and attraction, remains at the point in the

Universe where it was at the exact moment of death, of the separation of the fluid soul from the material body.

"Can you imagine the human soul, placed thus, without transition, in the environment of astronomical space? If it is not prepared, by a profound study of sidereal phenomena, for the splendid flight through the worlds, then, mad with terror, it might returns to its cradle and easily find a new incarnation on this globe, recommencing a new terrestrial existence. If, on the contrary, by virtue of the knowledge of great stellar laws, it is on the path of progress, it might disdain our Earth, and go elsewhere in search of new sensations and a gradual spiritual elevation.[9]

"This, Mesdames et Messieurs, is all that we ought to say to you today: that the soul is a fluid, manipulable, thanks to science, like other fluids. That is very little. Let us hope that, among the multitude of scientists occupied with the question, one of the more fortunate will discover the key to the obsessive mystery..."

A thunder of applause underlined those final words, and the doctor descended in the midst of a general ovation. He increasingly resembled a clown who had just astonished a circus, but no one was unaware of the elevated and marvelous thought hidden behind his smile. Rapidly, he shook a few complimentary hands, and went out immediately.

Outside, a group of snobs of both sexes, seduced by his picturesque and legendary status, were waiting to acclaim him. Ordinary people who were passing by, having heard his name pronounced, had also stopped, and they all formed a temporary crowd, bizarre and enthusiastic, typically Parisian.

A tall dark-haired man in a nicely-tailored jacket and a silk hat that was very chic in its design and shine, of aristocratic appearance, with extraordinarily beautiful and fascinating eyes, was in the process of accompanying to her auto a very elegant young woman, Comtesse Simone d'Armez, and a cameraman was in the process of filming their departure for the benefit of Gaumont cinemas.

"*Au revoir*, Madame," said the superb cavalier, who seemed to be continuing and concluding a flirtation—his bold and magical gaze was going straight to its target and penetrating it easily, like an invisible and powerful desire. "Without any need for other words, you can read my profound admiration in my eyes, *a bientôt*, lovely Comtesse. I shall be close to you in spirit—and, in truth, closer than you think and more intimately than you imagine."

But Jean Fortin appeared. Numerous hands were extended toward him. Disengaging himself with difficulty, he was getting ready to climb into a car

---

[9] This notion of the cosmic liberation of the soul was popularized by Camille Flammarion in *Lumen* and several other works of speculative fiction and speculative non-fiction, although the notion had earlier been broached by Louis-Sébastien Mercier in "Nouvelles de la lune" (1768; tr. as "News from the Moon")

when he stopped and shuddered; the tall man with satanic eyes bowed to him. Fortin ran toward him.

"Marc Vanel! You, here! I recognized your ardent eyes immediately!"

Their hands gripped effusively. The gentleman with the demonic eyes explained: "Master, I was among those who were listening to you just now, and am impassioned, as I was before, when I was your pupil..."

"My best pupil! How long ago that was! But where did you spring from? Everyone thought you were dead?"

At that moment, Dr. Fortin perceived that the man with the extraordinary eyes was not alone. A person of modest appearance was standing beside him. Clad in a light suit, with the jacket buttoned up, he was not attracting much attention, seeming somewhat paltry beside the bronzed athlete whose presence was dominating his. Nevertheless, the small man's eyes were shining intensely in a slightly swarthy face, in which one sensed an obscure valor. Dr. Fortin was too observant not to notice that silent, grave and self-effacing individual.

Vanel made the introductions. "Comrade Tchitcherine, commissar attached to the Soviet Ministry of Foreign Affairs, in Paris incognito."

The foreigner bowed. "I salute you humbly, Master."

Dr. Fortin was impressed. "Well, since, in finding one friend, I'm collecting two, you'll do me the pleasure of dining with me! Good, it's agreed—I'll take you away. I know someone who'll be delighted to see you."

"Your daughter. How is Jeanne?"

"Astonishing! Compared with her, I'm nothing, my dear friend—yes, nothing but a weakling."

"I'll be delighted to see her again," said Dr. Vanel, slightly emotional at the memory of the distant past—of his entire youth—that was rising in his heart.

"And you'll also find Garnier. Alexandre Garnier, the professor whose lessons you loved is a highly-respected practitioner today, and makes a great deal of money—he's gone to the bad!—but his son Georges, with whom you once kept company, is collaborating with us...oh, it gives me great pleasure to see you again!"

A splendid limousine had drawn up at the sidewalk. Vanel said a few rapid words to the Hindu chauffeur, whose bronzed face with ascetic features was surrounded by a silk turban, and whose ears were ornamented by gold rings; the latter got out and opened the door. The scientist, followed by his two guests, climbed into the automobile, which drew away and immediately sped in the direction of the Porte de Saint-Cloud.

It carried away three men seemingly similar, and yet very different. One, Fortin, had just been striving, so to speak, to Renanise,[10] physically and quasi-

---

[10] The verb *renaniser* [to Renanise] was derived from the name of philosopher Ernest Renan (1823-1892), most famous for his account of *La Vie de Jésus* (1863; tr. as *The Life of Jesus*), which dismissed all the supernatural and miracu-

materially, the problem of souls. The second, the ardent Russian communist, was synthesizing, very clearly, the vague aspirations of a great human mass, muted and inert: a nation long immobilized in age-old decrepitude, which had proclaimed in Moscow, with Lenin and his comrades in folly, the republic of the wretched. As for the third, Dr. Vanel, more powerful and more Mephisophelean in appearance, with aggressive, mysterious and hallucinating eyes, he had something of the magician and sorcerer about him.

Who was this Marc Vanel? Like the other two, Jean Fortin and Tchitcherine, he had the illuminated brow of those who frequent the temple of eternal truths.

And this book will display that Man-God.

---

lous elements as embellishments; the term was therefore used to describe similar arguments reducing the seemingly-supernatural to the natural.

III. The Red Nest

Dr. Fortin's house was hidden on the heights of Saint-Cloud, in the middle of an immense, exceedingly unkempt property in which the most beautiful plants and the most magnificent trees mingled with monstrous, vivacious brambles like the lianas of a virgin forest.

Once through the entrance—a modest Norman gate sheltered by a thatch roof—one found oneself in a park run wild, where the pathways, never raked, resembled those vague tracks that one follows in the desert, obstructed from time to time by brushwood. In the place where there had once been lawns, doubtless green and well-trimmed, there were now wild grasses, tall nettles, and an entire frantic vegetation of weeds, from which projected, here and there, the strong stem of a beautiful iris.

All along a ruined wall of stones covered in dense shoots, brambles had grown, which climbed proudly toward the sky, clinging to the trunks of nearby trees and the asperities of the enclosure. As if Beauty had wanted to preserve her rights even so, however, the stems of rose bushes climbed up even higher than the brambles; above the wall, dominating the ruins, the mosses, the weeds and the nettles, magnificent roses blossomed, all the prouder and more beautiful for having defeated the stifling brambles. For years pines had strewn the ground with their needles, falling every autumn, making a beautiful soft carpet in which splendid ferns had grown. Sometimes, in a bushy clump, a syringa branch sprang forth, and the heady odor of its flowers mingled with the scent of pines, embalming the vesperal breeze that slid through the foliage of the trees, rustling the leaves.

Dr. Marc Vanel's automobile traversed that nature freely. It passed beneath centenarian branches from which twigs of dead wood fell, skirted a pool of murky water covered with nenuphar lilies, brushed superb arums with immaculate calices as it swerved, and then emerged into a clearing in the midst of which the house stood.

It was dilapidated, as seemingly wild as the park. The walls were decrepit in places, the shutters had lost their paintwork, and in one corner, a piece of broken guttering hung down lamentably from the eaves.

It was bleak and sad, but infinitely delightful, for the ruined house and the abandoned park, the crazed and splendid vegetation like a fragment of virgin forest, a few minutes away from Paris—Paris, whose gray, squat mass was visible here and there through a gap between the branches—all gave the illusion of a distant, chimerical country to which civilization must have come one day, but from which it had withdrawn, perhaps vanquished by the indomitability of dreams.

Above the central block, a belvedere was outlined against the sky like the lantern of a lighthouse; it was a glass cage, octagonal in form, covered with a green-tinted copper dome and ringed by a light gallery to which the doors of two divided panels gave access.

As the automobile stopped in front of the dwelling, where no life seemed to be manifest, an enigmatic being, a household god, appeared at the top of the perron. On the threshold of such a house, he evoked the idea of a phantom, a revenant of yore, a valet of some defunct epoch, for it was impossible to believe that such an edifice was inhabited.

"Frédéric," said Professor Fortin, "there'll be two more people for dinner. Do you have the necessary?"

At that news, the domestic's face did not reflect any astonishment. The house was welcoming, the master prodigal, and it was not rare for people from various worlds to be guests at the "Red Nest."[11] Frédéric merely thought that they did not always come by auto; it was an unusual sight.

"Well," Fortin added, as he got down, "You're used to these unexpected occurrences. Don't look so glum."

Without replying, Frédéric hastened to the door of the limousine, his eyes filled with a sudden joy. "Monsieur Vanel! Oh, how glad I am…!"

"Frédéric! Still the same, you old rascal!"

Marc Vanel held out his hands to the domestic. He seemed slightly emotional.

Dr. Fortin noticed that. "Aha!" he said. "It does something to you, eh, to see the old family again?"

"Yes," Marc replied, in a dull voice. "One deceives oneself; one imagines that one is armored, rendered insensitive, because one has suffered in the midst of anonymous faces, far away, and has voluntarily raised barriers between oneself and the past. One thinks that one has abolished sentiments; one imagines that one has become skeptical and misanthropic, and is glad of that new state of mind, which protects against dolor…and then, one evening, it's sufficient to see an old abandoned park, similar, save for a few weeds, to the old park in which one once dreamed, to stir the heart. It's sufficient to see a tumbledown house in which one once spent laborious hours, to upset the soul. And the bonjour of a worthy servant who remembers you moves you, without meaning to, in the utmost depths of your being…"

"A proof, my dear chap, that you loved us dearly," said Dr. Fortin.

"And that we loved you, too, Monsieur Vanel," added the domestic. "That's why you're moved, on finding the age-old park, the old roof it hides, and your friends."

---

[11] The term "Nid Rouge" (Red Nest) had been used in newspapers before and during the Great War to refer to various locations searched by the police in search of seditious materials, all of them the residences of reputed anarchists.

While Frédéric took possession of Vanel, Tchitcherine, slightly astonished to find himself in the décor of that lost land, turned to Dr. Fortin, smiling.

"I've just come back from America, where I spent, for propaganda purposes, days and nights of feverish activity in the bosom of populous and airless cities, in the sad workers' districts of San Francisco, New York and Chicago—everywhere I could win a few souls to our cause—and it's only today, near Paris, that I can admire a veritable virgin forest."

Marc Vanel interrogated Frédéric while looking at him. The domestic was a curious individual. Physically, he was a sort of mountain giant, dark and stiff, with the sunburned face of a Pyrenean shepherd. There was not a gram of fat on his muscles, as tough and long as ropes. His eyes seemed to be full of a mild and distant nostalgia, in which one divined all the primitive poetry of the Basque country.

The man was sober in all things. He had never committed any excess, and spoke very little. Endowed with the strength of a brown bear, if which he retained the somewhat abrupt manners, perhaps because he had once done battle with them when he lived in the mountains, it was sufficient for him to have the care of this well-isolated house. He was a kind of legendary devoted domestic, a figure from a distant past, an old friend of the family—*domi amicus*—who had his immutable place at its hearth.

"Where's Jeanne, then?" asked Vanel. "I don't see her."

"When she's busy with her inventions, the devil couldn't make her come out. I think that if the house caught fire, she would only save herself when she'd finished her experiments. Oh, she's not like the rest! Georges Garnier knows something about that—here she comes!"

A young woman has just appeared on the perron: a blonde beauty, healthy and harmonious, resplendent with life and intelligence. All of her external appearance, her gestures and her gait, revealed a slightly girlish grace. She advanced toward Marc Vanel, her hand extended.

"*Bonjour*, Marc; I'm very glad to see you again." She addressed her childhood friend, the collaborator in her first endeavors as *tu* without the slightest embarrassment, like a comrade.

Animated by similar sentiments, Vanel explained, in a few words, how he had returned to France in the company of the Muscovite revolutionary. He was silent about what he had done during the years he had spent abroad, but he enthused over his friend, whom he introduced warmly to the young woman.

In a few phrases pronounced in Russian, Jeanne Fortin told Tchitcherine that the cause he was defending found echoes in her. Something of a revolutionary by temperament, and even an anarchist in her ideas, she fully understood the audacity of having brought down the formidable edifice of the Tsars, whose foundation rested on the oppression of so many centuries.

"I admire you," she said, holding out her hand to him. "My good wishes accompany you." She turned to Marc Vanel. "And you? You left one day because nothing in France interested you any longer—neither your contemporaries, nor science, nor your collaborators. You could only have chosen as a friend a man of great worth and an immense ambition for upheaval."

Marc Vanel tried to protest.

"Don't defend yourself. I know your misanthropy, in which there is probably more egotism than you think. Fundamentally, I understand it: our contemporaries aren't amusing, I agree, and only the study of their souls, their vices and even their amours incites me to seek a source of pleasure in the frequenting of human beings—but you were wrong to leave, Marc, for there are…other things."

"Such as what, Jeanne?"

"Science—the search for the great mystery of life and death. Oh, if you knew what excitement we've felt here, sometimes…what incomparable minutes we've lived…"

Vanel smiled strangely. "How do you know, Jeanne, that I haven't lived unforgettable minutes myself?"

She looked at him long and hard, and then said: "Indeed, why would your marvelous intelligence have rested? With you, does one ever know? Perhaps, Marc, you've learned more than we have…"

He made no reply. His gaze fixed upon a sunbeam caressing the leaf of a nenuphar on the glaucous water of the pond; that kiss of light posed like a drop of molten gold on a gigantic emerald.

In the fading daylight, the garden resembled a forest in a distant country, a troubling evocation of a corner of an uncultivated paradise. A pheasant passed through the branches of the tall trees, above the wild grass of ancient lawns; as it had bright plumage, one might have taken it for a bird of paradise, a fabulous creature born of the tropics, virgin lands beyond the sea.

Everyone had now fallen silent, and Marc Vanel contemplated Jeanne as one studies an enigma, for Dr. Fortin's daughter was, in physical terms, an extraordinary and disconcerting masterpiece. At twenty-seven, she was a flower of flesh divinely blooming: beautiful, with abundant short blonde hair, gilded like the sun, cut short at the nape in a tomboyish fashion, red lips, rather tall with a full figure, simple and rhythmic in her gestures. Desire stretched out toward her. Quickly, however—even very quickly—one revised that impression, caused uniquely by the generous splendor of an excessively beautiful body and a face that was too perfect. The eyes had a cold, rather hard gaze, in which nothing amorous was reflected. It was in vain, too, that one would have searched there for the clear radiance of happy thoughts, girlish frivolities and puerile ingenuousness—those subtle and delightful details, the adorable grace of young women, of which Prince Charmings still dream.

She no longer had anything of the slightly perverse seductiveness of the demi-virgin, uneasy, anxious and bold. Nor was there anything in her eyes of what is usually readable in the irises of young women; all that was manifest there was the power of a profound and serious mind, and the flash of a superior intelligence haunted by an elevated ideal. The lips were red, to be sure, but they remained cold. The visage, harmonious and pure, retained, in spite of its physical beauty, the gravity of the laborious study of arduous and indecipherable scientific problems.

And the ensemble of that singular flowering was combined in a being as complicated, magnificent and powerful as the great sphinx of Egypt near the pyramids, but dazzling with youth, gleaming with freshness, and all the immortal beauty of Aphrodite.

Marc Vanel, whose profound, sharp eyes, charged with radium, scanned the perfections of the troubling statue boldly, found there the soul of a committed scientist with unignited senses in the impeccable body of a tennis player or a Greek courtesan. He recalled the last words of the domestic Frédérique and understood now, on contemplating the intelligent visage that seemed to carry the imprint of arid preoccupations, why Venus did not smile on those exceedingly cold lips. And yet, what beautiful flesh for amour! Involuntarily, he imagined the magnificent and supple forms agitated by the emotion of tender sentiments, but the firm and gentle assault of a lover—himself, Vanel. Himself!

A tall blond fellow, the same age as Jeanne, appeared: admirably well built, with pink flesh, whose face revealed a cheerful nature but a slightly complicated soul, all generosity.

"That's Georges Garnier," said Dr. Fortin, in a low voice, to Vanel. "As he doesn't lack intelligence and good will, we took him on to please Alexandre Garnier, an old friend of the family. Georges is, in any case, a pleasant collaborator, who renders us many services."

Marc Vanel shook Georges Garnier's hand effusively, and could not help feeling a certain compassion in catching a dolorous glance directed by the young man at Jeanne Fortin, who was deep in conversation with the revolutionary Tchitcherine. Georges went toward them.

Now Jeanne Fortin and Georges Garnier formed a group whose silhouettes stood out against the green of the trees in a kind of luminous atmosphere gilded by the rays of the declining sun.

Frédéric came to announce that dinner was served.

"What about Garnier?" exclaimed Fortin. "Where's Alexandre?" He turned to Georges. "Hasn't your father arrived? He's always the same—turning up late for dinner and finding reasons to justify himself." Then he turned to the group of friends. "I'll show you the house: the Red Nest."

They went in. On the ground floor there was a kitchen and storerooms containing accessories and chemical products, along with Frédéric's lodgings, a bathroom with the supreme comforts of hydrotherapy, and the foot of a broad staircase leading to the upper floors.

On the first floor there was the dining room, the library, Dr. Fortin's laboratory and a kind of multipurpose room full of complicated accessories of mysterious form.

On the second floor there were bedrooms: the doctor's, his daughter's and three others without assignment, in which friends slept when it was too late to go back to Paris after prolonged meetings or passionate endeavors that were sometimes prolonged until dawn.

Above that was the belvedere.

Going back down to the first floor, Dr. Fortin ushered his friends into the dining room, whose large bay window overlooked the immense park.

"Well," he said, indicating the spectacle of the hectic foliage around them, "don't you think it's more beautiful than the trimmed lawns and symmetrical well-graveled pathways?"

The view was, indeed, splendid. Instead of flowerbeds and neatly ordered shrubs, magnificent irises grew amid the grasses. Beneath the trees there was an astonishing undergrowth in which, among the flowering thorn bushes and nettles, the yellow note of clumps of primroses sounded. Wood violets timidly dotted their bright patches at the feet of oaks, alongside lilies of the valley, and in the high branches, birds' nest entertained a delightful and noisy life. In the abandoned park, returned by humans to nature, it seemed that the furtive beasts of the surrounding area had taken refuge, for rabbits were playing on the edge of a warren and birds of every species, reassured and conscious of being in their own domain, were singing recklessly in the foliage, as if to salute the splendid firework display that the setting sun was creating in the thickets.

"On certain evenings in Java," Marc Vanel said, "isolated in clearings at dusk, when the brush was moving all around me, doubtless traversed by some fleeing animal, and a wing gleamed in the fire of the last sunbeam in the branches of a nearby tree, I thought of you, Jeanne, and this park, and also this family table beside the open window. I regretted, then, being so far away..."

Jeanne Fortin considered Vanel curiously. She had known him as a disillusioned misanthrope in the epoch when he had fled, but now a strange sensibility was manifest in him, after years spent among people of all races. Why? Was it because he had grown a little older? Because he had meditated, far away, on the dangers of the absolute? Or had he known frightful miseries, previously unsuspected, that made him appreciate, this evening, the simple charm of the dwelling and the amity of his hosts?

"Oh," she said, "you must have learned a great deal in the course of your travels. You'll enrich me with your experience and your acquisitions, won't you?"

"The avidity to know everything still grips you, Jeanne?"

"Yes, Marc. Don't worry—I'll get you to talk."

The sun had disappeared now behind the hill. Oblique, violent, almost red rays slid beneath the trees or nested in the clumps of wild plants. A play of day-

34

light fused, like phosphorescence, with the golden dust between the branches of a magnolia, and it seemed that the red rays were fixed in the calices of the superb flowers. A bird suddenly flew through the beams where the golden dust was dancing, its wings so rutilant and sparkling that one might have thought them facets of a diamond.

Already, though, behind the trees, a light gray mist was rising slowly from the Seine, extending like a veil of dreams over the valley through which the river snaked.

At that moment, the electric doorbell announced a visitor.

Georges hurried away. "It's my father. He's not so very late today."

Indeed, shortly afterwards, Dr. Garnier shook everyone's hand cordially.

"Just in time, Papa Garnier," said Jeanne, gaily. "This time, we'd only have left you the bones, because there are too many of us."

"Bah!" replied the doctor. "Frédéric would have found something for me."

"Let's go to table!" said Fortin. "That lecture at the Académie des Science has hollowed out my stomach."

IV. A Marriage Request

Dinner had just finished.

"Messieurs," said Jeanne Fortin, "we have the habit of taking coffee in the belvedere, and as the spring night is beautiful this evening, the location won't lack charm, as you'll see.

Already, Georges Garnier had hastened after her to the little staircase that connected the first floor to the terrace of the house. He was followed by Vanel and Tchitcherine.

Alexandre Garnier held Dr. Fortin back. "Listen," he said. "I have something serious to say to you. We'll join the young people in a little while."

"It must be very grave, what you have to say to me?"

"Yes, my friend, it's important."

"Speak, then, but speak quickly, for, after having said goodnight to Vanel and his friend, I'm going to shut myself away to work."

Alexandre Garnier adopted a contrite expression. "Don't rush me, because I'm slightly emotional, and as I'm afraid that I won't succeed in my request..."

"A request, you say? And you fear failure? Is there something, then, that I can refuse you? You intrigue me, Garnier. Let's go into the library."

When they were installed in the tranquil library, facing one another, Garnier said to Fortin: "My old comrade, our friendship has lasted for thirty years. We knew one another when we were interns at the Charité, and since then, no shadow has ever tarnished the sentiment that unites us."

"Is something going to change that?"

"Not between us, no, but we have to think about our children."

"Our children? But Jeanne and Georges are the best of friends."

"They can't always be friends."

"What do you mean?"

"Oh, don't you see anything? You haven't noticed that my son is in love with your daughter?"

Dr. Fortin rose to his feet in a single movement. "Georges is in love with Jeanne?" he exclaimed. He went to Garnier and took his hands. "My poor friend," he said, "that's a great misfortune. I feel sorry for you, and I feel sorry for Georges."

"Why is it a misfortune? You're refusing us Jeanne's hand?"

Fortin smiled palely. "I have no say in the matter, alas. But Jeanne is perfectly well able to refuse by herself."

"Why? If she doesn't love Georges now, there's no reason why she might not allow herself to be seduced by his qualities in time. And if you help us a little, if you put your paternal authority at our service..."

Grumbling philosophically, Fortin protested: "My paternal authority? Can any authority whatsoever be exercised over such a nature? Oh, one might think that you didn't know Jeanne—but my poor friend, she'll never marry, because she'll never love a man. Jeanne? She has no heart—not, at least, a heart for love…love as other women understand it."

"She's not a monster, though! And she's so beautiful! She's not insensible, either, since she has a great deal of affection for you, and in a temperament where there's room for affection, there's room for love."

"You're mistaken. Jeanne doesn't love me as a father. She has a great deal of amity for me because I'm her collaborator. We've lived the same fevers, the same torments, in pursuing similar chimeras, and we've shivered with the same pleasure in the face of a problem finally resolved. That has created powerful bonds between us, which didn't exist before. Look, I'll amaze you: if I weren't the researcher who has done much for science, if I were an insignificant cretin, as her father, I'd only have her utter indifference."

"Is that possible, Fortin?"

"Yes, old man. She loves us—you, me, Vanel, Georges and, this evening, that extraordinary Russian—because we're elite individuals with whom she can speak a familiar language, but she has no sex. She has an amity for Georges, who helps her in her work, but she'll never perceive that he's a male."

"But don't you think that, by virtue of that constant intimacy…"

"No, I repeat that Jeanne is utterly ignorant, and doubtless always will be, of all the emotions of her gender. We can't do anything about that. She's a woman who has but one ideal: science, and one passion: study. The rest doesn't count."

Alexandre Garnier became exasperated. "But you seem to be rejoicing in a monstrosity, wretch. One might think, damn it, that you're proud of having raised that abnormal, amoral creature."

"I'm not proud of it, but I don't regret it. Of what am I guilty? Having had an elite intelligence at my disposal, I haven't sought to turn it away from the sublime goal that seemed to impassion her as soon as she was at an age to think: the research of the great mystery and the conquest of the Unknown. For what are you reproaching me? For not having made of her a ridiculous doll, a pretty mannequin, painted and prettified, who sings, dances, laughs and chatters like a parrot, like her mother, who caused me so much suffering? For not having dressed her up for the satisfaction of some Monsieur, probably an unknown, who would have debauched, toyed with her and corrupted her? That's doubtless what would have happened, since my daughter has a considerable dowry. Well, no, I preferred to maintain her like a virgin plant, and she's grown up here, in this wild nature, solely at the whim of her instincts—which are pure, I give you my word on that!"

"The plants of the virgin forest couple and reproduce."

"Well then, don't worry—if Jeanne ever feels the need to marry her flesh to a complementary flesh, she won't come to me to ask permission, and she'll accomplish the act very simply and sanely, in the manner of beings who only depend on themselves."

Alexandre Garnier leapt to his feet. "But you're insane! These are callous theories you're putting forward now—you, a member of the Institut! Doubtless for the sake of paradox and to take all hope away from me! Do you think, then, wretch, that it's possible to live differently than other men? You and I are part of a civilized society, whether you like it or not, whose laws and customs we've accepted. Let's leave these absurd ideas and get back to reason. Jeanne is of an age to assume a position in the world. She's rich and beautiful, undoubtedly, but Georges isn't a bad match."

"Let's not talk about interests," Dr. Fortin replied, curtly. "I repeat that Jeanne is entirely her own mistress. If your son can conquer her, which I doubt, she'll give herself to him freely, but I believe that there's no need to discuss, at present, the question of money."

"You're terrible!" exclaimed Garnier. "And you and your daughter make an extraordinary family. Oh, I'm no longer astonished now, by the singular ideas that I've discovered in my son. In truth, I'm wondering whether I don't have the right to address reproaches to you."

"I don't believe so. What harm is there in a new social estate? Have we, then, to be proud of the present one? We see nothing around us but adulteries, divorces and patched-up arrangements. Children have one mother and several fathers. It's a mess of flagrant immortality, and you want me to adhere to it? No—a hundred times no! But shall we leave this painful conversation? There are questions that nothing in the world can cut through. Here, we're in the presence of an irreducible fact: Jeanne isn't marriageable."

"She's not marriageable? Why? I'll tell you why—it's because your frightful egotism has made her into a kind of asexual monster, an astonishing prodigy who's necessary to you to resolve your hard scientific problems. Come on—you're afraid of losing your pupil!"

"My pupil? But, you poor fellow, I'm only a child by comparison with her! Jeanne is my master! Do you understand that? She's not a woman, she's a genius, an incarnation of thought. The most seemingly inaccessible summits where the secrets of nature lie, she will attain, on her own. She'll astonish the world! So, would you care to tell me, what can the petty passions and miseries of our perishable flesh and the sufferings of our vanity matter to her? The amorous sighs of a naïve young man who wants to imprison all that life, that immense life, in a poor kiss?"

Vanquished, Alexandre Garnier was content to murmur: "We don't have the same comprehension of our roles on this earth; me, I'm only an old man, a trifle sensitive, who would like to embrace his grandchildren..."

Fortin put a hand on his shoulder. "There are women appropriate to those needs. My daughter is pursuing another goal. Let her follow her destiny and advise your son to seek elsewhere for an ideal creature who will understand him."

"He'll have to do that—for, with your theories, it would soon be the end of the world, and there'd be no more family and society."

"So much the better!" exclaimed Fortin, rubbing his hands. "If the imbecilic, hypocritical and corrupt old world disappears, another will be born, in a splendid aurora of beauty and truth! In the meantime, in order for the race not to become extinct, I don't want all women to resemble my daughter. Let others make a vow of fecundity, but intellectual virgins are necessary for the races and cities of the future, as the Messiah once was for the great religious swell that stirred the peoples..."

Alexandre Garnier bowed his head. He felt that he was confronted by different, irreducible beings, and he understood that all obstinacy would be vain. He murmured: "I understand, in fact, why you said to me just now that love was a misfortune. But what would be ever sadder would be to see my son infected by the chimeras that your daughter and you defend."

Abruptly, Fortin said: "Take that back."

"Too late—the harm is done."

"What's the conclusion, then?"

Resigned, Alexandre Garnier stood up and said: "Let's go join the others in the belvedere."

"Ten o'clock! Animal, you've made me waste my time!" He opened his hands, with which he threatened Garnier: "I could strangle you!" Then, hugging him to his bosom, he said: "My poor old friend, let me embrace you..."

V. The Center of the Universe

Eleven o'clock in the evening. Dr. Alexandre Garnier, saddened by Fortin's refusal to give Jeanne to his son Georges, had gone back to Paris. As for Georges Garnier, the poor infatuated fellow was preparing anatomical specimens in the laboratory for the moment when the young woman came down.

In the glass cage of the belvedere overlooking the sleeping park, while the surrounding area, the hills and the countryside were melting away into the night and the silence, Jeanne Fortin, Marc Vanel, Tchitcherine and Jean Fortin were talking.

"So," said Jeanne to the Soviet commissar delegated to Foreign Affairs, "you're going back to Russia? And you're confident?"

Tchitcherine's face became animated.

"Yes," he said, "I'm confident. Yes. If our Revolution were to perish, it would have happened a long time ago. Your capitalists constantly throw our long terror and military imperialism at our heads, but they don't want to understand that we were forced to that. Here, in 1793, you had to sustain a terrorist regime for fifteen months, and that might have saved your Revolution temporarily; nevertheless, when repression got the upper hand, you had the Directoire and the Empire and years of wars. Fortified by the examples of history, we want to avoid that reversion, because a reaction in our country would be terrible.

"We're confronted by thirty million people, the majority of whom don't know how to read, with a large number of intellectuals to guide them. In our country there are more than a hundred million peasants, not only illiterate, but almost brutes, curbed by a long atavism of slavery and alcoholism. And how many of us are there at the head of the revolutionary movement? Scarcely a hundred veritable purists, and perhaps a thousand ambitious opportunists behind and around us, who are faithful to us because we give them a meaningful identity. If a reactionary movement powerful enough to buy them and promise them pardon and impunity comes along, they'll go over to the enemy. Do you believe, within those circumstances, we can hold on other than by terror? No, it's impossible.

"As for our military spirit, we're forced to that by several reasons. First of all, it's necessary to enable the workless to live. And if Russia isn't working, whose fault is it? Europe's! In any case, without military force, the immensity of Russia would disaggregate, fragmenting into an infinity of petty governments in which all manner of regimes would find directors, guided principally by their own interests. In sum, we need an unshakable military force to keep in check the capitalist states of Europe interested in the restoration of a State similar to theirs. I'm even leaving out of account the fact that a powerful army is necessary to our propaganda, and against the Russian nation itself, which, being ignorant, only understands, as yet, the reasoning of the greatest strength...

"The muzjik combines with that ignorance the egotism of his natural idleness. The possessor of the land, he only wants to work for his own need. It is thus necessary for us to take back that land, little by little, by roundabout means and only to leave him the tenancy. One day, it will be the Land of All, and it's already no longer the Russias of the Tsar and the Land of a few boyars. It's also necessary that the peasant should nourish the soldier, since the soldier defends his land. Oh, we're not yet at the end of all these complexities. And, as I've told you, there are not many honest men back there."

Tchitcherine said these things very simply, but with illuminated eyes and in a tone in which the immense faith that guided his actions was sensible. His listeners had the impression of being face to face with a prodigious and irresistible force condensed in that simple man, physically insignificant—puny, even—but whose gaze full of flames betrayed a grimly willful soul.

Fortin, his daughter and Dr. Vanel pictured the hundred million various subjects camped, it seemed, in immense areas composed of several countries that were almost ignorant of one another, and whose languages were still dissimilar. And in the belvedere, in the middle of a pure spring night, in that cage of glass, a calm individual of anonymous aspect, clad in a clerk's suit, presaging and advertising a Society of Nations of incalculable range—the Universal Republic—seemed to be holding a considerable fragment of the universe in his gesture...or at least of our Earth, our minuscule world.

"When you're out there in the midst of the storm," said Jeanne, "remember that we're thinking about you."

"But you also, for Dr. Fortin and you," the illuminate exclaimed, "are accomplishing by your science an admirable work of life. What you are doing involves more grandeur than there is in my role as a precursor. Me, I want to destroy and annihilate the past. I want to render life to the dormant, immobile strength of a people that, thus far, has been rendered formidable only by its mass. But this afternoon, sitting at the Académie des Sciences with my friend Vanel, when I saw Dr. Fortin capture, dominate and enslave souls, I understood that I'm only an atom compared with him, and I almost had a desire to weep. To be the master of the soul! Of that mysterious personality that one believes to be one's own, and entirely one's own, into which no one else can intrude! To be the master of the soul, until now an inviolable and inaccessible tabernacle! Dr. Fortin, capable of procuring us that wealth, the most precious of all, is a god!

"As for me, one of the petty agitators of a great slumbering people, what am I by comparison with Dr. Fortin? In the course of that session I knew the anguish of suddenly sensing myself deprived of my personality, of my will. I was suddenly afraid of seeing my brain vanquished, of no longer being anything but a slave in the hands of a superior being."

Dr. Fortin smiled. "Reassure yourself—I'm not as far advanced as you think. Although my speech to the Académie des Sciences impressed you, the problem isn't yet resolved, alas! Certainly, I believe that I know many things concerning the mysterious fluid that is within us. I can succeed in experiments that seem fabulous, but I cannot yet create a soul, nor resuscitate or recover a dead soul in the immortal state. Nevertheless, I feel that I'm on the right track. Soon, perhaps, thanks to Jeanne, I'll succeed in the fortunate experiment, for my daughter has found something more astonishing than my bagatelles..."

"What is that?" said Marc Vanel and Tchitcherine, in unison.

"She has almost succeeded in the miracle of reanimating life in a cadaver."

The Russian opened his eyes wide with alarm, and Vanel looked at the young woman admiringly.

"You've resolved that problem, Jeanne?" asked Marc.

"Theoretically yes, but practically, I'm stopped by stupid material difficulties, and I have to wait..."

"For what?" asked Vanel.

"The opportunity! For I'm at that point; I feel that my observations are correct and my formulae accurate. I've discovered the secret of the formation of cells, deciphered the enigma that permits the reconstitution, phase by phase, of the evolution of life in an inanimate body. Yes, I know all that, I'm sure of not being mistaken, and, having finished with banal and facile laboratory experiments, I find myself halted because it isn't permissible for me to operate on favorable human material. I can procure cadavers in the amphitheater—I've had that authorization for a long time—but I can only work there on specimens that are completely dead...which is to say, when all the organs, tissues and cells are advanced in decay, having become humus, nothing: when it's too late. And it's not in my power to reverse nature to that extent."

"So?" interrogated Vanel.

"So, I'm waiting. One day, perhaps, I'll have the means of operating on a body that is still warm, from which life has only vanished for a very brief time. If I have the opportunity to set to work before the invading army of destructive microbes, I'll answer for the success: the cadaver will become a living creature again. He will walk, he will talk, he will think with his brain, and if that is no longer viable"—she paused momentarily, seemingly thinking about something else—"with one that I shall graft into him...

"Three or four imbeciles, because I'm beautiful, have offered me love, fortune, flowers...flowers! I ask you, Vanel, what could I do with them? Flowers! Like a little girl or a dancer. Why don't they offer me that for which I hope with all my heart: a beautiful adolescent body abruptly scythed down by death? That is the splendid bouquet capable of moving me. Who is the male who will offer me that?"

Marc Vanel looked Jeanne Fortin squarely in the eyes and said, quietly but clearly: "Me."

"You?"

"Don't worry," said Vanel. "However much I might desire to please Jeanne, I wouldn't immolate a victim to bring to her—but I, too, have made my discovery, the power of which will permit me to satisfy her."

"Marc!" Jeanne exclaimed. "I was sure that you, too, had not remained inactive."

"I have only told my secret to my friend Tchitcherine, offering him the support of that force, because he's leaving for Moscow tomorrow."

In a grave voice, the Russian said: "It's a prodigious discovery."

"Really? I'd like to know what it is," said Jeanne.

"Not yet. Any revelation brings a responsibility. Fortin juggles with souls, you reanimate cadavers, and I possess a power whose range is incalculable. Well, frankly, Jeanne, Master, do you believe that it's appropriate to put our discoveries in the public domain?"

Fortin expressed his opinion. "That would be frightful. We don't have the right. The world would be modified; its harmony would become a terrible anarchy; the earth would quickly resemble an immense battlefield, more violent and savage. You're right, Vanel; I shan't reveal my secret; Jeanne won't confide hers to you; and we won't ask you to tell us yours. Only your friend Tchitcherine has told us what he wants: the fundamental transformation, from top to bottom. From the social point of view, of a country that is vaster than Europe in itself, far out there beyond the Urals, straddling Europe and Asia."

The mover of men said: "No, very close and very small: an atom of dust"—he pointed up at the stars—"in the infinity of the heavens."

Gravely, impressed, all four were absorbed in contemplation of the firmament indicated by the Russian's gesture. Through the open windows, in the divided panes of the glass cage of the high belvedere, they perceived the immensity around them, all the way to the horizon fused with the darkness. At the bottom of the hill on which they were situated, a thick curtain of mist indicated the valley, the sinuous course of the tranquil Seine. Further away, there was the somber mass of the Bois de Boulogne, and a kind of fantastic giraffe, with the neck and head like a steeple: the Eiffel Tower. Then, something low, widespread, squat, specked with innumerable blinking eyes and dominated by a luminous white dust, a Milky Way in suspension over a monstrous darkness: Paris! That gigantic accumulation was displayed down below, close by, imprecise in the blackness, like an abyssal chaos. From the symbolic height where the belvedere was profiled, one could only see a form reminiscent of the tentacles of an immense octopus on the seabed, reflecting the glimmer of stars.

No sound came from the City, but the people gazing at the luminous anthill in the plain pictured nevertheless its troubling nocturnal life. They thought about all the things that might be happening in the chaos glimpsed during that moment of silence.

Marc Vanel, the misanthrope, evoked the dramas, the dirty deeds, the hypocrisies, visions of interiors and intimacies delivered from all constraint. He went, in thought, through the streets swarming with society, the amused crowds, where anonymous dolor was indistinguishable. He penetrated into the luxurious houses of aristocratic quarters, and witnessed conventional happiness, the manifestations of vain or improper amours. He perceived, amplified, the gasps and the lusts, the cries of love and hatred, the caressant or deceptive murmurs, the fits of anger, the threats, the tears, the triumphs and the sighs: all the verity, the horror, the joy, the pleasure, the despair, the celebration and the divinity of life.[12]

Marc Vanel also thought, suddenly: *She's very pretty, Comtesse Simone d'Armez, whom I met again this afternoon at the Académie des Science. Oh, how delicately blonde and white she is, like a beautiful fruit of sensuality! What is she doing now? Eleven-thirty. She's still at the Opéra; her husband is gambling at the club, as he does every evening. He'll come home late—very late—and won't pay any heed to her. The imbecile! Am I in love with her? No, but I think about her and I desire her. Am I indifferent to her? Why did hazard place me beside her this afternoon? Why did she seem glad to see me? Why did I find her pretty, and tell her so? Why didn't she say the words to me that dispel all hope? And yet, she's indisputably honest and faithful.... What if I were her lover, tonight?*

A strange, enigmatic smile wanders over Marc Vanel's lips, while his eyes fix upon a light that is shining more brightly than all the rest in the somber and brilliant mass of Paris.

Tchitcherine, for his part, is thinking about the millions of people who are living under the yoke of liberty out there in Russia, and the starry octopus that is extending its tentacles over the plain reminds him of that immense country over which the red wave is breaking.

All four of them contemplate the monster, over which a luminous halo is floating, and, proud of feeling that they are above Paris and its miseries high up in the pure atmosphere, they raise their eyes toward the sky, which has no secrets for them. They recognize, as familiar image, the splendid constellations and the distant planets, where they divine another life. Then, the names of the

---

[12] This passage is strongly reminiscent of an earlier classic of French literature which makes use of invisibility as a literary device: *Les Diable boîteux* (1707; tr. as *The Devil upon Two Sticks*) by Alain René Lesage, in which the amiable limping demon Asmodée [Asmodeus] takes the protagonist on a nocturnal trip to reveal to him the hidden vices of a great city. That, rather than any of the recent stories about technologies of invisibility, might well have been the text that Champsaur had central in his mind while planning his own variation on the theme, and the phonetic similarity of the Latin "Homo-Deus" and "Asmodeus" is probably not coincidental.

star formations they have identified sing within them. Over there is Leo, Regulus, the Great Bear...then Coma Berenices...further away, Cygnus, Lyra, Aquila...and lower down, the quadrilateral of Orion with the Three Kings in the middle, and, in one corner, the scintillating and mysteriously colored dot of the splendid Andromeda.

In spite of everything, they are moved. Down below, there are turpitudes, battles, passions, hatreds, villainies, thefts, prostitutions and crimes. But they, themselves, are in this illuminated belvedere, which one sees from Paris as a star like the others, a point of light scintillating in the sky, lost among the others in the dark blue, dotted with gold, swarming with stars, lost in the myriad of heavenly bodies that pursue their immutable and rhythmic course around them.

Further away...very far away...higher up...much higher...in all directions...everywhere...in infinity...appear and move, in accordance with the eternal laws, thousands and thousands of fiery globes, each traveling with its escort of worlds and satellites following orbits of which they are the center, like our Sun. There are thousands of suns like ours.

Dr. Fortin, his daughter Jeanne, Marc Vanel and his friend are no longer terrestrials but superhumans, and they are experiencing at that moment the sensation that it might not be chance that has brought them together in that spot. They are there by virtue of the obscure power of destiny, which, without the absurdity of a Myth—the Creator—regulates human existences; the force that, outside of any religion, impersonal and unconscious, manifests itself upon them, beneath them, to the North, the South, the East and the West, in the brilliant night, in pursuit of a hectic course of which they know the goal and the mathematical tempo, being the equals of the One who, if he existed, would have ignited the stars and set them in motion, since they understand and can explain the infinite.

The true gods are the great men, Homer, Caesar, Jesus, Attila, Molière, Voltaire, Napoléon, Hugo, Edison, Fortin and Vanel.

Was there, perhaps, at that moment, on one of the inhabited worlds of our solar system or one of the stars scintillating in that spring night, another belvedere in which were gathered four individuals as superior—different, no doubt, but as worthy to represent, with the synthesis of four magnificent brains, the intellectual center of the world, its thought, its consciousness: to depict, so to speak, the eyes and divine face of the Universe?

Soon, the four individuals went downstairs and parted, each one returning to their task, their ideal, their destiny. They would not see Tchitcherine again, and for that reason, Fortin and his daughter made their farewells more profound.

Finally, Jeanne approached Marc Vanel. "You'll come back soon, won't you?"

"Yes, because your work interests me, and I'm avid to know whether you'll succeed..."

"Stay, then; I'll be working tonight."

Vanel appeared to reflect in response to an intimate thought. "I have another rendezvous tonight." Then, as if talking to himself, he added: "Yes, a rendezvous I've arranged with myself."

With those words, he left in the company of Tchitcherine. The luxurious automobile that had brought them was waiting in front of the perron. Vanel climbed into it with his friend, and the limousine, in accordance with an order given to its chauffeur in a bizarre language, sped way toward Paris.

While chatting to the Russian revolutionary, Vanel, if he had a few of the privileges of God or Satan, was thinking, on that ideal spring night, about being only human.

First, Marc Vanel took Tchitcherine back to his hotel. Afterwards, he said to the chauffeur: "Rue de Varenne."

VI. The Invisible Satyr

Half past midnight. Comtesse Simone d'Armez is coming home from the Opéra. How pretty she is this evening, and how troubling! Her theater dress ornaments her with a sumptuousness that gives her charm a more precise and more aristocratic savor. Delicate white fabrics, into which gold puts a joyous note, mold her adorable contours, the fresh flesh of an impeccable and splendid patrician.

In her bedroom, into which she has entered—her bedroom, with its familiar antique furniture, its blue fabrics of a soft, attenuated shade—her pure beauty, a piquant sprig, blooms like a beautiful flower of France. She takes off her evening mantle, a long supple fur that terminates, at the bottom, in fine overlapping fringes, and she appears in the bright radiation of her aristocratic and mutinous youth, in which is mingled a spice of discreet sensuality. Her shoulders are bare and white, delicately designed and attractive; her neckline, slightly audacious, betrays the ideal form of her firm breasts, uplifted by a vague emotion.

For Simone d'Armez is dreaming, and sighing. She sees her beauty in a full-length mirror, capable of troubling an artist; she also sees the smile of caressant and velvety eyes, profound yes in which resides the disquieting mystery of a timid voluptuousness, and she glimpses, in the faithful glass, the adorable arc of her amorous mouth, as red as the mouth of a lover who has bitten recklessly into the heart of her beloved.

Now the large cherry-colored mantle, laid out on the bed, resembles a spray of violet flowers. Alone, having sent away her chambermaid, Simone undresses herself. One by one, the delicate veils fall, the soft and impalpable tissues, precious leaves of a jewel case that slowly opens. And now, here is the splendid jewel of flesh, the warm and sensitive gem, a complex and living jewel, harmonious in its details, its innumerable delicacies discovered in every corner of the rosy, satiny, delightfully emotional skin.

Lovely but forlorn, the Comtesse thinks about the husband who does not know her. Oh, the imbecile! Stupid preoccupations deflect him from a duty that would, for any other man, be a deliciously pagan worship, a paradise of incredible, burning and refined joys.

Where is her husband? At his club, naturally, gambling and losing his income, and hers. Then the Comte d'Armez will go on to the abode of his mistress, a thin and provocative cabaret singer with short-cropped hair and a shaven nape. But she, so delicately lovely this evening in her semi-nudity quivering with desire and fervent aspirations, is all alone, like a flower awaiting a butterfly.

In the bathroom with marbles covered with small thick rugs, where the water sings in the white bath, the choice perfumes mingle with the healthy odor of a young body whose nudity has disappeared, for the moment, into the bath water, resembling a splendid alabaster tinted by the light of dawn.

Suddenly, Simone d'Armez shudders. In the movement that she is sketching in order to step out of the bath, she remains motionless for an instant. It seems to her that a warm draught, like a breath, has the strange warmth of approaching kisses that cause a frisson before one feels the contact of lips; something—nothing—has caressed the back of her neck. Feverishly, she stops and turns round.

Nothing! God, how nervous and sensitive she is! Her imagination is stirring. Did she not believe—only for a second—that her husband might have returned, stealthily, and that he wanted to surprise her in her troubling intimacy? No, nothing. She lifts the curtain of the bedroom: her husband is not hiding there. She was dreaming, then; she was dreaming, because her desires have eventually become exasperated in being unsatisfied.

Now, her body appeased by the caress of the water, she returns to her bedroom and looks at herself again in the full-length mirror before enclouding herself in the delicate short chemise of lacy batiste, the nightdress in which her beauty nests for sleep—for sleep, and nothing more.

"I'm beautiful, though," she murmurs. "And that skeletal bitch of the revues and operettas is taking the pleasure that ought to be reserved for me! If I were beside her, I'd eclipse her, and anyone but my husband would choose me without hesitation. Why does he prefer her to me?"

She falls silent and looks at herself for a long time.

"Oh my God!" she cries, abruptly. She had thrown herself backwards, frightened. There were, in the mirror, *two eyes*, irises shining like emeralds.

Trembling, her expression haggard, she retreats to the bed. Then, modestly, she envelops herself in a peignoir and makes the sign of the cross. And the emerald irises fade away, melting into the pure water of the mirror. Fearfully, the young woman looks around; there is nothing in the room, nothing but scattered vaporous whiteness: her lingerie, scattered like morning mists, and, on the coverlet of the bed, the shade of old ivory, the huge red mantle, like a spray of red flowers, a magical product of the hothouse.

"What's the matter with me this evening?" she sighs. "Am I becoming timorous? It seems to me that an invisible faun is prowling around me...coveting me everywhere...

Then, the Comtesse d'Armez thinks about the afternoon session at the Académie des Sciences. She shivers at the memory of the striking experiment carried out by the illustrious and eccentric Dr. Fortin, and explains her astonishing impressionability.

Women ought not to witness such spectacles, that's all, she concludes. *Our minds take fright in confrontation with phenomena reminiscent of sorcery. And because I've seen souls wandering from one body to another, I'm imagining that a soul has come to spy on me, threatening to violate my brain, and even my...*

She goes to bed very quickly, but as if pursued by a suggestion of caresses, desiring and fearful of something unknown.

My nerves are exacerbated; something non-existent is making me vibrate like a harp string. I'm crazy! And yet, what if those green irises reflected in the mirror were the eyes of a soul?

She blames Fortin, the celebrated scientist, for having put her into such a state that afternoon, in the astonishing session at the Académie des Sciences. Immediately, however, by an association of facts that imposes itself on her memory, she thinks about her neighbor on the bench while Fortin was devoting himself to that prestidigitation of experimental psychology.

What a strange man that Dr. Vanel is! Already, when I was a little girl, when I met him in the Marquise de Virmile's house, he made an impression on me. He had a profound, magnetic gaze that caused a singular disturbance to pass through me. Why did he disappear from Paris like that, for years? People thought he had died a long time ago, and then I meet him again at that session, curiously changed but as handsome as a god! And his gaze is even more pro-found and magnetic! He has satanic eyes, magnificent and adorable!

She utters a long sigh, and, as if she were ashamed of having thought about Marc Vanel, she blushes, and, confused, after having switched off the electricity, hides her head in the hemstitched embroideries of the batiste sheets to try to go to sleep.

However, Comtesse Simon d'Armez does not fall asleep. She spells out all the troubling words that Marc Vanel dared to say to her a few hours ago—to her, so profoundly honest; to her, whom he was seeing for the first time as a woman after having known her as a child. Why did she not have the strength to take offense? She can still see the doctor's smile, that diabolical smile, and his Eyes, full of warm gleams, caressant and willful…the Eyes of a voluptuous tyrant.

Her thought frozen under the mastery of that image, her flesh moist with anxiety, a strange warmth now infiltrates Simone's body.

Gentle and slow caresses travel over her flesh: invisible, expert, insistent caresses of bold fingers, and then, fluttering, returning again and again in light touches, furtive and suddenly skillfully precipitate. Something breathes on her lips, like the ardent exhalation of a faun.

Simone swoons. She is doubtless asleep, she is dreaming, and, a faithful spouse until then, she submits to an ineffable dream, without having the con-sciousness and responsibility of the sensations she is experiencing, nor sufficient will power to be troubled by the emotion that agitates her…until the burning sensation of two avid lips wakes her up entirely.

She sits up, supporting herself, breathlessly, on her elbow, her wide-open eyes gazing into the blackness. Nothing, still nothing—except that it seems to her that she can hear the beating of a heart. Married, what caress, what legiti-mate comfort of tenderness could she expect? Her husband? Perhaps, if the grace of love touched him…

She would certainly have welcomed that: sincere kisses would have stoked up the old ardor and reignited the embers beneath the ashes. But there were a great many ashes, such a mass that, in raking the depths of her being, Simone could no longer find a glimmer.

What hazard, what mysterious dream, had resuscitated joy in her? For Simon d'Armez, however, hazard was named God—a Man-God.

Now, she took a book from a shelf and read:

Poor creature who believes yourself to be alone, seek the invisible companion of your route through the world; invoke his help in the depths of your soul; he will manifest himself in you and in things. First of all, the believer ought not to imagine herself alone: a powerful gaze follows her actions, the gaze of the invisible...

Those words, from a book of devotion, those usually consoling words, evoke the words of that bizarre scientist Marc Vanel. The sarcastic eyes, mocking as well as tender, light up in her mind. She pictures them there, dwelling on her every gesture.

"Stupid!" she says, aloud, to criticize and to reassure herself.

Having a warm sensation beneath her dermis, she goes into the nearby bathroom, hung with bright satinette whose marble tiles appear between the rugs, and the water sings, pouring from the crystal ewer. Fresh perfumes expand, mingling with the heady odor of a splendidly young, blonde-haired body, the pure contours of rosy flesh: alabaster tinted by the dawn. Simone d'Armez is naked again, her tresses loose, a kingdom of living gold over her shoulders.

At the moment, however, when, bending over, her legs flexed, refreshing the nervous secrets of her white and pink flesh, she feels once again, on her shoulder and her neck, a warm breath.

Feverishly, the young woman has turned round. Again, nothing, no one! For the second time, she perhaps hoped that her husband had come in stealthily and, wanting to surprise her pleasantly, had hidden behind the floating door-curtain.

Reassured, while rebuking herself for her childish renewed fear, the Comtesse goes back to bed, extending her lovely body in the conjugal bed, and switches off the electricity…in order that the dream might return.

And, falling back into semi-sleep, abandoning herself to the libertine dream, she no longer attempts to react against the extraordinary pleasure, to which her shuddering body, legs parting, surrenders itself entirely.

She no longer makes a movement and resolves not to think any longer, and yet, someone is stroking her all over, searching gently. Enervated and feverish, she has thrown back the blankets and sheets, and remains there, prostrate, penetrated by a delicious vampiric tongue. Sometimes inanimate, then vibrant with ecstatic terror, she swoons, gripped, finally, adorably, in that conjugal intercourse, unknown to her until now, coaxing, sometimes relenting, and then resuming at the gallop, and fluttering, in a fantasia of interminable lust, which has already caused her to expire of pleasure twice.

Is she dreaming? Is she, on the contrary, living an incredible reality? Once again, she opens her eyes, and only perceives vague whitenesses. Then, quickly, she closes her eyelids again. Immediately, the more rapid stroking becomes vivid, more real, and she utters a long sigh of ineffable contentment.

But the bed yields a soft sound, revealing the presence of a sliding body, and Simone wants to cry out. The strength is lacking; she is caught. A form has suddenly seized her, is pressing upon her, dominating her with its force, in a mysterious and profound contact. Upon her parted lips an Erotic cyclone descends: another mouth, willful and penetrating, takes her mouth prisoner and an incomprehensible enigma glides over her, a double and supreme frisson, in which her last energy is exhausted. At moments, she thinks that she can see, gleaming in the darkness, the satanic eyes glimpsed in the mirror.

Dream? Reality? How can it be determined?

She weakens again under the unknown caresses, and her entire body capsizes in a voluptuous ecstasy, which shakes her spasmodically, and draws puerile squeals from her, gasps in which loving words are mingled, alternately or simultaneously, which declare her pleasure—and also another pleasure. It is the cry of a man upon her mouth, while the supernatural grip makes her vibrant corolla the sheath of a powerful and artful lingam, the spouse of an unknown flesh. In an utterly moist agony, she faints.

For a long time she remains in that state of prostration, which makes her as white as a corpse, a masterpiece of alabaster, Aphrodite lying on a confused bed, her long hair scattered, her visage ecstatic. Then, slowly, she raises her eyelids and smiles at her dream.

Immediately, though, she sits up, haggard. In the quasi-darkness, the strange eyes glimpsed in the mirror are shining: the Eyes of Marc Vanel, the fascinating Eyes of the man that she had nicknamed that afternoon "Dr. Satan."

She straightens up, frightened by the reality of her dream. The memory of demonic minutes imposes itself brutally on her thoughts; she is suddenly conscious of the fact that she was not asleep.

In the dazzle of an abrupt dawn, an intense glare descends from the ceiling; Simone has flicked the light switch. But every detail is in place within the room. The doors and windows are closed, the hangings do not display any bulge of a dissimulated body.

So?

"But no one could have gotten in here," she murmurs. "There's no one here. Dr. Vanel, a god made man, isn't here; it could only have been the thought of him, the memory, and the radium of his unforgettable Eyes."

Simone gets up; momentarily, she contemplates the large bed, reminiscent of a battlefield in which singular ardors have clashed, and she shivers from head to toe. She looks at herself again in the full-length mirror; she is naked, her chemise lying on the floor amid her vaporous lingerie. It seemed to her that her body retains, almost everywhere, the trace of passionate kisses, and her flesh the emotion of a faunesque and profound intercourse, an intimate straddling, an unknown lubricous fantasia. And the evident stains of her sins, in the dream of a spring night, cause her to blush and to weaken.

Quickly, she hastens into the bathroom and the contact of cool water soon restores a little calm to her being.

"What a dream!" she murmurs. "But perhaps it wasn't only a dream, it's necessary for me to confess. I'm as tired, exhausted, bruised and ashamed as if I really had committed an incomparable adultery..."

Anxious, tremulous and fearful, she wanders around the bedroom now, clad in a white Byzantine dalmatic embroidered with gold and ornamented with roses. The examination recommences; for a long time she goes back and forth, troubled and unquiet, examining the furniture, the drapes, sensing a king of presence.

Having lain down again, however, Comtesse Simone d'Armez succumbs to amorous fatigue, and goes to sleep immediately, heavily, still evoking— why?—the intense gaze, the magnificent Eyes, of Dr. Vanel, and the singular apparition of the two emerald pupils, the satanic eyes in the depths of the mirror.

A profound sleep, like that of a baby, her lips closed in a blissful moue, removes her from life, from the remorse of her involuntary and fatal sin, inexplicable and so deliciously real.

Homo-Deus, the Invisible Satyr, had fled, taking insomnia away.

VII. The Eternal Declaration

After the departure of Marc Vanel and his friend, Jeanne Fortin had remained in the high belvedere, contemplating the beautiful sky and the placid landscape. She was thinking about Marc's ambiguous words and his singular attitude. What fantastic surprise did he have in store for her?

Dr. Fortin came in. "Jeanne," he said, "do you know what Père Garnier asked me this evening?"

"Yes—for my hand for his son. What did you reply?"

"That you weren't thinking of quitting your father or your work. Was I wrong not to consult you?"

"Oh, you don't know your daughter if you could suppose that love could disturb me. The two of us have better things to do. Let's say no more about it."

They both fell silent, and remained for several minutes—a long time—in mute contemplation of the splendid spectacle of the magnificent May night.

Between Fortin and his daughter, sentiments existed that bore little similarity to those that parents and children habitually possess for one another. No excessive sentimentality was mingled there, even though sensibility was not absent; the tenderness was a trifle rude, although frank and sincere. Those two individuals, so curious, were essentially comrades, united by a serious and powerful amity, cemented by common endeavors, shared joys and difficulties, by the same desire to penetrate the arcane of a science that gave them new emotions every day.

Jeanne's allures, in any case, were not those of a young woman. Neither in her speech, nor the intonations of her voice, nor her gestures, nor her gaze, was her sex evident. In an adorable envelope, dazzling in its beauty, was the masculine soul of an Apollo, which had a wild passion for the most forbidding toil. She manipulated the most improbable mixtures like an old laboratory scientist, deciphered the text of the densest works, and neatly dissected the flesh and limbs of a human body with the expertise of the most skillful surgeon.

She spoke to assistants and comrades with a verbal rudeness that astonished them, and the liberties of language that men sometimes employed in her presence did not shock her any more than they seduced her. Absolutely indifferent to the game of love and passion, moonlit reveries were time lost to work, and novels—those that she had read before launching herself into scientific research—only left her with the memory of uninteresting futilities. Since she had been a little girl, having only devoted herself to sport and study, she had not even perceived that she had feelings. She relegated the act of love to a natural function, of which she only knew the scientific causes and effects, without any suspicion of its attraction, much less its delirious sensuality.

The fashion in which she had been brought up explained her character to some extent. She had lost her mother at an early age, when she was only six years old, and had retained the somewhat blurred image of an elegant, vaporous and rustling individual, perfumed like a flower, always in a hurry, never in the house, scarcely finding time to give her hasty kisses devoid of real tenderness, two or three times a day.

She was a kind of pretty little bird, light-headed, who did her best to squander Jean Fortin's money, while the scientist, stunned by her chatter, her sparrow-like fluttering and her futilities, locked himself in his study in order not to suffer the spectacle of that charming nullity. He did not detest her, but she exasperated him.

They only had really serious quarrels about money. Dr. Fortin made a great deal of it, but Madame Fortin dressed herself from the Rue de Paix and needed a car of her own to run around between her hairdresser, her shoemaker, her couturiers and her afternoon teas from five to seven, where she found smart individuals of her own species. Then, every time the scientist permitted himself a large expenditure to purchase an item of apparatus or for the construction of the instruments necessary to his research, she screamed and stamped her feet in rage, because it represented clothes, hats, furs of jewels that she would never have. It seemed to her that her husband was stealing a part of her happiness in that fashion, and she wanted him to sacrifice the sums that became dynamos or retorts, instead of changing into sparkling fripperies—and horns.[13]

She had died suddenly of pleurisy following an excursion by car in a light flesh-colored dress, of the kind then in fashion, which were worn without any underwear at all, even in the depths of winter. In losing her, Dr. Forbin had experienced neither bitter grief nor slight joy—he had been indifferent to her for a long time—but he had thought, not without pleasure that he would finally be able to devote considerable sums of money to his studies.

Little Jeanne had thus grown up in an atmosphere of egotism, which slowly numbed in her the treasures of tenderness that she might have concealed. As she enjoyed an unbridled liberty for the development of her intelligence, however, she grew in the fashion of wild plants, in accordance with her instincts.

At twelve years of age, her father perceived, to his amazement, that she existed—and existed in a rather unexpected manner. She rode a bicycle and a horse and climbed trees in the garden—for at that time, Forbin lived in a small town house near the Porte d'Auteuil with a park. She swung, trapeze-fashion, like a boy, and sometimes fought with the urchins of the neighborhood, unembarrassed about going out onto the Boulevard de Montmorency when a comrade of her old age challenged her through the gate.

---

[13] There is an untranslatable pun in this sentence relating *cornues* [retorts] to *cornes* [(cuckold's) horns].

What was more amazing, however, and which troubled her father delightfully, was to learn that she had, since the epoch when a vague instructress had been charged with teaching her to read, read a great number of the science books in his library. To be sure, she had not understood very much of the majority of the works she had deciphered, but she had found enough in her reading to impassion her. When she told her flabbergasted father that her greatest pleasure was to plunge into Haeckel's clear and simple *Histoire de la Création*,[14] the doctor wondered where that bizarre little phenomenon, to which he had previously paid no attention, had come from. Not for a second had he imagined that his scatterbrained wife could have given him an interesting child.

And when he had suddenly recognized the fact that his own somewhat primitive instincts, independent nature and prodigious intelligence had been revealed in his daughter, he experienced an immense joy, in which there was pride—perhaps the first he had ever experienced.

From that day on, he occupied himself with Jeanne. He put a brake on her escapades in the street, her free-and-easy behavior and her perilous gymnastics, and orientated her, without roughness, toward the sciences accessible to her mind. Understanding that it was first necessary to give her an education, he enrolled her in a school whose director, Madame Berton, was a first-rate educator, and took her back when her studies were concluded in order to teach her the great problems that he and his colleagues had been deciphering relentlessly for a long time.

In the interim, he had bought the vast property in Saint-Cloud, because the house in Auteuil was much too small and the owner, in any case, wanted to demolish it in order to build an apartment block on the site.

In the new dwelling, the father and daughter collaborated usefully and joyfully; and the life that they spent deciphering redoubtable enigmas and piercing thick darkness appeared to them to be ideal, for the work maintained in them the continuous appetite for the struggle and the desire for discovery in which they found the most complete and easeful satisfaction. They had learned to love one another, and that tenderness was no less real and profound for being exempt from banality, in conformity with their original hearts and their exceptional souls.

Dr. Fortin was the first to break the silence.

"We have to work to do, you know, Jeanne."

"Yes, Father, but I'd rather stay here for a while, reflecting on my own."

---

[14] *Natürlichte Schöpfungsgeschichte* (1868; tr. as *The History of Creation*) was a popularization of the theory of evolution by the German biologist Ernst Haeckel (1834-1919), which became a controversial best seller in France as well as Germany. French speculative fiction refers more frequently to Haeckel than to Charles Darwin, Darwinian theory being known to most of its writers (in a modified version) via Haeckel's popularization.

He did not insist; when his daughter thought in that fashion, the result of her meditations was always translated into astonishing research or discoveries.

"Well," he said, "I'm going down to the basement. You can join me there when you wish."

And he went.

Soon, however, Georges Garnier came into the belvedere.

The young woman turned round. "There you are, Georges. I have a reproach to address to you. For the sake of an inconsequence, you've brought disturbance into our amity, and into our work—that ideal collaboration whose charm I appreciated. You've sent your father to ask for my hand. You now, however, that I can't, in any circumstances, marry..."

"Jeanne," he stammered, "I didn't ask my father to take that step, the inanity of which I knew in advance. The worthy man decided to do it on his own, knowing that I'm madly in love. Forgive me for that. But why, though, forbid yourself so harshly sentiments in conformity with the eternal law of existence. Love governs humankind."

"Because, my poor Georges, we are beings outside humankind—I am, at least. The law of which you speak is not for the refractory individuals who have voluntarily withdrawn from the banal society in which others move. I belong to science, to my work."

"Never, then?"

"If, one day, nature and life no longer have any secrets for me, perhaps I would look at amour with other eyes, since it would then be the only mystery that I had yet to penetrate—but it's doubtful, my poor boy, that my lifetime will suffice to complete the studies that occupy me, and you wouldn't want to embrace me when I'm old and ugly, would you?"

"Oh, Jeanne, my passion for our intelligence and your beauty can only die with me, and time, I swear to you, will not diminish its sincere ardor. But we would have spoiled our best years, our youth. To love, Jeanne, it's necessary not to wait for the twilight of life. You don't know what felicities you're rejecting and, without suspecting it, what happiness you're scorning..."

She was leaning her elbows on the wrought iron rail that made a circuit of the belvedere, contemplating the tranquil beauty of the night. One might have thought that she was no longer listening to the young man.

After a few minutes, she said: "My dear Georges, I'd like you to understand fully that if I refuse to be your wife, it's not because you displease me. You're young, handsome, healthy and good. But love doesn't tempt me. I don't understand it. While you're pale, emotional, prey to violent emotions that betray the state of your heart, I remain cold, insensitive, distant and astonished. No, Georges, I don't experience anything, anything at all, except for a slight annoyance at causing you distress.

"It's necessary not to hold it against me if I'm like that, and above all, not to accuse me of cruelty. I don't ask whether I'm right or wrong, whether I ought to suffer or rejoice in my physical impassivity; it suits me very well. At the mere idea of marriage, I sense something bizarre in which there is perhaps repulsion, for I see the coupling of creatures, the act of reproduction as a rather unappetizing operation. I therefore have no merit, my poor friend, in promising you never to be anyone else's wife. And, having said that, as these conversations cannot lead to anything, and are time stolen from science, allow us to leave the matter there, so that I can go to work."

She was about to go downstairs when he blocked her way and took her hands.

"No," he said, "stay here and listen to me. It cannot be that a woman as dazzling as you, that a virginal splendor so perfectly made for love, is deaf to the singing voice of spring in fête, in joy, of all the rising sap and all the lusts of everything that crawls, walks, runs, flies, swims and respires in the meadows, the woods, the waters and the sky as all the solicitations of nature are renewed."

Gently, he led her on to the platform, at the very edge of the belvedere. Down below there was the immense park with its vigorous trees covered in leaves, from which did indeed rise up, in the gloom, a kind of intoxication of saps, continuing the work of universal fecundity.

Further away, the sleeping countryside extended, and the dome of the sky, above the spring, resembled an inverted goblet carved in precious stone, with a clear and splendid transparency, the bottom of which was encrusted with diamonds.

Georges indicated the magical panorama with a gesture.

"Look," he said, in a warm, ardent voice. "See how beautiful the night is. Listen—can't you hear the nightingale, out there, in the tall acacias? Can't you see the branches quivering? That joyful song is a concert that the bird of lovers offers to other birds hiding under the leaves. An imperceptible murmur is exhaled from the earth and troubles the night: it's the mysterious toil of saps ascending in the branches, causing the buds to expand and the flowers to bloom. In that marvelous night, everything seems to be asleep but nothing is; everything is loving. Spring exalts the fevers of life, with which generate frissons in animals, plants, insects…everything submissive to the eternal charm of renewal."

Jeanne turned to George, her face impassive. "Forgive me, my friend, but I don't hear the murmurs that you grasp through your excitement; I only see the need to reproduce animals and plants. Beyond that, nothing."

He wrung his hands in despair. "Oh, Jeanne, Jeanne! How can you be as insensible as you are to so much beauty, so much poetry? Don't you understand, in the face of the prodigious example that nature gives us, that there is something monstrous in abstracting oneself from the sublime duty that the smallest beings accomplish in which spring palpitates? Everywhere around us, Jeanne, the accomplishment of acts of love continue life, and we, too, young, handsome, vigorous and healthy, will be alone, like monsters, in remaining cold, uselessly and culpably sterile…"

He stopped, and considered the young woman's astonished face at length. And when she did not reply, he continued: "Scents are rising up to us, Jeanne. They intoxicate me, excite me—and they're the perfumes of saps, the odor of the earth, like a stimulation compounded out of all its effluvia. You don't sense that, Jeanne?"

She looked at him, rather wearily, with pity. "No, Georges, I'm not troubled at all, because I'm a stranger to that genetic folly. I understand you, but I'm doubtless essentially abnormal, for my flesh doesn't quiver at all these manifestations you point out to me, and isn't moved in the slightest by gestures complementary to the perpetuation of species, the observation of which only interests me as a problem. What do you expect, then? We're not speaking the same language. I'm only impassioned before a scientific mystery, a primitive unknown, but you're talking about banal, simple approaches...so simple...as old as animality."

Bitter and despairing, he replied: "Why live if we have to abstract ourselves from the laws of nature, if we have to abolish within us the noblest instincts?"

"In order to work, to pierce the thick darkness of rebirth and death, and to produce, to know, to create animal life—the causes of the acts before which you're ecstasizing—scientifically. Isn't that much finer that carrying them out ourselves, bestially?"

"Always study! Always that avidity to know that persecutes you. Oh, Jeanne, if you could read in me, if you were able, one day, by means of your science, to perceive the devotion, the idolatry, the immense love that there is in my heart, you'd be so astonished that you'd melt..."

She laughed, and said: "Read in you...examine your heart, your amorous brain. That's an offer not to be refused!"

"Oh, Jeanne, why mock? You're mocking, and yet, if you asked me, if you really wanted it, I'd tell you to take this brain, and this heart, since my entire being belongs to you. I love you, so I'm yours. In any case, after your refusal to respond to my love, perhaps it would indeed be better for my wretched body to become laboratory flesh. In sum, I belong to you; dispose of my body, my brain, my entire being, whenever you wish and however you please."

She looked at him coldly and thought: *The fool. He's quite capable of it! Oh!*

So it was true: there were men ready to sacrifice everything, to make an abstraction of their own joys, their dearest ambitions, their human envelope—their life, in sum—to make an imbecile holocaust offered to a beloved woman! It was, then, possible that love, the superior power whose domination she hoped never to suffer, had the power to transform superb males into slaves, generous forces into nothingness?

She shivered and mentally congratulated herself on feeling invulnerable. But as she had accorded the subject too much time, she thought that it was necessary to go to work, and that her father was waiting for her.

"Go to bed, Georges," she said. "You're in no state to aid me this evening."

She pushed him in front of her, down the stairs. And she went without looking, at least in a poetic sense, at the magnificent nocturnal landscape of the banks of the Seine, the magic of the sky, all of nature in heat, under the most scintillating stars, without listening to the end of the song of the nightingale, launching its trills into the trees, without breathing in the intoxicating odor of saps and the fecund earth, and without seeing that two fireflies were chasing one another over the windows of the belvedere, in the caressant breeze.

VIII. The Talking Corpse

Jeanne went down to the basement of the house and went into a large room, entirely white, in which her father was already working: the secret laboratory where Fortin and his daughter studied together in the quiet hours of the night, propitious to meditation. The walls were covered in ceramic tiles and the flagstones gleamed, immaculate and neat. A dazzling light descended from arc-lamps hanging from the ceiling, as white as a reflector. To one side, continuing the laboratory, a large space was reserved for electrical machines. The powerful current furnished by the city served to activate the special apparatus installed by the doctor for the needs of his research.

"Well, Father, "said Jeanne, "are we finally going to get some rest?"

For her, in fact, everything that had happened since dusk had been a social chore. Only now was she about to know the veritable joys, the rare sensations that caused her—so cold ordinarily—to vibrate like a lover in an embrace.

An anatomical body was lying on the marble tale that occupied the middle of the room. The chest was open. She approached it, leaned over the dead organs, and took the man's heart in her hands.

"So," she said, contemplating the bizarre object—hypertrophied, because it was the body of a sick man—"this, if one can believe sentimental verbiage, is the sacred tabernacle in which that incomprehensible sentiment resides. This one belonged to an unfortunate who committed suicide last week over the body of the wife he'd just murdered: a drama of jealousy. It's the heart of a great lover, then, a passionate man?"

She turned it over and back again, and then, having discovered nothing in the bloody viscera but repugnant defects, threw it into a corner, disgustedly.

"To serious things now," she said.

She put on a long white smock and leaned over the cadaver prepared by her father. They were continuing research begun a long time ago with a view to the great discovery that impassioned their lives; for a few days now they had sensed that they were on a profitable track. All the merit for that reverted to the young woman. Thus, she was nervous and excited, for she had glimpsed a little light in the cold darkness of the Unknown, and had been seeking ardently every day and every night.

She wanted, quite simply, to make the dead man live. She had taken pleasure in deciphering the enigma of human existence.

For a long time, the cellular life of living matter had no longer had any secrets from her. She had traced the most mysterious organic functions back to their sources; but what remained to be regulated and put in order was the functional mechanism of animate bodies and, above all, the harmony of actions with the brain: thought.

She had the impression—the certainty, even—that it would be possible to reanimate a corpse. She could make the blood circulate in the arteries again, make the heart beat, activate the nerves and muscles, but the resuscitated individual would only be an automaton, whose slightest actions would, alas, be manifestations of her own will, reflexes of her own brain.

All that she thought as she rummaged in the flesh of the cadaver displayed on the operating table. She had put the encephalum of the individual in contact with electric wires, and she studied the reactions provoked by the current in various instances, but obtained nothing conclusive.

Oh, she thought, *if only, instead of a man dead for four days, I could have a warm body, recently taken like a loaf of bread hot from the oven of life, I sense that I could attain the goal easily…but how can I procure one?*

It was not the first time that she had been preoccupied by that idea. Already, in fact, she had tried to obtain a provision of anatomical flesh other than through the intermediary of the amphitheaters. With the blithely amoral and slightly cynical carelessness of fanatical researchers she had had no compunction about making contact with a shady gang of night prowlers, to whom she had promised five hundred francs for every body found on the public highway. There were more of them than one might think. The popular quarters were often the theater of brawls that ended tragically. There was also the occasional recalcitrant drunkard stabbed to death by an apache on some street corner for his wallet. A prowler, perceiving the cadaver before the police, might easily be able to load it into a fiacre and bring it to her.

That had happened, in fact, three times, but the anatomical specimens were in too poor a state to be useful. They were the bodies of sick people, alcoholics undermined by tuberculosis and venereal disease. The organs were not healthy, and that complicated the research instead of facilitating it. She had promised, then, a thousand francs for a brand new cadaver, of an individual of sound constitution—and that was the cause of an adventure whose memory embarrassed her now, and which had, moreover, nearly attracted the worst annoyances.

One of the apaches in her pay had found no better means to satisfy her and get hold of the large reward than to attempt to murder a boxing champion as he was returning to his domicile in Levallois-Perret one evening. He had only been saved by the sudden arrival of police cyclists, who had captured the bandits. To explain his action, the apache, confident in the intervention of the celebrated Dr. Fortin, had told the police Commissaire the whole story. Naturally, the latter had not believed the unexpected justification but, simply in order to acquit his conscience, he had had the famous scientist interrogated by an agent of the Sûreté. After an energetic denial from Fortin, the case had been closed. The apache was given a few months in prison, but the doctor and his daughter had decided to do without the help of those dangerous collaborators in future.

Which doesn't alter the fact, Jeanne thought, *that if I could get my hands on a recent cadaver, I could attempt a decisive experiment.*

She was standing gravely and meditatively over the man displayed on the table when precipitate footsteps were heard outside the door. Fortin opened it, and found himself facing Frédéric, the domestic—but a Frédéric in great distress, whose face expressed an immense terror.

"What is it?" exclaimed the doctor. "What's the matter with you? And why are you disturbing us at this hour?"

"Oh, Monsieur, Monsieur, someone rang the doorbell of the house a little while ago, at three o'clock in the morning. It's not credible..."

"Well, did you go to see who it was?"

"Yes, Monsieur. I opened the door cautiously, of course, for a visit in the middle of the night didn't suggest anything good to me..."

"And?"

"There was a sort of individual at the top of the steps, bent double, limp, with eyes capsized, like the eyes of a corpse. His arms were dangling alongside his body, his soft legs seemed hardly to be touching the ground, and I thought—forgive me, Monsieur—I thought I saw a dead man come in!"

Fortin and his daughter started. Together, they said: "He came in, you say?"

"Yes. He came down the stairs behind me, bumping into the walls. Ah! There he is..."

A strange apparition was, indeed, framed in the doorway: the dead man of the Avenue Henri-Martin.

Jeanne Fortin and her father were too familiar with cadavers, and also with the secret of life, to believe in hallucinations or ghosts. All the same, that unexpected spectacle impressed them strangely.

The dead man, still similar to a grotesque marionette, with his head hanging down, his arms dangling and his legs unsteady, seemingly dragging his feet, with his body like a deflated waterskin, or a carnival dummy empty of stuffing, was frightful, tragic and menacing...

"What does this joke signify?" said Jeanne, in a harsh voice, advancing toward the tottering cadaver.

Then the dead man stopped, facing her. He ceased to tremble; his swaying arms became still, stiffening against the body, and the nodding head was raised up. The livid face, with terrified eyes, appeared in the harsh light and the young woman, at that moment, acquired the absolute certainty that he really was dead.

Grimly skeptical, but interested nevertheless by the troubling problem, she waited.

And the cadaver, whose lips were exceedingly hollow at the junctures, as if iron fingers were digging in there, displayed clenched teeth, between which words nevertheless emerged dully.

"Didn't you wish, as a splendid bouquet capable of moving you, for the body of a dead young man, still warm? I'm the flowers, Jeanne; I'm the dead man you asked for."

Two eyes, at that moment, shone beside the dead man: two intelligent, opaline irises, but alone, not belonging to any visible human being.

"Ah! Is that you, Marc?" the young woman interrogated. "Is it really you, Vanel?"

The two emerald irises were extinguished; the eyes vanished, and the dead man resumed walking, tottering, the head and arms dangling. When he reached the marble table, he seemed to bend double, and to raise himself up. For a moment, the horrible marionette seemed to float, suspended in midair, and, after two or three grotesque lurches, he fell full length onto the marble table, with a soft dull sound of fresh meat.

IX. The Marvelous Automaton

Alone in the secret laboratory with the white ceramic tiles, Dr. Fortin and his daughter were meditating beside the cadaver. Frédéric, on their order, in spite of his emotion and the strangeness of the event, had gone to bed. In the room violently illuminated by powerful arc-lamps, there were now only two individuals, sincerely troubled by the adventure, but glad of the windfall, and also transfigured by the new problem of which they might perhaps—who could tell?—find the solution that night.

Where did the cadaver come from? It does not matter much to them. A single exchanged glance has reassured them, and they had immediately set to work. It was a surprise. Contrived how? By whom? Marc Vanel? Why bother wondering? For the moment, the windfall was sufficient.

Jeanne is very pale, shivering with hope. Clad in her white smock, beneath which her firm breasts are revealed, with her arms bare to the elbows, also as white as alabaster, and her hair full of gilt reflections under the arc-lamps, she resembles some virgin priestess of an infernal religion on the point of accomplishing a frightful sacrifice.

And yet she is beautiful, with the cold beauty of an antique statue. Her movements have the harmonious suppleness of a sacred dancer, but there is a disquieting and formidable determination in her eyes.

She leans over the body lying on the marble table, the naked body splendid now in its young and vigorous form.

"What a pity!" she says. "He was a handsome fellow. But the luck, for us, is that he isn't yet cold."

She palpates him, examining him attentively. Of what did he die? Avidly, the doctor and his daughter search, exploring the young man's nudity.

Finally, Jeanne exclaims: "What a curious wound! An expert in jiu jitsu has broken the vertebral column at the base of the neck."

The father and daughter look at one another. Then, having reflected, Fortin asks: "What are we going to do? There has obviously been a crime. Merely by the fashion in which he was dressed when he arrived here, it's easy to deduce that strange hands have put his clothes on. Thus, the man was killed while he was in bed. That's curious. In what bed was he lying? The whole problem is there: a drama of love, of adultery, perhaps? It's a sensational affair. What do you think, Jeanne?"

"The same as you've supposed. But I don't suppose you have any intention of alerting the law?"

"Obviously not. Even so, I'm anxious. This young man—to judge by the clothes he was wearing and a detailed examination of his person—is wealthy. His disappearance will make the devil of a row..."

64

But Jeanne had to intention of being separated from a body so miraculously found, propitious for an audacious experiment that she had been waiting for months for an opportunity to carry out.

"A search?" she said. "Come on, Father—how could anyone suspect us? You know the singular fashion in which the cadaver was presented to us."

They looked at one another. The same name was in their minds: Marc Vanel. But how had he done it? Certainly, the dead man's words betrayed his work, since they had made allusion to a desire that Jeanne has expressed that same evening. There was, however, no explanation for that macabre, supernatural, impressive scene.

Responding to her intimate reflections, Jeanne said: "He's strong. We need to attach ourselves to that precious collaborator, Father, at any price. Anyway, let's not hesitate to make use of the gift he's made us. Then again, that doesn't prevent us from occupying ourselves with the poor fellow, whatever happens, and even of seeking to punish those who have murdered him. Are we not administrators of justice ourselves, with formidable forces at our disposal, more powerful than other men possess?

"Besides which, listen: I'm going to try the decisive experiment of which I've dreamed day and night, for which I've prepared everything, studied everything and foreseen everything. I'm going to restore life to this cadaver. If I succeed, he'll be able to strike those who've killed him on his own behalf. If I fail, and I'll soon find out, we can figure out a way of returning his body to his family without compromising ourselves, and we'll be his avengers. It will take the devil himself to prevent us finding out who he is and discovering his murderers."

Dr. Fortin knew from experience that it was not easy to make Jeanne renounce an idea. In any case, he was very curious himself to know what would become of his daughter's attempt. He did not persist. Furthermore, as if she were about to accomplish some fabulous rite, the strange Valkyrie was already preparing bizarre instruments, with surfaces as bright, beautiful and shiny as jewels.

"Quickly, Father!" she said, in a slightly emotional voice. "You have to set up the big battery. In the meantime, I'll finish preparing the culture of artificial blood that we developed together, which has given such marvelous results on various animals."

The scientist disappeared briefly. In the next room the singular hum of machines became audible, and two or three sparks spurted forth abruptly, illuminating the doorway with their blue flames.

While those preparations were going on, Jeanne worked on the cadaver. She had soon laid the unfortunate young man's neck vertebrae bare, for it was necessary, before anything else, to repair the fracture with the aid of a solder whose secret she alone knew. The bones were quickly set back in place.

While she was operating, a large sealed glass jar was warming in an immense waterbath placed on the stove. From time to time she checked a thermometer indicating the temperature of the artificial blood contained in the jar. All this was accomplished with precision, like the phases of a priestly ritual.

Now Dr. Fortin helped his daughter open the subject's chest, because it was necessary to expose the heart in order better to supervise the artificial labor they were about to demand of it.

While operating, Jeanne said: "Presently, the subject is out of any danger, since he's dead. We can, therefore, act without fear, until the moment of resurrection."

Her movements were confident and precise as he went about her difficult work, and her face was calm. Only her gleaming eyes testified to her impatience to get to the end of the attempt and discover the result. Now, aided by her father, she devoted herself to a curious task, introducing into the vena cava the extremities of two glass tubes linked by rubber tubing to two pumps, one aspiring and the other expelling; she thus established a flow that set the blood that had already decomposed in motion again, expelling it from the veins, the heart and all the organs, which would not take long to be poisoned. Soon, she sent the artificial blood into the empty conduits, mixed with sodium chloride, in order to wash the vessels more thoroughly and purify them.

She stopped.

"It's going well," she said. "The body is rid of toxins. One more irrigation with seawater."

When that was finished, she began pumping the artificial blood, suitably warmed, into an artery. Soon, the cadaver warmed up in its turn, while the pumps maintained an incessant artificial circulation.

"Touch the feet," said Jeanne to her father.

"They're warm."

"It's working, it's working. Let's try now to get the heart moving again by stimulating the action of the muscles."

They applied electric shocks supplied by the batteries at the appropriate places. Fortin supervised them while Jeanne put pressure on the heart in a rhythmic fashion. After half an hour of effort, they observed joyfully that the organ of life was beating by itself, normally. When the stimulators were withdrawn, the heart continued beating. Jeanne breathed deeply.

"Now," she said, in a anxious voice, "we need to know whether it will continue when the pumps stop."

"Let's try," said Fortin.

They were nervous, however, and their hands were trembling. Already, the result was miraculous. They wanted to enjoy the success and prolong it, for neither of them dared believe that the result would surpass what they had obtained. So they hesitated before withdrawing the glass tubes from the orifices through which they were infusing the warm blood—but it was necessary to act. While the doctor removed one of the tubes, abruptly, Jeanne applied a fibrin tampon to the lips of the incision. Then, skillfully, she made the necessary suture, and they went on to the other tube.

As she stopped the pump, the young woman could not help feeling a real oppression. Her face was frightfully white, her features drawn and her lips pursed. It seemed that the life was ebbing away from her own being as it reappeared in the inanimate being that she was trying to resuscitate.

"Victory!" proclaimed Fortin. "The heart's still beating. Let's close all this up, quickly!"

"Yes, said Jeanne, breathlessly. "The blood's penetrating everywhere. Life is animating the body. Let's try to maintain it there."

They had soon sewn up the chest. Then, without pausing, they moved on to the lungs. Operating as on a drowning victim, they opened the subject's mouth, pulled his tongue by means of forceps and carried out rhythmic tractions, combined with pressures on the chest and movements of the arms. In her impatience to discover the result, Jeanne did not hesitate to put her mouth over that of the cadaver and blow into it, desperately, the air of her own feverish breath, into which she injected all her will.

And that frightful kiss, at that sublime hour, that virgin kiss given to the corpse of a stranger, was terrible and magnificent. Jeanne Fortin resembled an admirable goddess learning over the inert matter, creating life after the fashion of God. And the father, confronted by that scene, admired his child.

Suddenly, however, Jeanne threw herself backwards. She had just experienced the disturbing sensation that the dead man was returning her kiss,

"Oh, Jeanne!" cried Fortin. "He's alive, he's breathing. Oh, my daughter! You've vanquished death!"

"Not yet," said Jeanne, in a muted voice.

Her face anxious, she remained in dolorous contemplation of her incomplete work. Mute and somber, her face striped by a hard crease, her eyes filled with a frightful desperation, she gazed at the being laid out on the marble table, the warm flesh, like that of other men, in which the blood was circulating beneath the skin: the body in which a heart was beating, the lungs of which were inflating with pure air—and which, however, was not alive.

Fortin understood to—but he was hopeful even so, and was distressed by the sight of Jeanne's face.

"Look," he said. "The chest is rising and falling like that of a living man."

"This one is still dead."

"The heart, the source of life! The heart, Jeanne—listen to how it's beating!"

"Like a machine. The man is still dead."

"But what about the eyes? The eyes, which are looking at you, Jeanne—the eyes, which are blinking in the excessively bright light!"

"Those eyes aren't alive."

"But Jeanne..."

"Oh, shut up, Father. Shut up! I'm too unhappy!"

And for the first time in his life, the old scientist was witness to an extraordinary event, which he had never imagined: he saw his daughter weep.

He leapt forward then, took her in his arms like a child, and rocked her, coddled her and covered her with kisses. Before those first tears he was utterly astonished, and also distressed by his inability to put an end to such sadness, whose cause he knew.

Jeanne was like a little girl who had irredeemably broken a beloved doll—and he, in order to console her, found the words of a father who suffers because his child is suffering. He discovered, at his age, a puerile tenderness that he had not suspected.

Calmed, Jeanne resumed her grim expression. In brief, curt phrases proffered in a dull, anxious voice, she moaned: "We're mad! Yes, mad...poor lunatics. We've had this stupid dream...us, humans...of creating beings similar to us...or, rather, of reviving the dead, which is the same thing. Creating life! Well, father, how crazy are we, eh? We were fabulously proud and stupid to think that we were capable of accomplishing God's work! God—which is to say, the synthesis of the mysteries that surround us...for that's what we wanted to do, isn't it? We, miserable mortals, vain and pretentious beings, wanted to create a man, to be a god. God! Do you hear, Father? God!"

She burst out laughing—strident and tragic laughter—and Fortin looked at his daughter with fearful eyes.

"Jeanne, my daughter!" he cried. "You're going mad!"

She understood his anguish and reassured him.

"Calm down, Father. We've only had one folly: that of supposing ourselves capable of doing divine work. At this moment, however, I am, unfortunately, too lucid, for I can see and understand the inanity of our research, of our experiments, even of our science, and everything. Yes, the inanity of everything, since it can't lead to anything. What have we done? We've taken a cadaver, we've given it new blood, after having repaired it, removing the cause determining death. We've succeeded in making its heart beat, making its lungs function, and its limbs—all its organs, in sum—and we've arrived at this lamentable result: we've fabricated a machine! Yes, a machine: a machine that can walk, of course, but which only walks when it's made to walk. People have been making machines for thousands of years, Father, more or less."

The scientist protested, reluctantly: "With inert matter, yes—with wood and metals, I'll grant—but no one, before you, has ever made one with dead flesh."

"What does it matter? What good does it do us to have half-resuscitated a cadaver? It exists, that's certain. If we make it eat by stuffing it with food, it will continue to exist. So long as we carry out the necessary actions in its stead, the natural functions of its body will be accomplished. It's even probable that I'll succeed in making it speak—but it will only say the words that I think, for it has no thought of its own."

"However, Jeanne, if the brain is healthy, if it functions, why shouldn't the man live again, veritably and completely, since the brain creates thought, will, movement…since the entire body obeys it?"

"Why, Father? You haven't understood, then? I've given the man blood again, I've reanimated his breath, I've repaired, if you wish, the fracture that could have annihilated the brain, but I haven't been able to give him what it isn't in my power to create…"

"What's that?"

"A soul."

The old scientist started. "The soul," he muttered. "The mysterious, impalpable fluid of unknown origin, of which the brain is merely the mechanical interpretation? And to think that I made a sensational speech to the Académie yesterday on that subject. What irony! We've been stopped by the deceptive enigma, and we know nothing about it…nothing, except the little society game that I permitted myself that afternoon."

Grimly, implacable logical, Jeanne Fortin continued: "The priests are right; we're double beings, composed of a mortal envelope and a mysterious, impalpable spiritual fluid. Look at that man. What a proof he is of that affirmation! The brain commands, that's understood, and the brain obeys thought, which creates movement, action; the brain is only the switchboard, the recorder, the book of memory. But don't forget, Father, that the brain is an organ itself. Thus, as an organ, it receives life from a force we don't know—the soul, if we give it that name. And if we don't accept that thesis, we fall back into the heart of mystery, of chaos.

"Why are we beings accomplishing logical, coordinated action? Because we have a spirit that decides and regulates actions. Why does our bran command one action rather than another? Because our soul orders it to do so. And that's why I'm despairing. This dead man is no longer dead. The organs of life are functioning, including the brain—but he'll only live again if I give him a soul. Now, Father, I ask you—where am I going to get a soul?

"And if it were possible; if one could miraculously procure the soul of some individual in order to give it to him, what purpose would it serve, since the other body, deprived of its spirituality, would no longer be good for anything? Oh, I feel discouraged, weary, in the face of that impenetrable mystery, this void…"

Having said that, she sat down, and put her head in her hands. For a long time she remained like that, in a meditative attitude, and her father did not dare trouble her reflection.

Suddenly, she stood up, uttering an exclamation: "That's it! That's it, Father! Eureka! Come with me—we're going to wake Georges."

Fortin did not understand. A secret anguish caused him to stiffen, to hesitate instinctively, without knowing why. But the terrible young woman pushed him in front of her. So, leaving the living corpse lying on the marble table, where it remained immobile, its visage cold, its eyes not reflecting any thought, they went out of the laboratory.

X. Of What a Young Woman Dreams

Georges Garnier was sleeping peacefully. Jeanne and her father came into his room, and contemplated him for a moment before waking him.

He loves me! thought the young woman. *Poor fellow! But is his love as great, as absolute as he claimed a little while ago, when he made me such brilliant confessions? We shall see...*

She touched him on the shoulder and called "Georges! Georges! Come on, Georges!"

He opened his eyes, closed them again, and then opened them wider, amazed to see her there beside his bed.

"What is it?" he asked, anxiously sitting up.

"I need you, Georges, for a great sacrifice. Are you awake? Do you understand me?"

He considered her. "Yes," he said, "I'm awake. What is it?"

She placed her hands on his shoulders, looked into his eyes, and, putting all her soul into a gaze that made the young man shudder, she said, in a breathless voice: "At this moment, Georges, downstairs, I'm interrupted in a decisive experiment for lack of an element that you alone can give me. Listen: a little while ago, the cadaver of a man arrived, still warm—young and healthy, the windfall, in sum, for which I've been waiting for such a long time, and of which I was beginning to despair. You know what a proof I can attempt with that, how sure I am of the result..."

"Yes, Jeanne, you'll succeed. So?"

"Well, I've begun the proof. The cadaver has been reanimated, new blood is circulating in its veins, the heart is beating, the lungs functioning..."

Georges Garnier looked up at the young woman ecstatically.

"Oh, Jeanne! You've succeeded?"

"Yes, but it's a paltry result. The man thus resuscitated is only a marvelous automaton, incapable of doing anything by himself, unable to make the slightest reflective gesture, because he doesn't have, and can't have thought. The soul has fled the corporeal envelope at the moment of death, and the body that I've reawakened is nothing more than a bazaar puppet."

"Well?"

"Well, Georges, I need a soul, you see! I know that my father, solely by an effort of his will, can cause that of any living human to pass into the body of the unknown man, but that's not a solution. The unknown would no longer be himself; he would think and act as the person whose spirit he has, temporarily, under the cerebral domination of my father, and the other, during that proof, would be fixed in the immutable attitude of a cadaver."

His throat tight, Georges Garnier asked: "What are you getting at, Jeanne?"

"This. You're familiar with my discoveries relating to the life of organic cells. I take a living cell, I place it in a favorable medium, I treat it by means of electrical procedures, and it soon duplicates itself rapidly, multiplying until it forms a complete organ, similar in all respects to the organ from which I took it. By that means I've made skin, hearts, livers, lungs and brains. I'll go even further—and this is where it's necessary for you to give me your serious attention.

"Down there, I have a healthy human body, absolutely complete. The encephalum has no lesions, but the subject isn't thinking, isn't acting, because the spirit no longer inhabits the body, and doesn't imprint its will on each of the 'centers' of the brain whose reflexes constitute life, strictly speaking. What is necessary to restore life to that dead brain? An impulsion coming from a living brain, from which the spirit has never been separated."

At that moment, Dr. Fortin emerged from his mute role and came forward. "Jeanne," he said, gravely, "I don't suppose you've woken Georges up to ask him to offer you his brain?"

"Yes."

"Wretch...are you mad? And you, Georges—are you naïve enough to continue to listen to her?"

But she exclaimed, in a harsh voice: "Enough! Let me finish. Suppose that I take a part of the brain of a living individual—which is to say, the precious material, still inhabited by the fluid of the spirit, and I take away in that living parcel a part of that spirit. By my care, the centers that I've removed from the man, which will not have ceased to live, will take the place of the corresponding centers of the resuscitated man, and thus I will have brought life, along with the spiritual fluid, into what was only an automaton."

"But your automaton would think like the individual who furnished you with the living substance," said Fortin.

"No, I wouldn't touch the centers of thought, intelligence and memory. I would only take the motor centers from Georges. That would suffice to animate my subject."

"Well, he'd walk, that's all."

"He'd live! Because, thanks to my electrical method, the fluid of the motor centers would expand through the brain, and soon, every circumvolution would be impregnated by it. The centers of memory, thought and intelligence, merely asleep, would wake up again, but they wouldn't lose the benefits of sensations and images recorded during the first phase of life. Friends, the man revived in that fashion would be as he was before his death."

Dr. Fortin shook his head. "After all, what you say there is possible—but what would become of Georges in the meantime?"

"Deprived of motor centers, he'd scarcely be valiant, poor fellow, and perhaps, for long days, the other circumvolutions, affected, would be insensible—but thanks to the discovery of the reproduction of cells, I'll quickly repair the damage. It will only be a passing moment."

"Some moment. Well, Georges, that's what's being proposed to you. You heard. In your place, I'd refuse. In any case, I refuse to associate myself with such an experiment."

The young man was pale, but a grim resolution was legible in his eyes.

"It would give you pleasure, Jeanne? Well, dispose of me as you wish. I love you, and I've told you a hundred times, my life belongs to you. Take it."

She was touched by the simplicity of tone accompanying such a generous, sublime and foolish offer.

Fortin, for his part, could not help saying: "That's heroism!"—but he added, in a lower voice: "Unless it's simply suicide... Well, my children, you're counting without me: I won't let you do it."

Georges Garnier had stood up, though. He put on a long dressing gown, and said to Jeanne Fortin: "I'm my own master. You've expressed a desire that only I can satisfy. I love you, Jeanne, and I give you my life." He added, with an ineffable smile: "No, because, personally, I have confidence. I know that you'll succeed."

Those simple words touched the young woman more than all the beautiful amorous phrases. She flung her arms around Georges' neck. "Kiss me," she said. "I've never regretted so much not being like others, in order to give myself to you—for you're my hero, Georges, and I adore you."

He went pale, hearing that confession. Mastering himself, however, he replied calmly and gravely: "I'm ready. Do with me what you will."

Then the three strange individuals went downstairs. Jeanne marched ahead, Fortin brought up the rear, and Georges Garnier, between the father and the daughter, naked beneath the long white dressing gown—almost a shroud—resembled a victim being led by executioners to the sacrificial altar, to be immolated to the gods: to the god of Love, the cruelest of them all.

XI. Death Vanquished

Before Georges, stretched out on the marble, asleep, the young woman thought: *He's mine, completely and irredeemably. I was unjust to Love, since that's what has given me Georges' life—which is to say, the means of attempting the impossible, the unprecedented experiment that will make me akin to a creative genius!*

She leaned over the splendid naked body. *But doubtless I'll return to you what you've offered me with so much heroism. Am I mistaken? Why would the soul perish? The spirit is a fluid contained within our individual. It can be liberated, as my father's experiments prove. So, I can take yours, or only the quantity necessary to my experiment, for I'm in the presence of two bodies and only one soul. I need to remake a soul!*

Remake a soul! Jeanne shivered, slightly frightened by the audacity of her own conceptions. She approached the resuscitated individual, whose cranial cavity she had opened.

"There," she said, "is the center of memory. In that container, the images of the past are permanently inscribed. If I restore the spiritual fluid to that lifeless compartment, the man will remember; he won't cease to be himself in spite of the foreign origin of the fluid that has reanimated him. It will be the same for all the containers, the various centers of the encephalum. But how long will the evolution take? How many days will be necessary for the mysterious fluid to reach every center and resuscitate it?"

She was tremulous with hope, slightly nervous and also anguished, for, in spite of her great confidence, she could not know, fundamentally, whether the experiment would succeed.

Dr. Fortin was staring at her strangely. "You're hesitating, Jeanne, reflecting—so you're in doubt. It's necessary not to be in doubt, Jeanne. Before trying such a formidable thing, one must be absolutely certain of the result. Listen: there's still time. Renounce this folly, let's wake Georges up..."

"No," she said, duly. "The die is cast; destiny will decide. Help me."

Immediately, she set to work opening Georges' cranial cavity. When the brain was laid bare, the young woman said to her father: "It's time to put the mass of the encephalum in contact with the wires transmitting the electricity, because it's necessary to avoid the parts in contact being isolated, even for a second, from the rest of the brain. The vitality of the fluid must remain entire, and we can only sustain it by maintaining a permanent contact between Georges' brain and the dead man's."

The doctor, understanding Jeanne's intentions marvelously, started up the battery, fitted the wires to Georges' cerebellum, others to the cerebellum of the dead man and others to the motors of movement that the young woman was preparing to remove.

"Perfect," she said. "Now we can go ahead. No break in continuity is possible. The individual's brain will receive Georges' fluid; it's just a matter of acting swiftly."

Rapidly, she connected Georges' centers of movement with those of the automaton. Then she seeded the brain of her admirer, making use of her cell culture, and when the operation was complete she replaced the two sections of skull.

"Now, the electricity will do the rest, with time…but we'll be able to see the first result right way."

"And what if the experiment has failed, Jeanne? Have you thought about that?"

"Yes, Father, I've thought about it. If Georges dies, and if this one isn't completely resuscitated, nothing will any longer attach me to this world. I shall disappear."

"Me, too, then," he said, with an intent expression.

They looked at one another, and then threw themselves into one another's arms. Their embrace was prolonged.

Jeanne finally broke away. "The time has come, Father," she murmured. "The connection in the stranger's brain is sealed. We're going to attempt the final experiment."

In the entirely white laboratory, the spectacle at that solemn moment became tragic and emotional. The doctor and his daughter were no longer speaking, but in the silence of the room, the sound of the machines became more emphatic, making it reminiscent of some diabolical workshop where atrocious tasks were being carried out.

Outside, daylight was coming. A white, opaline dawn was spreading over nature, slipping into the basement through the high-set barred windows. The arc-lamps became paler, their light seeming diffuse and weak, for the whiteness of the invasive dawn rendered the artificial light unnecessary.

In a milky halo, Jeanne's face stood out very palely, with immense eyes: avid eyes fixed on the two supine men, on the lookout for the expected movement indicating life. The machines were still turning with a lugubrious, oppressive noise.

Activate the current, Father," said Jeanne, in a strangled voice.

A crackle followed the doctor's gesture, and blue flashes, in a magnificent sudden flamboyance like those of a stormy sky, filled the laboratory, mingling with the soft whiteness of the nascent dawn.

"Look out!" said Jeanne, "A little more…that's enough!"

"Anything abnormal?"

"No."

"The heart?"

"Beating regularly. The body temperature is constant."

A long silence followed these words.

Then, a sudden cry: "Father! Oh, Father! Look at his eyes!"

"Jeanne!"

"And his lips are moving, the skin's quivering, the fingers clenching…the centers of movement are accomplishing their natural function. Victory! The man is resuscitated; he's no longer, now, a vulgar automaton. This time, death is vanquished!"

It was true. Dr. Fortin, leaning over the body of the unknown man, watched the slow, progressive return of life. The eyeballs were now moving in their orbits. The mouth opened and closed without any words emerging. The legs and arms moved of their own accord, giving the impression that it was not a matter of simple nervous reflexes, but of the true, real movements of a living creature.

Finally, the subject's right hand was lifted to the nape of the neck. Together, the doctor and Jeanne seized the arm and returned it to its position alongside the body.

Jeanne explained: "He felt the pain resulting from the injury to the vertebral column. It's the reawakening of sensibility, and as he's able to move, his first impulse is to touch the part of his body that hurts. Perhaps the awakening of the other senses will proceed more rapidly than I dared to hope. Who can tell whether he might not already be able to hear us, to understand us?"

She tried to question him: "Who are you?" she asked.

There was no answer.

"No," she continued, he doesn't have any other faculties, for the moment, than that of movement. However, as his actions, unguided by any intelligence, might be disastrous for his dressings we'd better tie him down. When life has returned to all the containers in his brain, we'll liberate him."

"And Georges?" asked the doctor.

"We'll wake him up."

A short while later, the laboratory presented a singular appearance. The resuscitated dead man, lying on a bed set up in a corner, with his arms and legs bound, resembled an unfortunate victim of dementia, a creature devoid of thought, but incapable of any extravagant action. Georges, the bewildered lover, sitting in a chair set against the tiled wall, looked like a poor idiot. Stiff, in the immutable attitude of a marionette, like one of those wax figures seen in museums, he evoked the lamentable vision of an inert being, a parcel of futile flesh forever deprived of his faculties.

Jeanne, on considering him, could not help smiling. "That's the image of love," she said, sarcastically. "That's where passion gets you."

Dr. Fortin was distressed. "Don't joke, Jeanne," he begged. "I assure you that it pains me to see the poor fellow in the attitude of a grotesque puppet. Look, I'll tell you what I think. On looking at that one, plunged in an inertia akin to paralysis, and the other tied up like a dangerous lunatic, I'm wondering whether, instead of creating life, you haven't destroyed the sure and marvelous harmony of nature permanently."

At that moment, the unknown man made an effort before being restrained by his bonds. His body was seen to stiffen, and his face to contract, and then a long sigh, like a groan, escaped from his mouth.

"Did you hear?" Jeanne exclaimed. "A sound came from his throat. The work of the fluid is taking effect. Soon, it will be words that the man is proffering, and the great work will be complete. Oh, Father, I can feel my heart swelling, my bosom inflating. I need air. Let's go outside, shall we?"

Her face illuminated by joy, she darted one last glance at Georges, still plunged in his lamentable prostration, and stroked his jaw, smiling. "Come on," she said, "you'll soon be reanimated, puppet, and you'll be proud of having collaborated in this magnificent discovery. But what will the other say when he perceives that he isn't dead?"

"Indeed," said Fortin. "We'll learn interesting things then."

"Probably. But what prevents us from seeking information already, and penetrating the mystery of his death? Might we not find some clue in the pockets of his garments that might facilitate the task?"

They explored his clothes that they thrown onto a bench. There was nothing in the pockets, or almost nothing.

"Of course," said the doctor, "if it was to rob him that he was murdered, nothing is more natural than him being without any possessions…hold on…there's a piece of paper. What is it?" He read it, and said: "A jeweler' invoice."

"Made out to whom?"

"Julien de Vandeuvre. That must be him? The jeweler is Massin, Rue Saint-Honoré. Nothing easier, with that, than to identify our man."

"Remember, though, that the fellow, having mysteriously disappeared, is going to be the cause of quite a fuss in Parisian society—and you want us to go, just like that, and give ourselves away, by asking this jeweler for information?"

"That's true."

"The investigation, I can see, involves some danger. Marc Vanel will take charge of it admirably. I suspect that he has prodigious means at his disposal, compared with which ours are child's play."

"What makes you think that, Jeanne?"

"This cadaver came here *on its own*. Then again, to tell all, I have a suspicion."

XII. Dawn Light

Five o'clock in the morning. The doctor and his daughter went back up to the belvedere in order to offer their burning faces to the fresh breeze.

"Oh," said Jeanne, as she arrived on the platform. "Look at that splendid dawn rising on the horizon! Wouldn't one think that nature is celebrating?"

The countryside was, indeed, colored by the first gleams announcing the sun. Above Paris, from one end of the horizon to the other, in the landscapes divided by the sun, a light mist was floating, gray and transparent. Red and gilded sunbeams plunged into it, making curious long streaks in which the nascent brightness of the star quivered. Then the mists dissipated, as if melted by the ever-increasing irruption of daylight in the sky and over the earth.

Thoughtfully, Jeanne murmured: "It's a dawn of future times. Thanks to us, the sun will henceforth illuminate a life triumphant over death."

But the doctor bowed his head. "I'm afraid, Jeanne, of our foolish presumption. Before this grandeur of nature, in this minute when the victorious daylight is chasing away the shadows, I'm thinking about the power of a sublime harmony that nothing can destroy. The sun is rising in the sky, as if in triumph, but this evening, night will reclaim its rights. Everything has to take its turn, and whatever we do, we can no more defeat death than the sun can defeat darkness. Have you thought, Jeanne, that our ambition is trying to correct and remake the work of the Unknowable, whose name signifies the sum of mysteries?"

"It only completes it, Father," she said, in a soft voice, "for if I resuscitate a dead adolescent, full of vigorous sap, created to accomplish a role assigned by nature, I won't be going against the laws that had regulated the young man's life in advance. I'll only be repairing an accident."

"It doesn't matter; I'm afraid of usurping a power that might turn against us."

They fell silent, emotional. Outlined in the enchantment of the sky, now pink and blue after that fantastic night, was the red disk of the ascendant sun.

BOOK TWO: A TWENTIETH CENTURY SORCERER

I. The Absolution of the Dream

Ten o'clock had just chimed when the lovely Comtesse d'Armez woke up in her elegant blue and white Louis XV bedroom. One of the vanities of the family, the bed, made by Boulle and decorated with exquisite panels by Watteau, caused the privileged to marvel. Simone stretched her limbs, rolled this way and that, seeking the freshness of the fine fabric, and then, making an effort, rang.

Rose, the chambermaid, who was waiting for her mistress to wake up, came in immediately and went to open the blinds and curtains. Ardent May sunlight irrupted into the apartment, illuminating everything with a jarring glare.

"You're blinding me!" Simone exclaimed. "Close the curtains. What time is it, then?"

"Ten o'clock, Madame."

"Already! Very well! Leave me alone—I'll call you shortly."

Lying back on the pillows, Simone d'Armez meditated. She recalled the strange night that she had just spent. What a bizarre dream! Was it really a dream? She felt physically weary, and her flesh was still quivering at the memory of throbbing caresses. Was it possible for a dream to leave such precise memories? She darted a glance over the strangely disturbed bed. She got up, took off her nightdress and stood naked in front of a mirror with three panels.

Oh, how pretty she was, the young Comtesse, before the mirror, which reflected three Comtesses in slender silhouette—worthy of the brush of Fragonard! How pretty she was, blushing slightly as she inspected her lush body. A sudden anger turned her cheeks crimson: traces of the storm on her genteel and fleecy blonde Flower, changing that dream into a reality. So, a male had dared, and she, in the unconsciousness of her voluptuous dream, had submitted, without resistance, to intoxicating caresses whose gentleness still troubled her flesh on awakening.

She thought at first of accusing Rose, but the introduction by her of some gallant into her room was inconceivable. The words of the strange magician returned to her memory. Was it he, Marc Vanel, Homo-Deus? But by what means had he been able to succeed in reaching her? She was no longer her own mistress, then? She was that man's—that god's—"thing." She showed her fist angrily, and, throwing herself face down on the bed, wept for a long time, without taking account of whether she was suffering in her pride as a woman, or whether it was the shame of desiring a cyclone like the one that had just passed.

If he loves me—and he told me that he loved me—that type can't love like other people. He told me that: for him, time is precious, and he couldn't ever undertake a courtship that threatened to last a long time. Because, not for anything in the world would I have given in to his advances, He understood that, and that's the explanation of his conduct. She could not help smiling. *In any case, it's not my fault.*

She repaired the disorder of the bed somewhat, and rang for Rose.

Serene again, she began her toilette, took a bath and dressed in order to go down to the dining room, where her husband was waiting. They ate lunch when noon chimed; that was the custom.

After the meal, Monsieur d'Armez took his leave of his wife and left. Immediately, Simone had herself taken to the church of Sainte-Clotilde. The senior curate, her spiritual adviser, unable to admit a suggestion at a distance, concluded that it was a dream in which concupiscence had been awakened by unhealthy conversations. After a few indulgent pieces of advice, he obtained a thousand-franc bill for his good works and gave absolution, his fingers raised, smiling in the penumbra of the confessional.

II. The Erection of the Reality

Her spirit lightened, the young woman went to see her couturier, and then reflected that she might as well finish her day, recalling that Mademoiselle Alexane had invited her to tea at her house. The celebrated dancer's "five-to-sevens" in the Place Malesherbes were highly reputed for the elite individuals one encountered there. It was one of the places where the Parisian spirit sparkled in all its verve.

Her visit to the church had lasted a long time, so it was almost five o'clock when she arrived at the Place Malesherbes. When she went in, those present included the Baron d'Escarbes, an old habitué of the foyer Opéra, the journalist Michel Georges-Michel—only one of whose two Michels was serious, but whose writings were lively—among others.[15] After having touched on various topics, the conversation naturally turned to the sorcerer of the day, to whom three great dailies had devoted articles that morning.

The Baron d'Escarbes, whose age permitted him to speak frankly, said: "All these phenomena of more-or-less white magic, suggestion and somnambulism have been known throughout the ages. I'll remain skeptical, until one of these sorcerers has experimented on himself."

With those words, Marc Vanel came in. Brought up to date, he turned to d'Escarbes. "You're right, Monsieur. The marvelous doesn't exist. There's only science and the manifestation of physical laws—except that the person who knows how to make use of them can obtain effects that even subjugate the incredulous."

Alexane stopped him, in the casual manner of an illustrious and eccentric dancer to whom everything is permitted. "In the homes of my friends, my dear Doctor, you are a diviner, a famous sorcerer. In my salon, shall I have no more than a perfect gentleman?"

"The spirit blows where it will, where it can, Madame. It's a question of atmosphere; inspiration is necessary."

Meanwhile, Marc Vanel drew nearer to the pretty blonde Comtesse Simone d'Armez, in order to greet her.

She looked at him, somewhat troubled. Simone had tried hard to forget her dream. Dr. Vanel's face caused it to revive in her mind, and she felt like an in-

---

[15] Michel Georges-Michel (c1886-1985) eventually became more famous as a painter than a journalist and novelist, but his fame was still nascent in 1924. His novels of Parisian social life—most famously *Les Montparnos* (1924)—have much in common with Champsaur's, who might have thought him an imitator; indeed, Champsaur's next novel, translated along with this one, features his own appreciation of "the Montparnos," which surely has Georges-Michel's in mind.

génue of adultery, pious and tortured by remorse, who never wants to see her lover—the cause of a temporary weakness—again, but who meets him unexpectedly.

He took her to one side, laughing and mocking imperceptibly.

"Did you have pleasant dreams last night, my dear Madame?"

Simone d'Armez feigned levity. "Yes—you even played an absurd role in them."

"You lack indulgence—or should I say charity?" he said, maliciously, gazing at her. Whatever the circumstances, I would always reproach myself for appearing absurd to you, my dear Madame, even in a dream. All in all, though. I cannot complain if I have had the joy, even chimerically, of your company."

"The worst thing is that you frightened me terribly. It's for that reason that I'm critical of you; I have no other reproaches to make. You had, however, announced your visit, and I was forewarned."

"Oh! Do you truly believe in that power, then? Have I misused it?"

Mark Vanel, while fixing the young woman with his gaze as if to read the depths of her mind and penetrate her thoughts, had asked the question in a soft voice, with the anxious expression of a lover fearful of having annoyed his idol.

"No, since it was a dream," replies Simone. "It was an imagination, a phantom made of memories—of chic, to employ fashionable parlance. You're not culpable, since it could not have been your person."

"Who can tell? Who can tell? Who can tell?" He said it three times, as he had acted during the night.

She was visibly emotional. Her slender white hands, very long, with fingernails as bright as rose petals, were trembling slightly. She wanted to hide her disturbance, and deployed her fan over her face.

Marc Vanel imposed on her the vision of the true flesh of the luminous nocturnal mask. A frisson ran through her entire body. The eyes were similar to those of the phantom lover. Was that polite, respectable socialite, similar to all the rest in the uniform modern costume, the Devil, then? She submitted once again, as in the dark, to the mysterious grip. Was that man the invisible faun who had taken and possessed her so completely, in spite of herself?

"I've seen someone who resembled you," she said, "but he didn't speak."

"He acted. Perhaps it was I."

"Hey, over there!" shouted the journalist, his voice teasing. "We're reclaiming you, Comtesse; it's necessary to be suspicious of sorcery in little corners."

III. The Fortins' Investigation

Jeanne Fortin and her father had taken a few hours rest, leaving the laboratory and the two patients in Frédéric's care. They came together again at one o'clock in the afternoon in the dining room, with an appetite that was justified by the fatigues and emotions of the night.

After the meal, not having anything to do, for the moment, with regard to the two new subjects—because, for Jeanne, they were only subjects of study—the young scientist resolved, by way of distraction, to pursue the investigation of Julien de Vandeuvre. Consulting a social directory, she had no difficulty finding his address: 20 Rue de la Comtesse-de-Noailles.

She got dressed and went down into Paris.

Addressing herself to the concierge of the luxurious building, Jeanne Fortin was rewarded for her audacity.

"We've been sent by the agency. You have a furnished apartment, it seems?"

"Yes, Madame, in the fourth floor. Antechamber, drawing room, dining room, two bedrooms, bathroom, and a maid's room on the sixth."

"That's perfect. How much?"

"A thousand a month plus charges. Three months in advance."

"Can we move in immediately?"

"If you wish. The tenancy agreement won't be ready until tomorrow, though."

"That's annoying! We'll have to spend the night at a hotel."

"Oh. I can see who I'm dealing with. You can settle things tomorrow with the manager. I'll go telephone him."

Dr. Fortin slipped a hundred francs into the porter's hand. "Take that for now. I'll give you the *denier à Dieu* tomorrow.[16] Would you like to show us the apartment now?"

They took the elevator, reaching the fourth floor in a matter of seconds.

"This elevator functions marvelously," said Fortin. "I'm interested in such things; I'm the director of the Société Locomobile de Montlevoy, in the Indre."

"Yes, it works very well, but it doesn't please everyone. The tenant on the third claims that the noise, although it's very quiet, as you can see, prevents him from sleeping. It's true that he has his bed directly behind the elevator shaft."

"Can't he move his bed?"

---

[16] A *denier à Dieu* [literally, God's penny, derived from the Latin *Denarius Dei*] is a French legal formality, whereby someone renting a property gives the other party to the contract a token sum as evidence of a provisional agreement, which either party can still annul within twenty-four hours.

"Yes—he even has a beautiful room on the far side, but then he'd be directly over Monsieur Vendeuvre's bedroom on the second-floor, and as Monsieur Vandeuvre socializes a great deal and comes back at all hours, he'd still be woken up. Bah! He's a maniac—an eccentric."

While talking they had looked over the apartment.

"It's exactly what we're looking for—so, we can sleep here tonight?"

"If you want to."

"We'll go fetch our suitcases and come back after dinner."

When the doctor and his daughter came back, the concierges, put in a good mood by another hundred-franc bill, were untiringly obliging, and put themselves at the disposal of "Monsieur and Mademoiselle Grandeau."

At about one o'clock in the morning, when everyone in the house was asleep, the two new tenants went down to Julien de Vandeuvre's floor and, by means of his keys, entered it honestly. Jeanne went to close the curtains hermetically, and then switched on the light. First they made a tour of the five rooms comprising the apartment. After the antechamber there was a small drawing room, a dining room, two bedrooms and then a large drawing room, cluttered with works of art, paintings, bronzes and trinkets. Having glanced at it all, they returned to the antechamber and began a minute inspection.

Fortin was the first to make a discovery: "There's a *louis d'or* here on the carpet."

"And another one!" said Jeanne. "Are there always *louis d'or*, then?"

"We're not the first to come in here since the tenant's death. This is the proof."

"What did you find out from the porters?"

"The Vandeuvres are old Touranian nobility. Julien only came back four days ago from his estate in Vandeuvre, where he went to collect his mother's legacy. Nobody knows how much—about four million, they think."

"They're not surprised by their tenant's absence?"

"No, he's often absent. Hunting parties or long excursions by automobile with his friends."

"Who takes care of the apartment?"

"An old family maidservant—on holiday with friends since her master's departure, which is to say, for ten days. She probably doesn't know about his return, and, consequently, his death. That explains why she hasn't come back."

"What relations does this Vandeuvre have?"

"Numerous and aristocratic."

"An elegant imbecile."

"A very chic microbe."

"If he has any important papers, they ought to be here. The concierges don't know about any serious liaison?"

"In the last few months Julien has been visited several times by a veiled woman. The young man takes all sorts of precautions to bring her in."

"I think we're on the right track. Let's sum up: Julien has a liaison with a married woman. He comes back from the province with an inheritance. On his return he goes to buy some jewelry for his mistress, and, the following evening, he's murdered and his body is 'found' on the public highway. It only remains for us to discover the name of the woman and the money from the inheritance."

"The two louis dropped in the antechamber lead me to believe that our resuscitated coffers have already received an interested visit."

"The game's afoot!" said Jeanne. "Very amusing, the occupation of detective."

After having inspected the drawing room without any result, Jeanne said: "Let's take a look at the bedroom. "There's an old writing desk, and I believe this is the moment to use the little bunch of keys we found in his waistcoat."

"Click...clack!" muttered Fortin. "This is the one. Ah! Whoever searched this put the papers back pell-mell. Here are two drawers that are full, and the other two are empty."

"Look—a considerable number of title deeds..."

"What about Julien's personal fortune? Or the inheritance?"

"Look, here's another heap of deeds and bonds."

"Not important. Note that we're only finding deeds—no banknotes or gold."

"There are some letters. They might put us on the track of the woman."

Having made two piles, they began reading them with minute attention.

"Nothing!" said Jeanne Fortin, after an hour of research. "You?"

"Let's look elsewhere—the cupboard near the fireplace. The key? Here it is...damn! What a mess!"

It was a kind of Japanese cabinet; when the two front panels were open, they were confronted by ten drawers. They, too, were in great disorder. Little packets of letters, ribbons, dried flowers, perfumed handkerchiefs and small grooming implements were stuffed in and piled up.

"Some of these objects must have been disseminated over the furniture. During the visits of the woman in question, Julien must have put all the relics of former amours that he didn't want his current lover to see in here."

"In that case, if there are any to do with that lady, they ought to be in evidence."

"They ought to be—but the posthumous visitors have made them disappear..."

Dr. Fortin lifted up the sheet metal screen shielding the fireplace. "Ah! Burnt papers!"

"Don't disturb the ashes," said Jeanne, swiftly.

Both kneeling in front of a small piled of blackened papers, they examined it attentively.

"It sometimes happens," said Jeanne, that when one burns papers written in ordinary ink, that the charred sheet remained intact. Then the letters, once black, show up white on the carbonized sheet. Here's an example..."

Displaying a fragment of a letter, she succeeded in deciphering a few words. "It's the top sheet of the letter," she said. "*Tuesday 17 May*...it's May now. It was, therefore, prior to Julien's departure... Lower down: *My dear friend...depart...vexes me...* Evidently: *Your departure vexes me...* That's very little help to our investigation."

"There's another fragment," Fortin said.

Jeanne took out a visiting card, and, with infinite precaution, succeeded in disengaging the new fragment without causing it to disintegrate. "*And think of your Sophie often...*and a P.S.: *Write to me every day...* That's all. Now let's search the ashes. Look—what's that?"

"A piece of a picture frame."

"But I recognize that...yes, it's like the one I have in my bedroom—the one containing the photograph of the pupils at the Berton school."

"There must be lots of similar frames."

"That's where you're mistaken, for those frames were made by a wood-carver who worked at the school for a month. He repaired Madame Berton's old furniture, and when the photographer came to bring the photos, he offered those who wanted one to make frames with the fragments of a rosewood cupboard that was being thrown out."

"Hum! Were there a lot of pupils at the Burton school?"

"I remember that he ran off a hundred photographs, because several pupils asked for two or three for relatives."

"Then we can easily go astray."

"No, Father, so far as I know, there were only eight of us from Paris. Taking away me and Simone d'Armez, that only leaves six. Well, the woman we're looking for is named Sophie, and of the six pupils presently in Paris, there's only Sophie Jenson, who married the député Arsène Vauclin. Now, I know that Simone sees her sometimes. Sophie married Arsène Vauclin three years ago, a former clerk of her father's, a former journalist and businessman, who went into politics. I believe that couple to be capable of anything in order to make a fortune. She's already invited me, via Simone d'Armez, to go to her soirées. As a child, Sophie Vauclin was much feared because of her critical temperament, and was somewhat inclined to bad behavior, but she interested me because of her inexhaustible cheerfulness and her insouciance—of good as of evil. Such a woman, in association with an arriviste like Vauclin, might be very dangerous. Furthermore, it seems to me that I recognize Sophie's handwriting in the fragments of the burned missives. I ought to have a note from her, in which she asked me for the formula for some cologne. I'll look for it when we get back to the Red Nest."

"In that case, we have nothing more to do here."

"Let's make one last tour of inspection and then go to bed. Tomorrow—or, rather, this morning—we can go home to look after our patients. If I have time after dinner, I'll go to see Simone d'Armez."

"By the way," said Fortin, "shall we put Marc Vanel in the picture with regard to our little investigation? I think he shares our ideas in many respects."

"Yes," said Jeanne, "he's certainly very strong. Try to hang on to him. I repeat that I think he'd be a splendid collaborator for us."

IV. The Love of a God

The afternoon was beautiful, sunlit and perfumed, and Marc Vanel yielded to the charms of spring as he went through the Bois de Boulogne, green with all the young leaves.

He was on his way to the Fortins' house at Saint-Cloud. Since the evening when he had dined with them and his friend Tchitcherine, he had often taken the road to the wild property. He felt irresistibly attracted to it by the ever more cordial welcome he received and the experiments pursued by the scientist and his daughter.

To tell the truth, though, neither the strangeness of the dwelling, in which he rediscovered corners of distant nature, nor curiosity regarding the extraordinary endeavors of his friends, nor the calm, restful evenings he spent with them dreaming in the belvedere would have been enough to attract him in isolation. The real cause of his frequent visits to the Fortins was the cherished image of Jeanne, which haunted him, and which he could no longer rid himself.

He loved her. That was it: he had thought that all that was finished; he had thought himself sheltered from the dangerous charm of women; he had arranged his life so that the human species could never again cause him any concern or chagrin—but he had found in his path the only creature who could trouble him.

However, the genius of the young woman—which rose to his own level—exasperated him. Jeanne Fortin, his equal, scientifically, certainly admired the scientist in him, but did not take an interest in the man. And the man was vexed, because Marc was a sensualist, and what he loved above all in women was their possession. Then again, he had a rival, all the more powerful because Jeanne owed him a great deal, and he thought her perfectly capable of giving herself—who could tell?—without love, to pay her debt. Furthermore, he sensed that to act with Jeanne Fortin as he had with Simone d'Armez would close the door of the Red Nest to him forever.

He had initially been subject, without being aware of it, to the special seduction that emanated from Jeanne when she spoke about her science, her fabulous discoveries. She communicated a sort of fever, a sacred fire, of which one retained the influence for a long time—and Vanel experienced the effects more than anyone else because he understood her better. So he, Vanel, had fallen madly in love with her, sensing that she was his equal, a higher being placed among women as he was, among men: a magnificent superhuman.

He found her in the abandoned garden, clad entirely in white, gathering nenuphar flowers, leaning over the edge of the old pond with the tranquil murky water. She seemed thus to be an enchantress or a princess of legend in a park of another century—and Marc Vanel watched her for some time without revealing his presence.

Finally, he showed himself.

"Bonjour, Marc," she said. "How kind of you to come to see friends, instead of accepting tea with the beautiful ladies who pay court to you. Do you realize that you might unwittingly be disdaining enormous fortunes?"

He approached, slightly emotional, because he had decided to speak to her very seriously. The décor incited him to do that. The two of them were alone, in a frantically wild nature, far from the noises of the timid life that they hated; it seemed to Marc that the moment was fatal, and complicit.

"My greatest fortune, Jeanne, is to be in your company."

"Yes, we're good comrades; we like one another all the better because the hours we spend together don't lack originality—but even so, Marc, a handsome man like you can't be content with the pleasures of science..."

"Indeed, Jeanne, there are very sweet pleasures, intoxications of which I dream. But it's not with anyone but you that I can form the divine project of letting my heart sing its delight..."

"You aren't paying court to me, I hope, Marc?"

"No, Jeanne, I'm too honest, and my love is so great that I have no hesitation in telling you that I want you for my wife."

"You?"

"Yes, Jeanne; I adore you."

She linked her hands, which dropped the nenuphars, whose white corollas spread out over the grass, and she looked at Vanel with an indefinable gaze. "My poor friend! Then you, too, in spite of all your intelligence, your admirable determination, your misanthropy and your emancipation, have fallen into the miserable error in which the others are so grotesque? My poor Marc!"

There was such a nuance of scorn in her pity that Vanel was offended by it. He became almost vehement.

"I love you! Yes, I love you as no one else has ever loved you, as I myself have never loved. Jeanne, don't you sense all the difference there is between my sentiment and that of Georges Garnier, for example? So, I've lived on the margins of an imbecile humankind that I abhor, traveling the world, along barbaric peoples and refined civilizations; I've bent my body and my will to the harshest sacrifices; I've studied hermetic souls, penetrated inviolable secrets; in sum, I've raised myself up by means of a heroic life to fabulous discoveries, to be the equal of a god—only to hear myself treated by you today as if I were a naïve student confessing his inexplicable disturbance to his cousin. What annoys me, Jeanne, is not that you don't accept my love, but that you're scornful of it."

She was slightly nonplussed, and vaguely understood the magnitude of the sentiment that possessed Marc Vanel.

"What do you expect?" she said. "It's not my fault. Can I make you a response any different from the one I made Georges Garnier? And he, poor fellow, had a tender lyricism that didn't lack beauty."

"I shall prove to you that you could not know love before my arrival. The others were too far from you, unworthy of your superb intelligence, your genius, for you to be able to make a misalliance with any other them. I, on the other hand, am your equal, at least—and I can be your master."

He had planted himself squarely in front of her, and was so handsome at that decisive moment that she was impressed—but she did not lower her gaze before his.

"No one, you understand, will dominate me. And even if I were to listen to you, if I really thought—as, in fact, I do think—that you're worthy of my love, where could it lead us?"

"To the most beautiful passion that has ever plunged two beings into intoxicating voluptuousness."

"There you are. So, no matter in what form it's expressed, and no matter what man proffers the avowal, whether he be a god or a manual laborer, the end to be attained is a bestial act? Marc, you talk like the others. Well, I don't understand that language. What do you want? I appreciate your intelligence, your knowledge; I'm your best friend. You interest me, and I'd gladly spend my life by your side—but the idea of you and me behaving like a cook and a valet...no, Marc, I beg you; allow me to laugh!"

Homo-Deus drew nearer to her and took her wrists. "Don't laugh. If I wanted to do you harm, if the whim took me to possess you in that manner, no one, not even you, could prevent me from doing so."

She shuddered, for she suddenly had the certainty that he was not boasting. And then, without her being aware of it, the young woman's instinctive modesty awoke within her. The threat of a wild desire so close to her flesh caused her to shudder, and for the first time, she was conscious of a danger.

"What do you want me to say?" he said, her voice trembling.

"If I wanted to...yes, if I wanted to, tonight...every night...I could be in your room and I would see you naked, in spite of your forbidding it, in spite of you. If I wanted to, I could wait for the moment when you fell asleep, and then..."

She recoiled instinctively.

"Ah!" he said. "You're no longer so proud. But don't worry. If I only desired a brief pleasure savored on your marble flesh, it would already be done."

"You're lying!"

"Do you think so? Do you recall, Jeanne, the desire that you expressed one evening, in the belvedere, to have a bouquet such as no man had ever offered you. Before the day was out, I offered you that bouquet."

"The dead man," she stammered. "Yes, I remember; how did you do that?"

"Having found him on a bench, I picked him up in order to bring him to you."

"To bring him to me? But he came by himself! Oh, Marc, I'm afraid of understanding. You've discovered that? You have the faculty of making yourself invisible?"

"Yes, at will. Do you understand now the frightful power that makes me the master of destinies of souls, of intimacies, of the most impenetrable secrets? Do you understand, Jeanne? Do you appreciate my love, now? Have no fear: I won't abuse that power with you. It gives me the possibility of delivering your body to my instincts; it doesn't give me that of possessing your soul, your brain, your thought, your genius—and it's with all that that I'm in love. Oh, Jeanne, divine Jeanne, if I ever I have you, consenting, in an embrace in which your flesh vibrates with your heart and mind, that would be an embrace that would make us lovers worthy to command the universe."

She lowered her head. "Forgive me. Am I abnormal, a creature of a race different from the race in which lovers are recruited? I don't know—but for me, whatever you say, amour is an inferior act. I regard it as a function of the specimens whose mores I study, and the act doesn't interest me any more than the frisson of a microbe. In addition, it's a malady, since one dies therein, and it's a weakness, a degrading state, since those who experience it lose their reason. Marc, shall we not talk any more about that ignoble contact?"

He sensed, then, the inanity of a speech that she would endure with annoyance. He looked at her dolorously and said, his voice suddenly changed and sad; "Remember, Jeanne, that Amour is stronger than we are. You've gravely offended it. One day, perhaps, it might take its revenge."

No, Marc. You speak of Amour as if it were a god, having a power of action over beings, a god that avenges himself if one resists enslavement to him. But science proves to me that amour is a function, the obsession that all beings have for the reproduction of their species. I'm not a little white goose, my friend. If I haven't yet submitted to the sensation, it's because I haven't yet had the desire, or rather the curiosity to study it. For even then, I wouldn't be in love, but merely a student, and in that case, your role would be almost ridiculous. Come to your senses, Marc. We're anomalies, people like us; we only belong to humanity in an intellectual sense. Let's leave it its animality. There remains the voluptuous sensation you mentioned just now; I know one of those of which I make use sometimes; it contents me, and doesn't have the dirty aspect of the sexual act."

Marc was astonished. That young woman, who spoke without hypocritical prudishness, was overturning all his ideas. Once again the idea of a brutal possession crossed his mind, but that would be the rupture of a relationship that was full of charm for his intellect.

"Perhaps you're right," he said, "from your point of view."

"It's the only one that interests me. Look, I'll make you a promise. The day when love sings to me, I promise that it will be you…that I choose. But what a stupid topic of conversation! Let's go inside."

Pensively, Jeanne and Marc went into the Red Nest together. Dr. Fortin saw them coming in and went to meet them.

"Well, Master," Vanel asked, "how is your resuscitated man?"

"He's coming along marvelously. He remembered his name three days ago, and the circumstances in which he was killed. Curiously, enough, though, he refuses to say a word about that, even to his intimate friend Georges Garnier. And that's not the most singular aspect of the struggle of those two intelligences put in common...but I'm expressing that badly; it's nothing, in sum, but Georges' intellect augmented by Julien's memory."

"I don't know any more about the drama you've asked me to clarify, and about which your man refuses to enlighten you, than what I'm about to tell you: Julien de Vandeuvre was the lover of Madame Vauclin, the wife of the socialist député..."

"Sophie," said Jeanne. "An old school friend."

"Well, she accommodates her lovers poorly."

"We'll return this one to her in excellent condition. Georges' cerebral cells are renewing and making good progress; in a little while, I'll return his soul to him. As for Vandeuvre, the cure being complete, I'm no longer interested in him."

"I'll continue my report," said Vanel. "It concurs perfectly with the investigation that you've already carried out. That pretty woman, for reasons that aren't absolutely clear to me, either because she's frightfully desirous of shining in Parisian society or because she's subject to the domination of a ferociously ambitious husband—in any case, that amorous creature—after having enticed the young man into her home one evening, lent her hand to the crime committed by her husband. Vauclin, who is as strong as a bull, bent Vandeuvre, who was lying on his back, over the edge of the bed and broke the vertebrae in his neck. Afterwards, he carried the cadaver to a bench on the Avenue Henri-Martin, and must then have gone to the young man's domicile, where the greater, liquid part of an inheritance of four million was."

"That Sophie!" murmured Jeanne. "Already, at school, she troubled us with her intelligence of evil and her strange perversities.

"The unfortunate Julien de Vandeuvre must love her a great deal, since, now that he's out of danger, he refuses to say her name for fear of compromising her."

"The imbecile!" said Jeanne. "I'll wager that if we set him at liberty, his first concern would be to see her again, in order to throw himself at her feet and renew his oaths of tenderness."

"I'm sure of it," said Marc, "and it might even be interesting for us to attempt the experiment. If we favored that folly instead of preventing it, don't you think that the spectacle might be piquant, for those of us who know the truth?"

Dr. Fortin smiled. "Vanel, you're diabolical. To put the resuscitated victim in the presence of the murderers would, indeed by sensational. I won't oppose the project. I'd find it repugnant to inform the agents of the law of what we know, but that refined chastisement doesn't displease me. What do you think, Jeanne?"

"You'd be confounded by the result of that confrontation. It isn't a victim that you'd be bringing face to face with a criminal, but a man in love, who, instead of chastisement, would talk about caresses. Yes, I'd like to attempt the experiment, to show Marc what love makes of a man, to what miserable submissions and shameful baseness it constrains him."

"You misunderstand the sentiments of the fellow, Jeanne," protested Marc. "He's a hero!"

"He's an idiot! An idiot!"

With that peremptory declaration, they went down into the basement. Lying on a chaise-lounge, a pale, thin young socialite was resting with his eyes open.

"Well, Monsieur de Vandeuvre," said Jeanne, "how are you today?"

"Very well." It was the soul of Georges Garnier that was replying, through Julien de Vandeuvre's body. "But are you going to leave me in the skin of this imbecile for much longer? This condition is increasingly uncomfortable for me; it seems that another individuality is mingled with mine, that I have memories that aren't my own. I have thoughts that are in combat with mine, with my tastes. I feel narrowly confined in this fellow's skin. He's a socialite, an idler. His love for that whore is stupid. She had me murdered; I have the proof of it now, but I only ask to excuse her. After all, perhaps her husband forced her and…sacred thunder, that's what I still think with his mind! Oh, Jeanne, Jeanne, give me back my skin, my garment!"

Everyone burst out laughing.

"Come on, Georges, a little more patience. My cerebral culture is going well enough; it's justifying my presumptions. It isn't necessary to leave you in Julien de Vandeuvre's brain. He has enough brain now to continue his previous life. As you can sense, my dear Georges, your intellectual fluid has revivified Vandeuvre's. A few more days and I'll return you to yourself."

"Hurry up, Jeanne, hurry up! I'm afraid, afraid of going mad, me or the other...me or the other; I no longer know!"

The three witnesses of his emotion looked at one another in a singular fashion, and then went away. Just as they were leaving the laboratory, Vanel perceived Frédéric, in the process of spoon-feeding a lamentable individual who was slumped against the wall, supported by straps passed under his armpits.

"Poor Garnier!" said Marc.

He stopped to contemplate the young doctor. He was bleak and dejected, his eyes staring, his lower lip slack. Frédéric had fastened a bib around his neck and was cramming him with white pap, as he would have done for a little child.

The domestic turned to Marc. "He's no trouble. Except when he's hungry, he's as good as gold. But every time he needs nourishment, he wails terribly."

Jeanne had drawn closer. She smiled as she pointed to the poor fellow.

"Another victim of amour! Georges Garnier makes a fine pair with the other, Vandeuvre, the idiot who's dreaming of getting himself murdered for a second time. So, Marc, these lamentable victims don't cure you? All the same, what if you resemble them one day—you, a god!"

She burst out laughing.

"You have no compassion," he said. "When will you restore life to poor Garnier?"

"Don't worry—soon. The artificial cells have finally decided to reproduce. Within a month. Georges' brain will be normal again."

"And his father?"

"He thinks he's still traveling. He cursed us a little, because he accused me of being the cause of the abrupt expatriation, but it will all work out."

Upstairs, at the door, she extended her hands to Marc. "Adieu, Marc," she said. "Remain yourself, my friend, remain a good comrade and don't look at me any longer as a possible satisfaction for your carnal frenzy. Be my brother, Marc, my brother in intelligence, in knowledge.

He did know how to respond, but as he went away he traversed the wild garden, where the blooming flowers of spring were growing, full of vigorous sap, and he murmured; "Nature and life ordain amour, however."

Around them, in the branches and the leaves of the park, a sylph, borne by the wind, caressed Marc Vanel's temples, beating the chamade there, whispering in his ears that the genius of the species, the pressure of germination, commanded that amour in everything that breathes—from the insects to the birds, from the small minnows of the streams to the whales, from the brutes to those who, among humans, are gods.

V. A Social Soirée

The Hôtel de Virmile, situated at the extremity of the Rue de Varenne, was certainly one of the most alluring of town houses. A high wall with an arched reinforcement framed the enormous door of sculpted oak, ornamented by superb heavy bronze knockers, a marvel of casting; above it were the Virmile arms, a hand holding a sword: *Vir*, brave, *miles*, soldier.

Once through the entrance one found oneself in an immense paved court-yard, with the porter's lodge to the left; at the back stood the house, in the pure Louis XIV style, behind which was a garden that extended all the way to the Rue de Grenelle.

That evening, there was an extraordinary reception, and the elite of Parisian society was crowded into the vast drawing rooms. There was a time—that of Mesdames de Sévigné and Deffand, and later, that of Mesdames Geoffrin and Louise Ancelot—when the nobility of name and the nobility of letters had gathered there quite naturally, forming circles of sparkling and durable conversation around those charmers; but today, when the need to change location, in automobiles and airplanes, is making itself increasingly felt, by virtue of a kind of madness, or rather vertigo, of speed, what is the point of the life of the hearth, conversation both intimate and critical, in which the works of the day are judged? That difficult problem, however, Hélène de Virmile had solved, and very much in the swing of things, she had been able to make her salon a covered walk in which all notability was proud to be counted.

That Marquise had been born Hélène Fortin; by virtue of her grace, her intelligence and a dowry of a few millions, she had married the Marquis de Virmile. Royalists rallied to the Empire, the Virmiles had remained on the good side of favor; in the same way, Christian Virmile, a former servant of the Empire, had become a senator under the Republic. In the Senate he played a rather unobtrusive role, just sufficient not to be forgotten. He had had the good fortune, in marrying Hélène Fortin, to encounter a woman capable of maintaining his rank with marvelous tact. Thanks to his wife, he was able, very gently, to detach himself from intrigues, to devote himself to his taste for the sporting life and leave the direction of political matters to the Marquise—for the latter, by virtue of her tradition, launched herself into the opposition and for that reason attracted to her salon all the notabilities of nationalism. A certain number of illustrious litterateurs, a trifle indispensable, mingled there in the hope of finding an outlet, or at least maintaining the awareness of their names.

The sole fault of that exquisite woman was an excessive vanity relative to everything connected with the nobility she had acquired by marriage and luck. Aristocratic tradition was a veritable obsession in her, to the point that she broke off all communication with her brother, Dr. Fortin, of whose scientific glory she was nevertheless proud, because of his excessively advanced scholarly ideas. It was, in consequence, very painful for her to see her son Antoine affect a great disdain for the traditions of nobility.

Antoine, who was certainly not stupid, devoted his youth to poetry, but a poetry that was very much his own, along with a few other petty decadents, pessimistic and mannered, affecting a style in which locations of the fifteenth and sixteenth centuries were preferred to modern ones. He had obtained and retained antique mores and effeminate manners from his education with the Jesuit priests, which shocked his parents, and especially Monsieur de Simiane, who held the position in the Hôtel de Virmile of omnipotent arbiter.

Evil tongues also suggested that Monsieur de Simiane had been the beautiful Hélène's lover for a long time, since the fall of Troy; others contented themselves with thinking that he was the titular fiancée of Huguette de Virmile. That young woman of twenty, brunette and Tanagrean,[17] was due to connected the name of the Virmiles with the ancient blazon of Simiane, descendants of a nobility less ancient than that of the Virmiles, but going back nevertheless to the sixteenth century, when Tiburcio Fabiani, the squire of the Constable du Bourbon, had surrendered his daughter to François I, who had ennobled her and given her a fief. It had since been one of the specialties of the family to furnish favorites to kings or princes of the blood. Fortune had augmented the domains and income of the Simianes.

Unfortunately, the father of Jacques de Simiane had been ruined under the reign of the excessively bourgeois Louis-Philippe, by virtue of giving a warm welcome to Lord Seymour. He had only left his son the name and the debts. The Second Empire would gladly have lent its aid to such a great name, but Jacques had too many links with the legitimist party to move in that political direction and had preferred to accept the aid of a devoted and very rich friend; he lived more in the Virmiles' home than his own, and simultaneously filled the functions there of steward and cavalier serving "la Belle Hélène."[18]

Jacques de Simiane, although he had reached sixty, did not look, when heavily made up, any more than forty-five. Thus the projected marriage had nothing ridiculous about it, and many young men would not have had the success still carried off by that Lauzun.[19]

In accepting the invitation of the Marquise de Virmile, people were curious to see the magician Marc Vanel, about whom all Paris was talking. Present were,

---

[17] i.e., reminiscent of a "Tanagra figurine": an ancient Greek terracotta statuette, simulacra of which were manufactured in Paris as contemporary *objects d'art*.

[18] The formulation conventionally used in French letters to refer to Helen of Troy.

[19] The notorious courtier and soldier Antoine Nompar de Caumont, Duc de Lauzun (1633-1723).

first of all, as prestidigitator, the President of the Council, Claude Barsac,[20] who, by virtue of the rallying of the Republican government to the Court of Rome, had conquered all of the noble faubourg; the wily chameleon Louis Barthou,[21] president of the Commission for the Reparation of Devastated Countries (four hundred thousand francs per year), his ferrety eyes behind a binocle, on the lookout for captures; the députés Vauclin and Baruyer and many others, of the right, naturally—Vauclin and Baruyer belonged to the socialist left, but the unscrupulous left that eats in all troughs—and finally, artists, journalists and anyone who had a name: all the peacocks who circulate in order that people will talk about them.

The conservatory, a magnificent winter garden in which the most beautiful specimens of tropical flora grew, was open to the elect. In the main drawing room, the Marquise had had chairs and armchairs set out. In front of the large marble fireplace, the work of Falconet,[22] a vast Louis XV sofa formed the central point of the most intimate circle. In the intervals left to her by her social duties, the Marquise de Virmile took her place there between her young and intimate friend, the exceedingly blonde and seductive Comtesse d'Armez and her daughter Huguette. Behind the sofa, the Marquis de Virmile and the requisite Simiane went back and forth in front of the fireplace.

"My dear friend," said the latter to Virmile, "Who is that beauty coming forward on the arm of d'Orsennes?"

"His sister Geneviève, emerged from the convent last week. D'Orsennes introduced her to us recently."

"Amaury is counting on his sister," Antoine put in, "to get him afloat again."

"Pooh!" said Virmile. "He'll marry her off to some *nouveau riche* exploiter of finance and the cost of living. Money has no odor today."

---

[20] Claude Barsac is the protagonist of a trilogy of novels by Champsaur first published in 1895-6 under the collective title *Le Mandarin* and subsequently reprinted in an omnibus as *L'Arriviste*, which describe the rise to fame and fortune of a corrupt politician. He crops up in several of Champsaur's later novels in the same archetypal role, usually in the more distant background than in the present instance.

[21] Louis Barthou (1862-1934) was a real politician, who served a brief term as President of the Council in 1913 before acquiring a reputation as a hero during the Great War and being elected to the Académie Française. He was still active in politics in 1924 and was surely annoyed by the snide remarks included in the present novel (this one is not the last or the worst), if he was aware of them, but must have been battle-hardened by the relentless maulings of the opposition press.

[22] Étienne-Marie Falconet (1716-1791), the foremost of the French rococo sculptors.

"Today as yesterday," riposted Antoine. "Our ancestors espoused some king's bastard. It's always been the same."

"Shut up, Antoine!" said Madame de Virmile, dryly. "You know, my son, that we don't like to hear you say such things."

Antoine shrugged his shoulders and dived into the crowd. Meanwhile, Amaury d'Orsennes, having seen gazes fixed upon him, had approached.

"Come on, Geneviève," said Huguette. "I've saved a place for you."

She sat down beside her, and a joyful babble was not long delayed, mingled with little bursts of bright laughter.

"Well," said Amaury to Madame d'Armez, "are we going to see this famous charlatan?"

"He's Joseph Balsamo, Comte de Cagliostro," she said. "Yes."

"This magician impresses you when his eyes weigh upon yours."

At that moment, a new arrival came to greet the Marquise: Albert Baruyer, the brother of the famous socialist leader Georges Baruyer. Of tall stature, built like an athlete, with broad massive shoulders and powerful hands with knotty fingers, over which brown hair grew, Albert had short-cropped hair, a bushy moustache descending slightly in the Gallic fashion, and cruel and sensual lips. One single defect: the inferior jaw, protruding and overlapping, made the mouth of the notorious commercial advocate resemble a foot bath. His prestige among women, however, was legendary. He was a highly regarded and feared Parisian figure. He had, moreover, the halo of his bother Georges, who might be a Minister one day, or even President of the Council.

"You know, Monsieur Baruyer, that you promised me to be indiscreet with regard to your play at the Théâtre de Paris. Will you tell me its subject?"

"Certainly, my dear Madame—but you alone."

"You're wrong, Baruyer," Antoine de Virmile interjected, reentering the circle with the genteel painter Jaquelux[23] and Michel Georges-Michel. "It's necessary never to confide anything to a woman."

The word "woman" was emphasized with a scornful disdain for the sex. Addressing himself to the chronicler of the good and bad places in Paris, Albert Baruyer took him by the arm and drew him into the elegant crowd, hunting for femininity.

"Do you know who that appetizing young woman on the sofa is?"

"The daughter of the house, Huguette de Virmile. Antoine's only eighteen and his sister is twenty; she ages la Belle Hélène too much, and everyone in Paris, including you, knows that Simiane has been the Marquise's lover and factotum since…well, forever…and Huguette's fiancé."

---

[23] Lucien Jaquelux was the illustrator of several of Champsaur's books, although he became far more successful in the 1930s and 1940s as a designer of stage and cinema sets.

"That's appropriate!" said Baruyer, without conviction. "The mother's lover marrying the daughter!"

"But the mother is sure of keeping her beloved close to her, and the marriage stabilizes Simiane's situation. It's necessary to pay the jazz band. As long as the creditors are content."

"Look," said another besuited individual, joining in, "Vauclin and his wife, the beautiful Sophie Vandeuvre can't be far away. You know Arsène Vauclin well, don't you, Baruyer? What do you think of him?"

"A man of action without silly scruples; he'll be a Minister before long. Look at him, with Barsac and Barthou. Birds who flock together..."

At that moment, there was a stir in the crowd; Dr. Marc Vanel, Homo-Deus, had just been announced. Madame de Virmile hurried forward.

Above medium height, he looked a trifle heavy in his regulation formal attire; his broad shoulders and muscular neck did not seem made for his cramped and uncomfortable garments. His head, a trifle massive, with strongly accentuated features, had a fantastic expression of power and authoritarian intelligence. In his slightly dark face, his steel-gray eyes had an unsustainable glare. His forehead, very high, was crowned with thick, almost frizzy metallic brown hair; one might have thought it a crown of bronze. He advanced with casual ease and kissed the hand that the Marquise held out to him.

"Be welcome, my dear Master. Everyone is dying to meet you."

Madame de Virmile had an armchair brought forward, for, even though Vanel was not unaware that she had solicited his presence in order to interest her guests with the story of a few previously-unpublished adventures, it was necessary for her to mask that desire under the pretext of an introduction to Parisian society: an introduction that began immediately. The audience filed past Vanel, who, standing beside the armchair, found an amiable word for everyone. Then he sat down, and Madame de Virmile, leaning toward him, went into action.

"Are all the fabulous tales told about fakirs true?"

"The fabulous, Madame, is only so for those who do not understand its causes."

"And you can produce the same phenomena as the fakirs?"

That dialogue, in a loud tone, could be heard by everyone in the profound silence of that Parisian assembly.

"My friend, the fakir Ahmasithamani had himself suspended by his feet, head down. He remained like that for several days without taking any nourishment. You wouldn't want to hang me from your chandelier, I suppose, so that I could do likewise. For one thing, in this costume, I'd look ridiculous, and then again, you'd find the experiment long and tedious. Similarly, my other friend, the fakir Sahamaki, kept his arms raised for many years, each holding a handful of soil containing a sorghum seed, with the result that the seed germinated; a plant surged forth between his fingers, its roots surrounding his wrists, and the fakir thus became a kind of man-plant, to the most bizarre effect."

"What suffering he must have endured!"

"No—for the good reason that, although the fakir was present so far as the profane were concerned, in reality, he was not."

Since the beginning of the conversation, a prelude to the occult séance, everyone had drawn nearer, bringing their sets as silently as possible, with the result that a large circle of listeners surrounded Marc Vanel. Quite simply, Homo-Deus went behind his armchair, which he thus made into a kind of podium, He was facing the sofa that now accommodated Mesdames de Virmile and d'Armez, Huguette and Geneviève, while behind it stood the Marquis de Virmile, Simiane, Claude Barsac, Louis Barthou and Albert Baruyer.

"What do you mean?" asked Madame de Virmile.

"This: you're not unaware of the work on hypnotism carried out by our eminent doctors, the Charcots, the Dumas, the Richets and the Férés,[24] suggesting the most implausible things to subjects naturally prepared by an unhealthy state of neurosis or hysteria. Well, what our doctors obtain from subjects predisposed by an abnormal mental state, the fakirs, subjects predisposed by practice throughout their lives, are the most hypnotizable beings that it is possible to encounter, and they practice on themselves what our doctors practice on others. They can suggest to themselves whatever they wish; thus, by the force of their will alone, they force their spirit—or their soul, as you please—to emerge from their bodies and travel where it will. In the same way, during sleep, our own spirits roam and wander. The fakir, by virtue of daily training, is eventually able to command his spirit; that is why he can submit his body to the worst tortures; he does not feel them, any more than if he had been put to sleep by an anesthetic."

That's incredible!" cried Her Blondeness Simone d'Armez. "So, the soul of a fakir can escape his body and roam at random."

"*At random* is not the term, for the spirit half of our being, and one is only veritably oneself when one is unburdened of the uncomfortable envelope known as the human body."

"What a singular theory!" said Albert Baruyer.

"Not at all," said Vanel, henceforth addressing his gaze more particularly to Simone d'Armez. "A little reflection would enable you to agree. You must have perceived, many a time, that there is a discord between our bodies and our minds, and if that demon obtains the upper hand, it's at the price of real physical suffering. For example: you plan some excursion, promising yourself the pleasure of contemplating some location or some effect of the light at sunset, but in order to get there, the sun has burned you, the stones of the road have lacerated

---

[24] The psychologist Georges Dumas (1866-1946), the physiologist Charles Richet (1850-1935) and the physician Charles Féré (1852-1907) all carried forward Charcot's work on hypnosis, the latter two extrapolating it into the field of psychic research.

your feet and insects have bitten you; sweat is streaming over your body; your legs are fatigued, your forehead burning—everything is against you—but you go anyway, because the spirit wills it. What would be more agreeable would be to leave that wretched body behind and go alone, solely by means of the imagination, to wherever one desires to go. Well, among the fakirs, the body is abandoned, like an accessory."

"Shall we have the chance to see a few phenomena of hypnotism with our own, thanks to you, Master?"

"The clinic at the Salpêtrière offers numerous cases to us every day. They would merely seem more striking if they were presented in the marvelous frame that is the Orient, with its ardent sunlight and its simultaneously starving and neurotic population, undermined by a five-thousand-year fever. There, hypnotism reigns as master, and every Indian is a marvelous subject. Out there, the European is submissive to the ambience and becomes an impressionable subject himself. Hence these phenomena, which are seen and heard everywhere, and which, in reality, only exist in the mind of the spectator. For example, a fakir places in front of him a kind of lyre, and that lyre plays whatever the fakir desires. Do you think that the lyre is really playing? No—it is only playing in the suggestible mind of the spectator."

Homo-Deus paused for a few moments, and then resumed: "Nevertheless, Madame la Marquise, I should like, in order to thank you for your welcome, to show you a phenomenon of fluidic emanation at a distance, of which I confess that I have not yet made a scientific demonstration. It can perhaps be seen as an instance of the influence of mind on matter. Would you care to have that sidetable brought here and to give me a simple piece of letter paper?

The Marquise hastened to a bell, and gave the order for the requested objects to be brought. Marc Vanel had the sheet of paper passed from hand to hand, and asked Madame d'Armez to place it on the table herself. Then, going to stand with his back to the fireplace, he seemed to absorb himself in profound contemplation.

There was a rather long pause, and a few mocking gazes were beginning to drift away, when Marc's steely eyes opened again and fixed their gaze on the table. Then, to the general amazement, the sheet of paper rose up a few centimeters above the tabletop. It remained immobile momentarily, and then, with a single surge, fell onto the knees of the Comtesse d'Armez, who could not suppress a cry of fright.

A frisson had passed over every pair of shoulders, and a little timid applause was heard. The Comtesse, emboldened by the bravos of the audience, picked up the sheet of paper.

"Read it," commanded Vanel's curt voice.

Her Blondeness Simone d'Armez looked down at the paper. Immediately, an ardent blush covered her face and shoulders.

"Oh!" she cried, in a squeal of offended modesty.

"What's the matter?" asked those nearest to her.

The Comtesse had dropped the piece of paper. It was de Simiane who picked it up.

"But there's nothing there," he said, passing the piece of paper to his neighbors.

"Madame, however, read something," Vanel replied. "An effect of suggestion produced by one free spirit on another."

"What was it?" whispered Huguette in Simone's ear.

"But…you can see, there's nothing there." And she darted a glance at Vanel that was both fearful and imploring.

De Simiane had taken the piece of paper back. "What about me?" he asked. "Can't I read something?"

"Perhaps," replied the hypnotist. "Look."

De Simiane looked down at the sheet of paper again, where there was a picture of a mackerel.[25] A few other members of the audience saw it, too. He went pale, then wadded up the piece of paper and threw it away, angrily.

Turning toward Vanel, he said: "Do you know what I've just seen?"

"I have absolutely no idea, Monsieur, any more than anyone else."

The Marquise de Virmile had picked up the crumpled sheet.

"But there's still nothing…nothing at all…"

"Give it to me! To me!" clamored several voices.

Mademoiselle Alexane, the star dancer of the Opéra, had just arrived, and, not having witnessed the two experiments, had them related to her by Michel Georges-Michel, who had seen the fish. So, Vanel being beside her, she said to him: "You merit the pyre, my dear sorcerer."

Then the conversation moved on, and Vanel took advantage of it to go into the conservatory, toward which he had seen the Comtesse d'Armez heading.

Simone was sitting under an arbor of magnolias with Geneviève d'Orsennes. "Every man for himself!" she exclaimed. "It's Balsamo."

Geneviève, under the suggestion of the satyr, understood that she was excess to requirements, and stood up, giving the excuse that she had something to say to her brother, and left Simone and Marc Vanel alone.

"You find my manner of action bold, but I'm nonetheless sincere; allow me to hope that the keen attraction that you inspire in me merits reciprocity."

"You're forgetting that I'm married."

"Very slightly…so very slightly!"

"What do you know about it?"

"I know everything."

"What strange conceit!"

---

[25] The French *maquereau* [mackerel] is a slang term for a pimp.

"No—conceit is unknown to me, but I'm conscious of my means…and I make use of them…with your permission, I'll resume this conversation, tonight, in your own home."

"In my home! You're mad!"

"Mad with love, a little, yes."

Homo-Deus took the Comtesse's hands and planted a long kiss on it. Then he drew away, leaving his victim and his prey troubled, pensive and enervated, tracked everywhere by the suggestion of the faun.

Meanwhile, an aristocratic and Tanagrean virgin, Huguette de Virmile, Jeanne Fortin's cousin, was also thinking of him, dreamily, captured by the emprise and domination of his gaze.

VI. Genius Akin to Madness

Frédéric, the scientist's factotum, was pacing up and down in Dr. Fortin's laboratory, in the company of the victim of amour, Georges Garnier, whom he was guiding, holding him under the arms like a puppet of flesh and bone.

"Come on, Monsieur Georges, a little further—there! There! I'm going to let go of you..." He let go, and only just had time to catch the marionette. "Oops! A moment longer and he'd have been on the floor. Oh, I'm beginning to have had enough of the society of this young man. To think that a few weeks ago he was reasoning as well as me, and now, like a child a few months old, he can hardly stand up. Come on, sit down. There...bend your knees. What a simpleton! He doesn't understand anything about anything. What the devil have they made him swallow to put him in this state?

"It's a fine thing, Science; like Amour, it brutalizes a man. And in the meantime, the other one, the former dead man, is walking, coming and going, speaking and acting in his stead. Truly, there's something to be proud of in that rascal, for it would make all the sly swine in the Faculté des Sciences swallow their tobacco if they could see that Mr. Punch!

"Come on, it's necessary to feed him now. What a chore! I'd rather have a dozen nurslings. They wail and whine, but that's understandable, whereas he, damn it...! It's necessary to stuff the grub into him. And he's no help! On the contrary, he's the most stu...pid... Come on! Open your beak! Now, swallow!"

Frédéric forced George Garnier's mouth, introduced an esophageal syringe into it, and made him absorb the contents. "You're looking well, old man," he continued. "You're even putting on weight—but that doesn't mean that I'd like to be in your shoes. There! Now go bye-bye in your corner..."

At that moment, Jeanne Fortin came in with the double man—which is to say, Julien de Vandeuvre's body playing host to Georges Garnier's soul—in the company of Marc Vanel.

"Leave him there, Fred," said Jeanne. "We might need him. You've earned a break. Go get some rest, my friend."

"Bah! It's not very tiring, after all, and I'd prefer it if he were a little more turbulent, for it hurts me to see Monsieur Georges this way, like a wax figurine."

"Be patient a little longer, Fred. I hope to be back in my skin soon," said the mind of Georges Garnier, via the smiling mouth of Julien Vandeuvre. "Thanks, old chap."

After Fred's departure, the three strange individuals surrounded Georges Garnier's body.

"Nothing new," said Marc Vanel, after having examined the lamentable human wreck attentively.

"What are you waiting for in order to return me to myself?" said the double George-Julien, irritatedly. "The body of this Vandeuvre is horribly embarrassing..."

"Do you find it ugly, then?" said Jeanne Fortin, teasingly.

"On the contrary. I'm afraid that you'll get too accustomed to this face and end up falling in love with it. This lady-killer I'm living in is odious to me, and I'm in haste to get back to my clothing of an honest man. This Vandeuvre, in whom you've installed me like a hermit crab in someone else's shell, has committed regrettable actions—not those that society reproves, but ones of which a conscience like mine cannot approve. When, on your order, Jeanne, I recovered possession of my...of his...apartment, the sight of familiar objects, and the reading of a journal that he kept quite regularly, filled in all the lacunae that subsisted in my memory, and the mind of Julien de Vandeuvre was entirely revived within me. Since then, these two souls have been influencing my actions, often against my will. The spirit of Julien de Vandeuvre steers me and draws me toward ideas that my own spirit, Georges Garnier, only envisages with scorn and repulsion. The life and character of that socialite, infatuated with himself, his birth, his fortune, his appearance and his chic, accustomed to find flatterers and accomplices among other men and easy conquests among women, are antipathetic to me.

But it seems to me," Jeanne said, "that your thoughts don't always have that inclination, since you're criticizing them yourself."

"That's because I'm in the presence of my own self here, collapsed in a corner, and that presence drives de Vandeuvre's spirit away, temporarily."

"Although you're in haste to recover possession of your envelope, I'm not yet ready for that restitution. I still need Julien de Vandeuvre's body for the realization of a certain project."

"Why aren't you telling me what you want to do?"

"If there were only Georges Garnier's spirit in you, I'd tell you right away, but it's still mixed, in your fleshy enveloped, with Vandeuvre's, like water with wine."

"And that," cried Georges-Julien, the double man, "is why I'm in haste to quit this accursed carapace. Do you think I can't see that you're no longer treating me in the same way? I no longer have your confidence. You don't trust me."

"Not you, Georges—it's the other, Julien de Vandeuvre, who serves as your host, that I don't trust."

"But you know full well that it's not him who's talking to you at this moment."

"Remember what you said a little while ago," Marc Vanel put in. "Would it be reasonable for Jeanne to confide her secrets to a man who, once out of here, under other influences, can become the man that Georges Garnier despises?"

"You're right—but this partly double existence is weighing upon me. Hurry up, Jeanne, for I'm afraid... I'm afraid...afraid..."

"Don't worry," Jeanne assured him. "We'll succeed." She indicated Homo-Deus and added: "There are three of us now."

"It's not just a lack of success that I'm afraid of. You know, Jeanne, how much I love you. Well, I'm jealous—jealous of the other, this ladies' man." He slapped his chest. "Do you understand?"

"My poor Georges!"

"How could it be otherwise, when it's a Don Juan you're talking to, while I can see myself, my wretched body, forgotten in a corner, like a living pile of rags."

"Don't say that!" said Jeanne. "Your body is of inestimable value to me. For me, it's the means of succeeding in the discovery and capture of the human soul."

"Yes, what does my suffering matter? Science—which is to say, the love of the unknown, the search for the impossible—fills your soul and renders it insensible to any other passion."

"Words, words!" said Jeanne, impatiently.

"You're cruel."

"No—at least, not unnecessarily. But that's enough time wasted in idle chat. Have you done what I told you to do?"

"Yes—I'll come to collect you this evening, at nine o'clock, and I'll bring the evening suit that you commanded."

"Thank you." She added: "Go, my friend, and don't be annoyed."

"Annoyed, no. Sad, yes."

Jeanne held him back. As the conversation was going on too long for the liking of Homo-Deus, he had gone back to the lamentable body of Georges Garnier, reminiscent of a broken marionette, and appeared to be examining it attentively.

"Sit down here beside me," said Jeanne to the elegant young man harboring the soul of Georges Garnier. "You think I'm cruel. I can prove to you that I'm nothing of the sort. You detest Julien de Vandeuvre, whose actions and thoughts are so different from yours. The revelation of the fellow's resurrection is impossible for us. You know the circumstances in which his cadaver fell into our hands. His death hasn't been officially recorded; as far as Parisian society is concerned, he isn't dead. No matter! Once I'm certain of success, I'll repeat the experiment on another subject. But since I have an initial subject of observation in my power, I want to utilize him to the profit of our social projects, since I can't use him as a subject of demonstration.

"The character of Julien de Vandeuvre inspires disgust in you; that's because it's despicable. We're going to punish him, Homo-Deus and I, by making him repair, with your help, the evil actions of his past life. Do you understand, now, why I need your envelope?"

"I'd prefer it if you abandoned Julien de Vandeuvre."

"And think, my friend, how interesting the study might be, for us, of your two such different natures combined in the same individual, and what results we can extract from it in future."

"Study!" sighed the young man. "Always study! In the end, though, studying together might trigger the commencement of love."

"I promise you," Jeanne said, gravely, "that on the day when you resume possession of your body, I'll give you my virginity to thank you for your sacrifice."

"And that would be, in your turn, a sacrifice. That promise, which ought to give me joy, almost drives me to despair. You'll give yourself to me, Jeanne? Do you not know yourself? You only love science, and that nuptial gesture would be one more physiological study."

"What if it is?" said Jeanne, impatiently. "What more can I offer you?"

"The impossible, alas. Your love."

"Again!" exclaimed the young woman. "Oh, what do you understand by that ludicrous word, Love? What sentimental dream is driving you? Hey, over there, do you hear, Marc? You, who are strong, tell him that he's the dupe of all the poetic drivel spouted since the dawn of civilization for the deification of woman. Do those sighs, those tears, those dreams disguised as poetry, lyric dramas or whatever, composed for the sublimation of lust, have any other goal, any other result, than the final spasm, the need imposed by nature for the fecundation and reproduction of the species?" She turned back to Georges-Julien. "You love me? You say so; if necessary, like David, you'd sing the Song of Songs. You weary my ears with oaths, amorous protestations, and your imaginary eulogistic comparisons, in order to elevate and embellish, in your own eyes, a little slit, and poeticize the materiality of the repulsive final act."

"Jeanne!" murmured the young man. "Dare you blaspheme like that?"

"I'm offending you, I know; but you've learned to know me, and if I expressed myself otherwise, you'd be convinced of my hypocrisy. Although a virgin, I'm not innocent. The true name of chastity, at my age, is ignorance or imbecility, and as the majority of young women are far from stupid, it's only, on their part, a false ignorance, which they exploit to the advantage of social conventions—conventions that serve to mask all the lies and the cupidity."

"Stop it, Jeanne!" exclaimed Marc Vanel. "I confess that you're right, up to a point, but amour is not, in humans, merely a carnal need; it's also a spiritual need, and that's one of the ways in which we're distinguished from the rest of animality. In that, I, too, share Georges' opinion. A man cannot be content with physical possession. What he wants, what he seeks, above all, is the communion of souls that is so very difficult, alas, to encounter."

"No," proffered Jeanne violently. "You're also a dupe of social convention. The amour idealized by men ought not to exist. Only material love, necessary to the conservation of the species, is useful. All other love, which seems designed to excite pride and vanity—*all* other love—is verbiage, poetry as hollow as a little bell, and futile. What ought the sage to think of the adulation pushed to baseness by certain lovers? Too many males sacrifice the most brilliant of their faculties to their passion for a being who is their intellectual inferior. How often does one see notoriously stupid women enchain to their caprices men of an infinitely superior intelligence and judgment, and who, bound by the conventions admitted on the subject of amour, shamelessly allow themselves to be duped by dolls devoid of intelligence?

"Look, let's take for example this conversation: it's an hour wasted in idle words. And you, Georges, how many hours that might have been usefully employed has your foolish amour wasted in hollow dreams? Confess that, out of pity for you—note, Vanel, that I don't say for his love, which I reprove—I shall give myself to you. Do you think me capable of responding to that love, such as you understand it, of following you in your poetic ramblings, of encouraging a pastime unworthy of us? You understood just now when you, whose scientific brain I esteem and appreciate, said that I would give myself to you out of curiosity. I shall give myself to you bodily, yes, but spiritually, never."

"So be it," said Georges-Julien. "I thank you for your frankness."

At that moment, Dr. Fortin came in. He saw Marc Vanel leaning over the wretched puppet devoid of his soul.

"So, you're at the Red Nest again? What's new?"

"Georges is asking to move house, to go back to his former dwelling."

"Bah!" said Fortin, laughing and pointing at Julien de Vandeuvre. "Isn't he satisfied with this one? Don't his trousers have an impeccable crease?"

"Don't joke, Master—you who are making use of me in an experiment that might have cost me my life. I daren't regret it, since it's Jeanne's will, but I'm suffering by virtue of lending myself to it for so long, and by virtue of your prolonging that situation excessively."

"Patience, my friend. Your ordeal is reaching its conclusion. A few more days and we'll attempt a definitive operation."

"Can't you tell me what you're up to?"

"What do you think, Jean?" asked Dr. Fortin.

"My first idea was to act in secret with regard to Monsieur de Vandeuvre, but our conversation just now has changed my mind. At the point that Georges has reached, he might as well know everything."

"To work then," said Marc. And, going to fetch Georges, he lifted him up, brought him to the worktable and, having sat him on the floor, maintained him there between his knees. The double man, Julien de Vandeuvre with Georges Garnier's soul, was following all the movements of his body with anxious interest.

Jeanne and Fortin had drawn nearer.

Homo-Deus lifted up the apparatus sealing puppet-Georges' skull.

"Look: the encephalum, initially depressed, has resumed its ordinary volume, and the cells their activity. We've going to assure ourselves of their functioning by influencing them separately...pass me the Voltaic pile. We'll commence with movement." He touched one of the circumvolutions of the brain; George raised his right arm and rubbed his eyes. "You see—the first instinctive gesture is directed toward sight. Look, he's gazing, and this time, his eyes can see..."

Indeed, the patient appeared to recognize the familiar faces; he smiled at Jeanne, who was leaning toward him.

Marc Vanel changed the location of the electrode.

"The voice," he said.

Georges pronounced, distinctly: "Jeanne! Jeanne!"

"Enough!" cried Julien-Georges, the elegant socialite. "This spectacle is terrifying for me."

Marc reclosed Georges' skull. "You see, my dear Georges: your body is in good condition; a few more days of patience..."

"But will that reconstituted brain have the same qualities as the old one?" interrogated Julien-Georges, the chic Monsieur.

"I'm sure of it," said Jeanne. Matter is one, but its combinations are incalculable. By decomposing particular substances we eventually obtain the universal synthesis. That's what I've done for blood. Today, from combination to combination, I've obtained the culture of the cerebra cell. Step by step, Homo-Deus, my father and I will study the entire human body, and obtain by means of a molecular culture the creation of an artificial being, alive and thinking."

"Be careful!" exclaimed Georges Garnier, via the mouth of Julien de Vandeuvre, the chic Monsieur. "Be careful—such conceptions lead to madness."

"Get away!" replied Jeanne, excitedly. "Why hesitate? Why hesitate? The goal, the only honorable goal of life, is the work, the research that, until now, has been insoluble, but which the future race will discover. Then, humans will have conquered immortality, and will identify themselves with God."

"God?" Marc queried, with a certain irony.

"God!" Jeanne exclaimed. "God, which, in spite of the indifference, the deceitful indifference of matter, I sense in everything and everywhere: God, the creative force of the universe; God, which created the primordial atom; God, the force, the impulsion that makes everything out of everything, the organic from the inorganic; God, not a being similar to a human but the ensemble of all the physical forces. Intelligences are numerous; God is their sum: the all, the goal, the self!"

"Pan," said Marc, disdainfully.

"Well yes, since humans have put a name to everything: Pan, the God of All; but that name doesn't render it any more comprehensible."

"Time's passing," said Fortin. "Let's get back to Georges. Today, we're going to attempt the first experiment to render life to him completely. This is a human body from which the soul is absent—which is to say, deprived of thought-fluid. It's inadequate to any function. The organism, abandoned to itself, operates uniquely by molecular labor. The cellular material reconstitutes itself mechanically, following the universal laws that reign over matter on the surface of the globe. The body of this Georges Garnier is incapable of action; it only obeys external impulsions. It's impossible for it to act by itself. It can neither move, nor see, nor hear; it's therefore necessary to return its soul—which is to say, the motor of its actions"

"By decoupling the double soul of George-Julien?" asked Marc Vanel.

"That was my first idea," Jeanne replied, "but I haven't yet found it practical to bring about that separation. How, in the brain that, although it contains two such different spirits, has not increased in volume, can the mind of Georges or that of Julien be collected for separation? I was obliged to renounce that, and, unable to do it, thought that it would be preferable, for our synthesis, to create or revive Georges' empty brain. I have, therefore, by means of a similar substance composed of the same elements, reestablished the molecular action in the skull. Today, that reconstitution, as you can see, is perfect, to the point that it's impossible to distinguish it. The proof that we have the secret of the cerebral molecule is that in the fresh state of the organ, which, in the month that it has been exposed would have decomposed if it had not found the conditions necessary to its life and its molecular reproduction."

"What do you mean?"

"That molecular life is independent of our will; that all the parts of our organism are eliminated and renewed incessantly. Not one remains immobile, in the current of the arterial and venous torrent; all the debris and new elements are removed and replaced relentlessly; and it's that life, independent of our sensible life, in which I shall confide in order to complete our experiment successfully."

"Go on!" said Marc. "We're following you."

"That molecular life," Jeanne went on, "has never ceased to exist in our friend George Garnier. It's sufficient for us to reconnect it to the…let us say, spiritual life, to distinguish the normal state of a living body…and that's what I hope to obtain by using the fluid agents: magnetism and electricity."

"Go on! Go on, then"

"In removing from Georges' brain what was necessary for my study, we chose the part relative to movement. Thus, all the rest of the cerebral matter has remained as it was—which is to say, imprinted with all the knowledge acquired by Georges before the operation. I assume that you think, as I do, that the cerebral mass is nothing but a kind of receptacle, in which all the recordings—auditory, visual and so on—are maintained indefinitely, ever ready to file before the objective lens of Thought. Let us therefore animate the encephalic mass, by means of the Voltaic pile, and intellectual life will gradually be reborn.

"But what about the motor?" asked Georges-Julien. "The soul of the receptacle?"

"The soul is nothing other than the sum of the notions acquired. If I observe the soul of a new-born child, it is only slowly—very slowly—that an ordered mechanism of movement, sight and natural needs becomes manifest; then comes work and study; and later still, the individual property, judgment, comparison, invention..."

"Ah! You've arrived!" said Homo-Deus. "It's the triumph of materialism."

"It's the triumph of the spirit over matter," Jeanne replied, "or rather, the alliance of the two. Is not anything, in nature, tightly bound? Why demand, scientifically, a division that logic shows us to be impossible? In sum, there's neither materiality nor spirituality: there are only natural laws to which everything is submissive."

She turned to Georges-Julien. "Now leave us, Georges, and don't worry. Your clothing of flesh and bone will be returned to you soon."

"But what about me? Me...? Anyway, it's not important. Haven't I given myself to you, body and soul? Dispose as you wish of the man who loves you."

Jeanne Fortin held out her hand to him. "Thank you—but think over what I've said."

"Yes. Until this evening, then."

The elegant man went out, with his two souls, and Jeanne Fortin said: "I have a means of utilizing Julien de Vandeuvre. I'm going to marry him to his former victim, Julie Berton."

"What's this story?"

"An amorous adventure of de Vandeuvre's, which we discovered while sorting through his papers. Madame Berton, our schoolmistress, had a daughter, Julie, who obtained a position as reader and lady companion to Madame de Vandeuvre, Julien's mother. The latter was smitten by the young woman and succeeded in making her his mistress by a dishonest means: he got her drunk and profited from her drunkenness to abuse her. It's necessary to add that Madame de Vandeuvre was her son's accomplice. In brief, Julie, having become pregnant, disappeared, and no one knows what has become of her. I want to find her and make Julien de Vandeuvre marry her."

"You have a taste for punishment. Me, too."

"It's a means of making use of that socialite. Afterwards, we'll make use of him for the success of our projects."

"It amuses you to make these puppets move?" asked Marc Vanel.

"Yes, it amuses me, and relaxes me—as it does you," she added, looking fixedly at Marc, who shivered. She went on: "Let's get back to our study. We'll activate a powerful battery; we'll try to animate our automaton. I didn't want to do an experiment front of Georges that might have been too painful for him."

"The battery's ready," said Dr. Fortin, resuming his place.

"First, we're going to electrify the part of the encephalum that we've reconstituted, in order to assure us of its general functioning. Afterwards, we'll submit the ensemble to a regular and continuous excitation, to which we'll abandon the subject... There! Pay attention!"

Georges' body sat up, and recovered its equilibrium.

"Stand up!"

Georges stood up.

"Sit down!"

Georges sat down.

"He can hear! He can understand!" exclaimed Dr. Fortin, radiant.

"It's more probable that it's just an effect of habit. The human body, habituated to obeying certain impulses, acts mechanically; but this proves, at any rate, that the brain has heard…anyway, we shall soon see…"

She called: "Georges! Georges!"

Georges turned round.

"Do you recognize me?"

Georges made no reply.

"You see—his movements are instinctive, but he has no judgment."

"What do we do now?" Dr. Fortin asked.

"What I said, and nothing more."

At that moment, someone knocked on the door. It was Frédéric, carrying a letter. Fortin took it and, recognizing the handwriting on the envelope, said: "Damn! From Père Garnier."

He opened it and read:

My old friend,

I've been called to see one of my clients who lives in your neighborhood. I'll take advantage of it to dine with you. Embrace our daughter.

"An unfortunate inconvenience!"

"Yes," said Jeanne. "He's going to ask us for news of his son, Georges, again."

"Fortunately, I received letters from my correspondent in Istanbul this morning, drafted in the fashion that I indicated to him."

"Then all's well," said Jeanne.

"You've understood, Fred," Fortin went on, addressing the servant. "Not a word that might betray us."

"Don't worry, Monsieur. But will Monsieur be good enough to give me news of my nursling?"

"You'll soon be relieved of your chores."

"It will only be a matter," Jeanne said, "of making him drink the contents of flasks that I'll prepare for you, every four hours. In the intervals, you can leave him alone."

"Very well, Mam'zelle Jeanne."

"Are you dining with us, Marc?" Jeanne asked, making a sign to Frédéric to wait. Then, seeing Marc hesitate, she added: "Yes. So, this evening we shall have Papa Garnier and our friend Vanel. Distinguish yourself, Frédéric."

"Have no fear; one will do what is necessary."

VII. The Revelatory Jewel

Slightly nervous, feverish and anxious, as she cast one last glance over her drawing room, Madame Vauclin testified to the particular state of agitation of women getting ready to receive guests.

Sophie—Fifi to her intimates—was very pretty, and the refinement of her intelligence earned her a quantity of relationships that she had subjected to a strict triage, in order that her house might be classified among those that it is useful to frequent. Because he was always, and systematically, party of the redoubtable opposition that prides itself on representing in the Chambre the country avid for a new era, Député Vauclin was on the best of terms with the leaders of the government, whoever they were, and the elect of the turbulent group that obtained more favors than the most notorious government supporters. His wife knew how to utilize that influence with tact and discernment, so effectively that a number of people of rather elevated position were obliged to her.

Incessantly on the lookout for novelties, and avid for social renown, Madame Vauclin never let any opportunity escape to put herself or her husband on show. Thus, she had arranged for Dr. Vanel, who was causing a sensation in Parisian society by his legend and his allure, to come to her home, as he had been to the Marquise de Virmile's.

Madame Vauclin inspected her drawing room nervously, going back and forth, a trifle feverishly, moving a vase of flowers or a trinket and then stepping back to view the ensemble, like a general disposing his batteries on the eve of a battle. Then, satisfied, she examined herself in a mirror, smiling.

She was rather petite, nervous, supple, with an admirable figure, splendid black hair, a warm and milky skin, long-lashed eyes, profound, dark and enigmatic, her blood-red lips always tremulous, as if perpetually bruised by recent kisses.

In spite of her voluptuous beauty, however, she lacked the confident, slightly languid charm that adds a divine aura of likeability to pretty women. She was disturbing, disquieting and seductive, but people resented that seductiveness, for they sensed that she was dangerous and cruel, grim in her determination, and had the instinct of stiffening themselves and slipping away when they were subjected, in spite of themselves, to the attention of those intelligent and caressant eyes. A fluid seemed to emanate from her similar to the one that snakes use to fascinate the prey that they are about to devour.

That afternoon, she had put on a dress that was rather simple in its lines, but tailored in a supple golden fabric that molded her, revealing her contours with all the immodesty that can be permitted to a woman known for her beauty and originality. A thick black stripe ran along the edge of the discreetly low neckline, emphasizing the whiteness of her neck; it then descended along one hip, to lose itself in the skirt in a pretty movement. Similar stripes terminated the ends of the sleeves, tapered like those of a kimono, composing an artistic ensemble in which the warm white flesh seemed framed in gold, like a valuable gem.

Four o'clock. Sophie Vauclin chose a monstrous carnation from an array, crimson in color, so dark that it tended toward black. Having contrasted it to her hair and to the snowy skin of her neck, she admired the harmony of tones, and fastened the flower to the gold of her corsage by means of a diamond clasp whose heart was a ruby. That precious jewel having taken the beautiful carnation prisoner, she murmured: "Let's go—I'm in form today."

The Vauclins lived, as we know, in the Avenue Henri-Martin, in a splendid building. But the socialist député did not receive his electors there. He had hired a modest floor in the Rue des Saints-Pères, where a lithe secretary was permanently stationed. The stairway leading to that obscure office was dirty and malodorous, as was fitting, in order that the political allies of the grim revolutionary would not be offended by an out-and-out luxury. That address was recorded in Bottin, under the name "Arsène Vauclin, député," while the other, in the Avenue Henri-Martin, was attributed to "Vauclin, man of letters"—for the political man edited an artistic periodical.

An automobile stopped outside the gate of the small garden.

"Albert! I'm certain of it," she murmured. She darted a final glance at her dress, at the mirror, patted her hair, and waited.

A few minutes went by; then a domestic opened the drawing room door and announced: "Monsieur Albert Baruyer."

He bowed respectfully and kissed Madame Vauclin's hand. While the advocate placed his lips on her slender wrist, she looked at the door, which the domestic closed again. Then Baruyer stood up, put his arms around her, and gave her a long kiss on the lips.

When they were disentangled, he said: "Your husband isn't here?"

"He won't be long."

"Since we're alone then, another kiss." He drew her against him, seeking her mouth.

"Albert, Albert!" she stammered. "Why must you dominate me thus?" She pulled free. "Let me be—I thought I heard someone ring."

She was not mistaken. The door opened, giving passage to the Marquise de Virmile, Comtesse Simone d'Armez and Jacques de Simiane. The curious were arriving with every passing minute, excited by the presence of Homo-Deus at the pretty woman's tea. In addition to the Baruyer brothers, there was the financier Walesport, Louis Barthou, and Mademoiselle Alexane, the principal dancer at the Opéra. There were socialites, sportsmen and deputes, Maurice Donnay[26] and several other Academicians, a Russian dancer, a professor of the Faculté de Médecine, the great surgeon Jean Bouchon and other personalities, the least of which had some title to being a notable figure in Paris.

"You know, my dear friend," simpered an American, Madame Gourard, whose house was the most original palace of Buddhism, "I was due to leave this morning for Venice—well, I won't go until tomorrow, because of this sorcerer. I'm sure that in a little while Homo-Deus will make us tremble with his demonic eyes."

"Please be quiet," said Madame Vauclin, smiling with her long-lashed eyes and carmined lips. "You'll sow fear in my salon—quite unjustly besides, for I suspect that Dr. Vanel is, in sum, a great scientist."

At that moment, the person who had provoked the sensation in question was announced. He advanced casually, with a supple, feline gait, an enigmatic smile on his disillusioned lips, and kissed the hand that Madame Vauclin held out to him.

"Welcome, Master Satan."

But député Vauclin, who had just arrived, took possession of him. Homo-Deus had immediately observed the affinities and attractions, secret or avowed, that presided over the formation of groups in that Parisian salon. He had seen, for his magnetic eyes were not unaware of anything around him, the adroit maneuver by means of which the elegant de Simiane had drawn closer to the Marquise de Virmile. He grasped the incredulous gazes of the Messieurs of the Faculté. He had noticed the narrow alliance of five individuals: Walesport, Barthou, the Baruyer brothers and Vauclin. Homo-Deus listened, and replied— in the manner of Rasputin, by means of vague images—to the threadbare fluency of the revolutionary député.

"I know," the latter said, "about the friendship that links you to a man I hold in high esteem, Tchitcherine, the Soviet commissar delegated to Foreign Affairs. Oh, that one has a brain! Where, among us, is the French genius, sublime and convincing, who will lift the popular masses to launch an assault on a democracy in the process of sinking in the muddy pools of a frightful egotism?"

Well, at least he doesn't lack cheek, Vanel thought, casting a glance over the supremely elegant gathering, rich, perfumed and useless. He saw the gilded decorations of the three sequential drawing rooms, and evoked the image of his friend, Tchitcherine, so modest, so effacing, with meager needs and an immense soul. A slight disgust came to his lips. Inventing a pretext, he slipped away from the politician. A cry of admiration uttered by Simone d'Armez caused him to turn round.

---

[26] The dramatist Maurice Donnay (1859-1945) had begun his acquaintance with Parisian literary life as a habitué of the Chat Noir, in the days when Champsaur used to hang out there.

Addressing Madame Vauclin, the pretty Comtesse said: "Oh! What a charming idea to attach that beautiful carnation by means of such a jewel. The man who offers that gem to his wife is a model husband."

Homo-Deus shuddered. Moving to one side, into the embrasure of a window, he took a piece of paper from his pocket, which he examined rapidly on the sly. It was a receipt:

To Monsieur Julien de Vandeuvre, a clasp, diamonds mounted in platinum, forming the corolla of a flower, with a ruby in the center. Ten thousand francs. Paid in cash.

Vanel's magnetic eyes fixed themselves on Madame Vauclin, studying her, seeming to penetrate her. The disquieting magician advanced toward her. After having bowed, he said: "Madame, to thank you for your welcome, I'd like to show you two amusing phenomena. The first is a manifestation of spontaneous generation, the second an example of fluidic emanation at a distance. You shall see how the spirit commands matter and spirit. For the first experiment, would you please send for a few seeds—of beans, maize, peas or wheat, as you please? I assume that your cook will have something suitable."

Madame Vauclin hastened to give the order. A valet presented a few grains of millet on a tray.

"Perfect!" said Vanel. "Please watch closely." He put a few grains in the palm of his hand, which he extended, while his eyes closed. The spectator saw the grains begin to stir, gradually, to move, and finally to burst, sending forth white shoots that seemed to go green.

Applause burst forth, and Vanel reopened his eyes. Homo-Deus, smiling, asked, as he had done before at Marquise de Virmile's house, for sheets of paper, which he set on an item of furniture beside him. He picked up one, and showed the audience that it contained no inscription. He placed it on the sidetable and then stepped back, seemingly absorbed in a profound spiritual contention.

Abruptly, the steely eyes darted their magnetic gaze at the piece of paper. The sheet rose slowly into the air; it became still, suspended there, and then, with a single surge, as had occurred at the home of the Marquise de Virmile, it flew across the room to fall on to the knees of the Comtesse d'Armez, who could not suppress a slight scream.

"Read it!" commanded Vanel's curt voice.

Simon d'Armez looked down at the piece of paper. Immediately, her forehead and cheeks reddened.

"What is it? What is it?"

"It's nothing," she said, passing the sheet to her neighbor.

The paper circulated. People observed that it was blank. Had the trick gone wrong?

"Madame d'Armez read something, however," Vanel affirmed. "I don't know what, of course—perhaps an effect of suggestion, of one free spirit on another."

Simone darted a desperate glance at the invisible satyr, fearful, imploring and somewhat complicit. For she had read: *I shall return this evening.*

"And me, Master?" begged Madame Vautrin.

The hypnotist plunged back into his meditation; the sheet of paper took flight again, to land on the knees of the mistress of the house. Madame Vautrin went frightfully pale, and her husband leapt to sustain her, for she seemed about to faint.

Both of them, then, saw the words: *Julien de Vandeuvre is not dead.*

His gaze malevolent, the député advanced abruptly toward Marc Vanel. "Do you know, Monsieur, what I've just read, at the same time as my wife?"

"I have absolutely no idea." Vanel's voice was cutting, and his attitude utterly disengaged.

Madame Vauclin did not lose her composure for long. Smiling, she held out the piece of paper to her friends. "How stupid we are! It's a reflection of our thoughts that we read on the blank sheet. Nothing, of course, can really be written there."

"You're perfectly correct, Madame," Vanel confirmed, with a diabolical smile. "What you read is merely a materialized translation of a grave preoccupation or"—he glanced at Simone d'Armez—"an agreeable memory."

From all directions, hands reached out. "To me! Me, Master, I beg you!"

Marc Vanel declared: "Pardon me, Mesdames. The little experiment will conclude there today."

He bowed to Madame Vauclin to take his leave.

"What a terrible man you are!" she said, looking him straight in the eyes.

But the glamour of those charming irises, the fluid of her gaze, collided with the steely arrow of the satanic eyes of Homo-Deus, who, leaning over respectfully, brushed her wrist with a kiss.

VIII. A Small Discreet House

Marc Vanel occupied a private house buried in verdure in the Rue d'Yvette, in the utmost depths of Passy. The garden was separated from the street by railings lined with a thick hedge of ivy. The house, white and cheerful, raised its silhouette in the midst of a grove of lindens and acacias.

Flowers dotted their bright colors in the bushes, and all along the enclosing wall lilacs were bowed down by enormous clusters of blooms, filling the surroundings with their scent. A perron of a few stone steps led up to the door. Above it, decorating the façade, the vigorous stems of superb wisterias ran. It was all lovely, in charming taste, like a love nest.

Marc Vanel only had two domestics: a Hindu maidservant and the chauffeur Mardruk, also Hindu, but very familiar with European mores. Vanel had once saved his life, and the man had attached himself to him, simultaneously fulfilling the functions of valet, mechanic and laboratory assistant—for if Mardruk's intelligence was prodigious, his faculties of adaptation were surprising.

Such was the tranquil lair of the invisible satyr.

IX. A Hypnotized Quartet

The last sunbeams of a splendid afternoon were playing on a stained-glass window. Having traversed the panes, they put dazzling gems onto the bright carpet of the hallway leading to the drawing room, along with monstrous moving flowers, like magical insects, red, yellow, emerald and lilac.

The door opened, and Mardruk ushered in a man who came forward, his gait stiff, his gaze fixed and his lips taut. Without hesitation, he went straight to a leather armchair backed up against the wall, sat down without saying a word, placed a briefcase stuffed with papers on his knees, and remained fixed in the strange attitude of an automaton.

Mardruk closed the door, leaving the enigmatic individual alone, solemnized by a long frock coat like those worn by notaries, a few old physicians and a few magistrates. Gray side-whiskers framed his thin-lipped face. His features seemed cold, reflecting no sensibility.

Soon, the door opened again, giving passage to a man who was still young, quite handsome, elegantly dressed, with a smiling face ornamented by a superb blond beard, slightly bleached. He was wearing a well-cut jacket; his hands, carefully gloved, were holding a top hat and a cane with a golden pommel. He advanced with the same stiffness as the first individual, with the same eyes empty of thought, the same jerky gait and the same indifference to his surroundings. A former drummer at the Chat Noir, he had once made numerous connections in that mixed artistic milieu. Thanks to successful protections, he had been able to get a job in the administration after the closure of the famous cabaret, and was presently the most Parisian of Commissaires de Police. In his spare time, he composed little ditties and amiable satires. He was also—although he had no suspicion of it—an auxiliary of Homo-Deus.

The second person did not sketch the slightest salute to the first; he did not even seem to have perceived his presence, and went to sit down beside him; the other remained immutably nailed to his seat, his hands placed on the black briefcase.

For a third time, Mardruk opened the door. The visitor who advanced was dressed in a velvet suit of an indefinable color. A bowler hat with a very narrow border partially concealed black hair, strongly pomaded. His nose was long, hooked over a mocking mouth, from which a cigarette end was hanging. He was limping slightly, his hands in his wainscot pockets. He went to sit down in a third armchair beside the previous arrival, set against the same wall, and waited, with the jaundiced cigarette end still dangling from his violet-tinted lip, to which it appeared to be stuck.

Finally, Mardruk ushered in a short and stout individual, very red in the face, his calves in leather leggings. He was holding a flat cap in his hands. He also took his place against the wall, on the fourth and last vacant armchair, next to the apache. The four individuals sat motionless, like statues, looking straight ahead of them with strange, haggard eyes.

Brought together mysteriously under the effect of inexplicable causes and unknown forces, they were a notary, a police Commissaire, an apache and a taxi-driver.

Without a line of their faces twitching, they remained there, as if asleep with their eyes open, rigorously aligned against the wall, mute and indifferent. They gave the impression of marionettes devoid of thought or will, inert, moved by a singular and obscure power.

After a few minutes, Marc Vanel came in. He considered the immobile individuals momentarily. A smile of satisfaction appeared on his lips; then he sat down at a desk, facing his four visitors. His steely eyes darted singular gleams, which seemed to penetrate the eyes of the marionettes, who shivered.

Homo-Deus addressed the driver first.

"Have you followed my instructions, Claude Chamot?"

"Yes, Master."

"What information did you collect at the wine merchant's?"

"Madame Vauclin is the mistress of Albert Baruyer, the advocate. She also had a young man who disappeared mysteriously, Julien de Vandeuvre."

"I know all that. I need precise, vigorous and, above all, little-known details concerning the Vauclin household."

"That's not easy, Master. The domestics with whom I've clinked glasses, who are well-paid, don't say much. I can tell you, however, that the husband is certainly not unaware of his wife's affair with Baruyer any more than he was unaware of her relationship with Julien de Vandeuvre."

"What is the Vauclins' financial situation?"

"Hum! They gave the impression of people who have their ups and downs, but for some time it seems that money has been abundant in the house."

"Is Albert Baruyer genuinely rich?"

"An advocate who'll do anything, a spendthrift and a gambler."

"And what do you know about the dancer Alexane?"

"She leads a very regular life. No entitled protector for a year, but she's playing at true love with a young foreigner, as handsome as a god. She's madly smitten and hides him away as if she were afraid of losing him."

"What is his name?"

"Don't know yet."

"I need precise and detailed information about him. You can go."

The driver went out, without paying any attention to the remaining visitors, and without departing from his strange stiffness, giving the grotesque impression of a strolling marionette.

"Your turn," said Homo-Deus, addressing the notary. "You know, Maître Gaderne, what I instructed you to do?"

"Yes. The Vauclin inheritance is a pure legend. The household was living, until recently, on the député's salary and Vandeuvre's largesse. Although I haven't discovered any trace of an inheritance justifying the sudden fortune of the Vauclin household, I have discovered that young Vandeuvre had inherited four million immediately before his disappearance. He had entered into that sum at the moment of his abrupt plunge into the unknown. It's that coincidence that makes the young man's family believe that he's been murdered in order to rob him, unless he's sequestered somewhere."

"That's possible. Try to tell me, next time, on what day Vandeuvre collected his legacy."

That won't be difficult. Maître Parisay, the family notary, is one of my best friends."

"All right, go. Do you need money?"

"No, Master. Business is picking up. The gap in my finances will soon be filled in, and I'll be able to pay you back the sum that you've advanced me. My clientele, momentarily anxious, has confidence in me again."

With that, the notary left at the same automatic pace and with the same grave and cold expression that he had had when he came in.

"Your turn, Molard," said Vanel, addressing the Commissaire de Police. "My congratulations on the elegant manner in which you buried the affair of the cadaver found in the Avenue Henri-Martin the other day."

"Oh, Master, I have no great merit in having obeyed you on that occasion. You told me that my agents had had a spring night's dream. But I believed it, since my subordinate's report was more like a hoax. Then again, I remembered that Shakespeare had written a delightful fantasy called *A Midsummer Night's Dream*, and I composed a Montmartrean song called *The Mystery of a Spring Night* on the theme furnished by the two merry agents. Thanks to my friends in the Sûreté, I know that no one is getting steamed up about the matter. It's not worth the trouble, is it, since the newspapers aren't talking about it? As the press wasn't interested in the young cretin's probable flight, in spite of the family's persistence, the investigation was only continuing as a matter of form. In those conditions, one can consider the case as closed. All the more so as the police have discovered an intrigue between Vandeuvre and Madame Vauclin."

"I know that."

"Yes, but as Vauclin doesn't want that to be spread around, he's approached the magistracy in order to prevent the annoyances that an indiscretion might occasion him. One more reason for the affair to be buried."

"Very good. Now, what do you know about the relationship between Georges Baruyer and the American Walesport?

"Walesport is a rather enigmatic individual, whose past is lost in an obscurity impenetrable to us. It would be necessary to go to America to be better informed. All that is known is that his origins were modest, perhaps wretched. Former cowboy, probably, then gold prospector, he must have committed a crime that made him rich and obliged him to quit his country. Very intelligent and very strong, he's an interesting figure. One finds him mixed up, since the beginning of the exploitation of the bank he created, with a mysterious affair of Rumanian mining shares, in the course of which the prime mover, a certain Baron Rodock, died suddenly, seemingly not of natural causes."

"And Georges Baruyer is in the life of that bandit?"

"He's his associate! The bank is a partnership—but because of the political situation, Baruyer can't put his name to it. That doesn't prevent the député from lending the most active collaboration to the enterprise, for he's a remarkable financier. Furthermore, as he's admirably placed, thanks to his connections with Claude Barsac, the President of the Council, he's been able to benefit before anyone else from reliable information about exchange rates, by means of which the bank has succeeded in bringing off several nice coups on the Bourse in the past year. Vauclin is also involved in the affairs of Walesport and Baruyer."

"Keep watch on the whole clique, and try to discover their plans. Inform me about this Rodock, who died at the outset of the Baruyer-Walesport enterprise."

"Understood, Master."

"Here's a thousand francs, Molard. Be generous with the Sûreté agents you employ."

Stiffly, the police Commissaire went away, and Marc Vanel finally addressed the picturesque criminal.

"Your turn, Merluche," he said. "You haven't been much use to me thus far."

"Not my fault. Give me jobs that are in my area of specialty."

"Let's see—I instructed you to introduce yourself, by the means habitual to people of your species, into the unoccupied apartment of Julien de Vandeuvre and bring me all the tenant's papers. Do you have them?"

"Yes, Boss. Here they are."

Merluche unbuttoned his dirty jacket and then his shirt, and Vanel saw the wads of paper wedged against the burglar's dirty skin. The criminal placed them on the desk."

"That's good," said Marc. "I'll look at them later. Is that all?"

"Y...es, Boss..."

Merluche's voice seemed uncertain. Moreover, his gaze avoided Vanel. The latter stared at him.

"You're lying! Merluche, when I give you a mission, it must be executed scrupulously. If I send you to burgle an apartment in order to procure me useful documents, I don't want you to profit from it to work on your own account. Come on, out with it—what have you stolen?"

The burglar trembled like a leaf, without making any reply, but Homo-Deus never stopped fixing him harshly with his eyes that seemed to be emitting flashes; he ended up extracting a packet of bonds from a hiding-place situated between his belly and the belt of his trousers, which he set down before the Master. Then he rummaged in his trouser pockets and took out some gold coins, which he set beside the bonds.

"There," he said, "minus three ten-franc pieces."

"Good. You can keep the gold, but leave the bonds there; you can put them back from where you got them tomorrow evening, with the papers I haven't kept. You must be careful to work neatly, so that no one will suspect the clandestine visit to the young man's apartment."

"Yes, Boss."

While the apache took back the louis with evident satisfaction, Vanel darted a glance over the bonds that Merluche had stolen.

"Damn!" he exclaimed. "There's one for seven thousand francs. It's hard, eh, to be obliged to surrender that? Well, old chap, thank me. You have no suspicion of the favor I'm doing you."

"What do you mean, Boss?"

"These are bearer bonds, of course, but they're shares in a great industrial enterprise constituted by only half a dozen individuals. If you sold them, they wouldn't have any difficulty, thereafter, in finding you."

"So?"

"And as Julien de Vandeuvre was murdered, who could the murderer have been except the possessor of these bonds? You could struggle all you liked, my poor old chap, but you wouldn't get out of it, and you'd be espousing the Widow one morning."

The burglar's teeth chattered at the idea of a brush with the guillotine. Homo-Deus burst into laughter: the singular, slightly nervous laughter that he emitted in moments when the spectacle of life took on interesting aspects.

How that unexpected solution would have suited the Vauclin household's affairs, he thought. *Yes, it would have settled everything. This sinister brigand taken for Vandeuvre's murderer—for he's doubtless committed murder—would have explained the crime. The Vauclins would have breathed easy, tranquil for the rest of their lives. The police would be glad to close a troublesome case, and the Vandeuvre family would declare themselves satisfied, having avenged the death. I would have contrived the entire comedy, and it would only have cost the life of an uninteresting individual who is doubtless already a criminal.*

He uttered another bust of nervous and mocking laughter, and studied the apache pityingly.

"You don't know how much you owe me," he said. "Go on, get lost—and come back tomorrow evening to take what I give you. Everything must be back in place as soon as possible."

"Yes, Boss—tomorrow evening."

Merluche left, slightly less stiffly than the other collaborators, but with the same fixed gaze—in which, however, a certain dread or submission was fuming.

Left alone, Homo-Deus examined the booty brought by the apache. As he went along, an expression of contentment was painted on his face. Soon, he had finished. Everything was placed in a safe, and after having closed it, Marc Vanel rubbed his hands together.

"That's it!" he said. "Tomorrow, the Fortins will be up to date, and when Vandeuvre wakes up, he'll have nothing to tell us." Once again he uttered his nervous, staccato laughter, and his face took on a curious expression reminiscent of a misanthropic Mephisto contemplating life as a humorist.

X. Entr'acte

    Dinnertime had arrived. Marc Vanel went into the dining room, adjacent to the hallway, sat down at the table and rang. Mardruk appeared.

    "I'll be going out this evening at nine o'clock."

    Mardruk bowed and disappeared. And Vanel, while waiting for the Hindu servant to bring his soup, meditated.

XI. !?! Homo-Deus !?!

Marc Vanel, alias Homo-Deus, was a bizarre and complex being whose life surpassed the most fabulous novels. He was the son of an admirably beautiful creature whose nationality remained as dubious as her social status. She was living in a luxurious apartment in the Rue Marbeuf when she brought into the world the child whose father was unknown to anyone. Calling herself Princess Nadinska, French and Russian were as perfectly familiar to her as German, Turkish, English and all the Latin languages. She only received individuals of note in her much sought-after salon, especially scientists, litterateurs, artists and many diplomats. The insistence that she put into making connections with the latter ended up causing her to be accused of espionage, at least in jealous conversation, and that version was supported by the obvious luxury and the expensive lifestyle—inexplicable things, given that she was not known to have any protector, in spite of the army of exceedingly rich suitors ready to throw their fortunes at her feet.

That went on for years. Princess Nadinska, leaving her son in the care of an experienced guardian, made long voyages abroad. Then, for a while, she seemed fatigued. Eventually, she became involved with a very distinguished chemist, Pierre Vanel, who married her and recognized her son. The princess brought not a sou of dowry to her husband, but she furnished the regulation papers, which established indisputably that she was a Russian princess. She died not long afterwards, and no one ever knew what she had been, nor whose son Marc was.

By virtue of his attachment to the supremely intelligent and beautiful wife that he had adored, the chemist Vanel devoted himself entirely to young Marc's education. The child, moreover, was astonishingly precocious, and amazed his adoptive father by his love of study and avidity for scientific matters. More than anything else, the chemist's work caused the boy to marvel, and the lovely Russian's former husband was flattered by having awakened in his stepson a passion for the science in which he had made his name.

Unfortunately, the scientist had not been long delayed in dying too, leaving his friend Fortin the care of watching over the child. The fortune he possessed at this death permitted Marc to be given a very advanced education. The remainder, about a hundred thousand francs, was to be handed over to him when he came of age.

At twenty-three, having finished his military service, Marc was superb, overflowing with strength and intelligence. He had devoted himself to medical science, but his brain was so avid for knowledge that one branch was not sufficient for his activity. That was why Marc, while climbing the usual steps of medicine, had made parallel studies in chemistry, the first notions of which had been given to him by his father. Soon, chemistry no longer being sufficient for him, he turned to mechanics and ended up becoming passionate about electricity. Then, combining those studies with the ones he was accomplishing in the medical domain, he had made, while still young, astonishing discoveries regarding the properties of high frequency currents and ultraviolet radiation.

Encouraged by Fortin, whose research was in the same area as his own, he announced himself as a future genius. That was the era when Jeanne, having returned from boarding school, was already taking part in the scientific endeavors of her father and Marc. The latter had immediately noticed the young woman's extraordinary intelligence, her cold, splendid beauty and her genius for discovery. But as she did not go to the expense of any coquetry toward him, they only became comrades and true friends—and life had continued like that for some time.

One day, abruptly, Vanel had fled. Having become somber and choleric, European humankind disgusted him, and he had resolved to deprive himself of its contemplation, at least for some time. He had gone to India.

There he had lived unforgettable years. He recognized the enervating perfumes of an old magic, and, closing his eyes, saw once again the Brahmins, the Hindu gods, the bayaderes, the corteges of warriors and the sacred elephants. He became the companion of fakirs, and lived their life for three years, speaking their language, thinking their thoughts, and subjecting his body to cruel necessities. He learned secrets that justified the mortifications he endured.

With their science he combined his own science, and he obtained amazing results—but he dreamed of new skies, new décor, unseen faces and launched himself, avid for sensation, through the most varied races. He traveled across Africa, where he found nothing to interest him, reached South America, and then, heading northwards again, lived for some time among the last Sioux tribes. He finally washed up in San Francisco.

In that city he made the acquaintance of Sun Yat-Sen, a small Chinaman of prodigious intelligence, who subsequently became the founder of the Chinese Republic. The two men had immediately reached an understanding; as they were both doctors of medicine, they recognized common scientific preoccupations and affinities that testified to the identity of their aspirations.[27]

By that time, Marc Vanel no longer had any money. He knew days of poverty and tasted the bitterness of hours of hunger. Living in the Chinese quarter with his friend, he helped him in his slow work in favor of a future republic that would liberate the ancient Middle Kingdom. The two men, nourished on a little rice and tea, spent days preaching to the yellow men and caring for them. Still together, they were able to reach London by obtaining employment as stokers on

---

[27] The Chinese revolutionary Sun Yat-Sen (1866-1925) was only in America briefly during his years of exile, but spent some time in San Francisco in 1910, where he published a newspaper; it is presumably during that interval that Homo-Deus supposedly encountered him.

an English cargo ship. Then the Chinaman left him in order to go to Peking to realize his dream, an astonishing ascension.

In London, Marc Vanel lived on his medical art. He took advantage of it to install himself in a small house near Kew Gardens, not far from the capital, where he found the calm he had long sought. His desire for that calm was ardent, because an idea was now haunting him: a mad, presumptuous, grandiose idea, which, if he realized it, would make him the equal of a god, finally permitting him to be, beneath the most agreeable form, the sarcastic misanthrope that he intended to remain.

Liberated from material cares, rich in scientific treasures accumulated over the years, he had attached himself to a formidable endeavor whose success would give him the means to withdraw from humankind but to remain an amused, arrogant, *invisible* spectator.

XII. The Mesmoth Experiment

Invisible! To be invisible! Could a man ever find, in the resources of his science, the fabulous means of abstracting himself from the gaze of his fellows? And yet... humans had invented the telephone; they had succeeded, thanks to wireless telegraphy, in manifesting life at a distance—a great distance—in spite of obstacles: mountains, seas and abysses. Thirty years before, could anyone have supposed that a day would come when a discharge of electrical force, propagating through space by means of waves, would be realized wirelessly beyond the oceans? Would anyone have had the temerity to think that human beings, mounted in machines of canvas and steel, would surpass the speed of a royal eagle soaring over the mountains? That a Frenchman would travel by air, in forty days, from Paris to Tokyo?

Why, then, should he, Vanel, be insane to devote his youth, his intelligence, his Mirandolaesque knowledge and his marvelous divination of the secrets of chemistry and electricity to research the supremely precious discovery of invisibility? What a dream! To participate in actions without betraying one's presence! To be—like a god—the unknown cause of punishments and recompenses; to know the worst secrets; to see crimes being prepared and prevent them, or allow them to be accomplished in accordance with his own moral law; to savor coldly and impassively the joy of witnessing hypocrisies, humiliating baseness, degrading misery, improper favors, ignoble ploys, debaucheries, passions and vices! To be, in sum, the invisible observer of the human comedy...yes, what a dream, and what enjoyment!

In his little cottage near Kew Gardens, Marc Vanel had installed a secret laboratory hidden in his basement. The room was clean, well lit by powerful electric lamps, and no one knew of its existence except Mardruk, the faithful Hindu who had followed Vanel ever since the doctor had left Asia.

Thanks to bold surgical operations carried out on his clientele, Vanel had earned some money with which he was able to complete his installation and procure the indispensable instruments. Now he dedicated himself entirely to his problem.

He worked relentlessly, seeking by means of calculations, mixtures, analyses and syntheses. Always coldly scientific, even when his probing led him to seemingly-incoherent trials, Marc Vanel spent months equilibrating formulae, attempting experiments on substances equivalent to those making up the human body. He ended up finding the right track. He had acquired the mathematical certainty of the discovery; the figures, the mixtures, the voltages—everything ended up being checked, coordinated and harmonized, and he was convinced that the hypotheses were faultless.

Among solid invisible bodies there is one—glass—that is only betrayed by the reflection of light from its surface; and yet, glass is only vulcanized sand. The human body, naturally, could not be subjected to a similar proof or a similar temperature, but it was necessary to find an equivalent, and it was primarily in the radiation of the obscure rays of the spectrum that Dr. Vanel searched.

The rays in question have chemical properties, some of which are known; x-rays, which render a part of the human body invisible, only allow the bones and certain parts of the viscera to appear. Thus, the flesh, muscles, blood—life, in sum—is blurred and effaced. Marc pursued his research in that direction; he discovered that, far beyond the ultra-violet rays, invisible rays exist which nevertheless leave marks of their existence on ultrasensible plates. One day, he had the idea of combining those obscure rays with the fluidic influence of magnetism and electricity. Then, when he projected certain rays, he observed, depending on the substances struck by the rays, gaps—which is to say, parts that became invisible. Once, an entire section of his operating table disappeared, along with the objects placed on it. He searched for them, and they remain invisible in his hand. He was in possession of the theoretical verity.

One day, Marc Vanel felt that his ideas were clear and luminous, to the point that he astonished himself, with slight anguish, with his sudden enlightenments after so many painful hours spent before the deceptive enigma, after so many false hopes in which he had thought that he had grasped the secret pursued. Now, obscure formulae, painfully elucidated and extracted from the Limbo of science, emerged from his groping, bursting into magnificent radiation.

There were surges of joy, and then grave anxieties took hold of his questing soul once again. Finally, in the closed laboratory with the padded windows, under the glare of a powerful lamp, among the acrid odors escaped from overheated vessels, the biological chemist Marc Vanel sensed that he was the rival and the peer—even the master—of the most ancient doctors. He was conscious of being a Flamel or a Lull, an elucidator of mysteries; he understood that he had a terrible force at his disposal.

The previous day, he had procured anatomical specimens, entire limbs conserved by freezing. Patiently, with a prodigious skill, in spite of the trembling of his excited hands, he had treated them in accordance with his definitive formulae—and his eyes had ceased to make out the form and colors of the inert flesh that he knew to be present, whose frigid, gripping reality his fingers were touching. Feverishly, Marc started pacing back and forth in the laboratory. He listened to the silence, and then made sure that the door was bolted and checked the fabric covering the ventilation shafts.

The breakthrough troubled him, without, however, taking away anything of his exacerbated faculties. He thought hard. Dead flesh had served for the experiment; doubtless it was identical to living flesh, but it was, even so, inert, useless matter. It was necessary to attempt the experiment on a living animal. His cat was prowling around.

Marc Vanel was still thinking. For him, the experiment was not decisive; might not the warmth of blood, of life, along with the army of microbes inhabiting the organism, oppose the combined action of the drugs, vapors and currents? Might not the palpitation of tissues, the moistness of living skin and the continuous transformations of juices interfere with the work of the mixtures? Might not the various liquids and gases distributed throughout the human body, the majority of which were unknown and fulfilled ill-defined roles, such as the secretions of certain glands, disrupt the effects of foreign external applications?

"No," he said, aloud, "because the electric fluid will penetrate everywhere. There is not a single atom in nature that is not to some degree electrified. Oh, the marvelous vehicle…!"

He wanted to begin again immediately. He activated the plates of a strange machine, and sparks suddenly blazed forth, spurting in a crackling firework display and striking blue and red reflections from the polished steel of the supports.

On a copper stand, Marc isolated a woman's arm, delicate, white and inert. The stand rested on a large disk of thick glass. Then the operator closed a contact. Immediately galvanized, the fingers clenched convulsively, and then, rhythmically, struck the insulator, stretching and moving. Marc then communicated heat and life to that artificially living flesh.

The cat, which was watching, sitting in an attentive attitude and purring, did not miss any of his actions. From time to time it turned its head as its master passed from the right to the left of the machine, or blinked its eyes when excessively bright sparks blinded it. When it saw the fingers of the dead hand taping the glass disk, it thought it was an invitation and moved closer. Suddenly, wanting to play, it leapt onto the stand—but a blue spark sprang forth, and the frightened cat fled to a table in a distant corner and curled up into a ball, its fur bristling, swiveling its eyes, yellow and green by turns.

Marc Vanel now applied the necessary lotions, the action of which, under the effect of the current, ought to provoke invisibility.

In the calm atmosphere, in which the mysterious souls of the fire, liquids and ether were singing, the delicately pink-tinted white form of the arm melted away. It was the exact opposite of what happens during the development of a photographic print, the same operation carried out in reverse.

A misty mass, soon similar to a transparent gelatin, replaced the human limb. Then that homogeneous mass apparently disintegrated, beginning with the edges. The tips of the fingers disappeared completely, and nothing any longer remained but a kind of fleecy gray nucleus, around which a halo remained, similar to mist. The nucleus melted in its turn; the light gray fog remained visible for a few seconds above the glass disk, and then, definitively, no trace of matter subsisted. Nothing of the human debris was any longer manifest to vision, and a mirror placed nearby reflected nothing but emptiness, or jars, alembics and retorts.

Marc Vanel sighed then. He was pale and anguished, but retained all of his grim determination. He perceived the cat, which had taken refuge in a corner of the laboratory, gazing at him fearfully. He approached it, and caressed its black, curved back, whose magnetic fur crackled at the touch.

"Be good, Mesmoth!" he murmured. "You're going to have the first fruits of my glory, old chap!"

He stroked the animal, but the cat remained anxious, even though it raised its head so that Marc could tickle it under its chin. Then, in an imploring and resigned manner, in response to its master's touches, it set back its delicate ears, instinctively sniffing trouble.

Adroitly, Vanel had brought the animal to the machine. While multiplying his caresses, he prepared the experiment, and Mesmoth, amused, was reassured. Mischievously, while the operator was setting up the contacts, it bit his hands. And then, as in the experiment a short while before, the form of the animal became misty and shrank.

Soon, the cat no longer had a head, nor feet, nor a tail; all that remained of its image was a gelatinous center surrounded by transparent mist. And, as with the woman's arm, everything eventually disappeared, quite rapidly, and no appearance remained of Mesmoth, now absolutely invisible. Marc Vanel could feel the supple fur beneath his hands, the warmth of the body, and could hear the animal purring.

At that moment, Marc felt a profound anguish; he was about to do something that might shatter all his illusions, destroy his considerable effort or procure him the most delirious joy, and the pride of the most striking triumph. He was, in fact, about to remove Mesmoth from the apparatus, abstract him from the effect of the currents, the cause of the cat's invisibility. And he feared that, after that fatal action, he might see the image of the cat abruptly reappear.

He hesitated for some time, wanting to enjoy his initial success first, and then made his decision. Mesmoth was lifted up, carried to a table, and finally released. And Marc Vanel uttered an exclamation: the cat was still invisible. Then, strangled by emotion, he collapsed in a chair.

Suddenly, from a crucible forgotten on the fire, vapors rushed with a whistling sound. A pan fell from the table where Marc had placed Mesmoth, and further away flasks were knocked over. The noise and the odors had doubtless frightened the animal, which had run away, bounding. The sound of light muffled footfalls became audible in the laboratory.

Although it was the consequence of the work he had intended, the presence of an invisible being was disturbing. The moment was grave and disquieting. The animal leapt about, uttering hoarse *miaow*s as he pursued it at hazard. He sought with his hands, where he believed he had hard it, the fabulous being superior to him—to him, who had given it its astonishing power. Objects fell, knocked over in passing by the frightened cat. The master's extended hands seemed to want to seize it in order to administer punishment, and the frightened animal fled those haggard hands. Retorts broke; the contents of an entire shelf laden with flasks and various utensils crashed down with a frightful noise, accompanied by a dolorous plaint uttered by the terrorized Mesmoth. Sweat was running down Vanel's temples.

"Mesmoth! Come here, Puss!"

Nothing moved. Now, silence reigned in the laboratory. No further sound of muffled footfalls could be heard. The electric machine had stopped. All that Marc could perceive, with his anxious ears, was the beating of his heart and the slightly hoarse sound of his respiration.

He looked around; neither on the table nor among the numerous objects scattered around the basement was there the slightest movement betraying the presence of the cat. It was doubtless huddled in a dark corner.

Abruptly, in a corner, two emerald phosphorescences appeared: *Mesmoth's eyes*.

Quickly, Marc extinguished the lights. Then, the green gleams in the blackness hone more intensely, and the master moved, softly, toward the irises.

Just as he was about to seize it, the cat bounded away, mewling lugubriously and desperately, knocking over other objects, which broke. Angrily, Vanel ran after the animal; it escaped him incessantly; now, its diabolical irises, moving in the darkness of the laboratory, sometimes appeared to the right and sometimes to the left, high up and low down—everywhere—and Marc thought he saw dozens of them, which stared at him anxiously or danced in the darkness like fire-follets in a cemetery.

He sat down and collected himself momentarily, in order to discipline his thoughts, and, without any longer making any movement, called out in a soft, insinuating voice: "Mesmoth! Mesmoth! Come here, old Puss!"

He remembered that there was milk in a bowl at the back of a cupboard. He switched on the electricity, fetched the bowl, sat down again and set it on his knees.

"Come on, Mesmoth, come here..."

When he's calmed down, Vanel thought, *he'll come. Hunger will make him drink the milk, and at that moment, I'll grab him—and there'll be nothing more to fear!*

He was slightly ashamed. What phenomenon could have made him, Marc Vanel, who had never trembled in his life, fearful? Thus, the power of invisibility had something diabolical or superhuman about it, which even frightened the man who possessed its secret!

Soon, Marc Vanel distinguished the footfalls of the animal drawing nearer; he perceived the lapping of a tongue, causing the surface of the milk on the bowl to stir. Gently, he reached out, felt the warmth of the magnetic fur, shivered at the unanticipated contact, and lifted up the cat.

Serene, maintained once again on the glass disk while the electrical machine was activated again, Mesmoth, under the effect of the new currents and appropriate practices, soon became apparent again. His eyes were fearful, imploring, and Vanel breathed out, triumphantly.

Invisible, he could penetrate anywhere, see everything, without betraying his presence.

Invisible! That was, in sum, to withdraw from the world of the living without dying; it was no longer to be part of a despicable, vain, insipid society, while remaining in its wings—better than that, in the action and also in the souls of the actors, for he could penetrate at will into the most hermetic intimacy of others.

"Now," he said, aloud "I believe I can return to Paris."

He would have liked to go right away, but in the ardor of his enthusiasm he had not perceived the imperfections in his extraordinary discovery, and experienced, to begin with, a few snags that obliged him to do further research to complete the solution of the problem. It was thus that he was able to find the means of communicating a durable invisibility to inert objects in contact with its body, without which he would have been forced to go about the streets naked, which was not exempt from dangers. In the same way, he had experienced a great disappointment in discovering that the invisibility only lasted for an hour or two, and he was obliged to work for a long time to prolong the state. Thanks to powerful machines and new methods, he eventually succeeded in abstracting himself from human sight for ten hours at a time.

Now, he was the master of his discovery, of which he made use as a consummate dilettante. Having only been back in Paris for a month, Invisibility had manifested itself on two picturesque occasions, one of which had been the despair of a policeman in the Avenue Henri-Martin, the other the joy of a lovely woman who believed that she was living a dream of love. They were only petty amusements, however; Vanel was thinking about the profound joys, tragic or comical, with which the human comedy would provide him.

XIII. In Quest of the Unexpected

Marc Vanel had finished dinner. He emerged from the dining room, took a cigarette from a case in the drawing room, and smoked it reflectively.

A quarter of an hour later, he descended by means of a hidden stairway into the basement of the house. A model laboratory was installed there. Having traversed a room floored with white flagstones, he opened a small iron door by means of a secret mechanism hidden in the wall. After crossing the threshold, Homo-Deus found himself in a kind of cellar entirely decked out in black fabric; even the floor disappeared beneath a thick carpet of the same color. In the center of the room, an exceedingly thick crystal disk about a meter in diameter rested on the carpet. On the disk was a copper framework.

Although no light bulb illuminated the cellar it was not entirely dark; a white, slightly milky glow surrounded the crystal disk, seemingly floating, but it was impossible to tell how that opaline gleam emanated from the apparatus. Marc Vanel undressed, and then donned a black three-piece bodystocking made of a special silk, which even covered his head, only leaving two holes for the eyes, and put rubber slippers on his feet. Then he started up the electric machinery placed in a corner and lit the fire under a crucible. Soon, strange vapors filled the room.

Marc consulted his watch and placed himself on the disk.

Immediately, he seemed to melt, apparently mutating into a dense mass of gray vapor, initially almost solidified. Soon, as the extremities became vague, unreal and transparent, the mass of vapor disintegrated, the mist dissipating. Nothing remained but a slightly darker nucleus at the center of a scarcely-perceptible halo.

Homo-Deus followed the phases of the operation in a full-length mirror placed facing him. After a few minutes, he observed the complete disappearance of the light mists reflected by the mirror; there was no longer anything in the limpid transparency of the mirror but the image of the black wall, with two luminous green dots, which were his eyes.

The master increased the current; sparks sprang forth; then the gleam of the pupils vanished.

The fluid had penetrated the utmost parcels of his being, carrying the agent of complete discoloration, of invisibility. Now, the man could come and go among other humans; no longer belonging to their world, he would be above them, powerful and terrible, like a god.

Abruptly, the machines stopped, seemingly of their own accord. The small iron door opened and closed again, with a sinister click. Footsteps climbed the staircase, whose steps creaked, and traversed the hall—the carpet was crushed beneath invisible feet—and then, on the threshold of the entrance door, a voice asked: "Are you ready, Mardruk?"

"Yes, Master."

The Hindu driver opened the door of the automobile. The footplate was depressed, and then, after a moment, the door closed again. In the limousine, the cushions were hollowed out and the same voice commanded: "To the Opéra!"

The engine roared, and the vehicle pulled away smoothly and rapidly, apparently empty.

XIV. The Wings of the Opéra

At about nine o'clock, Marc Vanel's auto stopped outside the Opéra. A door-opener hurried toward the limousine's footplate, but he let go of the handle that he was about to turn: the car was empty. The Invisible opened the door himself and got out, closed it again tranquilly and climbed the steps of the immense perron. He went past the ticket collectors, smiling. Soon, Homo-Deus was in the tiled corridors that surrounded the boxes.

It was the first time that he had come to the Opéra in those implausible conditions. It was necessary to place himself where he was safe from accidental collisions, under the penalty of creating a certain alarm among the people who might bump into him. A favorable opportunity presented itself in the form of the Vauclin household.

Look! They're searching for a box number. Now, lodges have six places, and there are only two of them. This is the moment to install myself in their company.

The usherette opened the door for them. While they were taking off their coats, the Invisible, who had slipped in behind them, took note of the disposition of the place. The large box, preceded by a small reception room, had a sofa in an obscure alcove. The spouses sat down in the front row and Vanel sat in an armchair behind them. He had before his eyes the white nape of the pretty brunette. He breathed in the intoxicated odor of that well-treated flesh.

That evening's performance was Gluck's opera *Armide*—and Mademoiselle Alexane was to feature in the ballet. When the curtain fell, the Invisible rapidly quit his armchair and installed himself in a corner of the little reception room. Vauclin and his wife went to sit together on the sofa; the Invisible only just had time to huddle in the corner.

"No need to go out, is there?" said Vauclin. "Let's wait here for Albert Baruyer."

"Yes—all the more so as I'm tired."

"Indeed, I've noticed over the last few days that you seem weary and anxious...worn out."

"It's not my fault. Since that sorcerer came to the house, I can no longer sleep."

"Marc Vanel? What can that fellow know about the story of Vandeuvre?"

"There are moments when I wonder whether he's dead."

Vauclin's face took on a mocking and ferocious expression. In a low voice, he said: "It was certainly a cadaver that I deposited on the bench in the Avenue Henri-Martin."

"Then why wasn't it found there? Who took it away? Why have they kept the body?"

"Shut up."

"I'd like to—but how can I calm my anguish? And then, why does that damned Vanel trouble me so much with his tricks? I wasn't hallucinating that day; I read on the piece of blank paper: *Julien de Vandeuvre is not dead.*"

"I read it, too."

"That sorcerer knows more than you think."

"What makes you think that? His experiment is explicable. He suggested to us that we translate our most intense preoccupations; we had to read the name of our victim—it was fatal. There's no proof that Vanel had any suspicion of what was written."

On seeing the two accomplices admit their terrors in low voices in the little reception room, the Invisible, in his corner, could not suppress his customary sarcastic snigger. Vauclin and his wife stood up, haggard. The député had brought out a revolver, instinctively; he aimed it in the direction of the dark corner from which the odious laughter had come, but his wife reassured him.

"How impressionable we are! There's no one there!"

"That laughter, though?"

"It came from the box next door."

It was a plausible explanation. Next door, cheerful people were amusing themselves during the entr'acte. At that moment, in any case, the bell indicated that the performance was about to resume, and the couple took their seats again at the front of the box. The Invisible resumed his place in the armchair behind Madame Vauclin's attractive nape.

The act that followed was rather short. The homicidal household got up and the Invisible only just had time to step aside in order not to collide with the Beauty. He took advantage of Vauclin's exit to go into the corridors, which are very broad at the Opéra, and it was without difficulty that the Invisible, avoiding any impact with the strollers, reached the small door connecting the auditorium to the stage and the wings.

A Cerberus was guarding that door, reserved for faithful subscribers and individuals known to be friends of the house. Marc Vanel, in his invisible bodystocking, went past him proudly, not without irony. After the narrow corridor leading to the stage, he found himself on a kind of immense arena whose floor was formed of joined planks hollowed out with groves and pierced with holes. An army of scene-shifters were changing the set, carrying out their tasks silently with sure, practiced actions. Suddenly, he felt an impact and a curse erupted; someone had just bumped into him while carrying something. Vanel was momentarily amused by the bewildered expression of two scene-shifters searching in vain for the obstacle they had encountered.

Having traversed the stage, he found himself in a vestibule still cluttered with planks, frameworks and ropes; it was the entrance to the dancers' foyer. The Invisible went in. Immediately, he experienced a considerable disappointment. For him, as for many others who have doubtless intoxicated their imagination with the exciting evocation of the magical words "dancers' foyer," the sadness and desolation of the room with the fugitive parquet brought a regret. What—is that all it was? He had imagined numerous ballerinas, slender and light, in their arachnean tutus, with slim, muscular legs. He had seen them smiling, sketching supple gestures and audacious curves before the eyes of admirers come to intoxicate themselves with their sensuality. Instead of that there was a kind of jolly party, three dancers leaning on exercise bars, in earnest conversation with five men in black suits.

Homo-Deus understood that there was little chance of running into Alexane in this desolate place. At hazard, he headed toward a glazed door with two slats, leading to a dirty corridor with gray walls, which ended in a stone stairway. Dancers dressed as shepherds and shepherdesses were coming down for the fourth act.

The Invisible went up the stairs, but on the next floor he ran into an embarrassment when he heard a familiar voice behind him; it was Albert Baruyer, the advocate, in company with Barsac, the President of the Council. From their conversation, he learned that they were on their way to the principal dancer's dressing room. Vanel was certain that Albert Baruyer was infatuated with Alexane; he had learned that from the reports of his four hypnotized agents.

Vanel followed the two black suits, wondering: *Why doesn't Alexane appear to experience revulsion for that advocate with a vile reputation? Doubtless he's well-known in the theatrical world, and powerful, thanks to his brother Georges, whom he plays, for his own account an interested solo after the fashion of Paganini. But I'm sure that Alexane detests Albert. Why?* The little group arrived at the star's door. The dresser let them into the room, which was large enough for the Invisible to slip in behind Barsac.

At the sight of the Prime Minister, the dancer got up, smiling.

"Welcome, Seigneur," she said, bowing to Claude Barsac.

An admirable handsome young man also stood up. *The lover!* Vanel thought.

Alexane introduced him. "Hans de Bliggen, Messieurs. A very devoted friend for whom I have a great deal of affection. An orphan in consequence of dramatic circumstances, he's worthy of your interest."

The President of the Council sniffed a probable request for his influence. In a good humor and disposed to give pleasure, he smiled, raised himself up like a fighting cock and said: "If I can do anything for him..."

"Later, yes, perhaps later..."

Hans de Bliggen intervened, however: "My dear Alexane, I beg you..."

Albert Baruyer, sensing a rival in the admirable Antinous with the slightly Oriental complexion, said sarcastically: "I'm an advocate, Monsieur, and if you wish, I can contribute, graciously, to rendering you justice..."

Homo-Deus caught the brief glance exchanged by the two lovers. *Well, well,* he said to himself, *the problem is clarified. Perhaps, before long, the com-*

edy will be more amusing than I thought. What was going to emerge from this chaos? Madame Vauclin, the mistress of Albert Baruyer; the latter infatuated with Alexane; Vauclin and Baruyer accomplices in still-mysterious affairs; the dancer's lover full of hatred—that was obvious—for Baruyer: the situation did not lack spice.

Now Barsac was complimenting Alexane. She was in a state of extreme undress, ready to put on her stage costume, displayed on an armchair, and revealing, beneath the thin cloth of a peplum, the harmonious splendors of her body. Albert Baruyer never ceased staring at her. Hans de Bliggen perceived that. He went pale. Alexane, seeing him suffering, having met his imploring gaze, obeyed his prayer.

"I can express how agreeable your company is to me, Monsieur le Président, but it's time for me to get ready for the ballet."

"We'll leave you to it," said Baruyer.

She allowed her hands to be kissed, pretending not to see the amorously flashing eyes of Albert Baruyer. "Don't go so quickly, Hans, Messieurs, he can take charge of a few insipid commissions for me. Don't be jealous—the time to explain what I need him to do, and he'll be leaving, like you."

Closing the door behind Claude Barsac and Albert Baruyer—without, of course, suspecting the presence of the Invisible—she ran to the young man, who embraced her ardently, crushing her lips with a long kiss.

"My love!" sighed Alexane, finally.

"My queen! My mistress! Oh, I thought I wouldn't be able to control myself! I nearly strangled him, that Baruyer."

"Oh, my love, you know what you promised me. Wait a while, and I'll deliver him to you, disarmed."

"The wretch! He's robbed and killed my father. And that whole gang…his brother, his mother, that sinister Walesport…all rich on a fortune that belongs to me. My father's blood has made them powerful, formidable, and I, I have nothing, nothing!!"

"Are you not my lover?"

"I owe you everything. You've given me love, the most captivating voluptuousness, and you're helping me to recover the wealth that was stolen from me. What an enchantress you are! And why, tell me, why?"

"Why?" she said, pressing herself against him. "Because you're young, as handsome as a god! Because you're pure, healthy, honest and unfortunate! In my love, along with so many perverted and pagan sentiments, there's a little maternal love. You're my child…I adore you!"

She caressed his forehead and his eyelids, and the invisible Vanel, who was watching the scene, thought: *Well, I want to be on the side of the lovers. I'll take them under my protection and enable them to triumph. But what the devil have the Baruyers, Vauclin and Walesport been able to do to him? I'll find out via my hypnotized instruments.*

At the first opportunity, after having contemplated the dancer in the nude, he went out and went back to the corridors of the auditorium. He had been wandering briefly outside the box where the Vauclin household were, without being able to get in, when the fourth act ended. The usherette took advantage of that to open the door and offer her services, and the Invisible slipped in behind her. This time, however, the box was full of black suits; he wedged himself in a corner.

The usherette left. Marc Vanel identified the people present: with the Vauclins, there was a Minister, Prosper Crémiot, the two Baruyer brothers, and Walesport. The Invisible was poorly placed to grasp all of the whispered conversations, but a few phrases reached him.

"Then you think that Germany..."

"...Is only waiting for an opportunity. She's still too weak, but when she's stronger, she'll take advantage of any circumstance not to pay. Every time, it will be a warning, and we'll always concede something. With every conference, our pledges and rights over Germany are diminished. When we're despoiled, the French victors, definitively transformed into the vanquished, will settle the mode of payment of the hundreds of billions furnished to us during the massacre and devastation in our territory by England and the United States. There alone, our allies, stuffed by the war, won't diminish anything. What will become of poor France?"

"It's not a matter of what will become of France, but what we ought to do ourselves in order to take advantage of what might be a uniquely profitable opportunity."

"Yes," added Walesport.

"Come on, Messieurs," said Crémiot. "This isn't place to discuss that. I've just told Walesport that he should reach an agreement regarding a plan in conformity with our interests, but let's not talk about it anymore now."

"Very well," said Vauclin. "Let's meet at my place then—9 Rue des Saints-Pères—next Saturday."

Madame Vauclin's voice made itself heard. "No, my friend, on Saturday we're hosting a grand soirée."

"Well, Monday then, at three o'clock. Is that agreed?"

"We'll be there," said the Baruyers and Walesport, in unison.

I'll be there, too, the Invisible said to himself.

They fell silent, because the curtain had just gone up for the fifth act. Homo-Deus was able to get a little closer, in order to admire Alexane in the ballet. The dancer, supple, light, pert and cheerful, spun among the other ballerinas, and her beauty stood out in the midst of the bouquet like the most beautiful rose on a flowery bush. She turned and leapt, graceful, enchanting, as if intoxicated by voluptuousness, drunk on amour, and her artistry was, for the Invisible, a public confession, in exquisite leaps, in which she seemed to be laying out for the public all the reminiscences of her passion for her handsome young lover.

BOOK THREE: THE BLIND SEE

I. A New Assault of Love

On emerging from the Opéra, Marc Vanel, Homo-Deus, was simultaneously intrigued and delighted by the secrets he had just discovered. The disinterested love of Alexane, in particular, enticed him. What a difference of temperament and mentality from Jeanne Fortin! *What good is that scientific madness of a genius, if it annuls amour? The dancer is in the right: life, and its enjoyments, before everything.*

Well, he would attempt the adventure. Jeanne was only vulnerable in the direction of science; it was necessary to attack her by that route. His decision was made. He would reveal to Jeanne the technicalities of the secret of invisibility. By that means, undoubtedly, he would succeed in moving her.

As soon as he woke up, after a rapid breakfast, he had himself taken to the Red Nest.

Jeanne was in the laboratory, in the process of examining the exposed brain of Georges Garnier. The marionette doctor was sitting on the ground, his head between the knees of the young scientist, who was leaning over her fiancé's open skull. Jeanne was attentively observing the progress made by the encephalic culture. When Marc came in, she looked up, saluted him with a gesture, and beckoned to him to approach.

"Look," she said. "I believe that before long, our friend will be able to move. The encephalum has recovered its normal volume. There's no trace of any disorder. The reconstituted cells appear to have the same constitutive elements. So, I think we should interrupt the stimulating current in order that the patient can rest before the final experiment."

"And what will you do with Georges Garnier?"

"I'll keep my promise. I'll marry him, if he still wants that. Yes, if he demands it."

"You love him, then?"

"No, I don't love him, and I don't believe I'll ever love him—neither him nor anyone else. But he surrendered himself to the fiancée; what will he do for the wife? I'll surely have need of him for further experiments—among others, the formation of spermatozoa, of which I'm also ambitious to make cultures in order to attempt the artificial creation of a human being."

"Leave your marionette and put him back in his place. He's had enough for today. I have something important to tell you. What do you think about invisibility?"

"I know that you've realized the problem, but I don't see the utility of it, except for the satisfaction of an indiscreet curiosity or your stolen faunish pleasures."

"You say that you know that I've solved the problem. What makes you think that?"

"The revelations of my friend Simone d'Armez. She consulted me on the subject; she confessed to me. But why this confidence today?"

"Because I, too, am in love with you—and I hope, by means of this mark of confidence, to bring you closer to me."

"You dare not act the pig with me, then, as you did with Simone?"

"No, because you, I love—your body, certainly, but also your questioning intelligence, your genius. What might the two of us not accomplish?"

"Indeed," said Jeanne, thoughtfully. "You're much stronger than Georges Garnier, and, by that entitlement alone, you have the right to preference. But refrain from talking drivel about your boundless love, and we'll work together as allies, intellectual to begin with. By the way, we have Papa Garnier this evening. Are you dining with us?"

"If that would please you."

"We still have an hour ahead of us. How did you discover Invisibility?"

Homo-Deus recounted his experiments with anatomical specimens and his cat, Mesmoth, and then continued: "I invented and constructed an accumulator of light, storing the ultra-violet rays and condensing them, and enclosed them in a bronze jar buried in the ground and covered with a thick crystal plaque. It remained to fix the invisible fluid in myself—which is to say, to prevent its evaporations when I'm impregnated with it. Thinking that silk might play the same role in that as for electricity, I attempted the experiment with that fabric. Good results, but not absolute. I coated the fabric with various rubbery gums, and finally succeeded, after multiple trials, in obtaining a weave that would not allow any fluid to pass.

"So, having put on a bodystocking made entirely from that special silk, and a mask of the same, with holes for the eyes, I place myself on the plaque of my accumulator, activate a powerful electric battery that excites the energy, and in a matter of minutes, I become invisible. Only the eyes, which, not being covered by my fabric, allow an infinitesimal quantity of the fluid to escape, and can become slightly fluorescent after a certain time, or in certain circumstances. Well, Jeanne, what do you think?"

"I'm listening with admiration."

"I've calculated that it requires at least fifty hours for the invisible fluid to lose its virtue detectably, but I hope in time to be able to double the duration of the invisibility. Thus, invisible myself and clad in a black garment equally invisible, I can circulate for two days and more without needing to recharge my body. To resume my visibility, I have only to place myself on my plaque again and activate the battery in the opposite sense. The invisible fluid drains away as it entered, only causing me a sensation of intense heat when I store it and cold when I empty myself. In a few minutes, though, equilibrium is restored and I find myself in a normal state again. That's it. As for the chemical formulae, I'll write them down for you."

"You're an ace, Marc. The two of us might do great things."

"Then I've truly interested you?"

"A great deal." Laughing, she added: "So, poor Simone...?"

"Excuse me. She's only a replacement."

"Yes, I excuse you, Marc, for if you truly loved Simone you'd have respected her as you respect and will respect me...and then, a regular courtship would have wasted your precious time, satyr."

II. Important Affairs

There was a meeting at Vauclin's that evening, not in the Avenue Henri-Martin, but in his political residence in the Rue des Saints-Pères—the meeting arranged during the evening at the Opéra, where the Invisible had discovered the time and place of the rendezvous in Vauclin's box. Present were five conspirators who wanted to bring down the Ministry of which Claude Barsac was the President of the Council, to wit: William Walesport, the two Baruyer brothers, the député Prosper Crémiot, the Minister of Public Works—which are not Herculean labors—and Arsène Vauclin.

Walesport was the first to speak.

"Messieurs, I have no need to remind you of the motive that brings us here. This time, we're undertaking an affair of great breadth, which a fortunate hazard has thrown our way. Summarize the scheme, Crémiot."

"Everyone in the Chambre knows that my ideas are sometimes at odds with Barsac's. That earned me a visit and a proposition from Grandjean, the editor-in-chief of the government's official newspaper, the *Malin*.[28] Grandjean is ambitious and highly intelligent, a clever arriviste. He knows that Claude Barsac has always had a weakness for pretty women, and Madame Grandjean is a veritable beauty. The Boss has been carried away by a routine flirtation. It's a matter of a diplomatic post for Antoinette Grandjean's father, the Comte de Morges. The perfidious woman can thus enter the Ministry of Foreign Affairs by the front and the back door, and Barsac's study therein. She's had the skill to filch the documents in question, the originals of which Walesport bought, yesterday, for the round sum of a million."

"A million well spent," said Walesport, "for it will bring a hundred others into our net."

A gleam of avarice was shining in all eyes.

"In brief," Walesport continued, "according to the latest agreement with the allies, Germany has to make a payment on the fifteenth of this month of a billion in gold. I have, from a reliable source, the certainty that a bribe of fifty millions has been offer to Barsac for a postponement of the payment of that billion, the anticipation of which is maintaining prices on the Bourse. If the gold isn't forthcoming on the agreed date, shares will certainly go down, and will rise again after Barsac's fall, because the scandal we'll provoke will force Germany to make the payment eventually. But we need to bring Barsac down to bring about the rebound: the next day, or a few days later, the advent of the new Crémiot-Vauclin Ministry, which, having the advantage of realizing the German

---

[28] A joke, playing with the name of one of the leading Parisian dailies, *Le Matin* [The Morning]. *Malin*, of course, is the equivalent of the English "malign."

payment, will have all the favor of the Chambre and the credulous. What do you say? And we'll take full advantage of the movement in prices."

"I say," said Vauclin, "that it's necessary to be very sure of bringing down Barsac and his Ministry."

"You'll take charge of that, Vauclin, equipped with certain documents that I'll give you." He opened his briefcase and took them out, reverently. "Firstly, a coded telegram."

"Hmm!" said Albert Baruyer. "A dispatch is disputable, even if it's in cipher."

"Indeed, and I anticipated that objection. But this is what will guarantee our Premier's acceptance." He displayed an official German document, with the heading of the Great Chancellery. "*To His Excellency Claude Barsac, Minister of Foreign Affairs and President of the Council of the French Republic. In accordance with the desire expressed by Your Excellency to possess a guarantee, we hold on your behalf, through the intermediary of the Reich's ambassador in Paris, the following document: 'Between us, the representatives of the government of the Reich and His Excellency Claude Barsac, it is agreed that: given the difficulties of every sort for the government of the Reich in assembling, for the due date, the sum of a billion in gold; and equally recognizing the desire of the French government represented by Monsieur Claude Barsac, to bring about cordial relations between the two peoples, which perhaps can only be achieved by forgetting the hatred of old and the humiliating reparations consequent upon it; in recognition of the services rendered and acquires, the government of the Reich believes itself to be authorized to offer Monsieur Barsac a payment of thirty million gold marks, which will be deposited in whichever bank and whichever account he pleases.'* Followed by signatures..."

"Barsac is stuffed!" said Vauclin.

The Baruyer brothers nodded their heads.

"Now," said Walesport, "it's a matter of knowing what we can put into the affair; there's a profit of three or four hundred per cent to be made."

"Good business!" said one voice.

"Certainly," said Vauclin, without knowing which of his fellows had spoken. The others, after having looked at one another, also attributed the remark to one of their number, and attached no further importance to it.

Walesport continued: "It's certainly enough to lead me to attempt the grand coup: the operation is excellent, I'll put everything at my disposal into it."

"Two million for me," said Georges Baruyer.

"I thought you were better supported than that, Brother."

"No—and that's your fault; you cost me a great deal."

"I can only put in a million," said Vauclin.

"That's a lot for a socialist député," said Crémiot. "I can't do as much, Minister though I am."

"In return for services rendered and to be rendered," Walesport continued, "it's agreed that a share of ten per cent will be reserved for Messieurs Albert Baruyer, Prosper Crémiot and Arsène Vauclin."

"Perfect" said the men in question.

"So," Albert Baruyer went on, "since the affair is concluded, what if we pass on to a little compromise between ourselves?"

"Why?" said Walesport. "None of us could make any use of such a document."

"Not from the legal point of view, obviously, but it seems to me that it wouldn't be a bad idea for us all to be linked together between ourselves, by a signature."

"All right, if you wish."

The five accomplices drew up a kind of legal document, which they signed—and the electric light went out.

"A short-circuit," said Vauclin. "I'll go find the candles."

Suddenly, however, the lights came on again. Georges Baruyer proposed that they put the paper in a sealed envelope and confide it to a notary, who would be instructed only to return it to the complete group, after the conclusion of the affair. Everyone approved—but as the député was reaching out to pick up the sheet of paper, he stopped, and went pale, his eyes fluttering and his hands trembling.

"What is it?" Vauclin and Albert Baruyer asked.

With his finger, Georges Baruyer pointed at the piece of paper. Beneath the five signatures, a word had been written in red pencil, in capital letters: SCOUNDRELS.

"Damnation!" howled Vauclin. "There's a spy among us—a traitor!"

For a moment, there was a great tumult. The five men hurled insults at one another, attempted to interrogate one another, and to obtain explanations. The doors, having been examined, were all found to be locked; no one had come in or gone out during the meeting. So?

The five retained, individually, the conviction that one of them was suspect, but as the practical joker had signed the document, there was little to fear. Georges Baruyer erased the fateful word with a rubber, folded up the piece of paper and put it in an enveloped, which was immediately sealed.

The five men went out. Outside, they continued to walk together, chatting, among the Rue des Saints-Pères.

Jokingly, in order to dispel the final cloud, Albert Baruyer said: "The five pères are us. And in Latin, *Semper*: always. Between us, in life and death."

And as they made the resolution to go immediately, all together, to the notary, in order to confide the envelope to him, they accepted Walesport's invitation to climb into his powerful limousine, which was following the little group as they went along the sidewalk, slowly.

The American made a sign to the chauffeur, who stopped the vehicle. Then, just as the accomplices were preparing to get in, strident laughter burst out behind the gang.

They turned around abruptly—but there was no one there.

II. The Report of a Hypnotized Individual

It was the time for reports at the house of Homo-Deus. The four hypnotized men had come, as usual, on the master's orders, to give an account of the missions with which they had been charged. It was an amusement that Marc Vanel offered to his smiling misanthropy: he took delight in causing to march, under his mental influence, individuals inspired by his dominating thought: adroit servants launched forth by him on tasks appropriate to their natural faculties or their social status, and maintained by him, Homo-Deus, in hypnotic slavery. He had sent away the first three rapidly, retaining the Commissaire.

"Well," he said, when they were alone, "do you have the information concerning Alexane and her lover?"

"Yes, Master. Alexane met Hans de Bliggen in Cairo at the beginning of last winter. He was working as a dancer in a grand palace where the star was appearing. Madly smitten, she brought him to Paris. Hans de Bliggen is not his real name. His real name is Hans de Rodock, and he belongs to one of the oldest families of Dalmatia, today completely ruined."

"For what reasons?"

"That's quite a story. The father, Baron de Rodock, was a rich Dalmatian lord, the owner of immense estates. A very handsome man, courageous and passionate, Karl had been the hero of gallant scandals that had forced him to quit the court and exile himself to his estates, at the manor of Rodock-Eskinen, when he was only forty-five years old. His wife, a dutiful creature, gentle and modest, accompanied him in his retreat with Hans, who was twelve years old. At that time, a French engineer, who had come to Eskinen to build an aqueduct designed to supplement the manor's water features, discovered in the course of his endeavors an important deposit of platinum. For the Baron, that was the greatest misfortune of his life."

"Why?"

"Dazzled by his unexpected fortune, the Baron glimpsed a magnificent future. He saw himself pardoned by his king, immensely rich, enjoying once again the good fortune he had thought he had lost forever. He departed for Paris, in order to confer with businessmen and bankers, who would give him the means to exploit his windfall."

"Ah! I can scent the consequences."

"It's quite simple. The Baron, completely trapped by the financiers to whom he had addressed himself, consented to put the affair in the hands of an anonymous company. An enormous fraction of the shares was attributed to him in remuneration for his contribution. Once the company was formed, however, the Baron died mysteriously. His heirs, of course, came to Paris for the liquidation. How amazed they were to learn that the company was legally constituted on a basis very different from the one that Rodock believed to have been agreed. By virtue of trickery, it transpired that not only did the Baron have no claim on the anonymous company, but that he owed money, perceived in the form of advances, to the Walesport bank, the promoter of the operation."

"I recognize the method of Walesport and his associate, George Baruyer."

"They are, indeed, the names that have been communicated to me, with those of Albert Baruyer and their mother, the widow Baruyer."

"Hold on—I don't know that individual!"

"Madame Baruyer remains in the wings, but she guides the operations of her children. Endowed with a prodigious intelligence, a subtle flair, and a powerful instinct that one might think to be multiplied by her infirmity..."

"What infirmity?"

"The mother has been blind for five years. Widowed very young, she was one of the most beautiful and spirited women in Paris. Her blindness, Master, doesn't prevent her from divining, so to speak, better than anyone the hazards, dangers and favorable opportunities of life."

Homo-Deus was listening with extreme attention to the hypnotized man; he found this story prodigiously interesting. "So," he said, "this blind woman is an old rogue? If she guides her sons and one judges them according to their actions..."

"I inform you; I don't appreciate."

"That's true. Let's get back to Rodock."

"Having returned to Dalmatia with little Hans, the Baronne saw a flock of vultures descend upon the castle. Creditors unknown to her surged forth from everywhere, obliging her to defend herself. She confided her interests to a rapacious businessman who cheated her, causing her to sustain lawsuits in which she lost everything that remained to her. When everything was sold—the land, the farms and the manor—she languished for three or four years, and then died, scarcely leaving enough for her son to continue his studies. He was charged by her with avenging his father, finding his despoilers and demanding a settlement of accounts—for the platinum mine, now being exploited, produces enormous profits. Madame de Rodock had no idea what had happened, but she had remembered the names..."

The hypnotized man seemed fatigued. Sweat was streaming down his temples, even though he was sitting down and not moving. Homo-Deus knew, however, the effort he was demanding of the automaton. He passed his hands above his forehead once again and ordered him to continue his story.

"With his mother dead," the Commissaire went on, "the Rodock son, with no experience, and probably also because he had his father's penchant for gambling, began by squandering the few thousand francs of patrimony that remained to him. When he was completely broke, he lived somewhat at hazard, allowing himself to be loved by mature women ecstasized by his beauty. Then he became ashamed of that life, and found employment as a dancer in a very chic hotel in

Cairo, where he happened to be. It was there that he made the conquest of Alexane..."

"Quickly! The end of the story."

"Hans confessed to the dancer all the misfortunes that had befallen his father. On learning that Walesport and the Baruyer brothers were the authors of the spoliation, she was gripped by a ferocious joy, for Albert Baruyer is in love with her, and she scented the possibility of rendering justice to her lover by means of some trap. If he were rich, she would be able to show Hans de Rodock on her arm proudly."

"From which you conclude?"

"The Baruyers and Walesport must certainly have murdered Rodock, after having robbed him. Alive, he would have protested too much on learning that he had been cheated. But they have no suspicion of the enemy lying in wait for them. A woman in love is terribly dangerous, and that one has vowed to make her lover happy, at any price."

Homo-Deus reflected momentarily, with his eyes closed in order to concentrate his thoughts, and with his head between his hands.

IV. *From Four to Eight o'clock in the Evening*

When the dancer Alexane went into Albert Baruyer's apartment, four o'clock was chiming on the wall clock in the dining room. The advocate and dramatic author, who had sent his valet away, had come to open the door himself. He took the hands of his bellissima and, while kissing them devotedly, said: "I'm happier than I can say."

He had introduced her into a small drawing room. Without embarrassment, the dancer took off her hat and looked for somewhere to put it down.

"Don't trouble yourself," he said, radiant—and getting up, he hastened to take the delightful hat, her gloves, her handbag and her scarf. Then he took her to sit down on an Arab divan by a dainty Moorish table, bearing everything necessary for a light and delicate snack.

Alexane looked around. "Your home is charming," she said. "The mere sight of it would be sufficient to attract many daughters of Eve. Where is this famous collection?"

"Next door. But allow me to believe that you have also come, a little, for the collector."

"Conceit!"

"Come on, Alexane, we're no longer children. I don't want to flirt with you, as with just anyone. My affection for you is more than a banal fancy. I won't tell you either that it's the great immortal passion, but it's a very profound and sincere sentiment of true love and admiration."

"I believe you, and that's why it's repugnant to me to become your plaything, because afterwards, you'd have less esteem and admiration for me."

"With a woman of your intelligence that could not be. It would be the veritable communion of two minds, united by the senses, two souls brought together by the same artistic tastes. Listen, Alexane, until now, I've lived alone. I've arrived at the age when one feels the need to be supported by an affection."

"Ah! Is that a proposal of marriage? That sentiment would raise you considerably in my esteem."

"What? Am I, then, so low otherwise?"

"Well, I'm neither deaf nor blind, and I know a certain Madame Vauclin."

"La la! My dear, you're straying from the point. That mundane liaison, virtually non-existent, has nothing to do with the love I feel for you. Certainly, I desire to possess you. It would be an insult to you not to have that attraction of the human antenna, but what I want in you is, above all, a kind of amorous amity, quasi-fraternal but incestuous, solid and durable."

"It seems to me, my dear, that I've already read that speech in one of your plays. I hoped for better of your imagination. Come on, honor me with something unpublished."

"Unpublished or not, I desire you ardently and I want you madly; I love you, in spite of the face that you insist on treating everything as a joke. Love me, my darling, and let's not concern ourselves with literature."

"Nor childishness, my dear."

Seizing the young woman, Albert Baruyer pushed her down on the divan. To his great astonishment, she put up scarcely any resistance, contenting herself with deflecting too direct a movement on the part of the dramatic author. She started to laugh, very lightly.

"Like that, then? Immediately, in the fashion of a hussar? Why the classic preamble, then? Be careful—you'll upset that pretty table where I can see so many nice things. You haven't even asked whether I'm hungry or thirsty. Amour, amour, amour and more amour! What brutality!"

"You're mocking me, Alexane," he said, somewhat disconcerted.

"No, but I don't see us quitting the entirely appropriate position that we occupy before this table in order to deliver ourselves to the amorous struggle the idea of which is bludgeoning you. Come on, friend—you look so good in that elegant indoor costume. And how do you like me in this nice summer dress?"

She got up, profiling her elegant figure against the somber Cordovan leather drape covering the wall of the drawing room.

"You're adorable!" he exclaimed, seizing her arms and allowing his adventurous hands to take their course.

"Adore from a distance, and don't touch," she said, pushing him away gently but firmly. "Don't you know how annoying it is getting dressed outside one's own place? I won't play the prude with you, but I hope that you'll share my opinion. Remember that it's five o'clock, and at six I have to be at the Opéra, where I have a meeting with Ida Rubinstein,[29] and if we behave foolishly, I won't have the time to dress myself decently... You should have come sooner, then," she said, rather stupidly.

"I only came to see your collection," he mocked, "and not to...the term embarrasses me a little...to...help me out a little, my dear...you're more accustomed than I am to drumsticks."

"Damn it!" she swore. "To make love, simply, as two individuals who feel the desire."

"You daren't say *bestially*, like two animals."

Escaping his grip, she burst into laughter, with the result that he did not know how to react. Angrily, he poured himself a glass of port, which he drank in one gulp.

"That makes you feel better, eh?" she said, still laughing. "I'd like a little myself."

---

[29] The Russian dancer Ida Rubinstein (1885-1960) appeared in Léo Staats' ballet set to the music of Vincent d'Indy's *Istar* at the Paris Opéra in 1924, where Champsaur presumably saw her while writing the present text.

"Alexane, Alexane! You're making fun of me."

"Do you think so? I wouldn't dare." She became serious. "My friend, my dear friend, I have a horror of these unexpected bodily tussles. But now that I know your Don Juan's lair, I'll come to surprise you here one evening, when I leave the theater."

"Good! Tonight?"

"No, my dear author. I have a great deal of work to do—remember that it's as much for you as for me."

"All right! On the day of the première of my drama, which you'll make illustrious with your dance in the second act..."

"All right—give me a key to your apartment. And when you've escaped the congratulations, you'll find me here, waiting for you. And I'll be more at my ease for that première."

He was obliged to settle for that. For a long time he had coveted the artiste, who truly had the gift of enticing him, especially by means of a long resistance full of promises, which never ended. He had inserted a dance scene into his next play, and it had required his brother's great influence for the Académie de Musique to consent to lend its principal dancer to the Gymnase. Obliged, therefore, to be careful of the artiste, he conducted himself as gallantly as possible, and, taking on the air of Bluebeard, he said: "This is the key to Paradise. If you forget to make use of it, a terrible punishment awaits you."

And as Alexane politely offered him her cheek, he kissed her lips, while sliding the key into the artiste's handbag.

If he had been able to see the star, once she was on the staircase and out of sight, wiping her mouth with disgust, he would have been rather anxious about the consequences of that gallant conversation.

After leaving Baruyer's apartment, Alexane hailed a cab and had herself taken, not to the Opéra, but to number 56, Rue de Douai. Rapidly, she went up to the third floor and rang the bell of the door to the left, which opened immediately, and then fell into the arms of a young man, who carried her rather than guiding her into the bedroom. In an instant, the artiste had taken off her coat, her light dress, and appeared in elegant underclothing that made her seem more undressed than nude.

"Do you love me a great deal?" said the dancer, taking the young man's head in her hands, kissing his eyelids and then his tongue.

The latter's only response was to clutch her to his heart.

"I adore you," she repeated.

He was handsome, that son of the Orient, as handsome as the males of the Lands of the Sun are. The Dalmatian could have served as a model for an Apollo, so reminiscent were the harmonious proportions of his body of the most beautiful ancient marbles. His head, especially, was a plastic poem, with the great dark eyes, luminous and soft, with the languorous appearance of women's gazes; the imperceptibly hooked nose; the full cheeks as hard as amber, of which

154

they had the color; the well-designed lips revealing magnificent teeth; and the blue-black hair and eyebrows.

When the first outpourings were past, Alexane told her lover the result of her conversation with Baruyer junior.

"I know that he has to go to Lyon tomorrow to meet the director of the Théâtre Municipal to discuss a series of performances of his play. He won't be back until Saturday for the première of his new play, *All for Love*. It's probable that his valet will take advantage of it to go out. Watch the house, and as soon as you're certain that the blackguard is out of the way, come to find me..."

"Oh, my love! How much trouble you're going to for me! But I swear to you that if we succeed, you shall be the Baronne de Rodock."

"No, my child, I love you—love me, that's all I ask of you."

"My dear Alexane! My..."

"Love me! Love me for as long as possible, and it's me that will owe you gratitude."

Drawing the young man into her arms again, she hugged him passionately. Hans returned her caresses, and night surprised them in amorous frolics in which prodigal youth flourished.

"Eight o'clock already!" sighed Alexane. "I have to leave you, my darling. When shall I see you again? I have to work at least until eleven. Come to pick me up at the Opéra. We'll have supper together, and afterwards..."

Eventually, the two lovers separated. The last kiss never wanted to be the last.

V. The Fall of a Ministry is Prepared

The député Georges Baruyer was working in his study. It was nine o'clock, and the financier had been at his desk since seven a.m. He was undoubtedly pleased with his work because, putting down his pen, he rubbed his hands and uttered an "Oof!" of satisfaction. He sat back in his armchair, daydreaming.

Well, he thought, *that Grandjean is a precious man. Thanks to him, I'll make at least five million from the Barsac affair. But why the devil is he betraying him? Is it a matter of vengeance?*

He rang.

"Ask Madame Baruyer to come," he asked the usher who presented himself, "if it's not disturbing her."

A few minutes later Madame Baruyer came into the banker's study. Although she was blind, she knew the house so well that she moved about there confidently.

Madame Baruyer was now fifty-eight years of age, and still retained, in spite of her cruel infirmity, the traces of a magisterial beauty. In spite of her precociously white hair, her complexion had retained the freshness of youth. Her eyebrows were black; her eyes, once brilliant, were now misted by a light misty veil. Her lips were flesh; the lower one, slightly emphatic, gave her a rather disdainful expression, quickly effaced as soon as she smiled. She had smiled often, once upon a time.

Such was the individual who had been, for a long time, the beautiful Madame Baruyer. Her husband, a former Undersecretary of State, had owed the rapid advancement of his political career more to the beauty of his wife than his own capacities. He would have risen higher if an unfortunate duel with the Comte de Simiane had not cut his career short. The motive for the duel had always remained obscure. In any case, his wife, free henceforth, had not abused that liberty overmuch, and although she was credited with many intrigues, she was clever enough to avoid scandal. She devoted herself entirely to the education of her sons, as she had worked for the rise of her husband.

She did not have the fantastical love that some mothers have for their sons, but, being ambitious, she had been able to profit from their aptitudes, and even their faults, to make use of them. Thanks to the high status achieved by their father, they had only to choose their targets, their trajectories assured. Georges Baruyer had followed the political track and soon entered the Chambre. He had already founded a bank, with difficulty to begin with, but which, after a few well-handled affairs, had acquired a renown that was still increasing. He made use of his political connections adroitly to carry out operations whose fluctuations were regulated in accordance with certain indiscretions emanating from ministerial offices. Although he sat to the left, he had numerous friendships among the reaction, and knew how to serve them and make use of them when necessary.

Albert Baruyer, lighter and more Parisian in his character, had never been able to take the thousand tribulations of political life seriously, and his less flexible character did not lend itself to kneeling before and fawning upon the electorate. Very intelligent and a lover of the high life, the career of the bar and letters was the only one that attracted him. He would rapidly have accumulated a fortune by those means had his tastes, very luxurious and very artistic, not always led him to spend more than he earned. Thus, he was often obliged to have recourse to his brother, with whom, in spite of the difference in their character, he was always on the best of terms. They lent one another mutual support; malicious gossip even alleged that Georges, the député, had more that once had recourse to his brother in affairs to which he did not want to commit himself personally. Physically as well as morally, Albert was a man to take on any scabrous affair.

"You have need of me?" said Madame Baruyer, as she came in. She went to take her place in a comfortable English armchair placed next to the window. "I assume that it's to tell me about your meeting at Vauclin's," she said. "How did it go?"

"Very well. Vauclin's putting in a million. By the way, I'm wondering where he's found that money. He was living on expedients only ten months ago."

"It doesn't matter—money has no odor."

"Crémiot's with us, ostensibly."

"Let's get back to the affair. This Grandjean doesn't inspire me with complete confidence. Have you seen the letters?"

"Indeed—they're in our hands."

"How did the journalist get his hands on documents of that importance?"

"It's quite a story. His paper is backed by the government. Barsac often remembers that he was once a journalist, and poor. He noticed Grandjean, who's a very capable fellow, and gave him the editorship of the *Malin*. But Grandjean's wife interested him even more; it appears that the former Antoinette de Morges has a particular entrée to the Quai d'Orsay. It's from her that Walesport got the documents."

"So they're damning for Claude Barsac?"

"Judge for yourself. You know all the tricks that the Boche are using to avoid payment. There's a settlement of a billion marks in gold due at the end of the month. The letter in question indicates a transaction between Barsac and the Chancellor of the Reich granting Germany a delay of two years, in return for which Barsac will receive a trifling fifty million."

"Marks?"

"Francs."

"And you've seen the letters? They're not fakes?"

"No, nothing to fear on that side. Besides which, Grandjean has every interest; he's already been paid a million and promised ownership of the paper where he started out as a junior reporter."

"A clever scoundrel, this Grandjean. Where does he come from?"

"A notary's clerk who became an officer during the war, and then a journalist. He married the exceedingly pretty daughter of the Comte de Morges."

"De Morges loved the high life—and his daughter married that adventurer?"

"The father is glad to be rid of her; he no longer has a sou."

The blind woman smiled; she knew a little about where the Comte's fortune had gone. "If the papers are authentic, the affair is excellent. There's a big coup on the Bourse to bring off on Barsac's fall."

"You advise me to go ahead boldly, then."

"Certainly. You can dispose of five hundred thousand on my behalf. What about your brother?"

"He's still holding the devil by the tail."

"I'll put in a hundred thousand francs for him."

There was a knock on the door and a domestic came in, carrying a card on a tray.

"Hans de Bliggen," the banker read. "Don't know him—refer him to my secretary."

"The Monsieur insisted," said the usher. "A private matter, on behalf of Monsieur Albert Baruyer."

"Oh, that's different. Show him in."

"I'll go," said the blind woman. "You can tell me what it's about later."

VI. A Settlement of Accounts

Georges Baruyer looked at the man who was presenting himself on his brother's behalf, who was unknown to him. He indicated an armchair with a gesture, and straightened up in his own.

The visitor, a chic fellow, quite tall, with the appearance of a perfect gentleman, sat down, after moving his chair closer to the financier's desk. While Baruyer waited, he carefully adjusted the impeccable crease in his trousers before speaking.

"Excuse me for making use of a subterfuge in order to get in to see you."

"I don't much like my door being forced like that, Monsieur. I hope that the motive that led you to act thus is at least susceptible of interesting me."

"It will interest you—too much, perhaps, for your taste. My name is Hans de Rodock."

"What's that?"

"Hans de Rodock. I see that the name isn't unknown to you. You knew my father well."

Hans' attitude and gaze, as well as his tone of voice, warned Baruyer that he ought not to treat the matter lightly, and that it was necessary to take this adversary seriously.

"Indeed, Monsieur. If you're the son of Karl de Rodock, I have no reason to hide the fact. To what do I owe your visit?"

"The desire to have some information regarding the mysterious death of my father and the present state of his affairs."

"Listen, my dear Monsieur. You're young, and your behavior is pardonable because it's justified by the love you have for the memory of someone dear to you. I understand that the death, far away from you, of the head of the family might appear troubling and enigmatic to you, and if it were in my power to edify you, believe that I would not fail to do so. Although I have no ability to inform you in any precise fashion about your father's last moments, however, I believe I can tell you that he died entirely naturally, doubtless of chagrin. The affair that brought him to Paris only caused him disappointments. He had built up his hopes thereon, and it was, alas, a lamentable fiasco in which I lost a great deal of my own money."

Hans stared coldly into Georges Baruyer's eyes. "I possess a few letters proving that there was a very close relationship between your brother and accomplice, Albert Baruyer, and my father."

Georges Baruyer came to his feet. "Letters?" he stammered. "You have letters?"

Hans de Rodock, also standing up, took a thin sheaf of transparent sheets out of his pocket.

"Here they are," he said—but added, smiling: "Or, rather, these are only copies, for I've put the originals in a safe place, as you might imagine. Would you like me to read you one of these documents?"

Georges Baruyer made no reply. He sat down again, while, still master of himself, the visitor read:

"Why, my dear Monsieur, did you not come yesterday evening to La Broue's? I found myself alone with Walesport and those ladies. Now, I'm beginning to be very anxious, because I don't understand very much of this American's dealings in the affair of the Eskinen mines. The company has scarcely been constituted when there's talk of dissolving it. And I, the originator and holder of a great many shares, haven't even been consulted.

"I hope that you will not be long in giving me reassuring explanations, for I have vague anxieties that I would be glad to dissipate.

"Always believe, my dear Albert Baruyer, in my dearest sentiments, Karl de Rodock.

"Well, Monsieur," Hans concluded, "what do you say to that?"

"*That* informs me of a more intimate relationship than I thought between your father and my brother, but I don't see..."

"I beg you, Monsieur," Hans continued, "not to manifest impatience. You may congratulate your brother, for his correspondence was carefully filed, and my research has been greatly facilitated."

"In fact, Monsieur, how do these letters come to be in your possession?"

"I don't believe I can tell you. However, I confess that I procured them against the will of your brother."

"A theft, then? Continue, Monsieur."

"I am continuing, Monsieur Député. This second letter is from Walesport. It also mentions you.

"My dear Albert, are you not coming back to Paris soon? I'm beginning to have had enough of Rodock, who is getting more and more agitated. Your brother got rid of him by telling him that the entire business is between you and me, which means that I have him on my back all the time, and it isn't amusing. Georges Baruyer, moreover, is too stingy with him. He's only given him forty thousand francs since he's been in Paris, and you know that the fellow won't get far with that. Now, his affair will make us enough money for us to permit a little more generosity.

"I repeat to you that he's very agitated. Lacking funds, he might become dangerous, and I can't urge you too strongly to come back to Paris in order to take measures with common accord. Yours truly, Walesport."

Georges Baruyer had got a grip on himself.

"I can see, in fact, that you need an explanation, and I'll give you one. Undoubtedly, I would have preferred to hide these painful facts from you, and I would have preferred to recount everything to someone other than Baron de Rodock's own son, but since your suspicions oblige me to speak, I won't hide anything from you. Know, then, that when your father arrived here he was entertaining considerable illusions about the profits that he might obtain from the mines discovered on the Eskinen estate. I, too, made my first investment in the affair, and gave proof of a naivety almost equal to his.

"Both of us, because we were inexperienced, made the mistake of building up excessive hopes of the exploitation of a deposit about which were not well enough informed. Engineers sent out there came back with disappointing reports. They had ascertained that the return per ton of the mineral was insufficient to pay the expenses of extraction and produce a profit. The affair had been launched, however, and the company constituted. What could be done? A great deal of money had been sunk into it, uselessly; the day came, alas, when it was necessary to liquidate.

"In order to avoid the bankruptcy of a company in which my name was involved, I consented to put in an enormous sum, and your father, engaged for eight hundred thousand francs, died with that debt unpaid. Your mother sold the manor house, and all the land, and I agree with you that that was lamentable. But what do you expect me to do about it, my dear Monsieur? Those letters prove your father's anxiety—a justified anxiety, alas—but I'm not responsible for that."

Harshly, Hans de Rodock replied: "How is it that the Eskinen mines are presently flourishing, and that their exploitation is enriching those who own the shares?"

"That's the hazard of business. The original company was ruined in the operation. A second bought the entitlements of the first, and favored by good fortune, discovered new deposits rich in platinum. There are banal surprises. Some are lucky, others unlucky; some are ruined, others succeed."

"Are you not one of the major shareholders in the new company?"

"What does that prove?"

"That you're a bandit."

Very pale, Georges Baruyer stood up, menacingly—but the steely gaze of Hans de Rodock nailed him to the spot.

"Listen," said the young man, in a terrible voice. "Listen to this. We'll talk afterwards."

Again he opened the sheaf of papers and read the rough draft of a letter from Albert Baruyer—a draft written on the back of the letter that he had received from Walesport.

"*My dear Walesport, I share your opinion; Rodock is becoming a dangerous encumbrance, and I'm afraid of what he might do when the company is liquidated. If he realizes our intentions he's capable of making a legal complaint. My mother has been to see him, and you know what an extraordinary influence she has over him. Nevertheless, she hasn't be able to calm him down, and we still have to fear a scandal on the day we file for bankruptcy—even more so if he suspects that we're going to buy back the entire enterprise afterwards. What are we going to do?*

"*The best thing would be to put an end to it categorically. The Baron is apoplectic; he loves good food and amour. Don't you think that might favor an abrupt but plausible end after a good supper in a private dining room with the young person who is very devoted to you, and of whose talents you've already made use? You can tell her that we consent to the sum that my brother thought, initially, to be a little high. As is our custom, however, we don't want to get mixed up in anything, and it's up to you and Jane to arrange the final plan. We think, in fact, that your part in the scheme justifies your collaboration, and you know the confidence that my brother and I have in your skill.*

"*I shall be in Paris on Tuesday and will see you then, your A. B.*"

When he had finished reading, Hand de Rodock looked at Baruyer.

"I hope that now, Monsieur, we're not going to waste our time in idle disputes? My father died in a private dining room in the company of a certain Jane, in the circumstances foreseen by your brother; it's beyond doubt that my father was poisoned."

Georges Baruyer was astounded—but since Hans de Rodock had not addressed himself directly to the law and had come to see him, he must have an interesting objective. Nothing was lost as yet! Already, he had glimpsed the fabulous profits that the Barsac affair was going to bring him; he had received great dividends from the exploitation of the Eskinen mines: a considerable bleeding, on due reflection, would not sink him. But how had that imbecile, Albert, allowed those letters to be filched?

For a moment, he had a suspicion. He knew his brother; the blackguard, squandering money, was always up against it. Perhaps this handsome fellow was only an accomplice, and had nothing in common with the Rodock son? Albert was perfectly capable of having concocted this scheme in order to blackmail him. Why, after all, had he kept the dangerous letters?"

"Oh, the bandit!" he muttered, between his teeth. "This will cost me dear..."

Having looked at Hans de Rodock again, though, he recognized the eyes and features of the father, Karl de Rodock."

"In sum, what do you want?"

"Three million."

"You're mad!"

"I estimate that that's the sum you owe my father. It is after all, only a matter of restitution."

"And if I refuse?"

"When I leave here, I'll recount everything to the public prosecutor."

Baruyer passed his hand over his forehead. It was hot.

"Why haven't you brought a complaint?" he asked.

"I want, if possible, to settle the affair myself."

"But Monsieur, one doesn't have three million at one's disposal just like that, in one's safe. Give me time."

"You have a large liquid reserve at this moment, for an operation that you're planning on the exchange."

"How do you know?"

"It doesn't matter. To prove to you that I won't come back for more in the future, I'll return all the letters to you. Your brother had filed them so methodically that he can be certain that I haven't kept any."

Georges reflected momentarily, and sighed.

"All right," he said, finally. "Come back tomorrow at the same time, with the originals. I'll give you the three million myself, in my brother's presence."

Hans stood up, placed the thick sheaf of papers on the desk and took a revolver out of his pocket.

"I'll give you a quarter of an hour. I have the originals of the letters I've just read you in my wallet. A straight swap. Give me a certified check for three million. Call one of your employees. Order him, in my presence, to take it to the Banque Orientale, where I have an account, asking him to deposit it immediately to my credit. I'll wait here for the proof of deposit, in exchange for which I'll return your papers to you. I warn you that any trickery would be futile; at the slightest suspect gesture, I'll shoot you like a dog. The Assize Court will judge us, if necessary. So, do it."

Then, hiding his weapon in his overcoat, the chic young man installed himself in an armchair—and waited.

Subdued, Baruyer wrote the check with a tremulous hand, and did what had been demanded of him so peremptorily. An hour later, the employee came back with the receipt. Hans verified it, threw his wallet down in front of Georges, who was livid with rage, and went out, still calm, correct and impeccable, while the banker-député collapsed into his armchair, uttering a frightful oath.

VII. The Blind See

For a long time, Georges Baruyer remained pensive. That was a hard blow! Now, it was a matter of repairing the vast hole made in his fortune by means of the profits of the fall of the Barsac cabinet—but he did not intend to be alone in paying off young Rodock. He sniggered.

"You'll cough up, too, my dear Walesport. You profited from the windfall; it's necessary to take your share of the responsibility. And Albert? Where has he squandered the profits of which he was the beneficiary?" He groaned again. "Women will be his doom, and we'll be sunk by the repercussions. Oh, the fool!"

He rang.

To the domestic who came in response to the summons he said: "Send Vincent to my brother's place and tell him to come immediately. Telephone to warn him to be ready—needed for an urgent matter. Is Maurice Carnaud here?"

A few moments later, the chief cashier of the Walesport & Co. Bank came in. Every day, at the same time, he came to the député's private domicile to receive the instructions of the anonymous co-director.

"Has Walesport given you instructions regarding liquid capital to be assembled with the briefest possible delay?"

"Yes, Monsieur; I've occupied myself with it, and you can see, by virtue of the check for three million made out to Hans de Bliggen, which I gave instructions to pay just as I was setting out to come here, since it was written, signed and certified in your hand, that the work is proceeding very rapidly."

"What do you have remaining in my name?"

"Two million two hundred and fifty thousand francs."

"Here are three checks totaling eighteen hundred thousand francs. Deposit them this afternoon"

"Yes, Monsieur."

"And as you go out, call on my mother. She'll give you a large sum, which you'll put into her current account. You'll receive instructions shortly concerning the employment of those funds, as well as those that remain to us."

"Understood, Monsieur."

"Now sit down here beside me, and note down these shares as I read them out to you. It's necessary that they should all be deposited with the brokers today, before noon, so that we can work with the receipts tomorrow. As they accumulate, you'll send them on deposit to the banks I indicate to you, the largest sums to Rothschild and the Lyonnais. By the way, you'll make out the receipts to the bearer; it's necessary that the sellers retain their anonymity."

"Yes, Monsieur—understood."

For two hours the two men worked hard. At the end of that time, the voluminous piles of shares had been converted into a hundred parcels.

"Take them all away and bring me the receipts."

Carnaud went out. Two hours later he came back, bringing Baruyer the receipts for the shares placed on deposit. The député checked them, and threw them into a drawer in his desk, which he locked with a key. Then he sent his secretary away.

"Until tomorrow. It will be the day of a major drop."

Maurice Carnaud left, and the député plunged into profound meditation.

Suddenly, he shook the table with a mighty blow of his fist. "Bastard!" He was thinking about his brother. "But for that swine, who kept ammunition against me, none of this would have happened. Everything was going marvelously. Now, it's necessary to risk the lot! And what if it goes awry?"

At that moment, he heard a rustle behind him. "Is that you, Maman?" he said, without turning round. Having received no response, however, he looked over his shoulder. Nothing—he was alone in the room.

"However," he murmured, "I thought I heard footsteps. This business is agitating me too much!"

He started making calculations, covering large sheets of paper with figures. Already, he had estimated what he would gain from the fall of the cabinet, independently of the portfolio that he would obtain in the scheme.

It was at that moment that Albert Baruyer came in.

"You sent for me, Georges—what's up?" he said, his voice a trifle hoarse.

"You don't have any idea?"

"Not the slightest. I've just gotten back from Lyon—you might have given me a little time to rest."

The sincere response increased the député's irritation.

"Of course!" he howled. "You don't know anything, and you don't suspect anything! And because of you, we're in a fine mess! Wretch! You didn't trust me, and you kept ammunition to use against me. That's nice! Because of your knavery, you imbecile, we've risked prison or the labor camp."

"Georges!"

"Oh yes, you're in a funk now! And it's me, yet again, who'll have to bail us out. But have I never refused you anything? In spite of our follies, in spite of your imprudence, which has made me tremble a hundred times over, haven't I always sustained you, with my cash and my influence? Did you think I'd betray you?"

"But after all," exclaimed Albert, exasperated by these reproaches, "what have you got against me? Why this quarrel and these insults, the reasons for which I'm completely ignorant?"

"Here—read these."

At the sight of the letters, the advocated became livid. He could scarcely stammer: "The letters of the Rodock affair! How did they get here?"

"You can't guess who gave them to me?"

"No."

"The Rodock son. Yes, our victim's son. It isn't worth the trouble of pulling that face."

"But...where did he spring from?"

"Oh, I don't know! What's certain, however, is that he's an energetic fellow."

The député marched backed and forth across the room, and then turned to his brother and planted himself in front of him, his fists clenched.

"But why, you triple idiot, did you keep these dangerous letters? And what's Walesport going to say? Oh, I see your game! You were waiting for the propitious moment to bring them out and blackmail me! You don't change; you owe me everything, and you were thinking of turning on me, like a cut throat."

"Georges..."

"Shut up! Without me, poor wretch, what would you be? If you have a name at the bar, it's because I've given you sensational cases, and almost compromised myself obtaining favors for you that you don't deserve! And your part in the Eskinen mine company, who gave you that? If you still had those shares, you'd be able to contribute to the restitution of a sum of three million that he demanded of me, but you squandered the lot! How insatiable are your vices, your needs? Tell me, then—do you think I haven't done enough for you? Have I threatened to refuse you my collaboration? So why did you keep those letters? To have a hold on me, wasn't it? To doom me, if I no longer wanted to be blackmailed? Child! Don't you think that I know about the filthy crimes that you've committed, and of which I haven't taken advantage?"

The advocate stood up, menacingly.

"Georges, you're going too far. Oh, I've had enough, finally, of your imbecilic reproaches and your grand airs. If I'm a criminal, what are you? And then, if you've given me money, you've only paid me for my collaboration, for my work. You have a head for business, I don't dispute that—but when there's dirty work to be done, Georges, there's no danger of you showing yourself. You're too cowardly and too wary; you leave me to do the difficult work. It's just like this Rodock business. You throw in my face the few shares that I had in the mining company, but you forget that they were to remunerate me for the fellow's murder, arranged with that whore Jane Héling and Walesport. You imagine and you plan in the tranquility of your study, but when it requires energy to carry out your plans, you're glad to have us—mother and me—because it's only us who can carry your diabolical ideas through to the end. So what are you reproaching me for? If you've given me money, I've worked for you. We're quits. You don't have the right to bawl at me." He lowered his voice, and went on: "Anyway, what's this Rodock son that you're throwing at my head? What does he want?"

166

"Three million! I told you—he demanded them in exchange for the letters. He's gone."

"Well, pay him. The affair has brought you double that, and will bring you more."

"I have paid. Otherwise we'd have be arrested—but you're going to pay your share, and Walesport his."

"That's all right, Georges," said Albert, sniggering. "You can put it on the slate, since I haven't a sou."

"But into what unspeakable well have you thrown your money? I'll wager it's your dancer that we've enabled to dance! Imbecile! Look, it's like these letters—would you care to tell me where you put them?"

"At home! Carefully hidden, I assure you."

"Yes, well hidden," Georges sniggered. "And who do you receive in your home?"

Albert Baruyer went frightfully pale. He remembered the key he had given to Mademoiselle Alexane, and he also remembered the handsome young man glimpsed in her dressing room on the day when he had introduced the "star" to Barsac. No, it wasn't possible!

Suddenly, he perceived, on a corner of the desk, the card left by the young man.

"Ah!" Albert roared. "It's Alexane that has brought off the coup! So Hans de Bliggen, her lover, is Rodock's son!"

He was unable to say any more and collapsed into an armchair, but his brother had understood.

"Cretin!" he said. "Such gaffes at your age! Letting yourself be fleeced by a whore, like a student!"

But the advocate rebelled. "Well, yes, I have an excuse: passion. Oh, it's not you who'll make gaffes of that sort, for you only love your strong box. Leave me, in peace, now! And since you're holding the purse strings, pay up. Pay for yourself, for me, for Walesport, for our mother—for all of us who've acted in your stead and risked our necks or prison to make you rich! You say that I need you? And don't you need my audacity and my courage? You talk about Rodock, but I'm the one who got rid of him, and the others who were in your way. Do you want me to name them?"

"Oh, shut up!" cried Georges, advancing on his brother with his fists raised. "Shut up!"

"No—I'm not afraid of you! There's no point in putting on your grim air of authority; we're not in an electoral meeting now and your attitude doesn't scare me. You've mocked my love, sullied the woman I adore with a nasty name—I won't forgive you even if you can prove to me that that dancer of genius is a prostitute. Haven't you lived throughout our youth on our mother's prostitution?"

"Swine! At least respect the woman who gave birth to us!"

"No, old man, don't expect me to play the respectful son. Remember that you went partying with the painter Fabio Danti for three years, and you knew full well that he was one of our mother's lovers..."

Livid, George Baruyer hurled himself upon his brother. "Shut up! Shut up! If she heard you, wretch...!"

"She can hear these hard facts, because she's welcomed many others. Oh, we're a fine family: thieves, murderers, pimps...the whole spectrum!"

He started to laugh nervously, like a madman, and Georges Baruyer seized his brother by the throat. "If you say another word, I'll strangle you!"

But Albert had suddenly fallen silent. He remain still, petrified, his eyes fixed on the connecting door to the next room, the curtain of which slowly rose up to reveal the haughty silhouette of his mother—and the son's gaze contained a haggard expression of sincere terror, for he divined that she had been there, behind the curtain, for some time, and that she knew everything about the ignoble dispute. He started to tremble like a leaf, and Georges, beside him, was consternated.

Then, as they did not say another word, or even make a gesture, the blind woman advanced.

"Imprudents," she said, in a deep, strange voice. "I heard your raised voices."

Albert's anger had suddenly faded away before that apparition, which imposed itself upon him. Timid and ashamed now, facing the invalid, he felt crestfallen and heartsick, like a naughty child caught in the act.

"Excuse us, Mother," he stammered. "We were quarreling, stupidly, because we've suffered a great misfortune."

The blind woman replied, bitterly: "You've pronounced painful words. If I've sinned in the past, it was for you; I've always wanted you to be rich and happy. You ought not to have forgotten that..." She stopped speaking abruptly and turned toward the window. In an anxious tone, she said: "But who's the confidant in front of whom you're displaying the family's dirty linen? Is it an intimate? Walesport? Why isn't he saying anything?"

Astonished, the two brothers stared, without comprehending. The blind woman was still looking toward the window, and her extended hands seemed to be feeling the air and shivering."

"Speak, then Monsieur. Who are you?"

Her voice was hoarse, strangled, and Georges, astounded, grasped his brother's arm.

"My God, Albert—Mother's gone mad..."

Although he had whispered, the blind woman had heard. "It's you who've gone mad to shout out your secrets in front of a stranger. Come on, Monsieur, who are you?"

Now, with her arms extended, she advanced toward the window. With the curious divination of the blind, she substituted for her infirmity a means of an astonishing perception of the slightest sounds, even the most muffled, and the tactile sensations she experienced were of such finesse that she had only to extend her hands in front of her to "see," so to speak, a person or object several meters away. In the vicinity of an object, the air no longer had the same density of temperature; the differences were infinitesimal, to be sure, but sufficient nevertheless to guide her.

Suddenly, she cried: "The door! Lock the door!"

Instinctively, Albert obeyed. He ran and turned the key, without knowing exactly why he was doing it.

Meanwhile, Georges had launched himself forward toward the blind woman.

"What can you see, Mother?" he said, in a tremulous voice.

"Oh, it's you, my sons, who are blind! He's there, now, in front of the desk..."

Georges leapt forward. He did not understand any of what was happening, but he was subject to the distraught will of his anxious mother. Subjugated by her conviction, held launched himself, arms forward; he encountered nothing but empty space.

However, a chair that no one had touched was knocked over, and fell in the middle of the room.

Then the two men felt their hair bristle, and an icy chill ran through them.

"There! There!" cried the blind woman, increasingly frightened as she indicated the approach of the mysterious being, divined in the darkness, followed in his slightest movements by her senses, sharpened by the perpetual night into which blindness had plunged her.

"But where?" articulated the advocate, with difficulty. "You're mad, Mother—there's no one here."

She became angry at not being understood, and gasped: "I can see him! I can hear him, I tell you! There—look! He's discovered our secrets—don't let him escape, or we're doomed. There! There! There!"

Her gestures indicated a precise, definite point, and the two men followed the direction of the blind woman's fearful hands with their eyes, but nothing appeared to them. No one, no dangerous presence, was revealed, and yet their mother's affirmation was so convincing that it acted, terribly, upon their consciousness and dread of their past crimes. Now they feared the unknown, the Invisible, whose presence was revealed to the blind woman's refined senses.

"No, Mother," said Georges, who, in spite of his assurance that he had neither heard not seen anyone, was looking fearfully behind the furniture. "I swear to you that we're alone..."

"Yes! Yes! I tell you...there, behind you, Georges! Oh, there! I can see him! Catch him, then—he's slipped between the two of you. He's hiding behind the curtain, there, to the right...look! Albert, he's beside you—get hold of him, then! Oh, I'm scared! I'm scared! What does this mean, my sons? Albert,

Georges, my children, why can't you see the man? Oh, my God, I understand! Are you blind, too?"

And her face suddenly took on an expression of awful terror. She uttered a heart-rending scream, and the two brothers leapt forward in order to sustain her.

They had to calm her down, to reassure her.

At that moment, the roll-top of the American desk rose and fell with a dry click—but nothing had changed behind them; they were still alone with the blind woman.

Now, gripped again by the terrible conviction that was taking hold of them, in spite of the testimony of their eyes, the rival brothers, allied by instinct against the unknown peril, began to hunt through the room for the invisible being that the blind woman could see with the superhuman gaze of her soul, with the eyes of her exalted senses.

The same atrocious fear was making the two men tremble, for they sensed the certainty gaining on them of a supernatural presence divined and betrayed by the tragically extended hands of the blind woman, whose tarnished, empty pupils were swiveling, peering into the darkness. And they were afraid of that being who was watching them, listening to them, but whom they could not see. They sensed him, as an invisible watcher of their actions, spying on their movements, perhaps waiting for the moment to strike a sure blow!

Rustling, the vague sounds of footfalls were now manifest to the ears of the two men, and they even perceived at moments, a human respiration, here, there...then elsewhere... And the respiration became noisier as the hunt became more active, in pursuit of the strange enemy that they could not reach.

They sensed him now, like dogs flushing out game, and tried to catch up with him in the void with leaps and bounds, with hands abruptly projected forward—but the invisible prey continued to evade them.

There was no longer any doubt about it: chairs were knocked over as the mysterious, supernatural being passed by, that violator of secrets who now knew everything about them, their infamous past, and of whom they did not know the form, the face or anything else.

There was no more doubt about it because, suddenly, Georges had bounded at a drape that moved and, when he had grasped nothing but fabric, strident, sarcastic laughter burst forth, freezing them all in tragic stupor.

It was true then: an enemy of superior essence, stronger than them, was spying on them. What did he want? Who was he?

Albert Baruyer uttered a cry of rage. On the desk, a Japanese dagger serving as a paper knife was overlapping the edge of a blotting pad on which it had been placed. He seized it and slashed the air around him with demented gestures, reminiscent of the American boxers who, in the course of straining, battle a shadow, their phantom!

Georges, for his part, had taken hold of a heavy candelabrum and was poised, ready to hurl it at the slightest movement of an object.

The blind woman was still guiding them.

"Quickly! Quickly, Georges! To you, Albert—between the safe and the fireplace! Over there, now, in that corner! You have him! Strike, strike quickly! Strike, then! Oh, escaped again!" She uttered a scream. "He touched me! He's touching you, Albert, to your right, there!"

Soon, the battle became more precise, because a curious phenomenon occurred, which aided the two brothers considerably. Without perceived the slightest human form, the two brothers nevertheless saw green fulgurations sparkling, here and there, in the tribulations of the terrible chase: emerald gleams, like bulging, living irises; a gaze that did not belong to anyone.

"There! There!" cried the blind woman. "Can't you do anything? Don't let him escape! Yes, Georges, you have him..."

With a terrible crash, the heavy candelabrum broke against the marble of the fireplace, and the blind woman moaned: "Oh, he's escaped again!"

Suddenly, there was a frightful scream and then, immediately afterwards, a dolorous groan, a gasp of agony. Albert, who was close to his mother at that moment, recoiled against the desk, with which he collided violently, and his eyes were full of terror.

In front of him, the blind woman was nailed to the door by means of the Japanese dagger, which traversed her throat and made her resemble a great night bird, one of those owls that peasants crucify on the doors of their barns!

Her head bowed and her arms hung down. A jet of blood spurted, striking Albert full in the face.

"Bastard!" shouted Georges. "You've killed our mother!"

Crushed, Albert turned round, his teeth chattering. "What did you say?" he stammered. "What did you say?"

"Murderer! Murderer!" howled the député. "Help! Murder!"

Livid, his features utterly distressed, he made a rampart of the desk, moving around it in order to avoid his brother, who was pursuing him, trying to make him shut up. Albert, covered in blood, ran after Georges, who, mad with fear, continued to shout with all his might, while the mother, nailed to the door, seemed to be staring at them with eyes devoid of life.

People came running from outside. They were trying to open the locked door.

"Break it down!" shouted Georges, still circling the desk. "Help! Murder!"

Soon, the door split, shattering into splinters. People rushed into the room. They all threw themselves on Albert, because he was covered in blood, and because his brother, with his finger, was pointing him out to the crowd.

In a matter of seconds, Albert was knocked down, trampled and stunned, while Georges, exhausted, fainted and fell to the floor.

Then, there was an oppressive calm.

Albert laid in the middle of the room, tied up, an inert, lamentable mass. The domestics gathered around the député, while in the background, on the other door, there was a vision of horror. The old woman, retained by the dagger that traversed her throat, was hanging there, black and bloody, sinister and horrible, like a witch tortured by a mob.

Finally, someone approached the cadaver. He saw then that the door was open, and that there was blood on the key.

And on the denunciation of his brother, Albert Baruyer was arrested.

VIII. Storm Warnings

Claude Barsac was pacing back and forth in his study, very agitated. A press campaign had been launched against him, led by a newspaper, the *Malin*, which had previously been in his pay and under his orders, but was taking on an air of independence and turning against its benefactor. He had some suspicion as to why: he had, because of a liking for the man's wife, installed a certain Grandjean as editor-in-chief, who had announced himself in the press as a first-rate polemicist. Barsac had given into the temptation of pocketing fifty million, and, by virtue of that imprudence, compromised his political situation.

Le Malin, moreover, appeared to be very well-informed, for its allusions were sufficiently clear, and he knew that he would be questioned on the subject today. His political adversaries had been raising their heads for some time; he had entered into the Ministry as a man of action capable of resolving the question of indemnities and the German debt, but since he had been in power, things had remained at the same point. It was not that he had not tried to react against the administrative apathy, but he had had to contend with such a force of inertia that he had ended up renouncing the struggle, like everyone else.

And that was the cause of his imprudence. The instability of power—which might, from one day to the next, hurl him back into the crowd—had incited him to fill his pockets first, like everyone else. After him, the Deluge.

Claude Barsac was not a dreamer but a realizer of the gross desires of youth, and a positivist. He sensed that the financial situation of Europe was hanging by a thread. England, with the pound, and America, with the dollar, governed the world market, but that false prosperity was only a lure; unemployment reigned everywhere. Intensive production surpassed consumption, and the formidable egotism of nations, preventing an economic entente, was preparing worldwide bankruptcy.

He strode back and forth in the vast room for a while longer, and then threw himself into his armchair.

This isn't a moment for philosophizing. The future isn't anyone's, but the present is mine. If I recall the exact tenor of that accursed letter, I could try to subvert the meaning—I am, after all, an advocate before anything else; chicanery doesn't frighten me. Obviously, it's that bitch, Antoinette, who's smearing me on account of her Grandjean. Imbecile of a Samson—there's always a Delilah! I let the whore wait for me, alone, in my study. All the same, one can't play the Trappist. Oh, the cunning spider! Well, Claude, she's only done what you've done, and she hasn't killed anybody.

He passed his hand over his brow. *You're definitely getting old, Barsac, getting old. How to stand up to it? If it's the German letters, I'll fall into univer-*

sal scorn. Deny it? Deny it anyway, against the evidence, against the proof, and retire with dignity.

He burst into nervous laughter. *That's a good one! Yes, to go with dignity, shrugging the shoulders, without recriminations, leaving doubt in the minds of the faithful, and even the adversaries. A misunderstood, disillusioned, disabused brilliant man, going away...*

He sank more deeply into the vast armchair and let himself slip into a kind of somnolence while ruminating his projects. Suddenly, a creaking floorboard caused him to shiver. He opened his eyes and seemed to see something moving over his desk. But he was alone—quite alone!

He stood up mechanically, and shivered.

Someone had written strange words on his blotting pad while he was drowsy: *Look under the blotter.*

"So! People come in here as into a mill?"

Furious to discover that someone had been able to contemplate him in the torpid attitude of a defeated man, he delivered a terrible blow of his fist to a pile of dossiers, and reached out to ring—but he changed his mind, sat down at his desk and opened the blotting pad. There was a large piece of paper underneath the absorbent sheet, covered in bold, thick handwriting, in blue pencil:

Your political adversaries and, above all, financiers are aware of our relationship with Germany and have the proof. Député Vauclin will lead the attack. A scheme built by you will serve your enemies' plans, in bringing you down, and you will be ruined, sunk and shamed. Don't worry about anything. Deny everything, with all your might; have no fear of the letter that Vauclin will read in the Chambre. Proclaim loudly that it is a fake. I will answer for everything. Remember that, if you get out of this, you owe your salvation to me.

THE INVISIBLE

"Who is the trickster who's making fun of me?" muttered Barsac, suddenly feeling a prickling sensation.

He stood up, but, perhaps by virtue of some ludicrous association of ideas, recalled a sentence from Victor Hugo, the reminiscence of a drama in which Angelo, tyrant of Padua, says to Tisbe: "Often, at night, I sit up in bed, and listen—and I can hear footsteps in the wall!"[30] He scanned his vast President of the Council's study in all directions, darting suspicious glances to the right and the left, but nothing—neither an item of furniture nor a drape—could possibly be hiding a man, and he wondered, with anguish, how this singular piece of advice had reached him, for he was sure that the door had not opened.

---

[30] The 1835 play *Angelo, tyran de Padoue* [Angelo, Tyant of Padua], the basis of three operas written prior to 1924 and a fourth afterwards, plus a movie.

He reflected. What if it were true that an anonymous friend was sustaining him? But for what motive? And who could that person be? Some madman, no doubt; it would be very naïve, quite infantile, to clutch at some a chimerical hope. And yet, whoever had written those words was correct: he knew the truth. And he understood the whole affair. For Vauclin and his friends, his accomplices, the Ministry would be brought down tomorrow, and there was not the slightest doubt about it. Then the Bourse would panic, and the index would go down substantially. If he triumphed, on the other hand, it would go up, because an impending danger would have passed.

He divined the entire scheme, working out its details with astonishing lucidity. Of course! Crémiot would replace him, Vauclin would have a portfolio. He wondered whether the best course to adopt, with such scoundrels, might be to send for them and offer them more than Crémiot's party had promised them—but he was quickly convinced that it was too late, and that he had to let destiny take its course.

Suddenly, he sniggered. If, by some extraordinary twist, a miraculous hazard saved him, what a catastrophe it would be for the Baruyer gang! He could already see the collapse of Walesport & Co., the ruination of its associates, their rout—and he rubbed his hands. But what credence could he place in the simple declaration of a mysterious being whose name and face he did not know?

He dared not take advantage of the information himself. Oh, if he had been certain...! He would have given orders immediately to buy the shares that would rise again the following day. In twenty-four hours, he could make a fortune! He collapsed in an armchair placed in front of his desk, put his head in his hands, closed his eyes and meditated for a long time.

When he opened his eyes again, he started. There was another sheet of paper in front of him, covered in the same handwriting, in blue pencil.

You're wondering who I am, and why I'm helping you. Know, then, that I'm playing the role of a supernatural administer of justice, and that it's necessary that those who are leading the Walesport, Baruyer and Vauclin affair must be punished. On the other hand, I need money. My reserves are exhausted. I shall have a great deal tomorrow, if you do as I order.

THE INVISIBLE

Barsac stood up, haggard. He thought: *The person who can come in here without me seeing him can accomplish extraordinary exploits. What he says in therefore true, and I'll be saved. But why isn't this so-called administer of justice punishing me, who nearly sacrificed the prestige and interest of France to my own interest? Undoubtedly, it's to succeed in his own coup, since he'll get rich in saving me.*

Barsac trembled. He told himself that later, he would have the walls of the room sounded, which must be tricked out like a theater—but for the moment, it was necessary to be bold and play a straight game.

Raising himself up to his full height, he said, aloud: "Whoever you are, angel or demon, thank you."

A burst of sardonic laughter replied to him.

Then the Minister was shaken by a frisson, and he pressed the button to summon the usher who was on duty in the antechamber, in order to restore his sense of reality.

IX. From the Chambre des Députés to the Arc de Triomphe

In his office in the Rue de Saints-Pères, his political address, Vauclin, who was due to question the Minister on the matter of the impending German payment, was finishing off his speech. A man mutilated in the war had just come in to announce the visit of Walesport and Crémiot. Astonished, the député had them shown in immediately.

"Well, have you heard?" Walesport demanded, immediately.

"I haven't heard anything. I've been working on my interpellation since four o'clock yesterday afternoon, and didn't even go out yesterday for dinner. I had a bite here while I was working, and slept here on a camp bed.

"Read this." Crémiot threw a handful of newspapers in front of his colleague. In the evening and morning papers almost identical texts were displayed in enormous letters, at the top of the front page:

PARRICIDE
Advocate Albert Baruyer murders his blind mother.
Arrest of the murderer.
Député Georges Baruyer at death's door.

When Vauclin had scanned a few articles, all similar, he let himself fall into his seat, staring at Walesport and Crémiot in utter bewilderment.

"Well?" he asked.

"Well, we don't know what to do. I've tried to get in to see Georges Baruyer, but the imbecile is half-mad; entry to his room is forbidden. Fortunately, I was able to see his secretary, Carnaud; he told me that all our money has been divided between the banks, but he doesn't know whether the receipts have been sent to the brokers or whether they're still at his house. If the orders are placed, we're all right, but if the catastrophe happens beforehand, it's probable that the receipts are still in his safe, and Carnaud couldn't give me any certainty about that."

"What are we going to do, then? My interpellation has been announced. I can't dispense with making it."

"Bah!" said Crémiot. "Let's still bring Barsac down. If the financial coup fails, we'll get it all back when we're Ministers."

"But what about me?" asked Walesport.

"We'll find you something—and then Baruyer will get better, and we'll still have our money.

"For me, nothing's changed, then?" asked Vauclin.

"No," said Walesport, ill-humoredly, "Except that we're going to be working in the dark. By the way, you haven't mislaid my little papers?"

"They're here," said the député, opening his briefcase and shutting them in with his speech. He passed the padlock strap over it, which he locked with a key.

"Thank God! They haven't been stolen."

"It's time," said Vauclin. "I have to go."

He called the one-legged servant, wounded in 1916. "Go fetch me a taxi, Timothée."

"Before going to the Chambre, we'll try to see Baruyer again. If we have an assurance in the matter of the receipts, that will take a great weight off our minds."

The three men went downstairs together. They shook hands, and then Crémiot and Walesport got into the latter's auto, while Vauclin took the taxi that Timothée had procured for him.

Bizarrely enough, as the mutilated man got out of the vehicle, the other door opened. Vauclin installed himself in a corner. The driver closed the door again, and the other one closed at the same time.

Nestling comfortably in his corner, with his precious briefcase on his knees, Vauclin was thinking about what he had just learned, and thinking anxiously that the brilliant scheme that was about to make him rich was becoming problematic. Then, suddenly, it seemed to him that a veil descended over this thoughts; he was invaded by a kind of torpor, and lost consciousness of himself and his surroundings.

He woke up abruptly.

The vehicle stopped in front of the Chambre de Députés. Still dazed, he made sure that his briefcase was under his arm, got out and paid the driver. Then, hastily, he went into the Parliament.

"Are you free?" the driver was asked by a man of Hindu appearance, elegantly dressed, who already had his hand on the car door.

"Yes, sir—where to?"

"Place de l'Étoile, the Tomb of the Unknown Soldier."

Scarcely had the vehicle surged forward when Mardruk—for it was him—slid his hand under the cushion and pulled out a thin wad of papers. Having made sure that it was what he wanted, he tore them up into little pieces, then, putting his hand out of the window, allowed them to be successively carried away by the wind. When he arrived at his destination, he no longer had more than a pinch in the palm of his hand.

He got out, and paid the driver handsomely. The latter thanked him effusively. Then Mardruk headed slowly toward the Tomb of the Unknown Soldier, which was still abundantly covered in flowers and wreaths.

The driver followed him mechanically with his eyes. He saw him make a circuit of the Tomb, dropping little pieces of paper on it—the letter from the Chancellor of the Reich—which the swirling wind carried away under the Arc de Triomphe, around the flame rising from the sepulcher of the Victory.

X. The Parliamentary Weathervane

There was expectation in the Chambre of a *coup-de-théâtre*. From the viewpoint of the honorable gentlemen, if the President of the Council were defeated, that would mean a good dozen Ministerial portfolios up for grabs. From the viewpoint of the public, a crisis in a troubled epoch was the prospect of the worst possibilities. Among the audience, there were envoys of big banks and stockbrokers, who were waiting, not without anxiety, for a vote that might have incalculable repercussions on the Bourse.

At two o'clock, the President of the Chambre opened the session.

The Invisible, meanwhile, must have found a favorable corner in the national hemicycle.

Vauclin, invited by the President to make his interpellation, made a grave declaration in which he accused Barsac of being an accomplice of a Foreign Power, and having made, in secret negotiations, an agreement by which the dignity and interests of France were compromised.

Barsac having boldly accepted an immediate debate, affirming that he wanted nothing more than to explain himself, a ripple of excitement ran through the assembly, for everyone foresaw a ferocious, impassioned and also uncertain battle, in respect of which no one was sufficiently well-informed to offer a prognosis. It was rumored that Vauclin was in possession of terrible proofs, but no one had seen them; the feller of the Ministry had carefully refrained from divulging them in order to bring about a formidable *coup-de-théâtre*, by virtue of which he would carry the vote of no confidence, and even the accusation of treason.

In a thunderous voice, Vauclin let fall terrible precisions in his speech for the prosecution. He explained the bargain concluded between Germany and Barsac, and it was in the midst of a profound stupor that he said: "Now, Messieurs, it only remains for me to read you a document revealing the interest that Monsieur le Président du Conseil has in postponing, indefinitely, the payment of our former adversaries."

Barsac was pale and anguished, but he was able to remain upright, arrogant, almost smiling, in the midst of the tempest. In his distress, he still dominated the others and himself. And as he received a broadside of insults without flinching, he suddenly had the sensation of a whisper in his ear: "Deny the secret negotiations, deny the letter, deny everything—have confidence in me."

He turned round, stupefied, but saw that he was alone. His colleagues had quit the Ministerial bench, drawing way from him, as if he were infectious. Then, as he still did not say anything, the same incorporeal voice, close by, made itself heard again: "Deny, then. I tell you, Monsieur. I don't want you to fall today, or beware! Deny!"

That enigmatic voice, the echo of his imperturbable confidence in life, of his customary aplomb, his extraordinary nerve, responded to an interior voice that said to him, as to Danton: "Audacity, and more audacity!" He rediscovered all his cerebral strength, then, and gave his portfolio a mighty blow with his fist.

Barsac followed the advice of Danton, and of the man whose breath he felt but whom he could not see.

"You are a liar and a knave, Monsieur Vauclin!" he replied, in his magnificent voice, velvety but terrible and thunderous. "Your accusations are unworthy, and if I have not called you a liar sooner, it is out of respect for this assembly, for I do not suppose that it can add faith to your abominable slanders. Everything about your threats is false, and the pretended revelations that you have brought here are nothing but a heap of manure picked up by you in I don't know what gutter of gold and filth in which you have had the dismal courage to go fishing."

Nonplussed by such aplomb, Arsène Vauclin was momentarily shaken. Barsac's brazen attitude, meanwhile, regained him sympathy.

But the accuser pulled himself together and pounced. "How dare you give proof of such impudence when I have here a terrible document..."

"That document, I repeat, if it exists, is a fake!"

"Wretch! It's a letter from the Chancellor of the Reich, the conclusion of an ignoble bargain between you."

"Show it!" was cried from all directions. "Read it!"

Barsac had folded his arms, and, standing up, waited anxiously. Meanwhile, beneath the icy or feverish stares of the députés, Vauclin was rummaging in his briefcase.

He was seen to go white, agitate feverishly, shifting papers, and then suddenly cried: "Someone has stolen the letter!"

Volleys of whistles replied to him; it was a triumph for Claude Barsac. The assembly acclaimed his ironic and mordant reply, and a vote of confidence was carried by an enormous majority. All those who had moved away from him moved back, with little Barthou in the lead, vulpine and graying, watchful behind his lorgnon.

XI. The Vultures' Stupor

In the meantime, the delegates of the banks leapt into taxis and raced to the Bourse. With the Ministry having emerged from the contest victorious, there was a rally in prices. Walesport, who was watching the session from the public benches, was devastated. He could not diminish the catastrophe, since he did not have the receipts and did not know whether the brokers had the deposits. Prudently, he had charged Baruyer with making the disbursements, and that wisdom had turned against him.

He leapt into his car and was driven to the Bourse. The closure had seen a considerable rise in the index, which was for him and his associates irreversible ruination.

From the Bourse he was then taken to Georges Baruyer's house, where there was utter chaos. Journalists, curiosity-seekers and policemen were all trying to collect further information.

Finally, Walesport got his hands on Carnaud, Baruyer's secretary.

"You believe it was a murder, then? And that Albert is the murderer?"

"He was caught in the act."

"That story is absurd. That's all you know, then?"

"Inevitably. Oh—I forgot to tell you that I paid a check for Monsieur Georges Baruyer to the Banque Orientale."

"What's that you're telling me?"

"It must have been an old debt."

"What! What makes you think that?"

"The fact that I paid out three million to the Banque Orientale to the account of Monsieur le Baron Hans de Rodock."

That was another hammer-blow for Walesport. Bewildered, searching for some saving straw at which to clutch in the catastrophe, he was absolutely at a loss. Three million paid to the son of their former victim, preceding the drama. Perhaps that was an enlightenment; he sensed a connection between the two events.

In distress he left Carnaud and was taken to Vauclin's political address. He assumed that the latter, after the scene in the Chambre, was more likely to be there than the Avenue Henri-Martin. He did indeed find the député there, in the company of Crémiot, the Minister of Public Works.

On seeing Walesport come in, the two men ran toward him.

"Well," screeched Vauclin, "we're in a fine mess!"

"You've got a nerve!" cried Walesport. "Do you think I can't see through your game? You're in it with Barsac. Oh, you've done well—and you, too, Crémiot, you're in league with this blackguard!"

"Calm down, William—we haven't betrayed you. Isn't it you to whom we've given our money? One doesn't lose millions for a sham."

Walesport understood the justice of the reasoning. "What, then?"

"There's something inexplicable about this," said Vauclin. "I was sure, absolutely certain, that I had the letters in my briefcase. In any case, I showed them to you. I remember, now, that I felt drowsy in the cab that took me to Parliament, but I never usually fall asleep, and I was wide awake when I left you, in full readiness for the interpellation. I think I've got the thread: it was cooked up between Barsac and that cuckold Grandjean of the *Malin*. They must have found some means of putting me to sleep in that accursed taxi and taking back the letters."

"In that case, the fellow's damnable clever."

"I'll kill him."

"Violence is all very well," said Vauclin, "but it ought to be a last resort. What's important for the moment is figuring out whether there's a means of saving some of our cash, and we don't know anything about that, so long as we can't talk to Baruyer."

"I've been to his house," William snorted, "and I'm no further forward."

"I've got an idea," said Vauclin. "What if I were to send Sophie? She's clever—she'll be able to get to Georges."

Madame Vauclin did, in fact, succeed in getting to see Baruyer, whom she found in a state of utter depression. He recounted the tragic scene, and how his brother had murdered their mother.

"But that's crazy—completely crazy! Why would you think that Albert killed his mother, given that she was useful to both of you? There's something underlying this that's escaping us. What have you done since Albert's arrest?"

"Nothing. I've been brutalized, helpless, for hours."

"And the money for the affair—where is it?"

Baruyer stated. "Damn! The receipts are still in my desk."

"That's incorrect—they're circulating at the Bourse. Who has sold the shares, then?"

Baruyer got up and dragged Sophie to his desk—but he ran into an unexpected obstacle. The law had put it under seal because of the murder.

"After all," said Madame Vauclin, "it doesn't get us any further forward to acquire proof that you've been robbed. What we need is to find out who's attacking us. Walesport and my husband are accusing Barsac, but I don't think he's as cunning or as ferocious as that. There's someone very clever behind this. Try to get Albert released—I'm sure he's not guilty of his mother's murder."

"But we were alone with Maman. It must have been him or me."

"Remember that your mother could see someone—an invisible enemy."

"Shut up! Leave me alone! Shit! I think I'm losing my mind!"

With that, Madame Vauclin left him and went back to report the result of her visit to the two men. She made them party to her suspicions.

Walesport shrugged his shoulders, but Vauclin, with better reasons to believe her, shared his wife's opinion.

"In any case," Walesport concluded, "it's necessary to wait. For my part, I'll try to pick up the trail of the mysterious seller, and, above all, keep an eye on Grandjean."

With that, they separated. The faces of those great bandits, those superior blackguards, however, were anxiously marked by mistrust for one another.

All of that would finish with life becoming more expensive every day in victorious France by virtue of new taxes, which would be increased by twenty, forty or fifty per cent, by the revolution and the new war. At all times, the sheep are led to the abattoir while the vultures fly overhead. And when people change politicians, as when a man changes his trousers, there is always a backside—with gold, or something resembling it.

BOOK FOUR: THE INVISIBLE ADMINISTRATOR
OF JUSTICE

I. Claude Barsac, Statesman

On the day after the vote of confidence, when Vauclin read the account rendered of the previous day's session, he was astonished by the disdainful moderation with which Barsac had interpreted his conduct. He saw in that indulgence of tempered terminology the possibility of returning to Parliament without exciting too much mockery from his colleagues.

But why was Barsac sparing him? Was there something to fear? In any case, he would send his excuses and thanks to the President of the Council, blaming the error he had made on those who had procured the letters for him.

That, of course, was the nub of the matter. Barsac had gone easy on him because he wanted to know from whom he had acquired the famous letters.

That's all right, he thought. *It was diabolically clever to have them spirited away from me at the very podium of the Chambre. If it were only I, I might think I was going crazy, but it's Grandjean who gave them to Crémiot, who gave them to me, so they really existed. Thunder! It's damnably clever!*

Vauclin had more admiration than anger for the man who had rolled him over.

That was not all. The hardest part of the hard blow was that he was ruined. He had put the two million of the pseudo-inheritance into the conspirators' game, and all that was lost. That was the most serious thing because, already counting on the receipts, he had started negotiations to buy a house on the Avenue Kléber. He was gripped by rage against Crémiot and his acolytes. Barsac was a skillful wrestler; he and the others were imbeciles. For a practical man, the victor is always right.

Anyway, it was decided: he would write to Barsac. Since the other had spared him, he must need him. Vauclin therefore dashed off a letter in which he made it clear that the fault was less his own than those who had pushed him forward with fake documents.

Having done that, he waited.

The following day he received a note written by the general secretary of the President of the Council summoning him for the following day at seven a.m. *They light the fires early in the Barsac household!* Vauclin thought. *That's so I don't run into anyone; all well and good.*

At the appointed hour, he was introduced into the prime minister's study. The latter, sitting at his desk, was already working. He saluted Vauclin with a gesture and indicated a seat to him; then, having finished what he was doing, he turned toward him and said, abruptly: "Do you know, Monsieur Vauclin, how much I made financially from your attack the day before yesterday?"

"Judging by what I lost," Vauclin riposted, "you can't have done badly."

"I was in the process of drawing up my accounts when you came in. I realized exactly seventeen million eight hundred and forty thousand francs." He rubbed his hands together and looked at Vauclin with a mocking expression.

"I've rendered you a great service then."

"Add to that the influence regained over my colleagues; I've reinforced my majority."

"I don't suppose that it's solely to make me party to your triumph that you've summoned me. I thought you were too wily to take pleasure in mocking a defeated adversary."

"You're not mistaken. It's because I have confidence in your worth, my dear Vauclin. While you had me by the collar and were strangling me a little, I admired you. Mirabeau must have had those authoritative gestures. In truth, you looked very good."

Vauclin nodded silently, waiting.

"How much did you put into the enterprise?" Barsac asked, bluntly.

"Two million—the fruit of an inheritance by my wife."

"Ah! Madame Vauclin receives legacies like that?"

"Yes," he replied, dryly. "Her mother was a creole, and my wife has rich relatives in America."

"Then it won't astonish anyone if she comes into another. There are lugubrious weeks when there are successive deaths in a family. The thing is, my dear Vauclin, that I have a scruple. It seems to me that the enormous sum that I owe to your…eloquence…would weigh upon me less heavily if I were to make restitution of a part of it to the most deserving and most necessitous of our colleagues. The Ancients, you know, made sacrifices to the gods on days of success, in order to ward off evil destiny. The system has merit, and one should often follow their example…

"Let's see, I suppose that in your group there are a certain number of needy individuals. With your help, given that you know them intimately, might we not render them a few services? I hope that they might be grateful to me. I like round numbers; sixteen million will be amply sufficient for me, for I have simple tastes, and it would be a pleasure for me to offer relief to a few unfortunates.

"I have confidence in you. The indignation that you testified the day before yesterday against the vampires who, etc., etc…convinced me that I'm dealing with a deeply honest man. So I'm ready, if you consent, to give you the eighteen hundred and forty thousand francs that embarrass me, in order that you might be obliging enough to divide them between those of our colleagues who, having been deceived…like you…were able to launch themselves into bad speculations."

"I accept," Vauclin replied, although confused. "But were there not some among the members of the cabinet who were deceived, like me?"

"Crémiot is treacherous enough to bear the loss—but perhaps you know an intimate adviser who is not in the same situation?"

"In truth, no. Georges Baruyer? But he can support a loss."

"You got the famous letters from him?"

"No, from Crémiot, who got them from Grandjean."

"That explains everything. Grandjean, who ought to be grateful to me, fabricated the fakes. But let's leave these nasty stories aside and talk business. I believe you to be very capable, Monsieur Vauclin, and I like to surround myself with men of great value and the highest probity. I assume that had I been brought down, you would have had a portfolio in the new cabinet. You've compromised your situation in the Chambre somewhat as the leader of a group, but if you succeed in resuming your place on the extreme left, it might be that in a future cabinet—I mean a socialist ministry, and I'm presently orienting my politics in that direction—I'll reserve you a place there. Once this annoying question of Germany has been concluded, I intend to resign. I need rest, and I've been offered a lecture tour of the United States. A Ministry with socialist tendencies seems the most appropriate to replace me."

Vauclin looked at the prime minister incredulously.

"You think I'm making fun of you? Not at all, and I'll take the trouble to explain my plans to you—it is, in any case, necessary that you understand them in order that you can help me to accomplish them when the time comes. I believe I have a little experience of men; politics is based on the knowledge of men, and is the science, the clairvoyance, of possibilities. One fights for principles, but they're masks to disguise appetites. My dear Vauclin, I appreciate your worth; you're the man I need, and that's why I'm fishing you out and putting you back on your feet."

"I...?"

"No, no thanks, not even tacit ones. If I weren't sure of your collaboration, I wouldn't confide in you; it's not your devotion I'm counting on, but your self-interest. I'll go on. You can't believe that a man of my age and experience can retire from business when he's tasted power and had some success. Of all métiers, that of leader of men is the one that causes the greatest ennuis and has the least stability, but it's also the most desirable, and it is, I believe, the universal desire for a perilously high position that makes it attractive. I possess what multitudes believe to be desirable; now, of all human passions, vanity is the most overwhelming. Just think: those millions of men are my playthings, and with a little skill, I lead a country as I wish; nothing is more captivating, and, when one has stuck a little finger in the gears of power, the entire body passes through—until it reaches the summit, directing the struggle and the intrigue...

"But let's get back to my plan. The cartel of the leftists has contrived to have a few major reforms accepted, to prepare for the study a few questions that,

186

in the present state of the world, are virtually insoluble. A man like me can't waste his time. So, as I said, I'm preparing the way for a socialist Ministry, in order that it can founder and condemn itself to impotence. In France, we don't like people who can't get anything done. The socialist Ministry will last for three to six months; then it will collapse, along with the questions that it has raised, without resolving them. Then, I come back on stage, I become the providential man, I keep one or two of the socialist ministers with me, and I reign again for some years. After which, by way of retirement, the Presidency of the Republic....

"What do you think, Vauclin? Isn't that a well-rounded career? You're young—you can model yourself on me. A beautiful career is open to all intelligences liberated from scruples."

Like Machiavelli, Barsac thought that those who govern ought to strive to appear great in all their actions and to avoid in their sentiments anything that has the character of indecision or weakness.

Vauclin bowed. "If I'd appreciated you sooner, I wouldn't have tried to struggle against you. You are, Master, a veritable political genius."

"Perhaps. But I've only found, thus far, envious individuals to betray me or incompetents to serve me. You, I believe I understand; you can second me, to begin with, and succeed me thereafter. I'm not asking you for any oath of fidelity; your self-interest is my surest guarantee."

"Secret alliance concluded," said Vauclin. "What need I do to be useful to you? Barsac is great, and henceforth, I am his prophet."

"Thanks to that money, first of all, you're going to recover your preponderance at the head of your group, making them understand that I'm with them—that, disgusted with the continual procrastinations of my colleagues, I'm preparing a socialist Ministry. When the moment comes, I'll withdraw, while conserving, thanks to you, an occult influence over the new cabinet. After that, we'll see. In the meantime, my dear friend, I'm going to sign checks for you drawn on various banks in order not to attract attention to you."

He signed a dozen checks, for the sum of eighteen hundred thousand francs. He gave them to Vauclin, who, taking a step back from his chief, extended his right arm straight in front of him by way of a salute and said: "*Ave Caesar.*"

Then the two separated after a warm handshake.

Once he was alone, Barsac rubbed his palms together. *That's money well employed,* he thought. *Now, there remains my mysterious savior. That one will probably be more demanding. I won't haggle.*

He lifted up the famous blotter, expecting to find another message. There was nothing there. Barsac remained pensive for a moment; then, picking up his checkbook again, he signed ten for a hundred thousand francs each, drawn on five different banks, and placed them under the blotter. Then he rang.

Gérôme appeared immediately.

"Come in, my friend," said the Minister, affectionately. "I want to talk to you personally."

The usher bowed and approached the desk.

"My dear Gérôme, I'm very pleased—very pleased, you understand—with the manner in which you understand your service, and I want to testify to that in a more interesting fashion than compliments."

He took a wad of thousand-franc notes from his desk; he detached one of them and held it out to the functionary, who was dazzled by that generosity.

"By the way, Gérôme, I beg you to redouble your surveillance. Certain papers have disappeared, fortunately of little importance, which were in my desk. I believe that someone has introduced themselves here, without your knowledge, during my absence."

"Oh, Monsieur le Président, that's absolutely impossible. The antechamber commands the various entrances, and I don't leave it. The cleaning is done by reliable men, as reliable as me—and I've been at the Ministry for twenty years, and am incapable of any indelicacy."

"Nevertheless, observe, observe closely, Gérôme. Don't let anyone disturb anything in my desk, and if anything abnormal happens, alert me."

Gérôme bowed, and went out.

Evidently, the man knows nothing. Oh, if I could believe in God or the Devil, I could explain the mystery. In truth, there's nothing to do but wait.

Nevertheless, he picked up his checkbook again and made a mark on each of the last ten stubs. *If the checks disappear*, he thought, *I'll alert the banks on which they're drawn in order that they can have whoever cashes them followed, and perhaps I'll succeed in unmasking my unknown.*

The next day, the first thing that Claude Barsac did on entering his study was to open his desk. He made a gesture of satisfied astonishment. The ten checks were no longer there—but the checkbook had also vanished.

He shrugged his shoulders, carelessly. "Bah! I'm being ridiculous."

He had been saved; that was the main thing—and the savior wanted to remain invisible. That was his business.

II. Midnight Antitheses: Dance and Drama

One evening, a fortnight after the famous session that had nearly brought down the Barsac Ministry, Arsène Vauclin, his aplomb recovered and his parliamentary influence reconquered, was playing host.

Political men, magistrates, celebrated artists, socialites and sportsmen were all saluting his revival. Red-faced and congested, but triumphant, he was in formal dress, smiling, shaking hands with the men and kissing the hands of the ladies, amiable with everyone, for he was one of those people who thought that he might make use of anyone at a given moment.

Vauclin was exultant; he was riding his lucky streak, and he had a solid grip on it. Sophie Vauclin was also triumphant; this was the life of which she had dreamed. After the soirée, fifty intimates would stay for supper, including, naturally, Simone d'Armez, Jeanne Fortin and Monsieur and Madame Grandjean. Sophie was only too glad to dazzle her former school friends.

Everywhere, there was dancing.

During the fête and the tango:

"You don't appear to be having a good time, my dear Jeanne."

"My habits and tastes are so different from yours that it would be surprising if it were otherwise."

I'm all the more grateful that you've come; it's an unappreciable honor to have you here—you and your father—and I'll make many people jealous."

"You always like to make fun," said Jeanne, smiling.

"I'm not joking. When people read, tomorrow: *Brilliant party yesterday at the home of Madame Arsène Vauclin, etc., etc...we observed the presence of Monsieur le Docteur Fortin and his daughter. The illustrious scientist has left his studies for an evening, to permit the fine flower of Parisian elegance to admire the grace and beauty of Mademoiselle Jeanne Fortin. Needless to say, the presence of such illustrious guests was one attraction more...*"

"Add to that account my fiancé, Dr. Georges Garnier."

"You're joking in your turn. You're getting married! Is it possible? Your motto is: *Outside science, nothing.*"

"Certainly, but by marrying Georges Garnier, the two of us will be able to work and carry out research together."

"Where are you hiding that fortunate mortal?"

"Behind us. He's chatting to my father and other people."

Sophie turned round. On seeing her former lover, Julien de Vandeuvre, whose back was turned to her, she went livid.

"What's the matter?" Jeanne asked.

"It seemed to me...but this crowd, this heat...I don't feel very well. Come to my room. Come on."

Cutting a path through the dancing couples, with difficulty, she dragged Jeanne away.

Fortin was following the scene from the corner of his eye when Vauclin approached.

"My dear Master, I'm thankful for the presence here of one of the purest national glories. My wife has told me that your daughter was infinitely beautiful, and that you've deprived Parisian salons of her. You're a great egotist."

"In truth, I won't hide the fact that my best moments are those I spend in my laboratory at the Red Nest, with my daughter and Georges Garnier, my future son-in-law."

"Why haven't you introduced him?"

"I'll go look for him."

Dr. Fortin thought: *I'll bowl you over.* He went to join someone who was hidden by the large leaves of a latania palm in a corner of the room.

"Stay calm and try to recall your memories. Here, look in that mirror at the man I've just left. Do you recognize him? He's coming toward us."

"Yes—that's the man who killed me."

"Let's manage our effect. Don't turn round until I introduce you... Monsieur Vauclin, you wanted to meet my future son-in-law. Here he is: Monsieur Georges Garnier."

Vauclin leapt backwards, and collapsed, as if thunderstruck. The chemist Bernardot caught him in his arms. Everyone ran forward.

"What is it? What's happened?"

"Why, it...it's him, it's Vandeuvre," said several guests, including a general—and the general added, addressing Georges-Julien: "I would have been astonished not to see you here this evening, as one of the intimates."

"Messieurs," said the young man, "there's some mistake; my name is Georges Garnier."

"But that doesn't explain out host's fainting fit," said Dr. Fortin. "Everyone is astonished by the extraordinary resemblance, but no one else has fainted."

"Indeed," said Bernardot, who, aided by several other people, had carried Vauclin to a window, and had then returned to look for Fortin. "I was surprised, too, but not to the point of feeling ill. Fortunately, we're physicians, Come on."

"Go find Jeanne, and leave us to it," whispered Fortin in the young man's ear. "I'll take care of Vauclin." Aloud, he added: "Go quickly, Georges."

"I thought Monsieur de Vandeuvre was named Julian?" said a lady.

"Know, my dear Baronne, that that young man isn't Monsieur Vandeuvre."

"Get away!" said the Baronne. "It's a hoax!"

"No, Madame," Bernardot interjected, "And that's the cause of Monsieur Vauclin's fainting fit. In truth, it's remarkable."

"I greeted him just now, thinking that I was greeting Vandeuvre," said a guest. "I was astonished that he didn't stop for a chat. It's at least two months since I last saw him."

In the meantime, Fortin had devoted his cares to Vauclin, who had come round completely.

"Well," said Fortin, "How are you, my dear Monsieur?"

"Me?... Oh yes...I remember... Where is he? Get rid of him! Get rid of him! He's dead, I'm sure of it."

"What are you talking about?" Fortin interjected, swiftly.

"Is it Monsieur de Vandeuvre?" asked Bernardot.

"But Vandeuvre isn't dead, so far as I know," said the Baronne.

"Vandeuvre," said Vauclin, standing up. "Where is he? Have you seen him?"

"No," said Bernardot, "but we've seen someone who bears a striking resemblance to him—isn't that so, Messieurs?"

"Which I to say that I was convinced that I had seen Vandeuvre, and no other," said the general.

"In that case," Vauclin repeated, "I really saw Monsieur de Vandeuvre, or someone who resembles him strangely."

"You saw my son-in-law-to-be, Georges Garnier," agreed Fortin, "whom I was introducing to you at the moment when you were struck by a sort of congestion caused by the heat. I've just sent him to fetch my daughter, for we'll take our leave, thanking you for your welcome and the pleasure I've had at the party."

"Say that your presence was one attraction more. Henceforth, we hope to see you more often. My wife and your admirable daughter are old school friends. But permit me to go and repair the disorder of my costume. If your daughter, whose beauty equals her genius, is with my wife, I'll bring her back to you."

Vauclin went away in the direction of the private apartments. Fortin followed him at a distance, murmuring: "I'm not losing sight of you, my man."

At that moment he perceived Vanel, who was kissing the hand of Simone d'Armez, as if saying goodbye. In fact, Marc did quit the Comtesse. When he turned round, he found himself facing Fortin.

"Come with me," said the latter, "I believe I'm going to need you."

"At your orders, Master," said Homo-Deus.

III. The Recalcitrant Dead Man

Guiding Jeanne, Madame Vauclin had taken her to the first-floor apartments. There, all was calm and the sounds of conversation and music scarcely reached them. After passing through an elegant boudoir, they went into Sophie's bedroom, furnished with refined taste.

"Here, at least, we can chat at our ease without fear of being disturbed. Let's see, my dear Jeanne, you were telling me that you're engaged to your father's best pupil. Tell me about him. It's the first time I've see him, you know—and only from behind. I wouldn't have thought that such a great scientist could also be a man of the world." With her habitual versatility, she added: "Is he handsome, is he nice?"

"My father?"

"No, your fiancé."

"If you hadn't dragged me here, you'd know. But I hope you'll see him soon other than from behind."

"It's astonishing how his appearance reminds me of...someone you don't know. But come on, you, who knows everything, can give me some information."

"About what?"

"Oh, a very macabre subject. Every human body found on the public highway is taken to the Morgue, isn't it?"

"An odd conversation for a pretty socialite like you."

"Indeed, but can you answer my question?"

"Yes, unless papers are found on the body establishing its identity, in which case it's taken to his domicile. That, of course, is in the case of natural death, for if it's a murder, transport elsewhere is necessary for the autopsy."

"Is there a possibility that something else might happen?"

"The corpse might be picked up by people capable of making a profit from it—as, for example, by selling it to physicians for their anatomical studies."

"And has that ever happened to your father?"

"Oh, often. In fact, it happened about two months ago."

"Two months, you say—and what was that corpse?"

"That of a man of about thirty."

At that moment, Georges-Julien appeared, who bowed to the petrified Madame Vauclin.

"What's wrong, Madame?"

Sophie, terrified, had thrown herself backward on the divan and was hiding her head in the cushions.

"Julien! It's Julien!" stammered Madame Vauclin, still hiding her face.

"Do you recognize this woman?" said Jeanne to Julien de Vandeuvre, in a low voice.

"I didn't know her a little while ago, but on hearing her cry: 'Julien! It's Julien!' it seemed to me that a veil was torn apart in my brain. I remember…it was her and her husband who murdered me!"

Finally, Jeanne thought, *the mind of the other is beginning to resume its identity*.

Georges-Julien had launched himself toward Sophie and raised her head brutally. "Your husband and you…I remember, now... Wretch! While he broke my neck, you were holding my arms. But why that crime? Why?"

"To steal your mother's legacy."

"Ah! That violent love was only a lie? I, a poor fly, had fallen into the web of two spiders!"

"Pity, Julien, pity! I confess, yes, it's true—but it was my husband who drove me..."

At that moment, the door opened again and Vauclin appeared on the threshold, distraught. His bulging eyes were staring at Georges-Julien, unable to detach themselves. His terror was such that he did not perceive that two men had appeared behind him, seemingly ready to throw themselves upon him at the slightest suspect gesture.

"It's really him! It's not an illusion..." The dead man took several strides across the room. "By what frightful mystery have you emerged from the grave?"

"I am, in fact, dead," replied Georges-Julien, laughing. "Does that astonish you? Me, too!"

"I'm going mad," Vauclin groaned. "I'm going mad. Or it's an abominable nightmare. Sophie…say something! Speak, so that I can hear a living voice! I'm dreaming, aren't I? It's a dream, a frightful dream. Oh, I understand now. It's remorse. Did I know what that was, remorse? It exists, then, the conscience, as in novels and Shakespeare. Banquo's ghost... One thinks one is strong, one comes and goes, nothing stirs…then night comes, one goes to sleep full of confidence, and then…oh, then, everything changes! Conscience is there, the avenger, it takes you by the throat, it grips you, and the dead…the dead come back. They look at you, speak to you, laugh in your face..."

"Ha ha! You thought you'd killed me, imbecile. I'll always be alive for you, and every night—every one!—I'll come back. And every night—every night, do you hear?—until you confess, or…you go mad..."

"I'm scared! Scared!" howled Sophie.

His wife's voice seemed to reanimate Vauclin; his gaze became somewhat firmer, he straightened up, and his combative nature got the upper hand again.

"Anyway," he said, "dream or reality, answer me, specter—what do you want with us?"

"A detailed account of your crime."

"And if I refuse?"

"You won't refuse."

"Why?"

"Because if you refuse to make the confession that I'm demanding here and now, I'll force you to make it in front of the crowd that's filling your drawing rooms."

"Well, speak, you!" roared Vauclin, turning toward his wife, who was moaning on the divan. "You deserve your part of the punishment."

"I don't want to! I'm only a weak woman."

"Enough nonsense! Speak as if I didn't know anything."

A suspicion was dawning in Vauclin. He darted a suspicious glance around him, and suddenly perceived, in a mirror set in front of him, although not distinctly enough to make out their faces, two men of tall stature standing behind him, not missing a single one of his movements.

There are three of them, he thought, *they didn't dare come alone.*

Redoubling his attention, he observed the ghost and the other two phantoms by turns. As for Jeanne Fortin, as soon as Vauclin came in, she had hidden behind the curtains of a window. She was only visible to the living dead man, who was asking her with his eyes what step to take.

"I'd been married for two years," Sophie began, in a choked voice, "when I met you for the first time, at Madame Chambigne's. For two years, I'd been serving my husband's ambitious aims. I'd married him for love, but he had only seen in my beauty an advantage to favor the means of reaching his goals. Through him, I learned the métier of petitioner, and how one obtains that for which the ugly or prudish wait indefinitely. I was a coquette; you were amiable and attentive. My husband, absorbed by his political affairs, neglected me. I was bored; you were handsome, rich, gallant, much sought-after by women, and I was proud of having attracted your attention. I didn't take long to become your mistress.

"I thought my husband was unaware of our liaison; he was not—and it was then that he constrained me to solicit and obtain gifts and loans from your generosity, which, for him, were the sole means of rising above his mediocrity. Our relationship might have gone on for a long time like that. To your misfortune, you were summoned to collect your mother's legacy, and I was informed by you of all the formalities of the inheritance. I knew the manner in which you planned to collect your fortune, and, finally, that at a given moment you would have in your home about two million in cash, with which you were going to attempt a big coup on the Bourse.

"It was at the instigation of my husband, and on his advice, that you were going to attempt that supposedly-infallible coup, which had no other objective, for us, but to have the certainty of finding the desired sum in your home. Once the idea of the crime had been decided, we planned the details minutely and settled the procedure. Arsène had already put about the rumor of an inheritance in my family. My mother was creole, so it was a matter of an American uncle who had made me his heir. Then we waited for your return from Vandeuvre. As soon as you arrived, your first concern was to call on me and offer me a piece of jewelry. My husband had pretended to go away, but remained on watch here. I followed his instructions exactly.

"The following evening, you were to spend the evening with me; I'd prepared a fine supper and sent away my only domestic. I encouraged you to drink; you had no suspicions. Then, after supper, we went into my bedroom..."

"Go on," said the former dead man.

"The scene was arranged in advance. While teasing you on the bed, I succeeded in tilting your head backwards, over the head of the bed. My husband, hiding behind it, was waiting for that moment. I seized your arms and descended upon you with all my weight, while he, grabbing your head and twisting it backwards, broke your spine on the headboard."

Vauclin leapt forward and stood in front of his victim.

"I was sure that I'd succeeded. I can still hear the sound of breaking vertebrae, see the body falling limp and inert on to the bed. You're dead, Monsieur de Vandeuvre, really dead, and it isn't those two sorcerers behind you who've brought you back to life. Ha ha! You've played a trick on me! But I can see clearly now. Don't be afraid, Sophie, these Messieurs are playing a game."

Turning to the two astonished scientists, he said: "That's all right! You're very good. Fortunately, you've had the good taste to make me play this macabre comedy behind closed doors, for I recognize that it would have played as well in public."

He turned to Sophie, who was looking at him in bewilderment: "Come on, stupid," he said. "Can't you see that it's a matter of suggestion?" He let himself fall into an armchair. "That's all right! I've got the trick. But now, let's stop playing games, because it's becoming tiresome. Come on, my dear phantom, do me the pleasure of decamping from my mind—I've seen enough of you... As for you, Messieurs, I warn you that it would be dangerous for you to play this comedy any longer."

With lightning rapidity, he opened a drawer in the nightstand and seized a revolver. "I'm in my own home, in a case of legitimate self-defense. Free me from this suggestion, or I'll kill you."

He aimed his revolver at Marc Vanel, while making a rampart of his armchair.

"You're forgetting that your drawing rooms are full of people," said Homo-Deus, "and that at the first shot..."

Vauclin lowered his weapon.

"A poor means, you see. However, as the situation can't be prolonged, it's necessary to put an end to it. What should we do, Jeanne?"

Jeanne Fortin emerged from her hiding place and came forward.

"Mademoiselle Fortin!" the député exclaimed—and then immediately howled. "Oh, you swine!"

Taking advantage of his astonishment at Jeanne's arrival on the scene, Marc Vanel had leapt forward and, twisting Vauclin's wrist, had snatched away the revolver.

"Ah! Am I going mad, then? What does this mean? Is it a dream or an impossible reality? Who's alive? Who's dead?" He turned to Marc Vanel. "Well, kill me," he said. "Kill me. I'd rather die than live like this."

"It's up to your victim to do with you what he deems appropriate. Our role is concluded. Monsieur de Vandeuvre, you owe us our lives. Don't forget that."

With that, Jeanne went out, followed by her father and Marc Vanel. They went back down to the drawing rooms.

"Well?" asked the old chemist Bernardot. "I hope that Monsieur Vauclin…?"

"It's nothing," said Fortin. "We left him in the care of his wife and my pupil. You'll see him come down in a little while. We're leaving."

"Already?"

"You're forgetting, Bernardot, that for us, this social tumult is a veritable fatigue."

"For me, too," sighed the chemist. "But my wife…"

"Well, au revoir, my dear colleague. We'll meet again, one if these days, at the A.D.S."

"They slipped through the groups toward the exit.

"I'm going to run home," said Homo-Deus, "and I'll come back; amusing things are going to happen here tonight."

And Marc Vanel leapt into his auto, which departed at speed, while Jeanne and her father took a modest taxi to return to Saint-Cloud, to the Red Nest.

IV. The Wife, the Husband and the Puppet

The departure of the three scientists had left Vandeuvre somewhat at a loss. Until then, the presence of those who had rendered him life had sustained him and encouraged him. Left to himself he lost his self-assurance. Since, by courtesy of Sophie's story, his anterior life had been recalled, he had gradually returned to himself, and the mentality of Georges Garnier was soon completely effaced, giving way to that of Julien.

He hesitated for a long time, while the two murderers still remained under the influence of the terror they had experienced. Finally, he made a decision.

"Since I know, Monsieur, that you're not unaware of my relationship with Sophie, I have no fear that you will punish her severely. I won't say that I love her as I did before, but I don't feel the horror for her that I ought to have. Give me back the stolen money, and I'll leave you free to lead your lives as best you can. When one has passed through death, as I have, one is more indulgent to human weaknesses. Nevertheless, my indulgence for your crime does not go as far as abandoning my millions to you. I can't accuse you of murder, since I'm alive. The judges would take me for a madman, but it would be easy for me to prove the theft. So, make restitution, or I shall make the accusation."

While Julien was speaking, Vauclin had recovered his composure. Return the money? How? It had been swallowed up in the Baruyer catastrophe. As for what Barsac had given him, that was his money, and to return that would be giving it away. Never in this life! Rather kill again—but how could he do that? To murder him now, in the middle of a party from which he and his wife had already been absent for too long...

It was necessary to go back to the drawing rooms, and as soon as possible. He stood up. "You must understand, my dear Monsieur, that I don't have the money that I…abstracted from you…here, at the ready. On the other hand, I can't abandon my guests for too long. Will you give us until tomorrow to make the restitution?"

Sophie, who had also recovered her aplomb, said: "Monsieur de Vandeuvre is too gallant a man to drive us into poverty. He'll give us time."

"It would be impolite of me to refuse, inasmuch as I don't have the means. Given that I'm not pursuing you, it's necessary to accept your conditions."

Vauclin and his wife exchanged complicit glances.

"Well then," said the husband, "Madame Vauclin will bring you the sum of two hundred thousand francs every month, until the debt is liquidated."

Julien looked at the enchantress. She had a Circean expression in her eyes that caused a voluptuous frisson to run through the marrow of his bones.

"So be it," he said. "Tomorrow, then?"

"Tomorrow, I'll give you all that I can put together. Until tomorrow, at your home."

Julien looked at Sophie. "Until tomorrow—at my home."

Perhaps Vauclin would have let him go—but as Vandeuvre reached the door, he received a shock, recoiled, staggering, and bumped into Vauclin, who was following him. There was a cracking of broken bones, and Julien collapsed at the feet of the fearful député.

"What have you done?" cried Sophie. "You've killed him."

"Me? But I haven't touched him!"

They lifted up the body, which was limp, the head hanging inertly from the shoulders.

"It's enough to drive one mad!" roared Vauclin. "There he is, just like the other time, with his neck broken—but this time, it wasn't me! What demons are guiding this adventure?"

At that moment, someone knocked on the door. Vauclin grabbed the body and dragged it behind the bed. Sophie approached the threshold.

"Who is it?" he asked.

The voice of a domestic replied: "People are anxious about the long absence of Monsieur and Madame."

"We're coming right away. My husband is better."

"Let's take care of the most urgent matter," said Vauclin. "Let's go down. We'll see about getting rid of the cadaver later."

After having dabbed eau-de-Cologne over their faces to restore a measure of composure, they went back to the drawing rooms. As people gathered around them, Vauclin said: "It's nothing. A sudden malaise, but it's dissipated."

In order to get the party moving again they competed in gaiety and wit, so effectively that no one had any suspicion of the confusion of their thoughts.

As they left the tragic room, they had switched off the electric light. A few seconds later, the light came on against.

But the room was empty.

V. Swirls of Nightmare

When the last guests had gone, at three o'clock in the morning, there was no one left in the deserted main drawing room but the two white-faced spouses, their eyes wild and their faces anxious. Madame Vauclin had sent away the domestics, only retaining her chambermaid. Alone at last, the two accomplices looked at one another in anguish. The same thought was congesting their brains: what were they to do with Vandeuvre's cadaver?

They examined various means, one after another, but none seemed practical.

Finally, Sophie had an idea. "You remember, Arsène, that grain loft under the roof on the other side of the corridor leading to the maids' rooms. Three weeks ago, when I was showing the new cook to her bedroom, I saw the masons who were making repairs at the time storing sacks of plaster, bricks and various materials there. The work is finished now; months will go by before anyone sets foot in there. We can hide Julien's body there for a few days."

"Let's go take a look at it."

After rapidly changing their clothes they went up to the fifth and top floor of the building. Hazard favored them. The tenants on the third and fourth were on holiday and the bedrooms of the Vauclins' domestics were at the end of the corridor to the left, and consequently opposite the one that led to the grain loft in question—a kind of storeroom for all the lumber of the house, only closed by an external bolt. The six-meter-long redoubt extended beneath the roof, and the ceiling slanted down to the level of the tiles of the edge of the roof. There were three hinged panels in the roof, but they were closed. There were stacks of bricks and bags of plaster along the wall.

"Are you capable of playing the mason? With those bricks you could construct a kind of box. People might take it for a bench set deliberately along the wall. But it's necessary not to dawdle."

They went downstairs again. Sophie helped Vauclin to load the body onto his back. Fortunately, they had found some Japanese lanterns in the apartment, with candles. They went upstairs with the aid of that illumination.

It was a singular spectacle: the two night prowlers, dappled with red, green and blue reflections by their colored lanterns. When they arrived at the redoubt, Vauclin was sweating profusely, as much from fear as fatigue. When he had dropped the cadaver on the floor, he looked at his wife.

"Did you hear something just now? It seemed to me that soft footfalls were coming up behind us. I lifted the lantern, but it was an illusion—the blood hammering in our temples. No one."

"To work, then. We need water."

"Get everything ready. Look, here's a zinc bucket you can use to mix the plaster. I'll go get some water in this old sandstone pot."

"But I don't have any tools or a trowel."

"You'll have to make do—use that piece of slate."

There was a drinking fountain for the maids beside the water closets. Sophie found a zinc jug there, which was less heavy and more comfortable than the sandstone pot.

In no time at all, Vauclin had erected around Vandeuvre, who was in formal dress, folded in two, a little wall of bricks, which soon surpassed the breadth of the cadaver.

"There's no more to do than fill it with plaster."

In order to go more rapidly, he emptied several sacks over the body, sprinkled it copiously with water, and finished it off by smoothing over the surface. It was so hot that they had been obliged to open one of the roof panels. They were streaming with sweat. As they completed their macabre task, dawn was blanching the sky.

"Just in time," said Vauclin. "Here comes the daylight."

"Oh, the flunkeys won't open their eyes for some time yet. We've time to put things in order. Finish off your work while I tidy up."

"That's good," said the député. "I doubt that Vandeuvre will come back to bother us now."

"Who knows?"

"What do you mean, who knows? You'd do better to hold your tongue than say such stupid things."

"But it was you who said *who knows?*"

"Oh *zut!* Let's get out of here. I've got the wind up all of a sudden."

They headed for the door, which they had closed while they cleaned up—but just as they were about to open it, they saw a word traced in chalk: *Resurgam.*

"What does that mean?" asked the wife.

"*I shall rise again.*"

White and trembling, they looked at one another; then, gripped by panic terror, they ran back down the two flights of stairs. Having returned to their own home, they did not speak for some time, distraught with terror.

"Are we mad or hallucinating," she said, finally. "Perhaps we were dreaming. It's a nightmare that the three illusionists suggested to us."

But they could see that they were still white with plaster. The député yelped: "Damnation! Damnation! But what have I done, then, to the good God?"

Finally at the end of their strength and thought, they washed themselves and went to bed. It was not until late in the morning that they finally went to sleep.

VI. Albert Baruyer Goes Mad

In a cold and dismal prison cell, with wan daylight filtering in through the barred window, Albert Baruyer was waiting for the law to decide his case. He was not nurturing any hope. The presence of an invisible being in the room where their drama had unfolded had not encountered any credence in the examining magistrate; he dared not bring that subject up again, for the magistrate's gaze, that of the clerk, and even that of his own defender spoke clearly enough of the anxiety of men confronted with a madman. He had the atrocious fear of finding himself incarcerated in a lunatic asylum.

During the investigation, he had tried many times, in vain, to get his brother to come. Did Georges seriously think that he was a parricide? Get away! Their mother, in the course of that hectic chase, had made the two brothers share her conviction that an invisible being was spying on them. So...?

No, Albert Baruyer was not deceived. His brother would not have been himself if he had not seized that opportunity to get rid of a dangerous accomplice once and for all. And he understood that very well, feeling neither hatred nor despair; it was profoundly human, in conformity with their temperaments, and he would not have acted any differently.

He had chosen for his advocate Maître Henri-Robert, whose character and talent he admired. To the celebrated president of the bar and member of the Académie Française, exaggerating a calm that he wanted to be cold and logical, he had recounted the drama as it had happened. He had not asked him to believe him, but had begged for his help in deciphering the enigma by submitting the case to scientists.

Certainly, he had picked up the dagger from the desk, and that was the weapon that had been found in the dead woman's throat; but he told his defender: "If I had committed this odious crime, I would have denied it. There was only my brother and myself in the room where the drama unfolded. If I had shouted out first, accusing Georges, he's the one who would have been arrested. Remember that there was no witness to the scene."

That plausible, judicious reasoning had impressed the great advocate. When he came back from the homes of men of science to who he had recounted the tragic circumstances, however, he treated the accused with reticence. In spite of everything, Henri-Robert did not understand any more than anyone else.

Albert Baruyer could not sleep, and was forever thinking about the probable fate that was reserved for him. Parricide! Such criminals always went to the scaffold!

One evening, a warder making his round came into his cell, accompanied by a guard carrying the keys and another equipped with a lantern and a ledger.

Behind them, the door remained open. They had no fear, of course, that the prisoner might escape.

The warder made his inspection of the cell, cast the habitual glance over Albert Baruyer, and left. But it seemed to the advocate a moment later that an unexpected sound moved at floor level, though could not see anything abnormal.

The Invisible was there. Homo Deus did not like to leave tasks half-done. Continuing his role as an administer of justice, he was tracking the gang of frightful rogues.

Already, human justice had juxtaposed itself with his, and the enigmatic misanthrope was amused to observe that it was for a crime of which the accused was innocent.

He had therefore come into Baruyer's cell. For him, that was easy. And when he saw the man lying there, his haggard eyes open, his ears unquiet, he placed himself before him, invisibly, and, projecting his hands forward and murmuring incantatory words, he imposed his will by suggestion on Baruyer, without putting him to sleep, in order that he would remember.

Then, the fatigued prisoner, closing his eyes, lived a frightful dream. He heard a dull, distant rumor swelling like a tide. Then there were footsteps resonating in the corridor, before the door of his cell, and finally, the entrance of men in frock coats, bare-headed, with the faces of undertakers. Other silhouettes, black and curious, leaned around the doorframe.

"You appeal has been rejected. Be brave!"

A chaplain, whose face was framed with gray hair, shivering in his long robe, came forward.

"My child, don't forget that God pardons the greatest criminals for their sins, if they request it."

The prisoner recovered all his energy to cry out: "I'm innocent!"

"Have confidence, then, in divine justice, which is not deceived..."

Immediately, Albert Baruyer saw an individual whose appearance was reminiscent of a petty bourgeois in his Sunday best; it was the executioner. Then he felt himself seized by brisk and brutal aides; practiced hands turned down the collar of his shirt, and he shivered under the cold steel of the scissors sliding over the nape of his neck.

Outside, in a wan morning, a black and murmurous crowd was massed behind the soldiers. The clinking of weapons, the stamping of the horses' hooves and him, Baruyer, his hands tied behind his back, with the black hood of parricides over his head.

Stiffening with all his might in order not to seem afraid, he was placed beneath the blade of the guillotine, against the sinister plank, and in a rapid vision in which things were confused in the morning haze, he perceived in front of him a crucifix brandished by a priest.

Suddenly, there was a hard and icy impact on the back of his neck.

He uttered a loud scream and woke up, his eyes haggard.

And he heard strident, satanic laughter mocking him. His hair standing on end, he stammered: "But I'm not guilty."

"No, Albert Baruyer," said a voice, "You're not guilty of this crime. It was me, the Invisible, who took the dagger from your hand to cut your infamous mother's throat. No, you're not guilty, but you'll be guillotined all the same, because I, the Invisible, want to punish you thus for your other sins. You have merited the supreme punishment, Albert Baruyer, and it's of no importance that the law is imposing it for an erroneous motive. You'll pay on the scaffold for the evil that you've done in other circumstances."

There was a further burst of strident laughter. Livid and terrified, Albert Baruyer started howling like a madman, and warders equipped with lanterns came running.

"The Invisible!" he cried. "He's here! Lock the door! Don't let him get away…escape again…"

The warders looked at one another; they made signs and went out rapidly. One of them murmured, in a Provençal accent: "He's mad, po' fella! He'll never go to the Assizes."

VII. The Poorly-Sealed Coffin

The winter had passed very gently, and since the first days of March, a precocious spring had put buds on the branches of the trees. Albert Baruyer, interned for life, was a dead man. His brother, virtually ruined by the gamble on the Bourse in anticipation of Barsac's fall, was trying painfully, in association with Walesport, to shore up the bank and prepare a new operation. Vauclin, also afflicted by the disaster, blamed Georges Baruyer for it. Between all those modern conquistadors, a kind of mistrust had arisen, an obscure, imprecise hatred, for too many affairs had gone awry in a matter of months, and each of them was convinced that the fault lay with a traitor in their midst.

Meanwhile, Barsac, the man whose abrupt triumph remained an enigma for them, had finally been overturned; his politics of procrastination, prevarication and continual half-measures has ended up wearying public opinion.

Germany was smiling.

During a kind of lull favorable to the resumption of business, Walesport and Vauclin were thinking about reconstituting their lost resources. Already, the two men were elaborating a scheme, when an unexpected event occurred, a *coup de théâtre*: the cadaver of Julien de Vandeuvre had been discovered in the Vauclins' house.

One morning, the domestics, lodged in the attics, had noticed a frightful smell, and the frightened concierge had run to summon the police. When they went into the redoubt under the roof, after serious ventilation, they soon established that the nauseating odor was coming from a long rectangle of plaster elevated against the wall. No doubt was possible: a brownish liquid was running over the floor through a gap between the block and the red tiles: an unspeakable ooze that was spreading out in a semi-coagulated pool amid the dust in a corner of the room.

"What carrion is buried in there?" the Commissaire interrogated.

The concierges remained stupefied. Neither the man nor his wife remembered ever having seen that bizarre construction before. They knew when the masons had stored materials there; it must, therefore, have been constructed during the summer or the winter. By whom?

The masons, for whom the Commissaire sent, observed that the base of the construction had been undermined by accumulated liquids. One of the men explained: "You see, Monsieur le Commissaire, that skylight that has been left open? The rain has come in through there, and the water has spread out through the cupboard, accumulated in this corner, passing under the plaster block, inundating the tiling. We can easily remove that botched work."

Indeed, when two workmen put pressure on the construction, it slid into the middle of the room, leaving a fetid trail.

"You see, Monsieur le Commissaire, it's a cadaver that's been hidden in there, but the swine who built the tomb weren't in the trade."

"Why?"

"Because masons, before anything else, would have molded it to the floor, even sunk a few points in order to raise up an underlay on which to build subsequently. Whereas, operating as they've done, the murderers—for I assume that it was them—didn't know that the block wouldn't adhere to the floor. Then the rain, coming in through the skylight, penetrated inside the block from underneath, and that filth has leaked out."

At that moment, the Commissaire perceived the inscription in chalk traced on the door: *Resurgam.*

"If it's a human cadaver in there, the bandits didn't lack audacity. In spite of that macabre joke, we're going to find some big dog in there, or a litter of kittens. Demolish it."

With blows of a pick-ax, the block was broken up. A crack extended through the middle and the mass opened in two halves. The spectators recoiled, fearfully.

"Ah, so much the better!" the Commissaire could not help crying.

The formless, black, stinking mass that lay in the plaster, in the midst of stained fabric, was indeed a putrefying human cadaver. The witnesses of that vision had haggard, fearful expressions; the concierge's wife uttered piercing screams, and they all held their noses.

"Don't touch anything!" cried the Commissaire.

An agent having telephoned the Prefecture of Police on his order, less than half an hour later all the representatives of the law were there. Monsieur Sauliet, the examining magistrate, took the affair in hand. Hundreds of curiosity-seekers were already gathered outside the putrid house.

On perceiving all the people gathered in the Avenue, Vauclin and his wife manifested the instinctive recoil of people who do not have a clear conscience. Already, via the service stairway, the news of the macabre discovery had spread, and it was a chambermaid who informed the brunette Messalina.

Before the domestic, Madame Vauclin did not manifest any emotion, but once alone with her husband she assumed a distressed expression reflecting atrocious anxieties. The two accomplices, disorientated and fearful, wondered what they ought to do: brazen it out or flee?

Vauclin quickly made his decision. Before judging the situation, it was necessary to know more about it, and, in order to do that, to see. Boldly, he climbed the stairs and arrived at the corridor to the maids' rooms, which as blocked by an agent.

The representative of the authority did not want to hear any plea to let him pass; he was obeying orders. However, as the argument became heated, the public prosecutor came out of the attic to investigate the cause of the racket. Recognizing Vauclin, he advanced toward him, smiling.

"That's true," he said, "you live in the house."

The prosecutor shook Vauclin's hand, took him by the arm amicably, and drew him into the lumber-room before the astonished gaze of the policeman. The criminal, very cool and admirably self-controlled, nevertheless started abruptly in the presence of the horrible vision.

"Ah!" said the prosecutor. "It isn't pretty." And he put a perfumed handkerchief to his nostrils.

Vauclin looked at the cadaver, a putrescent mass of green-tinted flesh, with which plaster dust and shards of brick were mingled. The young man's white evening shirt was a frightful rag.

The murderer thought: *He's unrecognizable. It'll be a clever man who can identify the handsome Julien de Vandeuvre in those putrid remains. Come on, they won't get me this time, not me, Arsène Vauclin*. But he was suddenly transfixed by the word *Resurgam*, the chalk inscription on the door. *Well, the prophecy is realized; here's Vandeuvre, returned to the light.*

"Let's see," said the head of the Sûreté. "Workers carried out repairs in the house last spring. When the work was complete, they deposited the remains of the plaster they'd used here, along with the materials belonging to the owner. At that time, they didn't see anything abnormal, and the concierge affirms that when they left, the plaster cube didn't exist. So, in a window that we ought to place in June, according to the medical examiner, the crime was committed. Where? In the house, indisputably, for it's inadmissible that the cadaver came from outside. It is, therefore, among the tenants of the building that it's necessary to search for the key to the enigma."

The concierge, very worthily, thought he ought to protest. "The house is only inhabited by people above any such suspicion."

"Of course, my man; in any case, we're not accusing anyone."

But the examining magistrate, not wanting to give evidence of any less perspicacity that the head of the Sûreté, said: "I don't believe that that it's in the direction of the tenants that it's necessary to search. It's a drama of the sixth floor."

There was a sudden stir; employees dressed in long hospital smocks set about transporting the remains of the cadaver.

Before going out of the attic, Monsieur Sauliet made the further observation: "And then again, Messieurs, who, if not a domestic, accustomed to inferior work, would have had the idea of using that plaster to build the victim a sepulcher. I can't see a man of the world..."

Vauclin smiled. He was triumphant, but he regretted, even so, having been so maladroit. If he had known what he was doing, the cadaver would only have been discovered much later. In those conditions, however, it would have been mummified, and in consequence recognizable, whereas the water, coming through the skylight that he had forgotten to close, and subsequently penetrating the block of plaster had hastened the decomposition of the body, and it was scarcely probably now that they would succeed in identifying the victim. Thus, it had all worked out well.

Obligingly, he furnished the representatives of the law with numerous details about the house and the tenants, puerile items of information gravely recorded by the examining magistrate, the inanity of which Vauclin was well aware.

When he went back to his wife, who had retired to her bedroom, terribly anxious, he had a face so radiant that she stood up suddenly, also transfigured.

"You can be reassured. The law is going astray in silly paths, and Vandeuvre is unrecognizable."

"In spite of all that, I'm uneasy. There are obscure points in this inexplicable story whose rationale escapes me. That dead man, already dead once before and then resurrected, is outside the natural laws of logic, and I sense the hand of a mysterious being who is our enemy."

Vauclin remembered the word *Resurgam* written in chalk on the door of the attic. Suddenly, he stood up and started pacing back and forth in the room. In a dull voice, he said: "But what is this invisible being that is following us through life, hiding in the shadows? Who is it? Oh, it's all coming back to me now: that Vandeuvre who came back to life, that dead man who reappeared at a party in my house, that inscription of the door, the sarcastic laughter I heard coming down the stairs, other laughter—the same one—when we decided, with the Baruyers and Walesport, the famous coup on the Bourse, and then the debacle that followed, our fortune lost. Albert Baruyer mad, his mother tragically killed—all of it looms up as a bundle of evidence, in testimony of the hatred of this powerful unknown. But, powerful as he is, when I know who he is, I'll take responsibility for killing him! Who is he? Who? Who? Who?"

He was now in a state of extreme fury and his eyes were flashing. Then, his wife, calm and cold, said: "Why did the Fortins, whom we never see, and who never see anyone, bring Vandeuvre to us on the evening of that tragic night?"

At that reflection, Vauclin started. "You think," he said, his throat taut, "you think it's from that direction? What motive for hatred could the scientist have against us? I've searched hard..."

"But you haven't found anything? Me neither. Jeanne was a friend at school. She still was, I thought."

"So?"

"So, there's a mystery here that it's necessary to clarify. This afternoon, I'll go to Saint-Cloud in the auto, to the Fortins'—and I hope that this evening, I'll have indications that will permit me to fix my opinion."

Vauclin had a boundless admiration for the genius of his wife. Between those two individuals, in whom no real tenderness existed, but merely complicity, a link was suddenly sealed, for they sensed danger threatening—and in a moment of confidence, and perhaps gratitude, Vauclin took his wife in his arms and kissed her forehead.

VIII. Madame Vauclin's Astonishments

The lovely Madame Vauclin arrived at the Red Nest at about three o'clock. The March afternoon was delightful, for the extraordinarily precious spring was sensible, even though the trees were still bare of leaves. The old Norman gate to the vast park with the appearance of wilderness was wide open. The auto moved into the pathways scarcely traced through the undergrowth of the abandoned wood. When Madame Vauclin perceived the house covered in moss with its decrepit walls and its slender belvedere, she had the sensation of arriving at the dwelling of a sorceress.

She did, in fact, find Fortin in the company of the Sorcerer, Homo-Deus, who already knew the story of the discovery of the cadaver.

Well, she doesn't lack nerve. So much the better; I like adversaries who aren't afraid.

Jeanne and her father, brought up to date by the Invisible, who had come to have lunch with them, exchanged knowing glances.

The young woman came forward. "To what do I owe the pleasure of seeing you?"

Madame Vauclin could not give the true reason for her visit. On the other hand, at two o'clock in the afternoon, she could not maintain silence about the discovery made in her house. That omission would have been too conspicuous.

"No other motive than the joy of spending a little time with you, and the desire to savor the charm of a delightful afternoon. I was in the Bois and, perceiving the hills of Saint-Cloud, did not hesitate to come."

"How nice. But why are you so pale?"

"I'm still under the influence of a violent emotion experienced this morning."

Jeanne looked at her curiously, and Vanel smiled imperceptibly.

At that moment, Madame Vauclin sensed an uncomfortable atmosphere around her. An obscure intuition warned her of danger. The three individuals were attentive—perhaps more so than was appropriate—to what she was about to say. And on sensing them thus, simultaneously courteous and avid, their necks taut and their ears pricked, she experienced a vague instinctive terror.

They know! she said to herself. But she braced herself against the emotion that overtook her; a grim energy stiffened her, and she was able to assume a naturally fearful expression, without excess. To say: "Yes, can you imagine that a putrefying body was discovered this morning in the building where we live, on the flunkeys' floor."

"Oh!" said all her listeners, in unison.

There was nothing sincere about their astonishment, and Madame Vauclin pursed her lips. *Now I'm sure that they know.*

What should she do? She gave details, volubly, bravely pushing boldness to the point of saying that her husband had assisted the agents of law with their investigation, and that he had read the bizarre prophecy on the door of the attic.

Marc Vanel found her astonishing. Individuals of this sort were a change from the vague dolls encountered in society, and his misanthropy was amused by playing with an adversary of greater dimension.

He questioned her. "Do you know who the cadaver was, Madame?"

"I would doubtless know if, like you, I possessed the talent to divine everything. Personally, I'm not a witch, and it appears that the victim was in such a state of decomposition that it will be very difficult for the law to identify him."

"Oh! But perhaps the cadaver was dressed. In that case, his pockets might contain papers?"

"No. There's every reason to believe that the identity of the dead man can never be proven. That doesn't alter the fact that the drama, under my own roof, has distressed me somewhat."

"It's a sensational affair," Homo-Deus remarked. "The newspapers will take possession of it."

"My dear Madame," Dr. Fortin added, "Be sure that the law, with the aid of science, will be able to identify the dead man. A scientist finds clues where others see nothing. A preceding wound, the traces of an accident—a fracture for example—is more than enough to clarify the mystery. A fracture is never effaced; the trace remains as clear as a signature. It even reveals the date when it was repaired. Don't worry—the dead man found in your house will surely be recognized, and if the murderer lives there, the law will rid you of him."

Sophie Vauclin was as white as a corpse now, but she retained a clarity of thought and a lucid mind. The doctor's insistence reminded her that Julien de Vandeuvre's fracture was characteristic, known. Perhaps foolishly, she still wanted to fortify her certainty.

"Who knows," she said, "whether the poor fellow might not have been drawn into a trap by a soubrette?"

Coldly sarcastic, Homo-Deus seized the opportunity to amuse himself on the wing. "What would be even more frightful is that one of your guests might have been seduced by your chambermaid." He laughed, blithely, mockingly and stridently. "Pardon me," he said, when he had finished. "I'm amused by your terror, caused by the possibility that you might have a criminal in your service."

As he seemed veritably to be enjoying himself, casually, Madame Vauclin wondered whether he was sincere or whether he was mocking her—but she knew that laughter.

"Oh, how unkind you are!" she said, pulling a face that she wanted to be pert, but which was a trifle forced.

"Aren't I? Do you know what guest came to mind when you mentioned that supposition of a chambermaid? Julien de Vandeuvre!"

She went frightfully pale and bit her lip. Homo-Deus was still smiling, however, and saying terrible things with the most amused expression. Jeanne Fortin and her father had been unable to repress a shudder, however, for they were wondering exactly how far Marc would push his ferocity.

These people know, thought Madame Vauclin. *So why haven't they denounced us?* Ignorant of the role that the Invisible had played in those adventures, she did not understand.

Time passed. In order to help her old school friend, who seemed distressed, recover somewhat, Jeanne gave her a tour of the curious house: the dining room overlooking the magnificent countryside; the belvedere, from which the setting sun could be seen setting the horizon ablaze with its red fire. She showed her the laboratory in the basement, and made the electrical machinery throw off formidable sparks, so effectively that the frightened visitor emerged from the fantastic dwelling with the idea that those people were lunatics or geniuses.

Outside, in the liberated park, Jeanne and Sophie found the scientist and Vanel again. There was no further mention of the affair of the Avenue Henri-Martin.

As the afternoon was finishing with an agreeable atmospheric warmth, and the décor, although wild, incited mute contemplation, the criminal felt herself influenced by the calm and purity of the ambience, and suddenly thought that if she lived here, so far from human life, permanently, she would never know any torment again.

Here, everything was reposed and shielded by philosophical security. Soon, she would return to Paris, the furnace—and it would be necessary to recommence the struggle, the hard labor of society. It would also be necessary to defend herself against people, things and hazards. Then, even though she sensed that she was in the company of latent hostilities, she suddenly experienced the need to prolong the moment, and she accepted an invitation to tea, which Frédéric served on a table in the garden.

IX. The Man With Seven Faces

Among the faces that have figured in this story along with the Baruyer brothers, Vauclin and his wife, Barsac and the others, little has been seen, at least in the foreground, of Walesport's cold, tanned, clean-shaven visage, illuminated by two little gray eyes that pierced other people.

Like that other equivocal Manitou, Basil Zaharoff,[31] a resident alien with a murky past, the mysterious friend of Barthou, and a great dignitary of the Légion d'honneur for reasons of political economy, William Walesport liked to remain in the wings. Walesport, however, a vulture of smaller wingspan, could only sport around his neck on gala evenings the red cravat of a Commander. The government had established the difference in beaks and claws between the two raptors. And that was why events put the faces of Baruyer, Vauclin and Crémiot in the light, while leaving that of the foreigner in relative obscurity. And yet, he manipulated the others like puppets.

Walesport had not always had that name. It would certainly have been difficult to recover the name on his birth certificate. Where did he come from? Who was he? One day, Baruyer had nearly found out. As he came out of the bank in the American's company an emaciated man dressed in rags had approached them. At the sight of him, in spite of his sang-froid, Walesport had been unable to suppress a start.

"So," said the man, in English and in a mocking tone, "It's no longer Jimmy that you call yourself? It doesn't matter, I'm glad to see you again. What! You don't recognize your old friend Sullivan? We have, however, pulled enough stunts together."

"The man's mad!" Walesport exclaimed, white with rage. "He's trying to get money out of me."

At that moment, Albert Baruyer had the same suspicion. In fact, the pauper followed them. "Oh, very well, you're putting on a swagger, my old Jimmy—that's all right. But let me have a few dollars."

"You see—it's extortion. Anyway, the best thing to do, to get rid of the wretch, is to give him alms. Perhaps, deep down, he's worthy of interest."

---

[31] The Greek arms dealer Basil Zaharoff (1849-1936), notorious for making money from various conflicts by selling weapons to both sides, and reinvesting his money in banking and oil, made a vast fortune in the Great War. He subsequently took over the company that owned the casino in Monte Carlo, the chief source of income of the principality of Monaco, where he took up residence. Champsaur spent a lot of time on the Riviera and undoubtedly knew Zaharoff by sight as well as reputation, which doubtless helped Zaharoff become a particular target of his loathing.

With a terrible glare, he gave the man a twenty-franc bill, which he pocketed briskly.

"Well, you're not generous...but we'll meet again." As Walesport moved away with long strides, he added: "Go on then, cowboy, I'll find you again."

That scene had impressed Albert Baruyer, who, on reflection, regretted not having learned more. Always short of money, squandering his it gambling or to satisfy the caprices of women, he would have been delighted to possess serious and precise information regarding the sire who manipulated the bank's millions. One day, he read in the latest news section of the paper that a wretched foreigner in rags, carrying papers in the name of Sullivan and letters indicating that he had been resident in Chicago had been found on the road running alongside the Seine between the bridges of Pureaux and Suresnes, no longer showing any signs of life, having been run over by an automobile. Albert Baruyer understood the forceful decisiveness of William Walesport and the stupidity of attacking him.

He it was that Madame Vauclin judged capable of combating the danger that threatened them. She went to find him and made him party to her suspicions as well as the certainties she had been able to gather. For her, the obscure enemies who had aborted all the affairs planned in the most absolute mystery—the ones who had resuscitated Vandeuvre, killed old Mère Baruyer, provoked Albert's madness, saved Barsac and aided the Rodock son—could not be anyone other than Fortin and his daughter, those exalted geniuses who execrated triumphant society, the pick of the bunch, in sum, and were posing as redressers of wrongs.

Walesport's own suspicions were primarily directed at Marc Vanel. By his own experience, and that of his master Zaharoff, he knew how dangerous self-effacing individuals could be, and he had an instinctive dislike of the sorcerer in question.

Madame Vauclin explained why, in her opinion, Homo-Deus was a friend of the Fortins. She had caught a glimpse of the doctor's love for the young woman, and that was the probable reason for their intimacy.

"Ah!" said Walesport. "The charlatan is in love? He's vulnerable, then. Well, I shall have my revenge."

"How?"

The cosmopolitan adventurer had no desire to reveal his plans, but he had a terribly resolute expression. Their vengeance was in good hands.

X. The Mind of an Examining Magistrate

When the examining magistrate Amédée Sauliet went into his study that day, he hastened to pick up the file containing the mysterious affair of the Avenue Henri-Martin. Setting aside the less interesting cases, he went through the evidence already accumulated.

"It's very thin," he muttered, weighing the dossier in his hand, "but it will grow..."

Police reports had arrived that morning. He read them attentively. No clues. The tenants, all honorable, were above suspicion, and the most conscientious searches of the private lives of the valets, cooks and soubrettes had not turned up the end of any suggestive thread. It was, however, necessary at all costs to orient the investigation. Public opinion was impassioned. Monsieur Sauliet did not complain about that noise, which put him in the public eye, but the papers would tire of the mystery and another crime would take possession of the news. Monsieur Sauliet, a worldly and elegant magistrate, was enthusiastic for advancement and notoriety.

He started abruptly. On a sheet of white paper placed on the desk in isolation, the magistrate read two lines written in blue pencil: *The victim is Julien de Vandeuvre. Follow that trail.*

The magistrate stood up and shouted: "Bonichon, close the doors! There's someone here!"

The clerk rose to his feet slowly, because he had rheumatism, but the two men did not discover anyone, either under the green sofa placed at the back of the study or behind the heavy curtains of the windows.

"But that piece of paper didn't get here on its own!" stammered the magistrate.

He rang for the office boy and interrogated him. He had not seen anyone either; he was sure that the door of the study had not opened since Monsieur Sauliet's arrival.

The office boy withdrew. Then, the examining magistrate, weary of searching, went to sit down again, and uttered an exclamation.

"Monsieur Bonichon! Monsieur Bonichon! The documents from the file—where are they?"

They had vanished! All the police reports, the interrogations of the domestics, the indications collected and the information on the tenants of the building, had gone—stolen! As the frightened magistrate, with sweat on his temples, looked around with haggard and anxious eyes, he suddenly saw a flame springing up in the fireplace. It was the documents from the file that were burning.

The clerk and his boss ran forward, but they were unable to save the slightest fragment from the mass of papers, and as they stood there, mute with surprise and dread, strident sardonic laughter burst forth behind them, which made their hair stand on end. The door opened by itself and closed again the same way. They had the sensation that an invisible being had just gone out. They looked at one another without being able to say a word, and when, after several seconds, they were able to recover their composure, the clerk risked: "Perhaps, Monsieur le Juge, the advice is worth following..."

"Perhaps," echoed the examining magistrate. "Go right away, Monsieur Bonichon, to ask the Sûreté to make enquiries about this Julien de Vandeuvre. A file has already been opened on the occasion of his disappearance—I need all that information by this evening. We'll work on it tonight. Come to my house after dinner, because I'm in a hurry to clarify this dark affair."

Monsieur Sauliet adjusted his cravat in front of a mirror hidden behind a curtain. He filed his fingernails carefully, looked at himself once more, and went out, with a pale cane under his arm, the handle of which was carved from a moonstone.

XI. Banquo's Ghost

It had not been difficult, of course, to ascertain that the cadaver interred in the plaster was Julien de Vandeuvre. The height was the same, the death appeared to date back to the time of the young man's disappearance and—this was serious—the last time the latter had been seen was at a soirée at the Vauclins' residence, in the very building where his body had been found. In the matter of his identification, therefore, there was no possible doubt, all the more so as the family had furnished an indication—a fracture of the little finger, resulting from an old riding accident—that was easily discovered. Another fracture, however, of the vertebral column, repaired and then recently broken again, testified clearly enough to the cause of death.

What amazed the medical examiners, of course, and troubled the examining magistrate, were traces of a trepanation, of which the skull revealed the perfect sutures. Now, the family declared that they knew nothing about that operation, which had, according to the experts, been carried out by a skilled surgeon. What did that imply?

An autopsy, well-executed although difficult, also gave the rupture of the vertebral column as the cause of death. And Monsieur Sauliet had the declarations of the notaries and Vandeuvre's parents; he could not be in any doubt as to the motive for the murder: the vanished millions of his mother's legacy and the bonds representing the murdered man's personal fortune were sufficient explanation.

Who had struck the blow, then? The examining magistrate was not floundering for long; the Invisible returned to his study and deposited another sheet of paper on his desk, one which was written, simply: *Cherchez la femme.*

He had found her. Police reports recorded Julien de Vandeuvre's attentions with regard to Madame Vauclin. It was obvious that Julien de Vandeuvre was in love with Madame Vauclin, offering her gifts that she had accepted. She was, therefore, his mistress, for the reports did not affirm the virtue of the député's wife. They also identified her liaison with Albert Baruyer. And that had been bound to cause the examining magistrate some embarrassment. He was delving into very complicated lives, the lives of notorious, influential individuals, and it was necessary to proceed with tact and infinite circumspection.

Nevertheless, greatly intrigued, passionately attached to the case, which might bring him a real glory—he was congratulated for having identified the dead man so rapidly—he pursued his research methodically, without weakness. He would have liked to interrogate Albert Baruyer, but the man was mad. Then it had been necessary for him to summon the Vauclins under the guise of them being witnesses, of course, capable for furnishing useful information to the law.

Their deposition, however, had disappointed him. The député expressed astonishment, with a certain arrogance, at being disturbed on a matter of which he had no knowledge.

"However," the examining magistrate ventured, "Monsieur Julien de Vandeuvre was your guest on the evening of the disappearance."

"Pardon me, Monsieur le Juge, but there's no proof that he disappeared on that day."

"No one has seen him since."

"Have the domestics been interrogated? Are you sure that Monsieur de Vandeuvre did not return to his apartment after leaving my house?"

The investigation had revealed that Julien had only been back to his apartment once since he had been to Vandeuvre to collect his mother's legacy. His only domestic, an old maidservant, had not heard from her master since that return and she had not seen him since. On her advice, the family—a sister and a brother-in-law—had made enquiries, but with no result. The young man's enigmatic visit to the Vauclins was all the more singular because he had presented himself under another name—but no one had been deceived, and it really was Julien de Vandeuvre who had been at the house in the Avenue Henri-Martin that night.

Monsieur Sauliet smiled.

"Listen, Monsieur le Député, if I've asked you to furnish a few items of information, it's because I wanted to retrace the use of the victim's time from the moment that he left you. Do you remember what time he left?"

"In truth, no, Monsieur le Juge. There were so many people there that evening..."

"Evidently."

Suddenly, Vauclin slapped his forehead. An idea had just occurred to him, which might lead the law further astray.

"Now I think of it," he said, "Vandeuvre was in evening dress, naturally. Now you tell me that he hadn't been to his apartment. Where, then, did he usually live, since he must have dressed there in order to go out into society? Have you, Monsieur le Juge, discovered Vandeuvre's other dwelling, where the key to the enigma doubtless resides?"

"I'll find out—but that won't explain, in any fashion, why the cadaver was buried in your home."

"Pardon me," Vauclin corrected, "not in my home, but in the building that I inhabit."

The examining magistrate was unnerved. He was unable to retain the necessary calmness.

"Not in your home...not in your home? It's bizarre, all the same. No other tenant of the house was acquainted with Vandeuvre, intimately or distantly, and it's on the evening that he was seen in your drawing room that he disappeared..."

Vauclin cut him off with a harsh voice: "What are you saying, Monsieur?"

And without being invited to do so, Vauclin put on his hat and left.

"I believe," the examining magistrate stammered, "that I've just committed a gaffe!"

Monsieur Sauliet was increasingly convinced of the culpability of the Vauclins, but did not have the means of confounding them. *Cherchez la femme*, the Invisible had said to him, but if the woman were as strong as her husband, he would have difficulty making her confess her guilt.

Mechanically, he riffled through the dossier in quest of the piece of paper on which the mysterious advice had been written. He had no difficulty finding it, but beneath the phrase *Cherchez la femme* other lines had been written more recently.

Strange, the examining magistrate said to himself. This Invisible comes here as if he were at home. *Let's see—what has he written now?*

Adjusting his lorgnon on his nose he read:

During the excavations carried out at Pompeii, the diggers discovered bizarre cavities. An engineer had the idea of pouring plaster into them; he thus obtained an exact mold of human bodies buried in the ash for eighteen hundred years. Those molds are in the museum in Naples. Do the same with the plaster mold in which Monsieur de Vandeuvre was buried, and confront the guilty parties with the resuscitated specter.

"Well, well—the idea is original and will do honor to my imagination. It's a matter of finding a specialist. Well, I have the affair well in hand." He rang.

"Is Bonichon still here?" he asked the office boy.

"Yes, Monsieur le Juge."

"Send him to me, then."

Shortly thereafter, the clerk came into the study. "Monsieur le Juge has need of me?"

"Yes. If my memory serves me right, you asked my permission to attend your sister's wedding."

"Yes, Monsieur; she's marrying a molder from the Montparnasse district, Paolo Besani."

"Does he know his métier well?"

"He's an artist of his profession."

"Perfect. Well, I have a job for him, but it has to be done quickly. Take me to your brother-in-law's home."

The first result of the conversation between Monsieur Sauliet and the molder Besani was that a crew of workmen presented themselves with a court order to remove the debris of the masonry left under seal in the attic of the house in the Avenue Henri-Martin, which they did with the utmost care.

A week later, a large heavy crate was brought to the Palais de Justice and taken up to the examining magistrate's study.

The day after the receipt of that crate, the Vauclin household received a new summons to appear. The employee on duty said that he had orders to send in Madame Vauclin first.

With a gesture, the examining magistrate offered his visitor a seat. She was trembling somewhat internally, but was determine not to allow herself to be intimidated.

"I beg your pardon, Madame," he said, with the most exquisite courtesy, "but the Law is sometimes obliged, in order to fulfill its role, to penetrate the intimate lives of those with whom it is occupied, and I have proof of a liaison that existed between you and Monsieur de Vandeuvre. Don't hold it against me; I'm fulfilling a painful duty, and since it involves no other inconvenience for you that making the confession of it, be assured that I shall be discreet."

"Indeed Monsieur, the unfortunate man was in love with me. As my resistance drove him to despair, he went away—I don't know where—in order to forget, he said. One evening, he suddenly came back, in the course of a social occasion that I was hosting at my home. I did not see much of him, for there was no possibility for him to talk to me in private that evening; I belonged to my guests."

"At what time did he leave?"

"Between midnight and two o'clock; I don't know exactly. At any rate, he was one of the first."

The magistrate had just picked up a piece of paper from his desk. Suddenly interested, he read: *They're making a fool of you, and I don't have time for you to find the key to the enigma on your own. Use the work of your molder.*

Monsieur Sauliet got to his feet, troubled by that intervention of the Invisible. Smiling, however, he said: "I beg you, Madame, to lend yourself to one last formality—to put you in the presence of an important witness."

So saying, he marched to a curtain extended over a corner, and drew it abruptly. Standing there, with his arms folded over his chest, was Julien de Vandeuvre. With an indisputable artistry, the molder had painted the plaster and given his work an appearance that was frightening for the young woman, with the cadaverous tint of the face and the glassy eyes.

The accused had become livid, all her blood flowing back to her heart; nervously and mechanically, she rubbed her hands, as if to efface something. Her teeth chattered. She felt lost, but made a superhuman effort to overcome her terror.

"Well, what do you have to say?"

The magistrate's voice had the effect of an electric shock. She put her hands over her face and collapsed, with a terrifying scream. The député, who was waiting in the antechamber, bounded forward reflexively, opened the door and ran in. Bonichon tried to stop him, but in vain. Thrusting the clerk aside he was already in the magistrate's study.

The first thing he saw was his wife's body, next to which Sauliet was crouched, frightened himself by the effect produced by this funeral depiction.

"What's the matter Sophie? And you, what have you done?"

"Bonichon, fetch a doctor!" shouted the magistrate.

"She's dead!" howled the député. "Wretch, what have you done? What have you said to her?"

With a gesture, the magistrate showed him the accusing statue. The député fell to his knees, hiding his face.

"You confess, then?" said Sauliet, intent on his case.

"*Resurgam!*" said Vauclin. "He said it!"

"You confess?" Sauliet repeated, making a sign to Bonichon, who had come back in. The latter ran to his desk and seized his pen. At that moment, the Prefecture physician arrived precipitately. At a glance he understood, and, kneeling down beside the recumbent woman he examined her rapidly.

"Nothing to be done," he said, on rising to his feet. "The lady has suffered a shock so intense that the vessels of the heart have ruptured—a fatal aneurism." Noticing the statue, he added: "Why, what's that? I doubt that people will approve of that mode of investigation. You can see the effect."

"Bah!" said Sauliet. "I've caught an important murderer."

XI. The Hunted Beasts

Vauclin looked around, with the gaze of a wild beast. The three men had the intuition of a desperate effort; they threw themselves between him and the door. But Vauclin launched himself forward with Herculean force, battled momentarily, knocked Bonichon down, and stopped Sauliet, who was about to call for help, with a mighty blow of his fist. The physician moved aside in order not to be similarly struck down, and Vauclin ran out, pursued by the clamors of Bonichon and the physician, who ran after him.

Fortunately for him, the député was perfectly familiar with the Palais de Justice. By means of a few skilful detours, he was therefore able to evade his pursuers and escape from the maze. A taxi was passing by; he leapt into it.

"Twenty francs," he shouted to the driver, "if we're at the Gare du Nord in ten minutes."

The driver accelerated his vehicle and departed in a swirl of dust.

Once reassured on the matter of his immediate arrest, the député thought about what to do next. To go home was impossible; the police would get there at the same time as him. Take the first available train and flee? He had ten thousand francs on him; that would last for a few days—but afterwards? His description would be sent everywhere by telegraph, and his arrest would only be a matter of hours.

The taxi stopped. He paid the driver and noticed that the other was looking at him in astonishment. He was bare-headed. From a nearby hatter's shop, Vauclin bought an English cap; then, taking another cab, he had himself taken to the Gare de Lyon. There he took the Metro and got out at the Place de l'Opéra. From there he went on foot to Walesport's private apartment in the Rue du Quatre-Septembre.

Walesport was not at home, but Vauclin was known to the valet, who let him into his master's study. There, Vauclin had time to reflect on his situation, for Walesport did not return until six o'clock in the evening.

Rapidly, the député brought him up to date.

"Damn!" said Walesport. "You're not brilliant. Nor am I, though. I succeeded in seeing Georges today; he's still half mad, and swears that the receipts were stolen from him—which is to say that we're all in trouble. Oh, if I could get hold of the scoundrel who's rolled us over so comprehensively…Claude Barsac or George Baruyer…"

"The blow didn't come from them," said Vauclin, furiously. "It came from someone stronger than them—the Fortins and their friend Marc Vanel, the one that society now calls Homo-Deus. They all made fun of my poor wife a few days ago. When she told me that, I ought to have gone to Saint-Cloud, to the Red Nest, and massacred the whole gang."

"There's still time," said Walesport. "The more I think about the maneuvers of that pretended sorcerer, the firmer my conviction becomes. It was the Fortins who brought Julien de Vandeuvre to your house, and Vanel was there. Do you remember Fortin's communication to the Académie des Sciences, and Marc Vanel's experiments at your home? Those people can play with the soul, with the spirit, as they wish. Who can tell whether they might have hypnotized Albert into killing his mother? As for the certificates, they must have taken advantage of the confusion to steal them."

"But in that case," Vauclin put in, "our millions are at the Fortins' place, or Homo-Deus' home."

The two men exchanged a rapid glance. They had reached an understanding.

"You stay in hiding here," said Walesport. "My valet is a reliable man. Tomorrow, I'll obtain information about our adversaries' habits, and we'll act."

"What about me?" said Vauclin. "After the authorization of the Chambre, I'll still be under the threat of an arrest warrant."

"You'll have to change your identity. I'll get you a passport, and we'll go to America. Personally, I've had enough of the old continent of Europe, in war as in peace."

BOOK FIVE: THE INVISIBLE SATYR

I. A Virgin's Confession

Alone in his study, Homo-Deus was mulling over the events that had occurred since his return to Paris, and the sequence of occurrences by virtue of which he had arrived in the midst of intrigues that had put him in contact with individuals whose morality had only served to augment his natural misanthropy. In that entire society, there were few sympathetic individuals. Only the dancer Alexane had left him with a favorable impression, but on reflection, that woman, who was nearing forty in spite of her beauty and the miraculous youthfulness of her face, was merely an egotist fighting for amour and her illusions—for Hans de Rodock's twenty years could not be united for very long with the dancer's age, and her love for Hans was all the more ardent, because she could sense its last flames.

Suddenly, however, the radiant visages of Jeanne Fortin and Simon d'Armez appeared in his mind. Jeanne was certainly the woman predestined for him, as beautiful as an antique statue, with an intelligence equal to his own. What a mixed couple they would have made! But Jeanne did not love him and never would. Could his own sensual nature ever be in harmony with that mentality, which saw even amour as nothing more than another subject of study? As for Simone d'Armez, in the nights he had spent with her, he had encountered a nature according to his tastes, an amorous harp immediately ready to vibrate beneath his savant desires—but with Simone, he was invisible, and the lovely Comtesse believed that she was under the influenced of a voluptuous dream.

Weary of reassessing their sensualities, he got up in order to give Mardruk a few orders. At that moment, he came in with a card in his hand.

"What is it?" Vanel asked.

"A visitor. Pretty, I think—but she's wearing a thick veil."

"Show her in, old man."

As she came in, the visitor lifted her veil. Homo-Deus could not suppress an admiring exclamation.

"Huguette de Virmile? I'm proud to have your confidence, Mademoiselle. Please sit down."

A vivid blush reddened the young woman's exquisitely pure face. Finally, making a visible effort, she said, "What I have to tell you, Master, is a kind of confession, but it isn't pious. I'm confiding in someone who, by virtue of his intelligence, might perhaps be a better director of my soul than a priest, if he will deign to play the role."

The savant nodded. She continued: "You've been to the Hôtel de Virmile, and you've perceived the distinguished nullity of the head of the household, where an intruder reigns: the Comte de Simiane."

Marc thought that he ought to make a gesture of astonishment, although it was notorious in Parisian society that Jacques de Simiane was the maintained lover of Madame de Virmile.

Huguette continued: "Since the age of observation, I've perceived Simiane's attentions. He was, moreover, a veritable friend to me. He took an interest in my games and my studies, pampered and caressed me—and was, in sum, more caring and attentive in my regard than my father.

"Things might have gone on like that indefinitely without attracting my attention to relationships that time and social habits had consecrated, but Maman, seeing me grow older, increasingly avoided keeping me near to her, and confided me to the care and direction of Florine, her principal chambermaid. Then she thought that Florine was getting too old—she was forty—to maintain in that employment, and replaced her with someone younger.

"Florine, wounded in her self-esteem, and who was very attached to me, having known me since my birth, did not take long to take me into her confidence. It had been agreed that, in order to give our Simiane a position that would attach him permanently to his benefactress, I would give him my hand. As I said, I had a certain amity for Jacques de Simiane, and the prospect of becoming his wife did not frighten me at first.

"Florine, seeing that she had missed her aim, then told me that Simiane was my father, and furnished me with irrefutable proof by means of letters that she had stolen. An extreme horror and disgust took possession of me; I waited with anguish for my mother to make me party to her project. That happened three days ago; I threw myself at Maman's feet and begged her to spare me that union, preferring, even though I have a fear of religion, to retire to a cloister.

"The scene was terrible; having run out of arguments, I flung the revelations of her former chambermaid in her face. She burst out laughing, told me that I was old-fashioned, and that such ideas were no longer of our world. 'You have a bourgeois mentality, my dear child.'

"It was then that I appealed to Simone d'Armez. I asked for her help and protection, in case I fled the house. Then, Simon talked to me about you. She told me that you might be able, by means of suggestion, to bend my mother to your will and force her to renounce her projects. That's why I've come to see you, Master, to beg for your help."

The young woman stopped talking.

"I am, Mademoiselle, something of a Don Quixote, who has accepted a mission to right wrongs and punish the guilty. You can count on my help. But I'd like to have *carte blanche* to bring about a denouement according to my whim."

"Act as you please. I sense, beneath your skeptical and misanthropic attitude, a great love for the weak and the isolated. You called yourself Don Quixote just now; there is, in my eyes, no nobler figure than that seeker of the ideal."

Homo-Deus stood up; he gazed profoundly at the strange young woman. Since his return to Paris, he had not seen a type of beauty similar to Huguette's—who was Jeanne Fortin's first cousin, via her mother. Tall and slim, she had the torso and the figure of Diana the huntress. Her sparkling brown hair, cut short over the nape of her neck, gave her the appearance of a delightful ephebe. The face was perfect, slightly pale, the skin so finely-grained that amber and ivory would have seemed coarse by comparison, the ensemble animated by large dark gray eyes speckled with gold, and a calm and proud expression.

"And afterwards," said Homo-Deus, "when I've liberated you, what will you do then?"

"I'll come to ask you," she said, frankly, meeting his gaze.

II. The Slumbering Hog

It was the eve of the Grand Prix and the weather was particularly warm. As he went to Saint-Cloud to see the Fortins, Marc Vanel went through the Bois de Boulogne, gray with the dust raised in swirling clouds by rapid automobiles. When his own car had left the blinding road, it was almost noon. Homo-Deus suddenly found himself in the kind of virgin forest that surrounded his friends' house, and he experienced a sensation of restful calm and soft freshness, the verdant caress of which was very pleasant.

His arrival was greeted with cries of joy. Vanel thought that he would find his friends alone, as usual, but there, in front of the house, grouped around a garden table were guests chatting while waiting for lunchtime. He recognized, without displeasure, the lovely Comtesse Simone d'Armez and—with more amazement—Georges Garnier, very much in form. *Good*, he thought, *his brain's recovery of function has been accomplished promptly; Jeanne is a veritable genius. Too bad that it gives me a rival.*[32]

Jeanne seemed more beautiful than ever. Either because the success of her scientific endeavors had rendered her, normally so grave, more cheerful, or because Homo-Deus' declaration, coming after that of Garnier had disturbed her in spite of her rejection, there was less of a chill in her face, and her astonishing plastic beauty seemed to be animated by a new fever. Her eyes, in fact, had a vivid and warm gleam that made Marc shudder.

Simone d'Armez teased Vanel, however.

"Did you know, Monsieur Sorcerer, that your science has failed?"

---

[32] The time-scheme of the novel has gone seriously awry here; both this observation and Simone d'Armez' subsequent remarks imply that this scene is taking place only days after the afternoon tea at which Vanel caused Madame Vauclin to see the inscription informing her that Julien de Vandeuvre was not dead, whereas, in terms of the Invisible's eccentric pursuit of the criminals, more than nine months have gone by; the author has literally lost the plot, presumably because its various strands were composed separately—it seems likely that the point of origin of the story was the prologue featuring Simone d'Armez, and that the soirée described in Book Two chapter V was the original opening, with the subplot concerning the Fortins being filled in subsequently, and never really marrying up, even before the spur-of-the moment decision to kill off Julien for a second time and then follow the subsequent fate of the body threw the whole scheme into utter chaos. By this point, of course, the author/dictator's only priority is to get the whole exercise wound up as rapidly as possible, although he presumably still had two steamy scenes of invisible satyriasis to slot into the sprint finish.

"Bah!" he said. "Why do you say that, my dear Madame?"

"You've made predictions that haven't been realized."

"Would it be indiscreet to ask what they were?" asked Jeanne Fortin.

Embarrassed, Marc attempted to explain. "At Madame Vauclin's house the other day, Madame d'Armez asked me to carry out an experiment whose secret had been revealed to me by the fakirs. On a sheet of blank paper, an invisible spirit had written something—what, I don't know, of course—and which, I've just learned, was a promise."

"Oh!" Simone d'Armez protested, blushing. "That depends how one understands it. It could equally have been a threat. In any case, the prediction has not been realized."

Homo-Deus looked her directly in the eyes, and she blushed again. "Are you afraid of that prediction, Madame, or is it agreeable to you? I have no need to tell you that, if you demand it, I will take measures to ensure its failure."

This time, the Comtesse seemed very embarrassed. Her cheeks, colored a vivid incarnadine, and her eyes, in which a fever of pleasure gleamed, rendered her prey, piquant and flavorsome. Homo-Deus was suddenly invaded by a stupor that exasperated troubling reminiscences.

"Whenever the spirit visited me," she stammered, "it hardly seemed to care whether I was consenting or not. My God, let it do, once again, as it pleases. I dare not interrogate myself; I simply submit to its caprice—that of a very fickle spirit."

He moved nearer to the pretty Comtesse and whispered, so that only she would hear: "The spirit will come again tonight."

Meanwhile, upright and proud, Jeanne Fortin was staring at them. Georges Garnier created a diversion by taking Vanel away. When the two men were alone, not far from the house, waiting for Frédéric to announce lunch, Jeanne's first suitor said to the other: "You weren't expecting to find me in such good condition, eh?"

"In truth, no. I last saw you in a state akin to infancy."

And remembering the scene of the domestic in the process of spooning food into the poor fellow, Marc could not help laughing.

"I was ridiculous, eh?" Garnier remarked, philosophically. "Well, would you believe that I wonder now whether I wasn't happier when I was in a stupor? At least, then, Jeanne paid attention to me. She watched me every day, interested in my person, and the progress of the experiments she was carrying out on my body. I was necessary to her, precious, and I know that she was glad to have me. Alas, since she's restored my means, rendering me similar to other men, she no longer pays any heed to me. She's become completely indifferent."

Homo-Deus smiled. The young man's love, naïve and so absolute, touched him. He shook his hands forcefully, because he was conscious of the same misfortune into which both of them were plunged, but he also felt a kind of anger toward the beautiful young woman who scorned the young man's heroism and his own genius so casually.

He was about to say a few words of consolation when Frédéric appeared to announce that lunch was ready. Then everyone went to the dining room, with its large bay window overlooking the plain through which the Seine snaked. Beyond the slopes of the hills, where the villas looked like doll's houses among the woods and the meanders of the river, the gray mass of Paris was visible, over which floated an almost opaque halo formed of dust and smoke, which the midday sun caused to sparkle.

As he sat down, Marc Vanel remarked: "I like that view, that unique spectacle. We're in the azure blue, in the pure silence, and we're savoring the refinement of contemplating the monster, Paris, drowned in an immense dirtiness that makes the light dusty."

The afternoon concluded in the wild park, into which Vanel-Satan, at the whim of the powers of his charm, drew in Simone d'Armez and Jeanne Fortin. In the bosom of that free nature, unkempt but vivacious and odorous, those young and handsome individuals felt generous saps rising within them. Perhaps for the first time, Jeanne, because she was unconsciously subject to the contagion of an ambience supersaturated with amour, could not entirely defend herself against a vague, uneasy disturbance that sometimes sent frissons over her skin. She seemed thoughtful, anguished and discontented, without being able to identify the cause of her irritation. Furthermore, it was with herself that she was annoyed, because she could not see with the indifference she desired the eagerness with which Marc took advantage of the slightest opportunities to press himself against the lovely Comtesse.

When they went back to the house and Vanel-Satan took his leave, she held out her hand to him abruptly and went to her laboratory without responding to the emotional adieu that he addressed to her in a low voice.

Saddened by that attitude, Homo-Deus left, his heart anguishing, accompanied as far as the road by Garnier—who never ceased, poor fellow, talking about Jeanne and her insensibility. His unsuspected rival listened distractedly, because he was thinking about Jeanne Fortin and Simone d'Armez. Within the god, the hog that slumbers within every one of us was rising up.

III. Stark Naked Surprise

When he got back to Paris Marc, Vanel was still under the impression of that delightful day.

Jeanne's attitude had touched him. Might it be by means of jealousy that he could awaken love in that scientific heart, so far above human passions? Could it be tamed by such a banal sentiment? Perhaps. The human soul has its mysteries; had he not lost control of himself when he had felt a hateful anger against Julien de Vandeuvre when he interested the young doctor so powerfully, albeit scientifically? If Jeanne was jealous, it was because, unconsciously, she was beginning to love him.

After a beautiful day, already too warm for the season, it was as if the atmosphere were impregnated with electricity, and that state of nature acted upon the nerves of Homo-Deus. That evening, he felt entirely a man, and his passions were further exacerbated.

He risked his grand amour on an all-or-nothing gamble. Going down into the basement, he rendered himself invisible, and then, climbing into the automobile, he gave Mardruk the order to take him to the Red Nest. To enter the Fortins' home was not difficult; the gate was never locked; it was sufficient to turn the handle and push. He opened it just wide enough to slip inside, because he knew that it creaked frightfully. He was in the park, and was soon in front of the house. Light was filtering through barred windows, although it was eleven o'clock at night.

She's still working, he thought. *Over what arduous problem is her beautiful face pondering at this moment? Before what enigma are the eyes that I love so much open?*

It was better for the success of his plans, however, that she was in the laboratory. That circumstance permitted him to go tranquilly up to her bedroom and install himself there. He therefore climbed the stone steps of the perron and, having listened, certain that no one had any suspicion of his visit, he opened the door that those simple and confident folk did not even take the trouble to bolt.

When he was on the point of going into Jeanne's bedroom, a violent emotion stopped him. For a moment, he hesitated. He, who had braved so many dangers in the course of his adventurous life, found himself intimidated and anxious, his heart tormented, on the brink of an action whose consequences he could not envisage.

What was he going to do tonight? Was it an unhealthy curiosity that was driving him, a base sentiment of sensual covetousness, or the simple desire to contemplate Jeanne's image and then to go away, his eyes full of the adorable vision? He did not know. A singular force was guiding him, and he was obedient to its impulsions without being able to make out their exact implications. Crazy ideas, however, were haunting him.

He had dreamed of seeing the young woman in her nudity of a splendid goddess, of throwing himself at her feet, of gripping the white columns of her legs with his feverish arms and applying his amorous lips to her flesh of cold marble. And it did not seem possible to him that she could resist. The fire of his mouth would burn her, animate her body in spite of herself, in spite of her grim determination, and his caressant hands would electrify her being, and she would shiver—for the first time! Her senses were dormant—yes, dormant, like marvelous plants in the thick darkness of a cave—but they would wake up, quivering with delight; her femininity would blossom in her lover's arms, as a flower opens when warmed by the first rays of the sun.

Well, yes, he would risk the supreme audacity. In any case, it was his last hope of conquering her. If he did not succeed, she would doubtless be lost to him forever, but if he did not dare to make the irremediable gesture, she would be lost anyway. So, he decided on the adventure, and entered resolutely into the room of the woman he was about to outrage or seduce.

He immediately felt troubled on sensing himself within the atmosphere of her mysterious intimacy. He knew everything about her intelligence, her brain, her soul and her heart, but nothing about her femininity.

He looked around the room, at the smallest objects, the furniture and the lingerie, hoping to find a clue that would reveal a secret corner of her to him. The room was sober and bright, however, without delicate frippery, devoid of lace and ribbons, but nevertheless beautiful, carefully ordered, cheerful and comfortable. It was not the temple of an amorous woman, but nor was it the monastic cell that one might have feared in the redoubt of a young woman devoted to the most arid sciences. The brass-framed bed, with covers in pastel colors, was vast. Marc Vanel divined that Jeanne, after hard work in the laboratory, liked to rest her body completely, and that sleep, for her, must be a comfortable voluptuousness.

The bathroom astonished him. It was almost as large as the bedroom, admirably ornamented, with nickeled pipes running along white walls, adding the bright note of their gleam. The bath and shower were improved models, seductive in their lines, and he liked their precious fitments and the amusing complication of their taps. The pearl porcelain basins of antique design made Marc think of Rome, infatuated with water and hygiene.

And Marc Vanel understood that Jeanne must rest her body and her mind in that vast bathroom, where the caress of cold water calmed the anxieties of her flesh. He guessed that every evening, she must spend long intervals restoring the vigor to her muscles necessary for the hard work she did, and he also understood, on perceiving gymnastic apparatus on the walls, why the lines of her body were so pure, why she resembled a masterpiece of statuary, and why one sensed an astonishing suppleness in her gait.

"What an admirable creature of amour she would be," he murmured, "if she finally consented to abandon herself...if her grim will-power no longer defended her body!" He sensed the robust, vigorous and handsome athlete that he was himself. He imagined the embrace in which their ardors might be confounded, and thought: *What a love-making ours would be!*

He only just had time to plaster himself against the wall in a corner; Jeanne Fortin came in.

The Invisible then knew the joy of contemplating an individual who, thinking that she was alone, showed herself in the abandonment of her natural gestures and her tastes, and the frankness of her instincts. He watched Jeanne come and go, her forehead anxious.

What was she thinking about? What difficult problem was still pursuing her? At whom were her preoccupations directed?

Soon, however, the young woman made a movement of the head that seemed to chase away the efforts of her thought; her eyes shone with a sudden joy, and her face became radiant. She threw her garments recklessly onto a low chair and, in her chemise, turned on the taps of the shower. The steaming water spurted two or three times, at her whim, and then Jeanne undressed completely, appearing in the aristocratic splendor of a troubling, impeccable nudity.

And Marc Vanel shivered with his entire being. He had never seen such a perfect creature, so pure in form, so vigorous, full of muscles, blood and life! And the burning ardors of his passions flooded his skin and his brain so abruptly that he was momentarily dazzled, after which he nearly pounced—but he held himself back, obedient to the anguishing dread of the irreparable.

Now, he gazed avidly at Jeanne's resplendent beauty. Her hair was gathered into a kind of red bonnet, the bright color of which cut across the white skin of her neck, as she prepared to immerse herself. Her allure had an astonishing suppleness as she disposed the various objects necessary to her toilette, moving back and forth across the white room.

She stopped in front of a Sandow[33] attached to the wall, took the handles of the apparatus in her slender but sinewy hands, pulled the rubber extensors taut and, for five minutes, maddened Marc Vanel with insensate attitudes, difficult exercises and dizzying gymnastics to which her supple body lent itself. In doing so, she was, without suspending it, terribly immodest, and the gestures and attitudes adopted for the employment of the apparatus, executed standing up, with audacious flexes, or lying on her back, displayed everything to Vanel, so com-

---

[33] "Eugen Sandow" (Friedrich Müller, 1867-1925) was a German body-builder who became a showman, founded the magazine *Physical Culture* and marketed exercise equipment, including the apparatus indicated here, which consisted of a system of rubber straps intended to be stretched by the arms and legs. His career was the model for that of the American bodybuilder who called himself Charles Atlas.

pletely that the most intimate beauties of her body, including the most secret jewel, were offered to him in luxurious display.

Weary now, a delicate sweat pearling her skin, she stood up straight, breathing deeply, and Marc saw her firm upper body, like a statue, with round, hard-tipped breasts, the charming nipples of which still seemed like two rosebuds posed on snowballs.

She placed herself under the shower, pulled a nickeled chain, and a hot rain immediately descended upon her, almost scalding, which steamed over her skin, enveloping her with a gray mist in which her imprecise, fluid image appeared to melt like a desert mirage. And Marc, heartbroken to see her disappear into the fog, made a movement as if to approach the fugitive vision. But she had extended her hand and seized another chain, and now the water ran colder, devoid of vapor.

Jeanne was still pulling the chain; now the water was falling upon her in an icy rain, and she contracted herself, stiffening herself, offering her hips to the stinging caress, and over her arched body, stretching under the violent sensation, little cascades spurted, descending from the pretty abdomen over the curved thighs, along the slender and muscular legs.

There was an abrupt click, and the rain suddenly ceased. Then the admirable creature wrapped herself in a thick bathrobe, which absorbed all the water. Nude again, having taken it off, she rubbed herself with towels that were warming on an electric radiator. She sat down in order to rub her legs more forcefully. In that position she was directly facing Marc, who was maddened by exasperated desires as he contemplated the roguish spectacle that she offered him so freely.

Suddenly, she stopped, seemingly nonplussed. Her gaze, which had suddenly become very hard, was fixed on the corner of the room, which was less brightly lit since she had turned a commutator that was close to hand.

Into that corner, an item of furniture projected a shadow—and in that shadow, there were two luminous points of emerald phosphorescence: the irises of the Invisible.

Alas, the phenomenon had partly betrayed Vanel several times. He had studied the reasons for it, which he knew, but he had not yet found a means of remedying it. It was provoked when a violent desire took possession of him, or when he was possessed by veritable anger. During the few minutes that his paroxysm of passion or rage lasted, one might have thought that all his vital fluid was concentrated in his eyes. Then, the other fluid, the one that impregnated his body to render it invisible, no longer had sufficient power, and that is why the irises charged with gleams lost the acquired property, at least during the few seconds when the passion culminated.

Very calmly, uncomprehending, Jeanne Fortin remained in a fixed attitude, with her hard eyes staring at the eyes that were gazing at her. Then Marc was afraid, terribly, that she would guess, for he sensed the effort that her brain was making, and understood that she must not. Catching him in his dubious role, not knowing the motives that were animating him, Jeanne would banish him insolently and scornfully, never to see him again.

Coldly, not afraid but very intrigued, she was still staring at the green irises, and reflecting. Marc could see the moment coming when he would no longer be able to speak. He was still hesitant—but he sensed the necessity of making the all-or-nothing gamble. He therefore advanced from his corner and murmured: "Jeanne…"

She started. And stiffened, but her gaze said that she was not afraid.

Again, Marc Vanel said: "Jeanne…"

Then she suddenly understood, and burst out laughing. "Oh, it's you!" she exclaimed. "Well, my dear Marc, you have some nerve. Did you think you could take me while I was asleep?"

"No, Jeanne, since I'm denouncing myself before you sleep."

She seemed struck by the argument, reflected for a moment, and said: "That's true. Why did you come, then?"

He did not reply immediately, astonished by the tranquil calm of the young woman, who, naked before him, knowing that she was being violated by an avid gaze, and experienced neither embarrassment nor shame. He stood there, confused and troubled, but the flame in his eyes had weakened, and the two emerald dots had now disappeared.

"Where are you, Marc?" said Jeanne, in a voice that was slightly less firm.

Now that she could no longer perceive his eyes, she seemed less self-assured. Just now, something of the Invisible had been apparent to her, indicating his location, his movements, and even his intentions. Since the shining eyes had been extinguished, nothing revealed the presence of the mysterious being, and Jeanne, in spite of her composure, could not suppress a slight anxiety.

"Where are you?" she said again.

"Here, Jeanne."

She shivered, alarmed, because the voice had come from behind her.

"Why aren't you in front of me? Oh, it's my triangle that embarrasses you! But what does the sight of the human body signify for the two of us, my poor Marc? Am I not similar to other women? Souls, hearts and minds differentiate individuals; flesh is always flesh, and you don't possess any of me by contemplating my intimacy."

"No!" he exclaimed. "You're lying…you're embarrassed at this very moment, knowing that my eyes are violating you, possessing you, but you want to be brazen, to impose your scorn for love on me…and you're not succeeding, even in your own eyes. Look, Jeanne, you're standing up to me, at this moment, determined to remain nude in order to demonstrate your disdain for the modesty that a true love contains, but I'm sure that in a little while, when I'm gone from here, and I've proved to you that I've really gone, you'll immediately dissolve in tears, because you're suffering in your self-respect, in your pride, from knowing that I've contemplated you, for a whole hour, with the eyes of a lover."

"Marc!"

She grabbed a peignoir swiftly, and covered herself with it.

The Invisible sniggered. "You see. Why are your cheeks pink, why does your throat betray a curious emotion, which is perhaps fear?"

Laughing and affecting indifference, although her voice was trembling, she said: "Oh! I'm not afraid!" As she said it she stood up, straight and proud, facing the direction from which Marc Vanel's voice had come. Now they both fell silent—but they sensed that the situation was untenable.

Jeanne was the first to speak, asking: "What did you want—what did you hope for—in coming here? Marc, I want you to tell me frankly the motive that guided you. I don't think that we ought to expose ourselves to such scenes again."

"Well, then, I'll be sincere. When I decided to see you, I didn't know—no, Jeanne, I swear, that I didn't know exactly what I wanted. I came to you, driven by an obscure instinct, in which there was perhaps a fatal attraction, perhaps an irresistible need for your presence, perhaps also a vague hope. No, truly, I didn't have precise thoughts; there was only an instinct. But when I came in here, I confess Jeanne, my ideas suddenly crystallized into a wild, powerful desire, and I resolved that you would be my mistress."

"Marc!" she said, recoiling, crossing herself and tightening the peignoir about her upper body.

"Yes," he continued, forcefully, "I wanted you, ardently and passionately. I was sure of myself, and I had the conceit that experience gives. I would have waited until you were in bed, almost to the point of falling asleep, and then I would have slid toward you, and with subtle caresses, the pressure of knowing lips, slow and profound kisses, sexual insistences that you would have been unable to resist, I would have *had* you."

"Marc!"

"I would have had you in spite of yourself, in spite of your resistance, your vigor, your repulsion, and, having made use of a sensuality of whose power you're ignorant, I would have made you know, regardless, Pleasure...perhaps Love."

"Shut up, Marc! Shut up! You're horrifying me!"

"Vehemently, he continued: "Yes, that's what you would have shouted in my face when, lying on top of you, I would have crushed your lips under mine, and your sex would have yielded to mine. You would have insulted me, hated me, I know, but you would have swooned."

"You're lying! You're lying! It's not true! My flesh will never know the ignoble frisson of lust, my mouth will never utter the sighs that reveal the pleasure of women in heat. No, I'm not a beast, and I won't submit to the goat!"

She was panting, and in the ardor of her gestures, she had let go of the lapels of the peignoir, which opened up and revealed her, naked and starry.

Then, for a second, the green irises shone in front of her, and she recoiled.

Now, Marc Vanel spoke in an emotional, dolorous voice

"Jeanne, you're alone, and I'm only a man. If anyone else—no matter who—had offered me those enticing visions, those luxurious attitudes. I would have hurled myself upon her like a famished beast on a prey. Spare me your hatred, Jeanne, because I haven't told you the sequel to my thoughts. You know the sentiments, the savage determinations, than animated me when I crossed the threshold of this room. Well, Jeanne, my beloved, when I saw you just now, alone, and all my instincts were driving me toward you, a will more powerful than my own retained me, nailed me to the corner where I was huddled."

"Why?"

"Because I love you. I suddenly understood, then, the immensity of that love and its character. Jeanne, Jeanne, I adore you—don't you sense it?—and my lips will never take your lips, if your lips don't want them to. Oh, I'm so unhappy, for I can measure the time and effort necessary to conquer you. Well, I shan't be discouraged; I'll pursue my goal and await my hour; but I'll only have you now if you offer me the splendors of our body yourself."

She did not reply with the grim "No!" she had so often pronounced, because she understood, now, the sentiments of the man, and—for the first time—she saw the distance that separates Love from sensual desire. In an ill-assured voice, she said: "Marc, you need to go."

"Yes, Jeanne, but I need to take away the certainty that you won't hold this against me."

Softly, she replied: "I no longer hold this against you." She took a step toward the voice. "Give me your hand, Marc, or take mine, since I don't know where you are."

She felt the contact of burning flesh around her wrist, and perceived the sensation of lips pressing against her hand. She shivered, and pulled away, stammering: "*Adieu*, Marc."

"*Adieu*, Jeanne."

The bathroom door opened of its own accord, then that of the bedroom, and Jeanne Fortin, going out on to the landing, heard muffled footsteps going down the stairs...

IV. The Gathering Storm

Outside in the savage garden, the Invisible started in surprise. Instead of moonlight enveloping the bare trees with a soft whiteness, there was now dense, warm, feverish, almost tragic darkness.

In the far distance, on the horizon, a black band had risen very rapidly into the sky, extinguishing the stars one by one. Then large inky clouds, driven by a nascent wind, had passed over the earth, veiling the moon at increasing narrow intervals.

The storm was gathering now, and Marc Vanel had difficulty finding his way through the interlaced branches. When he reached the gateway to the road, a pale light suddenly flared, the forerunner of the phenomena that were about to ensue.

Mardruk was dozing on his seat.

He heard the door of the auto click, and then a voice speaking to him through the acoustic tube.

"Let's go back. At the Porte Maillot I'll tell you where we're going."

V. And Now, Simone d'Armez

On leaving Jeanne Fortin, Marc Vanel was in a state of extreme overexcitement.

All his desires, flowing over his burning skin, were torturing him with imperious needs, and his eyes were phosphorescent again in the auto that was piercing the darkness. He remembered Simone d'Armez, the enticing little Comtesse, and her fiery kisses, the passionate embrace of her perfumed arms. What a flame there had been in her eyes when she had asked him, as a sorcerer, to bring back the libertine dream that had troubled her so much!

Oh, dear Simone! Now he was dreaming about her, her ideal, muscular body. Once again, he sensed the taste of her peppery lips, her soft throat, her amber skin. She was sincerely amorous, and Marc Vanel decided that because of that, tonight, she would be the Substitute.

He picked up the microphone that he used to communicate his orders to Mardruk, and gave him the address. They went through the Bois in a fine rain, falling from heavy clouds that obscured the sky, in which streaks of fire appeared from time to time, preceding rumbles of thunder.

"Quickly!" Marc commanded.

Mardruk pressed the accelerator of the sixty-horsepower, which bounded forward like a fantastic beast.

It was one o'clock in the morning, perhaps later.

Marc would not have any trouble getting into the little Comtesse's apartment. In anticipation of future visits that he was certain of making, one night or another he had obtained impressions of the locks from the hypnotized apache, which had permitted him to have keys made, by means of which he could enter Simone's home as easily as his own.

Marc had the auto stop fifty meters away, got out, instructed Mardruk to wait, and, as usual, had no difficulty at all getting into the house. The concierge, profoundly asleep, did not notice the service door opening. Vanel went through the silent rooms whose floors were covered with thick carpets, and was soon in Simone's bedroom. It was very dark, and he had to remember the layout of the room in order not to bump into the furniture and wake the sleeper.

Fortunately he remembered that a switch near the bed illuminated a discreet nightlight with a pink silk filter. He switched on the feeble light, for he feared that illuminating the large electric lamps would make the lovely Comtesse open her eyes. She was sleeping in an adorable attitude, forming a picture of the purest eighteenth century, her face very rosy, her sensual lips slightly fleshy, her upper body bare, the flesh appearing through delicate lace, her plump white arms like the wings of a dove.

Marc contemplated her for a long time. She had less nobility of contours, fewer muscles and less blood than Jeanne Fortin; she was no antique statue, but her child-like face was charming; everything in her spoke of the joy of love, the pleasure of pleasure. The Invisible saw her smile; her lips exhaled an imperceptible plea, while her features betrayed an emotion of contentment.

What was she dreaming about? What passionate idea was haunting her? Doubtless, she was ardently amorous, and a cold husband neglected her. But as she was naturally honest and rejected the idea of treason with horror, she must know tiresome evenings in which her forsaken, unquiet flesh, summoned dreams that deceived her desire.

So many honest women, so many faithful spouses are like that! How many times, their head buried in the pillow but their eyes wide open, have they not wished, with all their unemployed ardor, for a culpable embrace? They commit their sin cerebrally, and even physically, all alone, and—in minutes of illusion—they live perverse, violent joys, the kisses of the damned, extraordinary caresses. But it does not go any further! On awakening, exhausted and weary, undated, education and social limitations tame them, and they continue to be honest women and faithful spouses.

Oh, if, when they were asleep, a silent male came to visit them, disappearing thereafter forever, returning to the darkness, perhaps their virtue would be less intangible! And if, returning to the question of the Mandarin, a simple pressure on a button could make a powerfully virile, robust and anonymous being surge forth, who would depart once their appeal was satisfied, into the mists from which he had come. Doubtless not one of them would resist the desire to press that button. And, for want of an invisible satyr, more than one contents herself with the caresses of a beloved dog.

Marc Vanel, who was reading Simone's face as he made these reflections, murmured: "I shall be a first class mandarin." He put out the night-light.

Outside, the thunder and rain were raging; the atmosphere was heavy with electricity. Suddenly, a clap of thunder following a fantastic bolt of lightning caused the windows, the furniture and the crystal of the ceiling-light to shake. And soon, another, longer streak of lightning, similar to a firework, lit up the room.

Then Simone's wide open eyes saw an unusual individual beside her, and she uttered a scream—the scream of a woman who perceives a danger and is frightened.

Instinctively, Marc Vanel straightened up. He had just experienced the intuition of an obscure menace that he did not understand. Simone, meanwhile, bravely switched on the ceiling-light. A blinding glare fell from above on the individuals present, and the Comtesse, very pale, considered the somewhat bewildered man before her, Marc Vanel.

"You!" she said. "You!"

She let her head fall back on to her pillow and sighed. "It could not, in any case, be anyone else..."

Marc had the habit, when he was invisible, of never speaking. But this time, someone was speaking to him, and seemed able to see him. A sincere, anguished amazement was painted on his face.

Simone went on: "I thought you more a sorcerer than you are, and my disillusionment saddens me, because it puts an end to our relations. Yes, the first time, I thought that a supernatural power gave you the means of only being, at times, a creature of dream. Alas, here you are in the flesh and bone; you're only a man, just like the rest, and I, now, am an adulterous wife."

She dissolved in tears, and Vanel, stupefied, considered her without the power to make a gesture, the one that was required.

"A man just like the rest," he stammered, repeating Simone's words.

He looked down at himself and understood. He was visible.

While the young woman sobbed, he remained pensive. The adventure caused him real pain, for it resulted from a failure of his invention, and his own failure, too—and that truly did him harm.

He quickly divined the reason for that avatar: it was the fault of the storm. His body, charged with electric fluid, had not been sufficiently isolated in an atmosphere charged with ozone. A contact had been established between the ambient electricity and that which ensured his invisibility; thus, an event had occurred akin to the abrupt discharge of an accumulator in the middle of a storm; all his fluid had abandoned him and he had become visible again—exactly like other men, in fact. And now he found himself in the ridiculous situation of a man caught in a fault, and weakening.

Marc Vanel was too intelligent not to understand that it was finished between Simone and him. He leapt out of the bed, and said in a faint and dolorous voice: "Pardon me, I'm a very poor sorcerer. I had the power that you supposed me to have, but a furious nature has reminded me, tonight, that the power of God always exceeds that of human beings. I should not have come tonight."

Ashamed, she was still hiding her face in the pillow. He headed for the door, slowly, head bowed, defeated.

As he was about to go out, she sat up.

"My friend, how will you leave?"

Marc Vanel thought sadly: her reputation. He smiled palely and said: "Don't worry. No one will ever know anything about our adventure. It will remain in my memory as a strange flower too briefly bloomed, and although no human being will ever know about this amour, I will always retain the delectable perfume within me."

"Thank you."

As she said that, the manner in which she looked at Marc betrayed her regret—and he went away less sadly.

Mardruk, on seeing him, uttered an exclamation of amazement.

"Yes, my poor Mardruk," Vanel said to his chauffeur, in a melancholy tone, "the science of love has proved bankrupt, this time. Let's go home."

VI. Huguette de Virmile

It had been a bad night for Marc Vanel; the two amorous failures he had just experienced put that passionate nature into a state of nervous tension that the memory of the two beauties he had contemplated in the course of the night was not calculated to calm. Unable to sleep, he got up and went down to his laboratory, haunted by the accident that had just occurred.

Unless he were to renounce his marvelous discovery, it was necessary to find a means of avoiding a further catastrophe, for some such adventure could have happened to him at the Baruyers' home, and then he would have been the murderer caught in the act—and he, the superman, Homo-Deus, would have been arrested and guillotined like a vulgar bandit.

With his head in his hands, he thought hard. He envisaged new chemical procedures, means of isolating himself more completely. Daylight surprised him still at work, mentally, on the perfection of invisibility. An idea had taken form in his mind.

"I'll talk to Jeanne about it, and the two of us will be able to solve the problem."

That resolution calmed him, and gave him confidence. He saw in that revelation made to Jeanne Fortin a means of getting closer to her, and that baroque thought brought a smile to his lips. *It would be amusing to make love, both of us invisible; the trivial aspect of the act, which Jeanne finds repugnant, would thus be avoided.*

He was about to throw himself on the bed in order to get a little rest when the sound of an auto pulling up outside the house caused him to stay where he was.

Almost immediately, Mardruk came in.

"Master, it's the veiled lady who came before..."

"Huguette!" exclaimed Marc Vanel. "Show her in."

The young woman came into the studio where he was meditating, and immediately came toward him, nervously. "Excuse me for disturbing you so early, Master, but I left the house at dawn in order not to be seen by the servants."

Marc sat her down on a divan and took her hand. "I told you that I would be at your disposal when you needed me. The moment has come?"

"Judge for yourself. My marriage to the Comte de Simiane has been arranged to take place in three days. My mother had pushed forward so actively with the preparations for the celebration that the sinister incest would have occurred sooner than I expected."

While she was speaking, Marc looked at her. The animation into which her singular situation had plunged her gave her features an expression that embellished them further; her hand shivered in the savant's, and she suddenly withdrew it.

"I came here to find a protector," she stammered.

Marc was slightly embarrassed. As he gazed at the splendid young woman, desire had gripped him, and unwittingly, his expression had betrayed him. He collected himself.

"Forgive me," he said. "In spite of my science, I'm only a man, and as such, submissive to the impulses of my temperament. I'm still too young to play with beauty with impunity. I would not want to take on the appearance of a Don Juan in your eyes and abuse your confidence, but believe me, it's a hard proof."

Huguette stood up. "I'm not, alas, the ideal young woman of whom poets and fashionable novelists sing. Life has been hard for me. Although pure, I know what vice is. Around me I've seen nothing but depravity. Like all children abandoned to themselves, I've had unhealthy curiosities. I've spied, I've seen, I've learned, and if I've remained virtuous, it's because my pride had set me above certain sins. The ermine, it's said, dies of a stain on its fur; I'm similar— I'd die of a stain on my dignity."

"And yet you came back here, to the home of a man you don't know?"

"I came back because I judge you to be above other men, almost equal to a god—at any rate, far above the mundane society of which I have a horror."

"Ah! What dream have you had, then?"

"A dream, alas. Can one live, if one doesn't dream? I live, since I have a hope, a goal. My dream is to liberate myself from this ridiculous life and leave—to go where? I don't know, but to flee, to flee recklessly toward the new, toward the ideal."

"And you'll flee alone?"

She blushed. "Yes, at first. Afterwards, I don't know. I'm only a woman…just as you said, a little while ago, 'I'm only a man, in spite of my science.'"

Marc stood up and paced back and forth across the studio for a few moments.

"Listen to me, Huguette," he said, stopping in front of her. "If I had known you sooner, perhaps I would have asked for your love. Oh, don't worry, I'm not going to talk to you as an amorous man, but as a friend. I'm in love with a young woman who, in all probability, will never be mine. If that amour were not my entire life, my entire hope, I would say to you: 'Let's leave together,' because you have everything within you necessary to be adored, and I deserve to be loved. But beside that impossible love, there is room for physical love—I'm speaking to you brutally, you see. If, once liberated from the caste that horrifies you, you have need of an affection, a desire for a man, think of me, who is worthy of you."

"You do well to speak to me like that," said Huguette, her voice trembling slightly. "The reply I shall make to you has something of the air of a bargain, but

242

events have overtaken my modesty and my will. On the day I am free I shall give myself a master, and that master will be you."

Homo-Deus took the virgin in his arms and kissed her forehead chastely.

VII. A Spring Night's Dream

It was the night following Huguette de Virmile's visit to Marc Vanel—which is to say, two days before her marriage to Monsieur de Simiane, her mother's aged lover and the father of the bride: an Edenic night on the middle of June.[34] After several days of storms and squalls, the calmed atmosphere was definitely set fair, and the end of spring seemed to promise a splendid summer. It was a warm night, with a dark sapphire sky studded with a diamante star named Huguette, a svelte brunette intoxicated by her blooming youth, who was further inebriated by respiring all the pollens of renewal.

After the contract dinner, the young woman, offering the pretext of a slight fatigue, retired at about eleven o'clock to her own apartment, a kind of pavilion attached to the house by a small gallery. In that fashion, Huguette had her own abode, which she had occupied since childhood. Madame Virmile, unconcerned with maternal duties, had thus rid herself of a child who had aged her, putting her in the shade by virtue of her beauty. Huguette had gained in strength and health in consequence. She had lived in the vast garden, almost in the middle of nature, without disturbing overmuch the artificial existence and worldly habits of her mother. It had required the necessity of establishing her lover on a solid footing and keeping him closer to her for the Marquise to consent to bringing their daughter out of that penumbra.

Huguette was not fatigued, but she was in haste to be alone. In her room, the windows, with turquoise curtains, overlooked the garden, and the sculpted woodwork, lacquered with pale lilac heightened by silver threads, was a princely vestige of olden days. Huguette de Virmile, an only daughter, dreamed that evening in her solitude, and her gaze often encountered, on a small rosewood Louis XV desk, in an outrageously modernistic frame garnished with green lizard-skin, a portrait of the fashionable sorcerer Homo-Deus cut out of an illustrated newspaper: a monochrome image, an agreeable obsession. She murmured: "Marc, I love you..."

The firmament, infinite in its purity, scintillated with the innumerable dots of the constellations. A light wind brought a breeze through the wide open windows embalmed by new blossoms: lilies of the valley, syringas and violets. The garden—one could have said park—in which vagabond fireflies were clustering, had tall chestnut trees, clumps of box-trees and elders, and a row of old linden-trees for a backcloth.

---

[34] Again the time-scheme is awry; it was March only yesterday—but this scene was obviously not composed, in the first place, immediately after the preceding ones.

The magnificent trees are quivering in their thousands of emerald leaves. A perfume of fresh sap inundates the room; one might have thought that all the sticky efforts of the vegetation have been captured there, in order to stimulate the young and forceful senses of the sensitive child. Yes, the entire nocturnal and mysterious spring is buzzing and singing at that belated hour. The malicious zephyrs are dancing a hectic farandole, drawing the songs of birds and crickets, stimulated themselves by the lusts of the new season. The red, yellow and crimson roses are embalming the entire park and the sacred hymn of the flowers, from the enormous proud poppies to the white lilies, appeal amorously to the young virgin; on the edge of a stream, black irises, speckled as if with flesh and a furry down, are heavy with torpor.

Huguette de Virmile, who has undressed, as usual, without the aid of her chambermaid, has put on a white lace nightgown, retained at the waist by a silver cord. With a sigh, she comes to lie down on the sofa facing the French windows in the middle; thus placed, she can see the marvels of the sky through a wide gap in the foliage, and abandons herself to the caresses of the breath of the park, in which the active fermentation of seeds and saps in full activity is sensible. In her, there is no anxiety concerning the marriage that is being prepared around her. Homo-Deus has promised to watch over her, and that promise is sufficient, from the man she adores as a god. She therefore allows her prayer to be borne away toward the One in which she has placed all her confidence, all her hope: the one whose masculine and intelligent visage is central in her mind's eye: Homo-Deus.

The supple creases of the nightgown emphasize all the harmonious beauties of a faultless body. Sometimes, her dream lights up in a smile; then, her eyelids open and her pupils launch a kind of luminous ray; she tilts her tomboyish head with short black hair backwards. Chastity and purity, in a young woman, are not always completed by stupidity or hypocrisy. Huguette, thinking about Marc Vanel, anticipates the impetuosity and gentleness of his embrace; finding ordinary life flat and despairing in its monotony, she loves the dream.

That dream, in which Marc Vanel bathes her with his thoughts, is soon mingled with an entirely external impression. What human fluid is mingled with the vesperal night breeze, the aroma of corollas, the acrid odor of rising saps and the magnetism of the vegetable lusts? A male is advancing. Who?

Him.

And, hidden in the shadow of the branches, a nightingale sings, giving with its crystalline trill a definitive quality to the different scales of the spring melody. For Huguette, all the little winged composer's notes spell out the three syllables of the divine name: Marc Vanel. Then, in the phantasmagoria of the dream, the emanations of things and the individuality of the beloved man whose approach corporealizes the spring and amour are combined. All the lust of the world fuses in an imaginary being who, insensibly, becomes real, while remaining invisible. She feels the friction of a masculine force close at hand, imposing itself on her purity, which no longer desires to be, impressing her entire being, in the utmost intimacy, like a material presence—as if, in sum, he were there.

It was true. The invisible satyr—the skeptical and the disillusioned—had had that fantasy. Everything in that night in which June was bursting forth with a fantastic exuberance celebrated the triumph of life and sexual intercourse: not only the romantic love created by humans in order to idealize the grossness of that reproductive act, but the brutal and sensual love ordained by nature, with the unique objective of the propagation of the species.

Homo-Deus sensed the intimate communion that links all beings together, everything that is, from the infinitely small, the constitutive atom, to the innumerable suns that populate the universe. And Marc Vanel told himself that every star has a soul, a directive spirit, that each of those globes circulating in space lives, like a human, like an animal, like a plant, a special life, and that all of them have a birth and a death, like the humblest insect.

What is time? A lapse that humans measure by their own existence—but in the universal life, the star that lives for thousands of centuries, and the ephemeron that lives for a few hours, have lived the same amours, the same needs for reproduction. Of what humans do not know, that which is can be deduced. The domain of human knowledge expands incessantly; one day, they will understand the language of plants, of inferior beings, and on that day, they will be very close to knowing that of planets and suns.

Saturated by an extraordinary magnetism, Homo-Deus sensed the soul of worlds palpitating within him, and, wanting to share that act of communion with the young woman, with suggestive movements and rhythmic movements, as rhythmic as a dance, he imposed the divine poem of universal love upon her.

Huguette de Virmile's eyes were closed, but she was not asleep. Possessed by an invisible being, in an ineffable intellectual penetration, which had nothing terrestrial about it, she floated above humanity, receiving without any possible control the suggestions of the Initiator.

Now, the tension of Homo-Deus was such that he feared for his state of invisibility, and he was afraid of seeing the charm broken, as on the night of his visit to Simon d'Armez. Meanwhile, Huguette had drawn closer to the windows. The rays of moonlight, sly and curious, undressed her entirely beneath the veil of transparent silk. All of nature, at that vision of a virginal enchantress, quivered and whispered: "Love…! Love…!"

Over that vegetal orgy, in the increasingly profound sky, the stars are multiplying. What God is throwing into infinity his mantle of azure sewn with myriads of diamonds? Huguette is excited, and in a spasm, would have liked to give herself entirely to that mysterious nature, to be the queen and spouse of that immense perfumed debauchery.

Troubled, the Virgin, comes back into the room. The zephyr follows her, Nature surrounds her, intoxication bewildered her. All the roses quiver toward her. Then, with a previously-unknown sensuality, she undoes the silver cord of the lace night-gown, which falls around her and forms a snowy lotus on the soft carpet. The virgin is naked, beneath a chemisette of white muslin.

Huguette, her senses confused, throws herself then onto her adolescent's bed. The sculpted amours seem to be continuing the amorous frolic of that delirious nature. Homo-Deus approaches. She divines his presence. The moon is already veiling herself at the nascent spectacle, but soon returns, curious. And suddenly, in the great silence, the nightingale trills repeatedly, spelling out the syllables *Marc Vanel*. And the entire orchestra of spring resumes playing a languorous waltz, in which the perfumes of roses twirl.

Homo-Deus crosses the room with a light step, smiles, and, like a radiant sylph, shapes around the virgin awaiting the eternal dance of the stars.

He dances around the bed, where that human lily awaits the kiss; pausing, he contemplates the supine Huguette for a long time, and then, in a mad leap, turns round, bounds toward the window, toward the park whose orchestra is accompanying his invisible nuptial mass. From the depths of the garden of Eros, the arbor of Apollo, he returns swiftly in a waltz of fantastic adoration to that young body of pale marble, transparent and radiant through the light muslin, his arms laden with multicolored roses, which he strews around the room, drawing with him, like Pan, all of nature drunk on voluptuousness, lust and germination, and, with a conquering gesture, stops at the foot of the virginal bed.[35]

And the moon smiles.

The birds, the crickets and the flowers are anxious.

Homo-Deus, with grace and devotion, plucks the petals from roses over the adolescent with the short hair, exquisitely naked, in repose and dreaming. Then, very gently, religiously, he applies his lips, flushed with ardent blood, to those of the svelte young woman's sacred flower.

Huguette, with a smile of appeasement, seems to wake up. Her beautiful eyes of jet black gaze into the dark room. Promise passes enchanted fingers over her face, and then her gaze widens with fear of pleasure. What can she see? Two opal-green eyes: translucent emerald eyes staring at her.

"Marc," she murmurs, "is that you?"

His eyes are about to betray Homo-Deus. He resolves to recoil in a retreat. The emerald eyes draw away, are extinguished, after a final glance at the young woman whose arms are extended toward the invisible lover.

Then, with a gesture of superhuman amplitude, Homo-Deus gathers and condenses the combined fluids of the universal forces and impregnates the brain of the young woman, saying mentally, with his formidable power:

Huguette, no matter at what moment, nor wherever in the world you might be, you will come at the mere appeal of my thought.

---

[35] This scene appears to be based on the famous Michel Fokine ballet, based on music by Hector Berlioz, *La Spectre de la rose*, first performed in Monte Carlo in 1911 and first staged in Paris in 1917, with Nijinsky in the leading role.

Yes, she says, her eyes wide open, as if she could see the Invisible.

They were, henceforth, fluidically linked to one another. No human force could any longer break the bond that united them.

Meanwhile, silvery clouds hid the fat, round moon, under which roses in folly opened their calices.

A huge lily swells up—and wakes up—in the first light that is pricking the sky, while Homo-Deus reaches the window and launches himself, with a prodigious leap, into the garden.

Huguette has an impression of that departure; standing up on her bed, her face ecstatic, she blows a kiss, with both hands, toward her dream.

VIII. The Surprises of the Invisible

Marc left the Hôtel de Virmile shortly before dawn. To his astonishment, he did not find Mardruk's limousine at the rendezvous. It was the first time that the Hindu had ever failed in his duty. Marc had an inkling that something extraordinary had happened at his home. From the Hôtel de Virmile it was scarcely half an hour's journey to go home on foot. The Invisible set out.

At that early hour there were only street-sweepers and rag-pickers about. Without any fear of colliding with a passer-by, he was able to accelerate his pace. As soon as he entered the Rue de l'Yvette he perceived the automobile parked outside his house, without having attracted the attention of a policeman in that remote corner of Passy. He could not retain a cry on perceiving the inanimate body of Mardruk lying inside the vehicle.

First of all he put the car in the garage. He closed the door of his house—which he found ajar—behind him. Then he carried the Hindu into the studio and examined him.

He's not dead, but I'm just in time.

The body, laid bare, allowed the sight of two wounds, both in the chest. Rapidly, the savant lanced the wounds in order that the blood could run out and would not choke the injured man. A few minutes later, the two projectiles had been extracted, the wounds were bandaged, and the victim was lying on the divan. The most urgent thing done, Homo-Deus went down to the invisibility room and came back shortly thereafter, returned to his normal appearance.

He back went to the injured man, and made him absorb a cordial, which must have had astonishing properties, for the invalid opened his eyes two minutes later.

"Don't worry," said Vanel. "You're safe. Just tell me what happened, as briefly as possible."

"I came back from the Hôtel de Virmile, where, according to your instructions I was to return in order to wait for you at daybreak. I stopped outside the house and was about to open the door when men surged forth and shot me. I fell, losing consciousness."

"Did you recognize them?"

"Only the voice of one—Walesport."

"Ah! The bandit suspects me? The other must have been Vauclin, then."

"It seemed to me that there was a third."

"Ah!" Marc sniggered. "The complete trio. They must have burgled the house, then."

He made a rapid examination, and observed that locked drawers had been broken open. Papers were scattered. Three Hindu daggers were missing from a panoply.

Suddenly, a terrible suspicion crossed Marc Vanel's mind.

At that moment, the telephone that he had linked directly to the Fortin house rang. He bounded to the receiver.

"Hello! It's me, Fortin. Come quickly, Marc! Quickly!"

"Jeanne!" cried Marc.

A faint voice replied: "Help me, Marc! Help!"

Homo-Deus uttered a roar of dolor and wrath..

"Oh, damn them!"

"Go, Master—the car is full of fuel."

Homo-Deus darted a glance at the wounded man. He could wait.

Two minutes later, the limousine was speeding along the road to Saint-Cloud, toward the Red Nest.

This is what had happened.

Walesport judged that by striking swiftly, he would surprise his enemies in total safety. In the course of the evening, he went to Georges Baruyer's house. As on the preceding days he found the député in a confused state, completely at a loss, devoid of ideas and energy, his mind wandering. At the sight of his accomplice, a gleam came to his eye. Walesport had promised to discover those who had caused his ruin, and that thought alone had sustained him a little.

"Well?" he demanded.

"I've identified the bastards who rolled us over: the Fortins and Marc Vanel."

"But I don't know those people."

"That's possible, but they know you. I don't know them either. Diabolically strong types, scientists who have marvelous means, they resuscitated Julien de Vandeuvre, whom Vauclin and his wife had killed. It was them again who turned the Barsac affair against us and pocketed our millions."

"Our millions!" Baruyer roared, leaping out of his armchair.

"Ah! That's woken you up—yes, and doubtless those accursed scientists caused Albert to kill your mother by suggestion. Dr. Fortin has been seen in a full session of the Académie accomplishing disconcerting feats of suggestion. These people are diabolical. They appear to have a bee in their bonnet about punishing rogues and great thieves like us."

"So? What do we do?"

"Hit back! If not, we're already ruined, hunted and driven into a corner. They'll do with us as they please, as they killed your mother, your brother—very nearly, as he's mad—and as they killed Vauclin's wife yesterday. Are we going to offer our throats to be cut, like sheep? Before they strike us, let's strike them first."

"I'm in."

"Good! Vauclin's hiding at my place. The three of us will see it through to the end."

At about eleven o'clock, three shadows slipped along the garden walls of the Rue de l'Yvette, where Marc Vanel lived. Walesport, prudent and fearful that the scientist's dwelling might be protected by electricity, had equipped himself with rubber gloves. No lights were burning in the house. Marc Vanel had left in the car for the Hôtel de Virmile. After having driven the Invisible there, Mardruk was to come back in order to get some sleep before going to collect him at daybreak. The Hindu maidservant had been in hospital for a week, having caught flu. Marc Vanel was caring for her, but as it was inconvenient for him to have a sick woman in the house, he had installed her elsewhere. The house was thus absolutely empty when the three villains arrived.

"Too quiet!" said Walesport. "Let's be wary."

They went along the railings that surrounded the house.

"We could force the gate," the American went on, displaying a heavy crowbar that he had brought with him, "But I think it's more prudent to climb over. There might be tricks in this box to snap back. Vauclin, keep watch, and you, Georges, help me to climb over."

As the three of them were getting ready to attempt the venture, an automobile came around the corner of the street.

"Look out!" said Walesport, who was directing the expedition. "If it's his car, we'll jump him."

It stopped in front of the house, and the unsuspecting Mardruk got ready to get out.

"Shoot!" commanded Walesport.

He and Vauclin fired at the chauffeur, who fell onto the sidewalk.

"The windows! Fire at will!"

All three rapidly took up positions at the vehicle's windows, but it was empty.

"No luck!" said Walesport. "We'll have to wait in the house. Shh! No noise."

They hid in the shadow of the vehicle. A window had just opened in a nearby house. Two heads appeared, looking into the street.

"It's Dr. Vanel's car," said a voice. "A tire must have burst."

They went back in; the window closed again. Now they were tranquil and masters of the situation. They searched Mardruk and found the keys to the house. After having put the inanimate body back in the vehicle, they went into the house.

"Georges! Stay behind the door, and at the slightest alert, come to warn us. The two of us, Vauclin, onwards!"

They made a conscience search of the furniture, but found no trace of the millions. In fact, the deposit receipts from the various banks in which Vanel had placed the millions were on Homo Deus' desk before their eyes, under a crystal paperweight, but the modern sorcerer had rendered them invisible.

"The money must be at the Fortins' place," said Vauclin. "We're wasting time here. It's probable that Vanel is there now."

"It's more than probable, in fact."

"Well, it's only one o'clock. Shall we go to Saint-Cloud?"

"Yes. If Vanel isn't there, the others will be, and when he sees that we've been here, he'll come running."

"Let's go, then. By the way, we'd better equip ourselves with less noisy weapons."

"You're right. The Hindu daggers there, in that panoply, will suit our purpose very well."

After having chosen three of them, they went out and made Baruyer, who was guarding the door, party to their new plan.

A few minutes later, they found a taxi, one of those on the lookout for a windfall, whose drivers make a specialty of working by night. In return for a hundred francs he took them to Saint-Cloud.

On the stroke of two o'clock, they were outside the Red Nest. Walesport turned the handle of the gate automatically. It opened.

"These people are splendid—they have no fear."

"They're wrong," sniggered Vauclin. "And so much the better for us."

Walesport pushed the gate gently, but in spite of his precaution, it emitted a long creak, which made the hearts of the three villains lurch.

In the laboratory, Jane, her father and George Garnier had been working for a long time. They were in the process of completing a major work, which would comprise a synthesis of all their endeavors, a scientific history of the earth.

The various adventures in which the Fortins and Marc Vanel had been involved had slowed them down, and now they were trying to make up for lost time. Georges Garnier was consulting an enormous parcel of notes and calculations; he was passing them to Fortin, who was dictating to Jeanne. While writing, they were discussing obscure points.

Suddenly, outside, two gunshots rang out.

All three bounded to their feet, turned in the direction of the park, and listened. There was a third detonation, closer this time.

"Oh, the swine!" cried the voice of Frédéric, from the park.

"What's that?" said Jeanne, seizing a long pair of compasses from the table.

Already, Georges Garnier had armed himself with a poker, and Fortin with a heavy steel ruler.

Another gunshot shattered a windowpane, and a bullet whistled over Fortin's head.

"We'll be shot down here," Georges exclaimed. "Let's retreat into the cellars." He shoved Jeanne in front of him

Outside, on the steps of the perron, there was the sound of a fierce struggle. Frédéric, wounded, was still shouting.

"Look out! Save yourselves!"

"We can't leave Frédéric to die! Go downstairs, Jeanne—as for us, forwards!"

A further cry of agony resounded outside, and then Frédéric's gasping voice: "Ah! Brigands! I'll have you all!"

Jeanne had already set foot on the cellar steps, and Fortin and Georges were running toward the door when it opened violently.

Walesport, distraught and bloody, appeared on the threshold. He was holding a blood-stained dagger in one hand and a smoking Browning in the other. He was wounded, and had to support himself on the door frame. He assessed the situation at a glance and took aim at Jeanne, who, amazed and fascinated, had remounted the step.

"I'm done for," croaked Walesport, "but at least I'll die avenged."

And he fired at Jeanne, who lost her balance, hit in the shoulder.

Georges Garnier had leapt forward, brandishing his weapon. Walesport fired again. Hit full in the chest this time, Jeanne collapsed on the floor. At the same time, Walesport fell, his skull fractured.

Fortin and Garnier had raced to Jeanne, lifted her up and laid her on the divan. The wound in her shoulder was not serious, but the one in her chest was mortal; already the blood was spreading out internally, choking her.

Fortin stuck his lips to the wound and sucked forcefully. That caused the blood to flow outwards. They positioned the victim so that the flow would be maintained in that fashion. Eventually, Jeanne opened her eyes. She collected herself momentarily, and judged her own condition.

"Doomed! She said. "Nothing to be done. Call Marc."

Let us go back. That night, Frédéric, who had gone to bed early, had woken up at about one-thirty. The worthy fellow could not stay in bed once he was awake. He remembered that he had set a few snares in the thickets, and had an impulse to go see whether any rabbits had been caught. After having dressed summarily, he had picked up a big canvas bag and gone out.

The sky was clear, and it was bright enough for him, habituated as he was to all the meanders of the park, to be able to steer without hesitation to the place where the snares had been set.

"Damn!" he said. "There's one, a beauty. It must weigh at least five pounds."

He stuffed the rabbit in his bag and continued his exploration. At the end of a path he saw that the house was still illuminated.

"Not in bed yet," he muttered.

At that moment, he heard the creak of the gate behind him. Astonished, he threw himself into the shadow of a bush in order to listen, without moving.

There were muffled footsteps in the grass; then, three shadows slid along the path, heading toward the house—and, in consequence, toward him. Frédéric had no other weapon than a fairly sturdy knife, which he always kept in his pocket, and which served various purposes. He opened it, at hazard. The steel made a dry click as the blade was fixed by the spring, and the three shadows stopped.

"Did you hear that?" whispered a voice.

"Yes—look out!"

On either side, there was immobility.

Softly, one step at a time, Frédéric began to retreat toward the Red Nest. A branch cracked underfoot.

"There's someone there," said the former cowboy, Walesport. "Forward—before he raises the alarm!"

Seeing that he had been discovered, the good servant turned round, and the three men fell upon him, daggers in hand.

Frédéric had the darkness in his favor; he avoided in impact, and hurled his bag at the head of Baruyer, who happened to be nearest. While the villainous advocate[36] rid himself of the bag, the other two fired at their adversary. Frédéric felt the wind of a bullet on his face.

"Ah! Pig! He exclaimed, and, diving at Baruyer, he plunged his knife into his breast all the way to the hilt. He had struck so forcefully that the député, as he fell, dragged him down with him—which saved him, for two more bullets whistled over his head.

"To the house!" said Walesport. "The alarm's been given now. There'll be obstacles."

He and Vauclin ran toward the Red Nest, guided by its lights. They had reached the perron when a gunshot rang out behind them. Vauclin, hit in the back of the neck, collapsed, uttering a lugubrious cry.

Walesport turned round. Frédéric ran forward, armed with Baruyer's Browning, and shouted at the same time to warn his masters. Walesport fired at him.

Hit in the thigh, the valiant servant continued to advance nevertheless, re-turning fire. Walesport, hit in the right side, uttered a cry of rage.

Ah! I'll have you all!" cried Frédéric.

Another bullet hit him. He made a superhuman effort to get up, but had been hit in the skull, and the blood running down his face blinded him. The ad-mirable guard-dog fell again, unconscious this time.

Mad with rage and pain, Walesport ran to the door of the Red Nest and opened it, furiously...

We know the rest.

The humble Frédéric, the arm and heart of the people, had finally brought down and punished, without even knowing that he was making a symbolic ges-ture, the financier Walesport: a raptor of international wingspan, maneuvering puppets, petty matamores and scaramouches, just as the vulturissimo Zaharoff, the frightful Basile, employs the Barthous in his designs, and the députés Vauclin and Baruyer, two wild beasts disguises as shepherds, representatives of the packs of wolves and jackals of the jungle of politics, who govern while nib-

---

[36] The author appears to have forgotten that it was Albert Baruyer, not Georges, who was an advocate.

bling, gasping and devouring, each in accordance with his claws and fangs, at the immense French flock, driving them toward the abyss.

X. The Transmitted Soul

The sun rose in a sky radiant with pink clouds. At the zenith, it was a blue of infinite delicacy. Jeanne had asked to be taken to the belvedere, and the two men had transported her there with infinite precaution. Fortin was under no illusion; his daughter was doomed; her death as only a question of hours, perhaps minutes. Lying on the divan, her torso supported by a pile of cushions, Jeanne watched the sunrise.

"There it is," she said, in a low and halting voice, "the Immortal: it is unconcerned with our agitation, our dreams, of sages or madmen. Where is the wisdom? One believes oneself to be above humanity, and a fragment of metal reduces us to nothing. No, not nothing! I want to live, to survive! Marc's taking a long time. He'll arrive too late." Her eyes fell upon Georges Garnier, who was sobbing helplessly, prostrate in a corner. "No, not him—he's not strong enough. I need a Master!"

At that moment, Homo-Deus' limousine came into the garden in a whirlwind. Marc leapt out, and Frédéric, his head swathed in bandages, greeted him.

"Jeanne?" cried the savant.

"Go up quickly—she's asking for you! You're her only hope!" With a gesture, he indicated the belvedere.

In a matter of seconds, Marc scaled the staircases. In two bounds he was beside the moribund, and collapsed at her feet.

"Finally," said the dying woman. "There you are. Don't waste any time."

"I'll save you!" Vanel cried.

"If it were possible," said Fortin, "I'd have done it. My daughter, my colleague, my master! Oh, what a loss for science!"

"Silence! Listen to me. I won't die. I don't want to die. Father, you've carried out transmissions of the soul in public, at the Académie des Sciences. You're going to help me; it's necessary to transfer my soul into Marc's. You, Homo-Deus, wanted to possess my body—see what a fragile thing you would have had. The gesture of a wretch sufficed to make this beauty you desired so much into tomorrow's pinch of ashes. But I, more proud, want to give you something better than this perishable flesh—to give you my soul, Marc, my mind, the intelligence that you loved as well as my body. *Is that not love, Marc?* Are you content?"

"Jeanne, I want to die with you."

"But what, then, is this love, which you prefer to immortality? Wretch—you tell me that you love me and you want to let me die, *entirely!*"

She stopped, exhausted, a trickle of bloody foam running from her mouth; she was having difficulty breathing.

Georges Garnier leapt up from where he was crouched.

"What kind of man are you, then?" he cried. "And you say that you love her! But whatever she asked of me, I would obey without reflection, without regret…as I have done already, without hope."

Fortin had made the dying woman take a few drops of an elixir; she reanimated gradually,

"So be it," she said. "Since he doesn't want it, I'll go. Anyway, I shall know. If Marc had wanted it, I would have remained on your Earth a little longer. The mystery's there, in the afterlife. Have we sensed the truth? Or is it only a lure of our pride? I shall know. Oh, Father, I'm afraid. What if we were mistaken? What if the soul can't survive the body? What if the fluid that animates us and directs us is only a combination of matter, and I'm truly about to die? What good is life, then, if it has no other objective than to ferry us to death?"

"Death doesn't exist," said Fortin. "It's a mere modification."

"If I have to be reborn in an inferior form, what would be the point? And it's death anyway, since the memory of the anterior life doesn't remain."

Gradually, Vanel, brutalized by grief, came to his senses. The sound of words that had initially struck his ears as mere noise, without leaving any intellectual impression, and which cradled his grief, ended up allowing him his true sensibility, and his grief died down to give way to admiration. What kind of beings were these two to debate, at such a moment, the greater or lesser chances of immortality?

Jeanne went on: "Don't forget, Father; as soon as I've ceased to live, to put yourself at the receiver of the apparatus we've constructed. It's so sensitive that if the soul can dispose of an atom of fluidic force, the machine will register it. You'll thus have the assurance that I'm not entirely dead, and I'll thus be able to help you, still, in your future work."

"I'll try," said Fortin. "But without you, I'll be very little. Why not make me the gift that you wanted to offer Marc Vanel?"

"*Because I love him!*"

The Invisible straightened up, while Fortin and Georges took a step backwards.

"You love me? You're mine, then! Now, I accept your superb offer. I couldn't double my spirit with an indifferent soul, but you love me! What is the union of two sexes in comparison with that of two pure minds? Come, my bride, my wife, give me your lips for our first and last carnal kiss."

"Not yet. Help us, Father! I'll help you with what remains of my energy."

At that moment, mental strength dominated physical strength in the dying woman: the last flicker of a flame ready to be extinguished. Her voice had become firmer and, lifting up her upper body, she drew Marc Vanel's head toward her and plunged into his eyes all the fluid power that remained to her.

Above her, Fortin, his eyes bulging, his hands open, concentrated all his magnetic effort on their two heads. Jeanne paled gradually; her eyes became dull and lost their radiance. By a supreme effort of her will, she drew Vanel's face toward her own, and their lips met.

Marc shuddered to the utmost depths of his being, and then, suddenly, the young woman's lips became icy. He had the impression that Jeanne had just expired in that kiss.

He allowed his forehead to fall upon the breast of the dead woman, and did not move again; he sensed the final frigid impression spread through her entire body.

Exhausted, Fortin, sitting down on the divan beside the corpse, contemplated it with avid attention.

For what was he hoping?

Further away, Georges Garnier, on his knees, was giving no other sign of life than the tears trickling down his face, without a muscle moving.

The glacial impression sensed by Homo-Deus dissipated slowly. A reaction set in; his blood gradually warmed up and a warmth rose to his brain, in a kind of fever; it seemed to him that a new force was born there, that a fluid of a previously unknown quality was inundating the cells. Thoughts that had not previously been his own surged forth. His remembrance was doubled, and he had memories that were not his, which were not of his sex.

A power stronger than his own will made him open his mouth and words that he had not thought emerged from his lips: "Victory! Father! Georges! I'm alive!"

Fortin, who was monitoring the movement of the needle of the soul-transmission apparatus, leapt forward. His eyes were ablaze with enthusiasm. He seized Marc in his arms and hugged him to his heart. For the first time in his life, his eyes moistened.

"Oh, Marc—my daughter is resuscitated in you!"

Georges had taken possession of one of Vanel's hands and kissed it. On the threshold, Frédéric—who had arrived, breathless, in quest of news—rubbed his eyes, wondering if he were seeing things.

"Yes," Homo-Deus went on. "It really is me, Marc Vanel, it's *us*. Oh, there will be fine days yet for terrestrial science..." He resumed: "Yes, I'm now a formidable duality, and I sense that two intelligences are fused in my brain. It will doubtless require a few days for complete harmony to reign between us. But what problems the two of us are going to resolve!" He took Fortin's hand. "Henceforth, my dear Master, let me call you Father. As for you, Georges, what do you want to be to us?"

"What I've always been: Jeanne's servant."

"As for me," said Frédéric, "I don't really understand what I'm seeing and hearing, but I'll always be part of the household."

"Don't try to understand, my dear Fred. Give us all your devotion, as you were devoted to the One who lives again in me."

And, moving forward, he revealed the body lying on the divan."

"Dead!" cried the faithful servant—and had to lean on the wall in order not to fall over.

"Dead?" repeated Vanel, in a vibrant voice. "No. One does not die here! What would be the divine value of humanity and love if they did not triumph over death?"

XI. Toward the Summits

Order has been restored to the Red Nest.

After having discussed the course to follow, the three men decided to continue settling their affairs without recourse to the law. The noise of the gunshots had not attracted anyone's attention; the house is isolated and the park large enough for the sound not to reach the nearest neighbor.

After the catastrophe that has just occurred, Fortin has decided to go traveling for some time. That is also the intention of Marc Vanel, who has political concerns in Russia and Asia. He will go with him, and Georges Garnier, who does not want to quit Jeanne—whose soul Homo-Deus has assimilated—will accompany them.

An entire grandiose plan has germinated in the brain of Homo-Deus-Jeanne-Fortin. They desire the emancipation of the world and an end to fratricidal wars; thanks to the invisibility that Homo-Deus will share with his companions, they will thwart all the conspiracies of diplomatic politicians, the leaders and parasites of society.

"When shall we leave?" asked Fortin.

"The day after tomorrow," said Homo-Deus. "I need that time to realize the millions we've recuperated; I need to transfer them to Asian banks in order for us to have them accessible."

After a pause, he continued: "Our first stop will be Russia. If we can bring about an effective alliance between China and Russia, that's nearly four hundred million people who will stand up against old Europe. India will awaken; its closer contact with the young world will permit it to establish parallels and to be counted. There, too, it will be necessary to spread progress and enlightenment in floods. A people enmired for thousands of years in an exuberant fantastic mythology will be difficult to bring back to reason and verity; we'll reach that end by awakening the idea of independence among the Hindus. I've attracted followers in the past even among the Brahmins and fakirs.

"Woe to the poor in spirit! No ridiculous sentimentality! Intelligence and work must be masters, but it's necessary to do everything possible and even the impossible to diminish the number of the ignorant. Everything in terrestrial life cries out to us: Woe to the weak!" It's necessary to diminish the number of the weak. Will we resolve the problem of happiness for all? I don't think so—but it's noble and great to try. We ought to: we're marvelously equipped for it.

"Perhaps we'll see the result ourselves! But *He* will see it!"

"Who's *He*?" exclaimed Fortin and Georges.

"Our son: the one who will inherit our two conjugated intelligences, who will be, mentally, the son of Jeanne Fortin and Marc Vanel."

Two days later, the bodies of the three murderers and Jeanne's having been buried in the park, a large touring automobile, driven by Vanel himself, came to collect Fortin and Georges, who helped Frédéric, still weak but on the way to recovery, to climb aboard. He was hoisted up along with Mardruk, who offered his hand to his colleague in misfortune. Then Dr. Fortin locked the gate of the Red Nest for the first time, and took his place in the vehicle beside the young woman that Marc introduced to him.

"My fiancée, Mademoiselle Huguette de Virmile, Jeanne Fortin's cousin, who will soon be her wife and mine."

As they went past the post office in Saint-Cloud, Homo-Deus stopped and put two letters in the box. They were addressed to the Commissaires de Police of his quarter and Saint-Cloud, informing them of their departure and putting the two houses under the protection of the police. A considerable sum of money was enclosed with each letter to ensure the surveillance.

Then, at top speed, the huge red automobile, with the pilgrims—Homo-Deus, the radiant Huguette, Dr. Fortin, Frédéric, Mardruk and Georges Garnier—headed toward the East, where the Sun was rising:

the Sun, which, tomorrow would rise, in the course of their journey toward the light, over the fraternal steeples of the cathedrals of Strasbourg and Cologne, over the Rhine, the river of the bloody beard with the imbecilically disputed banks;

the Sun, which would soon illuminate Moscow for them, dreaming around Lenin's tomb, standing up like a religious altar in front of the palace of the Kremlin, more radiant for peoples than its famous antique golden cupolas;

the Sun, which would offer the newcomers its flamboyant and joyous host, the source of life, in Constantinople, in an unforgettable communion of the lips of Homo-Deus and Huguette, resplendent with love and the enchantments of the Bosphorus;

THE SUN, which, in a few months, eternal and almost indifferent, the nearest of the millions of suns scattered in infinity, would shine its lamp, in India, over that egalitarian, amicable group of rich and poor, humble and privileged, ascending toward the summits, in the course of a magical voyage, of the most vertiginous and most inaccessible slopes of the Himalaya and the Ideal.

It is necessary to have a taste for summits. It is necessary that, disdaining frontiers, abolishing them by the union of peoples determined no longer to sent to be massacred in the great national abattoirs, the poets, the thinkers and the orators of progress—the precursors, courageously scaling the mountain in spite of the smiles, the insults and the threats—will raise up, tomorrow, on the summits that are lost in the clouds of a petty globe in which human beings are still killing one another, and never be extinguished again, this humanity, torches of peace and love.

Paris, 1924

KILL THE OLD, ENJOY!

BOOK ONE: A WAR-HERO AND PARRICIDE

I. A Boss who wants to have Complete Control

In every great city, certain quarters are singularized by specialties. In Paris, Grenelle has that of metallurgy. One sees numerous factories there producing all the equipment concerned with telegraphy, heating, electricity and locomotion. There is not, certainly, the intensive and formidable fabrication of the agglomerations of Saint-Etienne or Creusot, but at Grenelle, a very active portion of the iron and steel industry employs thousands of workers.

The Aubert-Coutan Company, founded in 1904 by Firmin Aubert, the father of Antoine Aubert, the present owner, the associate of Sixte Coutan, was in 1923 one of the oldest and most prosperous in the arrondissement. The factory of automobile components and small machinery occupied, in good years and bad, six hundred workers.

Between the two associates the work was thus divided: Antoine Aubert, a man of the métier, was principally occupied with the day-to-day running of the factories, and Sixte Coutan with external affairs, the quest for and the augmentation of orders, publicity, etc.

The factory occupied a vast rectangle in the Rue des Entrepreneurs; the property was terminated on the edge of the Quai de Javel[37] by a rather elegant detached building; it served as a habitation for Antoine and his son Etienne, a hero of the five-year war, with several citations and the Croix de Guerre, now liberated from military servitude and murder, one of the eight hundred thousand Chevaliers de la Légion d'honneur. (The inflation of the red ribbon equals that of banknotes, but honor and money are going down and down.)

That detached building, separated from the factory buildings by a long set of railings, had a side door opening on to a small and neat garden behind the proprietorial abode, the principal entrance of which was on the Quai de Javel. Another gate, tall and beautiful, with two battens and two lateral doors, gave

---

[37] The Quai de Javel is now known as the Quai André-Citroën, after the car manufacturer whose factory actually stood on the site attributed to the fictitious Aubert-Coutan factory in the present novel.

263

access to a broad sandy driveway going around the master's dwelling, leading to the garage, situated to one side and invisible from the Quai.

Half past six—corresponding to eighteen-thirty in regulation terminology—had just chimed on the factory clock. The workers had all abandoned their tools and quit the workshops half an hour earlier.

Antoine Aubert was in his office, in the company of a tall man dressed in blue overalls, like those mechanics wear, while the boss was settled in his armchair.

"So," said the latter, getting to his feet, "I won't get a definitive response today?"

"Wait a little longer, my dear Lafon. You know that Coutan promised to be here at six. He must have been delayed."

"Your associate is doing everything possible, it seems to me, to avoid concluding this business. It requires all the devotion I have for you, Monsieur Aubert, to prevent me from taking my invention elsewhere, to a rival company."

"Thank you, Louis. It's certain that Coutan doesn't look at this contract with a favorable eye, but I've explained to him that it's in our interest to make a deal with you first, and all your comrades thereafter. Between your two employers, my dear friend, there's a profound difference of opinion. I, as you know, Lafon, have always lived with the workers; I've handled the iron; I'm a craftsman; I can see the advantages and disadvantages. Because of that, I understand that workers ought to benefit from the enterprise whose success is, to some extent, their making. That participation in the profits will create competition among them, make them more interested in their work, improving it and finding means of making it more efficient, by unearthing, like you, inventions that merit consideration.

"Yes, that's my opinion. Coutan, however, considers the industry to be first and foremost a source of profits for its shareholders; he only sees the brutal financial returns, and the manual labor carried out by human hands is considered by him as mechanical work. According to him, a worker has no need to think. *Think? About what? Let him do what can't yet be done by machines, but don't let him imagine that he's anything but a machine himself.* By proposing to Coutan that we pay ten thousand francs for your invention and give you a share of the returns, I'm completely overturning his biases. But he'll come round to it. It's necessary that he does—and to all the rest, too."

"Undoubtedly, undoubtedly, Monsieur Aubert, but you must understand that I can't wait indefinitely. It's necessary to reach a conclusion. Today is the fifth of April. I'll wait until the end of the month—but if I don't have a favorable response by then, consider our conversation today as giving notice of my departure."

Monsieur Aubert did not have time to respond. The door of the office had opened softly. A pretty young woman had heard the worker's final words. Advancing swiftly toward the desk, she said: "Well, I've arrived just in time." She turned toward Aubert and added: "Yes, it's me. Sixte wasn't able to come, and as this business annoys my husband, he's sent me in his stead." She turned back to Lafon. "You're putting a knife to our throat, then? Pay up or I go? Well, get lost, my friend. We won't keep you. And you tolerate his language, Antoine? But my dear Aubert, the Coutans still count here!"

Antoine Aubert had stood up. Nonplussed at first by that flood of words, he interrupted. "My dear friend, you're interfering with matters that you don't understand. We'll discuss it seriously with your husband, who is my associate, as I haven't forgotten. For today, your intervention is, to say the least, unnecessary, and I beg my old comrade Louis Lafon to disregard it."

"What? What?" stammered the young woman. "You talk to me like that, Antoine?"

"Would you like to go in there? I'll explain later, my dear friend." Drawing the svelte prettiness away, gently but firmly, he pushed her into a room adjacent to the office and then came back.

Lafon, in his blue overalls, was quivering with anger. Aubert patted him on the shoulder.

"Henceforth, it's a question of honor and the future for me. It's necessary that reason holds sway over fantasy, if the association isn't to be broken, for I now regret no longer being the sole master. I wanted to become a great factory owner instead of the petty manufacturer that we were in my father's time. That's where ambition gets you."

"Don't regret anything, Monsieur Aubert. It's necessary to move with the times." He laughed and added: "And that's what we workers are doing, too."

"And that's justice. Come on, my old Lafon, I'll see you soon. I hope to have good news to give you shortly.

He showed the worthy workman to the door, and parted from him with a cordial handshake.

Then, anxiously, he went into the room where Josette Coutan was waiting for him—a kind of retreat where private or very intimate business was conducted. There was a small eighteenth-century desk, a large divan and four Louis XV armchairs; on the mantelpiece there was a Clodion terracotta and two candlesticks.

Sprawled on the divan, Josette Coutan, very modern with a tomboyish appearance, her black hair cut very short and neatly over the shaven nape of her neck, was twisting her sleeve furiously. Antoine Aubert, plump and good-natured, came to sit down beside her and took her hand.

"You're angry with me, then, Jo?"

"Of course I am. Such an insult, in front of a worker."

"It's not for want of asking you not to get involved with factory matters, which only concern me and your husband. Content yourself with emptying him out."

"Oh, that's you all over! If I'm ruining Coutan, you laugh about it, and it amuses you, but if I put my nose in your office, that displeases you. All the same, I don't regret what I said to that Lafon. Yes, let him get out, with his superior airs. Good riddance."

"Do you know what would happen if Lafon left the factory at the end of the month? All the workers would follow him."

"Get away! You'll swallow anything!"

"I'm sure of it. A rival company, which wants to expand its manufacturing, would take them on immediately. Your husband is skillful at winkling out orders, I'll give him that; he can't make things, but he brings work in."

"Today, that's almost everything." After a pause, as he remained impassive, she said: "After all, it's humiliating for us to give in."

"There's a means of settlement," said Aubert, coldly. "Let's each take our share. I estimate the value of the factory at eight million. I'm ready to pay him half."

"Really?" said Josette, amazed. "Four million?"

"Neither more nor less. Think about it, Jo. What you want, your husband will want. Seven years ago, during the war, when he brought me two million, the enterprise was only half-fortunate. Doubling his capital, after pocketing considerable profits, which you've played your part in spending, isn't a bad deal."

Josette thought about it, to the extent that she could. Fundamentally, the factory didn't please her. She kept company with exceedingly chic dolls, whose husbands were vaguely "in business," and those worldly households lived on an income of five or six hundred thousand a year. Her husband, so artful, so clever and so enterprising, could make whatever he liked, especially with an initial capital of four million.

"And you'll carry on?" she said, already decided.

"Certainly—my son Etienne will help me. Is it yes, then Jo?"

"And afterwards—the two of us?"

"You'll come from time to time, when you spare me a thought."

"Yes, I see now—it's a matter of breaking it off between us. Pig!"

"No. If I want to separate myself from Sixte, it has a great deal to do with my affection for you. Your husband adores you; he listens to all your caprices and acts in accordance with them. If, one day, he learns that he's been cuckolded, especially by me, it would be a terrible blow for the factory."

"That, for want of other scruples, is a consideration that's stopping you a trifle belatedly. As for me, if I've deceived my husband, it's the fault of the war. Mobilized, he was on the Eastern front, while I was mobilized to your factory. I've been weak."

"Don't reproach yourself, my dear. I'm the guilty one. Your temperament did the rest."

"You arranged our love in your own fashion. Anyway, we'll see what follows. Four million, you said?"

"Would you like to see the books?"

"I don't understand any of your figures. Do you know that you haven't kissed me yet this evening?"

"That's your fault. You wanted to talk business. Four million—think about that. Plus a hundred big blue bills for you, my little Jo."

II. Widowers who Remarry Don't Deserve to Be

The amorous relationship between Josette and Antoine Aubert dated from May 1918. In spite of what he believed, Aubert had not started it. Eleven years older than his associate, he had not given the slightest thought to Josette, an arrant coquette, who had always striven to provoke him by playing the flirt with him. Josette was then in the full exuberance of her beauty. The husband, always infatuated with his young wife, had only seen playfulness in her lively treatment of an associate at least twenty years old than her. For the spouse blinded by Eros, she was a child teasing her Papa. So when, in a surge of patriotic enthusiasm, emulation and vainglory, he had renounced the tranquil post where he was tucked away to leave for the Eastern Front, he confided his young wife to the care of Aubert, a widower of thirteen years, after the wife he had adored was carried away by a cardiac arrest, leaving him with a small boy of six.

The industrialist, entirely given over to work and money, had placed his heir with an aunt in Touraine, and then the lycée, destining him for the École Polytechnique. Too young when the war broke out, Etienne remained at the factory at first, with his father. It was the only free time he was to enjoy. In 1916, at the age of nineteen, he left to play his own part in the immense slaughter. Having passed from the artillery into the air force, he won the Croix de Guerre after three citations, and in October 1918, the red ribbon. That is quite an achievement, when one is scarcely more than twenty years old.

The more or less tender liaison between Antoine and Josette had, therefore, been going on for five years, and was sometimes far too much for Aubert, ever faithful to the memory of the lost saint, adored as she deserved to be. What was the frivolous Josette compared to that perfect wife and mother? The excellent widower had supported it, until the end of the war, with resignation, for he was certain that his pretty protégée, left to her own devices, would have fallen into easy gallantry with the Allied combatants, French, English and especially American.

The affair of the Lafon patent was, therefore, an opportunity for which he had been waiting for a long time—not to mention that there was another reason for breaking with Josette. A friend of his wife had returned from the province where she had married. Her husband had been killed in the vicinity of Verdun. A young widow, as rich and pretty as she was good and intelligent, Madame Jousselin had conquered the industrialist with the infinite, sovereign, prodigious charm that emanated from her—and he did not displease her.

The frequentation of Aline Jousselin rendered Josette's intense libertinage and silly gossip even more insupportable. Aline's ten-year-old daughter, an exquisite child, had all of her mother's character. Was not an instinctive aversion to be feared on the part of the little girl for the man suspected of wanting to steal her beloved mother from her? No, Ulette, who had befriended him warmly, gaily threw her arms around his neck when he went to visit.

One day, Ulette put on a blue sash and gravely asked: "Monsieur Antoine Aubert, do you take for your wife Madame Alice Jousselin, here present?"

"Yes," Antoine hastened to say.

"And you, Maman, do you consent to take for your husband Monsieur Antoine Aubert?"

"That requires reflection," said the seductive widow, laughing.

The sentiments of a widower in the process of wanting to marry again were there on the evening when Josette Coutan reminded her husband's associate, her paternal lover, of his lack of urgency in soliciting kisses.

III. An Adorable Octopus

Meanwhile, Josette returned by automobile to the conjugal domicile. She was thinking and calculating, in her minuscule head framed with black hair, cut short over the nape, which covered her forehead and descended flatly to either side, advancing over each cheek with an enticing curl, while blowing out large opaline puffs of smoke, tomboyishly, from an Egyptian cigarette.

Four million! Four million! That's surely better than continuing this stupid life. When I think about all the fuss I had to make this year in order to go to Deauville with the Marchands, those show-offs and braggarts, ready for anything, who probably only have a hundred thousand francs to their name and spend twice that per year by running a bluff that brings in big rewards! My husband isn't stupid; with four million, he could roll them all over. But I need to convince him. And then, Antoine might change his mind. What a softy with his workers! Instead to making them use my method of a big stick...Aubert's got the wind up, that's obvious. All the more reason to let go... Four million! Oh, with that I could make them dance...and then again, I've had my fill of Antoine. Less amusing than a telegraph pole, he's getting old...I've noticed that several times... As for his son Etienne, oh, I was forgetting him. He keeps me waiting, but attacks hard, him, solid as a post...and then, I'll always have, via him, a hand in the house. Oh, Père Antoine, if you're playing the pig with me, you'll pay me for it...

She broke into song: "*Etienne, Etienne, Prends le mien! Rend la tienne!*"

Four million! Twenty seven years old and good teeth! It'll be a laugh...provided that my husband doesn't resist! Go on—has he ever wanted anything other than to give me pleasure? And then, he'll work; it's necessary that he work, otherwise, I'd always be on the go or on my...Froutt! Get a move on, old man, it's your age and your sex. Do Business, with a capital B, big Business! It's in schemes, slippery operations of luxury and bluff that one fishes up millions as easily as lobsters... Four million! Four million! Four million! A big blowout!

They lived in the Rue Mozart, in a kind of town house with three tenants.

On the ground floor was Georges Moudy, the author of a volume of blank, amorphous and colorless verses, *Silences*, and a surrealist novel, *La Lueur du Diable*, winner of the Prix Goncourt. After those two births, he was resting, like God after having created the world, on the laurels that were heaped upon him in the newspapers and magazines by columnists, critics and other runts of letters. Prematurely balding, meticulously clean-shaven and thin, he had an annual income of thirty thousand francs, which, in these times of inflation and the high cost of living, permitted him to live modestly and pay at the Café de la Rotonde in Montparnasse for the consumption of his incense-bearers and to let himself be tapped for a fifty-franc note for every printed eulogy.

On the first floor lived Comtesse du Rouvre de Molkoët, born Anaïs Roupiot. After having been a sub-Prefect in Brittany, his province, her husband had recently died as a senior administrator at the Ministry of Public Education and Religion. Her legs open all her life, having been able to underpin her gallant adventures with the fortune and salary of the functionary, at sixty-nine she had pretentions to fresh flesh and subsidized a young actress at the Odéon. A Voltairean and revolutionary, she allowed it to be seen occasionally, but she remained alert, tidy and well-made, youthful in her mannerisms but full of nobility.

The second floor was the Coutans'. Sixte, a man of taste, had furnished it in the modernist style, with a flair for harmony and comfort: an ensemble of bright tones, agreeable to behold, in a spectrum sympathizing with Josette's beauty, of which she took full advantage.

The entrance to the small building did not permit the introduction of an automobile. The car was kept in a garage nearby.

Josette Coutan found her husband sunk in a vast and comfortable English armchair. He was reading *Le Temps* and yawning over an article by Paul Souday.[38] Getting up and coming to meet his wife, he said: "There you are, Jo. Finally! I was beginning to get worried. The wild beasts of the factory haven't devoured you?"

"You know that I'm a good lion-tamer. All the same, another time, you can run your own errands. It's noxious, that odor of a mixture of oil and soap. I still feel like retching."

"And Antoine?"

"He was in conference with Lafon. Nothing to be done—he's making a deal with him. It'll be necessary to give in...unless..."

"Unless what?"

"You know, my darling, this scrap iron is too dirty; it smells too bad."

"But I never set foot in the workshops."

"That's not the point, my dear. You're too elegant, too fine and delicate, the object of my adoration, so active and rapid in your intelligence, to live in that environment. The Comtesse du Rouvre de Moëlkoët, who I met the other day in a dance hall where she was giving tea to her lovely protégée, said to me: 'Your husband's aristocratic face clashes with his factory in Grenelle.'"

"Do I really have the honor of pleasing that old camel?"

"The old camel has good connections. That might be useful. But that's not the point. I think the role of factory owner—half-owner—is beneath you."

---

[38] Paul Souday (1869-1929) was a noted literary critic; he fulfilled that function at *Le Temps* from 1912 until his death.

"I'd certainly rather be a Minister. It doesn't last as long, but it pays much better."

"Why not? Later…who knows?"

While talking, she had taken off her dainty hat and coat, and sat down on her husband's knee, seductively.

"My darling, you ought to give up the scrap iron and *do business*. It would be more in your line, and you'd earn far more. Look at the Bidards, the Marchands and even Toto—you can see they have plenty of free time, seem never to have any worries, and yet they make a lot of money along the way."

"The Bidards yes—not Toto, who's always broke."

"Because he hasn't got the initial funds—but you, with your cash?"

"I've invested in a factory. It's necessary to carry on."

"But what if Aubert wanted to dissolve the partnership?"

"That would be different—in fact, I'd like to do something else."

"Aubert's offering us four million for our share. Are we going to accept it?"

Nestling against her husband, with her two rosy buttocks, of whose charm she was very well aware, in the hollow of her husband's lap, exteriorizing the fluid of her sex, interiorizing the awakening and the frisson of the male, she captured him, winding her bare arms around him To an observer entering without being perceived, some invisible satyr penetrating on a whim without betraying his presence, she would have been reminiscent of an adorable octopus.

We retain in our bodies a little of all the animals of which we are the most perfect mixture and result—our nose, for example, is a bird's beak. Don't some individuals evoke a wolf or a jackal, Clemenceau a tiger, others a dog, a beast of burden or a lion?

Josette, like any pretty woman, awoke the idea of a voracious octopus, the attractive chasm of which is hidden in the center, served by the snare of the navel, the forward bastions of the breast and those of the rear; for tentacles, the bewitching arms and the magical legs. The octopus has only one orifice, and the woman has three. The octopus is horrible with its suckers, which such the blood and the life out of you; Eve is molded of lilies and roses, of ideal flesh. Adam, enchanted, always goes toward her, toward amour, ruination and sometimes death, captured by the smile and the snares of the eternal seductress.

Josette, on Sixte's knees, as if naked beneath her short, light dress, her hairy and perfumed flower hidden between her Tanagrean thighs, drawing desire magnetically toward it, with one arm around her husband's shoulder and the other hand caressing his cheek, advanced an amorous mouth toward her husband's, momentarily calm and indifferent: Sangsue and Delilah.[39]

The adorable octopus repeated: "Aubert's offering us four million for our share. Tell me, big man, are we going to take it?"

---

[39] I have left *Sangsue* [leech] untranslated in order to conserve the scabrous pun.

Tranquilly, Sixte Coutan replied: "It's eight o'clock, my dear. I'm hungry."

"Me, too—but I thought you'd invited Toto."

"We can't wait for him indefinitely. To the table, Josette! We'll talk about the four million later."

They went into the dining room. Standing up, the valet waited to read out the menu. He made the newspaper disappear immediately.

"Serve, René," said Josette. "If Monsieur Thomas Keysar comes, he'll catch up."

The door opened. Two young men came in, both with red ribbons in their buttonholes.

"One setting more!" cried Thomas Keysar, joyfully. "I met Etienne and I've brought him along. I've got a box at the Casino de Paris. We'll go after dinner, all right?"

The belated guest was a fellow of medium height and impressive physique, Thomas Keysar. Very well-versed in the practices of occultism, graphology and palm-reading, he had written a small book, pillaging ideas that were not new, but skillful pastiches of Péladan, Stanislas de Guaita and others. His visage served him well in those occult practices: a Mephisthophelean mask illuminated by magnificent yellow eyes—at the Café de la Rotonde he was known as the golden-eyed Caesar. A juvenile tone occasionally contradicted his infernal laughter.

He was correctly dressed, his shoes always polished, his linen impeccable, but an artful eye would have been able to discern in the detail of his costume the artifice inspired by penury. He had slipped into a daily paper as a literary critic, and that gave him a platform, an alibi and the prestige of a façade, the appearance of making his living with his pen, when he was nothing but the envoy of the books that he resold.

A dozen satirical portraits of ancient celebrities in an ephemeral periodical, the *Canard Sans Nom*, had made him briefly fashionable in a vague microcosm of arts and letters. It was entitled *Les Morts de Demain*. Almost everyone, beginning with Hercules, who had not accomplished his famous labors, Homer, who had never written the epics of the *Iliad* and the *Odyssey*, and Shakespeare, who acted in and appropriated Bacon's or Rutland's dramas, had stolen their fame, having merely signed the works of genius bought from poor devils for a few sous. Others had made their way by marrying rich courtesans.

It was unproductive blackmail. For artists, everything is advertising. Poets are only known and slightly esteemed because they are thought to be pederasts. All that blackening of character, Bohemian life and ink composed for Thomas Keysar a shady notoriety, and earned him, along with the books sent by editors and sold on for twenty sous apiece, the dedications erased or the page torn out, to a local second-hand book dealer, or the occasional box at the theater or the cinema.

That effortful existence was nothing but a continual seesaw between embarrassment and strokes of luck, blackmail or publicity. There were dupes, too, on occasion: a superstitious or weak-minded woman on whom he cast a spell and exploited to the best of his ability, and the profits of chiromancy.

That was only slightly the case with the Coutans, however; Thomas Keysar, very cheerful and lively, in addition to his magic tracks, pleased Sixte and Josette, who treated him as a friend. He did not take too much advantage of them, knowing how to remain moderate, and, no matter how much difficulty he was in, he never borrowed more than a paper louis from Coutan. He thus avoided the appearance of a social parasite. Furthermore, the fellow was one of the eight hundred Chevaliers de la Légion d'honneur.

His companion, invited by a fluke, was Etienne Aubert—yes, the son of the factory owner, who, naturally, by virtue of that fact, experienced no embarrassment in the home of his father's associate. And Josette was their mistress.

Tall and strong, Etienne had something hard and brutal in the expression in his gray eyes that contrasted with his father's, which were sympathetic and benevolent. He had acquired authoritarian habits in the war and in the Air Force, and an absolute disregard for social conventions.

"We have a hare sent by Bidard today," said Josette

"I knew that," said Thomas Keysar. "He's been hunting in the Poitou, and the bag was so heavy that the guests carried away fifty kilos of venison each. There hasn't been a shoot at Sauvageac for eight years and the game is pullulating."

"That reminds me of a night in the trenches," Etienne said. "I believe it was..."

"You've already told us that one. You mistook rabbits for the enemy and ordered blanket fire; all your barbed wire was cut up by bullets."

"That's right," said Etienne, ill-humoredly. "But why cut me off in order to appropriate it?"

"Your heroic actions? To replace mine?"

"That's true," said Josette. What did you do in the war, Toto? You never talk about it."

"For good reason. There's nothing bellicose about me, you see, and I didn't have the slightest motive to hate anyone foreign, so there was nothing to tell me to get myself stupidly killed for reasons far beyond my comprehension. My thinness and pale complexion served me well. I played the invalid and avoided the abattoir until 1917. Then it was necessary to march—but not far. I employed influences so well that I was dismissed definitively as unfit."

"You ought to say dishonest," snorted Etienne.

"If you wish. I have no vanity."

Coutan and Aubert looked at one another.

They remembered the suffering they had endured, and those former heroes by obligation could not help admiring, disdainfully, the man who had found the means to escape it.

"I couldn't do that," said Etienne, swelling his chest, "with an athletic torso like mine."

"And Sixte's." said Josette proudly. "It's agreeable all the same not to be a shirker."

"Oh well," sniggered Keysar. "I've failed often enough since."

"By the way, Etienne," said Coutan, to change the subject, which had acquired a certain chill, "Have you heard your dear father talking about wanting to break our partnership?"

"Oh, that's what it's about? For some time, the Old Man's had a funny look. I wondered what he was ruminating."

"Yes," said Coutan. "He wants to give the workers a share of the profits, and there's also Lafon's invention. I think all that's idiotic."

"If I were running things," Etienne said, clenching his fists, "If I were the boss, the workers would be tamed. Those swine were earning enormous wages while we, the combatants, were risking our lives at every minute. I'd teach them to take an interest in the profits."

"So, to avoid falling out and quarreling," Coutan went on, "I'll gladly agree to take out my share. And after that, I'll do business."

"There, at least, you'll have elbow room, my dear," said Josette. "What about you, Etienne, do you like the life of a factory owner?"

"Yes," said the young man, dryly. "I love the factory. I have the temperament of a leader of men—but softness, oh no! *Look out!* as the *poilus* used to say, and if the workers go on strike, bring out the machine guns..."

"Bravo, Etienne!" said Josette, blowing him a kiss. "I like masterful men."

"Unfortunately," sighed Thomas Keysar, insidiously, "Etienne isn't the master, and his father's still young, as stout as an oak. You aren't anywhere near to being the master at the Quai de Javel. Give me your hand, Etienne, and I'll read your future."

"Go to the Devil with your foolery" he retorted—although his *l* had a suggestion of a *c* about it.

"You're wrong, Etienne," said Josette gravely. "In that regard, Toto's a marvel."

"Yes, I know: he'll tell me: *Macbeth, you shall be king.* When, though? In forty years?"

"For my part," said Coutan, who believed that he was making a decision that his wife had actually suggested to him, "I'll go to tomorrow to have things out with your father, and if he persists in his ideas. I'll take out my share: four million."

"Four million!" repeated Thomas Keysar—and a wild gleam lit up his golden eyes. "*Zut!* Four million. That's also your father's share, Etienne."

275

"Yes, plus the factory and the machinery."

Thomas Keysar, the magician, leaned toward the young man's ear. "Etienne Macbeth, it's necessary to want it."

"Well," said Coutan, "it's necessary to get a move on if we're going to the Casino de Paris. The show is idiotic, it's said, but in the splendid décor there are a hundred naked women..."

"Completely," concluded Keysar. "Apart from little cache-sexes of roses or feathers, which, according to the dances and the poses, expose a few of the hairs of all those nests of pleasure."

"Nude or lewd, we're on our way," said Josette, laughing.

IV. The Brain of Montparnasse and the World

On emerging from the Casino de Paris, the quartet—Coutan and his wife, Etienne Aubert and Thomas Keysar—consulted one another. Where should they finish off the evening? Josette, excited even more than the males by all the feminine nudes, wanted to continue the party.

"I'd like nothing better," said Etienne. "Montmartre's run out of imagination somewhat—always the same songs and the same singers. Anyway, it's midnight; there's no longer anything but cellars and dives where one can be bored to death with champagne at a hundred francs a bottle and ten francs for roasted nuts.

"Well, the time has come," said Sixte. "Toto's always boasting about his Rotonde. Show it to us, my dear Keysar."

They piled into the Coutans' auto, bound for Montparno.

In the same way that certain quarters seem reserved for certain industries, there are certain points in the brain of Paris where the spirituality of the capital seem to be concentrated. In 1923, that was still Montparnasse. The mind of Paris has evolved, along with its morality and everything else; it has amalgamated, among so many brutalities and so much foreign intelligence that it has become global without progressing.

Where are the snows of yesteryear, the mind that reigned in 1880 from the faubourg Montmartre to the Opéra, the brilliant epoch of Aurélian Scholl, the Tortoni, Le Brébant, the Café Anglais and the Maison Dorée? The "brain of the world" moved to the Butte, by courtesy of Rodolphe Salis, to Montmartre, to the theater and cabaret of the Chat Noir, to the Café de la Nouvelle Athènes, into the lofty studios perched in the wilderness, and on the far side of the butte, into a den with the appearance of a little country chapel, the Lapin Agile—because of its sign, painted by the caricaturist André Gill…but time effaces all glories.

Today, the Mind of Paris has no domicile, sparse premises, undiscoverable apartments, always running in the streets, tracked by boors. For want of a dwelling worthy of it, there are still a few talking-shops where tongue-lashings are handed out, to give the illusion of wit. One of those evil artistic and literary spots, the most fashionable—until when?—is the Café de la Rotonde, at the corner of the Boulevard Montparnasse and the Boulevard Raspail.

It did not have for its founder an ironist like Salis, the charlatan of the Chat Noir, but a worthy kind of liquor merchant, debonair and benevolent. Libion, without the truculent verve of the Montmartrean cabaretier, welcoming and obliging, had the skill to retain a few gangs of young men pregnant with novelties. Before 1912 Lenin and Trotsky often dreamed sitting at its tables, editing some minuscule Bolshevik newspaper there, which they printed themselves on cigarette paper and sent to Russia inside plaster casts of Tsar Nicholas II, in order to set fire to the old edifice. And they did it. The painters who were regulars at the establishment exhibited ludicrous canvases at the Rotonde. If Libion had had any inkling of the future fashionability of decadent daubs, the imbecile would have made a fortune.[40]

During the Great War, the Rotonde was a refuge for the cosmopolitan youth who came to France to study arts, letters or the law. There were police raids on suspicion of espionage, and poor old Libion was obliged on several occasions to see his establishment closed by order, and almost always, in addition, labored under the threat of consignment to the army. Since then, the Rotonde, considerably enlarged, has become primarily a restaurant and dance hall. In expectation of the vogue moving elsewhere, the clientele has already changed. Some have emigrated to the Café du Dôme opposite, others to the Café de Parnasse.

In the car, the quartet talked about the show they had just seen, the plastic and decorative revue, and Thomas Keysar said that one could still pick flowers from living gardens in the corners of the Folies-Bergères, the Casino de Paris and the Moulin Rouge: supine young women with their legs in the air, the stems of whose blossoms were plunged into two natural vases; original bouquets for the buttonhole or the corsage. There was loud laughter in the auto.

When the Coutans, Etienne Aubert and Thomas Keysar went into the café, the Rotonde was packed on the ground floor and the first, the booths and the dance floor alike. They went back down and found seats with great difficulty. There were extraordinary Japanese faces there, with hooded eyes, the savage masks of Sioux Indians, Malays, Egyptians and Russians, specimens of the humanity of all lands, the most picturesque types and the most emphatic.

Thomas Keysar called out to a pretty negress: "You're still here, so late, Aïcha?"[41]

"I'm waiting for Rinaldo. He owes me for fifteen posing sessions, and promised to have the money for me this evening."

"If you pose as a rabbit," Etienne put in, "would you like me to go home with you, on payment of the fee?"

"Is this Monsieur a friend of yours, Thomas? Doubtless he doesn't know who he's talking to. Inform him, if you please."

---

[40] Victor Libion founded the Café de la Rotonde in 1911. He often accepted paintings as pledges by impoverished artists unable to pay their bill and hung them on the walls; he could, indeed, have made a fortune if he had known which ones to keep; Picasso and Modigliani were among his regulars.

[41] Aïcha Goblet was painted by several of the artists who frequented the Rotonde, including Modigliani and Tsuguharu Foujita. She appears as a character in André Salmon's novel *La Negresse du Sacré Coeur* (1920), and published her memoirs in the magazine *Mon Paris*. She danced on stage, sometimes naked, but also acted in serious dramas and did retain an impeccable reputation.

Keysar leaned toward Aubert. "A gaffe, my dear. Aïcha's not what you think. A model only, and a virgin."

"That's a joke!" said the young decorated boor, brutally, while Josette Coutan laughed at his setback. "If it's necessary to be a painter to see her pubic hair, as frizzy as hard wool, I can do as well as that." His gesture designated the canvases stuck on the walls, from the wainscot to the ceiling.

"I don't doubt it. Did you know that someone exhibited here a picture splattered by a donkey's tail?"

Josette cackled joyfully with affectation, in order to attract attention to herself, thinking that Etienne was neglecting her.

"By a donkey? And did it sell?"

"For a lot of money, my dear. It was signed Cézanne."

"The Master!" cried a voice. Some people stood up, greeting the new arrival. The individual in question, full of conceit, clad in an artist's smock that was brand new, and yet speckled with patches of every possible shade of blue and splashes of blood red, advanced negligently between the tables and shook the hands extended toward him. He stopped in front of the pretty negress.

"Are you waiting for Rinaldo, my beauty?" he said. "Don't waste your time here. He's not coming. I took him to Saint-Anne this afternoon."[42]

"He's mad," said the young negress. "That doesn't astonish me. He painted me with green hair and orange breasts."

"That's not a reason," Picasso said. "I've done you with a green Veronese cat, but I'm not mad."

"Perhaps," she said, showing her exceedingly white teeth in her brown mouth, "but you drive others mad."

Laughing like a gong, Picasso said: "So what? If no one can overtake me, it's stupid to follow me."

"Indeed!" cried Someone—at least, he had the attitude of being Someone—of about sixty: Guilleret, a member of the Institut, insulting the celebrated cubist. "What do you hope to get out of your challenges to common sense, Art and Beauty?"

"First of all, common sense has nothing to do with Art, and we've seen too much of Beauty. I want to rehabilitate ugliness. And if I made beauty, I'd die of starvation like you."

"I'm not dying of starvation—that's obvious from my appearance. There are still art-lovers whose heads retain intelligence, fortunately. If you wanted to, Picasso, you could be a great painter. Why depict horrors? Because you find people madder than you are to buy them, avid to run after innovators. Look what's happened to your pupil Rinaldo. Never mind, let your conscience rest. Sit down here, old man, and let's chat."

---

[42] The psychiatric hospital de Sainte-Anne, established by Napoléon III, had established a free Centre de Prophylaxie Mentale in 1922.

"My conscience, old fellow—for you're the old man—is a mad cow. If I leave her tranquil, she lets my painting alone. When Cubism has had it day, I'll invent Conism. In art, as in amour, the cone comes after the cube."[43]

"Bravo!" cried one of Guilleret's and Picasso's neighbors. "Keep up to date. Enough of the old game, Guilleret. Novelty, even idiotic! We've had enough of style, nature, beauty and women. We've had a bellyful of old masters."

"Yes," said the eccentric genius Picasso to Guilleret, laughing, not even sparing his partisans. "That's obvious from the old queer's backside."

"Down with the old!" cried another. "They're cluttering up the world. It's not enough to have kissed our chicks during the war—they don't have the decency to make way for us now, we who did the fighting in the meantime. It's the turn of those who saved the world, but the old men are still running it. They're the dirty swine who wanted the war, in order to get rid of the young men. We need the government of youth. We need to kill the old, to enjoy—not in our turn, but right away."

"He's right, you know," whispered Thomas Keysar in Etienne Aubert's ear, who shuddered.

The other went on: "After thirty, the mind and the body diminish more than they're augmented, and retreat more than they advance. The old occupy all the elevated situations, all the superior posts, all the highest stages, and youth, which wants enjoyment after having suffered in the trenches and the sky, remains an immense unemployed force.

"On all sides, the old contains us, dominates us and cuts our throats. Cambronne, get down from your horse, you old fraud, to say the word.[44] Already, one ace, Paul Raynal, in a sublime piece, *Le Tombeau sous l'arc de Triomphe*,[45] has put a father on his knees before his son, who has come home on leave from the front—yes, *on his knees*—to beg his pardon. Young people can't always regard their parents, stupidly, as demigods, as they did when they were small, or with the gaze of a dog looking at its master. The war and the victory have emancipated us; we've grown up. We are the masters of the war! Us!"

---

[43] The French *cône* [cone] is also the term used to refer to the mouth of a volcano.

[44] The "word of Cambronne," falsely attributed to the general of that name when he was surrounded at Waterloo and invited to surrender, was "Merde," which could be construed, depending on the way it was said, as the equivalent of either "Oh, shit!" or "Fuck off!" Victor Hugo started the literary fashion for using "the word of Cambronne" as a euphemism for any unprintable expletive.

[45] The cited three-act tragedy by Paul Raynal (1885-1971) had its première at the Comédie Française on 1 February 1924, so this reference is slightly anachronistic

"Death to the old!" howled Keysar, standing up. "To suppress them, quietly, let's put a glacial silence around the old, the night and the tomb in advance. It's up to us, friends, to use the intense advertisement, the you-scratch-my-back-and-I'll-scratch-yours, untiringly, of all the newspapers and all the magazines that we've invaded, as a swarm of ants falls upon a rich treasure. Unlimited publicity for us, the claps on the back of all the comrades for all. It's necessary to bring down the gerontocracy, to annihilate it, to destroy it. We've won the right to live, to live well, and to enjoy all that we've protected for five years with our breasts. It's necessary that the old don't get in our way, eating, breathing, living and fucking away our right to happiness, to wealth, to love—our right to everything."

"No more!" said Guilleret, the member of the Institut, getting up in his turn, brave and alert, his white moustache twitching.

Another group had just come in: the Painter of the Sun, Fabio Canti,[46] and another man, accompanied by a very pretty girl.

"They bore us, the old! Down with Guilleret!" howled twenty voices. "What's he coming here for, the immortal? Under the cupola! Into his cellar! Hang him! Throw him out! Out the door!"

Guilleret stood his ground in mettlesome fashion. "You want to throw me out! You know how to bark, but that's all."

"Calm down. Messieurs, calm down!" said two waiters, intervening. "What can we get you?"

"Reason and beauty!" cried Fabio Canti, on the threshold of the big room, raising his right arm like a Prophet

"Fabio Canti!" shouted Guilleret. "Fabio Canti! You've arrived in a timely fashion, my dear. At least there'll be two of us to stand up to these lunatics."

"We'll be three!" That was Picasso, surging forth in his turn, radiant in his multicolored smock, like some Olympian Jupiter come to calm the storm—and it calmed.

"Damnation!" said Etienne Aubert. "There's one who could replace the negress advantageously. What an adorable face, with her long black tresses! The face of a Madonna!"

"Etienne's decidedly amorous this evening. There's nothing extraordinary about that woman except that she's behind the times. She's a Botticelli. In any case, my dear, you could dissimulate your desires a little more when you're in society."

"Bah!" said the husband. "Pardon me, Josette, but Etienne has no need to be reticent with us. He's a bachelor. It's quite natural at his age."

---

[46] The painter Fabio Canti appears as a minor character in several of Champsaur's novels, rarely playing as significant a part as he does in this one. It is possible that the "Fabio Danti" mentioned once in the previous novel was intended to be him, but suffered a misprint.

"He's a boor," said Josette, dryly.

"I'm giving my opinion," replied Etienne, shrugging his shoulders.

The truth is that the hundred naked women at the Casino de Paris had excited him considerably, and he had drunk a little too much.

Meanwhile, peace having been reestablished, Picasso shook hands with Fabio Canti and Guilleret, and the man to whom he had just been introduced—"Monsieur Raynaud, the Commissaire de Police of the Grenelle quarter"—bowed to the pretty lady with the Botticelliesque hair, to whom he had also just been introduced—"Madame Jousselin"—ceded his place at the table to her, and went away triumphantly.

While a waiter hastened to ask the newcomers what they wanted to drink, the smiling Madame Jousselin said to Guilleret and Fabio Canti: "Messieurs Righters of Wrongs and Stupidities, you'll have a great deal to do in this evil place; the society seems a little too mixed to me."

"That's why I brought you here, my dear Madame," said Fabio Canti, "to satisfy your curiosity."

"What I've seen and heard," she replied, "justifies the idea that our friend the Commissaire has given me of artistic and social anarchy."

"Listen" said the Painter of the Sun. "There's a young poet I know. He's going to recite one of his productions for us."

In fact, at one of the nearby tables, a clean-shaven young man with shiny, pomaded, slicked back hair and a cold American expression—in order to appear very up-to-date—stood up and announced a modern poem: *Tall Factory Chimneys*.

"Good," said Guilleret. "He's going to pour smoke over us."

The poet coughed, cleared his throat, and with majesty of an oyster—which is to say, of a mouth from which a pearl is about to emerge—began, using long pauses to mark the end of each line of his amorphous work, with assonances here and there for rhymes.

> *Recklessly looming up beneath the autumnal cloud*
> *They are*
> *Three, and more further away, black, rigid and mute as*
> *Mountains;*
> *Intestinal tubes of the turgescent lair.*
> *Just as, untiringly, their plumes extend, curving and thinning,*
> *So, I, in my inclusive mind,*
> *Pour out recklessly an impure sexual dream,*
> *Colorless, with the reek of gum and eau de Javel,[47]*
> *Fecund.*

---

[47] Eau de Javel is a kind of bleach.

"Like you," put in a joker.
The poet, without blinking, continued more loudly:

Oh! you who, like me, dream of being,
By day or by night, perhaps—
No matter!—let's ejaculate!
I want no more of love, the orchid, the banana,
Nothing. And yet,
No matter! Still,
They are three, superb, black, rigid, and mute as
Sounds,
Or telegraph poles.

The poet sat down in the midst of bellows of enthusiasm from the cenacles.
"Well, Madame Jousselin, what do you think of the Rotonde?"
"It's a madhouse."
Meanwhile, at the quartet's table, Josette sighed. "I've had enough. It's worth the trouble of being seen, but that's all."
"The only interesting thing I've caught," said Etienne Aubert, becoming boorish again, sincerely and to annoy Josette, "is the pretty lady with the long black hair over there, with the little girl eyes. It's a pity she's not alone."
"What? Really!" exclaimed Madame Coutan, whose crystalline laughter rang out. "A hero like Etienne can't carry off his beauty in competition with two old monsters?"
At that moment, a customer who was dozing at a nearby table sat up straight and called the waiter. "Has Gottfried arrived?" The latter leaned over and winked in the direction of the table where Guilleret, Fabio Canti, Madame Jousselin and Monsieur Raynaud the Commissaire were. The customer got up immediately and the waiter went out behind him.
"A lover of narcotics," said the Commissaire de Police. "I'll point him out to my colleague. These drug dealers lead us in the devil of a dance. The more we arrest, the more there are."
"Business must be booming."
"I know that at least half the regulars here are habitual users of cocaine, morphine addicts, etheromaniacs or opium smokers. I can make verses, too:

Smoking rooms are very much in fashion
But coke dealers are those who really cash in."

Madame Jousselin was listening to the conversations going on around her.
A dreamer with bulging eyes was saying: "I'm working on a symphony in which I want to put the present soul of the Globe. The sounds of the overture mingle with the cacophonies of a jazz band, evoking the United States preaching

the disarmament of its neighbors, respect for the Bible and the Dollar, the mewling of Japanese kotos and the moaning of shamisens singing the horror of volcanoes and earthquakes, Italian accordions attributing Fiume to Italy, and German violins, under the thrusts of Wagnerian bows, sighing after universal peace. And then, for you know that by means of a microphone enclosed in a steel box and then dropped to the bed of the ocean, after having linked it to a telephone place in a launch, one can collect the noises, and even the language, of fish, recognizing their species and quantity, I'll add the maritime symphony to the terrestrial symphony, the *pip-pip* of herring, the *coo-coo* of cod and the light whistling of mackerel. Throughout my symphony, I also want to make audible, mingled with all those noises, all the souls of the world, the flapping at the top of the Eiffel Tower of the starry flag of the United States of the Earth."

An aged artist was there with his daughter, exquisite and spring-like, her hair cut in the page boy style, smoking a cigarette. Thomas Keysar pointed out the father amorously gazing at his green fruit, and said to his friends: "He practices incest."

Etienne looked intently at the pretty sixteen-year-old. "He's lucky."

Josette stood up. "That's the third time, my dear Etienne. Saint Peter was no more boorish denying his master. Let's go."

"I ought to have gone home when we left the Odéon," said Madame Jousselin to Fabio Canti and the Commissaire—Guilleret had already gone. "Bizet's *Arlésienne* was a lot healthier than what one can see and hear here—and I'm only listening to the conversations going on around us."

"It's necessary to know all to appreciate the best," pronounced Fabio Canti. "Here there are failures, the envious, liars, slanderers, calves and cows, a viler humanity than anywhere else, but I'm certain that there are future great artists, poets whose verses will remain in human memory, perhaps a great novelist of tomorrow."

"It's possible, but what do you expect? In my estimation, this society isn't tolerable. Don't look at me with so much surprise. I'm simply a good Christian and an honest woman, perhaps a little too bourgeois, but without affectation, I beg you to believe, in spite of the declaration I've just made. Look, I shall only ever belong to a man who'll take me in marriage. My own art is knowing how to run a house, to be thoroughly versed in French cuisine—and I can make at least thirty different dishes. Above all, I have respect for my person, my body as well as my soul."

"But doesn't our mind, Madame, like poets—Musset, for example, Gérard de Nerval and Verlaine, who said:

Here are flowers, leaves and branches
And there is my heart, which only beats for you.

"And what about Baudelaire? Balzac? Anatole France?"

"You're choosing poorly, Fabio, my friend. Musset, too often drunk on absinthe, recounted and made money out of his affair with George Sand, who also marketed her adventures; Gérard de Nerval finished up hanging himself; and your Baudelaire died syphilitic and aphasic in Honfleur—all after disorderly lives. Verlaine, doubtless delightful, a Socratic vagabond, wandered drunkenly from prison to the hospital—and so many others; I'd rather admire them by reading them."

"But what about Balzac? And Anatole France?"

"Balzac? Forty to fifty tons of coal, in which one finds diamonds. A genius, but he lived in his chimera, incessantly harassed by creditors, hiding in his domiciles under the baroque name of an old lady. And on the very night of his death, that genius was deceived by the woman whom he had married because he thought she was rich, in the room next door to the one where the illustrious cadaver lay, with the sculptor Préault. Another artist, who boasted about that dirty trick, as Sainte-Beuve once did with regard to his friend Victor Hugo. All those celebrated men are picturesque, like Villon, La Fontaine, Jean-Jacques Rousseau; I admire them, I repeat—but that's all.

"Anatole France, a hypocritical satyr, extraordinarily intelligent, destructive without seeming to be, of all moral beliefs and boundaries, pillaged ideas and even sentences from old books, which he sharpened and honed, which he presented and resold in a work of his own in which every perfidious thought and phrase flowed, clear as spring water. Sick and tired of being a reader at Lemerre's, he became the third wheel in the opulent house of a multimillionaire couple; and that clever faun with the face of a horse recounts, by order of their hostess who still furnishes not the water but the yacht for his voyages to the Orient, and recites in that academic salon, stories in that he modulates over and over, threaded with anecdotes, continually improved to the point of perfection, like an actor skilled in monologue.[48]

"Anatole France excuses himself to Lucien Guitry that he begs over a magnificent lunch at the lady's home, with a plaintive smile: 'But there are also the expenses...' And that parasitic aristocrat, a lover of Medieval and religious antiquities, is also a revolutionary, a nihilist. I astonish you, Fabio, a young woman behind the times, not at all of the twentieth century. And if I express myself thus, my dear master, in regard to men who are justly glorious, what do you expect me to think about all those in this inferno of art and mind to which you have brought me, wanting to be my Virgil, who are merely extravagant fetuses, a mass of pretentions, vices, the dung-heap of the capital?"

"Then a writer or an artist of merit, if he loved you, would have to renounce all hope of marrying you?"

---

[48] Anatole France had died in October 1924, shortly before the present text was published, so Champsaur was running no risk of being sued for libel in offering this extremely uncharitable and unwarranted assassination of his character.

The adorable woman with the face of a Madonna pretended not to understand, and without taking the polite hint, said: "The wife of Alfred de Musset or Baudelaire? Of Rousseau or the worthy Le Fontaine? Why plunge so far into the past, with my outdated principles? Of Verlaine? Why not Félicien Champsaur, then? What horror! And why are you listening to me like that, and looking at me with that anxious expression?" She laughed. "Oh, heaven preserve me from such misfortune, marriage to an artist—and preserve my daughter, too! Yes, my dear friends."

"So be it," said the Commissaire de Police, who was also something of a poet.

Meanwhile, on the first floor, without occupying themselves with the cost of living, the ever-accelerating depreciation of the franc or the blue peril,[49] enlaced couples were whirling, in close company, scarcely brushing the carpet of the dance floor, but brushing one another in flight. Grave and sensual tangos, frisky one-steps and voluptuous foxtrots with infinite variations, crazy disarticulated shimmies, plastic intoxications and illusory spins—feminine couples here and there leaping up, supple, as if plastered with the makeup of dreams and the ideal, forgetful, for the moment, to all the fantasies of life, as ephemeral as the minutes, impelled, twirling lightly, swayed and caressed by the music, submissive to the laws of rhythm, in successive images of amour.

And the Earth itself is dancing, transporting through space all our wisdom and all our folly, dancing—so minuscule that it must be invisible from Sirius and a multitude of Suns—transported in the universal dance of millions of beings.

---

[49] *Le peril bleu* [the blue peril] does not refer, in this instance, to the classic Maurice Renard novel but to a well-known cartoon from 1910 signed T. Bianco, entitled "Le Péril Bleu: Le Papier Timbré," in which the phrase refers to the deadly effects of official paperwork in much the same way as the Anglo-American phrase "red tape." It can still be purchased as a poster.

V. The Temptation of Macbeth and Barsac

In the detached house on the Quai de Javel, Etienne Aubert occupied two rooms on the ground floor, with a bathroom fitted with a shower. It was the siren of the factory that woke him up at seven o'clock in the morning. He had gone to bed late and slept badly. Sleep? It was necessary not to think of it any longer; the machines were commencing their racket. He leapt out of bed in a rather bad mood, and with a slight headache. He took a shower and felt better. He got dressed and then, ready to go out but out of sorts, let himself collapse into an armchair, and started thinking. Keysar's words rang in his ears:

"It's necessary to want it."

What did the accursed sorcerer mean by that? And the attacks against the old, so clear and so just, at the Café de la Rotonde?

"Death to the old!" They're the ones who wanted the war to get rid of the young men. We need the government of the young, and to kill the old, who are cluttering everything up, in our turn...

To want it? That's not the same as being able to do it...if the desire were sufficient, humanity would be decimated again by murderers taking no risks...

If I were the master of the factory, it's certain that things would work here very differently, but I'm not, and my father is still too young to retire from business. And I, in spite of my red ribbon, am only an accessory here—the boss's son, as they say. A scamp, for many of them who knew me as a child, and regard my father as a demigod. The scamp is a man now, formed completely by the war, with an immeasurable Napoleonic soul. What can a man expect after fifty?

Yes, to want it, like Macbeth. But I'm alone, there's no wife to push me. Claude Barsac, the arriviste, acted alone though. What idea has that miserable Thomas Keysar, with the chamber-pot forename,[50] put into my head? Kill the old? Fair enough—all the young want that. But one's father? That's frightful.

Come on, they're no longer of out era, those classical tragedies, those family murders only acceptable for ancient Greek theater. And yet, we've only just emerged from an immense tragedy with innumerable acts. How many fathers of families, heads of households, factory owners, industrialists, sons and sons-in-law perished in that war? But that was war. Well, it's still war, in peace-time, where the war goes on, perhaps more pitilessly, no longer giving, in the struggle for money, succor to the wounded, the vanquished...

It was war then, the hazard of shells, the accident, the accident that might strike at any moment, when one least expects it. What a thunderbolt! If my father

---

[50] The fact that "Thomas" is a Parisian argot term for a chamber-pot or lavatory, much like the American "John," crops up repeatedly in references to this character, sometime obliquely.

were the victim of an accident, I'd be the master of the factory, without having done anything for it, from one day to the next...

Someone knocked on the door: a servant.

"Monsieur Etienne, Monsieur Aubert asks you to call in at his office."

"All right. I'm on my way."

Etienne rose to his feet, extracted from his meditations. He felt exhausted, more mentally than physically.

A few minutes later, he went into his father's office.

"Well, Etienne, how are you this morning? I know you went to bed late, so you've scarcely slept. Amuse yourself, my boy, but look after your health."

"I didn't know that I was monitored so closely. I'm no longer a kid, though."

"Don't criticize the interest I take in you, my friend! You're annoyed with me. It's a matter of chance. It's Baptistin who, when I asked him to go, replied without my asking him: 'Monsieur Etienne might be still asleep; he came home at about three o'clock last night,' You can see that there was no ill intention on either side."

"Then it's me who should apologize. I do so humbly."

"You don't sound sincere, my son. Anyway, let's pass on. I have serious things to tell you. Sit down."

"I'm ready to hear them."

Antoine Aubert hesitated momentarily, and then made his decision.

"This is it, my son. You're now a man. You fought in the war so magnificently that your conduct was rewarded with a red ribbon, which I only obtained after twenty years of work. You know what life is like; you understand all its necessities. I'm nearing fifty, but I'm solid enough; my health is good. You must understand that my home, in spite of your presence, seems a trifle empty. I would have been able to live and to die alone, as I have done since the death of your mother, whom I loved passionately—but time effaces everything, sadnesses and joys alike, and I've met a woman..."

"In brief," said Etienne, "you're thinking of giving me a stepmother?"

Aubert frowned. Patience was not his dominant virtue, and his son's aggressive attitude irritated him.

"That's right. The widowed Madame Jousselin would be an excellent mother for you."

"Madame Jousselin? I've never heard mention of her."

"Etienne, please be polite with the woman I've chosen."

"What have I to do with it? You're remarrying. That's your right. I have no more to do with that than your factory. I'm a zero"—he glanced toward his red ribbon—"and merely have to bow down to it."

The father went pale and lowered his head. "It's painful to have to explain, to excuse myself. You doubt my affection, because you've been parted from me for a long time. The demands of business have forced that upon me. Then again, you were better cared for in your mother's sister's house in Touraine than you would have been here in the factory on the Quasi de Javel. I kept you with me, when you left the Lycée, for as long as I could—but the war took you away from me as an adolescent when our relationship might have become closer, as good comrades.

"When you returned, especially because of that red ribbon you earned, I had the intention of putting you in my place, running the factory, with Coutan, but you both came back with authoritarian ideas that are untimely. Today, my lad, the workers have a solidarity; to strike one is to strike them all. They've understood that work, like capital, is a force. In numbers, they use that, and sometimes abuse it; that's why I've decided to attach to me, to my factory, the elite workers that I've been able to gather, by enabling them to profit, with me, from the rewards of our enterprise.

"Coutan doesn't want to understand that, and I've decided to separate myself from him, paying him four million. Do you feel capable of replacing Sixte? You'll take care of the external affairs, having no more contact than him with the workers, which will avoid dangerous frictions. You won't be putting in any money, but you're my son, and you'll benefit from the same advantages as Sixte. Does that suit you?"

Etienne was forced to admit that his father was acting nobly with him. For sixty seconds he sensed that the old man loved him, and was striving to get closer to him, and was sincerely moved.

"I'll do as you wish, Papa, and I thank you for your wisdom and generosity. I'll try to be worthy of it."

"Well said, my son. The two of us will do good work."

"Then it's settled, Papa? You're breaking with Coutan."

"Yes. I've seen his wife, and Josette will persuade him to agree."

"I dined with them yesterday evening. They talked about it. I think it's done."

"And I thought I was telling you something new!" exclaimed Aubert, cheerfully.

"All the same, I didn't expect to succeed Coutan, and I believe I'll be as artful in the job as he was. I'll even say that the war will be useful to me, from that point of view, for I've made connections in the Artillery and the Air Force; I'll find it easy to obtain orders."

"So much the better! You'll have an equal share in the profits."

"And you still have the intention of involving the workers?"

"If I've delayed so long, it's because of Coutan, who didn't want to see my point of view."

"Me neither. Since the war, the workers have been living better than the poor rentiers, and they still want to lay down the law to us."

"What do you expect? The worker is no longer the beast of burden of old. He can count and compare. There are six hundred in our employ who make a good enough living, but they're not unaware that the two bosses make five or six hundred thousand a year. It's the labor of six hundred men that procures that profit for two. The balance isn't equitable. Let's say that I accord them a third of the profits; they'll be satisfied, and I'll still make as much because, having an interest in it, they'll put more care into their work and consequently produce more. They'll have the stimulation of competition and find improvements, even inventions like Lafon's, whose triple-socket connecting rod is a marvel. While having the appearance of posing as a philanthropic socialist, I won't lost anything."

"Why have you made me an engineer, then?"

"Although education produces engineers for us, manual know-how gives us, from time to time, workmen of genius, who, having the practical knowledge of their métier, immediately envisage the practical applications of what they find."

"You're right, up to a point—but all these concessions to the workers excite them to further demands, augmenting their ambition to be masters. What will become of the bosses then—of us? Anyway, there's no point arguing."

"Yes, let's argue. I'd like you to share my ideas. You're called to succeed me, and I'd like to leave in your hands the means of continuing my work. Fortunately, I'll be able to last long enough to see your mind evolve, and recognize, by virtue of the prosperity of the factory, the justice of my anticipations."

"I hope so," said Etienne, getting to his feet. "When do I start?"

"As soon as I've paid off the Coutans."

Etienne shook his father's hand and withdrew. Having gone back to his apartment he recapitulated what his father had just proposed to him. Although glad to be associated with the enterprise, he perceived that he would not be its master, that he would not be able to satisfy his hatred and disgust for the workers, that he would not have any opportunity to put his theories of mastering the common herd into application for a long time. Thomas Keysar's sentence began hammering his brain: "It's necessary to want it."

To want what? His father's death. The old man wanted to marry again. At fifty, he might still have children. Then it would be necessary to share. He clenched his fists angrily.

Oh, zut! Let's go out. Movement and air will do me good.

He was walking aimlessly when he saw the railings and verdure of the Jardin du Luxembourg. He looked at his watch. Eleven-thirty.

"Well, I'm close to Thomas' place. If I bought him lunch, I'd be welcome."

VI. Flirtation with Crime

Thomas Keysar lived in a rather bizarre ground-floor apartment in the Rue Joseph-Barre. It was a transformed sculptor's studio. After a little antechamber there was a vast studio with a sufficiently high ceiling that it had been possible to erect, at the back, a closet that would serve as a bedroom for a man of letters. Having had a job for some years while at the Colonial Ministry, he had been able, by virtue of intrigues and clever manipulations, to persuade his protectors to pay for its decoration, on the occasion of a colonial exhibition, of which he had also taken advantage to procure, for his own account, planks, mats, curtains and rugs—all for three hundred francs, which he had never paid.

With the planks he had constructed a three-step platform, on which he had perched a rather pitiful mattress, but the platform was covered with moquette, and the mattress with the freshest of silks from the same lot. A large packing crate took the place of a table. He had fabricated stools and painted them violet. A few planks attached to the wall formed bookshelves, which he garnished and degarnished as he went along with the books sent to him as review copies by authors and editors, as the literary critic of an unimportant daily and an avant-garde periodical devoted to the arts—the *Canard Sans Nom*, in which Thomas had published a famous series of vitriolic portraits, *Les Morts de Demain*. The volumes brought in a franc each from a neighborhood bookshop, and in view of the quantity of novels that were published, that commerce paid to some extent for the criticism and articles he provided free of charge.

The rug and mats tastefully distributed on the floor, and a few unframed pictures by Cubist painters on the walls, made it quite pleasant. Although he possessed nothing of real value, the ensemble was agreeable to the eye.

Thomas Keysar, like Etienne Aubert, had got home late—even later than the son of the factory owner—because he had gone to prowl around Les Halles, where he met up with an intermittent mistress, who was as hard up as he was. Fortunately, he went three times a week to the residence of Dr. Jaworski on the Boulevard Malesherbes, near the Parc Monceau, who rejuvenated and prolonged human life, regenerating the human organism by giving injections of young and vigorous blood to old people. Thomas Keysar was a blood donor.

The doctor extracted blood from his arm into a glass ampoule, and then immediately injected it into the arm of the person, of either sex, who was in the process of being rejuvenated. The quantity of blood removed was insignificant, less than needed for an analysis—for a Wassermann reaction, for instance—and it was a fifty franc bill every time for the donor. Thomas Keysar had earned fifty francs that way the day before, before going to dinner with the Coutans. He did not tell anyone about his traffic in human blood, appearing to live on his poorly-remunerated pen, and not compromising his dignity as a magician and lit-terateur.

The woman that he had brought back that morning was, like him, in quest of adventure. Not very pretty, but enticing, she lived with Thomas Keysar from time to time, when he had money. Well dressed and styled, she sometimes rendered him a service when he added magnetism to the hundred ways that he had, like Panurge, of earning a living. Berthe Jafaux played the role of somnambulist so well that Thomas allowed himself to be taken in by it, doubting Thomas as he was, and almost lent credence to it.

When Etienne Aubert came to knock on Keysar's door, the latter was still sleeping profoundly in the company of Berthe. When no one answered, Aubert shouted: "Thomas! Thomas! It's me, Etienne. I've come to take you to lunch."

Keysar put on a dressing gown, an old market gardener's overcoat stolen from Les Halles, which Berthe had decorated with all sorts of braid and embroidery. It was part of his magical apparatus, along with an old felt hat whose rim he had cut up in such a way as to form a bonnet with earflaps. The magician's robe and bonnet harmonized with the furniture.

"It's the guy I told you about, Etienne Aubert," he whispered to Berthe. "Hurry up and get dressed."

He jumped out of the closet and went to open the door, smiling.

"What good wind brings you here?"

"There's news, my dear."

Etienne sat down on a stool. He was familiar with Thomas' abode, having been in the Magician's home several times before. "Oh—you're not alone?" he said, on hearing the planks creak in the closet.

"It's nothing. Berthe. I met her after leaving the Coutans and you. You can talk in front of her. I only have to put her to sleep. She won't hear anything." And Keysar, darting his fluid toward the cupboard commanded: "Sleep! I wish it."

A moment later, Berthe came down, stiffly, her eyes closed.

Keysar went to take her by the hand, and sat her down. "There," he said. "Say whatever you like. It's as if she weren't here."

"Are the two of you making fun of me?"

"What, you still doubt my power? You don't believe in the occult sciences? I believe in them because I know, because I'm an initiate. Look, would you like Souriah to tell you what's going through your mind? Afterwards, perhaps you'll believe."

"Souriah? Who's that?"

"It's Berthe's occult name, as mine is Assaouah."

"You're annoying me—all that's a joke."

Thomas Keysar turned round imperiously and raised his hand over the young woman's head.

"Speak, Souriah! What are the two sentences that Monsieur Albert is ruminating? Speak, I wish it."

"Macbeth, you shall be king. To be king, it's necessary to want it."

Etienne started. "You amaze me. But I don't believe—I can't believe."

"As you wish. The evidence is there, though."

"And yet, I have no need to want it. My father's giving my Sixte's place; so I'm already king."

"Hmm! As Coutan was. Boss—but at the first sign of resistance, your father got rid of him. He'll do the same with you. Although he's sharing the profits with you, he wants to remain the master of the factory. Nothing to say, though. It's a nice gesture he's making. You're content?"

"On that side, yes. But now my father wants to get married again."

"To whom?"

"Don't know. A widow, Madame Jousselin. Thirty years old."

"Your father's only twenty more. That's the standard rule for a woman: half the age of the man plus five. And your father must be a sturdy fellow."

"I don't know. I don't care about that. But no children. Share with them—no."

"It's probable, though..."

"I want the factory all to myself."

"You want! You want! You're getting there! But it's not only necessary to desire. It's necessary to *want*. To want is to be able to."

The Tempter looked at Berthe. Souriah, her eyelids closed, was as motionless as a boundary-stone. Nevertheless, he stood up and drew nearer, and whispered to him: "There might be an accident. It's necessary to want it, and the accident happens."

The son could not suppress a frisson. "No! I could never do that."

"You, perhaps. But someone else? Don't worry about it—but when you want it, the accident will happen. You have only to say to me: *'I want.'*"

Etienne looked at him fearfully. "You're trying your magic tricks on me. Let's go to lunch. It's time."

"Are we taking Souriah? That magnetic sleep is very tiring for the subject."

He made a few passes over Berthe's head; she uttered a profound sigh. She got up, and seemed astonished to find herself in the presence of Etienne, but bowed graciously.

"Say, Aubert, what if, instead of going to a restaurant, we eat lunch here. Berthe will go to get what we need, and we'll be more comfortable here."

Etienne took a hundred-franc bill from his wallet and held it out to the woman. "Is that enough?"

"Certainly," said Thomas. "You'll see that nothing is lacking. Go on, Berthe—I'll set the table while you're gone."

293

He escorted his mistress to the threshold and gave her a sign of intelligence. Ever practical, he thought that there ought to be, for him and the improvised housekeeper, an adequate surplus for the following day.

Meanwhile, Etienne was reflecting, his wallet still in his hand. What Thomas had said to him on the subject of his father established a kind of complicity between them.

"Listen, Toto. Since I'm going to share in the profits of the factory, I want you to retain a good memory of the event, too. Look, take this thousand-franc bill. It will give me pleasure—and you, too, I think."

"Thanks, old man. You're a true comrade. I hope that everything succeeds as you desire."

"When I'm the master of the factory, there'll be good days for you, you know."

Without saying any more, they had understood one another. It was a pact, on which the life of Antoine Aubert now depended.

VII. The Chagrin of Love Doesn't Last a Lifetime

Madame Jousselin lived in a simple apartment in the Rue d'Hauteville near the church of St. Vincent de Paul: two bedrooms, a kitchen, a bathroom with a tub, a dining room and a drawing room. Her first marriage, a union arranged by the two families and accepted by the young people without great enthusiasm, as without regret, had not exactly been a love match, but it had become one. Pierre Jousselin, a modest manufacturer of automobiles, had had some success—hence his relationship with Aubert. Then the war had come. Jousselin, having departed as an officer in the engineers, was killed at Bois La Prêtre, where he was installing the emplacement of a 420 battery. Aline's chagrin was real, for tenderness had been born in the young household with Ulette, who was now ten years old. The little girl adored her father, and it was the resemblance—not physical but moral—between her Papa and the factory owner of the Quasi de Javel that had led the child to trust the two relicts.

Seven o'clock in the evening had just sounded on the wall clock in the dining rom. Madame Jousselin, aided by Ulette, was completing setting the table in order that the maid could give all her attention to the dinner. Wednesday was Aubert's day, for, since the engagement, Aline had decided that Antoine should come to dinner once a week. The marriage was to take place soon, at the end of July. That was generally the slow season at the factory; Aubert would leave the direction to his son and Lafon, and the newlyweds would go to spend their honeymoon at Plounevez in the Côtes-du-Nord, where Madame Jousselin had a property.

Aubert arrived with a superb bouquet of roses and a picture book for Ulette. He kissed Madame Jousselin frankly on both cheeks, and then kissed the little girl, and they sat down at table. As they dined, Aubert told her about the position at the factory given to his son Etienne. Aline, naturally happy, simple, honest and cheerful, with not spirit of vanity or domination, approved, but she added: "How is it that you haven't introduced me to him yet?"

"My son has a slightly abrasive temperament. When I told him about our marriage, his initial reaction was one of evident discontentment. It was only on reflection that he understood, but when he saw that I was giving him a large share in the factory, he softened."

"I would have preferred it if he'd understood his father's desires with his heart."

"What do you expect? That accursed war had spoiled many minds, falsified many characters. ME—in capital letters—is the sentiment that dominates everyone, and one of those frank egotists, Jean Sarment, has titled a play that's still on at the Théâtre Français *Je suis trop grand pour moi.*[51] It's the motto of a generation that thinks itself greater than it is. *Me first* is everyone's watchword. Many relationships—as many as possible—but few friends. One has friends, but not a true friend among them. There's no longer anything but people running after money and personal pleasure.

"People no longer come together, like us, out of love and mutual esteem, but out of common interest, to seek pleasure and sensations together. Then, they go their own way, where their whims or vices lead them. Etienne, like many others, has seen death at such close range that he feels, even today, that indifference to all humanity. On seeing, in addition, so much injustice and boorishness between nations as between individuals, one wonders at present if one isn't stupid to remain honest and good.

"Then again, there's no point in hiding the fact that this generation of old combatants considers itself as having every entitlement henceforth. In their eyes, they're the saviors of France...what am I saying?...of the entire world. They're the heroes; everyone who isn't one of them has no value. Past forty, one's no longer human, one's old, and the old ought to have the good manners to disappear. Etienne, unwittingly, is subject to the influence of the milieu, an ambience that certain writers are trying to exploit. But signs are abundant of that boorishness of youth, that savage amorality devoid of pity for the weak, which mocks all honesty with barbaric laughter."

"In that case, my friend, the sight of our household will be the best education for our son. Bring him here. I'll try to make the house agreeable for him, and one day, we'll find him a wife. Family life will do the rest."

"I hope so. The sight of our happiness will make him desire something similar, and he'll become again what he was before: a mild and worthy fellow."

"And then," said Ulette, "I'll tell him myself that he has to love all three of us—and he won't be wicked enough to make me cry."

---

[51] Again, this reference is slightly anachronistic; *Je suis trop grand pour moi* by "Jean Sarment" (Jean Mellemère, 1897-1976) had its première at the Comédie Française on 26 March 1924.

VIII. Etienne's Introduction

The annulment of the Aubert-Coutan partnership was complete; Etienne had taken Sixte's place. Entirely given over to his new role, deploying a feverish activity, he had begun by obtaining, easily, a large order for components for military aircraft. That success had put him in a good mood. He was obliged to make the acquaintance of his future mother-in-law, albeit unwillingly, and he accepted Madame Jousselin's invitation without too much annoyance.

At eight o'clock on the dot, the doorbell rang, announcing the father and the son, both bearing flowers. Etienne started slightly on recognizing, in Madame Jousselin, the adorably lovely woman who had not sacrificed herself to the fashion for the pageboy hairstyle, whose long black tresses gave her the air of Raphael's most exquisite Madonnas: the lady who had struck him like a thunderbolt with a formidable desire for her possession. He repressed his surprise, and when the momentary emotion was past, he complimented the young woman in a banal fashion, without telling her that he had admired her before, and kissed her hand. Then his father kissed her without ceremony.

Madame Jousselin smiled when they sat down at the table. "Now, I beg you to be indulgent to my old Madeleine, who has done her best."

"It will be excellent, then," said Antoine, "for she's a true *cordon bleu*, and as I'm sure that you've added your touch, we'll be eating a meal fit for the finest gourmets."

Everything was perfect, in truth: the food, the organization and the wines. Aubert, glad to see that the ambience pleased his son—along with everything else, beginning with the mistress of the house—did not miss any opportunity to praise his future wife and little Ulette. The young man, however, while following the general conversation, could not help occasionally letting his thoughts follow their natural inclination, which was the desire, the need—stronger than ever—for possession and authority. Mentally, he drew a comparison between one of his mistresses, Josette Coutan, and Madame Jousselin, the former frivolous and peppery, artificial and vicious, a flower of evil, and the latter as seductive as possible with her old-fashioned tresses, whom that exception made original—yes, delightful, intelligent and refined, while remaining natural.

My father has all the luck, he grumbled, internally. *All the luck. But she's much younger than him—too young. It's not right. It would be more logical if it were me she loved.* The desire that he had felt as soon as he saw the woman, so tempting, clawed at him.

During dessert, with all malaise having dissipated in the triumph of the dishes and the wine, Etienne said, a trifle maliciously: "Would I be at fault, Madame, in telling you that, if I'm conquered by your grace, your charm and your beauty, it isn't the first time. You impressed me recently one evening, around midnight, at the Café de la Rotonde, where you were accompanied by three old men."

"Three old men?" she riposted, swiftly. "One is Fabio Canti, who had taken me there after an evening at the Odéon, where *L'Arlésienne* was playing: Fabio Canti, whose celebrated paintings are so luminous, evoking Egypt, Palestine and Syria, not to mention the magic of Venice, where he was born; Fabio, always young in attitude, verve and talent, and well brought-up; Fabio Canti, known as the Painter of the Sun. The others were Antoine Guilleret, the famous portrait artist, a member of the Institut, whom I was meeting for the first time, and Monsieur Raynaud, a simple Commissaire de Police, but who wasn't out of place in that environment of more-or-less failed litterateurs and more-or-less insane artists. I gave my impressions of that evening to your father the following day, and believe me, my dear Etienne, I shall not be returning to that evil place, even in good company. You were there?"

"Your beauty, however," Etienne went on, "ought to be more indulgent to art, poets and artists."

"I like everything that is good, and everything that is beautiful: the arts, poetry, music above all—but too many artists today have quarreled with grace, morality and beauty. I was only passing by, admittedly, in the place where you saw me, and I'd like to be mistaken in my judgment, but all that I saw there, in an unhealthy steam bath of picturesque individuals devoid of faith or law, sacrificing everything to their fantasy in quest of the bizarre, capable of anything, with no religion other than themselves and their chimeras, was a cosmopolitanism of false, spoiled minds and rotten souls." She smiled. "I beg your pardon, my dear Etienne, I'm not in the habit of getting carried away like that. But I don't want you to retain the opinion of me that you might have formed that night."

As she stood up, Etienne kissed her hand again.

"Would you like to take coffee in the drawing room?" she said.

The old maidservant had brought the odorous beverage, and Madame Jousselin filled the cups with her customary grace, and presented them to her guests.

"You see, my son," said Aubert, "that I'm not giving you a stepmother who is too stupid or disagreeable. I hope that you'll willingly sacrifice one of your evenings to us. If you want to live with us when we're married as part of the family, you only have to say so." At a gesture from Etienne, he went on: "Oh, I know that at your age, one prefers more independence. But if, one day, your weary of that life outside, the house will always be open to you."

Ulette, the genteel gamine, advanced toward the young man. "You know, my friend Etienne, that it's me who married Maman to my friend Antoine. You can see that I understand such things. I'll marry you off, too."

"Agreed, Mademoiselle. In fact, why not marry me yourself?"

"Oh!" said Ulette, nonplussed. "But you're already my brother. You can't be my husband as well."

"That's a pity, because I already like you a great deal."

"Me, too. Oh, that's unfortunate. What can we do, Maman?"

"It's necessary to grow up first. Marriage will come, in time."

"Yes, if I were engaged to Etienne. Oh, too bad! I'll definitely call you Etienne, quite simply. Call me Ulette…you can pay court to me, bring me flowers, as to Maman..."

"Would you care to shut up, little hussy?"

"It's Etienne's fault—he talked to me about marriage."

"In any case, Ulette, I'll kiss you." He matched words and gesture.

The little girl allowed herself to be kissed and also kissed Etienne on both cheeks. Aubert and Aline, their eyes moist, squeezed one another's hands.

When they returned to the Quai de Javel in the automobile, Aubert, who normally drove himself, sat in the front beside his son, who had wanted to take the steering wheel himself this time.

"Well, is your future mother-in-law to your liking?"

"I believe you've found the ideal woman. It's sufficient to see and hear her to envy your good fortune."

"Why use the inappropriate word *envy*? In any case, she's a spouse of a kind that's now rare, not a doll like..." He hesitated.

"Like Josette, you were about to say. There was a time when you, too"—he adopted the tone and attitude of a comrade—"yes, you, too, according to the gossip, found something attractive in that doll."

"No, on that matter you're mistaken. I submitted to Josette. She never pleased me. It was loneliness and the circumstances of the war that brought us together. Especially since Sixte's return, however, that liaison has become a torment for me."

"You're doubtless not unaware that Josette is my mistress, too."

Aubert looked at his son. "Truly, I regret such a confidence. You should have kept that to yourself."

"A secret for a secret, Papa. It's to let you know that I understand the difference you're establishing between Madame Coutan and Madame Jousselin."

"I don't even attempt any comparison," said Antoine, dryly. "However, since you've brought up the subject, I'm astonished that, knowing, as you've just informed me that you do, about my former relationship with that whore, you've become her lover."

"Oh, in our epoch, and with Josette, that's of no importance. Me or someone else, Coutan would be cuckolded anyway. Anyway, I have the excuse that Josette was my wartime godmother.[52] That title has its impositions."

"What? Your relationship goes back that far?"

"Yes—but don't worry about it. I appreciate Josette for what she's worth: an amusing playmate, nothing more."

"I've always deplored the fact that Coutan's in that woman's hands. In spite of everything, he's a good fellow and an honest man. The husband's millions will be frittered away."

---

[52] *Marraine de guerre* [wartime godmother] was a phrase derived from the fact that many French women "adopted" a soldier during the Great War, to whom they sent letters and food parcels; the practice was officially encouraged in the interests of maintaining morale.

"He has good business sense, and so has she—perhaps more than him. He'll earn as much as he wants."

"You call that earning money? Deceiving and bluffing incessantly, taking advantage of dupes, stealing."

"Business? It's taking money from others. It's time has come."

"Etienne, if I thought that you, too, were thinking about getting rich by any possible means, I'd rather give you a million and not associate you with the factory. To live well by working hard, that's my ideal, but not be trafficking in dubious enterprises."

"Have no fear on that subject. The Aubert company will always be stainless and above reproach, like the knight Bayard of old."

"Thank you, my son; I am and will thus remain proud of you."

X. To Be or Not to Be the Master of the Factory

If Antoine Aubert had been able to read his son's thoughts, he would have been less reassured—not that Etienne was thinking of launching himself, like Coutan and Josette, into financial dealings; he had THE FACTORY in his blood and under his skin. In fact, since his early childhood, he had been obsessed with the idea, which had also been that of his grandfather and father, of the continued expansion and ever-increasing prosperity of the factory. The very term "The Factory" had a solemn and martial splendor of conquest in his eyes.

With a grip that was growing stronger every year, the workers were obtaining an superiority over the upper classes, the progression of a proletariat hoping for a nobler bourgeoisie than that comprised by a few merchants and state functionaries, an ascension similar to that of the military man beginning as a simple soldier and in the process of seizing the starry baton of a Maréchal de France—with the difference that industry leads to social amelioration while militarism leads to destruction, a retrogression of humanity.

There was, throughout the stages of life—apprentice, drudge, piece-worker or wage earner, foreman, overseer, director, boss—a natural competition of intelligent and honest men. Instead of envisaging, like his father, a union of workers and industrialists, Etienne Aubert only saw his egotistical domination over workers who would be exploited as ruthlessly as possible, in a sort of mild forced labor, over which he would reign as absolute master, a boss getting richer and richer, relentlessly, on the universal march. He wanted to become one of those autocrats of labor with whom Heads of State were obliged to reckon.

That was what the young man, lying in his bed, was mulling over vaguely, and which prevented him from sleeping. And with his ambitious dreams were mingled the faces—superimposed, as they say in the cinema—of Madame Jousselin and Ulette. The hypothesis of an eventual marriage with the ten-year-old girl did not displease him, but that was a long way off, whereas his future mother-in-law would make an adorable mistress.

When? Immediately.

He had retained from the uncertainty of life, the uncertainty of seeing tomorrow, during the Great War, the desire for immediate enjoyment caused by the apprehension of death. And that unhealthy obsession with immediate enjoyment, one of the fatal consequences of the spirit of war, was aggravated by a kind of morbid sadism, the unconscious and irresistible idea of possessing everything that his father possessed: the mistress, THE FACTORY, the wife.

It was that secret but tenacious envy that had driven him to reveal to his father that he, too, was Josette Courtan's lover; and now obscure meditations were opposing his restfulness.

Finally, very weary, he went to sleep.

XI. Le Bar des Barbeaux et des Tantes

In reality, the proprietor has simply baptized the Bar with his own name, which was Léon Barbeau, but the humor of the clients and their special qualities had inspired the true designation of the establishment, which was thus known in the quarter as *Le Bar des Barbeaus et des Tantes.*[53]

A few hundred meters from Père-Lachaise cemetery, on a corner, with a terrace on the Rue des Pyrénées, the place was divided into two parts: the bar, with a long high counter, and what was called "the café," a small part of which, at the back, formed a shady intimate back room, closed by a door with an interior bolt, fitted with a divan and a wash basin, and with no other exit than the one to the café.

Three o'clock in the afternoon: at that time, the only customers were those who justified the bar's appellation—when the nearby workshops emptied, the clientele became more honorable. At the counter, the idlers succeeded one another with the nonchalant and slothful air of pimps and rent-boys whiling away the time. Near the café entrance there were four, three semi-males and a woman, playing cards.

"Go on, shut your trap. You've lost. You're going down. You've lost, because it's your turn. If he doesn't have the cards, the cleverest player is stuffed. Are you going to stick it out?"

"In truth, no. What if we took a stroll to unearth Vizautrou? There was talk yesterday of a good tip, to make a stack of bills."

"Well, go with Tuemouche. I'll go back with Sans-Liquette.[54] If it's anything good, tell us about it."

The two rent-boys went out. Baudard and his wife remained silent for a moment, then Sans-Liquette said: "Why didn't you go with them? Vizautrou often has nice tricks, and I wouldn't be sorry to walk for a while. Goujot's chick is at the sea baths."

"If I haven't gone with them, it's because there's something on with the Petomane."[55]

"I don't like the Petomane. He shows off too much."

---

[53] The literal meaning of *Barbeau* is barbel, and that of *Tantes* is aunts, but in Parisian *argot* the name of the bar signifies "The Bar of Pimps and Pederasts."

[54] "*Liquette*" is a slang term for a chemise or nightgown, but "*Sans-Liquette*" also embodies a contemptuously feminized echo of "*Sans-Culottes*," the nickname applied to the Revolutionary rabble of 1789 and their later analogues.

[55] The reference is obviously not to *the* Pétomane, the celebrated performer Joseph Pujol (1857-1945), who had retired from the stage by 1923, but to some humbler "flatulist."

"Well, he's an artist. And then, he doesn't put on airs with me. We've known one another since we were kids."

"Lick your glass, then. We'll go up to the roost."

The door of the bar opened and a woman appeared, seemingly looking for someone.

"Berthe!" shouted Sans-Liquette.

Thus summoned, Berthe Jafaux—Souriah the somnambulist—came in.

"I had difficulty finding you."

"We moved house because of Armand—it's a long story. Are you having a drink?"

"Yes, a cognac coffee. Anyway, I've found you—that's the main thing. Are you free, Baudard?"

"Completely. Is there a job for me?"

"Yes. A big deal that could put us all in the sun for a long time, and no risk. Thomas is steering the boat, and me."

"You're still with that sorcerer, little sister?" asked Sans-Liquette.

"Yes, there's something in his noggin. It only needed the opportunity, and it's finally come along. Yes, a big deal, and I repeat, no risk. Remember that Thomas isn't one of ours. He needs me, and I need you. Especially you, Armand. You haven't forgotten your trade as a mechanic?"

"Oh," said Baudard, "I hope you don't have the intention of putting me to work?"

"Don't worry—not for long."

"And what's it worth?"

Five hundred thousand. Four hundred for Keysar and me, a hundred thousand for the two of you."

"Shit! You call that cutting the pear in two, do you?"

"We're the brains—you're only the arm. Take it or leave it. For twenty thousand I can find someone else."

"And what is there to do?"

"Go into a factory as a worker and cause an accident—an accident, you hear—that leads to the death of the boss."

"That suits me. Since I'm no longer working I'm sick of bosses. When do we do it?"

"They'll be hiring tomorrow, Saturday. You'll be signaled, you're sure to be taken on. Then, the rest is up to you."

"I'll try to work quickly, then. Fork out the information."

"The Aubert factory, Quai de Javel. You present yourself to the son, Etienne Aubert, on behalf of Monsieur Thomas Keysar. The boss's son will be warned by telephone."

"And the cash?"

"Within a fortnight at the latest, after the burial of Antoine Aubert, the father."

"Good. Is there any payment in advance?"

"The boss has to be dead in order to dip into the funds."

"I'll go to the Quai de Javel tomorrow. Kiss your sister. We're going."

And Berthe Jafaux—Souriah—went back along the Rue des Pyrenées as far as the Avenue Gambetta, which she went down as far as the Square du Père-Lachaise. There she met up with Thomas Keysar, who was waiting, buttoned up to the neck in a reefer jacket with a red ribbon. She sat down beside him on the bench, where he was reading a literary magazine.

"I was beginning to get worried. Did you succeed?"

"I had trouble finding them. The affair's in the bag. You still have your guarantee?"

"Here," said Thomas Keysar, taking a wallet out of an inside pocket and a piece of stamped paper from the wallet. "It's compromising for him if he doesn't pay up. Have no fear. He'll pay."

Berthe took the piece of paper.

"Give it here—I'd like to reread it.

"I, the undersigned, Etienne Aubert, industrialist, Quai de Javel, acknowledge a debt to Monsieur Thomas Keysar, journalist and Mademoiselle Berthe Jafaux, the sum of five hundred thousand francs, which I promise to reimburse them on the day when I enter into the employment as my father's succession.

"Signed, *Etienne Aubert*.

"Written from end to end in his hand. He can't refuse to execute it."

Berthe handed back the document. "Above all, don't lose it. You know what's agreed between us: we get married. If we were keeping a journal of our life, of which there's no need, we could write today: *Poverty ended*."

XII. The Workers on the March

A few days before the celebration of his marriage, Antoine Aubert gathered his entire workforce together on that Saturday evening. Lafon, who was in his confidence, had ordered the machines to be stopped and announced that the Boss wanted to talk to the workers.

At quarter past five, he appeared on the mobile walkway that overlooked the workshops. Without further ado he leaned over the side, supporting himself on the handrail, and began.

"Comrades—permit me to use that term, which has something amicable and familiar about it, between us. For you, until today, I've been a good enough Boss, but a Boss all the same—which is to say, someone who exploits the workers solely for his own benefit. Don't think that what I'm going to say to you is a sudden decision. No, for a long time, I've been thinking about it, and my father thought about it before me. I want to associate you all with the fortune of the factory, by giving you an interest in its profits. You won't only be my workers, you'll become my collaborators, my associates.

"Perhaps you're saying to yourselves, 'If he had these ideas, he and his father, why has he waited so long?' It's because, my friends, it isn't as easy as you think. To install a factory like ours, with its enormous equipment of machinery, requires capital. My father and I took forty years to build up that capital, which represents today at least four million. That four million isn't money, but the tools necessary to earn it.

"What I'm proposing to you, which I hope you'll accept, is very serious, capable of having repercussions throughout the metal-working corporations. You're all, as things stand, members of trade unions, and by virtue of that fact, united with your comrades in similar trades. Now I can't, by myself, convert all the factories of my colleagues overnight. It's necessary for you and me to be the fundamental nucleus of a vast future association.

"For a long time, I've been living with you; I know you all, and I can boast, not without pride, of having gathered in this factory a veritable elite of good and wise workers. The man who wants a fruitful crop must choose his land and his seed well. Reflect maturely on the proposition that I'm making to you. Tomorrow, Sunday, there'll be a meeting at three o'clock. Discuss it in complete liberty. If your response is favorable, the new exercise will begin in Monday, in the afternoon. These are the broad outlines of the pact to be concluded between us.

"Firstly, the annual profits will be divided into three parts. The first is to be divided among the workers, in equal shares. Only the daily wages will be dependent on capacities. The second part will be devoted to the augmentation of the company's capital, in order that it will always be making progress and expanding. The third part will be attributed to Antoine Aubert as the interest on the capital invested by him.

"Secondly, each worker's wage, in accordance with capability or skill, will be fixed by a workers' council elected by you. Given that competition between all is a law of progress, that workers' council will meet every three weeks in order to judge disputes between competing workers and then decide them in all conscience. The workers' council, elected for three years, will be re-electable.

"That, comrades, is the basis of the initial statutes to be established. It is up to you, thereafter, to ameliorate anything that is faulty, and to create conditions susceptible of leading to progress, first in your association, and then in your corporation."

This proposal was so unexpected that the workers remained mute, as if stupefied. Louis Lafon, who had been informed in advance, took it upon himself to reply.

"Monsieur Aubert, your proposition comes from a great heart. It ought to bring about a veritable revolution in the factories and the minds of all our comrades. On behalf of all of us I thank you from the bottom of our hearts. Long live the workers' revolution! Long live its prophet! The cause of the workers is on the march, and it won't stop. Long live Antoine Aubert! You're the model of Bosses."

The audience was unfrozen. Everyone applauded and cheered.

The next day, at the meeting held in the great machine hall, the workers, who had had time to reflect, were discussing the factory owner's proposals. The trade union, having been alerted, had sent delegates; that was the opposition, for the great majority sided with Antoine Aubert. But to separate from the trade union was a serious step, in fact. Lafon went up onto the stage, a few planks place on trestles.

"Comrades of the union, until now we have been perfect syndicalists, and have always paid our subscriptions. However, at your head offices we see, not workers like ourselves but well-paid delinquents of the bourgeoisie who, having not succeeded in liberal functions and taking advantage of their educations, have infiltrated our ranks, and, being better educated, have easily taken the place of ignorant workers.

"That's not a bad thing. The worker easily extends his hand to anyone who shows him amity. But often, these bureaucrats, to legitimate their functions, propagate arguments among us. It's even said that they conspire with the bosses to stimulate strikes at times when orders are slack. In those cases, they're only serving the interests of the bosses, by making them close factories for a time, inasmuch as the workers are content to return to the same conditions as before the strike, when it isn't with a reduction in wages or a selection of workers. A double advantage for the bosses: they've avoided the lay-offs of the slow season, and the workers capable of making trouble are put on the bosses' blacklist.

"Well, comrades of the union, an exceptional opportunity has been offered to us to become the masters of our heads and our arms. Are you going to stop us? This experiment we ought and are going to undertake. It's a step forward in the direction of industrial communism, the means of creating, with time, a single organism for labor and capital. If the union abandons us, too bad! It will lose more by it than we will."

The delegates cried: "We'll close your factory!"

"So be it. But we're several hundred strong man to defend it, and when the comrades in the trade union know why we're accepting the battle, I doubt that you'll find many combatants for your side."

Unanimously, the factory workers applauded Lafon's proposition, and the representatives of the trade union went away, disappointed. But the union preferred to pretend to know nothing about it, and to continue collecting the subscriptions that Lafon and Aubert, in order to avoid a conflict, advised the workers to continue to pay, anticipating nevertheless that in the event of a strike, the Aubert factory would remain outside any difficulties, and would not close its workshops.

XIII. The Attraction of Forbidden Fruit

With the satisfaction of the duty accomplished toward his workers and associates, Antoine Aubert had celebrated his marriage with Aline Jousselin, which his personnel had already decided to celebrate, a month before, with the gift of a bronze bust, cast by the lost wax method, by La Monaca.[56] In a few sessions the sculptor had made a clay image of the factory owner, a striking resemblance, astonishingly expressive and quivering with life. A wind of good fortune seemed to be blowing that July over the factory on the Quai de Javel, and the joy of the big boss, whom love had rejuvenated, as he prepared to leave for Brittany the following week with his young wife was also radiant in the faces of the workers.

Only one, among all those happy men, was not satisfied. Etienne Aubert had been forced to capitulate with what he called his father's social lunacy, and he was already feeling the beneficial effect, but, disturbed in his authoritarian theories, he was suffering, understanding that he would never be able to treat the workers of our era as he wished. To take them backwards, when they were increasingly glimpsing the possibility of an elevation in their conditions would be difficult. The bosses were too few in the face of the laborious masses, the multitudes of workers, and Antoine Aubert's example, and that cowardice on the part of a boss disgusted his son.

Not being able to oppose it, Etienne thought it wiser, for the moment, to go with the flow, to march alongside his father and even if necessary, to appear to be marching ahead.

In addition to the factory, however, there was the new household. Affectionately treated by the new Madame Aubert as a son, and by Ulette as a brother, Etienne could not help coveting the woman, so lovely and exquisite, whom he had desired so ardently when he had seen her for the first time without knowing her. The libertine relationship that he maintained with Josette Coutan, who had become entirely the great socialite, did not cure him of that lust. Etienne combined the two different characters of his parents; from his father he inherited intelligence and a love of work, but the discontented and critical spirit of his mother was far more accentuated in him, along with the need to dominate.

The young and pretty wife who seemed to give his father a conjugal exaltation, in a sensory frenzy, was for him a nonsense, a sacrilege against nature, a spoliation. Was he, Etienne, veritably in love with her? No—but he desired her madly, recklessly, with an irritated passion, further exasperated because his fa-

---

[56] Francesco, or Francis, La Monaca (1882-1937) was mostly working in ceramics in 1923, but might well have been tempted back to his old métier by a suitable commission.

ther possessed her. He knew that the factory would be his one day. But when? And what about the possible children of that damnable marriage? Other heirs to the factory? Brothers and sisters?

Meanwhile, his new family did everything possible to be agreeable to him—but envy burrowed into him, a sentiment that he could not drive away or extirpate. He was being robbed, he, who had fought, had risked his life for long months while the old man, on the Quai de Javel, had amassed all the benefits of the war and distracted himself with Josette Coutan, the wife of his partner, who was at Salonika on the Eastern front. He had been robbed, yes, of that factory and that young widow, a miracle of grace and beauty, whose husband had also been killed in the immense massacre. And it was the old man, who had remained sheltered, who profited from everything.

Decidedly, his generation was a sacrificed generation, which the old had sent to death for five years, and which they had condemned afterwards to renunciation, to waiting for years, when it was necessary to enjoy the roses of life right away, without allowing them to fade and pass.

XIV. The Death of the Boss

It had been sufficient for Etienne to recommend the fitter Armand Baudard to his father as an old comrade of the war for the apache to be taken on in the workshops. Armand was a little out of practice, but he could have been incompetent without the factory owner dismissing him; it was sufficient that he had shared deprivations and dangers with his son.

Baudard promised himself that he would not spend very long at the factory. He intended, as soon as he was in possession of the large payoff, to retire to the province, near a river full of fish, where he could devote himself to his favorite pastime. Sans-Liquette was nearing thirty, and her charms were beginning to demand a great deal of artifice. Like the majority of Parisian women, she had a hankering for a cottage with chickens and rabbits, and a garden with flowers and butterflies in summer.

She had once worked as an assistant to a naturalist; she knew how to make the most magnificent butterflies of the Indies and Ceylon, which arrived in Paris mummified, almost come back to life between her fingers, by leaving them for a few days on a damp bed where their crumpled wings gradually recovered their suppleness and dazzling colors. She then extended the superb Lepidoptera on a board, flattening the dead and revivified wings and fixing them adroitly at the edges, delicate in hand, with minuscule pins, without damaging them. Skillfully, she repaired a slightly ragged wing with similar fragments taken from the damaged wing of another butterfly of the same species. Then she enclosed the marvelous resuscitated butterflies between two plates of glass, one flat and the other convex, and they had the prestige of life in their crystal coffins, minus the movement.

Since then, Sans-Liquette had become a prostitute, taking off her chemise so often that she hardly ever had it on—hence her nickname. But the butterflies of the Indies, which she had once caressed for nearly a year, had reinforced her appetite for nature, for flowers and fields. Baudard had hastened to offer to Sans-Liquette and himself a quiet existence, the repose, security and happiness of which they dreamed.

To gain all that, what was required? The death of Antoine Aubert, a boss—a treat, in fact. But how could it be done? However simple it might seem, arranging an accident in a factory is not easy. The boss spent a lot of time in the workshops every day, but was almost always accompanied by Louis Lafon or an overseer, and all the dangerous locations were carefully protected by guard rails and grilles. On the very first day, Baudard had seen the immense wheel providing impulsion, at the far end of the factory, but that flywheel, which was five meters in diameter, was half-buried in a metal frame and surrounded by a powerful grille rising to shoulder height. To be sure, anyone who fell beneath the rim

311

of that formidable wheel would be rapidly crushed, but how could a robust man be made to fall there?

The mechanic could not see any better means of achieving his objective, however. The mesh surrounding the flywheel had a gate in order to permit the gears and the axletree to be cleaned and greased while the machines were stopped, and it was one of the overseers who had the key. For Baudard, the duplication of that key was the ABC of his métier. Furthermore, at the back of the factory, immediately behind the machinery, were the storage bays of the raw materials for the manufacturing processes, with the consequence that the boss, in order to go home to the detached building on the Quai de Javel, had to go past the machinery.

That gave rise to a plan. It was necessary for Baudard to coincide a moment when he was able to go to the stores to fetch a metal bar with the time that the boss was going home; and every day, the factory owner left his office at quarter to noon to go to lunch.

Baudard fixed the day of the execution for the following Friday.

That very Friday, Aubert, having received a well-filled basket of bass, lobsters and oysters from a friend who had retired to Dieppe, had invited Etienne to lunch. The latter had accepted, arranging his travels in order to be at the factory at lunchtime, for his father liked punctuality. The last of his business meetings was at Saint-Cloud, so the young man, after having obtained a fairly substantial order, came back joyfully by automobile—and, as the day was fine, the July sun splendid but not yet too hot, he stopped for an aperitif at the Pavillon d'Armenonville. At that moment, he was certainly not thinking about the recognition of debt for half a million that he had signed on stamped paper.

At eleven-twenty he climbed briskly back into the auto and took the wheel with his gloved hands, in order to be at the Quai de Javel for quarter to twelve. His intention was to arrive at the office in time to deposit the new order there. Entering by the communicating door behind the machinery, Etienne saw his father, who was heading in his direction after having crossed the factory floor.

What happened then was rapid and horrible.

Just as Antoine Aubert was about to go past the great wheel, Armand Baudard emerged swiftly from the metal storage room with a heavy iron bar on his shoulder. Antoine recognized the recently-hired worker, his son's protégé; delighted by the prospect of the good lunch that he was about to have with his young wife and grown-up son, he gave him a friendly salute and stood aside to let him pass.

Baudard returned the salute with his free hand, but at the moment when he passed the boss, he swiveled, with lightning-fast movement, and the heavy bar struck the old man violently on the back of the neck.

Knocked unconscious, he collapsed without a sound.

Having put down the bar alongside the grille, Baudard swiftly took a key out of his pocket, opened the gate, seized the old man and shoved him under the enormous wheel. There was a dull thud and the cracking of crushed bones. Having closed the gate without locking it again, the murderer headed unhurriedly toward the workshop and resumed the place at the lathe where he was working at the moment.

The horrible crime had been committed before the eyes of Etienne, who was its instigator. Trembling in every limb, he stood there for some time, frozen, as if crushed.

It was the factory siren signaling midday that wrenched him from his daze. In the distance, at the extremity of the galley, he heard the hubbub of the workers running to the washbasins before going out to get their meals. Then, shaking himself, he passed his hand over his forehead several times, as if to efface a bloody stain, and then slowly retraced is steps.

As he went into the house, Ulette flung her arms around his neck. "Bonjour, Etienne, have you seen Father? He's late today."

"I've only just arrived, and I haven't been to the factory, Ulette."

He had pronounced those words with difficulty, his jaws convulsively clenched.

"What's the matter, big brother? You're all pale."

"I'm not feeling well. I've got a bout of fever coming on—a relic of the war."

The door of the dining room opened. Madame Aubert appeared on the threshold. "It's you, Etienne! What—your father isn't with you?"

"No, I've just gotten back. I haven't seen him yet."

"Perhaps you'd be kind enough to go and see what's keeping him."

Relieved to escape the presence of the young widow, Etienne hastened back to the factory. "I'll go with you, big brother!" shouted Ulette. And she ran ahead of him, skipping.

He felt faint at the idea of going past the flywheel, now stopped. He went alongside the terrible groove, not knowing what he ought to do, but following the little girl.

Suddenly, something cold and sticky fell onto his forehead. He put his hand up to it and brought it back covered with blood. A tragic howl escaped from his contracted throat, and he fell to his knees.

Ulette, who had turned round, stared, petrified, her frightened eyes going from the young man to a transmission belt above them. Held by the shred of a garment was an arm, or rather a bloody, hideous rag from which heavy drops of blood were dripping.

Etienne collapsed, and remained collapsed, under the somber debris that was staining him with coagulated blood.

Etienne's frightful, Aeschylian scream had been heard. A number of fathers of families who lived too far away to go home for lunch, had been authorized to bring their food in and eat their meal in a refectory next door to the washroom. Lafon, who detested restaurants, and whose wife was away visiting her sister, was among that number. Soon they all surrounded Etienne and Ulette.

"A man has fallen into the flywheel!" cried Lafon. "How could that happen? But the gate isn't locked!" He addressed two workers: "Carry Monsieur Etienne away—and you, Jouvenet, take the child home. I'll go down into the well. You, Bernard, run to fetch the Commissaire de Police. I'm afraid that it might be the Boss."

"Monsieur Aubert!" said the workers, horrified.

"He's the only one who passes this way at this hour. Let's go! The matter needs to be clarified."

And, lifting the steel trapdoor, Lafon set foot on the steel ladder descending to the bottom of the pit. An odor of blood was mingled with those of oil and soap. Through the open trapdoor, the bright daylight illuminated the bottom of the concrete well sheathing the gigantic wheel. A mass of flesh and fabric appeared, ripped, torn apart and crushed. Only the head, as if it had been cut off deliberately, lay in a corner.

"It's really him!" stammered Lafon, when he had climbed back up the ladder. "What a terrible misfortune!"

"The door must have been left open," said a worker. "The boss must have wanted to close it. He had a dizzy spell, and fell under the wheel."

XV. The Door to Oblivion

At that moment, the group parted, giving passage to Madame Aubert. Warned by the worker who had brought Ulette back, the young window had come running, frightened.

Lafon threw himself in front of her. "Don't come any closer, Madame! It's too horrible. Alas! We've all suffered an irreparable loss."

"Antoine! Antoine! I want to see!"

"I beg you, Madame—it's a frightful spectacle. Monsieur Aubert has fallen under that wheel and has been literally crushed."

Fearfully, the unfortunate woman looked alternately at the murderous wheel and the men surrounding it. Suddenly, her eyes encountered the arm suspended from the belt, projected. Her eyes revulsed and she collapsed, prey to a nervous crisis.

"A physician! Quickly, a physician! It doesn't matter who."

Three men, glad to escape the atrocious scene, ran outside. Aided by four others, Lafon carried Madame Aubert to the house, and left her in the care of her chambermaid. As they went past the dining room they could see the places elegantly set, the opened oysters awaiting the diners in the beautiful light of midday. The contrast struck them all with horror, and although they had only had a few mouthfuls of their meals, they felt their stomachs clenched by an ever-increasing anguish.

The Commissaire finally arrived, in a rather bad mood. His secretary had come to fetch him from his home, where he was in the dining room. The affair was too important to be handed over to a subordinate. Cursing, he had answered the call of obligatory duty.

In the hall, the workers, returned from lunch, were talking in low voices about what had happened. The overseers were interrogating one another, wondering what to do. Finally, Lafon proposed going to obtain instructions from Monsieur Etienne.

For some time already, the son had recovered consciousness of the situation, but he was still feigning weakness in order to give him time to recover the necessary composure. When Lafon appeared, he seemed to make a great effort and sat up on the divan where he had been laid down. He extended his hand toward the senior overseer.

"Oh, my friend…my friend…! This blow has broken me. My poor Papa!"

"Courage, Monsieur. We're all at the mercy of an accident."

"I've found myself as weak as a little girl. But where's my stepmother? What a hard blow for her, too!"

"I left Madame Aubert prey to a nervous crisis in the hands of her chambermaid and sent for a physician."

"Thank you, Lafon—a thousand thanks. Fortunately, my friend, you were here."

At that moment, two physicians summoned by the workers arrived. They were taken to the boss's wife. Meanwhile, the Commissaire, having established the customary details, seemed to have concluded that it was an accident due to lack of surveillance. The overseer in charge of the keys had affirmed that the gate was securely locked. The machinery had, as usual, been inspected the previous Saturday, after the departure of the workers at noon—they worked the English week. That afternoon, under his direction, the manual workers had proceeded with the general cleaning and greasing. The cage of the flywheel had definitely been locked, since no one had perceived in six days that it was open.

"The undeniable fact is, however, that it was open today. Where is the key?"

"In my drawer, Monsieur le Commissaire."

"Well, I want to see whether it's still there."

They went into the workshops. The key was found in its place. At that moment, Etienne, supported by Lafon, joined the group around the Commissaire.

"Permit me, Monsieur Raynaud, to release the workers. I don't think you need them all for your investigation."

"No—only those who were present when the funereal discovery was made."

"Very well, Monsieur le Commissaire." He turned to the overseer. "Would you please send everyone home, my friend. Tomorrow, Saturday, they'll be paid as usual, and this week will be paid in full, as will next week. We'll fix a time for the return to work tomorrow."

Lafon bowed and went out to fulfill that mission. Privately, he was rather surprised by Etienne's sudden amiability. Previously, the esteem that Antoine Aubert had had for him had never had the approval of the son.

After all, the worthy man thought, *I was here at the appropriate time. Great sadness bring hearts together.*

The Commissaire had resumed his investigation. The open gate was still the enigmatic element of the drama. After enquiring about the work in progress, it was concluded that the accidental opening had been caused by the repeated shocks of the pile driver that had been used the previous day. Monsieur Aubert, passing the gate, had tried to close it. A sudden dizziness perhaps caused by the charming fatigues of his marriage…and that was that.

As there was nothing left to do after that conclusion but to remove the Boss's remains from the well, when that frightful work had been done, Louis Lafon and Pierre Engelard, the overseer with the keys, left together, their hearts aching.

"Do you believe in the conclusion of the police, Lafon?" asked Engelard.

"Hmm! We've made use of the pile driver millions of times, and the gate has never opened on its own because of the vibration. It's true that that's not conclusive. Things that have never happened before do happen."

"No—a thousand times no. Vibration can't release a five-centimeter bolt, especially when the gate fits tightly, as this one does."

"So what are you thinking?"

"That's exactly what bothers me. I can't think of anything."

They parted—but Lafon, as he walked back to his home, repeatedly turned over all the possible hypotheses with regard to the fatal gate. None of them satisfied him. His thoughts returned to Etienne. There was no reason to suspect that he might be culpable, and his thoughts did not dwell on that possibility. But now, Etienne was the master of the factory. Previously an adversary of his father in the matter of the social reforms, would he continue the work begun in favor of the workers, or would he reverse it?

The accident, the stupid accident, troubled Lafon. That gate opened? To oblivion? And which profited the son...?

BOOK TWO: THE SPICES OF INCEST AND DANGER

I. Evil Well Done Never Goes to Waste

If one throws a bomb into a tranquil stream in a lovely rural area, or even into a foaming mountain torrent, when it explodes, it will kill a few fish, but it will not prevent the water from flowing into the river and toward the sea. Life follows its course, like the wave.

After the departure of the Commissaire and the official verdict of an accident, Etienne went to obtain news of the young widow—a widow for the second time—and sent for a medical authority.

A famous physician declared that Madame Aubert's condition was serious, as was Ulette's. The mother's brain had received excessive commotion, and though her body had recovered, her mind was floating in a mist. It was only when she had recovered sufficient self-consciousness to remember her daughter and understand the danger that the little girl was in, and that maternal love can work a miracle. In order to care for the flesh of her flesh, she became herself again, and in that upcoming care she would have to give, found a distraction from her own grief.

It was the little girl's imagination that had been struck and afflicted rather than the material substance of the brain. The child's well-developed intellect had been subjected to a kind of frantic horror on finding itself brutally face to face with the enigma of death. Until then, for her, it had only been a word. Her father had been killed, had died for the fatherland, for what was right, as all the dithyrambs and tall stories proclaimed, and that incense gave it a sort of grandeur of apotheosis. But Papa? When Ulette had understood death and had confronted the horrible remains of the father that she loved more than the first, whom she scarcely remembered, the child had had the sensation of a tearing apart of her entire being, and the result was a sort of mental paralysis: a complete indifference to material needs and a forgetfulness of the past that went as far as not knowing her mother. There was a patient reeducation to undertake. It was to that task that, in accordance with the indications of the doctor, Madame Aubert applied herself, and which saved her, personally.

Both of them, the mother and the child, having no relatives, were cared for by devoted subalterns: old Madeleine, the maid-of-all-work; the chambermaid Annie; the concierge of the factory, Madame Langlois; and Madame Lafon, who had come to render assistance to the other three, bewildered by the catastrophe. Etienne Aubert, who did not know his overseer's wife, mistook her at first, and for some time, for a relative of the concierge, and in any case, only occupied himself with all that in order to put at the disposal of the latter, who was more resourceful and wiser in her initiatives to obtain the money needed for the invalids.

In spite of the twenty-year difference in their ages, Madame Aline Aubert had loved her husband sincerely and profoundly. In the old man, during the fortnight of their union, she had discovered, along with an elite intelligence capable of directing hers and elevating it, a vigorous male, expert in lovemaking. Her thirty years, at the apogee of womanhood, which was then in its full sexual plenitude, had obtained the satisfaction of sensation and intelligence, with the consequence of a great cerebral and carnal love for the second spouse, which had revealed her to herself.

A being, still unknown, was already alive in her.

Where was Etienne Aubert in all this? In him, after the magnificent funeral of his father, whose hundreds of workers had followed a hearse laden with wreaths and flowers, the heavy task of the direction of the factory had been his means of forgetfulness. He did not know remorse in the romantic sense of the word. He knew that he had not killed his father. It was only at his instigation that the crime had been committed, but since the evil had been well done, and, in consequence, his keenest desire had been accomplished, it was necessary to accept the new situation and become, in the briefest possible time, a potentate of metallurgy. And his ideas changed. The course adopted by his father was the wisest. By associating the workers, they were not merely interested in the work, which they ameliorated in many ways, but also in the very existence of a factory that had become his thing, his goal, his hope of a continual amelioration of life.

So, he resolved to attach Louis Lafon, whom he sensed to be his equal, perhaps his superior, more closely to his fortunes. He made him the managing director of the factory, while he continued to search for orders. That move was very popular with the workers. Lafon was well-liked; he was an artisan like them, talented but so simple and so just that everyone applauded the decision. Antoine's name was eclipsed in all hearts by Etienne's—or, rather, the two were confounded in a single name that encapsulated all hope for the future: the Aubert factory.

There was one single black spot on that sunlit horizon: Thomas Keysar and Berthe Jafaux. He had taken care, when paying them, to recover the compromising recognition of five hundred thousand francs, written on stamped paper—but Thomas, who had talked beforehand about going to seek his fortune in America, had changed his mind. He had abandoned literary criticism, which had only brought him prestige at the Café de la Rotonde and the Café Napolitain, in order to set himself up, with the aid of amicable publicity, as a thought-reader.

He had installed himself in a new and solitary street, the Rue Huysmans, a little tributary of the Boulevard Raspail. There, he gave psychic consultations with the aid of the seer Souriah. The séances that he held every week in a large music hall, the Empire, had their successes magnified by his comrades in the press. Furthermore, he had published a book, with exemplars on Holland or Japanese paper, which he sold to the lower classes, and which had been plagiarized from a volume entitled *Le Satanisme et la Magie*, by a writer name Jules Bois, who had since disappeared in the United States, where no one knew what had become of him.[57]

At any rate, Etienne Aubert, after having paid him the large sum, the five hundred thousand, had broken off all, or almost all, communication with the dubious and compromising couple. Thomas Keysar did not care about that, but the seer, who attributed the success of the two enterprises to herself, harbored a resentment against that abandonment by Etienne, for whom she felt an inclination.

And that was how everything settled down. The old man was dead and buried. Madame Aubert had regained her charm, her beauty and her smiling gentility, and bore within her a living memory of that conjugal fortnight. Ulette was once again causing her laughter to ring in the house of the Quai de Javel, and the factory was working, formidably, all its machines driven by the great wheel that had devoured the boss, but had been cleaned of all that crushed flesh, that bloody clothing and those red clots.

In sum, life, ingenuous, amoral and cynical, continues as a clear or murky stream flows toward the sea, life always being stronger than death.

---

[57] *Le Satanisme et la magie* by the novelist, occultist and social commentator Jules Bois (1868-1943), which had a preface by J.-K. Huysmans (to whom Bois had supplied useful research materials for his novel *Là-Bas*), was published in 1895 by Léon Chailley. The comment that Bois had disappeared turned out to be a trifle premature, although he had indeed gone to the U.S.A., where he eventually died.

II. An Eclogue of New Wealth

Among the exquisite landscapes that decorate the Parisian suburbs, Vilennes, on the bank of the Seine, sufficiently elevated to be safe from floods, displays its habitations, more bourgeois than rural, in the sunlight. From the small town, the ground rises in soft undulations toward picturesque sites lavishly garnished with clumps of woodland and charming villas with flowering gardens.

On the road that goes from Vilennes to Médan, of Zolatre memory,[58] a gate with a massive lock opened to a long corridor, a grassy path a hundred meters long, narrowly confined between the walls of the neighboring properties. At the end of that path was a house, seemingly abandoned, like its garden: a ground floor over cellars and a single upper floor surmounted by a vast grain loft. That property, by reason of its isolation, had remained for sale or rent for more than ten years. The recent buyer had acquired it for forty thousand francs.

A cheerful September sun was shining down. At a first floor window, a woman darted a glance outside. Her hair was untidy and her eyes not yet fully awakened from her siesta; she was as naked as Eve in paradise, triangled with blonde hair. She stretched and yawned deeply; then, putting on a pair of worn slippers, went downstairs. In the dining room the table was still laden with plates and leftovers of all sorts. In the kitchen the sticky saucepans were keeping company with a bowl of soapy water and a washtub overflowing with dirty linen.

The Eve of that singular Eden, who was about thirty years old, made a weary gesture and, speaking aloud in order to keep herself company and make a little noise in the silence, said: "Armand has to hire me a maid. It disgusts me to wash dishes. And what are we going to eat this evening?"

She opened a cupboard. There were a dozen cans and jars of preserves on the shelves.

"That's great. Tripe, lobster and quince jam. Four bottles of rum. It's a shame there's no salad in the garden. Baudard could have grown some lettuce. He would have done better to plant some than go fishing."

She heard the bell on the gate to the road. "Oh, *zut!* There he is, already!" She stacked up the dirty plates in the dining room. "Eh! Boredom's driving him to talk to himself, like me…no, he's bringing someone…*zut alors!*"

Baudard shouted from the alleyway: "Hey, Sans-Liquette, put your clothes on. We've got a visitor."

Sans-Liquette darted a glance around, saw a camisole that was draped over a stool, slipped it on, tied an apron round her waist and considered herself dressed. Two men came in: Armand Baudard and an old acquaintance from the

---

[58] Émile Zola lived in Médan; his house—still a tourist attraction—is reached via the road in question.

Bar des Barbeaux et des Tantes in the Rue des Pyrénées, Arthur Fallot, alias Tuemouche.

"Bonjour to the loveliest," said Arthur gallantly. "You weren't expecting to see a mate from Ménilmuche, eh?"

"No, for sure. How did you find us?"

"Pure chance, I came to tickle the tiddlers at Vilennes. I'd been told that they were biting hereabouts. While I was fishing, I met Baudard. That's how it goes. I'm not inconveniencing you, I hope?"

"Oh no, we get bored to death in this hole!"

"Too bad! You're difficult to please. Me, I'd do the same old stuff."

"So, housewife," said Baudard. "What's for grub this evening?"

"Always the same: tinned stuff."

"I'll have to invite you to dine at the restaurant."

"At the restaurant!" protested Tuemouche. "You're not serious! You'd need at least fifty bullets." He groaned. "Filthy war! That's why everything's so expensive."

"So what? When one treats a mate, one doesn't spare the expense."

"Damn! You've got that much money? You're a rich man, then?"

Baudard frowned. "Maybe," he said, dryly.

"Oh, I'm not asking. Everyone to his own business. All the same, you're lucky. Me, I'm on my uppers. La Rouquine got nabbed. A fortnight in the Lazaro, and sick.[59] Rotten luck."

"How did you get here, then?"

"On foot, old chap, and Shanks's pony to go back. So, fork out a fry-up quickly. It'll give me the strength to go back. I haven't eaten anything since this morning."

"You can take the train," said Baudard, authoritatively. "I'll pay. Come on, my old mate, give us a hand cleaning up."

The two men went into action, while Sans-Liquette lit the gas and warmed up the tripe Caen-fashion and a tin of peas. The men wiped the plates with old newspapers, rinsed the glasses in the washtub, and everyone was soon at the table. First, they attacked a tin of lobster, then the tripe and peas; the four bottles were emptied.

As they digested the meal, Baudard tapped Tuemouche's belly and said: "That's better, eh? Never let it be said that I didn't help a mate in trouble. Look, old man, here's a hundred-bullet bill. Pay me back after your next affair." He took a dirty but well-stuffed wallet out of his pocket in order to extract a hundred-franc bill, which he handed to Tuemouche.

---

[59] The Saint-Lazare women's prison was where prostitutes picked up in police sweeps were sent, usually not for long—but they were routinely examined for venereal disease while there and prohibited from working until supposedly clear, thus inconveniencing their pimps. La Rouquine translates as "the Redhead."

"Damn!" said the pauper, tearfully. "As mates go, one can say that you're a mate. So, with all my heart, I hope you get another affair like the one you must have had."

"No thanks. I prefer something else."

"So," said Arthur, understanding that he had committed a gaffe, "you've installed yourself in this place for the season, eh? It's very chic. La Rouquine could do with something like this to get back on her feet."

"What do you say, Armand?" asked Sans-Liquette, nudging Baudard with her elbow. "Instead of hiring a maid? With these servants one's never tranquil—there are no more honest girls nowadays."

Baudard was a trifle drunk. The idea of dazzling old friends got the upper hand over prudence. "The property belongs to me," he said, self-importantly, "and I've retired from business. I have my income."

Arthur ecstasized: "Oh, I'm glad for you, old man. At least you've made it, and you're no snob. You still have time for your old friends from Ménilmuche."

"Say, Sans-Liquette," Baudard went on, pouring out three glasses of rum, "we'll walk Arthur back to the station. We'll have a drink at the buffet. Put on a skirt, for it seems that you're a little lightly dressed, and we'll be on our way."

Sans-Liquette sketched out a rather risqué cakewalk, given her summary costume, and ran up to the first floor to get ready.

"Yes," Baudard went on, in a vein of pride and confidence, "I'm a proprietor. Tomorrow, when you come back with the wife, I'll show you over the place. I paid forty thousand bullets for it. That's nothing, for the house and the land—eight hundred meters." Struck by an idea, he said: "Look—if you like, I'll take you on, the wife as maid and you as gardener. The two of us, we'll grow potatoes and salad."

"Me," said Arthur, gravely, "in your place, I'd have chickens and rabbits. That's not tiring and no fuss—crack, you break a rabbit's back or cut a pullet's throat, and you've got your stew."

"I'm glad I ran into you, mate. I was getting bored here all alone, and Sans-Liquette was missing Paname. The four of us will have fun. There's plenty of room—three bedrooms upstairs."

"Nice! We can go fishing and play cards."

The two friends embraced. Sans-Liquette came back, decently and attractively dressed. The three friends set out along the narrow path, staggering slightly. Before leaving, the newly prosperous couple gave Tuemouche two tins of preserves for La Rouquine, who was waiting for something to eat in order not to go to bed on an empty stomach. There were forty minutes to wait at the station. They went into the buffet and had a coffee and a liqueur. Finally, all three embraced like family members.

"Until tomorrow! Don't forget, Arthur—see you tomorrow!"

On the way back, Baudard and Sans-Liquette congratulated one another on their good fortune. Solitude and retirement were decidedly contrary to their temperaments. They were, therefore, going to have some fun.

III. The Consultation with Homo-Deus

Thomas Keysar's consulting room.

Since he had inherited four hundred thousand francs, Thomas had abandoned the gratuitous literary criticism, signed "A Savage," that he did for a daily with a modest print run. Anyway, literary criticism was undergoing a commercial evolution analogous to the one that had partially transformed art criticism. He had understood, as soon as he had a little money, that it was necessary not to count on Letters for a living, that glory is humbug and that only money counts. Installed as a thought-reader in the Rue Huysmans, with the aid of advertising, he exploited the extraordinary divinatory powers of his mistress. To impress visitors, there was a deck of tarot cards, a celestial globe and a crystal ball on the table. The ceiling was painted an intense blue and speckled with gilded paper stars.

Thomas was pacing back and forth when the gong in the antechamber rang. Keysar advanced rapidly toward the door, which opened, giving passage to a strange but correct man, Dr. Marc Vanel, who had been startling Paris for some time with his psychic experiments, and whose public demonstrations were astonishing all the scientists to a greater or lesser extent. Aged about thirty-five, he did not seem that old, and his visage, which as very handsome, maintained a marmoreal impassivity. Having come in deliberately, he made a gesture of salutation without taking his hat off. The somewhat theatrical and suggestive appearance of the reception room had caused him to shrug his shoulders slightly.

"Please, my dear Master. I know that the time of Dr. Vanel, Homo-Deus, is valuable. I wouldn't have asked you to disturb yourself if it weren't a matter of an extraordinary phenomenon."

"I'm listening, but be brief."

"I confess to being more of a clown in matters of somnambulism than a veritable scientist. I assure you, however, Master, that I've obtained results that I find stupefying with the medium Souriah, my mistress for three years. She's a daughter of the people, born of alcoholic and syphilitic parents. I mean that the fundamental organism of my subject is rather unhealthy, not only on the physical side but the mental side. As such, she's very apt to somnambulism, and, what is more, to a certain exteriorization of the spirit. What I mean by that is that Souriah's spirit seems at times to be endowed with dualism; she's herself and she's also someone else, who has not the slightest moral rapport with her own self. The enigma of that nature intrigues me, and I have faith that your aid might clarify the matter."

"Explain further," said Homo-Deus.

"In the last three months, since our financial situation improved, by virtue of a fortunate windfall, the young woman's psychic state has undergone a strange transformation. Until then, I utilized her clairvoyance to attract those that I previously considered to be dupes, but who are now veritably informed by a marvelous second sight. There's no longer any charlatanism in her revelations—which impresses me and disturbs me."

"Would you care to introduce me to her?"

"In a little while. I haven't finished. If that were limited to consultations susceptible of satisfying the clients and, in consequence, augmenting our reputation, I wouldn't have insisted, Master, on obtaining your advice. But in addition to that singular psychic condition, Souriah has been subject, for a month, to attacks of epilepsy, followed by increasingly long-lasting catalepsy. The first fit lasted four hours, the second nine, the third twenty-five, and this time—the fourth—she has been in a cataleptic state for more than two days, fifty-three hours to be exact."

"The progression is rapid. Are you feeding the invalid?"

"I'm entirely ignorant about her malady. That's why, Master..."

"You tell me that her spirit is double. When did you perceive that?"

"About three months ago—I repeat, in a state of somnambulism. It was as if she lost her personality and spoke with the spirit of another woman; and that intruder is surprisingly perceptive. You ought to understand that three quarters of the consultations requested are motivated by lost objects, amorous rivalries and family interests, questions of inheritance: rather banal matters. Always hopes for the future—and about the future, Souriah is no better informed than I am, so then it's the eternal game of simpleton traps. But with regard to the past, nothing—nothing, you understand—is hidden from her; it only requires some object to put her on the trail, and she sees it, even beyond the Ocean. Thus, she was able to give a young Brazilian from Montparnasse daily bulletins on the health of her father, resident in Rio. I could cite you twenty cases, which I can affirm as authentic. I don't understand it myself, I repeat, and it's completely different from how we began, when there was nothing but trickery. It's already surprising enough, but now there's this mental duality—yes, the junction of another being so different from Souriah that I'm almost frightened of her.

"Is it so frightening?"

"Frightening isn't quite the right word. *Alarming*. Can you imagine a being who is not of our Earth, who has lived on other astral worlds?"

"Come on! Are you mad?"

"Not yet. But that might come, if I follow my wife's fantastic dreams, in their deductions."

"That's all?"

"That's all."

Homo-Deus rubbed his hands, thinking that this really was an interesting subject for him.

"Take me to her."

Thomas Keysar took Dr. Vanel into the bedroom where the Seeress was lying. Souriah—Berthe Jafaux—was fully dressed, on the bed in the middle of the room, in her séance costume: an ample velvet dress secured by buttons of red coral. Her hair was cut to shoulder length. Thus extended, pale, with her eyes open and staring, as rigid as a corpse, the young woman was impressive.

Homo-Deus approached, felt for a pulse, placed his ear on Souriah's chest, and then touched her eyeballs lightly.

"Well, Dr. Vanel?" asked Keysar, anxiously.

"A perfect cataleptic state. The pulse is insensible, the heartbeat almost imperceptible. It's the fourth fit, you say? Two or three more, and it will be death."

"Death?" stammered Thomas.

"Unless I can master the malady. That chance seems to me to be problematic."

"What? You have no hope? You, whom they call Homo-Deus?"

"Believe me, I shall do everything I can to save her. Have you a poker, and a small gas stove?"

"In the kitchen, Master. If you'd care to follow me..."

Dr. Vanel found the poker. "This will do," he said. Then he switched on the gas stove and placed the iron rod on top of it.

"Watch the poker, Monsieur. When it's red hot, bring it to me swiftly."

He went back to the invalid and took off her shoes.

A few minutes later, Thomas Keysar returned, carrying the red-hot poker.

"Give it to me. Place your hands on her chest and put pressure on it rhythmically in order to reanimate her respiration. That's tight...keep going..."

Meanwhile, Vanel moved the poker rapidly back and forth beneath the young woman's feet. An odor of roasting, of burning, spread through the apartment. A slight shudder ran through Souriah's body.

"Put her to sleep," said Homo-Deus. "Magnetic sleep—you're accustomed to her temperament. By that means, we'll avoid a brutal awakening."

Three seconds went by; he plunged the hot tip of the poker a few millimeters into the middle of the soles of the patient's feet. This time she started, and uttered a slight screech—but as she felt the influence of the magnetic sleep, after a profound sigh, her eyelids closed, and regular breathing elevated her breast.

"Take the poker back to the kitchen," said Dr. Vanel. "We have no more need of it."

IV. The Mystery of a Double Soul

Leaning over the sick woman, Homo-Deus said, authoritatively: "Watch over yourself. I forbid you to allow yourself to return to that sleep, which might be mortal. Will you obey me, Souriah?"

"I'll try. But why do you want her not to die."

"Who are you talking about?"

"The other one. Berthe Jafaux."

At that moment, Thomas Keysar came back in. Marc Vanel signaled to him to be quiet.

"And what about you, who are you?"

"There are no sounds to translate it via a human voice."

"Are you not a terrestrial being like us?"

"No not me—the other, yes."

"The other? Berthe Jafaux?"

"Yes. Oh, the poor thing!"

"You feel sorry for her? Is she suffering?"

"More morally than physically, and she has no suspicion of it."

Dr. Vanel looked at Thomas Keysar. "A strange case, indeed. Unless we're dealing with a simulator. In the wake of a crisis of epileptic lethargy, however, that's unlikely." He turned back to Berthe Jafaux. "Are you aware, Madame, of the crisis you've just undergone?"

"Perfectly, but its gravity doesn't trouble me, because I don't want to live with the brain of a woman who has committed murder."

"Silence!" Keysar interjected, commanding the invalid. "Excuse me, Doctor, but Berthe Jafaux's secret is not only her own. Limit yourself, I beg you, to the penetration of the psychic mystery—the duality of a soul."

"If there is, in this woman's past, a crime that is influencing her mentality, I need to know about it, if only to combat the malady. What she says will remain secret for others—it's a matter of professional secrecy—but I must know everything."

"What's the point of charging your conscience with a responsibility that you can't infringe? I know Berthe Jafaux's secret, and I swear to you that the invalid doesn't want it to be divulged."

"You're her accomplice. Don't worry. I won't say anything, no matter what happens."

"As you wish, then. But the vulgar spirit of Berthe Jafaux, my mistress—and, yes, my accomplice—has no interest for you, while the spirit that animates her at present is utterly superior. Homo-Deus alone is capable of penetrating that psychological mystery."

Without replying, Vanel went back to the invalid, who was still seeming to be reposing in the same tranquil slumber.

"Can you see into my thoughts?" he said, placing her hand on his forehead.

"Yes. Would you like to have the key to this duality, this enigma?"

"Indeed. Do you have any objection to revealing it to me?"

"Not in the least. Know, first of all, that I have nothing in common with this wretch. If I'm making use of her organism, it's because I have no other means of existing on this globe, to which I have descended involuntarily."

"Your spirit comes from another world, then?"

"Far in advance of yours: a world of pure spirits—which is to say, existing without, as on your world, being enclosed in a carnal envelope. Although immaterial, we have senses that allow us to communicate our thoughts, unite with one another and procreate. Death, about which I only learned on the Earth, does not exist for us, and we replace that kind of metamorphosis of matter by exodus. The excess population of our world, obedient to some unknown impulsion of need, embarks in the ether, on the luminous waves of the nearest Suns, and spreads out through the sidereal universe. Hazard brought me to the Earth, and to my misfortune, I plunged into the brain of Berthe Jafaux.

"A rather repugnant detail of material worlds like yours—of which there are many—is that it is usually at the moment of copulation or genesis that our materialization takes place. Thus, many people on Earth have double souls, as there are double bodies, attached by a strip of flesh at the groin, double flowers and fruits, and double stars. I wanted to avoid that fundamental law, taking advantage of a syncope of an adult individual to violate her cranium, the domicile of her spirit, and install myself unknown to her. I had the ill fortune to happen upon this adventuress, and thus to be at the mercy of a villainess and her accomplice."

Dr. Vanel, astounded by this revelation, looked at Thomas Keysar, who put a finger to his forehead to indicate that his mistress was mad, adding: "For three months, Berthe's mind has been deranged. I, too, can feel my mind becoming unhinged. That's enough for today, isn't it, Master?"

"*Au revoir*, then. You can be sure that all this will remain between the two of us."

"Do you think that I can continue my usual experiments and consultations without any danger to the patient?"

"I don't see any reason why not. But make a careful note, for me, of anything that seems to you to be abnormal with regard to the somnambulist."

"I promise. Behind the charlatan that I appear to be, there's a writer who is very interested in psychic mysteries. With the aid of the illustrious Marc Vanel, Homo-Deus, a great discovery is possible."

"Amen," said the strange doctor. "I ought to tell you that I came here with a mind greatly prejudiced against you. I don't want to know anything about your past. This woman seals an alliance between us. Science above all."

V. A Pretty Bird of Passage

Having shown the famous scientist, Homo-Deus, on to the landing, Thomas went back into the bedroom and contemplated the sleeper for a long time. He did not have the courage to confront the unknown alone. He made a few passes and woke the sleeper.

Souriah—Berthe Jafaux—stretched herself, opened her eyes and said: "I'm hungry."

"Of course—you've been asleep for two days. After a consultation, you had an epileptic fit, which terminated in a lethargy, which would probably still be enduring if I hadn't called Dr. Vanel."

"I've never felt so well."

She jumped out of bed, but fell back onto it, uttering a scream of pain. "Oh la la! My poor feet!"

"I forgot to tell you. To wake you up, it was necessary to pass a red-hot iron over the soles of your feet. I'll bandage you up. You'll no longer feel it in a few days."

Thomas Keysar, who had done a little of everything, had been a medical orderly for six months during the war; he had just completed the dressing when the gong rang.

"Oh!" cried Berthe. "Whatever it is, after an affair like this, I'm not up to it."

"It's Madame Coutan, Monsieur," said the maid.

"Josette? That's different. Show her in. That little bird will make me forget my burns."

Clad in a magnificent sable fur, in spite of the mildness of the weather, coiffed in a hat that was a marvel of fantasy, and with her hands, neck and ears a firework display of jewelry, pearls and diamonds, Josette appeared.

"Bonjour, my children. Why, what's up? Is Berthe not out of bed? She doesn't seem to be ill, though…unless…am I interrupting you, lovebirds?"

"Nights are sufficient for us. But you're flamboyant, my dear."

"Aren't I?" said Josette, going to admire herself in the wardrobe mirror. "I was right to make my husband let go of his factory. Sixte has just made three hundred thousand francs. That's work for you. Since he's been in business, he earns what he wants. From his latest deal, he gave me a third. So, you see, I bought myself this coat and hat, to come to see you."

"How did he make all that?" asked Keysar.

"You're more curious than me. I didn't ask him. In business, you understand, it's never the same thing twice… Oh, we're going to spend the winter on the Côte d'Azur in our Rolls. There's a whole gang of big players out there. He rubs shoulders with the cleverest. Albert Dubarry, the editor and owner of the

Ere Nouvelle,[60] the godfather of Herriot, of Painlevé, the faithful friend of Caillaux, our future masters, is advising him to let himself appear on the lists of the Cartel des Gauches in the next elections, and he'll support his candidacy. There was a question, recently, of leaving for Russia with Charles Humbert.[61] It seems that there are millions to be made with the Soviets. This is the good life— he was vegetating with that old mussel Antoine Aubert."

That name caused a frisson to run down the spines of Berthe and Thomas. Untiringly, she continued: "What's become of Etienne? He needs licking into shape—we never seen him anymore. He's well-made for living amid scrap iron, that one, but he's always been welcome at the house. Do you see him some-times?"

"A fortnight ago," said Thomas. "Absorbed by the factory, Etienne doesn't have time to see his friends."

"I can do without him," said Josette, deliberately. "Do you know why I've come?"

To show off your jewels and your fur coat, whore, thought Berthe. Aloud, she said: "In truth no, but it's very kind of you."

"Well, here it is. Would you like to come to Nice with us? I'm offering you hospitality. We'll amuse ourselves with trifles and sorcery."

"We won't say no," said Keysar.

Josette went on: "If the Russian affair works out, Sixte will soon be leaving for Moscow and Leningrad. Then it'll just be us. We'll try not to get bored."

Berthe exchanged a glance with Thomas. The invitation was amiably ego-tistical. Josette would be able to show off her luxury and distract herself in their company. But the two wily accomplices also perceived something better than a distraction for Josette. In such a house, given her depravity, there would surely be gleanings, by virtue of her squandering. Then again, if one wants golden ap-ples, it's necessary to go to the Garden of the Hesperides.

"On reflection," said Thomas, my reputation as a thought-reader is made in Paris. In Nice, Cannes and Monte Carlo, I'd have a ready-made clientele. Count on us, my dear friend."

---

[60] The journalist Albert Dubarry, proprietor of a series of radical Parisian news-papers, most famously *La Volonté*, was a keen gambler and a regular visitor to the casinos of the Riviera, where Champsaur presumably met him. He was a key supporter of the Radical parliamentarians of the era, including Édouard Herriot (1872-1957), Paul Painlevé (1863-1933) and Joseph Caillaux (1863-1944), all of whom served terms as President of the Council.

[61] The entrepreneur Charles Humbert (1866-1927) was the proprietor of *Le Journal* during the Great War but was brought before a military court in 1918 for alleged financial improprieties; although acquitted, his reputation was irrepa-rably damaged.

"You're truly very kind, both of you. I'll telephone you the day before we leave and come to pick you up in the Rolls."

She was about to leave, but suddenly, as if she had forgotten something, she said: "By the way, if you see Etienne Aubert, I wouldn't be sorry if he were to learn about our new situation, since Sixte quit his dirty factory."

VI. Prey to an Intense Desire

On the same day that Josette Coutan invited Thomas Keysar and Berthe Jafaux, alias Souriah, to come and spend the winter with her on the Riviera, an intimate feast was held in the little house on the Quai de Javel in order to celebrate Ulette's complete recovery after her convalescence. Naturally, Etienne Aubert was to preside over that solemn dinner *à trois*. The ephemeral and still delightful Madame Aubert, who saw her daughter's recovery as a good omen for her new maternity, still invisible, had prepared a delicate meal and decorated the table with the last roses of September.

Madame Aubert had the intention of going to spend the final phase of her pregnancy at the home of her godmother, Madame Desambez, the well-off widow of a notary in Cannes, who possessed a villa at the bottom of the wooded slopes of Cap Estérel, at Théoule, that was far too big for her. It was a welcome pretext for the opulent widow to offer her goddaughter hospitality, an opportunity that permitted the old lady to play with dolls. Madame Desambez had had two sons, both killed during the Great War; the older one was married and the father of two children, a boy who was ten years old in 1923 and a girl of seven. Although they had a beautiful apartment in Nice, Madame Ossola,[62] her daughter-in-law, and her children lived with Madame Desambez almost all year round.

At eight o'clock precisely, Etienne presented himself, carrying a superb doll for Ulette and a bouquet of roses for the young mother.

"Thank you, Big Brother," cried Ulette, throwing her arms round his neck.

Then he kissed the hand of his stepmother, who said to him: "How can I express my gratitude, my friend? What would have become of us, in all the emotions we've gone through, without your attentive solicitude? Oh, if our Antoine could see us"—she pointed to the bronze bust on the mantelpiece of the drawing room, modeled for La Monaca before the accident and now completed—"he'd be proud of his son's conduct."

Etienne went pale at that reminder of the past. The bronze visage seemed to be staring at him, and the son occupied at the factory a place usurped by murder. To change the subject, he said in a strangled voice: "Let's think about the future instead. Have you had any news from Théoule?"

"Yes. Madame Desambez is awaiting us impatiently, as well as her daughter-in-law, Madame Ossola. Robert, her grandson, and Simone are asking for Ulette. We'll form a veritable colony of widows and orphans down there."

"Madame Ossola is a war widow?" asked Etienne.

"Yes. Madame Desambez lost her two sons at the front."

---

[62] It is not obvious why Mesdames Desambez and Ossola have different surnames, given that the latter is the widow of the former's son.

"It would have been preferable for a bachelor like me to perish instead of a man with two children."

"Oh no!" protested Ulette. "For one thing, you know that you're my intended husband."

Madame Aubert intervened. "You're still playing with dolls, and you want Etienne to marry you?"

"Ulette's right. It's necessary that I legitimate her doll. What are you going to call her?"

"Antoinette. That way, she'll remind me of my good Papa."

The maid came in to announce that dinner was served, and they went into the dining room. Etienne complimented the flower arrangement and neatness of the table.

"Go on, Big Brother," said Ulette, "sit down here. It's good Papa Antoine's place, and you're the master of the house now."

"We're really intruders at present," added the young stepmother.

"You're joking, I hope. If I'd had the good fortune of knowing you a little earlier, it's probable that you'd still be named Madame Aubert."

"It's you who are joking, Etienne," she said, blushing.

But Ulette chipped in: "That's not possible. If you'd married Maman, you couldn't marry me."

"That's true, but you'd be my darling daughter."

"Oh no, I'd rather be your wife. And then, Maman won't remarry again. She's going to buy me a little brother. She'll have enough to do then. You don't know, Monsieur, what it's like to bring up a child."

"And you do, Mademoiselle?"

"Of course. Before Antoinette I had many others."

"Damn it! That's not amusing for your future husband."

"Oh, but they're children to make you laugh. They're dolls. Real children are dolls to make you cry. Ask Maman if I haven't been the cause of worries lately. She was afraid of losing me, you know."

"Let's not talk about that wretched illness anymore," said the mother. "It's necessary to make up for lost time and get your strength back. Your future friends in Théoule, Simone and Robert, are very robust, and you have the air of a poor little thing."

"They live by the seaside, and they haven't been ill. Don't worry, though; I'll catch up to them. Can I have another piece of chicken?"

Etienne listened to that puerile chatter, directing all his desire at the mother. Before that marvel of beauty, grace and charm, and the cause of envy of his father, there was no other obstacle now than the will of the young widow. Etienne sensed that she was sympathetic to him, and he had sufficient self-control to conceal his envious and domineering character, hiding his faults and gaining in the estimation of his beautiful stepmother by exaggerating instead the qualities of his father.

He had no doubt about it; in time, a physical influence would awaken—if not love, at least a need for love—in the young widow's senses. The amiable and obliging woman whom he had initially mistaken for a relative of the concierge, was Madame Louis Lafon, and that was a further means of gaining ground in Aline's heart, for Adrienne Lafon had quickly become a friend for her, and Etienne's conduct with Lafon had completely won the confidence and esteem of the wife of the new director. She and her husband never tired of singing the praises of "Monsieur Etienne." So, everything was on the right track.

"Are you content, Etienne?" asked Madame Aubert. "Is the factory progressing as you would like?"

"Very well. I believe that we'll have a splendid year. If this continues, it will be necessary to expand. Fortunately, we have another plot of land on the Rue des Entrepreneurs, two thousand square meters, which only needs to be employed. My father would have used it already if it hadn't been for his discord with Coutan, the associate from whom he finally separated."

"What is Monsieur Coutan doing now?"

"'Business.' It's a rather vague word, which seems to astonish you. It consists of all the means of making money without practicing any industry of commerce. One can make money very rapidly that way. Sixte Coutan has everything necessary for that kind of business: an intelligence for intrigue and the luck of the devil."

"It can't always be very honest."

"Oh, honesty! A very relative word nowadays. If there were only honest people, life would probably be very difficult and tedious. Thus, for instance, last week I obtained an order for five thousand aircraft engines. The intermediary, a senior bureaucrat at the Ministry of War, knows very well that I only manufacture separate components. However, I got the order, to the detriment of the Penaud factory, not because I submitted a tender lower than our competitors, but because I gave twenty per cent to the bureaucrat, who passed on half of it to someone else—because in those sorts of bargains, the responsible party is unknown. Well, it's those types who do business, and it's the Princess who pays the commissions."

"Which is to say the taxpayers—everyone."

"Everyone—of which I'm a part myself. But I make a profit from it. Today, take note, there are thousands of people who do business and make a lot of money by such traffic, spending without keeping count and not finding anything too dear. Hence, the increasing price of everything and an exceedingly hard life for those who can't make money in proportion.

"To get back to the factory, though, I can say that the idea of associating all the workers was a stroke of genius. One can visit all the factories, but nowhere will you find the enthusiasm and activity of ours. At Penaud's, for instance, they do a lot for the workers: co-operation for food, premiums for the fathers of families, insurance against accidents, and so on. Well, when I'm hiring I can take my choice of his workers, and if I need a hundred, I can get them from him."

During that serious conversation, Ulette had become drowsy. Aline rang for Madeleine, who took the little girl away without waking her. In the meantime, Madame Aubert served the coffee and offered Etienne the use of his father's smoking room.

"With a little imagination," said the young man—who was still wearing his mourning clothes, as was his stepmother—laughing, "I could believe that I was with my wife and child here. How unfortunate it is that I didn't meet you sooner!" As Aline did not appear to have heard, he went on: "The two of us are almost the same age, whereas my father could almost have been yours."

"I never perceived that difference, for misfortune had formed a character well in advance of my years for me. You can't imagine how great my mental distress was at Jousselin's death, left alone with a five year old child. I needed then to learn to direct my own life, something my husband had done previously."

"You can marry again. You're still so young, so pretty, so..."

"You're forgetting that I'm going to have another child."

"Are you certain about that? Nothing is detectable."

"Quite certain."

"I've heard you say that it was a blessing for Ulette to have a second father like mine. You might meet someone who loves you enough to be a father to your two children."

"I don't want that. Two dead husbands gives me the impression of being a bringer of bad luck."

Etienne made a gesture of annoyance. She definitely did not want to understand. He decided to burn his boats and make himself clear.

"You're too intelligent, Aline, not to have realized that I love you, and have for a long time, since the day I first saw you. The second time, there was an insurmountable obstacle, and I had to lock away that passion. A catastrophe, as frightful as it was unexpected, has left us free, and I can admit, today, an amour that has ceased to be criminal. I can be happy, and you can share that happiness. I swear to devote myself entirely to that goal, of being a father to your children as affectionate as if they were my own.

"Don't reply to me immediately—think about it... Weigh up your situation and your future carefully; think what a woman as young as you might have to suffer in isolation. The love of children can't replace that of a husband, and Nature has laws that can't be transgressed. After my churching, I'll remind you of this evening and you can give me your response. Until then, let me hope."

The ephemeral Madame Aubert thought that she had a duty not to alienate the bold fellow any further, to smile pleasantly if she could, and not to annoy him, for one can only ever be reconciled with the indifferent, and some words let slip are irrevocable. She could not judge, as a tribunal, that hero who was unconscious of being a swine, that ambitious and amorous individual who was devoid of shame, scruples and remorse—and who was not even an artist. As a bourgeoise, she reflected that it was necessary to handle chimeras carefully, like stockings—and the valiant brute was really not worthy of suffering.

"I've always counted on your affection, my dear Etienne, so believe that I'm very sensible to your sentiment, but my character is too mature in relation to yours, which is very advanced. Realize your father's vague dream, and mine; you'll find later, if you wish, in Ulette, a younger, prettier Aline suitable in every respect for a sagacious hard worker, an industrialist like you. By then, I'll have become an old woman, for the years count double for the majority of women. Think about all that, my dear, and you'll understand that if I accepted your seductive offer, I'd be doing you a disservice." She laughed frankly and added: "And then, one can't marry one's stepmother."

"One..." He dared not say the rest, which could be divined—*one can sleep with her*—and rose to his feet.

"Love has no reasons, like the heart. It dominates everything, because it is love. If you loved me, no objection could stand up. I love you, and I listen to none. I love you, and to possess you, I'd do the impossible. Yes, if more obstacles loom up between you and me, I'll break them as..."

Disturbed and frightened by that sudden explosion of anger and the increasing vehemence of that frenetic excess, she said: "So be it. The future is unknown to anyone. Let's both hope. But after these emotions, I'm exhausted. You'd be kind, Etienne, to leave me alone and to think."

In the ancient tragedy and that of Racine, Phaedra, the wife of Theseus, falls in love with Hippolyte, the son of the king, her husband. In Paris, on the Quai de Javel, it was the other way around. Where, then, could that madness have germinated? During the five years of the war? Then, almost everywhere on the globe, people had been killing, stealing—every man for himself!—and raping, when it was necessary, but not often. What leaven had that wild firebrand of civilization...that international return to primitive brigandage with the most modern of means—aircraft, long range bombardments, poison gas—while taking shelter in trenches, as during the Caesar's Gallic wars and the warfare of insects...what virus had all that ignominy left in the veins of that young man?

A novelist, expert in analysis, cannot, in spite of his wishes, explore all the depths of the unconscious, to discover there, in the human mystery, the furious and compressed impulsions, the erotic desires, the unhealthy hidden dreams, all the unspeakable lumber swarming and buried in the meanders and subterrains of the soul, to uncover all the passions and expose them to the light of day in their chrysalides—to discover, in sum, in a heart laid bare, the being who ceases to lie to others and himself. On what viscous germs is mad love alimented? From what microbial miasmas, from what realities, sometimes filthy and sticky, do many dreams take flight?

VII. A Question Mark

Having returned to the drawing room, where the bronze bust of her husband was gazing at her from the mantelpiece, after sending the young man away gently, smiling at his incandescent eyes, and allowing him to kiss her hand, Madame Aubert thought:

I suspected as much, but I didn't believe that he'd ever dare to declare it. The window of Antoine Aubert become the mistress or wife of his son!? He's not entirely mistaken. His father awakened in me a sensuality that I believed to be dead. I'm suffering in my flesh. What does it matter? He bears little resemblance to his father. He's violent, impulsive, jealous, brutal. After the mother has refused him, will the daughter refuse him one day? What did he mean, 'if more obstacles loom up between you and me, I'll break them as...' Oh! What a horrible thought!

No, it was an accident...an accident...nothing more...

VIII. Suspicions Regarding the Crime

It was a Monday morning. Work resumed with enthusiasm at the factory—an enthusiasm a trifle mitigated by Sunday's little extras. Once, Mondays had been less active because a substantial fraction of the workers had stayed up late in the local drinking dens, debating at the counter or rolling the dice in games of Zanzibar, or sitting at tables and playing cards. Often, the morning, and sometimes the whole day, were afflicted by that, but since everyone now had an interest in the factory, defections were rare, and those who were tempted to go on the spree resisted, in order not to be treated as "shirkers" by the others.

Lafon made his tour of inspection, leading a hand or offering advice here and there. Everyone liked him and held him in high esteem, so he was welcomed more as a friend than the director. He arrived at the vice of a planer, who was smoothing off a piece of steel with the aid of a file and a great deal of elbow grease.

"Well, Albaret, was the fishing good yesterday?"

"Not bad. Three pounds of roach. You'll eat some at midday—I sent a plate round to your wife this morning."

"Thanks—you're really too kind."

"Bah! It's the least one can do to give a treat to one's friends. But guess who I ran into at Vilennes—for that's where it's necessary to go nowadays, if you want to bring something back."

"It's worth the trouble. Who did you run into, then?"

A fellow who didn't gather any moss at the factory, although one has reason to remember it, because it was the week that the boss was crushed. Do you remember the guy?"

"Yes—the one recommended to me by Monsieur Etienne. I can find his name in the books."

"Not worth the trouble. Listen—I was with my brother-in-law, a chairmaker who knows the guy; it appears that he's an old pike[63] from the Avenue Gambetta."

"What are you telling me? Did you talk to him?"

"I wanted to, but as soon as he saw me, he hopped it. That's what intrigued me—so, without appearing to, I followed him. He was suspicious, and looked behind him, but there were plenty of people about, and to put him off the track, I'd put on Octave's hat—Octave's my brother-in-law. Anyway, I saw him go into a property of which he had the key. For a former worker, I thought was odd.

"In brief, I went into the neatest bistro, ordered a glass and asked: 'Doesn't that property whose gate has the big iron nails belong to Monsieur Pigeollet?'—

---

[63] French pimps can be likened metaphorically to pike as well as mackerel.

that's my brother-in-law, Octave Pigeollet. 'No, it belongs to Monsieur Armand Baudard, a good customer.' I left. I knew enough to satisfy my curiosity. All the same, the clown's a boor. If he's a rentier today, that's no reason for him not to recognize an old workmate.

"With that, I went back to my pitch and I found Octave, who'd taken the other's place, and I told my brother-in-law what I'd learned. 'Yes, it's fishy, if you ask me. If that fellow's rich now, it's because he's brought off some nasty coup. Anyway, the main thing is that he's put out bait for us.' So, my old Louis, it's thanks to that Baudard that you'll be eating friendly fish today."

"But you're the one who fished it out and brought it. Thank you."

Lafon shook the worker's hand and went back to his office. Involuntarily, a thought was hammering in his head. *It's Monsieur Etienne who had that fellow hired, and he quit the factory immediately after Monsieur Aubert's death. He came to be paid that same Saturday, and we never saw him again.*

Lafon revived that tragic morning, and the enigma of the curiously open grille. *Let's see, did someone go to the storage bay that day?* Closing his eyes in order to concentrate his thoughts, Lafon made an effort to recall. *No, it was a Friday, almost the end of the week. Everyone had a job under way. Oh, I'll find out...*

He took a thick cardboard file out of a drawer, one which was written in large letters: *Metals Register June 1923*. It contained the records of the work benches, with the names of the workmen occupying the places, the work completed and the time that each job had taken. He flipped through the file until he found the name of Armand Baudard, bench 47. The sheets told him that benches 46 and 48 had been occupied by old hands of the factory with ten years' experience: Albaret, the man who had just recognized the former pimp in the rentier of Vilennes, and Jean Ouchy, a first-rate fitter.

At the meal break, Lafon waited for the two workers to emerge. "Would you care for an apero?"

Once they were at the counter, he said: "What you told me, Albaret, has been running through my mind. When Baudard was between the two of you on the day of the Boss's death, do you remember whether he left his workstation at about a quarter to noon?"

"For sure," said Ouchy. "The imbecile went to the reserve to fetch a bar he didn't need, forgetting that he'd gone to get one the day before. He put the bar down behind the bench, stated to laugh and said to us—do you remember, Albaret?—'Look at that! I'm going daft. I went to fetch a bar to make a piston-rod, and I already had one.'"

"What are you thinking, Lafon?" asked Albaret.

"I'm making connections between the recent good fortune of that individual and the Boss's death."

"It's impossible! Why would Baudard have done that? And who would have paid him for doing it?"

340

Lafon drew the two men outside. The street was deserted for the moment. He seized his two comrades' hands: "Your testimony, the two of you, might explain a lot of things. For the time being, don't mention this Baudard to anyone."

"You think he caused the Boss's accident?" said Albaret.

"I'm beginning to think that it wasn't an accident. Until further instructions, all this stays between us. It would be stupid to say anything before being absolutely certain. Complete silence."

The three men separated, and Lafon went home to eat the famous fried fish, the point of departure for new concerns. Madame Lafon did not take long to ask: "What's up? Something's bothering you."

Lafon knew that his wife was a good adviser, and very clever at seeing through many things. He had no hesitation about telling her everything.

"You understand now, my dear Adrienne, the horror into which these suspicions are throwing me? Who paid Baudard to commit the crime? You understand that the bandit couldn't have gotten any benefit from the crime, and the Commissaire's first thought, if I took it to him, would be to go back to whoever profited from the murder."

"To Monsieur Etienne, our benefactor."

"Anyway, there's no urgency. Baudard doesn't know that he's under suspicion. It's necessary to watch him, not to lose sight of him."

"For my part, I'll try to find out something from Madame Aubert. Without actually putting her in the picture, I'll try to find out whether she's ever suspected something worse than an accident."

"If you want—but be prudent."

IX. Women's Confidences

Since the death of Antoine Aubert, the devotion with which Madame Lafon had cared for Madame Aubert and little Ulette had linked them in friendship. Adrienne Lafon was of bourgeois origin and had received a good education. Her parents, ruined by an unwise speculation on the Bourse and reduced to black poverty, had been very happy to encounter Louis Lafon, to marry their daughter to him and be supported themselves by the mechanic. That was a hard time of furious labor for the young man, subsidizing the existence of the two old people. Adrienne had done as much as she could, giving lessons in French and English. When the two old people had died, however, life had become easier and the good wife only kept up English translations as mental relaxation. Adrienne who was only forty, was therefore not out of place in the company of Madame Aubert, and that explains the sympathy between the two women.

When Madame Lafon arrived at Madame Aubert's home, Aline embraced her.

"I've decided to leave for the Midi a little sooner than I thought, and I have a lot of purchases to make. Would you be kind enough to take charge of them?"

"Gladly. Have you made a list of what you need?"

"Here it is."

"Where can we get all this?"

"I always shop at the Galeries Mondiales."

"Well then, we'll continue. You've received news from Théoule, then?"

"Yes, Madame Desambrez and her daughter-in-law are awaiting me impatiently. That's why I'm hastening our departure."

"And what does Ulette think?"

"She's delighted to be seeing her friend Simone Ossola again, whom she hasn't seen for eighteen months, and that scamp Robert. Madame Ossola has a house in Nice. She'll return there while I'm in childbed, with Ulette and her children. That way, Ulette won't see her big doll until after my churching. It will work out very well like that."

"Does Monsieur Etienne approve of the arrangements?"

A cloud passed over the young widow's face.

"In fact, you're my friend. I sense that I can confide in you and that you'll keep the secret. Last Saturday, after a pleasant dinner to celebrate Ulette's recovery, after my old Madeleine had put the child to bed, Etienne and I stayed together, chatting by the fire. After a few banalities, he declared that he loves me."

"You, his father's widow?"

"Yes. I confess that his proposal frightened me. It's hastening my voyage. Etienne revealed himself to me in an entirely new light. He told me that he's

342

adored me since the first time he saw me, that he's suffered from my marriage to his father, that he's been jealous. But what's the matter, my dear Annie? You've gone pale, fearfully. Would you like a cordial?"

"Go on," said Adrienne. "It's a nervous crisis, to which I'm subject. It's passed. You said that Etienne revealed that he's passionately in love with you?"

"Yes, and in the end, with such violence that he frightened me, saying that if any new obstacles came between us, he'd be able to break them..."

"He's mad! What did you tell him? That such a marriage is impossible."

"No, he was too excited. I talked about waiting, the necessary reflection."

"Perhaps you were right. But what are you going to do?"

"Leave, first. Etienne is willful, violent. The factory is his life. I thought he was entirely absorbed by it. He became its absolute master by virtue of his father's death. And now, in a few months, a child will be born, a brother or sister, with whom he'll have to share. It will be necessary to appoint a guardian to whom he'll have to render accounts. All that frightens me, and if my godmother consents, I'll stay with her. My personal fortune permits me to live independently. I'll settle somewhere in the Alpes-Maritimes and raise my children in tranquility. Retreat to the sun."

"I won't see you any more, then?" said Adrienne, sadly.

"Why don't you and Lafon come next year? Your husband has the right to a month's vacation now, as director. You can spend it with me, and in the meantime, we can write to one another often."

"I accept," said Adrienne, "but perhaps you'll come back without anything to fear from your stepson."

"It's certain that he might change his mind...if he marries, for instance."

"He'll marry!" said Madame Lafon, recklessly, thinking: *The red widow, the guillotine.* "Now that the future's settled for you, let's think about the present. I have the list of all the things you need. I'll take care of it tomorrow."

The two women chatted for a little while longer about various trivia, and then Adrienne withdrew.

X. The Anxiety of Worthy Men

When the good woman found herself with her husband again that evening, she told him about her visit to Madame Aubert.

"There's no longer any possible error," he said, sadly. "Etienne had his father murdered in order to become the master of the factory, and now he wants to marry the pretty young widow. It's terrible! And it's to him that I owe the direction of the workshops! The man I considered to be everyone's benefactor. If I denounce him, it's the end of the factory and the workers' co-operative. In punishing a cowardly and miserable murderer, I'd be putting all those men out of work."

"Have we the right to do that?"

"I don't want to take that responsibility on my own. Albaret and Ouchy are already partly informed—I'll tell them everything. They'll give me their advice. What do you think, old girl?"

"You're right, and it will take some of the weight off us."

"I'll bring them here tomorrow evening, then. They'll have supper with us, and we'll chat at the end of the meal, or afterwards."

XI. The Factory Protects the Boss

The next day, the two comrades, rather astonished by the invitation, came to take their places at the director's table. The dinner was almost silent, Albaret and Ouchy divining that their friend had something serious to tell them with regard to Baudard.

After dessert, Madame Lafon brought a bottle of old wine, and Lafon related the result of his investigation briefly, evoking the consequences of the factory owner's arrest.

"I can't take this under my hat. Like me, you're old hands at the factory, you knew Aubert, the father, and even his father, the founder. You've shared in the grandeur of the company. Give me your opinion."

They reflected for some time. Finally, Albaret said: "The factory must come first. The severed head of Etienne Aubert isn't worth the livelihoods of a thousand households and progress in the corporation. Ought we to sacrifice that to judiciary vengeance? What advantage would we get out of it? It would even be a black mark for Socialism. Léon Daudet's clamoring that those who are leading the democratic movement are sectarians and murderers.[64] I think we should keep quiet."

"Don't you think," objected Lafon, "that to act thus is only to listen to your instinct?"

"Possibly. But it's in everyone's interest. If we could consult the comrades, they'd say the same as me."

"Perhaps. Everyone thinks of himself first. What about you Ouchy?"

"If it were up to me, I'd gladly see the Boss guillotined, but fundamentally, I agree with Albaret. It's necessary to sustain the factory, since the factory is us. I have an idea though. What if we were to profit from our secret by demanding further concessions from the Boss? For example, if we were to forbid him to marry and have children, so that on his death the factory would revert entirely to the workers. You can't say that's an egotistical proposition, since Etienne Aubert is younger than us—but it would be our children that would profit from it."

"From a parricide? That's frightful!" said Adrienne. "And then, you know, Madame Aubert is pregnant."

---

[64] Léon Daudet (1867-1942), who followed in the footsteps of his father Alphonse in becoming a novelist, had been a committed Republican in his youth, but had deserted that camp for the far right, serving as editor of the virulently anti-socialist *Action Française*. He was a député in the National Bloc from 1919-24. Like Champsaur, he dabbled in speculative fiction, for which he had an evident predilection.

"*Zut!*" cried Ouchy, naively. "In a fortnight of marriage!"

"That's sufficient, my dear," said Albaret, laughing.

Gravely, Lafon went on: "It's necessary to think hard about all this. I think we should put off a decision for a year. Who knows what might happen in the meantime? It might be that Etienne Aubert will indicate the way to go by his conduct."

"You're right. There's no urgency. In any case, mouths shut about our secret. Today's the tenth of October 1923. Next year, on the same date, we'll meet again—here, if you like, Lafon. We'll make a decision."

"In a year, to the day," said the director. "Once, it was the cathedral that provided sanctuary to the guilty. Today it's the factory."

Interlude: Silly Talk on the Mountain

Etienne Aubert, the protagonist of this book, appears in a very bad light here, and perhaps some might wax indignant, claiming that such a criminal son could not exist, especially one who is young and brave. Brave? He only risked death during the war, and was decorated for that, and merely paid in order to occasion a fatal accident for his father. But is not that excess of egotism—which very rarely goes that far, I admit—characteristic of the mores of the period after the Great War, of which no one is proud? Have you noticed that no one recounts his exploits; everyone hides the atrocities that were committed during those five years of trenches, in which human beasts had their instincts unchained, whereas the soldiers of year II, the Revolution and the survivors of the Napoleonic Era continued to recount their magnificent actions when the wars were over and they had retired to their hearths, drinking coffee with a dash or two of cognac—a "gloria"—under the casks that they still call "gloriettes" in Provence because of the tales of the battles that the veterans repeated there, in the shade of jasmines and bindweed.

Never has the quarrel and struggle between men under thirty—or forty at the most—and those above that age, been as sharp. The generation that was dressed in blue horizon cloth to kill and to die is in haste to live, to enjoy, intensely, and without waiting, everything that their elders possess. They manipulate them, push them, knock them over, as much as they can, while waiting to stick them in the ground by means of ruses, perfidies, deceptions, concerted filthy tricks and calumnies—in short, by all cunning means devoid of the risks that pilfering carried in the war—on the principle of every man for himself. The "heroes" jostle people with their elbows, rudely, in the street, on trams and in the metro—even women—without apologizing or begging pardon, as an old man would do instantly, as a reflex.

Indifference reigns, and the boor is king.

Will you say, young men, that Etienne Aubert does not exist? How do you know? Perhaps he will exist longer than you. In any case, he is representative of the soul of thousands upon thousands very like him, and if he is unique, art, in the novel as in the theater, only sees exceptions. He kills his father; moreover, he is in love with his father's wife. Well, I am only reiterating old stories, transforming ancient tragedies into a twentieth-century novel, renewing, by modernizing then, Aeschylus, Sophocles and Euripides—and the depths of the human heart have not changed much: civilization, with the telephone and wireless telegraphy has only put a varnish over eternal appetites; at the first tremors of interest or passion it cracks; during five years of massacre, pilfering, theft and hasty prostitution, it cracked everywhere.

And the young are marching more terribly than ever, on the heels of their elders. Certainly, the adolescent cannot remain the baby who regards his father and mother, those benevolent despots, as infallible and perfect beings; one has the right, between twenty and thirty years of age, to contemplate the terrain to be conquered with immeasurable ambitions. Besides which, it is necessary not to cure youth; it is necessary to maintain its incomparable prestige carefully. It is not an evil, but, on the contrary, the best of trump cards, it is the conqueror to retain within oneself, for it is necessary to be green with white hair, to be young for as long as possible, to be twenty as long as one lives.

The young, escaped from the abattoir, no longer have any courtesy. They act like savages forcing an old man to climb a coconut palm. If the poor man cannot climb the trunk, or if, having reached the top, he cannot hold onto the branches of the tree when it is shaken, if he falls, they kill him—and eat him, if they are cannibals.

Personally, I would bombard them cheerfully with coconuts.

"What can a man of fifty expect?" writes a young man, François Mauriac.[65] "We are only interested in him out of politeness and necessity." Paul Raynal, in his tragedy *Le Tombeau sous l'Arc de Triomphe*, designates the father by the insult "the Old Man" and makes him kneel down before his son to beg his pardon. And Jean Sarment cries, over the trestles: "I'm too great for myself!"— which is to say, less nobly. "I want to fart higher than my ass!" They are at least fellows of verve and talent—but what can one say about the insignificant and the failures, the pretentious innumerable who lay their fly-specks gratuitously in the newspapers and magazines? Literati who have printed, more or less at their own expense, three thousand amorphous novels a year, devoid of originality, style and imagination, competitors for and beneficiaries of a host of Prix Goncourts, Balzacs and Conrads, which are no longer anything, and are sometimes founded in order to be, thanks to complaisant and bribed juries, launch platforms and advertisements for some book or other, and are attributed to the abortions of donors. O public, how is it possible to select, without being duped, from that ever-rising ant hill of books that assaults railway bookstalls and the shelves of bookshops every day?

As for me, having arrived at the summit of the mountain a long time ago, and who must be on the further slope, if I had to recommence my career, I would choose another métier. "Does it still amuse you to write novels?" Henri Letellier the owner of the great daily *Le Journal*—to which he adds oil, international sleeper cars and the Train Bleu—asked me one day in Nice. And a sixteen-year-old shorthand typist with golden red hair to whom I was dictating a

---

[65] François Mauriac (1885-1970) was just hitting is stride as a novelist in 1924; Champsaur had no way of knowing that he would go on to with the Nobel Prize for Literature, but given what he thought of Anatole France, would probably have considered that one more reason to dislike him.

few pages, while occasionally hesitating slightly, searching for a phrase, turned round to say to me: "So you can't do anything except write novels, then?"

Alas, no—and I regret not having chosen finance! When I was twenty I went to see a banker, Monsieur de Lamonta, the director of a carriage company in the Rue Taitbout—fiacres in those days, yellow fiacres, the *Urbaine*. He had left the Digne, my homeland, with no money, and I knew that he had wandered around Paris with patched and ragged trousers. As he wasn't stupid, he said to me: "You know how I started out. Well, do as I did. I have six million now. I'm owed three. That makes nine."

Immediately, he gave me a lesson in business. If I had gone into a bank and had educated myself there, perhaps, if chance had favored me, I would now be someone, like the extraordinary pirate Zaharoff, Grand'croix de la Légion d'honneur, who, while clinging like a fantastic octopus to the rocks of Monte Carlo, on French soil, captures by means of speculations, in his florid tentacles, profits of a hundred and fifty million a year, having among his employees the Prince of Monaco, and in order to avoid any fiscal inconveniences in Paris—for he pays no taxes—a former President of the Council, Louis Barthou, and his brother, Léon Barthou, as administrators. Perhaps I would be in the place of that magisterial, hyperbalzacian businessman, and I would found, in honor of Balzac, a literary prize of ten thousand francs.[66]

I would regret not having listened to the banker Monsieur de Lamonta if I did not think, even long thereafter, that dreaming and women are the best and sweetest things in life, and if I did not have the care and the pride, in spite of everything, of joyful work and a well-made book.

However, there is an annihilation of writing.

Young people want to be rich immediately, to be leaders rapidly, without waiting to be beaten, reduced and compressed by life. And why not? During the Revolution and under Napoleon, there were beardless generals. With their superabundant strength, which knows no limits, they are not resigned, as the old are; quite simply, they want everything and they want it now. They're right.

But I tell them this parable.

A couple—a pretty blonde of twenty, a delightful cinema actress, and a fellow of fifty, I dare not say more; it's abnormal, disgusting and unjust, isn't it?—were traveling by car, with the old man, an expert and adroit driver, at the wheel along the road to Gonfaron, a village in the Var perched on a picturesque crag. They encountered an old man who was moaning. They stopped to ask the poor man what was wrong. Sobbing like a child, he replied: "I'm crying because my father beat me."

They continued on their way, and further on they met another white-bearded peasant, and told him about the old man in tears.

---

[66] Basil Zaharoff endowed the Prix Balzac.

"Oh, you listened to that young rascal, did you? I clipped the lad round the ear because he was disrespectful to his grandfather."

"What! His grandfather?"

"Yes. You can go ask him. That's him up the fig tree, picking the figs.

Soon, the Parisians reached the village, and in the house of the Maire, whom they were visiting, they met a green curé—black in his soutane, of course, but as white with age as Charlemagne. They told him the story, and the genteel Brabant said to the priest: "Do you know them, Monsieur le Curé, that sixty-year-old man who was crying by the roadside, his father and his grandfather?"

"Of course I know them, Mademoiselle. It was me who baptized all three of them."

Where would we be if macrobites had the right to go on as long as Methuselah? Old Montaigne—he would be three hundred years old and it would be necessary to poison him if he were still alive and continued to write—proclaims: "As for me I deem that our souls are denounced at twenty. Of all the fine human actions that have come to my knowledge, of whatever sort they might be, I would swear that the greater number of them, in the last six centuries and our own, have produced more before the age of thirty than afterwards."

Like Michel de Montaigne, I think that it is necessary to love youth, which is the charm of the world. Old age is the setting sun, the twilight, night, and youth the dawn and the light, a new sun rising. In spring, things are brighter, and youth—*Gioventù! Gioventù!* Mussolini and the Fascists chant in Italy—youth is the laughter, the straightness, the clarity of a land. Oh, how I love you, how I understand you, young people, handsome young people, the old people of to-morrow.

XII. The Womb and the Child in the Sun

That afternoon, in the gardens of the Villa Bellarosa in Théoule, Madame Aubert was sitting on a wicker divan in the shade of a clump of mimosas, the golden clusters of which were warmed and made to sparkle by the bright March sun—that month being, in the paradise of the Côte d'Azur, a furnisher of spring, like April in Paris—and the perfume of which was always delightfully pleasant, seemingly paradoxical with her black Botticelliesque hair amid the tomboyish fashion of women's hair cut short to leave the nape of the neck bare, was breast-feeding a new baby, three weeks old, garlanded with lace. Beside the young mother, a pram garnished with a pink silk coverlet awaited the nursling.

"Look at that glutton," said Madame Desambez, who was also sitting in a wicker armchair knitting a pair of dainty socks for the child. "And what a grip! You can say, without boasting, that you have the most beautiful child I've ever seen."

"He takes after his father, who was big and strong."

"Poor child. This is a house of orphans," said Madame Desambez, sadly. "Of the four children we have, not one will have known their father."

"Yes, Ulette remembers hers, because I've maintained his memory piously. Her true father was, for her, Papa, but Antoine Aubert was Papapa—a superlative. When will Marcelle arrive from Nice?"

"She'll be in Cannes at three o'clock. I've asked Marius to take the car to pick her up at the station, because the express doesn't stop at Théoule. You're impatient to see Ulette. She's adorable, your daughter."

"It's the first time that I've been separated from her—but it was necessary."

"I'm curious to see how she'll welcome her little brother."

"She'll adore him. He'll be such a beautiful doll."

"He'll be everyone's little brother. Simone and Robert will be content, too."

"Someone won't be, though. I'm a little afraid of Etienne Aubert."

"I understand, given what you've told me—so I'll renew my proposition. Don't go back to Paris. Your personal fortune is sufficient, and you'll be at home here."

"I accept as wholeheartedly as I sense that you're making the offer, but I can't disinterest myself entirely in the Aubert factory; I can't disinherit my son. He has rights that I need to safeguard out of respect for the father."

"You haven't received a letter from Etienne Aubert since the laconic telegram he sent you congratulating you on the birth of his brother Antoine, as he's been baptized."

"The name of brother, applied by Etienne, caused me to shiver involuntarily."

"It's necessary not to magnify the suggestion of bad thoughts. The boy fell in love with you. In sum, given his age and yours, there's nothing extraordinary about that—but absence leads to forgetfulness, and with forgetfulness passion calms down."

"I hope so with all my heart."

Madame Desambez put down her knitting and picked up a regional newspaper, the *Eclaireur*, which she began to scan. Having placed the baby in the pram, Madame Aubert rocked him gently, singing in order to send him to sleep.

"Oho!" said Madame Desambez, charming and rosy with her crown of white hair. "The paper's giving a lot of publicity to those two charlatans. Today there's an article signed by Georges Maurevert, who's a writer of merit."[67]

"Excuse me but I haven't read a line of print since my churching. This little monsieur has taken up all my time. Who are the two charlatans?"

"A couple of thought-readers. The man—the manager, it seems—is called Thomas Keysar, and the woman, Souriah. She is, it seems, astonishing, another Madame de Thèbes.[68] There are always diviners turning out dupes."

"The marvelous doesn't tempt you?"

"Yes, but not via superstition and mystification. These two new sorcerers practice somnambulism and suggestion, but they don't predict the future; they limit their research to the present and the past. According to the paper, they've enlightened the law with regard to the murder at Le Mas de la Pinède, and brought about the arrest of the murderer."

"Well, that rehabilitates your charlatans."

"My word," said the old lady, laughing. "I owe them an apology."

"If they come to Cannes," said Madame Aubert, "I'll go to consult them."

"You? Why?"

"On the subject of my husband's death."

"But since he was the victim of an accident..."

"I'm beginning to doubt that, my dear friend."

---

[67] "Georges Maurevert" was the pseudonym of the journalist and novelist Georges Leménager (1869-1964), who moved from Paris to Nice at the beginning of the century and wrote abundantly for the local newspapers, the *Petit Niçois* and *L'Éclaireur de Nice*. Champsaur would have known him for a long time.

[68] Madame de Thèbes was the pseudonym of the notorious Parisian clairvoyant and chiromancer Anne Victoria Savigny (c1845-1916).

XIII. It's Never Over

For three months, Thomas and Berthe had been the guests of Sixte Coutan on the Côte d'Azur. The new "businessman" had rented a beautiful villa in Nice, on Mont Boron, where he entertained politicians, bankers and schemers passing through the Riviera, all those who live on bluff and glamour. Josette was enthroned there in all her glory, doing her best to make a splash, and to dazzle the two former Bohemians with her luxury. By way of compensation, Toto, who had rapidly insinuated himself into the various large and small newspapers of Nice, was obtaining "echoes" of the parties and receptions at the villa on Mont Boron, Les Papillons.

Thomas Keysar frequented a tavern under the arcades in the Place Masséna in Nice, an environment of vague predators of letters, uprooted from Paris, old whores with theatrical connections, where a respectable man gone astray, despite being on the Côte d'Azur, indulging in pleasure and sunlight, would be miserly with his handshakes: an environment of emaciated corsairs, harpies and Parisian bandits run aground there, wrinkled, bald or painted, more venomous than old toads; merchants of publicity, who nevertheless believed in their wit, in the yellow press of the Riviera—which is publicity nevertheless. Keysar, the thought-reader, needed it, for himself, for Souriah and for the double-dealing household of his friends the Coutans. In that fashion, he paid for the hospitality offered to the murderous couple in the villa on Mont Boron.

So, the two thought-readers, by sprinkling that gang with aperitifs, had become popular. They had given séances at the Ruhl and the Negresco. Their success in Paris was nothing compared to the enthusiasm of the coastal population of the Mediterranean, or, rather, the dubious cosmopolitan society that comes every winter to parade in the sun.

"We needed the sun to put us in the light," said Thomas, one day.

"You wouldn't be here without me," Josette pointed out.

"You said it, my beauty," said Berthe, who now addressed Josette as *tu*, and had the compliment returned. "So, in recognition of your kindness, what would you say to a party at Les Papillons, for the benefit of the war-wounded of Nice, which you patronize, which will put you in the limelight on the Riviera— not to mention that it would be useful to your husband, to bring all the wealthy people in this paradise together. Coutan can give us a few tips about his guests, and we'll read their thoughts."

"Oh, yes! Thanks for the idea. I'll arrange it with Sixte."

A domestic came in carrying a tray laden with letters and newspapers, for the masters of the house and the magician.

"Look!" exclaimed Josette. "A letter from Etienne Aubert—I recognize the handwriting. It's addressed to you at the Rue Huysmans in Paris; it's been forwarded."

Thomas and Berthe exchanged an anxious glance. "Bah!" said Keysar. "It won't be anything interesting. I'll open it later." And he slid the letter into his pocket.

"Is my presence embarrassing you?" said Josette, vexed, getting to her feet.

"Are you joking?" said Berthe. "We don't have anything to hide from you. Read your letter, Toto."

Thomas had reflected. It was impossible that Etienne had been imprudent enough to write anything compromising in a letter, at the risk of going astray. He took the envelope out of his pocket and opened it. It only contained a few lines. Having scanned them, he held it out to Josette. "Here, look."

She took the piece of paper and read aloud: "*My dear Thomas, how are you? I've telephoned the Rue Huysmans in vain; I'd be obliged if you could arrange a meeting with me. I know you're very busy but I need to see you, the sooner the better. Cordially, Etienne Aubert.*"

Josette burst out laughing and continued: "Well, he'll have to wait. There's a good joke to be made, though. Tell him that you'll meet him in Nice, at my house..."

"What if he comes?"

"I've no fear of that. The dear friend's given me the cold shoulder since his father's death, since he has the whole factory. *Au revoir*, children, I'll leave you and go to talk to Sixte about this soirée."

Left alone, the two accomplices looked at one another.

"It must be a matter of the stepmother," said Berthe. "She must have given birth. Etienne, I'm sure of it, must have a little brother. So, naturally, he has need of us."

Thomas shivered. "A kid...a baby..."

"Exactly. It's less heavy on the conscience. Think about it. What we've done serves no purpose if the widow's succeeded in laying. It'll be necessary for him to share. Confess that that's annoying. So I know in advance what he wants."

"Me, too," said Thomas, darkly, "and I don't want anything to do with it."

She burst out laughing. "Don't be childish. I haven't made it clear. It's another job for Baudard and the slut. He's running short—it couldn't have come at a better time. Only this time, it's necessary to make him cough up a million. You can give two hundred thousand to them—after that, the beggars will leave us in peace."

"And we can go to America, to New York. France is chic, but the New World is better. I'm always scared now that in our somnambulistic double state you might say something stupid—and also afraid of Dr. Vanel, Homo-Deus."

"That nonsense again. Look, whether I'm asleep or awake, how it is possible that I'm not me? Me, Berthe Jafaux of Paname!"

"No, a thousand times no. It's no longer you—it frightens me. It's for that reason, more than any other, that I'm thinking of leaving the country. Perhaps, in traveling, you'll end up leaving *the other* behind."

"You're driving me crazy with all that. Don't put me to sleep any more, then. We'll take in the mugs as before, that's all. One more reason, anyway, for working for Etienne. With the big payoff we'll go away, and the devil with the trade. How do we arrange the meeting with Aubert, then?"

"I'll send him a telegram and arrange a rendezvous in Lyon. That way, we'll be meeting half way. Go fetch me the P.L.M. timetable and I'll take the dispatch down to Nice right away.

XV. One Crime Leads to Another

On the day after next, Sunday, Etienne and Thomas met in Lyon at the Hôtel Terminus. As soon as they were alone in a room, each with their red ribbons in their buttonholes, with the door closed, Etienne said:

"You have some inkling of what it's about? My stepmother has given birth to a son, and you understand my situation, at the point where I am. If I could correct the past, I wouldn't recommence what I've allowed to happen. You and Berthe have been the two tempters; you made me consent to and sign a horrible pact. Oh, I don't want to dramatize my sin, but in having my father killed, I made a bad mistake. I'm not posing as a man racked by remorse; my hatred of this miserable kid will efface it. And then, there's also the woman I love, in spite of everything, whom I desire, whom I want. And that toad, who has been baptized Antoine, will always be between us. The kid has to disappear. It's necessary."

"It'll be expensive," said the other, coldly.

"You consent?"

"For your happiness, I'll do the impossible. We need another accident. It will be more difficult."

"My stepmother has gone to stay for the birth with her godmother, Madame Desambez, at Théoule, between Cannes and Saint-Raphaël."

"Damn! That's annoying; I don't know anyone there. There are locations to study, my operator to displace. How much are you offering?"

"The same price."

"Impossible. There are too many risks. Then again, people who don't recoil before the death of a man hesitate before a child. It'll need double."

"A million! Are you mad?"

"What's a million today? You've inherited, without counting the old man's cash, a factory that's worth several. Go elsewhere, then; I don't need it. If I'm still willing to run the risk, it's purely to do you a favor. You know, anyway, that I won't do it myself. I'm an honest man. I can aid destiny, that's all. Times are hard and rogues are demanding."

"All right. How will you do it?"

"I don't know, and that's not your concern. Let us take care of it, Berthe and me—and Baudard. It's not my fault, or his, that you witnessed your father's accident. Chance did that."

"I won't be there this time; I won't be able to see anything, fortunately."

"One more reason; it's an advantage—and no risk for you."

"Understood, my dear. You'll take charge of the affair?"

"It's necessary, since I worked on the other. By the way, you'll have to make an engagement, like the first time. Here's the stamped paper. You can see that I suspected what was bringing you here."

Without responding, Etienne wrote, to the dictation of his accomplice:

I, the undersigned, Etienne Aubert, factory owner of Paris, Quai de Javel, declare that I owe Monsieur Thomas Keysar, man of letters and thought-reader, domiciled in Paris, Rue Huysmans, the sum of one million francs, payable in ten monthly checks of a hundred thousand francs (100,000 francs) each, from the date of the death certificate of my brother, Antoine Aubert, in the year 1924.

Lyon, 14 March 1924.

Etienne Aubert.

Then, handing over the fatal piece of paper, he said: "When shall I have news?"

"As soon as possible."

"And will I succeed in making the mother love me?"

"You're sick, my lad? You have that woman in your blood, then? What microbe has ruined your eyes for her to get under your skin like that? I'll leave you now; I'm in a hurry to get back to Nice, where I'm staying in a splendid villa on Mont Boron with your old friend Josette Coutan, who retains a fond memory of you. There's a pretty woman who wouldn't give you as much trouble as Madame Aubert. By the way, on my way back to Nice I'll stop off at Théoule to inform myself as to the lie of the land. But a baby is susceptible to so many maladies, you know. A young life is so fragile..."

357

XV. The Land of Golden Fruit

On returning to Les Papillons, the villa on Mont Boron, as soon as Thomas was alone with Berthe, he had her read the engagement signed by Etienne Aubert, written entirely in his hand and signed by the factory owner.

"That's it." said the seeress. "We've got the happy ending. Now, I think, poverty is well and truly over. I'll write to Baudard and tell him to come alone, without my sister. You've put the wind in my sail with your Marc Vanel, Homo-Deus. Let's get the money, leave for New York and exchange the land of oranges for that of dollars. When you go to Nice, book a room in a small out-of-the-way hotel for my brother-in-law manqué. When he's there you can give him the information about the Villa Bellarosa that you brought back from Théoule. You're an ace, and don't waste time—but Baudard's sentimental and he'll jib when he knows that it's a matter of a kid."

"I'll give him a hundred thousand francs, as for the father."

"Yes, that's reasonable. It's settled, then?"

Thomas Keysar, all the more delighted because magnificent sunlight was filling their room with radiance and adding a pink tint to the palm trees with ivy-clad trunks that were outlined against the blue sky outside the two windows, embraced his mistress joyfully; they sketched a dance step, while singing the final refrain of the carnival: *Nice en folie.*

XVI. The Painter of the Sun

At the Villa Bellarosa in Théoule, meanwhile, there was bliss. The arrival of Marcelle Ossola and her two children, Simone and Robert, and the mischievous Ulette Jousselin, in the life of the excellent and worthy Madame Desambez provoked a redoubling of joy. The three women were certainly not short of reasons to be melancholy, but the sight of the children running around them prevented them from being absorbed by it. Ulette, in her capacity as the eldest, also more intelligent and alert, had quickly obtained an ascendancy over Simone and Robert; she organized all the games, the fantasy of which often made the three women laugh.

The plaything *par excellence*, however, was the baby Antoine. Ulette had declared herself his little mother; she called him "my son" ostentatiously; but as the living doll could not go everywhere with his little mother, Ulette had changed the sex of her articulated doll, and called it Antony; it was lugged around to every corner of the grounds and submitted, without complaint, to all the caprices of its three tyrants.

Furthermore a guest had come: Fabio Canti, the painter of Venice, Egypt, Palestine and Syria, whose warm and vibrant canvases had earned him the nickname "the Painter of the Sun." Like Ziem,[69] who had a villa in Nice, he was a regular visitor to the Côte d'Azur. He had come from Saint-Raphaël to see Madame Aubert, and the proprietor of the Bellarosa, Madame Desambez, had declared herself happy and proud to offer hospitality to the great master for as long as he wished.

Fabio, who had been famous and fashionable for a long time, led the simultaneously hard and joyful life of a true artist among the charlatans and art dealers. Of tall stature, and a handsome man, he had always had, as compensation for the struggle, not merely the easy conquest of the pretty girls frequenting the studios, but a number of bourgeois women and socialites subjugated by the spirited artist's manners and smile. Fabio was neither a gambler nor a drinker; his one vice was women. Not a sentimental lover, but lascivious, he saw nothing in amour but pleasure and did not seek any other attractions than those it gives wise men who do not torment their minds in order to find a thousand irritations and sufferings. However, as the years had accumulated, he sometimes wearied of liaisons that were as rapidly loosened as knotted, and, while repeating to himself that prudent happiness existed there, the pollen-gatherer could not help

---

[69] The painter Félix Ziem (1821-1911) produced many scenes of Venice, which he visited every year, as well as other sunny landscapes. Champsaur probably knew him when he lived in Montmartre, and might well have modelled Fabio Canti on him.

comparing, on certain evenings, his adventurous life with that of his parents in Venice, who had formed a happy and mutually adoring couple.

At present, the impetuosity of early youth had given way to sometimes-hesitant and whimsical virility, and the obsession of conjugal love had imposed itself on his mind; he felt lonely. What is the point of fortune and glory, if it is uniquely for oneself? The young widow, the perfect model of the indoor woman, Madame Aubert, was like a crystallization of his familiar dreams. But without giving too much concern to trying his luck, he was taking the cure at the Bellarosa of a tranquil and restful existence, and his eroticism, on leave, was dormant.

He knew every detail of Antoine Aubert's frightful accident. The Commissaire charged with the investigation, Albert Raynaud, was a friend of his. They had once hung out together in the brasseries of the Latin Quarter, when the Commissaire was something of a poet, a singer and occasional contributor to periodicals, and they had remained friends.

The Commissaire was not entirely convinced about the accident of the Quai de Javel, and had said so to Fabio. But the policeman, who had imagination, sometimes told the painter stories about his métier that he brought to fantastic conclusions, with which he also amused himself. Raynaud, of course, would have thought that Fabio Canti could not spend a fortnight or three weeks at the Bellarosa, that nest of widowed pullets without playing the cock. Well, no, he was a cock on vacation, whose eroticism was resting.

They were on the terrace in front of the villa that overlooked the magnificent gardens, with a splendid view over the coast and the sea, a scene such as one sees elsewhere all along that magical shore. The sky was so pure, the atmosphere so clear, that the gaze embraced, with a delightful clarity, the ultimate slopes of Cap Estérel descending into the sea, forming, with their green firetrees and red rocks, a rutilant and tormented mass, and in the distance, the town of Cannes, voluptuously extended in the depths of the enchanting gulf. The terrace, paved with large slabs of alternating white and pink marble, was shaded by vigorous wisterias, which, supported by a pergola, painted vermilion, covered it completely with their violet clusters, and the pergola was encrusted with small mirrors that gave the beams the appearance of being perforated, amid the profuse cascade of flowers.

While the three women were admiring the landscape, without being fatigued by the quotidian spectacle, Fabio Canti, with the heart of a child in an old bachelor's body, contemplated the two little girls and young Robert. The children were running around, twittering like birds, in the pathways that descended in zigzags toward the beach.

"What a demon that Robert is!" cried Madame Ossola suddenly. "Robert!" she shouted. "Robert! Don't go off the path! He's going to pillage all the arbors, the monster."

"Let him go, my dear Madame. The damage isn't irreparable, and it amuses him. The cleared, well-sanded paths are only for grown-ups."

The conversation resumed. Fabio never ran out of anecdotes about a host of famous people, with finely-pointed punchlines, and that reminded Mesdames Desambez, Aubert and Ossola of Paris—where, however, they no longer had any desire to be. Then Fabio talked about the ambitious young who were appointing the leaders of their schools—Cubists, Dadaists, Conists—although they did not know how to draw or paint. They were, he said, like the artful individuals who make a living from music without knowing how to play any instrument, by making themselves into orchestra conductors.

"The newcomers reproach me," he said, "for copying nature slavishly. No, but at least I respect it and admire it, while adding my sensibility to it."

"You translate it magisterially," declared Madame Desambez, the white-haired grandmother, "and I love your admiration for Life. The young ones criticize you, you say, for imitating Nature, but your canvases render it even more living and harmonious."

"Your works, my dear master," said Madame Aubert, "are those of an Epicurean."

"You've understood me, my dear Madame. I only want to see in Life what it has of the beautiful, the picturesque and the agreeable. I'm alive, and I strive to be joyfully alive. It's very difficult in the present era."

"Alas," sighed the three widows, in unison.

"It seems, Mesdames," he went on, "that the war has changed the human heart, and the determined optimism that I follow is beginning to turn into pessimism. Never, in my opinion, have mores been so bitter and so brutal. Today's mentality requires immediate enjoyment. To tomorrow, one pays no heed, because one knows nothing about it: a race toward the abyss. Let's enjoy the morning dew without delay; one cannot know what the evening will bring. No confidence in the capital one possesses, which the old have saved up like imbeciles, in banknotes whose value is diminishing incessantly as prices rise. Handiwork devoid of taste, education, and even craftsmanship, earns thirty or forty francs a day. Bring back the equilibrium of exchange.

"How can these people be made to understand that it's high pay that makes the cost of living dear, and that a reduction of salaries would have economic repercussions? Our leaders, in order to conserve their electoral clientele, have enriched the agriculturalist; the worker isn't enriched, since he had to pay more dearly. That leads to an antagonism that will become increasingly accentuated. Hence, the enriched agriculturalist wants to come to town, where he'll find pleasure and comfort; in his turn he encounters the high cost of living and ends up lacking. It's doubtless the social seesaw; one goes up, another goes down.

"The adventurers of all lands ride the roller coaster of everyday life, and the intellectuals are led astray by businessmen and women, by those who make millions shifting the wind and making dust. Here on the Riviera, one sees the rich of the day and their parasites, contaminating our beautiful Provence, holding their Bourse of schemes and ambushes here, around the great gambling dens of Nice, Cannes and Monte Carlo. What remains for a philosopher or an artist to do? To struggle as best he can and laugh, laugh at everything in order not to cry, to forget that fifteen million men died in the mud so that they could live and amuse themselves."

"So, Master," said Madame Desambez, "in spite of your insouciant air, you're suffering."

"No, since you can see me laughing at those puppets, the profiteers squandering the benefits of the victory and ensuring that the victors are now, by virtue of America and English egotism, worse off than the vanquished."

"For that," Madame Desambez put in, "my two sons died, the elder in a muddy crater at Verdun where he was agonizing for two days, without his comrades being able to help him."

Under the florid scatter of the wisteria, whose mauve clusters the delightful March sun was peppering, Fabio Canti continued: "That war has killed the sentiment of personal dignity and human solidarity. The biped with the visage that gazes at the sky—*os sublime coelemque tueri*—as the Latin poet put it,[70] no longer has religious beliefs to put the brake on his passions and govern his appetites. Conscience? One is always at peace with it. The uncultivated and the brutal are unaware of it, in any case, and the intelligent, the arrivistes of every rank and every stripe have arguments to appease it. One lives on the margin of all morality, one tramples underfoot all the ancient commandments of the duty to respect oneself and others. No one believes that there's a social debt to pay, and every one of us is like the Gryllos whom Circe transformed into a pig, and was not ashamed of being a hog.[71] The crafty and the well-brought-up merely conduct themselves so as to save face.

"But then, *zut!* That's life, and life is struggle. Everything in nature devours one another, exists at the expense of others, and yet, life is beautiful. It's a matter of understanding it and not looking for midday at eight o'clock in the evening, when it's dark. I have my art to defend me, and you, Mesdames, have those darlings."

With a gesture, he indicated the insouciant trio, Ulette, Robert and Simone, who were coming back up the slope, shouting and laughing wholeheartedly.

The grandmother said: "They know nothing, and only experience the intoxication of living. They're children."

---

[70] Ovid; the full quotation is *os homini sublime dedit coelumque tueri jussit, et erectos ad sidera tollere vultus*: to man the gods gave an upright countenance, in order to survey the heavens and look up at the stars.

[71] In the philosophical essay *Bruta animalia ratione uti*, usually attributed to Plutarch, the transfigured Gryllos lectures Odysseus at length on the superiority of the animal condition to the human.

XVII. The Pont du Tournant

In a corner of the Bellarosa's gardens there was a shaped arbor of horn-beams, forming a kiosk of verdure, and three conspirators, Ulette, Simone and Robert. Ulette was the ringleader.

"You know that the Painter left by car after lunch, with our Mamans and with his outdoor easel and his box of colors, to work by the Pont du Tournant. We've been left behind because it's very steep out there and they're afraid of our imprudence."

"As if we didn't know how to climb!" said Robert.

"It's not very far way," said Ulette, "from what I heard, and from the Pont du Tournant one can see the most beautiful part of the stream. What if we were to give them a surprise?"

"They'll scold us because they left us behind."

"It's agreed, then," said Ulette. "We'll go to Tournant?"

"It's agreed," said Robert. "I'm a man. You can go out with me."

"And we'll take baby Tony."

"Oh, no. It's too cumbersome for your kid."

"I'll ask Madeleine to lend me Antoine's pram."

"All right," said Robert. "I'll walk. I have no desire to carry your doll every time you don't want to."

"You're always afraid of getting tired. You must have been born on a Sunday."

"If you're going to me, I won't bother with the stroll."

"Don't get annoyed; it was a joke. We'll get kitted out, then? We'll need our big straw hats."

"I'll bring my carbine," said Robert. "What if we run into brigands? And we'll go via the Porte d'Estérel. That's much shorter.

As it was not the first time that Ulette had asked the good Madeleine for Antoine's pram for her big doll, the latter raised no objection, and merely ordered: "Bring it back by three o'clock; you know that's the time when your little brother has his walk."

"I'm going to take baby Tony for a walk," said the artful little girl. "He needs a stroll, too."

To get to the Pont du Tournant, it was necessary to follow a path between the wood and the wall of the Bellarosa as far as the road, then go along it for a good half an hour and turn left on to a side road that went up through the forest of pines and firs as far as the gully at the bottom of which the torrent ran, and which was spanned by a bridge.

At first the three little travelers marched gaily, Ulette making Robert push the pram. After a quarter of an hour on the dusty road, however, their legs began to get tired.

"It's very hot," said Robert. "You call this a pleasure trip?"

"Get away, you wet blanket! Since we've started, it's necessary to go on to the end. Look at that man coming up the hill. He's walking at a good pace, that one."

"He's not local. I've never seen him before."

"Load your rifle then. Perhaps he's a brigand."

"I'd have done well to leave it behind. It's gets heavy, after a while, especially while pushing your pram."

The man arrived alongside them.

"Am I a long way from the Villa Bellarosa?"

"We're the grandchildren of Madame Desambrez, the owner of the villa," said Robert, sticking out his chest, "and this is the daughter of Madame Aubert, and her baby in the pram."

The individual started. "Then this baby...?"

"Is Antoine, Monsieur. The Bellarosa is the beautiful villa that you can see from here."

"Damn!" swore Baudard—for it was him. "This is made to measure."

From the direction of Théoule, however, a peasant's cart was slowly approaching. *It'll be here soon. I believe I was about to do something stupid. That's no good. I'll follow the kids. Perhaps an opportunity will present itself.*

He thanked the children, allowed them to get a start, and then followed them at a distance.

Meanwhile, the quartet had arrived at the road leading to the Pont du Tournant. They turned on to it without hesitation, Ulette declaring that it was the right road. The Luron, after having descended sinuously through the maritime foothills of the Alps, ran into a mass of granite there, which left for it such a narrow passage that the water accumulated against the natural barrage, and broke through it to fall down on the other side onto the rocks in foaming cascades. At the top of the path followed by the children, and old bridge overlooked the roaring rush.

That, however, was not the most marvelous viewpoint, for the one chosen by Fabio Canti was at the bottom of the falls, a hundred meters from the bank. From down there, he could see the ensemble of the cascades, of which he wanted to make a study, in a harmony of silver, gray, green and blue. The three little excursionists, having arrived at the bridge, had a disappointment, for, from where they were standing, they could not see the auto, the painter and the three mothers, and the noise of the falls would have prevented them from being heard if they had wanted to call out.

"*Zut!*" said Robert. "They can't be far away. I'll climb up in the pines above the Tournant. From there I'll be able to see the Painter and our Mamans. Wait for me, girls."

"We'll go with you!" cried Ulette. "We'll find strawberries in the woods."

"And I'm fearfully thirsty," said Simone.

"What about the pram?" said Ulette. "And Baby Tony?"

"Oh, he won't fly away. Is there any need to burden ourselves with that?"

"You know very well that he needed a little exercise. You're not very nice to Baby Tony."

"Look—to give you pleasure I'll kiss the dirty kid."

Robert matched action to his words. After him, Simone did the same, then Ulette, at length, instructing Baby Tony, in a loud voice, to be good. Then all three of them ran into the wood, toward the top of the hill, and soon disappeared into the undergrowth.

Hidden behind a tree trunk, Armand Baudard had missed none of that scene.

Thunder! I must be blessed! A stroke of luck like that, on arrival! That's a hundred thousand bullets very rapidly earned. Let's see...the kids have gone. Just a matter of throwing the little rat into the drink. He started to laugh. *Well, that'll cure his thirst. Then it'll be an accident for which the kids will get the blame. Let's go—double quick.*

He ran forward, grabbed the pram, having glanced vaguely at its contents, without paying much heed, and threw the whole thing over the parapet of the bridge.

That's at least thirty meters to fall. If he escapes from that, he'll be lucky.

And the monster immediately fled, at top speed.

At the bottom of the waterfall, Fabio Canti had finished his sketch, and was rearranging his colors and packing his bag while chatting with the ladies of the Bellarosa.

"Oh!" said Madame Aubert. "What's that coming toward us?"

"One would think," said the painter, "that it's the wreckage of a child's pram."

Carried by the torrent, it raced along through the rocks, having broken into pieces. Hanging by its wrappings, a baby deprived of its legs, its head fractured and dangling, was following it lamentably. The members of the group were looking at one another quizzically, wondering what it might be, when Robert, Simone and Ulette appeared, emerging on to the slop between the fir trees, preceded by a landslide of pebbles.

"What's this?" cried Madame Dambrez, severely.

Robert threw his arms around his grandmother's neck, knowing full well, the little imp, that she would not resist his caresses for long. Ulette and Simone each did likewise with the necks of their mothers.

"It's me who brought them," he said, bravely. "We heard you say where you were going, and I was vexed to be treated as a little girl. And then, Baby Tony wanted to come, too."

"Ulette's doll," asked the painter anxiously, or her brother Antoine."

"The doll. We left it up there, near the bridge."

With his hand, Fabio Canti indicated to the children the debris caught between two rocks.

"Baby Tony!" cried Ulette. "My child! Help. We need to rescue him."

"In the state in which the torrent's left him, it's hardly worth the trouble. I'll buy you another one, my little Ulette."

"I forbid you to do that," Madame Aubert interjected. "This disobedience deserves to be punished. What would your brother Etienne say if he knew how you treated his gifts?"

Ulette burst into tears.

"Don't cry, darling," said the painter, picking her up. In a whisper, he added: "Tomorrow, Maman won't be angry anymore; she'll let me do it and I'll buy you a doll even more beautiful."

"It won't be Baby Tony."

"But I don't understand how the pram could fall into the stream," said Robert. "We left it far enough away from the bridge that it couldn't have rolled there."

"Besides which," observed Madame Ossola, "the bridge has a trellised parapet. Someone must have thrown it over."

Madame Aubert went pale. In her mind, a connection was made between the mesh of the bridge and the factory wheel."

"If I'd seen that…!" said Robert, brandishing his rifle.

"That astonishes me," said Madame Desambez. "There are no nasty people around here."

"Did you meet any strangers?" Madame Aubert asked the children.

"Yes," said Robert. "A man who isn't local. He asked me if he was far from the Villa Bellarosa, and he swore when I told him that we were the grandchildren of Madame Desambez, the owner of the villa, and that Ulette and Antoine were Madame Aubert's."

The three women exchanged a glance full of anxiety. While consoling Ulette, the painter had not missed a word. He put his equipment back in the auto.

"Climb in everyone, mothers and children. Madame Ossola, whom I know to be a very good driver, will kindly take the wheel. Go back to the house. I'll climb up to the wood and see how the pram could have rolled into the torrent. Perhaps—for I can read a dread in Madame Aubert's face—I can find an explanation."

He helped everyone to climb aboard.

"By squeezing up a little, there's room for everyone. See you in a little while, Mesdames. It will do me good to come back on foot, and I'll reflect."

With that, the auto pulled away, and the painter, heading in the opposite direction, scaled the sheer hillside down which the children had come.

A few minutes later he was near the bridge. The road was covered with a fine white dust, the dust of the Midi. Very clearly, beside the spot where the children had left the pram, he saw the scuff-marks and footprints that had been made around it when Robert, Simone and Ulette had kissed Baby Tony. Over those light imprints, Fabio distinctly saw the marks of solid shoes heading, with the pram, toward the bridge. There was no doubt that the owner of those heavy shoes had lifted up the pram and thrown it into the Luron.

Having done that, the man had run for some time: that was written in the dust of the road. But why had he done it? Some maniac, fond of destruction.

Then the painter went down the path that led to the main road. In certain places the dust was so thick that the malefactor's tracks were imprinted as clearly as in clay.

Why would a stranger to the region have had the stupid idea of playing a dirty trick on the children? Fabio Canti resumed walking. The individual had stopped there, behind that bush. Evidently, he had been following the children. Why? It was the individual encountered by Robert, Ulette, Simone and Baby Tony, in the pram, who had asked them the way to the Bellarosa.

Uh oh! he thought. *The clown mistook the doll for little Antoine. That would be serious. After the father, the new-born. Who do those two crimes profit? Etienne Aubert. No! That's too horrible! But the more I think about it, the more certain I am that he thought he was throwing Madame Aubert's baby son into the torrent. When he finds out that he's made a mistake, he'll look for another means...but I'm forewarned. I'll watch out. As for Etienne, I'm going to write to my friend Raynaud, in order that he can keep an eye on the boss of the factory on the Quai de Javel...*

No longer having anything to study, he took the road to the Bellarosa at a rapid stride. He arrived an hour after the auto carrying the three women and the three children.

"Well?" asked the grandmother and the mothers.

"And accident, quite simply. Those blockheads had left the pram on the slope; it rolled to the one place where it was possible for it to fall into the Luron—a gap made recently on the edge of the balustrade. I'll have to notify the watchman. There's no reason to be anxious."

"I told you so, my dear Aline," said Madame Desambez. "You forge romantic ideas too quickly. We're no longer in an era when such crimes can be committed."

"That's true—but since my husband's death, I've thought of nothing but all kinds of machinations against me and my son Antoine."

"That will pass, with time, my dear Madame," said Fabio Canti. "Your nerves are in a bad way, but the sun of these blessed shores will soon dissipate your dark imaginings."

XVIII. Baudard's Triumph and Defeat

While Fabio Canti was trying to restore calm to Madame Aubert's mind, Armand Baudard had taken the train back to Nice.

When they knew the result that same evening after midnight—for their accomplice had telephoned the villa on Mont Boron to advise them of his prompt and fortunate return, during the party that Josette Coutan was living—Thomas Keysar and Berthe Jafaux looked at one another.

"Well," said Thomas, "that's much better than one would have dared to hope. That's work well done."

"Let's wait for tomorrow morning's papers," said Berthe. "The *Petit Var*, the *Eclaireur* and the *Petit Niçois*. It will be sufficient to send them to the boss, underlining the information in red pencil. Etienne will have nothing more to do than pay up."

In spite of the inertia of their conscience, the two associates had a rather agitated night. Waiting for the news, the night seemed interminable. When they were served chocolate in their rooms, they sent the valet to buy the Nice papers.

There was no mention of an accident on the Pont de Tournant or of the Villa Bellarosa.

"It's nerve-racking to wait. What if we were to hire an auto and go to have lunch in Théoule?"

And that was what they did.

"What a splendid view!" said Thomas to the pretty waitress—her name was Rose—who served them lunch on the terrace of the hotel, with the intention of making her chat. "It's a paradise."

"Oh, we're used to it, we don't pay any attention to it. Personally, I'd prefer the inferno of Paris. One gets bored in paradise. Nothing ever happens here…well, yes…yesterday, Monsieur Fabio Canti, a great painter, so they say, who's a guest at the Villa Bellarosa, the roof of which you can see through the trees, was making a study of the Luron, the local torrent, when a bad lot threw a baby's pram from the Pont du Tournant. Fortunately, there was only a doll in it." She started to laugh, showing youthful teeth. "It wasn't anyone from Théoule, for sure, who did that—doubtless a vagrant."

Thomas struck the table with his fist. Berthe bit her handkerchief angrily, and Rose the waitress, nonplussed, looked at them fearfully. Then they paid the bill, adding a good tip, without taking coffee, and set off back to Nice.

As soon as the auto started moving, Berthe said in a low voice, so that the driver could not hear: "That idiot Armand! To mistake a doll for a kid! That's a bit too much. I'll give him what for, the imbecile! And to think that my sister supports such a numbskull! No, I can't believe it!"

"Calm down."

"All the same, he'd have done better to look at what he was chucking in the water."

"Damn! He was in a hurry. Perhaps you'd have done the same in his place."

"Never in this life! He didn't even think to poke it in the belly to make it say *Papa, Mama*."

"I'll go to see Baudard this evening at his hotel, to get things going again and give him orders to follow: how to get into the villa and a means of killing the baby."

"Prussic acid."

"No. That's an old game and its effect leaves traces. I have a mate at the hospital in Nice, who can filch me a test tube of typhoid fever microbes. Only it's necessary that Baudard changes his face and treads warily, now that Fabio Canti, who's a smart fellow, is at the Villa Bellarosa."

"All the same, it will be hard."

"A million; that's the price. Shut up—we're going through Cannes. What if we were to go take coffee at Cornichet's, near the Casino. We'll find friends and chic people there."

BOOK THREE: ZIGZAGGING TOWARD PUNISHMENT

I. Resumption of Work

On the terrace of the Villa Bellarosa, under the wisteria pergola, Fabio Canti was daydreaming, contemplating the blue sky, so pure, where he had just seen a flock of swallows fly by.

What was he thinking about? Nothing. All the springs of his mind had relaxed under the hot sun of the magnificent morning. He gazed at the progressing and impressive spring, the eternal god in the process of giving the trees a new verve and teasing the buds, the ascending sun and the errant violet shadows. Devoid of reflection and thought, he perceived as an artistic animal the images of the end of March, which already had the visage of April, the perfumes, the bird calls, the colors, the slight movements of the leaves and branches in the breeze from the deep blue sea. The Painter of the Sun was bathing, so to speak, in the sun, both of them insouciant, in the waves of the ocean of light, when he heard Madame Aubert calling to him.

"Fabio! Fabio! Come quickly!"

In a few bounds he rejoined the young woman, who was running from the far end of the garden.

"What is it? The children?"

"No, it's outside. An unfortunate cyclist has just had a fall out there. He isn't moving! He must have been killed!"

He's doubtless only unconscious. Would you like to prepare a cordial, water and a cloth?"

While Madame Aubert ran inside, Fabio Canti hastened toward the sunken fence, climbed over the balustrade and jumped into the ditch.

The cyclist, still unmoving, was lying in the road. His head had struck the edge of a buried rock hidden by the grass, and blood was flowing abundantly from a cut on his forehead.

He raised the man up, bracing him against his knee, and dabbed the wound with his handkerchief. A few minutes later Madame Aubert arrived, with Madame Desambez and the old maidservant Madeleine, with everything he needed. Soon, the wounded man, bandaged and reanimated, opened his eyes and stammered a few incoherent words.

"We must carry the poor man into the house," said Madame Desambez, always excellent and charitable. "Madelon, go tell the gardener what has happened. Tell him to come and help us move the injured man."

Madeleine set off immediately. The man had closed his eyes again, and was visibly making an effort to pull himself together.

"Well?" asked the painter. "Do you feel better now?"

"It hurts, and I still feel very dazed. It was an accursed dog. I tried to stop to avoid it and my wheel stuck in a rut. I made a mess of my dismount and fell into the grass."

"Where you nearly split your skull on that stone. You might have been killed."

Baudard shivered.

Baudard had been transformed; with his hair newly cut and his russet moustache shaved off, he looked like a valet in some respectable house. He had not anticipated the sharp stone; the fall, which was only intended to be a simulated accident, had nearly cost him his life.

"Don't worry," said Madame Desambez. "Head wounds heal quickly. We'll telephone Dr. Gayraud in Cannes. He'll be here within an hour. You can stay here until you're better."

"Do you have anyone to inform?"

"No, thank you. I'm an electrician, and I was on my way to Saint-Raphaël, where I was told there was a job going."

"Well, you're hired," said Madame Desambez. "When you're on your feet again, I'll have some jobs for you to do. I have repairs to be done, and some electrical adaptations to make."

"That will be a means for me to repay your kindness."

"I didn't mean it like that, my friend. But here's the gardener with Madelon. He's bringing a ladder to use as a stretcher. It's a little primitive, but there isn't anything better."

The wounded man was laid on the rungs, and the gardener and Fabio Canti lifted him up. Everyone followed. Madeleine brought the bike, whose front wheel, out of kilter, was atrociously twisted.

II. Information from Dr. Gayraud

The plan improvised by Thomas Keysar and Berthe Jafaux had, therefore—with the assistance of chance—succeeded better than the three rogues had
dared to hope. Baudard had counted on faking a sprain rather than cutting his
face. Now that it was done, he congratulated himself.

The doctor would not arrive until the afternoon; he was on his round when
the telephone call came in, and he was so desirous of satisfying his clientele that
he would have had lunch before coming in his automobile, which he drove himself.

Short, very dark, with a deep red complexion, a moustache and beard like a
horseshoe on his jutting chin, Dr. Gayraud, a general councilor of the Alpes-
Maritimes, and also an alert and cheerful *bon viveur*, inspired confidence with
his perpetual cicada song to the most obstinate invalid: "Illness," he said "only
exists because one allows oneself to fall under the suggestion of some indisposi-
tion. Get it into your head that there's nothing wrong, and you'll be cured."

Departing from that principle, he used fewer pharmaceutical products than
cordials. When he had to care for an injury, however, his skill was incontestable;
no one could count the number of fractures he had repaired and dislocations that
he had undone instantaneously. He was, in consequence, known and esteemed
throughout the region.

"So," he said when he came in, "What's wrong, clumsy?"

Baudard only replied with a groan. The doctor unwrapped the improvised
bandage in order to examine the wound.

"Damn! Fortunately, my lad, you've bled abundantly—which doesn't
mean there's no internal hemorrhage. In five or six days you'll be able to get up,
and in a fortnight you'll be as good as new."

He turned to Madame Desambez and Madame Aubert. "Absolutely no
food today. Tomorrow, light nourishment and a glass of Mariani wine. After
that, whatever he wants. I'll make him a dressing that won't need to be renewed,
unless there are improbable complications—in which case, call me. So, everyone's in good health here. Terrible clientele! And the children?"

They went back down to the drawing room, where Madame Ossola had
taken the three heroes of the escapade of the Pont du Tournant. Madeleine was
holding little Antoine in her arms. Dr. Gayraud examined all the children carefully.

"Go on, it's not this time that you'll go to bed without supper. But keep an
eye on the baby. I've heard it said, Madame Aubert, that you have the intention
of staying with us. In that case, you and your children will become future clients."

"Indeed, Doctor, if my godmother wants to keep us."

"Don't say such silly things, Aline. Well, Gayraud, how is the little one?"

"I'm aware of your misfortune, Madame Aubert. I feared that the child might be feeling the repercussion of your emotion, but there's nothing there. He's solid. By the way, where did you pick up that parasite?"

"He fell in front of the sunken fence. He's an electrician who was going to Saint-Raphaël to look for work."

"Ah! That's odd..."

"Why?" said Fabio Canti.

"Nothing. An idea..."

The painter accompanied the physician, who had taken his leave of the ladies. When they were alone under the wisteria pergola, the doctor, with his Provencal accent adding a hint of garlic to his confidence, said:

"Your wounded man surely hasn't contrived his injury deliberately? The day before yesterday, in Cannes, I was at Césaire the barber's, in the process of being shaved, with my chin covered in soap, when the individual you're hospitalizing—whom I definitely recognize, even if he didn't pay any attention to me—came in, but not with the face he has now. No, with a curly shock of hair and a russet moustache. He came in saying: 'Cut my hair and get rid of the moustache. I'm going to be a valet. Give me the head of a flunkey in a big house...' That's why, turning my face toward him, half-hidden by the white foam, I noticed the fellow, who scarcely had the appearance of that employment. As he's given himself here as an electrician, I'm advising you, *illustrissimo signor* Fabio Canti..."

"Yes, that seems bizarre to me, all the more so as...one confidence for another..."

The great painter told the physician the story of the death of the doll, Baby Tony, thrown with the pram into the Luron from the Pont du Tournant, and concluded: "Perhaps there's no correlation, but thank you for your information, which seems to me to be of great importance. I suspect the man of having believed, when he threw the pram into the torrent, that he was drowning little Antoine Aubert. And if that were the same criminal who caused the accident that crushed his father, it wouldn't surprise me."

"You're an artist, with a rapid imagination. All the same, you're going a bit far, it seems to me, in the association of ideas. Who would profit from all these murders worthy of the Atreides?"

"The son of the first marriage, Etienne Aubert, now the master of the factory. I'll write to a friend in Paris, the Commissaire of Police at Grenelle. He was the one who made the report concluding an accident, without conviction but without immediate evidence to the contrary."

"What? The son of the victim! That's monstrous! He had his father murdered by this clumsy cyclist?"

"The war has put consciences so far out of joint...not a word of this to anyone, Doctor, until further notice."

III. Fabio Canti is on the Right Track

For three days, Baudard, cared for and pampered by his hostess, had been ruminating his plan. He was in place now, and had no doubt that he would succeed. The test tube containing the culture of typhoid fever microbes was in the saddlebag of his bicycle. He shivered. *What if the excessively obliging hosts have sent it for repair?*

When Madeleine, who was attending to him and bringing him food, next came to his room, he asked: "Where's my bike?"

"Still in the garage. They'll have it repaired for you."

"No, tell them not to bother. I'll be able to take care of that myself."

"You're a man who can turn his hand to anything, Monsieur Brémond."

As she was going out of the electrician's room, however, which was next door to Fabio Canti's, she ran into the painter.

"Well, how's our invalid?"

"Very well, Monsieur Fabio. He's even thinking of going."

"What, already? But he's supposed to do some work here."

"Oh, I only said that because he's just asked me about his bicycle. He doesn't want you to bother with it—he'll repair it himself."

Hey! thought the artist. *I didn't think of the bicycle!* He went to the garage where the machine had been deposited and examined it attentively. It bore the address of a hire shop in Cannes with a number: 271. *Bicycle on hire. Let's take a look in the saddlebag. The usual tools...but what's this tube? I'll find out.*

He slipped the test tube into his pocket and made a note of the hirer's address.

First, let's go see Dr. Gayraud.

He went up to get dressed and inform Madame Desambez.

"I'm out of silver white. I'm going to Cannes with the auto, and I'll be back for lunch."

Prudently, he had telephoned the doctor. Gayraud was at home, and he had asked him to wait for an urgent matter.

Twenty minutes later, the painter was shown into the doctor's study.

"What's new?" asked Gayraud. "How's your injured man?"

"It's him that it's about."

Fabio Canti brought the physician up to date and gave him the suspicious test tube.

"We'll see what it is."

He opened it, carefully took out some of the contents with a spatula, placed it under a microscope and examined it, and then said: "It's the typhoid fever microbe."

"Oh!" exclaimed Fabio Canti.

The doctor opened a medical textbook and showed him an engraving in which the microbe was represented, greatly magnified.

"Now take a look in the microscope and compare it yourself."

Slightly terrified, the painter looked and was convinced.

"I have the letter that I mentioned, to my friend Raynaud, the Commissaire de Police in Paris, in my wallet. Will you permit me to complete it before putting it in the post?"

"In the meantime, I'll replace the tube with another identical to it, but filled with something inoffensive, and I'll keep this one, with your permission, as proof in support of our testimony."

When he left the doctor's house, delighted with his debut as a detective, Fabio Canti went to the address of the bicycle hirer.

"I'm bringing you news of an accident to one of your clients," he said, "to whom you lent a bicycle numbered 271." And he gave him an account of the cyclist's fall.

"Number 271. Lent to Monsieur Adolphe Brémond for a month. A hundred and twenty-five francs, facultative, with a guarantee in the sum of twelve hundred francs, pledged by Monsieur Paul Granger of Bordeaux."

"Who is Monsieur Granger?" the painter asked.

"I know you by sight, just as everyone in Cannes knows the famous artist Fabio Canti, so I'll give you a frank reply. Whether his name is Granger or not is of no importance to me, from the moment he insured my bike for its full value, but my wife, who was present, recognized him as the thought-reader, Thomas Keysar, who gave a demonstration in Cannes last week."

Fabio knew Keysar vaguely; the latter had once talked about his paintings in his art criticism, lambasting them for their poor style, denying that they had any merit, color or poetry. His friend, Guilleret, the member of the Institut, and a number of pretty girls had pointed him out one evening in Paris at the Café de la Rotonde.

"Your wife is sure about that?"

"Damn! Ask her yourself." And the worthy man called his wife, who confirmed what he said.

"I swear that it was him. A sorcerer, a man who can divine what you're thinking, has a face that makes an impression on you. I only saw him once, in one of the three séances he held at the Casino, with the pythoness Souriah. He's quite tall, has a pale face with black hair and magnificent yellow eyes, like those of a cat."

"Thank you, Monsieur and Madame. I beg you not to say anything to anyone about my visit, and whatever happens, you know that your bicycle is at Théoule, at the Villa Bellarosa, in the home of Madame Desambez, whose guest I am."

"It can stay there if he wishes. It's paid for."

Fabio Canti saluted the two hirers and left. The affair was getting complicated. Obviously, the role of the wounded man was that of a hireling, an instrument. But then, what was Thomas Keysar? He remembered, suddenly, having seen the impostor at Monte Carlo, in the gaming rooms of the Sporting Club, in the company of two women, one of whom was Josette Coutan, a troubling and perverse svelte individual—that was why he had noticed her and asked her name—an expert seductress, the wife of a bluffer, Sixte Coutan. In fact, that was the name of Antoine Aubert's former associate. Now, the chain of connection was complete.

It was him, this Keysar, who was the instigator of the accidents, on behalf of Etienne Aubert, the master of the factory.

He went into a café, ordered a Martini and a piece of paper, and drafted a further postscript to his letter to the Commissaire, relating the conversation with the bicycle hirer and his suspicions of the critic and charlatan Thomas Keysar, thought-reader, and his mistress, Souriah.

That way, Raynaud can obtain more information, and act in consequence. As for my electrician, who has put on the mask of a flunkey, I won't lose sight of him.

He got back into his automobile, set his gloved hands on the steering wheel, and headed back to Théoule.

Fabio Canti's first concern was to replace the inoffensive test tube where he had found the one with the typhoid fever bacilli in the saddlebag of the bicycle. And then, now satisfied with his debut as a policeman, he rejoined the exquisite society of women and children, who had no suspicion of the danger lurking in the villa of roses, for lunch, a little late.

IV. The Commissaire as Humorist

Louis Lafon was at work in his office, in his capacity as head of personnel and supervisor of materials at the Aubert factory on the Quai de Javel, when he saw a tall, affable and smiling individual come in, after knocking.

He held out his hand. "Do you remember me, Monsieur Lafon?"

"Certainly—you're the Commissaire of Grenelle; it was you who made the initial enquiries after the accident to Monsieur Antoine Aubert."

"Exactly. And it's in connection with that matter that I've come to see you."

"Please take a seat, Monsieur le Commissaire."

"One of my friends, the fine painter Fabio Canti has sent me some singular news from Théoule. Someone has attempted to murder the little boy, the son of your former employer's second marriage."

"You've done well to come, Monsieur Raynaud. For my part, I have certain things to confide in you."

Lafon recounted what he had learned from Albaret, and the deductions that he had extracted, without daring to go any further.

"Would you recognize this individual?"

"Perfectly. His name is Armand Baudard. A well-built fellow, but of shady appearance—that of a pimp. Curly chestnut-colored hair, long russet moustache."

"We're getting hot. That's the individual whose description has been sent to me from the Côte d'Azur."

"Hmm. The net's tightening."

"Yes," said the Commissaire, "but it's necessary to have proof of the connection between Armand Baudard and Etienne Aubert. An intermediary has been identified to me: a former petty critic of art and literature, Thomas Keysar, now a thought-reader and graphologist, accompanied by a female chiromancer and clairvoyant. Do you know him as one of your boss's acquaintances?"

"No, I don't know any of Etienne Aubert's intimate friends now that he no longer frequents Sixte Coutan, his father's former associate...or rather, his wife."

"It's said that she has relaxed thighs."

"She was Antoine Aubert's mistress, and Etienne's."

"The father and the son, eh! What does Coutan do now that he's let go of the factory?"

"I don't know. 'Business.' He's very artful."

"Thanks. I think I've grasped the thread. This Thomas Keysar and the seeress are friends of Josette Coutan. They've been seen together on the Riviera. There's no doubt about it: the thought-reader knows Etienne Aubert. I've found the connection."

The Commissaire, Albert Raynaud, reflected momentarily. He was a humorist in addition to his functions; he liked fantasy, satire and farce, and exercised his whimsy under various pseudonyms in some of the best-known specialist papers, including *Le Sourire* and *Le Merle Blanc*. He transposed serious matters, and supposedly important men of the day, onto another plane, altering their proportions like a distorting mirror, concave or convex.

"Have you read *Macbeth*, Monsieur Lafon?"

"Shakespeare? Of course. My wife makes translations from English."

"You know that the two guilty parties, obsessed by their remorse and their imagination, see specters everywhere."

"That's not so common nowadays. Perhaps Etienne Aubert can only be irritated by the police."

"He will be—but before then, it's necessary to trouble his idle mind a little."

"What do you mean?"

"Who has the key to the wheel where Monsieur Aubert perished?"

"Me."

"That's perfect. Will you please have a duplicate key made, secretly?"

"I can do that myself. I've been a metalworker, like Baudard—and I think that he must have made a key to the gate, too."

"In fact, since it's you who'll keep the key, it will be sufficient for you to open the gate when you think that Etienne Aubert is going to go past it."

"He won't be going past it much longer. The annex he's building will permit him to go home without going through the machine-room."

"All the more reason to work quickly. So, you open the gate, and if possible, scatter a few drops of red ink here and there to strike the boss's imagination, create an unease in his mind, a suggestion that might make him do something silly and start him on the fatal path. From now on, I'll put him under surveillance. You understand, Lafon?"

"Yes—the boss is stuffed."

Gravely, the Commissaire said: "Everything that I've just learned corroborates my presumptions. What do you expect? Etienne Aubert is another victim of that infamous war: it's a case of a slightly unsteady mind unhinged by life at the front. Those men living under the continual threat of death, seeing friends and comrades fall around them, have come to see life as a battlefield in which everyone must boldly entrench himself, without outdated scruples. Devotion, honesty, fraternity are just words on parade. Strength or skill—and success justifies anything. But the man isn't a devotee of the high life: one gets lost following all the meanders and manifestations of human mentality."

"Etienne wanted the factory."

"He would have had it. But his father's new marriage and the birth of a son have eaten away at his share. Perhaps there's also something else—who knows?" The Commissaire rose to his feet. "But I'll find out, damn it! It's my job and my passion."

But Lafon was asking himself what was going to become of the factory in all this.

V. The Specter of Antoine Aubert

At the very moment that fortune was turning against him, Etienne Aubert was opening his mail. No part of his daily work pleased him more. Nothing in fact, does more to affirm an industrialist's strength and supremacy within his factory. It is the mail, the offers and requests, the commissions and orders, on which the ongoing life of workshops depends. There, he felt that he was truly the master of the twelve hundred workers awaiting his orders. As he went along, he sorted out the correspondence.

Among the personal letters, two were from the Alpes-Maritimes. Etienne Aubert had recognized Keysar's handwriting on one and Josette's on the other. However strong his desire was to read them, however, he judged it to be his duty to deal with the affairs of the factory before passing on to his own, often dirty business. Having finished with the factory matters, he was about to turn his own concerns when voices became audible in the office next door.

He heard: "…in Monsieur Antoine's time…" The rest was lost in a mixture of other voices, but three times the same piercing words were repeated: "…in Monsieur Antoine's time…"

His father's name, pronounced at the moment when Etienne was opening one of Thomas Keysar's "epistles"—as the rogue liked to say—caused him to shudder. Shrugging his shoulders, he read on. It was inconsequential. Thomas talked about his successes in Nice and Cannes, and concluded with the underlined words: "All's going well." He threw the letter into the wastebasket and opened Josette's, written on mimosa paper.

My dear Etienne, Sixte joins me in sending you a bonjour from Nice. Why aren't you with us? It's the good life, my dear. Sixte is working. He has a big deal in Rumania. Millions to be made. How stupid it is, Etienne, to remain buried in your scrap iron! Come then, with your cash. Sixte will multiply it for you tenfold in a year. Just think that I have seven or eight hundred thousand a year to spend. This life is splendid. Hurry up and come. I miss you. Come, friend, come. Come on, then!

Screwed up into a ball, the letter went to join the other in the wastebasket. *All that's swagger to draw me into the trap. Her husband makes millions…not astonishing, for such a cuckold…*

Lafon came in.

"What was the matter just now?" asked Etienne. "You were making a racket."

"It's Ouchy and a couple of others who came, in a panic, to tell me that when they were going to the storage they saw the door in the mesh of the flywheel open 'as in Monsieur Antoine's time.' I told them they were dreaming, since the key's in my office."

"So?"

"I don't understand it. I went with them. It was true."

"Come on, Lafon. I don't like people making fun of me."

"The gate's slightly free in its movement. It could be that the lock wasn't completely engaged and that the vibrations of the machine, by making it jump, opened it."

"In any case, give me the key. Someone can come to get it from my desk when it's necessary."

"As you wish."

Lafon went to fetch the key.

"There," he said, handing it to Etienne.

Aubert took it, but immediately dropped it in horror.

"What's the matter?" said Lafon, picking the key up and putting it on the desk.

"There's blood on that key!" said the decorated young man in a strangled voice. "There's blood on it!"

Lafon started to laugh. "Blood! That's a funny idea, Boss. It's just some red ink that I spilled just now, when we were arguing. Ouchy threw the key down into it.

With a hoarse sigh, Etienne said: "It's stupid, these stories! Isn't it enough to have lost my father in that horrible manner without awakening such macabre recollections?"

"I'm painfully impressed myself by these strange coincidences," said Lafon, hypocritically. "But one often gets disturbed mistakenly. Everything's explicable."

"It's certain," said Etienne, regaining his self-control, "that the fantastic doesn't exist. It's only our impressionable minds that create it..."

You're strong, Lafon thought, *but it touched you all the same. It's not going to stop.*

"Anything else in particular to tell me, my friend?"

VI. Shadows and Light

"The Arnal factory's on strike. A number of workers have come looking for employment. If you want my advice, you could take on fifty or so. We have enough room and work for them. I know almost all of them, Boss; we'd have the pick of them."

"Arnal's shares were on the rise, though. I don't understand why the board of directors is obstinate in not agreeing to the same pay rates as mine."

"The shareholders are forcing the hand of the board. Arnal's washed his hands of the matter."

"Arnal's too rich. It's unfortunate to have to say it, but there are very few industrialists who love their factory for itself, for the joy of seeing it prosper and grow."

"Like you, for instance, Monsieur Etienne—and like me, too."

"Yes, I love it fanatically. It's the work of the Auberts. If, in time, I have a son, I want him to love the factory more than anything else, like my ancestors and like me. A man who doesn't create an objective in life for himself is a sterile man. One needs a stimulus. Personally, I've forged a colossal dream: incessantly to augment the production of the factory until it encompasses all the specialties of metalwork; to create, in Paris, an iron industry district, to extend it further and further, to make it a second Creusot. Perhaps, my dear Lafon, my dream's too big for me. Before being the master of the factory, I was the adversary, almost the enemy, of the workers. I've recognized my error. I shall make them—I have made them—my allies. If, by chance—since that bizarre business with the key a little while ago reminded me of what happened to my father—something happens to me, open this drawer. You'll find my testament in it, in which I've taken measures for the work begun to be continued."

"You're much younger than me, Monsieur Aubert. I hope that I'll never have to fulfill that mission."

"Who knows? Today, the flywheel gate was open, just as..."

"Oh," said Lafon, swiftly, "an accident like that never happens twice."

"Yes, it's possible." *And I don't have a son yet*, he thought.

"Excuse me, Monsieur Aubert. I have a few instructions to give."

"Go, go, my friend. I have an important meeting at the Ministry myself. If I succeed in that adjudication, you can hire a hundred workers."

"Good luck, then."

The director of personnel and materiel left in order to go to the workshops. When he reached Albaret's bench, he said to the worker in a low voice: "We made a mistake, yesterday, with Ouchy, in telling the Commissaire what you know. I'll explain it to you. The Factory *above all*."

"No," said Albaret. "One can't keep that on one's conscience. What will be, will be. I can't hold onto it any longer. Ouchy feels the same."

VII. A Masterstroke

Baudard had reflected, in his bed, on the means of arriving at his goal. The next day, he was due to begin his work as an electrician. Although he was not precisely in the trade, a machine worker is not without some notion of all the métiers adjacent to his own. He had already installed lamps or bells for mates on numerous occasions, and since he had been living at Sans-Liquette's expense he had made a special study of electrical systems with operations of burglary in mind. In that sense, therefore, everything ought to go smoothly. To get close to little Antoine was more difficult; he was rarely left alone. When the child was asleep, however, his mother or old Madeleine sometimes absented herself for a quarter of an hour; it would be sufficient not to waste those few minutes. Once the blow was struck, he could flee on his repaired bicycle—but that would be awkward if a crime was suspected and an investigation opened.

In five days his beard had grown again, and his former facial appearance might recall him to the memory of the children. He would go to Cannes on his repaired bicycle in order to get electrical supplies, and come back with his chin shaven. There still remained the question of departure, which was the most embarrassing one. He could not, however, wait for the development and aftermath of a virulent typhoid fever. All things considered, though, the sum to be earned was well worth a few risks. Given that, his plan was made, and he resolved to put it into operation as soon as possible.

Two days later he had not yet been able find himself alone with little Antoine for a minute. A kind of cold rage was beginning to gnaw at him. In the afternoon, he was in the first floor corridor, installing the conduits to provide Madame Aubert's bedroom with electric lighting. The corridor served several rooms; it was the ideal post. So he worked slowly, watching out for an opportunity.

Madame Aubert had been breast-feeding the child. Suddenly, the door opened and the mother emerged with old Madeleine, holding armfuls of dirty linen.

"Let's take advantage of Antoine sleeping to get on with this washing," said Madame Aubert. "While you take this load down to the laundry I'll go to Madame Ossola's room to tell her that we're only waiting for her linen, Simone's and Robert's.

The two women disappeared.

Damn! Now's the moment!

And Baudard descended rapidly from his ladder. In three cat-like bounds he was in the bedroom. He took the stopper out of the tube that he believed to be full of microbes capable of causing a natural death, without him being the murderer, since that would be the typhoid fever.

A hand fell upon his shoulder. Her turned round, livid. The painter was standing there with a Browning in his hand.

"Hands up and walk. We're going to my room for a chat. Don't forget that, at the slightest suspect movement, I'll kill you."

Petrified, Baudard obeyed.

Once in his own room, with the door closed, the Browning still in his hand and the electrician's hands still in the air, Fabio Canti said: "Thomas Keysar and his accomplice are under lock and key at the present moment. You know that whoever confesses first will profit from attenuating circumstances."

The danger had fallen upon him like a thunderbolt. Bewildered, Baudard stammered: "I'm not the most guilty. I was only obeying orders."

"I know that, but your chief, a clever man, will put both crimes on your back. Reply quickly, and truthfully. How much were you given to inoculate the baby with typhoid fever?"

"What! You know about that? A hundred thousand francs."

"Damn—that's a tidy sum. And for the father?"

The murderer, stupefied and frightened, rolled his bewildered eyes like lotto balls.

"Come on, swine, you're in the bag. Charge your mates."

"Thomas Keysar and the seeress organized everything."

"On account of Etienne Aubert, that's as clear as crystal. Sit down there and write my dictation."

"And if I refuse?" said Baudard, pulling himself together somewhat.

"If you refuse, I'll shoot you, and say that I killed you in legitimate self-defense. If you accept, I, Fabio Canti, the celebrated artist, the Painter of the Sun, will testify to your repentance at the court of assizes, to obtain the maximum indulgence for you."

Without replying, the murderer wrote what the painter dictated.

I, the undersigned, Armand Baudard, admit to having received from Thomas Keysar the sum of one hundred thousand francs for having murdered, by means of a premeditated accident, Monsieur Antoine Aubert, factory-owner of the Quai de Javel, Paris, acting on behalf of Etienne Aubert, the victim's son; and to having been promised a further sum of one hundred thousand francs by the same Keysar, in return for making young Antoine Aubert swallow a tube of bacilli of typhoid fever, which was given to me with that objective by Thomas Keysar and his accomplice, Berthe Jafaux.

Believing that the painter already knew it, Baudard wrote the latter name, of which Fabio Canti was unaware, without paying any attention to it.

"That's perfect," said the painter. "Now the date: twenty-seventh of March 1924. And sign it..."

With his left hand, Fabio put the piece of paper into the right inside pocket of his jacket, and took out a pair of handcuffs, which he had bought in Cannes.

"Hold out your wrists."

As if dazed, the electrician, still under the threat of the revolver, said: "Well, if you're as good a painter as you are a policeman, you must be one hell of an artist."

"At any rate, I can confess to you that neither of your accomplices has been arrested, and that I wasn't sure of any of what you've just confessed in writing."

"Impossible! Bloody hell! Camel!"

"Go ahead of me, my lad. I'm going to lock you in the cellar and telephone the gendarmerie in Cannes."

VIII. Accomplices in Distress and Dementia

Meanwhile, Thomas Keysar, anxious at not having had any news of Armand Baudard, had put Souriah, the Seeress, to sleep and had instructed her to see everything that was happening in Théoule at the Villa Bellarosa.

When he had awoken her from magnetic sleep, he had told her what had happened.

In haste, they had leapt onto the first express train for Paris, where they arrived the following day at about ten o'clock in the Rue Huysmans. Leaving Berthe Jafaux, alias Souriah, there, he went to the Boulevard Raspail in order to take the Metro to go and warn Etienne Aubert.

An automobile driven by a Hindu chauffeur swept into the Rue Huysmans like a whirlwind, and he only just had time to jump out of the way. His mind absorbed, he headed for the Notre-Dame-des-Champs station, without recognizing the powerful car as that of Dr. Marc Vanel, Homo-Deus.

An empty taxi went past, and he changed his mind, flagged it down and gave the address of the Quai de Javel.

It was eleven o'clock in the morning when the magician presented himself at Etienne Aubert's home.

As soon as they were alone, the factory owner demanded: "What is it? You look devastated."

"There's good reason. We're stuffed."

"Eh? What do you mean?"

Briefly, Keysar related the recent events and the dangers that threatened them.

Etienne listened, livid, his features contracted and his fists convulsively clenched.

"Then I'm finished!" he cried. "And it's your fault!"

"How is it my fault? Wasn't it in my own interest to succeed?"

"Why did you employ an imbecile, then?"

"But he'd succeeded in…the first affair. Anyway, it's not a time for arguing. We need to take the situation as it is. What are you going to do? Try to flee with us? Berthe, asleep, with her second sight, will help us to avoid the pursuit. Or are you going to let yourself be arrested as the murderer of your father and your brother? Remember that the minutes are counted. They think we're in Nice, or we'd already be locked up. You want to hear my escape plan? Get to the frontier as quickly as possible and flee to Russia, where there's no extradition."

"That's one way," said Etienne Aubert, who pulled a face at the idea of Russia. "I have a splendid fifty horsepower, and I'm a good driver…but I have an account to settle. Blow for blow, I want to avenge myself!"

"On whom? For what? Our bad luck? You'll doom us."

"I'm not holding you back, if you've got a head of steam. Go wherever you want. All the same, it was a good move on your part to warn me."

"Have you got funds available?" Thomas asked. "I've very little myself—three thousand at the most."

"What about the money I gave you—the five hundred thousand bullets?"

"First I had to pay Baudard. The rest I put into Coutan's business deals, persuaded by him and Josette. But let's act quickly. Every minute counts."

"I can get together, immediately, what I have in my current accounts with various banks—about eight hundred thousand. But I'll need time to withdraw it."

"What if I help you? If you write me checks..."

Etienne looked at him suspiciously. "No," he said, dryly. "I'll get it myself."

"As you wish. But I repeat: remember that at any moment an arrest warrant might be issued against us. Then, to the East, and Russia?"

"No, to Théoule. Afterwards we'll see."

"After what?"

"After I do what I need to do. Do you believe that I'm going to run away like that, leaving behind the woman I love, that I desire, that I intend to have...? It's bad enough to abandon the factory, which I can't take with me, but the woman I must have."

"Are you crazy? You're insane! You're thinking about love at such a moment—an impossible love? It'll get you nailed. Yes, decidedly, you're off your head, insane!"

"Well, I have the right to be a little crazy. I have the right to my crime of passion! I'm a hero, a liberator of the fatherland, with a red ribbon, five citations and a *croix de guerre*. I've risked my skin enough for others; I can risk my head on my own account, and for a woman."

"Your stepmother!"

"So what? *I adore her*!"

"Oh, it's insane!"

"In that case, swindler, I'm not keeping you. Go, and *bon voyage*."

During that exchange Thomas Keysar reflected; he was not lacking in the desire to flee, as quickly as possible, but truly, he did not have enough money. For the moment, Etienne was the master of the situation.

Meanwhile Etienne was pacing back and forth in the drawing room, where the bronze bust of his father, on the mantelpiece, was gazing at them.

"I'll have that woman, willingly or by force. The brutal desires of primitive humans are stirring within me: the wild animals of prehistory, when man was still half-gorilla. So be it. We've known ancestral mores for nearly five years, hiding in the depths of caves, under the rain of iron and fire, like them and worse than them, who were only living under the menace of storms and wild beasts. It's necessary not to play with the human beast. They wanted to make murderers of us, and they succeeded. Conscience—what's that? Sagacity, morality? Did anyone think of those stupidities out there? Did anyone even remember that they'd once existed? The beast is unleashed now; it's howling and it wants its prey. I want it! I want it! I want it!"

"Come on, calm down. You'll have it, and I'll do my best to help you. But I beg you, let's not lose a second. You have to get moving, and so have I."

"You're right," said Etienne, passing his hand over his forehead. "It isn't a moment to mouth off; it's necessary to take action. It's already half past eleven. I have to withdraw eight hundred thousand francs before three o'clock."

He consulted a ledger, and began to write checks made out to himself, Etienne Aubert. Behind him, Thomas added the numbers up as he went along."

"That's the lot," said Etienne. "How much?"

"Seven hundred and sixty-five thousand," said Thomas.

"Good. Go home. At half past four, at the latest, perhaps before, I'll come to fetch the two of you and we'll leave by car."

"Don't worry. With Berthe, we'll avoid the search."

"You believe in that, do you? That's only good for others."

"You'll have the proof of it."

The accomplices separated, Etienne to go to the various banks before they closed for lunch, and Thomas to go back to the Rue Huysmans, to the Seeress.

IX. Homo-Deus Abducts the Seeress

On arriving in Paris, Thomas Keysar had not been without anxiety. To be sure, Berthe, when consulted, had not recognized any danger. The Rue Huysmans was not being watched by the police; obviously, they were looking in the riotous society—frightful, if one knew everything—of the winter residents of Nice and Monaco, and had not yet thought of setting up a mousetrap in Paris. Also, the capture of Baudard in Théoule had only occurred the day before, and the Law is not omnipotent, being far slower and lamer than is generally supposed.

"Ah, you've come back!" the concierge had exclaimed. "Clients by the score are waiting for you, impatiently. They've read about your successes on the Côte d'Azur in the weeklies, and all that publicity has served you well."

"We're only passing through Paris. We'll be leaving again this evening."

As soon as they had gone upstairs, the concierge had picked up the telephone.

"Hello Mademoiselle. Auteuil 14-108... Ah, is that you, Monsieur Vanel? It's me, Madame Piver, Rue Huysmans... Yes, Doctor, they've just arrived... They're leaving again this evening... Yes, Monsieur... Understood..."

She hung up. And it was Marc Vanel, Homo-Deus, whose path Thomas had crossed in the automobile at the corner of the Rue Huysmans and the Boulevard Raspail.

On passing by the lodge, he learned that the magician had gone out, slipped a hundred-franc bill into the concierge's hand, smiling, and took the elevator.

Having arrived on the fourth floor, the magnetizer placed himself at the threshold, and, seeming to concentrate all his will, he extended his arms.

"Sleep," he said. "I wish it."

Scarcely a minute had gone by before the sound of footsteps approached inside and the door opened.

Pushing the young woman gently, Homo-Deus went in, sat her down in the studio that was normally employed for occult consultations, and considered her, devoting all his attention to the marvelous subject.

"Well, do you still have your double personality? Reply to me, spirit from beyond the Earth. Have you made peace with the other?"

"With that infamous creature? Never. Oh, if I could only find a means of quitting this wretch! I sense that you alone are capable of delivering me."

"Will you follow me with trust, then, Spirit?"

"And with joy."

Come, then, without indicating in any way, in your attitude, your speech or your gestures, that you're under magnetic influence. Be Berthe Jafaux for a few minutes, and read my thoughts."

"Good—I comprehend and I approve, Master. I'm all yours."

"In that case, get your coat and your cigarettes, put on your hat, and let's go."

When they passed through the vestibule, Madame Piver bowed deeply to Marc Vanel, the man whose portrait she had seen in all the major newspapers with the caption *Homo-Deus*. And the Seeress, smiling, under the influence of a magnetism far more powerful than her own, said: "I'm leaving with Dr. Vanel. Tell my husband that he'll never see me again."

X. The Flight by Automobile

On returning from Aubert's house, Thomas Keysar went straight up to his apartment, to which he had a key. He went through it, astonished not to find Berthe. Had she been arrested? A thought reassured the optimist: *No, she's gone to lunch. We haven't had anything to eat since the restaurant car. That's all right—I'll do the same.*

This time, he went into the lodge. "Did my wife tell you where I could find her? I assume she's gone to lunch in the vicinity."

"Not likely, Monsieur Keysar. She left with Dr. Vanel, and she seemed quite content."

"Oh! Dr. Vanel didn't know we'd returned to Paris."

"It's necessary to believe otherwise. He's a sorcerer, so it's said."

"And he's abducted my mistress, my Seeress?"

"Abducted, no. She seemed very happy and very proud."

Thomas Keysar, the so-called Caesar of the Chamber Pot, went away in distress. The optimist was no longer thinking about lunch; his saucepan had been overturned. Homo-Deus, as he had let him understand during his visit, coveted the marvelous physiological and psychological instrument that the young woman was, and had not wasted any time taking possession of the Seeress.

He did not have the strength to contend with Marc Vanel, and Berthe might talk and doom him, confessing the crimes—but Keysar rapidly decided that he had nothing to fear from that direction. Vanel did not occupy himself in furnishing game to the Court of Assizes—which would, in any case, take Berthe away from him, for legal purposes.

Tranquilized on that matter, his thoughts returned to Etienne Aubert, who would amass today, in his wallet, nearly eight hundred thousand francs...to Etienne, who, in a fit of idiotic stupor, of incomprehensible vengeance, in order to satisfy a kind of incest, a brute passion, risked sacrificing their common salvation by a further crime. An idea whimpering in his mind began to take form. What if he were to kill Aubert in the course of the flight and take possession of the eight hundred thousand?

Anxiously, he took a taxi to return to the Quai de Javel, in order to make the tour of the banks with him and cash the checks.

It was five to two. The master of the factory was about to climb into his automobile when his accomplice arrived, leaving his vehicle in order to install himself beside Etienne, who said: "Where's your wife?"

"I'll explain later, when we've left Paris."

When all the checks had been cashed, making a lovely wad of blue bills, with Etienne at the steering wheel, they each put on a cap that they had in the pocket of their heavy traveling coat, and drive off at top speed. They had dinner outside Paris, as far away as possible, and set off again immediately, still traveling at top speed, without stopping, passing through towns and fields, on the highway, straight and white in the moonlight. It was a hectic flight. They had stocked the car with a provision of full gasoline cans.

They had not said much thus far, each ruminating his own thoughts: only a few words at intervals, regarding the route and the intersections. They headed toward the Midi, via Montceau-les-Mines, Lyon, Grenoble and Digne, through the modified darkness of the warm spring night, with a full moon.

Suddenly, Etienne said to his companion, who was absorbed in weaving a plan: "So, Berthe, your seeress?"

Keysar told him what had happened, recalling Souriah's cataleptic crises, and the visit of Dr. Vanel: "A savant of whom you must have heard mention, very fashionable in the salons, where he astonishes the snobs with curious experiments and whom they call Homo-Deus..."

"In brief, a charlatan like you."

"No, charged with science and a superior intelligence, and a halo of mystery besides..."

"So?" Etienne interjected, irritatedly. "Finish your story."

"Well, he abducted Berthe this morning, while I came to warn you that it was necessary to flee right away, because Baudard had been pinched."

"You're unnerving me, and I've already had enough of your sorcery tricks. With the result, if I understand you correctly, that we're at the mercy of this Dr. Vanel. Homo-Deus, as you call him, is a perpetual threat to us. Thanks to your Seeress, he can track us as if we were leaving an uninterrupted trail behind us?"

"Yes, but you don't have to worry. He didn't take my wife in order to trouble us, but in order to have a marvelous subject at his disposal, whom he won't want to lose by throwing Berthe into prison, and to the courts, along with us, in whom he has no interest."

"All your sorceries don't prevent you from being a great *couillon*,[72] as they say in Provence where we're going. Thomas Keysar, the Caesar of shit, nicknamed Chamber Pot. Oh, what a day yesterday was!"

"What did you do between noon, when I left you, and two o'clock?"

"I had lunch, cursing you, to gather my strength. Then I wrote a long letter to Louis Lafon, a worthy man, a former worker who became my director of personnel and materiel. I'm stuffed, thanks to you, but I don't want the Factory to die because of my dirty adventure. Louis Lafon now has my full powers. He'll steer the Factory toward an industrial co-operative."

"What? While everything was falling apart for us, you thought about philanthropy?"

---

[72] A Provençal dialect term, roughly equivalent to the English "bloody fool."

"I'd thought about it already, in advance. That factory, which I loved so much, was a living reminder of my crime. You remember last year, when, to incite me to murder my father—for it was you, wretches, who drove me to it— you were always clamoring at me: 'Macbeth, you shall be king'? Well, like Macbeth, I've been having hallucinations for several days.

"Who was playing with me? I don't know. Perhaps your Homo-Deus. But three times, when I went past the big flywheel, I saw the gate open. Another time, I saw blood on the iron catwalk. Another time, I heard something like the cracking of my father's flesh caught, broken and crushed...

"It was time to finish with it. I would have gone mad, denounced myself, but for the obsession with the woman with the long black hair, who excited me and who... I'm broken down, crazy. Well, I'm almost glad to be obliged to run away... But it's toward Her..."

To change the subject of the conversation, because Thomas could sense mental alienation with regard to that point, which he didn't want to contradict, he said: "So you've given the factory to your workers."

"What did you expect me to do? At least that way, the Aubert factory won't perish. Yes, I've left them the factory, and a reserve of four hundred thousand francs--for I only took out half the money in my current account while you were hanging about in my automobile at the doors of the banks. That way, in any case, I didn't awaken any suspicions by drawing it all out, and we have gotten out of Paris sooner."

Thomas, who had counted on taking possession of eight hundred thousand in banknotes—he did not yet know how—cursed internally, but he said: "You did well. See, over there, where the money moon is disappearing...and dawn's about to break. The sun will soon rise. There's still a chance of salvation..."

"You're boring me."

Etienne Aubert plunged back into funereal or lubricious thoughts, while watching the road and the steering wheel, and silence fell again, in the reckless fluid of a grim hatred between the two accomplices.

XI. The Young Man of 1924

On the morning when Etienne and Thomas were traveling at top speed toward the azure coast, in Paris, at the factory on the Quai de Javel, no one going about their daily work had any suspicion that the boss had fled. All the machines were functioning as if nothing abnormal had happened. At eight o'clock, when Louis Lafon, before his habitual tour through the workshops to inspect the work in progress, went into his office, he saw a letter deposited on his desk. He read the writing on the envelope, and recognized it as that of his boss: *To Monsieur Louis Lafon. Personal.*

He opened it. As soon as he read the first words, he seemed to be gripped by vertigo. Then, pulling himself together, he let himself fall into his chair and resumed reading.

My dear Lafon, when you read this letter I shall be in flight in order to escape, if that is possible, the punishment of a horrible crime. I did not commit that crime personally—I could not have done that—but I had it committed, which is even worse, since it increased the cowardice. I'm no more courageous today; I'm fleeing the responsibility for the sins I've committed. Without excuses to palliate them, I dare say that without that execrable war, which deformed the consciences of many young men, it's probable that I wouldn't have committed my crimes.

More than former combatants, perhaps, I'm thinking at present about the men of letters, lying in ambush then, sheltered, in the general staff at the front, when they weren't in the offices and formations of the rear, who have trumpeted at us too loudly, in the papers, that the man of today, who is not yet thirty, is the greatest in the world. I've learned by heart a passage from an article:

'I don't think there has ever, even in the youthful, abundant epoch of the Renaissance, appeared upon the earth a human being armed with so many resources and adorned with so many graces as the man of today. He is truly a fundamentally complete being, in equilibrium with his two bases. There is something formidable and intoxicating today in knowing that one is a man! War has simplified him, had made him barbaric in the new sense of the term, by rendering him his original purity. It has scraped away the layer of conventions and prejudices, laid his being naked. And naked, a man feels formidably strong.'

I, Etienne Aubert, in order to believe myself stronger than I am, still drunk on victory and demobilization, on the onanism of the trenches, on decorated murder, have not been able, inebriated and disequilibrated, to recover the road and make my way, hypocritically, by marching between the flat walls of habit and the law, without causing principles and prejudices to crack in their age-old bark.

395

But I don't have time for futile meditations, my dear Lafon. The moment has come for you to open the drawer that I indicated to you and take out the papers it contains. You are, in a way, the executor of my testament. Outside my instructions, I leave you full authority to make the Factory an industrial co-operative from which you will all profit.

I loved the factory too much, Lafon; it was to possess it that I became a criminal. It is necessary, at least, that the work that I am forced to abandon should not perish. What a mystery the human heart is! And how one cedes to its passions! Why did I allow myself to be drawn into killing my father? Is it because I saw, in an official theater, a poilu obliging his father 'the old man' to kneel down before his son and beg his pardon? Anyway, whatever you may think and say about me, honest Lafon, man of integrity that you are, will you have some indulgence for the sad culpable individual who is writing you these words?

In any case, my salvation depends on what you are going to do. Give me twenty-four hours advance on the police, if possible; that will be the means, for me, of escaping a scandal for the factory at the Court of Assizes. Do you have the right to do what I'm asking of you, though? It's up to you to decide. Adieu, Lafon; for you, I'm already a dead man. With this testament I leave you my soul: the factory. Make it immortal. Adieu, my dear Lafon. You are the only man whose respect I regret to have lost.

Etienne Aubert

The director of personnel could not hold back his tears. His heart was breaking. He remained sitting there for a long time, absorbed in bitter reflections.

Finally, his energetic nature got the upper hand. He stood up and went to open Etienne's desk. The young boss, foreseeing a catastrophe, had consulted a skillful advocate, Maître Albert Crémieux, and then had carried out all the necessary formalities, in order that Lafon had only to fulfill further legal formalities to transform the factory into an industrial co-operative of metalworkers. Lafon was legally charged with appointing a committee of direction and administration. Etienne Aubert's power of attorney was transmitted to Lafon for the covering funds and the reserve funds in the banks, about four hundred thousand francs. The former worker felt extremely flattered by that confidence in his probity.

XII. The Commissaire is Obliging

There remained the question of the revelation to the law. Ought he to do it immediately, or accord the delay requested by the murderer? If it had only been a matter of Aubert, Lafon would not have hesitated. Why make Etienne pay with his head for a moral malady, a disease of the time, the post-war morbidity of those under thirty who, mentally at least, were murdering the old? But there were also his accomplices, those who had suggested the crime to him. That merited reflection.

I can still wait until midday, he said to himself. *I'll ask advice from the wife. And I can let things go here until Saturday afternoon. We work the English week, and I'll put up a notice announcing a general meeting for the afternoon. The mates will be delighted to see themselves all becoming the masters of the factory.*

At lunch, Lafon told his wife about Etienne's flight and his decision.

"Poor fellow!" groaned Adrienne. "Our suspicions are fully justified now, alas. Notice, Louis, how evil actions sometimes engender good ones. Without Etienne Aubert's crime, the factory would have remained Antoine's property. From the death of one man, the wellbeing of hundreds of other will result."

"Yes, it's rather bizarre; the flux and reflux of life doesn't corner itself with morality. Then, you think that I should grant the twenty-four hours requested by the murder to let him get away?"

At that moment, the doorbell rang. Adrienne went to open up.

"I'm the Commissaire de Police."

"Come in, Monsieur Raynaud!" Lafon shouted, getting up and going out to meet him. "We're just finishing lunch."

"Sit down, my friend, and permit me to do likewise. I've come to reach an understanding with you, to avoid a scandal at the factory. Today, we have proof of the culpability of Etienne Aubert, and I have a warrant for his arrest. As you know, I'm not any ordinary cop, and when a guilty party renders justice to himself by means of a suicide, despite avoiding a long trial, morality's thirst for blood will still have been satisfied nevertheless."

"You've arrived too late. Etienne has fled. This is the letter that I found on my desk this morning, which Langlois, the factory concierge—as I learned just now when I left the factory—had only just deposited there, the boss having given him the order to do so yesterday."

Monsieur Raynaud read the letter.

"An odd fellow. A mixture of good and evil. It's the frantic egotism of his generation that has doomed him. Let's give the maniac, decorated in the war for his bravery, the delay he requests."

XIII. In Spite of Everything, Measures to be Taken

After an approving silence, the Commissaire continued: "Yes, but I'm forgetting that Etienne Aubert, who seems to me to be something of a lunatic, and in consequence irresponsible, might commit further crimes: raping his young stepmother...that would only be a pleasure for him...and killing little Antoine..."

"He's insane!" cried the husband and wife, in unison.

"Would you care to come to the Commissariat with me, Monsieur Lafon? I need to telegraph and telephone various people. I'll tell you what has happened on the way."

At the nearest post and telegraph office, Raynaud sent a telegram, which he showed to his companion:

Fabio Canti, Villa Bellarosa. Théoule, Alpes-Maritimes. Etienne escaped, Arrest warrant issued. Keep watch on Madame Aubert. Raynaud.

"What? You really fear that Etienne might attempt to harm Madame Aubert or the baby?"

"Him, or the bandits who are his accomplices."

As they arrived at the Commissariat, Monsieur Raynaud was finishing the story of the events that had taken place in Madame Desambez' house, which he had from a reliable source: the savior, the celebrated Painter of the Sun, Fabio Canti.

"Undoubtedly, it's all true. But I can't explain who was able to warn Etienne Aubert so rapidly. I know, however, that the boss was called home by a few words in pencil placed in an envelope, and that he came back to his office to collect papers, and then left again a few minutes before two o'clock, with the person who had come to meet him, giving, Langlois, the concierge, the sealed letter to me that I've shown you. They left in the boss' auto."

"Everything's explicable. The visitor was Thomas Keysar. Do you know the number of the car?"

"28.247—a superb Helios. Four seats and a trunk, convertible top, dark red in color, nearly new."

"Good. I'll send that description to the Prefecture. They've been on the move since yesterday; that gives them a start of eighteen hours. It will be difficult to catch them if they cross the border. Which one? Which way did they go? Italy, I presume. Let's try, anyway."

And Raynaud, the poet, humorist and excellent Commissaire, immediately telephoned his superiors.

When he had finished, he said: "I'll go with you to the factory, to make the obligatory observations. According to what you've just told me, you're now at home there. I don't, in any case, have to occupy myself with the factory's concerns, but I might find interesting papers in Etienne Aubert's house."

XIV. The Struggle Between the Accomplices

At daybreak, Aubert and Thomas Keysar were at Chagny in Saône-et-Loire, at the junction to Montceau-les-Mines and Creusot—a road that Etienne had taken several times. As the entire town was still asleep, they went to the railway station. At the buffet, they ate all the scraps that could be found for them, drank two cups of coffee each, and set off again immediately.

In Lyon, Thomas went into a grocery store and bought numerous provisions and four bottles of good wine, and bread from a bakery, before setting off again. After a further hundred kilometers on the road to Grenoble, however, they were obliged to stop. Aubert, the driver, and Thomas Keysar as well, were literally falling asleep.

Etienne decided to stop for a few hours. He drove the auto into a clearing in a wood that the road cut through, and they both lay down on the grass. The morning was superb, the breeze caressing the birch trees; rabbits with their ears laid back, scampered away into the cover of the bushes, and very near to the two profoundly sleeping murderers, little birds in a nest were screeching, demanding to be fed.

Finally, after four hours of leaden slumber, Etienne woke up first and shook his companion. They each had a copious swig of cognac, without eating anything at all. After consulting the map, Aubert set the car in motion again. He took the road to Grenoble, in order to reach the Estérel via Champsaur, the Col Bayard, Gap, Sisteron, Castellane and Grasse.

Everything went well as far as Grasse, but twenty kilometers further on, four armed men seemed to want to bar their passage.

"Gendarmes!" hissed Thomas in Etienne's ear. He had seen them.

The group had split up. Only two men were blocking the road, signaling them to stop.

"Too bad for them!" growled Aubert. "It's necessary to get through, no matter what the cost." And, putting it into fourth gear, he launched the automobile at the gendarmes.

Understanding that the vehicle was going to run them down, the two gendarmes leapt aside just in time not to be hit.

"Fire!" shouted the brigadier.

Four carbines fired. Two bullets were embedded in the bodywork, a third shattered the windshield. A second salvo was followed by a third, but the fugitives were out of range and not wounded, save for a few shards of glass that had flown into their faces, inflicting slight cuts.

"We're fried now," said Etienne. "The telegraph has circulated our description."

"Give up on Théoule. Head for the frontier, and we'll find a means of crossing over on foot, over the mountain paths."

"What's the point? No matter where, we'll be pinched. Might as well stick to my original idea. If I can reach Théoule through the woods of Cap Estérel and the Auberge des Adrets, I don't care about the rest."

"You don't care about anything. What about me?"

"You can look after yourself, bastard!"

Keysar did not reply. He thought about having himself dropped off on the road. But where would be go? To get caught, in short order. The thought obsessing his brain became more precise. If he could get rid of Etienne, take possession of the four hundred thousand-franc bills that were stuffed in his pockets, and reach some hamlet lost in the foothills of the maritime Alps, going to earth if necessary, like a wild beast, in the forest, to await a favorable opportunity…within a month, his beard would have grown back, and he'd succeed, thereafter, in getting himself out of trouble. But Etienne was stronger than he was, and had a Browning in his pocket, as well as the blue bills.

Meanwhile, the auto, still traveling at top speed, was burning up the road. On a bend, Etienne perceived that the vehicle was leaning to the right. They were out of danger for the moment and dusk was falling. He braked and leapt out to inspect the tires. A bullet had scratched one of the rear tires and the frantic race had enlarged the rip. The wheel needed to be changed. It was time lost, but there was no means of avoiding it. He took off his overcoat and jacket, and set to work.

Thomas Keysar felt cold sweat running down his back. Etienne's jacket, thrown on the seat, contained the wallet and the Browning. What a temptation!

Aubert, absorbed in his task, had removed the damaged wheel and put on the spare one. A bullet brushed through his hair and another tore his ear. Thomas, leaning over the side of the vehicle, was taking aim again.

Instinctively. Etienne parried with the heavy wrench that he was holding in his hand, striking hard, twice, at the murderer's hand and wrist.

Thomas dropped the Browning. Aubert picked it up.

Dazed, the two accomplices stared at one another with horrified eyes. Thomas threw himself backwards; then, leaping out of the vehicle on the far side, he threw himself into the undergrowth bordering the road and disappeared, while Etienne staunched the blood that was blinding him.

In sum, the wounds were not serious, but blood was running in abundance from the ear that was half torn away.

Still holding the Browning, he climbed up on to the footstep in order to get the handkerchief from his jacket. It was no longer beside the steering wheel where he had put it. Suspiciously, he climbed into the vehicle. His jacket was lying on the floor in front of Thomas's seat, and the banknotes had disappeared. He collapsed onto his seat.

Everything was turning against him. If he let him go, he was doomed.

Taking his handkerchief, he made a bandage of it, and knotted it around his head in order to support his ear. In the meantime, darkness had fallen over the deserted countryside. He sensed that the wretch could not be far away, cowering in a bush. There were not enough concerns, then, not enough alarms?

In the end, he found a stout branch of dead wood, set it across the road, and then, climbing back into the car, activated the engine. He pulled away at moderate speed, without switching on the headlights, and the sound of the automobile was soon lost in the distance.

Only then did Thomas Keysar emerge from hiding. It was now a matter of finding a place of safety for himself and the money. Had it been daylight he would have tried to make off through the woods, but by night he risked getting turned around.

He decided to go back the way they had come, primarily because in front of him, there was Etienne, who might have been stopped again by some new accident. He therefore started walking, limping, because he had twisted his foot in the leap he had made to escape Etienne's vengeance. Furthermore, the blows of the wrench he had received on the back of the hand and the wrist made it exceedingly painful for him to use his right hand.

He walked for about an hour and then, unable to do any more, he lay down in the grass of the ditch and went to sleep.

XV. The Anthill

He was woken up by a shock as disagreeable as it was dolorous. Opening his eyes, he uttered a cry of terror. Etienne Aubert, bloodied by laughing sarcastically, taking advantage of his slumber, had trapped his feet in the noose of a long slender cord, and was dragging him into the undergrowth. He uttered a scream that was half of agony and half of terror, and lost consciousness.

Etienne, after having traveled some distance in the car, had stopped; then he had gone back along the road on foot until he reached the branch that he had placed laterally as a reference point. He was sure then of having reached the spot where he had nearly been wounded. Was Thomas still hiding in the wood, or had he set out on foot?

With the aid of a pocket torch he explored the terrain. There was a narrow ditch on either side of the road. It was not difficult to find the place where Thomas had plunged into the bushes; he also found, very rapidly, the place where he had emerged again, for he had grabbed hold of clumps of grass with his uninjured hand, some of which had given way under the effort.

Thomas must have retraced their route; otherwise, he would have run into him. It was a difficult search under the moonless sky,[73] but the bright darkness of a southern spring was sufficient for him to distinguish something on the white road from some ways away. After an hour, Etienne perceived the tottering silhouette of Thomas Keysar, and followed him prudently at a distance, walking by the side of the road. Eventually, he had come upon him snoring, exhausted by fatigue and emotion, and had bound the joker's feet.

Like a good automobilist, he had had a long piece of string in his pocket, known as a "whip," for making minimal repairs. He was about to make use of it to strangle the bad advisor and traitor, having taken back all the small bundles of banknotes, when he spotted, some distance away, a mound about a meter in height, which he recognized at a glance as an anthill. Then, rapidly, he wound the cord around the legs and arms of the adventurer of letters, wrapping him up like a gigantic sausage. Having done that, in order to reanimate the unconscious man, Etienne Aubert pulled up a few clumps of grass wet with dew, and rubbed the face of the former critic and charlatan thought-reader vigorously.

Under that energetic friction, Thomas Keysar came round.

"Mercy!" he moaned. "Forgive me! Forgive me!"

"No, my lad. Look what you've done to me, bandit!"

Etienne Aubert projected the light of the torch at his own face.

---

[73] In the world of a novel, unlike the real one, it is perfectly possible for a full moon to be on the point of setting at the approach of dawn one night, and to be completely absent from the sky in the dead of the following night.

At the sight of the blood-stained face and the ear that was poorly attached by a handkerchief that was almost entirely red, he understood, by the coldly determined expression, that he was doomed.

"However," said Etienne, "I won't kill you. I had my own father killed, but personally, I don't kill. I shall simply leave you here in this wood. The morning's already paling the firmament, and you're only a hundred paces from the road. Your eyes are already shining with hope, eh, imbecile?"

He left Keysar in order to head toward the anthill, and, breaking off a green branch, he used it as a lever to open up a broad gash in the hillock. The ants, woken up, rushed out in all directions to investigate the cause of the disaster. Then he went back to pick up his victim and throw him onto the section he had opened up, and retreated a few steps, in order to avoid being attacked himself.

The sky became brighter, and the large trees emerged from the shadows first. Then, the light penetrating through the braches descended, still vaguely, to the ground, where Thomas was moaning.

He understood now, the horrible objective of his former friend, by the characteristic odor and the furious swarming of thousands of ants. He twisted in his bonds and rolled over in order to get away from the danger, but he felt the hordes of insects running over his entire body. The enemy was reconnoitering the prey before devouring it.

Etienne sniggered, seemingly greatly amused, and sniggered and sniggered...

Eventually, as Thomas, bound as he was, was moving too far, Etienne took out his knife. He started cutting branches from the bushes.

He carved points on ten of them, then, returning to his victim, who had ended up rolling some distance from the anthill, he shoved him back with kicks and thrusts of the sharp branches, digging into his ribs. Employing all his strength, he drove pickets into either side of the wretch, thus imprisoning him, in order to prolong the torture of being slowly devoured by the ants, enraged by the disturbance of their home.

Thomas Keysar, the so-called Caesar of the Chamber Pot, understood that the only help he might obtain was in the locality, and he started howling: "Help! Murder! Help me! Help me! Murder! Help!"

That animal's capable of attracting people, if there are any nearby. Necessary to shut him up.

He rolled up his sleeve, and picked up a handful of earth, grass and insects, which he stuffed into the mouth of his victim. The patient was suffocating; in order not to choke he had to spit out, or even to swallow, the repulsive mixture—but a second handful followed the first. Then, as he was still rejecting it, and as the ants were climbing the arms and legs of the torturer, Etienne Aubert cut out the wretch's tongue with his knife.

The ants, rendered audacious by the vain efforts of the victim, tied up like a sausage between the stakes, eventually penetrated into his mouth, his nose, his eyes and his ears.

Then Etienne, certain that it was impossible for the agonized man to escape death, and in order to escape the ants that were beginning to invade him, beat a retreat.

Having already recovered his wallet, he then thought about his car, and went back along the roadside.

At the moment when he was about to climb the embankment, however, he heard the roar of an automobile traveling at top speed and threw himself behind a bush—but he had had time to glimpse blue horizon uniforms, kepis with white braid and the barrels of rifles.

More gendarmes! It's a pursuit, then. They're tracking the wild beast. My car will be captured. I only have my legs to save me now. Better to finish with it...

He took his revolver out of his pocket and raised it to his head—but his arm fell back.

I can't...I could never...

He stayed there for a moment, stupidly, and the instinct of self-preservation got the upper hand. The roads were becoming untenable. Without following any path, he climbed into the brush of the mountain.

XVI. The Refuge of the Lost Pines

He walked through the forest all day—for it was no longer a small wood but a great forest, stirred by the breeze, emerald-tinted by the spring, mostly of oaks, pines and firs, with branches traversed by light in the enchantment of renewal and the sun. Where was he? In the Estérel? He did not know. By dusk, hunger was tormenting him. He found fallen chestnuts in a grove of Spanish chestnut trees, left over from the previous season, with which to give his stomach some satisfaction, and he had four hundred thousand francs on him. He could do no more. He lay down on the moss at the foot of a tree and went to sleep—a heavy slumber that as troubled nevertheless by nightmares.

Toward morning, in a frightful dream, he saw the anthill again. There was no longer anything upon it but a skeleton whose skull and hands were shining with a phosphorescent glow. He, Etienne, was sitting on the trunk of an oak, facing the cadaver, and it was absolutely impossible for him to move. He could feel his heart and his temples beating impetuously, but it was as if his limbs were petrified.

Suddenly, the skeleton agitated, with slow efforts; it slithered, disengaging itself from its clothing and its cords. Finally free, it sat down in front of Etienne and started to laugh. The mute laughter that emerged convulsively from the empty breast of the skeleton had something frightful about it. Etienne felt sweat running over his face; he made superhuman efforts to flee, but without being able to lift a finger.

That went on for a long time, an eternity for the sleeper. Finally, the skeleton stood up, came to crouch down behind Aubert and placed its hands on his shoulders: fleshless hands, each phalanx of which was glowing in the darkness, for it was dark now, and only the skeleton was visible in the gloom. Its hands seemed to be made of lead. He could not support their weight, and could not escape them.

Then there was a long whisper in his torn and bloody ear.

"I'm sniggering in my turn. One doesn't kill a man entirely. I, too, could deliver you as fodder to the ants, but I'd rather feel you gasping under my hands. I'm going to strangle you with these pretty ivory hands, and I'll feel them digging into your flesh very slowly, and the warmth of your blood passing into me, and we'll live the beautiful life of the dead eternally, the two of us bound together in death as in crime."

The fingers of ivory and ice knotted themselves around Etienne's neck. He uttered a frightful scream, and woke up.

It was not entirely a dream. A snake, attracted by the human warmth, had slid over him and coiled itself around his neck. He leapt to his feet, and hurled the reptile away, which disappeared, hissing. He shook off his fear, and, having slaked his thirst with water from a stream, he washed his hands and face. Then he resumed his journey in the direction of the rising sun.

He had been walking in that fashion for two hours—for he had a wrist-watch—along a rocky crest, when he shuddered. Smoke was rising through the foliage.

Within infinite precaution, he approached. It was escaping from a sheetmetal pipe emerging from the roof of a miserable hut made of dry stones stuck together with a daub of straw and earth. Around it was a meager enclosure where vegetables were growing. Attached to a long tether, a goat was grazing at its whim on the grass and flowering hawthorn bushes.

Who could be living there? Armed, Etienne was not taking any great risk in confronting the inhabitants. One hand clutching the Browning in his pocket, he went straight to the door of the hovel and opened it. A woman of about fifty was occupied in frying scraps on a small cast iron stove. She turned round as she heard the noise, more astonished than frightened. She was tall and strong.

Etienne Aubert's appearance was not at all reassuring. She took hold of a heavy piece of wood and said, unemotionally: "There's nothing to take from here, Man. If you come any nearer, I'll split your head with this."

"Have no fear—I don't mean you any harm." And he handed the woman a hundred-franc bill. She dropped the piece of wood in order to take it.

"That's different, then. What can I do for you?"

"I've gone astray in these woods. I'm dying of hunger and fatigue."

"You're lucky. I've made grub for two days. We'll share."

The worthy woman put two plates on the table, cutlery and two glasses, put the little stove in the middle and held out a spoon in order that the strange visitor could serve himself. It was a stew of potatoes and lard. The bread was black. To wash it down, a varnished pitcher full of delicious fresh water. To conclude the Spartan meal, there was goat's cheese spread with odorous herbs and a plate of walnuts.

His hunger appeased, Etienne interrogated his hostess. She explained how she came to inhabit the high mountain forest. She was the wife of an itinerant knife-grinder, Jean Chrysostome, who owed his name to the saint of the day on which he had been found by the roadside. Raised at the expense of the Assistance Publique, he had been placed on a model farm when he was old enough; but Jean had no taste for large-scale agriculture, especially on behalf of others; he preferred fishing and poaching. He did his obligatory military service, and later, even though he was forty-five years old, took part in the Great War. Liberated, he had wandered for a while from one coast to the other, and finally, in love with the Estérel and the Côte d'Azur, had undertaken the métier of itinerant knife-grinder. In the course of a tour he had made the conquest of Sauvageonne, who had been by turns a farm girl, a tavern waitress, a cow herder and a maid-of-all-work, and was fond, like him, of solitude.

The two of them had constructed their shelter on land that belonged to no one—or about which no one cared, at any rate—far from all communications. The two anchorites had gradually enlarged their domain, clearing land around their cabin. Jean Chrysostome set off in the good season with his old wheelbarrow and brought back the little money necessary to the maintenance of the household. At the present he was on tour, and his wife did not expect him back for a fortnight.

Etienne made his plan.

"So," he said, when she had finished her story, "you don't often see people."

"In the three years that we've been here, you're the first human being we've seen."

"But how do you get food supplies?"

"I ride our little donkey to Cambescure, a village eight leagues from Puget-Théniers. I find what's necessary there: bread, salt, oil, vinegar and lard. There's a spring of pure water a little lower down the slope. Our garden furnishes the rest. With the money you've given me, I'll buy chickens and a small pig if I can find one."

"Listen to me, my good woman: meeting me might be lucky for you. For certain reasons, I need to isolate myself from the world. This hut and your way of life please me. If you'd like to take me on as a lodger for two or three months, I'll give you five hundred francs a month."

Dazzled, the old woman accepted on the spot.

"So," said Etienne. "Forest guards and gendarmes never come here?"

"What would they come here for, since there's only us here? The rocky ridge where we're perched overlooks a stony valley, you see, only covered with brambles and thorn bushes, which is called the Lost Valley. The hill of verdant pines where we live, as if separated from the rest of the forest by that stony valley, is called the Lost Pines. To reach us, if they ever came, forest guards and gendarmes would have to traverse that rather bare valley, and we'd see them in plenty of time for you to go to earth in a grotto hidden by brushwood, which I'll show you. But I repeat: no one ever comes to disturb us. We're known in the region as the Savages of the Lost Pines. I'm La Sauvageonne."

"It's agreed, then, Sauvageonne. And I'll pay in advance."

"Henceforth, Monsieur, you're at home. Use it as you wish."

"Are you a good walker?"

"For sure. The donkey is capable of going to Puget and back in a day."

"Well then, this is what you're going to do. You'll leave tomorrow morning for Puget-Théniers, and bring me some provisions—a few bottles of wine, a liter of cognac—and newspapers from that day and the one before. You understand that if you bought that in Cambescure it would seem suspicious and might excite curiosity. In any case, even in Puget you must procure what I desire discreetly. As for the chickens and the pig, you'd do well, for fear of the same suspicions, to wait for my departure."

"You can be tranquil. I'll be circumspect, and I'll hide all that merchandise in César's saddlebags—that's our donkey."

Etienne Aubert smiled at the evocation of Thomas Keysar.

"The expenditures you're about to make are my responsibility, of course. My rent is in addition to all expenses."

The enthused Sauvageonne raised her arms: "Thank you, God, for this worthy man! Thank you!" Two or three "hee-haws" joined in chorus. She would have had herself cut into little pieces for her guest.

With that, Sauvageonne improvised a bed, to the detriment of her own, in a redoubt, with a threadbare old Japanese mordoré tapestry that someone in Cannes had given to Jean Chrysostome. Etienne went to sleep there, this time, without having bad dreams, under a worn silk coverlet with a white and mauve pattern of wisteria flowers.

XVII. Jean Chrysostome's Flair

The following morning, Sauvageonne, mounted on César, the little donkey, set out for Puget-Théniers. Left alone, Etienne occupied himself exploring the surroundings, congratulating himself on his luck. The hill of the Lost Pines, like a promontory of a higher mountain wooded with pines and firs, overlooked the valley of stones and bushes on one side, and on the other the torrent from which the two eremites drew their water. It ran a hundred meters from their cabin, and Jean Chrysostome had commenced the construction of a cistern.

Etienne admired the initiative of the two poor devils, male and female, and envied them for having no other desires than a modest and vegetative life, sheltered from the great moral or immortal passions that often lead only to disappointment and misery. On reflection, however, Etienne decided that such a life was not worth living. To be both a spectator and actor in the human comedy flattered his vanity—of which the young man had not yet lost the taste.

The murderer spent the day half in exploring and half philosophizing. Shortly before nightfall, Sauvageonne returned, with the donkey laden with food supplies. Etienne scanned the newspapers avidly, but his expectation was somewhat disappointed. He only found a short item included in the local news:

The gendarmes and police launched on the heels of the parricide Etienne Aubert and his accomplice have completely lost trace of the criminals. They are assumed to have crossed into Italy after leaving their automobile on the road in the vicinity of Grasse to put the searchers off the track.

That was all. Etienne felt humiliated not to have more importance. What did one have to do, then? Of Thomas Keysar there was no mention. Doubtless his cadaver, half-devoured by the ants, had not yet been discovered.

A sequence of monotonous days followed. To relieve the boredom of watching April give a new dress to the mountain and the forest, from morning till dusk, he was able to modify the terrain in order to divert water from the torrent into the cistern and establish and overflow for the excess. At the same time he observed that physical labor, in the salubrious open air, brought about alterations in his person. His hair and beard grew, graying prematurely, salt-and-pepper fashion. His face was tanned by the sun. His hands and arms gained a coloration and calluses from the difficult labor. The elegant city-dweller had disappeared.

Thus, when Jean Chrysostome returned from his tour a fortnight later, he found a guest who was not excessively out of keeping with the household. Sauvageonne explained to her man the good fortune that the presence of the refugee represented to them; Jean immediately sympathized with a man who was doubtless a victim of social conventions, while dreaming about the advantages that the situation might have for the couple. The few hundred francs provided by Etienne sufficed to awaken the knife-grinder's ambition; while making a pact with his guest, he judged that in time the other might have recourse to him, and that might be the moment to obtain a round sum.

He was not mistaken.

After the five months of spring and summer in that solitude. Etienne judged that he was sufficiently unrecognizable. His violent soldierly instincts had reawakened. What had become of Aline? She must be embellishing, with her brunette beauty and the originality of her long black hair, the Villa Bellarosa, its garden by the edge of the sea and the neighborhood of Théoule. And in that five-month chastity, hard to maintain for an ardent young man, he reached the point of no longer being able to resist the desire to embrace the woman who, for him, in that retreat where summer conspired with lust, represented all women.

Jean Chrysostome, at his ease thanks to the liberality of his guest, had augmented the comforts of the hermitage; he had extended it in order to establish a room for Etienne. By calcinating a kind of friable limestone, he had obtained a species of plaster which, mixed with clay, was sufficient to maintain hard stone. The thatch roof had been renewed and the cistern, completed, was full. Finally, in an enclosure, twenty chickens and six rabbits brought a variety to the diet, and two little pigs were grunting in a sty constructed for them.

In addition to taking part in all this progress, Etienne Aubert became an observer in order to distract himself like the shepherds who, while guarding their flocks, look around them, interesting themselves in the smallest creatures, which they study and to which they become familiar, in the course of a silent and motionless observation. He learned many curious things about the life of insects, bees, wasps, lizards and spiders. He became interested in herbs and trees.

One evening, when the sky was reddened by the flames of one of the frequent fires that are ignited no one knows how in the forests of the Estérel, Saint-Raphaël aux Trayas, and all the way to Théoule, Etienne said to Jean Chrysostome: "Instead of so many pines and firs, which catch fire like matches, why not import here a tree from New Caledonia, the niaouli, the bark of which is said to be incombustible.[74] That bark, composed of the superimposition of extremely thin leaves, presents when cut a book of three or four hundred pages separated from one another by an infinitesimal layer of air, continuing a marvelous insulation. The soil and climate of the Côte d'Azur would suit the niaouli. Why not acclimate it, as has been done for the eucalyptus that comes from Australia? That tree, gracious in bearing, would add its picturesque element to the Mediterranean landscape."

---

[74] *Melaleuca quinquenervia*, also known as the paperbark tree or broad-leaved tea tree.

Jean Chrysostome nodded his head, thinking that a man as learned as that must have extraordinary motives for being reduced to retiring to this verdant desert. Without replying to the idea of importing the niaouli, the knife-grinder followed his own train of thought.

"Boss"—that was what he called Etienne—"I wouldn't like you to take me for an imbecile. Don't protest...it's fine. You said to me the other day, when we weren't talking about it, that you were bored, and proposed that we both leave to make a tour of the shores of the Big Blue. At the time when you arrived here, the gendarmes were searching for a criminal from Paris, and I have good reasons for supposing that you're the man they were searching for. I haven't denounced you. For one thing, it wasn't in my interest; for another, I have a weakness for all those at odds or in difficulties with the social order. You could have stayed here indefinitely without anything to fear from me. But I've thought about what you asked me the other evening, about leaving together. That means that you want to go back to common life, and that you need me. I've become your accomplice, and in consequence, am running certain risks, for which it's only just that I should be proportionately remunerated."

"How much do you want?" asked Etienne. "Fix the sum clearly."

"Well, I thought that...five thousand francs..."

"You shall have ten, my friend. But it's necessary that I can count on your aid."

"Accepted...except, Boss, for a further crime..."

"Don't worry, it's not a matter of killing, but of having a woman in Théoule, of finding a way of getting into her room, of having her no matter what the cost, even by force, and escaping thereafter to Italy... The image of that woman tortures me every night. I love her furiously. I want her, and can't live without having possessed her..."

"All right, that's agreed. Since it's tormenting you so much, we'll leave. When, Boss?"

"Tomorrow. I can't think of anything but Her. I have on my person, ready, ten thousand-franc bills, for you to consent to my folly."

Joyfully, Jean Chrysostome, pretending to accompany himself on the guitar, started singing:

O Magali, my beloved aunt.
Listen to a song of the dawn
On the tambourine and violin...

XVIII. The Knife-Grinder

During those five months, nothing significant had happened at the Bellarosa. After having saved little Antoine by his perspicacity, Fabio Canti felt that Madame Aubert's affectionate sympathy for him was augmented by a profound gratitude. Might it become love? He, the pampered artist weary of feminine adventures, was attracted to her, the young and lovely widow who was a meritorious housewife with a repertoire of forty dishes. A wife conquers a husband via the heart, but keeps him via the stomach, and that great artist, long given to dissolute tastes, wanted a bourgeois companion. At any rate, he had not revealed that intimate project to Madame Aubert; he had promised himself only to talk to her about it when her mourning was concluded—and sometimes, the hardened bachelor trembled before that sentimental settlement date, and thought about recoiling.

Fabio Canti had returned to Paris at the end of March, but the little feminine colony had decided, on the amiable solicitations of Madame Desambez, to remain in Théoule, Madame Ossola with Simone and Robert, Madame Aubert with Ulette and baby Antoine. That decision had given joy to the children, who got along admirably, and they filled the villa from morning to evening with the enchantment of laughter, the turbulent intoxication of life and gaiety.

The summer had passed in that fashion. The gardens of the Bellarosa justified the villa's name; it was, beneath the blue sky, facing the blue sea shining in the sunlight, from which a refreshing breeze blew incessantly across a fairyland of roses.

And from the fifteenth of August to the fifteenth of September, Louis Lafon, the new quasi-boss of the factory on the Quasi de Javel and the Rue des Entrepeneurs in Grenelle, had accepted with his wife the invitation made in Paris by Madame Aubert and renewed by Madame Desambez.

On the ninth of September, a few days before the end of that vacation, at about three o'clock in the afternoon, Lafon was sitting in a wicker armchair on the shady terrace, allowing himself to drift blissfully in a wellbeing that was new to him. Madame Desambez and her guests, among them Fabio Canti, returned for the Provençal wine harvest, had gone by automobile to Valbone, for a tasting at the home of the Maire and notary, Maître Bermond, while watching the young men and women picking the clusters of grapes from the vines and actively filling the baskets. Lafon, slightly fatigued by an excursion made the previous day, had requested permission to rest.

He had heard the sound of a slightly cracked bell ringing on the road, and then the repeated cry of a *familiar* voice that made him shudder: "Sharpening knives and scissors! Here's the knife-grinder! Knives and scissors!"

Shortly thereafter, at the entrance door, the concierge replied to a graying and bearded man: "We usually give our sharpening to Jean Chrysostome."

"It's him that I'm working with. He's installed his grindstone down below, near the stream. Would you like me to go make enquiries in the kitchen?"

Louis Lafon told himself that he knew that voice.

"I'll telephone the servants' parlor. Come into the garden."

From his position, Louis Lafon had a good view of the entrance door, but could not be seen, masked by a giant screen of red roses. The concierge had gone back into his lodge, and the knife-grinder came forward, darting investigative glances around, especially at the habitation, along the rosy pathway that led to the villa. Louis Lafon watched him.

"Go on," said the concierge. "They're waiting for you."

Louis Lafon had a presentiment that he ought to hide, and went back into the drawing room.

The knife-grinder arrived at the kitchen, where the cook was chatting to Madeleine.

"You have something to sharpen?"

"What! You're not John Chrysostome."

"Yes, Mademoiselle—I'm his associate."

"Business must be good, then?"

"One can't complain."

"There: I have a chopper and all my kitchen knives to be whetted. Do you know, Madelon, whether the ladies have scissors to be sharpened?"

At that name the knife-grinder had turned to look at the old maidservant, who was staring at him intently. *I know those eyes*, she thought. But she replied: "Take those for now. When you bring them back, we'll see if there's anything else."

The knife-grinder took the chopper and the knives, and left.

As soon as he was gone, Louis Lafon, who was listening behind the door, came into the kitchen. "Did you recognize him, Madeleine? For me, that's Etienne Aubert."

"Yes, it's his eyes and his voice. But that beard and gray hair?"

"There are good reasons for that. If Etienne's coming here, it can only be with evil intentions." He turned to the cook, while Madeleine became tremulous: "Listen, Mariette, the man you've just seen is Madame Aubert's stepson. When he brings back the cutlery, it's probable that he'll want to make you talk. It's necessary to treat him politely. You see, my beauty, it's necessary for us to take advantage of the fact that the wretch is delivering himself, to finish this once and for all. Tell him that there are only ladies and children at the Bellarosa, and no other man than the concierge. Is that understood? Above all, be confident and don't show any hostility."

"Indeed! May my future husband be cuckolded if I don't roll the brigand over! A man who killed his father! What does he want now?"

When Etienne brought back the reconditioned knives he asked: "Well, have the ladies given you their scissors?"

"Here's three pairs, and tell Jean Chrystostome to be careful with them. It's for my boss and her goddaughter, Madame Aubert."

"Is that the pretty lady that I saw at a second floor window?"

"No, Madame Aubert has a complete apartment on the first floor—a bedroom at the corner of the villa, to the right, a small drawing room and a bathroom. The children sleep on the second, with old Madelon."

"You doubtless have a lot of staff?"

"No, just Madeleine and me. The ladies do their own housekeeping. There's only one man in the entire property, the concierge. If the locality weren't honest, we'd have the right to be anxious."

"Oh, you seem to me to be a strong woman."

"Certainly. Men don't frighten me." And, jogging his elbow and laughing, she put him out of the door, saying: "Look after the scissors, my lad!"

A quarter of an hour later, the knife-grinder brought back the scissors, well-honed, received his payment for the whole consignment, and drew away, darting one last glance at the façade and the window at the corner of the first floor.

XIX. What Now?

After dining at Mère Maréchal's down-at-heel eatery, on good soup, an omelet and a piece of cheese, having paid for their meal and an accommodation in advance, because they had said that they were leaving at dawn, Jean Chrysostome and his representative installed themselves in their hostess' barn, of which they had been granted sole use.

"Here we are," said one of them. "I, at least, have arrived where I need to be. You're going to come with me tonight to help me climb over the wall of the Bellarosa. After that, you're free."

"As you wish. I don't know what you want to accomplish. Nevertheless, it might be that you'll fail, and in that case, I might still be useful to you. I'll continue my tour, taking the route that the Luron follows—a stream like the one we've crossed several times in recent days, the Loup, which descends from Grasse to Cagnes. More modest than the Loup, the Luron swells up terribly, even so, when there's a storm, and I believe that we're going to have a bad one. Look at those dark clouds, Boss, coming from the south and heaping up, invading the entire sky."

"It's ideal weather for what I want," said Etienne, giving Jean Chrysostome a hand to get his grindstone out.

XX. A Stormy Night, A Night of Justice

In spite of the sky, which was becoming incessantly cloudier, but was still sufficiently bright, the two men followed a path on the edge a little wood, along the enclosing wall. Only the sound of the barrow's wheels troubled the silence. It was half past eleven. In the villa, everyone ought to be asleep. No light was shining in the windows.

"Stop here," said Etienne, in a low voice. "The shade of that big tree seems encouraging to me."

Jean Chrysostome placed his barrow next to the wall. At that moment, without him having had time to realize what was happening, the knife-grinder was seized by the throat and at the same time the barrel of a revolver was pressed to his forehead.

"Don't move, or you're dead," said a voice.

He did as he was told and did not budge, awaiting events. Etienne, who had already set foot on the grindstone in order to hoist himself up to the top of the wall was seized and violently thrown down on to the ground. Turned over by a kind of colossus, his arms were wrenched harshly backwards and bound with rope.

Fabio Canti, who was holding onto the knife-grinder, relaxed his grip. "What do we do with this one?" he asked.

"Let him go. I obtained information about him this afternoon. He's a vaguely worthy man. He must be unaware that he's the accomplice of a parricide. Yes, get away! And don't breathe a word—you'll compromise yourself, in any case, if you tell anyone what's just happened to you."

Taking hold of the shafts of his barrow, Jean Chrystostome disappeared into the darkness. And the man who had mastered Etienne, astounded by the rapidity of events, leaned over him abruptly, furious, with a concentrated anger, shining the light of a pocket torch onto his own face.

"Do you recognize me now, Monsieur Etienne?"

"Lafon! What are you doing here?"

"My duty, by preventing you from committing a new crime, while wanting to spare you the shame of the Court of Assizes. Your accomplice, Baudard, who denounced you, has been sentenced to twenty years hard labor, but you wouldn't have attenuating circumstances. You, guilty of parricide, incest and fratricide, wouldn't avoid the scaffold!"

"The scaffold!" stammered the murderer, changed in ten months, unshaven and graying.

"I'm not alone. There's your father's widow, whom I need to protect, and your young brother." In a dull voice, he added: "There's also the honor of the factory. It's better that you do justice to yourself."

417

"So be it," said Etienne. "Untie my arms. I have a Browning in my pocket. I'll blow my brains out."

"No," said Fabio Canti. "We don't want your cadaver found so near. We're going to take you to the Pont du Tournant, which spans the Luron, from which your accomplice Baudard, condemned to the labor camp, thought he was throwing your brother in his pram, and you're going to take a dive from there."

While speaking, the Venetian and very Parisian painter was exploring the exterior pockets of the young man's jacket. He brought out a revolver and a sturdy knife freshly sharpened.

"These are playthings that it's dangerous to leave to a fellow like you. Let's go—*en route* for the Tarpeian rock. And walk straight, because, at the slightest sign of resistance..."

"And what if I refuse? Your duty is to arrest me. That way, I'd have a few more months to live."

"Coward!" proclaimed Lafon. "Coward! I'm going be forced to kill you—me, who knew you as a little boy—like a mad dog." Calming down, he added, in a low and supplicant voice: "For the name of your father, for the honor of the Factory! Monsieur Etienne, I implore you..."

Etienne Aubert had got a grip on himself again. "Let's go," he said, hoarsely. "Show me the way."

The long journey, which seemed interminable to the two administrators of justice, between whom the condemned man marched at a pace equal to theirs, was made in silence. The storm was rumbling in the sky, which had become utterly dark, and in the hearts of the three men. From time to time, great flashes of lightning, in zigzags or frayed sheets, illuminated the mountain, the whole shore all the way from Cannes to Juan-des-Pins, and the glaucous sea, stirred by the tempestuous wind.

That temporary tragedy of nature enveloped and exasperated the storm that was agitating in the minds of the marching group. Louis Lafon, the old worker, his chest tight and his larynx gripped by the anguish of duty, would not, in any case, have been able to pronounce a single syllable.

Large raindrops were beginning to fall, a precursor of the formidable storm, the hurricane that was about to burst over the drama.

"Hurry up!" murmured the painter.

"Oh!" said Etienne, mockingly.

The artist perceived, in a flash of lightning followed by an enormous roll of thunder, a rock bordering the road, which overhung the torrent, in the abyss.

"No need to go as far as the Pont du Tournant. This precipice will do very well."

Bursting suddenly, with unusual violence, after the prelude of large drops, the storm that had been threatening for such a long time was unleashed. Several lightning-flashes, almost simultaneous, illuminated the black, seemingly venomous, sky and the entire landscape, resplendently—and with a terrifying crash, a lightning bolt struck one of the large firs bordering the gulf, and set fire to it. It burst into flames, like a gigantic torch.

"This is it," said Fabio Canti. "Will you please step forward, Monsieur."

On the narrow plateau where the three men were, the other fir trees, illuminated in a sinister fashion by their shattered, blazing comrade—which was burning, hanging down, suspended by its roots over the enormous hole of velvet blackness—were displayed at intervals by the lightning streaking the clouds.

In the depths roared the torrent, which, at that place, revealed the foaming turbulence of its flow in the flashing gleams and the black rocks protruding from the banks.

Etienne Aubert, whose bonds Louis Lafon had just cut, advanced slowly, darting reckless glances around him under the threat of the revolvers of the two administrators of justice, who had bared their heads in a frisson of horror, and were holding their hats in their left hands.

A flash of lightning dazzled them all for the space of a second.

Etienne had seen Jean Chrysostome clinging to another fir on the edge of the gulf, pointing his finger at the blazing tree, to which the young fir was adjacent.

It was as rapid as the lightning, but Etienne had understood. There, perhaps, was salvation. To leap in such a fashion as to fall into those tresses of flaming green needles, into that mass of branches, of vegetable cordage, and to hang on there, in spite of possible burns; to crawl along and reach Jean Chrysostome, who was ready to seize him...

After that, he hesitated no longer. The desperate man stepped back slightly in order to brace himself for his leap, waited for another flash of lightning, and launched himself.

A scream mingled with the tumult of the torrent, a clap of thunder and the rain that was falling in veritable cataracts.

In the calculated effort that the parricide had made to leap in his necessary fashion, his feet had slipped on the damp moss, interrupting his thrust and the momentum of his projection, and had sent him tumbling down the slope.

He was swallowed up like a drowned fly.

XXI. On a Better Planet

Finale. There are always, in this world, worthy and ignoble people in all professions, even among wielders of the pen and artists of all kinds, among whom everything is worse, and whose natural egotism, appropriate to any individual, is complicated and exasperated by disgust for the rest of humankind and its ridiculous vanities. God is dead, in the wake the gods of paganism, and morals are no longer anything but obsolete, frayed, deformed and outmoded masks, still good for hypocrites and backward villains to hide their interests. The arrivistes, who were a minority, if not an exception, thirty years ago, when I published the novel *L'Arriviste*, have now become almost universal.

Why not?

A child, as soon as he emerges from his mother's womb, opens his mouth to breathe, to take in as much air as possible. Afterwards, as soon as he has been cleaned of the primal impurities, free of pollutants, he clings to the nourishing breast with all the might of his little hands, and empties it gluttonously. That continues, until old age sates him, or he no longer has the strength to hold onto anything throughout life.

But let us return to the characters of this story, whose heroes are, more or less, syntheses of our times.

Under the diluvian rain, Louis Lafon and Fabio Canti went back, somewhat frightened by what they had just done. In the morning, however, at eight o'clock, when the villa woke up, in the perfumed enchantment of its September roses, the sky had become once again—as often happens in the land of the sun, where tempest pass rapidly—very pure, a cloudless vellum, extraordinarily azure.

Never, at any rate, in that nest among the flowers, did the women and children—with the exception of Lafon's aged wife—ever find out what had happened on that night of storm and justice.

Etienne Aubert's cadaver, moreover, was never found. The torrent, its waters formidably swollen by the storm, had carried it away, with its four hundred thousand-franc bills. Money is useless when we are dead—even the dollar, the master of everything.

He was a man in love; he was a man at sea.

Etienne Aubert killed his father: "the Old Man." But the State, too, after having decimated youth during the war, is killing old men, more slowly but surely, by reducing them to misery, without having anything to fear from them, because they no longer have the strength to protest. They have worked for forty or fifty years, only to see reduced by three quarters—and tomorrow to nothing—everything that they have saved up, by means of hard labor and privation, in order to provide for the winter of their existence. Unshakably confident, from

420

1914 to 1925, in the virtues and the guarantee of France, the petty rentiers have emptied their woolen purses to subscribe to all the national loans, while the artful, the *nouveaux riches*, have invested the profits of the war and their illicit gains abroad, transforming ill-gotten francs into pounds sterling or dollars.

The old men! The poor old men! They are robbed, they are ruined, and they are killed, pitilessly. While the young men, only aspiring to immediate and personal gains, form the syndicate of the under-thirties against the bearded, demanding all the high positions, all the well-paid jobs, for their generation, demanding, with the loud cries of savages, elbow room for their ambitions and their appetites, the old, downcast, do not dare to speak or act, clamoring silently, without daring to formulate the demand aloud, for SOMEONE who will reestablish order in minds, equilibrium in finance, master the great thieves and make them cough it up.

After the Directoire there was Bonaparte; after Painlevé, Caillaux and Briand, then, WHO?

Sixte Coutan, having become a Parisian député in the elections of 11 May 1924, borne by the triumphant list of the Cartel des Gauches, has placed himself, while waiting to lick the boots of the future tyrant—if he has boots—in the ranks of the party in power, in case public opinion wants to scythe down the fortunes of the most extraordinary profiteers.

At any rate, the skillful, uncertain about tomorrow, are, like the young people, putting into practice the formula: *Enjoy!* after having flattened, flung to the ground face down, in the distress justified by their stupidity, the fools of foresight and the cretins of thrift.

Enjoy! Enjoy!

Sixte Coutan has just bought a very well-situated villa at Beaulieu-sur-Mer, in that haven of idleness where the multicolored carpet of the flowers overflows from every terrace, the Little Africa where a general staff has installed itself who want to build another Gaming Palace—competition for Monte Carlo, more frequented by riff-raff and the vulgar—in a delightful decor, in Italy, two kilometers from the French border. Sixte Coutan, Parisian député, who is paying court to Mussolini for the supreme authorizations of the King and President of the Council of the Crown of Italy, is a member of the consortium. And Josette is an even prettier and more troubling octopus, whose adorable arms and legs are irresistible tentacles, which serve to capture prey for her smiling mouth and her secret mouth.

Sans-Liquette? What became of her?

Nobody knows.

Everywhere, there is dancing. Little Brother, it's necessary to enjoy; Mesdames, it's necessary to enjoy. And as Anquetil says, Satan is the conductor of the ball.[75] The jazz band symbolizes, for those escaped from the immense

---

[75] The historian Louis-Philippe Anquetil (1723-1808).

slaughter, and for the children of the great five-year beastliness, the clownish incoherence, the buffoonery and the uproar of society, the cynical and disjointed saraband of the human race.

What does it matter? After us, the abyss.

But before then, *smile*.

As for Berthe Jafaux, Souriah the Seeress, people were able to read in the newspapers, toward the end of the month of May 1924:

The young woman, whom the celebrated and mysterious Dr. Marc Vanel, known to his admirers as Homo-Deus, has been cared for in a cataleptic state, and whose crisis has lasted for fifty days, only emerged from that semi-death to die, veritably, a few hours later. Dr. Marc Vanel was able to observe a singular case of mental duality, which he had doubted until then, believing that he was dealing with a simulator, an extremely common circumstance among hystero-somnambulists, but when the sick woman—whom humorists called "the double banâme"[76]—realized that she was about to die, any imposture became improbable. She displayed a singular satisfaction at being liberated from an envelope that horrified her, and said:

"Finally, I can quit this slut whose body I'm sharing, and this dirty planet."

Nice, 27 April 1925.

---

[76] This improvised portmanteau term *banâme* is roughly translatable as "soul in exile"

Afterword
Homo-Deus, Don Quixote and Asmodeus

In one of the latter chapters of "The Invisible Satyr"—although one might reasonably assume that it was written before much of the text that precedes it, Marc Vanel compares himself to Don Quixote, not meaning to imply that he is a deluded madman, but suggesting that he sees himself as a knight-errant in pursuit of a sacred ideal of chivalry and romantic love. He is, of course, not being serious, although the lovestruck Huguette, to whom he is speaking, immediately replies that Don Quixote has always seemed to her to be the very model of nobility.

In fact, as the conventions of superhero fiction developed subsequent to 1924, especially in comic books—most especially of all when American comic books fell under the aegis of the "comic book code" in the 1950, following a moral panic about their possible effects on impressionable young minds—Don Quixote, in the sense of a knight-errant in pursuit of a sacred chivalric ideal, really did become a kind of proto-archetype on which superheroic virtue could and ought to be modeled, but Félicien Champsaur had no way of knowing that, so Vanel's comparison is not quite as ironic as it might seem now.

The narrative voice, of course, uses an entirely different standard of comparison repeatedly and consistently, describing Homo-Deus as "satanic," "Mephistophelean" and "Vanel-Satan," while Simone d'Armez calls him "Dr. Satan" and wonders, at one point, if her invisible haunter might really be the Devil—all of which supports the possibility that one of the initial inspirations for the story might have been Lesage's *Diable boîteux*, and that Homo-Deus deliberately echoes Asmodeus as well as translating as Man-God. At any rate, the satanic connection, even if it is merely metaphorical, might well help to explain the striking difference between Homo-Deus, in his guise as a freelance "administrator of justice," and all the superheroes who came after him. Not one of those successors ever employ a method of administration that consists of murdering people—one of them an innocent whose uniqueness arguably made him exceedingly precious and the other a blind old woman—and then framing other people for the murders. Don Quixote would certainly never have done any such thing, and nor would Superman, Batman, or any of their multitudinous clones.

Given that, on top of his activities as a murderer, thief and accepter of bribes—not to mention his exploits as a satyr, which begin with an effective rape that can hardly be excused one the grounds of the deluded victim's enjoyment—it is perhaps a trifle odd that his supposedly virtuous associates seem to see Homo-Deus as a hero to be admired rather than a villain as contemptible as those he fits up for his own crimes. They are presumably unaware of the full range of his activities, but not to the extent of being completely deluded as to his nature.

Perhaps the Fortins are laboring under the illusion that the Vauclins really did kill Julien for a second time, although their failure even to wonder or to ask about it seems a trifle negligent. They are, of course, inclined to forgive Homo-Deus almost anything, on the grounds of his being a scientist, just as they are willing to forgive themselves for some extremely dodgy actions, and they sympathize with his misanthropy and disgust for human fallibility, but they would surely agree that a line has to be drawn somewhere, and would certainly not find it easy to draw it in such a way that Homo-Deus remained on the right side of it.

It is perhaps worth noting that the male protagonist of Champsaur's previous novel, Ouha, was also an unrepentant thief, killer and rapist—but he really did have a sound explanation and a good excuse for his conduct, in that he genuinely did not know any better, and had no mental or moral equipment to allow him to suppress or deflect the terrible impetus of his instincts. Seen from an objective viewpoint, Ouha is clearly a better man than Marc Vanel, but that is perhaps not surprising, given that Ouha, although mostly ape, is a little bit human, while Marc Vanel is thoroughly satanic, even when he protests—as he does more than once—that there are times when he is only human.

Homo-Deus' intervention in the plot of the second novel, although slight, is equally morally dubious, in terms of what he does not do as well as what he does. In general, in fact, his inactions are even more questionable than his actions, although he seems inordinately proud of some of them. (How much moral credit can a man really expect for occasionally refraining from rape?) That record of culpable inaction is, of course, matched by his record of non-accomplishment; in the climax of "The Invisible Satyr" the humble Frédéric accomplishes far more in the matter of combating evil in three minutes than Vanel has accomplished in a year, when he unexpectedly stumbles on an acute danger of which Homo-Deus is the sole cause, having casually exposed his innocent friends to mortal danger by association.

When Homo-Deus finally does do something that might be construed as a virtuous action, in belatedly agreeing to save his beloved Jeanne from oblivion—after initially turning down her desperate plea—even that action seems a trifle peculiar, given that neither he nor anyone else has given a moment's thought to the glaringly obvious alternative. In a novel not short of amazing narrative moves, surely the most amazing one of all is the fact that when the inventor of a technology of resurrection is under threat of death, no one—including her—mentions the possibility of employing that technique, and quite simply bringing her back to life. Perhaps it could not be done, given that all the scientists in the plot seems to be far too paranoid to have made any reliable record of their work in order that others might duplicate it, and it would have been easy enough for the characters or narrative voice to discount the possibility as soon as it was brought up, but not even bringing it up is surely a massive dereliction of imagination on the part of the characters and the author alike.

In fact, the author does more than simply forget his/Jeanne's invention; he actually goes to the trouble of eliminating its consequences from the story in the single most inexplicable and morally atrocious action in the entire lot, when Marc Vanel—with no conceivable human motive or justification, and every possible reason for not doing it—murders the man that his beloved has worked so tirelessly, ingeniously and dangerously to resurrect. Why on Earth does he do that? No explanation is given at the time, and only one vague reference is subsequently made to an angry impulse, but that absence from the scheme of the story is surely a remarkable failure on the part of the creative hand that is, or ought to be, guiding and shaping the scheme in question. The simplest explanation is, once again, the probability that Homo-Deus is satanic, given to committing evil deeds for evil's sake, but neither he nor the narrative voice ever says that explicitly. Still, actions speak louder than words, especially when the words are content to remain unwritten.

Another way to look at that particularly bizarre plot-twist, of course, is to consider it as a natural consequence of the author's inability to cope with the challenge outlined in the introduction, of extrapolating the logic of his innovations. Having worked so very hard to describe the scientific miracle of a resurrection, it seems that the author simply did not know how to continue that plot strand. He had no idea what to do next with his resurrected character, or with the unsentimental genius who had proven her theory by means of the experiment, so he took the coward's way out: he simply killed the resurrected man and forced the hapless heroine to keep the secret of what she had discovered, effectively rendering it useless even to combat her own death.

One could argue that the failure of imagination in question qualifies as a massive moral and intellectual failure on the author's part, but it is one that cannot be held excessively against Félicien Champsaur, because it is a kind of failure endemic to the entire genre of speculative fiction as it has evolved under the double pressure of overdemanding extrapolative logic and the pattern of editorial demand. The latter has always strongly favored "normalizing" endings in which speculative innovations are destroyed or neutralized, in order that the typical conclusion of works of fiction can effectively and essentially restore the status quo. The pattern of imaginative, moral and intellectual failure is, therefore, far more widespread than the whimsy of one particular author, and there is a sense in which Champsaur might be complimented rather than reproved for making it so starkly obvious, thus highlighting a suppurating sore that most writers cover up cosmetically by all manner of authorial chicanery.

In any case, "The Invisible Satyr" does not have a normalizing ending, in that it ends with a peculiar kind of apotheosis, in the fusion of the souls of the two leading characters, who then set off on a messianic quest to save the world, even though theirs is not so much a marriage of heaven and hell as a marriage devoid of any detectable heavenly element at all. Although the mundane component of "Kill the Old, Enjoy!" is far more conventionally normalizing, even that novel, thanks to the involvement of Homo-Deus, concludes with a deliberate and transformative expansion of perspective, as well as leaving a clutch of plot-threads ominously dangling. It is not obvious that Aline, Ulette and Antoine have really achieved a "happy ending" in merely having escaped being raped and/or murdered while being left contemptuously off-stage, but it is obviously better than the alternative.

As for the mystery explicitly left unsolved in the second novel, of what happened to Sans-Liquette, we can, alas, be certain, that whatever did become of her, she, too, failed in her manifest moral duty. We must, of course, take it for granted that she found out that her little sister was in Marc Vanel's custody, and that he was keeping her in a coma—presumably for the benefit of the censorious extraterrestrial who was longing to be free of the carnal habitation she considered too disgusting for words. Given that, even if Homo-Deus could not simply have shifted the trapped soul himself, he definitely knew a man who could (Jean Fortin), and his failure to tackle that problem—a failure that, while liberating the extraterrestrial, ensured poor Berthe's death—should surely have prompted Sans-Liquette to play the avenging angel and administrator of justice, and borrow a revolver and blow the satanic bastard's brains out.

Obviously, she didn't—and she, not being in the least satanic, in spite of her loose morals, has no excuse at all.

SF & FANTASY

Adolphe Alhaiza. *Cybele*
Alphonse Allais. *The Adventures of Captain Cap*
Henri Allorge. *The Great Cataclysm*
Guy d'Armen. *Doc Ardan: The City of Gold and Lepers*
G.-J. Arnaud. *The Ice Company*
Charles Asselineau. *The Double Life*
Henri Austruy. *The Eupantophone; The Olotelepan; The Petitpaon Era*
Cyprien Bérard. *The Vampire Lord Ruthwen*
S. Henry Berthoud. *Martyrs of Science*
Aloysius Bertrand. *Gaspard de la Nuit*
Richard Bessière. *The Gardens of the Apocalypse; The Masters of Silence*
Albert Bleunard. *Ever Smaller*
Félix Bodin. *The Novel of the Future*
Louis Boussenard. *Monsieur Synthesis*
Alphonse Brown. *City of Glass; The Conquest of the Air*
Emile Calvet. *In a Thousand Years*
André Caroff. *The Terror of Madame Atomos; Miss Atomos; The Return of Madame Atomos; The Mistake of Madame Atomos; The Monsters of Madame Atomos; The Revenge of Madame Atomos; The Resurrection of Madame Atomos; The Mark of Madame Atomos; The Spheres of Madame Atomos*
Félicien Champsaur. *The Human Arrow; Ouha, King of the Apes; Pharaoh's Wife*
Didier de Chousy. *Ignis*
Jules Clarétie. *Obsession*
Michel Corday. *The Eternal Flame*
André Couvreur. *The Necessary Evil; Caresco, Superman; The Exploits of Professor Tornada* (3 vols.)
Captain Danrit. *Undersea Odyssey*
C. I. Defontenay. *Star (Psi Cassiopeia)*
Charles Derennes. *The People of the Pole*
Georges Dodds (anthologist). *The Missing Link*
Charles Dodeman. *The Silent Bomb*
Harry Dickson. *The Heir of Dracula; Harry Dickson vs. The Spider*
Jules Dornay. *Lord Ruthven Begins*
Alfred Driou. *The Adventures of a Parisian Aeronaut*
Sâr Dubnotal *vs. Jack the Ripper*
Alexandre Dumas. *The Return of Lord Ruthven*
Renée Dunan. *Baal*
J.-C. Dunyach. *The Night Orchid; The Thieves of Silence*
Henri Duvernois. *The Man Who Found Himself*
Achille Eyraud. *Voyage to Venus*
Henri Falk. *The Age of Lead*
Paul Féval. *Anne of the Isles; Knightshade; Revenants; Vampire City; The Vampire Countess; The Wandering Jew's Daughter*
Paul Féval, *fils. Felifax, the Tiger-Man*
Charles de Fieux. *Lamékis*

Louis Forest. *Someone is Stealing Children in Paris*
Arnould Galopin. *Doctor Omega; Doctor Omega and the Shadowmen* (anthology)
Judith Gautier. *Isoline and the Serpent-Flower*
H. Gayar. *The Marvelous Adventures of Serge Myrandhal on Mars*
Léon Gozlan. *The Vampire of the Val-de-Grâce*
G.L. Gick. *Harry Dickson and the Werewolf of Rutherford Grange*
Edmond Haraucourt. *Illusions of Immortality*
Nathalie Henneberg. *The Green Gods*
Eugène Hennebert. *The Enchanted City*
V. Hugo, P. Foucher & P. Meurice. *The Hunchback of Notre-Dame*
Romain d'Huissier. *Hexagon: Dark Matter*
Jules Janin. *The Magnetized Corpse*
Michel Jeury. *Chronolysis*
Gustave Kahn. *The Tale of Gold and Silence*
Gérard Klein. *The Mote in Time's Eye*
Fernand Kolney. *Love in 5000 Years*
Paul Lacroix. *Danse Macabre*
Louis-Guillaume de La Follie. *The Unpretentious Philosopher*
Jean de La Hire. *Enter the Nyctalope; The Nyctalope on Mars; The Nyctalope vs. Lucifer; The Nyctalope Steps In; Night of the Nyctalope; Return of the Nyctalope; The Fiery Wheel*
Etienne-Léon de Lamothe-Langon. *The Virgin Vampire*
André Laurie. *Spiridon*
Gabriel de Lautrec. *The Vengeance of the Oval Portrait*
Alain le Drimeur. *The Future City*
Georges Le Faure & Henri de Graffigny. *The Extraordinary Adventures of a Russian Scientist Across the Solar System* (2 vols.)
Gustave Le Rouge. *The Mysterious Doctor Cornelius* (3 vols.); *The Vampires of Mars; The Dominion of the World* (w/Gustave Guitton) (4 vols.)
Jules Lermina. *Mysteryville; Panic in Paris; To-Ho and the Gold Destroyers; The Secret of Zippeliu; The Battle of Strasbourg*
André Lichtenberger. *The Centaurs; The Children of the Crab*
Jean-Marc & Randy Lofficier. *Edgar Allan Poe on Mars; The Katrina Protocol; Pacifica; Robonocchio; Return of the Nyctalope;* (anthologists) *Tales of the Shadowmen 1-10*
Xavier Mauméjean. *The League of Heroes*
Joseph Méry. *The Tower of Destiny*
Hippolyte Mettais. *The Year 5865; Paris Before the Deluge*
Louise Michel. *The Human Microbes; The New World*
Tony Moilin. *Paris in the Year 2000*
José Moselli. *Illa's End*
John-Antoine Nau. *Enemy Force*
Marie Nizet. *Captain Vampire*
C. Nodier, A. Beraud & Toussaint-Merle. *Frankenstein*
Henri de Parville. *An Inhabitant of the Planet Mars*
Gaston de Pawlowski. *Journey to the Land of the 4th Dimension*
Georges Pellerin. *The World in 2000 Years*
Ernest Pérochon. *The Frenetic People*
Pierre Pelot. *The Child Who Walked on the Sky*

J. Polidori, C. Nodier, E. Scribe. *Lord Ruthven the Vampire*
P.-A. Ponson du Terrail. *The Vampire and the Devil's Son; The Immortal Woman*
Edgar Quinet. *Ahasuerus; The Enchanter Merlin*
Henri de Régnier. *A Surfeit of Mirrors*
Maurice Renard. *The Blue Peril; Doctor Lerne; The Doctored Man; A Man Among the Microbes; The Master of Light*
Jean Richepin. *The Wing; The Crazy Corner*
Albert Robida. *The Adventures of Saturnin Farandoul; The Clock of the Centuries; Chalet in the Sky; The Electric Life*
J.-H. Rosny Aîné. *Helgvor of the Blue River; The Givreuse Enigma; The Mysterious Force; The Navigators of Space; Vamireh; The World of the Variants; The Young Vampire*
Marcel Rouff. *Journey to the Inverted World*
Léonie Rouzade. *The World Turned Upside Down*
Han Ryner. *The Superhumans; The Human Ant*
Pierre de Selenes: *An Unknown World*
Angelo de Sorr. *The Vampires of London*
Brian Stableford. *The New Faust at the Tragicomique;The Empire of the Necromancers (The Shadow of Frankenstein; Frankenstein and the Vampire Countess; Frankenstein in London); Sherlock Holmes & The Vampires of Eternity; The Stones of Camelot; The Wayward Muse.* (anthologist) *News from the Moon; The Germans on Venus; The Supreme Progress; The World Above the World; Nemoville; Investigations of the Future; The Conqueror of Death*
Jacques Spitz. *The Eye of Purgatory*
Kurt Steiner. *Ortog*
Eugène Thébault. *Radio-Terror*
C.-F. Tiphaigne de La Roche. *Amilec*
Louis Ulbach. *Prince Bonifacio*
Théo Varlet. *The Golden Rock. The Xenobiotic Invasion; The Castaways of Eros; Timeslip Troopers* (w/André Blandin); *The Martian Epic* (w/Octave Joncquel)
Paul Vibert. *The Mysterious Fluid*
Villiers de l'Isle-Adam. *The Scaffold; The Vampire Soul*
Philippe Ward. *Artahe ; The Song of Montségur* (w/Sylvie Miller) *Manhattan Ghost* (w/Mickael Laguerre)

MYSTERIES & THRILLERS

M. Allain & P. Souvestre. *The Daughter of Fantômas*
A. Anicet-Bourgeois, Lucien Dabril. *Rocambole*
A. Bernède. *Belphegor; Judex* (w/Louis Feuillade); *The Return of Judex* (w/Louis Feuillade); *The Shadow of Judex*
A. Bisson & G. Livet. *Nick Carter vs. Fantômas*
V. Darlay & H. de Gorsse. *Arsène Lupin vs. Sherlock Holmes: The Stage Play*
Séamas Duffy. *Sherlock Holmes in Paris*
Paul Féval. *Gentlemen of the Night; John Devil; The Black Coats ('Salem Street; The Invisible Weapon; The Parisian Jungle; The Companions of the Treasure; Heart of Steel; The Cadet Gang; The Sword-Swallower)*
Emile Gaboriau. *Monsieur Lecoq*

Goron & Emile Gautier. *Spawn of the Penitentiary*
Rick Lai. *Shadows of the Opera: Retribution in Blood; Sisters of the Shadows: The Curse of Cagliostro*
Steve Leadley. *Sherlock Holmes: The Circle of Blood*
Maurice Leblanc. *Arsène Lupin vs. Countess Cagliostro; Arsène Lupin vs. Sherlock Holmes (The Blonde Phantom; The Hollow Needle); The Many Faces of Arsène Lupin; The Island of the Thirty Coffins*
Gaston Leroux. *Chéri-Bibi; The Phantom of the Opera; Rouletabille & the Mystery of the Yellow Room; Rouletabille at Krupp's*
Richard Marsh. *The Complete Adventures of Judith Lee*
William Patrick Maynard. *The Terror of Fu Manchu; The Destiny of Fu Manchu*
Frank J. Morlock. *Sherlock Holmes: The Grand Horizontals; Sherlock Holmes vs Jack the Ripper*
Jean Petithuguenin. *The Adventures of Ethel King*
Antonin Reschal. *The Adventures of Miss Boston*
P. de Wattyne & Y. Walter. *Sherlock Holmes vs. Fantômas*
David White. *Fantômas in America*
Pierre Yrondy. *The Adventures of Thérèse Arnaud*

SCREENPLAYS

Mike Baron. *The Iron Triangle*
Emma Bull & Will Shetterly. *Nightspeeder; War for the Oaks*
Gerry Conway & Roy Thomas. *Doc Dynamo*
Steve Englehart. *Majorca*
James Hudnall. *The Devastator*
Jean-Marc & Randy Lofficier. *Royal Flush*
J.-M. & R. Lofficier & Marc Agapit. *Despair*
J.-M. & R. Lofficier & Joël Houssin. *City*
Andrew Paquette. *Peripheral Vision*
Robert L. Robinson, Jr. *Judex*
R. Thomas, J. Hendler & L. Sprague de Camp. *Rivers of Time*

NON-FICTION

Stephen R. Bissette. *Blur 1-5. Green Mountain Cinema 1; Teen Angels*
Win Scott Eckert. *Crossovers* (2 vols.)
Jean-Marc & Randy Lofficier. *Shadowmen* (2 vols.)
Randy Lofficier. *Over Here*

ART BOOKS

Jean-Pierre Normand. *Science Fiction Illustrations*
Raven Okeefe. *Raven's L'il Critters; Rave's Faves*
Randy Lofficier & Raven Okeefe. *If Your Possum Go Daylight...*
Daniele Serra. *Illusions*

www.ingramcontent.com/pod-product-compliance
Lightning Source LLC
Chambersburg PA
CBHW020251030726
47499CB00001B/146